MIND OF A KILLER

MIND OF A KILLER

An Alec Lonsdale Mystery

Simon Beaufort

Severn House Large Print
London & New York

This first large print edition published 2018
in Great Britain and the USA by
SEVERN HOUSE PUBLISHERS LTD of
Eardley House, 4 Uxbridge Street, London W8 7SY.
First world regular print edition published 2017 by
Severn House Publishers Ltd.

British Library Cataloguing in Publication Data
A CIP catalogue record for this title is available from the British Library.

ISBN-13: 9780727893987

Severn House Publishers support the Forest Stewardship Council™
[FSC™], the leading international forest certification organisation. All
our titles that are printed on FSC certified paper carry the FSC logo.

Typeset by Palimpsest Book Production Ltd.,
Falkirk, Stirlingshire, Scotland.
Printed and bound in Great Britain by
T J International, Padstow, Cornwall.

For Ethel, Gertrude, Ada, Audrey, and Ma

This story could be true.

The quotations from news articles and many of the events described here were taken directly from *The Pall Mall Gazette*, *The Times*, and other London newspapers in 1882.

Prologue

Where do the paths begin that lead two people to come together at a specific moment? How far back in their lives, and in what corners of their minds, lie the origins of their convergent fates? Is the linking of destinies part of an all-knowing master plan, or is it driven by some unthinking, unstoppable evolutionary purpose that we do not yet comprehend?

I, of course, think the latter. And yet I discern no progress achieved from those circumstances that have conjoined our lives. In previous years, our footsteps trod different roads. More recently, however, we looked at each other, lied to each other, mistrusted each other. Yet each moment has led to an encounter that will have its final chapter tomorrow, when this man who has dogged my being ceases to exist. But I still wonder when precisely our destinies became bound together.

Perhaps it began on that early December night in 1869. How clearly I remember the rain pattering gently on the chalky walkway, as I stepped deeper under the cover of the lime trees. It was too dark to see my watch, but I suppose I had been observing the house for nearly two hours. It was not attractive, and had no social or architectural pretensions. Indeed, although the buildings and gardens were obviously well loved,

1

the owner's modifications – a flint-stone wall between house and lane, a hedge around the kitchen garden, and the orchard – had been in the interests of privacy, rather than in the show-manship so frequent in Kent's country houses. This desire for solitude was certainly convenient for *my* plans as well.

The evening schedule was as regular as clock-work – also to my benefit. It must be almost 10.30, I judged, meaning that the backgammon, played each night, would soon be finished, and the couple would retire. Then the study would be mine, as the servants never entered it at night.

The rain had eased by the time the drawing-room lights were blown out, and the ground floor became dark. Still I did not leave the shelter of the trees, but stood tormented by indecision. I knew that within the study were clues about the work with which *he* was currently concerned – perhaps an unfinished paper, which I could rewrite and publish myself. I smiled, because the master of the house was famous for the slow, methodical process by which he reached his conclusions – I could revamp the article well before he completed it. My career would be made overnight if *I* were the first to express the ideas that came from him.

But then my courage began to fail at the pros-pect of stealing from a man who had proven to be a colossus greater than Newton or Bacon. Would anyone seriously believe that *I* had devel-oped such theories? But why not? Was I not a Balliol man? Could I not be like its other giants?

I pulled on my gloves against the cold, watching

for the upstairs lights to be put out. I had not long to wait – since he rose at 6.30 every morning, the master did not stay up late. But I hesitated – was it an hour or minutes until my desire won out, and I approached the house? The window shutters were open, the owner believing that, sixteen miles from London, his peaceful home served as a citadel against the world. It was over in a moment, the crowbar splintering the soft wooden frame around the rear door beneath the central staircase.

Silently I crossed the hall to his study: the microscope on a board in the window, the revolving drum table with its samples and specimens, the notes and scribblings. I closed the door, lit a candle, and then froze as my feet set the floorboards creaking. Had anyone else heard? I paused, motionless, holding my breath. Then I moved the regency chair towards the table, sat down, and began to go through the papers. A new book was obviously in progress, and I read several paragraphs with mounting excitement. I had to force myself to stop – I could hardly steal an entire book!

I continued my search. And there it was – a copy of a letter written that very day. I read it, then again, and gazed at it with a mixture of wonder and enlightenment. I still smile at the image a photograph taken at that moment would portray: a young man, mouth agape; right hand holding the letter and left pressed against the long Dundreary whiskers that were so popular but so ridiculous; and eyes looking far away, yet inward.

I had just found the central meaning of my existence, for this letter was not just an article or a manuscript, but an instruction, a calling from on high. In it were answers not just about *my* future but that of many others. I put it in my pocket and blew out the candle. But I did not leave. I sat there, the profound awareness of that moment seeping into every part of my mind and soul. That one piece of paper had shown me that I would be a leader of men, a minister of a new calling, in fact, no less than a saviour to future generations.

17 January 1882, near Arras, France

William was dozing fitfully in the otherwise empty second-class compartment when the door from the train's inside corridor was thrown open, waking him with a start.

'Good morning,' said one of the two men at the door. 'I hope seven o'clock is not too early to discuss business?'

William swallowed hard as the man entered the compartment and fastidiously brushed off the seat opposite with a gloved hand. His companion closed the door from the outside; William heard him lean against it.

'So,' said the visitor as he sat down, 'what are we going to do?'

'I received a telegram from a friend who's ill,' blurted William, heart racing. 'I was going—'

'Hush.' The man held William's eye for a moment. 'Let's just sit quietly, shall we?'

William's mind whirled in panic, although he

4

knew he had to stay calm if he wanted to survive. The man facing him was more monster than human, and William had never been so terrified in his life. Of course, he did not look evil. His double-breasted morning coat and vertically striped trousers were impeccably pressed, his short, buttoned boots freshly brushed, and his walking stick shiny and clean. He looked like a man stepping out of his club.

'Why are you here, Nathaniel?' asked William, trying to keep the tremor from his voice.

'More to the point,' countered Nathaniel, 'why are *you* here?' He smiled; it was not a pleasant expression. 'You bought a coupon from Calais to Brussels, making such a show that even the cretin in the ticket office would remember you. But then you changed destinations at Ghent. Now, why was that? Not to escape from me, surely?'

'I can't do this any more,' whispered William, cornered. 'I shan't try to stop you, but I can't be a part of it.'

'You won't try to stop us?' snapped Nathaniel, his voice increasing in volume. 'Fool! This is the natural course of events. No one can stop it! You entered this business as and when *I* determined, and you will leave as and when *I* decide!'

William drew back at the venom in the words, but then Nathaniel smiled gently. 'Come, my young truant,' he said silkily. 'Neither of us should become overly excited. If you wish to leave, then of course you may. But let's talk first; we owe each other that.'

'But how did you know . . .' began William, not deceived by the sudden show of geniality.

5

Nathaniel wagged a scolding finger. 'Never try to fool the master, William. It was obvious that France was your destination.'

William hung his head, feeling stupid and wretched. 'So what now?'

'Mr Morgan and I hope that you'll accompany us back to London.'

'No!' said William, trying to press himself back into the seat. 'No, please!'

Nathaniel inclined his head. 'Then we shall travel to Boulogne together and talk as we go. I'll try to persuade you to come home, but if you remain firm in your conviction, then I shall bow to your will. At least you'll be easier of mind, having left with my blessing, rather than having stolen away. What do you say?'

William weighed his options, which he sensed were actually very limited. 'Very well – if I have your word that I may leave if I choose.'

'Oh, I guarantee it,' said Nathaniel. 'If you wish to go, we'll just drop you off somewhere along the line.'

He smiled again, but there was such malice in his eyes that William felt his stomach lurch, and he was suddenly more afraid than ever.

One

Alexander Lonsdale blinked soot-laden rain from his eyes as he slogged over the well-manicured but sodden fields of Regent's Park. The downpour came in sheets, beating against the butts as he walked through the area reserved for the Royal Toxophilite Society; on reaching the Outer Circle, the ring road around the park, he followed it to Clarence Gate.

A greasy, grey plume, darker than the clouds, lay across the rooftops in the distance. His assumption that there was a blaze somewhere was confirmed by the clanging bells of a fire engine, audible over the ever-present rumble of traffic. The cold, dreary weather meant London's Fire Brigade was busier than usual for April, as hearths were left burning whenever their owners could afford it. Lonsdale kept moving, feeling rain course down his neck and his trousers stick unpleasantly to his knees.

A row of hansom cabs waited at Park Road, their miserable drays standing with drooping heads and matted coats. Drivers stood in huddles, chatting together, or puffing on their clay pipes, waiting for the inclement weather to push customers their way. They eyed Lonsdale hopefully, and he considered hiring one, but he was

7

already sodden and still indignant at the way he had been dismissed at the Zoological Gardens that morning. Thinking exercise would help alleviate his bad humour, he kept walking, eventually reaching Harewood Square, where imposing grey mansions sat behind smooth stone pillars.

But his thoughts kept returning to the irritating business of his unsuccessful morning. It was the second time that week he had arrived for an appointment with the director of the Zoological Gardens. It was also the second time that, after a lengthy wait, he had been informed that Dr Wilson was unavailable, and would he come back another time. As it happened, Lonsdale was not particularly interested in returning, but a commission was a commission, and if the editor of *The Pall Mall Gazette* was prepared to pay for an article on London's magnificent zoo, then Lonsdale would provide him with one.

More rain found its way down the inside of Lonsdale's collar, and he increased his pace. He resented being treated in such an ungentlemanly manner, and he had declined to leave until Wilson's secretary had put a new date in his diary: between seven and eight the next evening.

Lonsdale decided that if Wilson was indisposed a third time, the article would be written without his input. Perhaps he would include a few home truths: that the lions were mangy rather than ferocious, that cramped conditions were probably responsible for the bizarre behaviour of the monkeys, and that most of the tropical inhabitants would probably thrive and would certainly be healthier if they were ever let outside. Wilson would be hard pressed to deny these charges, and would heartily wish he had spoken to the reporter.

Engrossed in his vengeful musings, Lonsdale stepped off the pavement to cross the road. A sudden yell and an urgent jangle of bells brought him to his senses, and he leapt backwards as a fire engine hurtled past, the horses' iron-shod hooves striking sparks against the cobbles. He watched the engine swing down one of the side streets, and the clanging faded.

He had just begun to walk again when a shrill cacophony warned of the approach of another engine. Lonsdale glanced up at the sky, and saw that the dirty grey streak was now a thick cloud of smoke, hanging heavy across the rooftops. He could smell burning, too. As the engine thundered past, its brass pumps gleaming, he thought how unusual it was for three fire crews to attend the same blaze.

He hesitated. There were few things he despised more than ghoulish spectators at the scene of a tragedy. Yet he knew that if he were ever to be hired full-time – something for which he desperately hoped – he should take advantage of any opportunity that came his way.

As he hovered indecisively, he saw others were not allowing fastidious pretensions of dignity to prevent them from indulging *their* curiosity and were converging on the scene of the fire. Some were servants, cloaks hastily thrown over uniforms, sent to find out what was happening for their masters; others were chance passers-by. Mentally shrugging, Lonsdale followed them.

9

The engine turned into Marylebone Road, then jigged right into Wyndham Street. Here, among the solid, unpretentious villas of the city's clerks, shopkeepers, and transport employees, was a row of tightly packed, two-storey terraced houses, each with a tiny, low-walled front garden. Halfway down the road, bright tongues of flame licked out of the windows of two of them, and smoke seeped through their roofs – spiralling upwards.

The reason three engines had been sent was painfully clear – the fire was spreading to the adjoining houses. It was obvious that the two homes were lost, and the firemen were concentrating on their neighbours. Clad in their uniforms of dark serge, they laboured furiously with pumps and hoses, and hoisted ladders to the upper windows to drench the rooms and create a sodden barrier in the hope of preventing the fire from advancing.

Lonsdale watched the tiny spouts of water hiss ineffectually against the leaping flames, before moving among the crowd, storing impressions in his mind and looking for someone to tell him who lived there and how the blaze had started.

Some of the spectators lived nearby, and fear that the fire would take their own homes induced them to scream orders and advice, all of which were ignored by the sweating firemen. There seemed to be a body of opinion that the terrace should be demolished before the fire spread further. This proposal was vociferously contested by a thin-faced, frightened man who stood amid a random collection of chairs, clutching a biscuit barrel. Next to him, a woman dazedly rocked a

10

screaming child in her arms, and said nothing. Lonsdale balked at intruding on their despair, and looked for someone else to talk to.

Near the back of the crowd was a man wearing the distinctive peaked cap of a railway guard and a woman with a beaky nose, her sleeves rolled up and her arms dusted with a film of flour. Lonsdale surmised that, unless she often walked around with dough on her arms, they were residents of Wyndham Street and that she had been baking when the excitement started.

'What happened?' he asked, as hot tiles began to slip from the roof to smash on the ground below. A harried policeman and brigade volunteers tried to prevent onlookers from surging forward to snatch a better look.

The railway guard shook his head, while the woman studied Lonsdale suspiciously, pushing a tendril of wet hair from her eyes and leaving a smudge of flour on her nose. Her gaze turned from his face to his clothes, as if assessing his respectability by the quality of the top frock he wore. Lonsdale waited politely, although he knew that any conclusions she drew from his appearance would almost certainly be wrong.

He had spent most of his adult life in the Colonial Service – one of Queen Victoria's faithful representatives in Africa, where he had passed the better part of nine years. He had then returned to London, where a year later he had horrified his family by informing them that he intended to become a newspaper reporter. So Lonsdale, whose clothes were of good quality but not at the height of fashion, was difficult to

11

assess solely on the basis of his attire. Even so, she decided he was sufficiently respectable to warrant a reply, and began to speak in a nasal, self-important voice.

'I was just putting the bread in the oven when I heard yelling outside, so I went to see what the fuss was about. This is a respectable street, and we don't pry into each other's business, so I didn't rush straight out, like some would have done.'

'What did you see?' asked Lonsdale, when she paused for – he assumed – an acknowledgement of her proper manners.

The woman coughed as a billow of smoke rolled over them. 'Mr Donovan was yelling something about his chimney being blocked and catching fire. Then he rushed back inside again. I didn't believe him – he'd had the sweep, you see, so I assumed he was . . . well . . . intoxicated.'

She pursed her lips in prim disapproval, and regarded Lonsdale with bright little eyes. Lonsdale was bemused.

'He called for help because his house was on fire, and you thought he was drunk? And what does the sweep have to do with it?'

She sighed impatiently, and when she spoke, it was slowly, like an adult to a backward child. 'Mr Donovan had his chimney cleaned last week. People's chimneys don't catch fire after the sweep has been, because he removes the soot that causes fires.'

'I see,' said Lonsdale, although he still failed to understand why Donovan's claim that his house was on fire had led her to conclude that he was drunk. Suspecting they would become pointlessly sidetracked if he pressed the matter, he moved on. 'So Mr Donovan's home is one of those burning?'

She nodded. 'Number twenty-four – the left of the two in the middle. Anyway, I went back in the kitchen and put it from my mind. Then Molly Evans from next door came running and said there was smoke pouring from Mr Donovan's roof. We sent her boy for the fire brigade, while her Bert tried to break down the door to get Mr Donovan out.'

'Did he succeed?' asked Lonsdale. The house now was little more than a dark silhouette among the leaping yellow flames. The breeze sent sparks fluttering towards the crowd, which stepped back with a collective gasp of alarm.

The woman scanned the onlookers, then turned back to Lonsdale. 'I don't think so. I can't see him here, and he wouldn't go off while his house burned, would he?'

'I imagine not,' replied Lonsdale, although experience had taught him that people did all manner of strange things in fraught situations. 'What happened next?'

Her husband took up the tale. He did not look at Lonsdale, but addressed his words to the flames, which reflected yellow and orange in the shiny buttons of his railwayman's uniform.

'I was coming home from work, when I saw Bert kicking at Patrick Donovan's door. By then, flames were pouring out of the windows. Funnily, the door was shut fast – locked or bolted. Then I saw the fire had spread to number twenty-two, so Bert and I ran to help Joe Francis with his chairs.'

He nodded towards the man who stood disconsolately with what he and his neighbours had managed to salvage.

'So Mr Donovan is still inside?' asked Lonsdale in horror, astonished that they should abandon their efforts to save a life in order to rescue furniture. 'What about his family? Are they in there, too?

He gazed at where the flames had seared the paint from the door, and envisaged the hapless residents crawling towards it with cinders and flames erupting all around them, only to find it blocked, and then dying in the knowledge that safety was but a few feet away.

'He lives alone,' replied the woman. 'He isn't married and his father passed away last summer.'

'You said you returned to your baking after Mr Donovan first raised the alarm,' said Lonsdale, considering her story in the careful, analytical way that had proven successful for him, both in the Colonial Service and at his newspaper. 'While he ran back inside his house.'

'Yes,' said the woman. Her voice became unfriendly. 'To salvage his belongings, I suppose. What of it?'

'So where are they?' asked Lonsdale.

The woman scanned the road, saw the proprietorial way each small pile of possessions was jealously guarded by its owners, and shrugged. 'He probably didn't have time to bring anything out.'

14

'But you suggested there were several minutes between him first shouting for help and Mrs Evans telling you the fire was out of control,' Lonsdale pointed out. 'Surely he should have managed to save something, even if only a painting or a book?'

The woman frowned, disliking his questions. 'Well, obviously he didn't.'

Lonsdale moved away, watching the firemen battle on as the steam engine on their pump spat and hissed furiously. Down the street, more residents were taking the precaution of dragging their belongings outside. Lonsdale went to help an elderly woman with a table, then stood by helplessly while she wept in distress and shock. He stood next to her, knowing he was supposed to be observing, not joining in, and wondered if he would ever possess the cynical indifference that seemed necessary to make a good reporter.

Fires were not uncommon in a city where coal and wood were used to heat homes, and London blazes regularly caused loss of life and possessions. Donovan's tale, though pitiful, was hardly front-page news. Still, W. T. Stead, the flamboyant assistant editor of *The Pall Mall Gazette*, was always on the lookout for thrilling, sensational, or tragic tales that would attract readers away from the dignified morning dailies, so there was generally a place for 'human interest' pieces.

Lonsdale rummaged in his pocket for his pencil and notebook, and began to write:

Tragedy struck today at the home of Patrick Donovan of 24 Wyndham Street, when a blocked chimney resulted in a fire so intense that it not only destroyed the adjoining house but threatened to engulf other homes as well.

He frowned at what he had written. Donovan's neighbour had said the chimney had recently been swept, so the fire being caused by a blocked flue was unlikely. So perhaps the sweep had left a brush in the chimney. It would not be the first time incompetence had brought about a tragedy. He continued writing.

Neighbours valiantly tried to smash through the door to save Mr Donovan's life, but to no avail.

He frowned again. Was Donovan still inside, or had he managed to leave via the back door or a window? That Donovan had escaped seemed more plausible than that he had rushed into the street howling that his house was on fire, and then allowed himself to become trapped inside. And if he had run back to salvage his belongings, the absence of so much as a stick of furniture was puzzling. It seemed unlikely that Donovan would have been completely unsuccessful, especially as the woman had assumed he was drunk specifically because she had seen no evidence of fire.

Lonsdale walked to the end of the street, turned the corner, and looked to his right. Running parallel to Wyndham Street was a narrow alley, where more firemen struggled in the swirling smoke. No belongings stood outside, nor – he ascertained from another neighbour – did Donovan.

16

Lonsdale returned to Wyndham Street. Dozens of spectators were there now – servants, street vendors, well-dressed gentlemen, and the respectable working classes who lived nearby. They stood elbow to elbow, winter-pale faces lit orange in the flames, their mouths hanging open as they gazed upwards. They oohed and aahed as the flames crackled and snapped. A few cast sympathetic glances at the bewildered victims, but most just watched with fascination.

Eventually, the firemen began to win the battle. The flames were less intense, and there was more steam than smoke. Most of the small, pleasant houses in Wyndham Street would be saved.

'You a reporter?'

The soft voice, close to Lonsdale's ear, startled him, and he turned around quickly. The woman who had spoken flinched away from his sudden movement, and looked as though she might bolt. She cast a fearful glance behind her. Lonsdale glanced at the pencil and pad in his hand and thought the question was spurious. Who else made notes at such an incident?

'I write for *The Pall Mall Gazette*,' he said.

'*The Pall Mall Gazette*? That's not a big paper, is it, not like *The Daily Telegraph*?'

'No,' he replied. 'It's aimed at an evening audience, not a morning one.'

She regarded him sceptically, as if wondering who had time to waste reading a paper at night, when darkness brought the opportunity for more interesting activities. 'Well, it doesn't sound as good for me purposes as one of them big jobs, but I suppose it'll do.'

17

She glanced around again, making Lonsdale wonder what 'purposes' could necessitate such furtive behaviour.

'Are you one of Mr Donovan's neighbours?' he asked.

It was a question designed to begin a conversation, rather than for information, as he already knew the answer: the Wyndham Street residents were solidly upper working class, decent, clean, and dogged adherents of social convention. The woman before him had a pale, thin face, plastered with make-up; her body emanated a stale, unwashed smell, and her clothes were cheap and ostentatious. She was not the kind of person who could afford a home on Wyndham Street, nor one who would be accepted by its residents.

'Never you mind,' she replied, and fixed hard, calculating eyes on Lonsdale in a way that made her seem older than her years. 'All you need to know is that I got sommat to tell you.'

'About the fire?' asked Lonsdale when she fell silent again.

'Donovan ain't the first,' she blurted. 'He ain't the first to die like this. And there'll be others. You have to do sommat! The police won't listen, so you got to help.'

'You mean other people have been killed in house fires?' asked Lonsdale, bemused by the tirade.

'No!' she cried, and then looked around quickly, as if concerned that her outburst might attract attention. 'In other ways. Donovan is at least the sixth.'

'Donovan may have escaped. Just because he isn't here, doesn't mean he's dead.' Lonsdale felt sorry for her; she was clearly distressed and frightened over something.

'He's dead,' said the woman firmly. 'But I ain't talking here. They're watching me. Meet me tonight. Regent's Park – between the drinking fountain on Broad Walk and the bandstand. Eight o'clock; it'll be dark by then. I'll bring someone who'll answer all your questions, and you can bring this to an end.'

'Bring what to an end?' asked Lonsdale, bemused by the stream of instructions. 'Why can't you tell me now? No one can harm you. It's broad daylight.'

She shot him a look that bespoke utter disbelief, and hurried away, head down. Not sure that meeting the woman and her associate in the dark of Regent's Park was an arrangement he intended to honour, Lonsdale followed, catching her arm.

'I have an appointment tonight,' he lied. 'Can we meet another time? Tomorrow perhaps, during the day?'

She grimaced. 'Tomorrow night then – same time and place.'

'At least give me some indication as to what it's about,' he said, smiling in the hope of reassuring her. 'You'll forgive me if I'm a little . . . cautious.'

A tired, sardonic grin tugged at the corners of her mouth. 'Most men don't baulk when I ask 'em to meet me at night. But if you're too scared to take a chance, while I risk me life, then you ain't a man I want to trust anyway.'

'What do you mean, "risk your life"?' asked Lonsdale. 'Is someone threatening you?'

'You could say that. Will you meet me, then, to hear a story so horrible that you won't believe it?'

'If it's *that* incredible, my editor won't print it,' retorted Lonsdale.

'We'll give you proof. Names, dates, places; whatever you need. Will you come? You won't regret it.'

Lonsdale nodded, although the rational part of his mind told him he was a fool to make an assignation with this fidgety, furtive woman in an area that was usually deserted after dark. She gave the briefest of smiles, then turned to stride away, but collided with a policeman, who had been watching their exchange with interest.

'Now, then, Cath Walker,' he said, regarding her coolly. 'Not plying your trade with me standing right next to you, are you?' He was a large man, broad-chested and heavy-bellied, with a livid scar slicing through one eyebrow.

She gazed at him in horror, backing away until she stumbled. Then she turned and fled, tearing blindly down the lane. The policeman watched her go.

'Brazen,' he muttered.

'She's a prostitute?' asked Lonsdale, although he had assumed as much.

'An *unfortunate*, sir,' corrected the policeman primly, using the expression coined for the thousands of women who sold the last resource they could call their own. 'However, she usually works south of the river. Did she proposition you?'

Had she? In light of the policeman's confirmation, Lonsdale found himself uncertain as to what her intentions had been.

'Not as such,' he hedged.

The policeman wanted to press him further, but was interrupted by calls from outside Donovan's house. Several onlookers were signalling for him to assist three firemen, who were passing something through the gap where the window had once been in the now-smouldering house. A second policeman appeared at the other end of the street and headed for the firemen.

Lonsdale turned back to the first officer, and was startled to see him hurrying away. He turned the corner and disappeared.

Lonsdale blinked. Why would he dart away from a place where he was needed? He considered giving chase, but something was happening in the street – a body being carried from the Donovan house. The crowd fell silent as it was laid on the ground.

'Is this him?' asked a fireman, looking around at them. 'Is this Patrick Donovan?'

'How can we tell?' retorted an elderly woman who clutched a shawl around her thin shoulders. The body – sizzling slightly as rain evaporated upon hitting it – was blackened beyond recognition. Its fists were clenched and raised, like a boxer defending himself, and its legs slightly bent. And the head had been crushed.

'What do you want us to do with him, officer?' the fireman asked the policeman, whose pale, youthful face made it clear that he had not had occasion to deal with such an incident before.

'My sergeant will be here soon,' he replied hoarsely, before stepping forward to cover the body with his cape. 'Then we'll take him to the mortuary.'

'Check his leg,' suggested the old woman. 'Mr Donovan lost a kneecap a few years back, when he was kicked by a horse. If that body has one kneecap, then it's poor Mr Donovan.'

The fireman raised his eyebrows at the policeman, inviting him to do it, but the youngster only produced his pocketbook and began to write.

'One kneecap,' he murmured. His hands were unsteady, and Lonsdale felt sorry for him.

'I'll look then, shall I?' asked the fireman mildly. 'We've got to do it now, because we'll have to look for another body if this isn't him.'

The policeman nodded, with his attention wholly fixed on his writing. 'Go on, then.'

'Which kneecap?' asked the fireman. 'Left or right?'

'Well, Mr North?' asked the old woman of the railway guard, who stood with his sharp-eyed wife at the edge of the crowd. 'You were in and out of his house, when he was laid up with his bad leg.'

North swallowed, uncomfortable with being the centre of attention. 'I don't know,' he muttered nervously. 'It was one of the two.'

The fireman bent to poke about the dead man's legs. Tactfully, he shielded what he was doing with his own body, while the crowd seemed torn between the desire to watch, and an urge to look elsewhere.

Eventually, he stood, wiping his hands on the sides of his tunic. 'Left,' he said, letting the cape fall over the black shape on the ground. 'Patrick Donovan was missing his *left* kneecap.'

'So, you were wrong then, Alec,' said Jack Lonsdale, eyeing his younger brother thoughtfully later that day.

They were in the morning room of Jack's house, a large, airy, first-floor chamber dominated by an elegant, but very scratched, table at one end, and a sofa and several worn chairs near the fireplace at the other. Books lay on the table and the floor, which was partly covered by a handsome red-brown rug. Lonsdale loved the morning room's shabby comfort, although Jack's fiancée loathed it, and he knew its scruffy, masculine décor would be one of the first things to go once she was installed as mistress of the house.

The second thing to go would be Lonsdale himself. He had moved into the house – a fine, six-storeyed affair in Cleveland Square, Bayswater – upon his return to London the previous year, after years of hopping around Africa: Zanzibar, the Gold Coast, the Cape Colony, Natal. Despite Jack's belief that working for a newspaper was an ungentlemanly occupation, he had insisted that his brother stay with him. But Lonsdale could hardly continue to live on Jack's hospitality once his brother was married, and Emelia would no more want him in her home than Lonsdale would want to impose. Lonsdale and Emelia were uneasy together, and only a mutual

23

affection for Jack kept them outwardly civil to each other.

Jack flung himself down in a chair, oblivious to the way it groaned under his weight. The family resemblance between the two men was immediately apparent, although Lonsdale had flecks of grey in his dark hair, while Jack's mop was solidly mid-brown. Their eyes were blue-grey and both had a sportsman's physique, although Jack had recently noticed a thickening around his middle, something he attributed to approaching the end of his fourth decade rather than the frequent and lavish dinners at his club. His fashionable sideburns were the only facial hair either wore.

'You were wrong,' Jack said again. 'You thought Donovan might have escaped through the back door, but he died in his house.'

'So it seems,' said Lonsdale. 'Although it makes no sense – if Donovan knew his house was burning, why did he die inside?'

'That's obvious,' said Jack, using his pompous barrister voice. 'He went to salvage his belongings and was overcome by fumes. This reporter business has affected your objectivity. You look for mysteries, when there's nothing but simple tragedy.'

'Donovan's neighbours said they tried to batter down the front door, but it was locked or bolted. Why would he secure the door when his house was on fire?'

'He probably didn't,' said Jack, picking up a morning paper and reaching for his spectacles. 'Some piece of timber, loosened by the flames, doubtless fell across it.'

24

'In that case, why didn't he escape through the back door?'

'Maybe he was unconscious,' said Jack, opening *The Times* and shaking it out. 'Smoke can render one insensible very quickly.'

'But Donovan's neighbours didn't notice the fire immediately, so it can't have been so serious when he first raised the alarm. That means that he *did* have time to do something. And if his possessions were so dear to him, why weren't any outside?'

'Just because he didn't succeed in saving his property, doesn't mean to say he didn't form the intent to do so,' said Jack, sounding much as he did in court.

He cast his eye down the morning's news. Lonsdale was sure his brother did not need to wear spectacles, but there was no denying that they lent him an air of authority. Jack looked like a barrister without them, dressed in sober suits and immaculate cravats, but with them he looked like the personification of the Old Bailey itself. Lonsdale supposed that if *he* had committed a crime and saw John Lonsdale QC coming to represent him, he would have high hopes of getting away with it.

'The more I think about it, the more I feel this prostitute really does know something odd,' Lonsdale said, tilting his head to read the back of Jack's paper.

The Times was lowered, and Jack's disapproving face appeared over the top of it. 'What she knows is how to rob foolish men who meet her in dark parks. I'm glad you are dining with

25

me tonight – it saved you from your own stupidity. If I'd known this reporting lark would entail meeting harlots in remote places, I'd have stopped you from starting it.'

Lonsdale was silent. Jack could not have stopped anything of the sort, but he did not want to argue. Jack's nose went back into his paper, while Lonsdale read on the back of it that the fatal shooting of Jesse James was deemed 'cowardly' by much of the American public.

The newspaper was lowered censoriously. 'Either buy your own paper or wait until I've finished,' Jack said stiffly, bringing up an ancient and familiar grievance. 'I can't stand it when you try to read mine at the same time.'

Lonsdale stood and went to the window, where he watched a group of children with their nannies career across the road to the gardens opposite, oblivious to the drizzle. He stared absently at the raindrops on the glass.

Jack was right, of course. There was no reason to suppose that Donovan's death was anything other than accidental, regardless of what Cath Walker had claimed. But it nagged him: a man running into a blazing house does not secure the door behind him if he intends to come out again. Perhaps *that* was it: suicide. But then why raise the alarm?

'Good God!' exclaimed Jack, suddenly sitting bolt upright. 'Have you read the obituaries today?'

'Not yet.' Lonsdale had been up early to visit the site of what was expected to be called Eastcheap Station, as part of a series he was writing on a new underground railway line, and then he

26

had gone to the Zoological Gardens. After the fire, he had only just finished rubbing the smell of smoke from his hair with a scented towel when Jack had arrived home, and he had spent the next hour in an unsuccessful attempt to convince his brother that Donovan's death was suspicious.

'Charles Darwin died yesterday,' Jack said. 'There's a blow! Few men have contributed as much to modern thinking as Darwin.'

'Not everyone would agree.' Lonsdale went to scan the story over Jack's shoulder. 'A good number of churchmen, for a start.'

'Ignorant men,' declared Jack, waving his paper dismissively, at least in part to prevent his brother from reading it. 'Individuals whose faith is too flimsy to withstand intellectual probing.'

Lonsdale tuned out what soon became a tirade and read for himself, reaching out to hold it:

Exactly a year to a day has separated the deaths of two of the most powerful men of this century. On 19 April 1881, the civilized world held its breath at the news of the death of former Prime Minister Disraeli. Not less must be the effect when the announcement of the death of Charles Darwin flashes over the face of that Earth whose secrets he has done more than any other to reveal . . .

'How true this is,' said Jack, tapping the paper for emphasis and jerking it from Lonsdale's fingers in the process. 'Natural selection is one of the most brilliant concepts in the history of science.'

'You approve, then?' asked Lonsdale wryly. For a man of law, Jack's world was remarkably black and white. Theories were either brilliant or worthless, and the men who postulated them either geniuses or drooling imbeciles.

'We shall never see another man of science like Darwin,' averred Jack with utter conviction. 'He was the greatest thinker in the country.'

'What about Charles Lyell?' asked Lonsdale wickedly. 'Or James Clerk Maxwell?'

'Them, too,' said Jack, realizing his brother could probably list another half dozen men, all equally significant. 'But you shouldn't be here – you should be at your paper, writing a piece on Darwin. After all, you met him once, which is more than your colleagues can claim.'

'Did I?' asked Lonsdale, astonished. 'When?'

'At the Royal Geographical Society outing two years ago,' replied Jack. 'How could you have forgotten?'

'Probably because I was in Natal at the time. You must have gone with someone else.'

Jack raised the newspaper again. The silence meant that he knew he had been mistaken, but was unwilling to admit it. Yet he was right about one thing: Darwin's death *was* a major event, and it was indeed time that Lonsdale made an appearance at the office.

The Pall Mall Gazette was located on Northumberland Street, a mean little by-way off the Strand that was more alley than road. Number Two was a tall, grubby building with the name of the newspaper strewn like a banner below the top floor windows. Lonsdale hurried inside, glancing uneasily, as he always did, at the huge lamp that hung over the dingy front entrance. He expected that one day it would fall and kill someone.

A dark, narrow staircase led to the first floor, where there were four offices: the editor's, the assistant editor's, one shared by the sub-editors, and one for all the reporters. The door to the editor's office was open, but the leather seat in which John Morley sat while dispensing orders to his minions was empty.

Next door, assistant editor W. T. Stead slouched with his back to his desk and his feet on the mantelpiece, tossing balls of paper at a stuffed bear head that hung on the wall. He looked as though he were idling, but his reporters knew that some of his most brilliant thinking was done while he appeared to be wasting time. As Lonsdale passed the door, one of Stead's missiles bounced off his shoulder.

'Lonsdale!' Stead leapt to his feet with customary vigour as Lonsdale poked his head around the door. 'The article on the zoo. Can it go in the last edition?'

Guiltily, Lonsdale realized that he had not given it a thought since the fire. 'I'm due to meet Dr Wilson at seven tomorrow evening,' he replied evasively. 'It'll be ready first thing Saturday.'

Stead cocked his head to one side and regarded Lonsdale appraisingly. 'You were supposed to meet him this morning. Did his secretary tell you he was indisposed?'

Stead saw his reporter's surprise and grinned teeth flashing white through the tangle of reddish-brown beard that had been growing wilder since Christmas. He twisted around and tossed one of his paper balls at the bear, scoring a direct hit.

'Wilson will be at his club tomorrow night,' he said, tearing up a well-thumbed copy of *The Morning Post* to make more ammunition. 'If his secretary said Wilson would meet you at the Zoological Gardens at seven on a Friday night, he was being naughty.'

'How do you know?'

'Wilson visits the Garrick Club every Friday,' replied Stead. He grinned again. 'Listen to everything you're told, Lonsdale, and forget nothing. That's what'll make you a good reporter, not the ability to pen a story – any monkey can do that. Make yourself familiar with the people you interview, so you always have the advantage.'

Lonsdale nodded gloomily. 'So I should stand outside the Garrick and ambush him as he enters?'

'No need! Ambrose Harris is a member of the Garrick. He'll sign you in.'

'He won't,' said Lonsdale, startled. 'I know him only slightly, like him less, and he would no more sign me into his club than I would sign him into mine.'

'Now, now,' said Stead cheerfully. 'Poor gauche Harris cannot help not having been raised as a gentleman.'

'Perhaps not, but he can certainly help being employed by *The New York Herald*.'

30

Stead laughed. 'It's a dreadful rag, I agree, but its sensationalism seems to be what makes a successful newspaper in New York. However, we digress. I shall arrange for Harris to sign you into the Garrick tomorrow, and you can tackle Wilson there. I want this zoo story – wild animals are popular at the moment, and people are of a mind to visit them in their time off.' He saw Lonsdale's distaste. 'I know Harris isn't a decent man's choice of company, but we all must make sacrifices.'

He sat at his desk and waved a hand to indicate that Lonsdale should sit also. There was no other chair, but there were piles of newspapers, so Lonsdale perched on one. Stead watched him thoughtfully.

The Pall Mall Gazette did not have a large staff, and one of its senior reporters had recently announced his intention to retire. It was common knowledge that there were three candidates for the post, but it was likely that the choice would be between Lonsdale and another freelance reporter – or 'liner' as they were known – by the name of Henry Voules. Lonsdale wrote well, was a meticulous researcher, learned fast, and was pleasant company. Voules was none of these things, but was the nephew of the paper's business manager and a friend of the owner, both of whom approved of Voules's social connections through his aristocratic mother. It would be a difficult decision, and Stead was not sure the right one would be made.

While he listened to Lonsdale outline the zoo article, Stead collected spent missiles from

31

underneath the bear. He appeared distracted, but he missed nothing that was said. He liked Lonsdale, and felt his experiences with the Colonial Service lent a unique angle to his writing. He had assigned him to cover several stories in a manner frowned upon by most British papers and that had drawn the derogatory term 'investigative reporter' from Morley, the editor. But Morley wisely allowed Stead ample independence in pursuing stories with social significance, and Stead used the success of these articles to support Lonsdale for the upcoming post.

'What about the weekly progress report on the underground railway?' Stead asked. 'Is it ready?'

'The chief engineer says it will open as planned, despite delays over some skeletons that were found. Apparently, the tunnel went through an old plague pit, and the men refused to work when they were uncovered until the bones had been removed. A whole day was lost.'

'Excellent!' exclaimed Stead ghoulishly. 'Buried corpses make more interesting reading than the tonnage of excavated earth.'

'They were reburied in the nearest churchyard,' continued Lonsdale. 'The vicar held a memorial service for them.'

'This underground train system,' mused Stead, fixing Lonsdale with his unsettling blue eyes. 'Will it supersede the hansom and the trolley bus?'

'Never,' declared Lonsdale with conviction. 'It drops you where there's a station, and you have to take a hansom to get where you want to go anyway.'

'True,' agreed Stead. 'We can safely say that there will always be hansom cabs in London.'

'And we've all been on the Metropolitan underground railway,' Lonsdale went on with a shudder. 'Not everyone likes the noise, steam, dirt, and darkness – especially when there are more comfortable modes of transport.'

'*I* most certainly haven't used it,' announced Stead vehemently. 'And nor shall I. I'm all for progress, but not progress into the bowels of the Earth on an infernal machine that stinks of oil and screams like a banshee. Besides, we must think of the social ramifications: what would our friend the tramcar driver do if his livelihood were stolen by steam?'

'Become our friend the underground-railway driver?'

Stead began lining up his paper balls on the edge of the desk. 'Would you ask them to exchange a life in God's clean air for one labouring in the conditions of Hades?'

Lonsdale saw the gleam of fanaticism in Stead's eyes, and decided not to mention that few places in the world were as afflicted by a lack of 'God's clean air' as London.

'Never!' cried Stead when there was no reply. He slapped the desk with his palm. 'I shall see that such a monstrous thing *never* happens! Don't forget, Lonsdale, the mission of the press is to lead the struggle for the betterment of our society. It should give voice to the aspirations of the inarticulate classes and guide public opinion. That's what God's purpose is for us!'

Lonsdale was used to these tirades. 'Your tram

33

drivers are safe enough. But where is everyone? Out working on pieces about Darwin?'

'Most of them,' said Stead, retrieving the balls of paper that had scattered when he hit his desk. 'Although Milner is interviewing Mr Parnell about the prospects of being released from gaol and what is being done to calm Ireland – you know Mr Morley likes to dedicate at least a page a day to the Irish Problem. But returning to you, tell me about the fire you witnessed today.'

Lonsdale blinked his surprise. 'Do you have spies in *every* quarter? Or is there still a smell of burning on my coat?'

Stead laughed. 'You reek of it. Was it a case of arson? I heard there was a tremendous inferno at a warehouse in London Pool.'

'Nothing so exciting – just a house fire in Wyndham Street.'

'What happened to attract your interest? Were there casualties?'

Lonsdale nodded. 'A man called Patrick Donovan died, although . . .'

He hesitated, recalling how Jack had dismissed his suspicions. But Stead nodded encouragingly and listened intently as Lonsdale outlined his thoughts, ending with the invitation by Cath Walker to meet her in Regent's Park.

'Will you honour this mysterious assignation, considering that you risked losing the story by being unwilling to go tonight?' asked Stead. He sounded critical, but he had ceased to collect paper balls, a sure sign that he was intrigued.

'I can't go tomorrow, either, if I'm to meet Wilson at the Garrick.'

34

'You will meet Wilson at seven and your lady at eight,' determined Stead. 'I'll send a message to Harris, warning him not to be late.'

'So you think I should go? I'm intrigued, but I'd almost decided it isn't worth the risk.'

'Only you can determine how important it is to follow a particular story,' preached Stead. 'Meanwhile, write your account of the fire. Don't speculate on foul play. When you finish, go to the Metropolitan Police mortuary and ask for Dr Robert Bradwell. He'll probably be doing the post mortem. Now go, or you'll miss the deadline.'

Lonsdale opened the door to the reporters' office, and headed for one of the tables. The office was stained brown from years of pipe- and cigar-puffing: its walls were brown, the floor was brown, and the ceiling was brown. It stank of tobacco smoke, wet overcoats, and ink, but a small fire cast a cosy glow around the room.

Lonsdale liked the reporters' office, as well as most of the people who worked in it. It ran on the same schedule as the newspaper. Before each edition was 'put to bed', it was a hive of frantic activity, as writers dashed off last-minute stories, while print-boys waited to snatch them away before the ink was dry, and tear upstairs to the waiting compositors. At other times, it had an air of jovial somnolence, as the reporters relaxed and told tall tales.

That day, only three others were there. Hulda Friederichs was writing furiously, Edward Cook was editing his copy while standing next to the

35

one small window for extra light, and Henry Voules was surrounded by an impressive pile of tomes, through which he was lethargically riffling.

'Our Cambridge man,' sneered Voules unpleasantly. 'Come to make sure we don't split our infinitives, have you?'

Lonsdale declined to rise to the bait and only nodded at the books. 'Catching up on natural selection?'

Voules scowled and failed to reply, so Hulda answered for him. 'He needs to summarize Darwin's scientific achievements in less than a page,' she explained, 'which means he must do something at which he does not excel – original work.'

'Then why don't you do it?' asked Lonsdale, surprised. 'You once told me you'd read most of Darwin's work.'

Hulda looked smug, and pretended not to notice Voules's glower of outrage that he was obliged to spend his afternoon wading though Darwin's works, when she might have dashed off a summary in a few moments. Gloatingly, she waved a piece of paper in the air.

'Do you think readers will be more interested in musings on Darwin's theories or in the confession of the murderer Lamson to his Wandsworth Prison guard last night?' she asked. 'A story exclusive to *The PMG*.'

Voules gaped. 'Is *that* where you were all morning? Interviewing the prison guard? And all the while I was stuck here, slaving away over the lunatic theory that we're all descended from monkeys?'

36

Hulda gave a superior smile, and flounced from the room to present her article to Stead. Voules watched her go, his expression murderous.

'Why Stead hired her, I'll never know,' he muttered. 'She cannot open her mouth without being rude and aggressive!'

'She's also a gifted writer and an astute, incisive interviewer,' Cook pointed out, drawing a firm line through two of his sentences. 'We're lucky Stead persuaded Morley to hire her.'

Morley had broken new and dangerous ground by taking on a female journalist, but no one could claim that his gamble had been anything but a success. The 'Prussian Governess' or 'The Friederichs', as Hulda was known to her colleagues, seemed well on her way to meeting her dream of becoming the first woman reporter to be paid the same as the men. Even so, ability was no certain passport to success in journalism.

Cook was, if anything, even more talented. At twenty-four, he was the youngest liner on the staff, and had only recently graduated from New College, Oxford. He had already shown remarkable abilities, and was the last of the three in contention for the upcoming position, although Morley was unlikely to hire him because of his lack of experience.

Voules, by contrast, was a careless researcher and an indifferent writer, whose only value lay in his family connections. Lonsdale glanced at him and saw greasy crumbs and a long yellow streak of egg yolk adhering to his cravat, while he moistened his thumb with a wet, red tongue

37

to flick through the pages of the book. Morley's personal copy of *The Descent of Man* would never be the same again.

All three were concentrating on their work when Hulda returned wearing a triumphant smirk – her article had been heartily praised. Lonsdale completed his report about the fire, and left as Voules and Hulda began an acrimonious debate about evolution, which Hulda was certain to win. He glanced at his watch. It was four o'clock, and he decided he had plenty of time to visit the mortuary before returning home to change for dinner.

Raised voices followed him down the stairs, and he heard Stead chuckling as Hulda began a ruthless and systematic destruction of Voules's arguments. He walked briskly to the Strand, where he hired a hansom to take him to the mortuary. Iron-grey clouds dropped a light drizzle, and as the wind blew sooty droplets into his face, he felt as though it were the perfect day for a trip to the House of the Dead.

Two

The northern branch of the Metropolitan Police mortuary lay near the River Thames, in an area of Westminster dominated by dirty streets and grimy buildings. To the south was Millbank Penitentiary, to the east the chartered gas works, and to the west the run-down Grey Coat Hospital.

It never ceased to amaze Lonsdale how such a seedy and unkempt area could be located so close to the homes of the upper classes along Victoria Street.

The mortuary was one of the most ramshackle buildings of all, and Lonsdale wondered whether it would survive another winter without some serious repairs. Black water trickled down its walls from leaking gutters, and its wooden door was flaking and rotten. Had it been anything other than a repository for the dead, he was certain thieves would have smashed the filthy windows in their decaying frames, and stolen everything inside.

The door stood ajar, and an oil lamp within threw a feeble yellow gleam into the gloom of a hallway. Wafts of death and strong chemicals billowed out, ranker than the ever-present stench of rotting horse manure and poisoned river that pervaded the city. When no one answered his knock, Lonsdale walked in, calling Dr Bradwell's name. There was no reply.

The hallway stretched away into blackness. Lonsdale took a few tentative steps, then froze at the sound of scrabbling claws on the stone floor. Rats! He was about to take the lamp to light his way, when it gave a sharp hiss and went out, leaving him in the dark. A quick shake revealed that it had run out of fuel. He considered lighting one of the gas lamps on the wall, but then decided against it, feeling that if they were in as poor repair as the rest of the place, he was likely to blow it and himself to kingdom come.

More rats skittered in the darker reaches of the

corridor as Lonsdale rummaged in his pockets for matches – he did not smoke, but he always carried a box of Alpine Vesuvians. He struck one, and began to make his way down the dismal corridor, noticing that the walls glistened with black slime, while insects moved this way and that over the foul, speckled surfaces.

At the end of the hall was a sturdy door, with a line of light gleaming along the bottom. Lonsdale's match went out, leaving him in darkness again. He stepped forward and rapped on the door. There was no reply, and he was just reaching for the handle, when it was flung open. A figure silhouetted against the bright light behind advanced on him menacingly.

'What do you want? We're not in the business of cat food, if that's what you're after.'

'I don't have a cat,' replied Lonsdale, wondering what sort of person usually visited the police mortuary. 'I'm from *The Pall Mall Gazette*. Are you Dr Bradwell?'

'One of Stead's fellows?' asked the shadow, the belligerence fading from his voice. 'And women, of course, because one mustn't forget Miss Friederichs. Is she with you?' He stepped forward to peer hopefully into the gloom.

'I came alone,' said Lonsdale.

'Pity,' sighed Bradwell, stepping aside to allow Lonsdale to enter his domain. 'Miss Friederichs is always welcome here.'

'That must be a comfort to her,' said Lonsdale. 'Do you have a specific slab in mind?'

Bradwell gazed at him blankly for a moment before giving a sharp bark of laughter. He was a stocky man in his late thirties, with neat black hair and lively brown eyes. He sported thick sideburns, and his face was prematurely lined, although with laughter or care Lonsdale could not tell. He wore a thick apron, like the ones favoured by the fish porters at Billingsgate, which was stained with ominous smears.

The mortuary's inner sanctum comprised a large square room with a low ceiling that Lonsdale could have touched – not that he would have tried, as it was dappled with all manner of filth. Pressed along three of the walls were waist-level tables, occupied by human shapes covered with grey blankets. He estimated that there were about thirty in all, although this was insufficient, as several were doubled up with occupants.

In the centre of the room were two more tables, larger than the surrounding ones, with a lever at one end to adjust their heights. A brightly burning gas lamp hung above one, while a trolley bearing a grisly selection of instruments stood to one side. The sulphurous, cloying stench of blood and decay was overpowering, but Lonsdale resisted the urge to cover his nose with his handkerchief, knowing he would grow used to the odour. It was not the first time he had visited such places, and, during his days in Africa, he had grown inured to the sight and smell of violent slaughter.

There was but one other living occupant in the room. He was an unkempt-looking man with a poor complexion, a scraggly brown-and-grey beard, and a head of long greasy hair, parted in the middle of a flaking scalp. He wore an apron

41

similar to Bradwell's, and slouched near the wall, picking his teeth.

'Have you come about the Hackney Road murder?' asked Bradwell, indicating the waxy-white figure that lay on one of the central tables. There was a wide, deep wound on the victim's throat, and bone and cartilage gleamed through the mess of red and black. 'There's not much to tell, I'm afraid. He was killed by a single slash to the neck. The killer has already been apprehended, so there'll be no hue and cry over the police not catching the culprit.'

Lonsdale opened his mouth to tell Bradwell that he had come about the Wyndham Street death, but the doctor was not easy to interrupt. Lonsdale imagined that the sullen assistant, who still poked at his long yellow teeth, was unlikely to be much of a conversationalist, and supposed the pathologist was taking advantage of different company.

'It's difficult to conceal a murder like this,' continued Bradwell enthusiastically. 'Blood spurts from the neck, and unless you know what you're doing, you'll end up as covered with it as your victim. It makes escape more difficult. Why's Stead interested in this case?'

'He isn't,' said Lonsdale. 'We'd like to know about Patrick Donovan – the man who died in Wyndham Street.'

'Really?' asked Bradwell. He shrugged in a way that suggested he considered Donovan's the last case in which anyone should be interested. He turned to the slouching man. 'Bring in the burned one, please, O'Connor.'

42

O'Connor gazed listlessly at the covered shapes as though he expected Donovan to sit up and identify himself. Bradwell sighed.

'We put him outside, remember?' He turned to Lonsdale. 'He was making the place smell.'

'Yes, I can see that would be unpleasant,' said Lonsdale, wondering how they imagined Donovan's body might make a difference to the choking stench that already pervaded the building.

O'Connor returned with a clanking trolley. It carried a burden that was an unusual shape under its rough, grey blanket. Bradwell whipped the cover off with a flourish, like a magician removing a handkerchief to reveal a golden egg, and underneath lay Patrick Donovan, fists still clenched, knees still bent, and head still a mashed pulp.

Lonsdale was aware of Bradwell watching him, and kept his expression blank. He knew perfectly well that the surgeon had hauled the blanket away in such a dramatic fashion in the hope of shocking him – as a form of initiation to the morgue that would cause the reporter to run from the room in horror. It was by no means the first time a pathologist had played that particular trick on an unsuspecting visitor.

'So?' Lonsdale asked, meeting Bradwell's disappointed gaze.

'Typical pose for a fire victim,' said Bradwell, turning his attention to the body and pointing at the fisted hands. 'The muscles contract to make the corpse look as though it's ready for a fight. So what do you want to know? It's pretty clear to me how he died.'

'Is it?' asked Lonsdale, surprised.

Bradwell's eyes narrowed warily, as though he thought Lonsdale was trying to make fun of him. 'Surely even a layman can see that he's been in a fire.'

'But did the flames kill him, was he overcome by smoke, or did he die from the injury to his head?' asked Lonsdale.

'Oh, I see what you mean. The police don't usually want that kind of detail. House fires are so common that we tend not to waste much time on them. The inquest will be little more than a formality, and the coroner will record the incident as death by fire.'

'You won't even perform a post mortem?' asked Lonsdale, surprised.

'I didn't say that,' said Bradwell. 'But it won't be the kind of in-depth investigation that I'd do for the Hackney Road murder. I'll look at his heart and lungs, and then I'll assess the degree of burning – which you can see is severe.'

'And that's it?'

'Basically. Whether the cause of death was smoke inhalation, burning, or injuries sustained from falling masonry is irrelevant. That he died in the fire is usually enough for the records.'

'And you say it happens a lot?' asked Lonsdale. 'People dying in fires?'

Bradwell looked grim. 'More often than you'd think. People underestimate fires, and they usually don't live to learn their lesson. The smoke overwhelms them and they end up like your friend here.'

'Is that what happened to him?' asked Lonsdale. 'Death by asphyxiation?'

'I can't say without inspecting his lungs. I was planning to leave him until tomorrow, but as you're here, I suppose I could do it now. I'll be late home, but my wife's used to it.'

He and O'Connor transferred the charred remains to the other central table.

'What's your bet?' asked the surgeon, selecting a short, silver knife from the trolley. 'I'll put ten shillings on smoke inhalation. We might as well have a little fun, if I'm doomed to spend an evening in the frosty silence of a wife who objects to my long working hours.'

'I'll go for the head crushing,' said Lonsdale, wondering how he had ended up in the police mortuary on a wet afternoon betting on the cause of someone's death with a man wearing a fishmonger's apron.

For the next few minutes, the room was silent except for moist sucking sounds and the cracking of bones. Lonsdale watched for a while, then began to wander around the room, first inspecting the rows of gleaming instruments and then studying a stained chart on the wall that showed the major muscles. O'Connor watched him intently, and Lonsdale sensed that if he tried to touch anything, the mortuary attendant would leap to slap his hand away.

'You seem more inured to this than most reporters,' said Bradwell, not looking up from his work. 'Yet I haven't seen you before.'

'I worked in Africa,' replied Lonsdale. 'Violent death is no stranger there.'

'Good God!' exclaimed Bradwell suddenly. 'Look at this!'

Lonsdale leaned over him to see where he was pointing, but could determine nothing from the mass of blackened tissue and bone that had so excited the doctor. He said so.

'Neither of us will be claiming that ten shillings,' said Bradwell, straightening and eyeing Lonsdale soberly. 'This man died from neither smoke inhalation nor a crushing of the head. However, someone *has* made off with part of his brain – his cerebrum.'

For a moment, Lonsdale was too startled to say anything. He gazed at the police surgeon in astonishment, aware that the mortuary assistant was doing likewise from a shadowy corner near the door.

'*What*?' he gasped when he eventually found his voice. 'You must be mistaken!'

Bradwell pursed his lips in annoyance, as if Lonsdale were questioning his professionalism. 'I assure you I'm not. Can you see a cerebrum in that skull?'

'I couldn't tell you one way or the other,' said Lonsdale, looking down at the mess that had been Donovan's head, 'what with the charring and the crushing. Perhaps whatever bit you mean leaked out or was incinerated.'

'The cerebrum is the largest part of the brain,' said Bradwell stiffly. 'It wouldn't just "leak out" and, even after burning, there should be some of it left.'

'So what happened to it, then?' asked Lonsdale sceptically.

46

'I have no idea. But it didn't disappear of its own accord. And since it didn't go naturally, I can only assume that someone took it.'

Lonsdale began to laugh. 'Stead! He told you to spin me some outrageous tale, so that I'll write it up and provide him with an endless source of amusement.'

'You don't know him very well, if you think that,' said Bradwell reproachfully. 'He might have an odd sense of humour, but he would never make a joke of someone's death.'

Bradwell was right, yet what the surgeon was suggesting was outrageous.

'But Donovan's neighbours saw him run into the street shouting about a fire,' argued Lonsdale. 'I need no medical expertise to assert that he couldn't have done that without his brain.'

'Then his cerebrum must have been removed *after* he returned to his house,' said Bradwell firmly. 'Intriguingly, the rest of the brain is still there, including the cerebellum, the thalamus, and the brain stem.'

'So you think someone followed Donovan into his burning house – unseen by the neighbours – whipped out his cerebrum, and left?' asked Lonsdale incredulously.

'I'm a physician,' said Bradwell icily. 'I leave that sort of speculation to the police. *I* deal in evidence and facts: and the fact here is that there is *no cerebrum in this skull*!'

Lonsdale rubbed his eyes. Although he had sensed something odd about Donovan's death, he had not imagined it would transpire to be anything as sinister – or peculiar – as a missing organ.

'Are you sure someone didn't take it while the body was out in your yard?' he asked. 'When I first arrived, you thought I was looking for cat food, so you obviously deal with some very odd people.'

'We have a high wall topped by broken glass. If someone were to climb over that, he'd want more than a cerebrum.' Bradwell gestured that the reporter should move closer. 'The skull has been smashed, as you so eloquently pointed out, but if you look here, you'll see that the line of fracture isn't jagged – it's straight. In other words, someone sawed carefully around the top of this man's head, much as I did to the gentleman over there, who died from a fall.'

O'Connor lifted a blanket covering one of the corpses to reveal that a circular disc of skull had been removed from the top of the head, allowing the brain within to be examined.

'This is becoming even more outrageous!' exclaimed Lonsdale. 'Now you're suggesting that whoever did this had a degree of medical knowledge?'

Bradwell did not reply but fetched a magnifying glass for a closer look. 'Hah! I'm right! You can see the striations made by the saw.'

Still sceptical, Lonsdale took the glass and noted that there were indeed marks that looked unnatural.

'But what really convinces me that this didn't happen accidentally,' said Bradwell, 'is that *every* part of the cerebrum is gone. It is normally anchored to the skull by membranes, and it's necessary to detach each one very carefully to remove it in one piece.'

'But what could someone want with a cerebrum?' asked Lonsdale, bemused. 'You can hardly put it on your mantelpiece.'

'The world's a queer place,' put in O'Connor sagely, speaking for the first time from where he leaned against one of the tables, his hand placed without any thought on the chest of the body under the blanket. 'Full of strange folk with strange customs.'

'This is scarcely a custom, O'Connor,' said Bradwell.

'I blame the newspapers, personally.' O'Connor cast a venomous glance at Lonsdale. 'They write about all those peculiar places, and it gives people funny ideas.'

'What sort of places?' asked Lonsdale, searching his memory for a report from one of the Empire's far-flung outposts about corpse mutilation.

'Scotland,' said O'Connor, making it sound more sinister than Hades. 'And Manchester. And let's not forget High Wycombe, that vile pit of filth and corruption.'

'Let's not,' agreed Lonsdale, struggling not to smile.

Bradwell returned to the blackened corpse. 'What I imagine happened was this: your man Donovan was killed, his cerebrum removed, and then his skull smashed so that it would appear as though it had been crushed by falling rubble – a ploy designed to prevent a busy, underpaid police surgeon from looking any closer.'

He picked up a knife and investigated further,

while Lonsdale watched, his mind teeming with questions. O'Connor busied himself at a sink. While Bradwell worked, Lonsdale studied him covertly. The tiredness in his face, his inexpensive clothes, and his harried air suggested he was a poorly paid hospital physician, forced to undertake additional duties as a police surgeon to make ends meet. He had mentioned a wife, and might even have children to support. Regardless, Lonsdale felt certain that his mortuary work resulted from necessity rather than choice. Eventually, Bradwell straightened up.

'If Donovan died from smoke inhalation, there would be soot in his lungs. There isn't.'

'I knew there was something odd about this,' said Lonsdale, more to himself than the doctor. 'Right from the start.'

'And I'd have missed it if you hadn't been here with your ten shillings,' said Bradwell. 'I had seven post mortems to do today – this makes eight – and I'm expected at St Bartholomew's Hospital for the night shift. I don't have time to waste on the obvious cases. Lord help us! I wonder how many others I've missed?'

'How many fatal fires have you had recently?' asked Lonsdale, thinking without enthusiasm about exhumations.

'Five or six.' Bradwell brightened a little. 'But I can quite safely state that none had a crushed head, and I'd have noticed if someone had taken a slice from the top of a complete one.'

'So, what happens now?' asked Lonsdale.

'I inform the police about my findings, and you

tell them why you suspected Donovan's death was not all it seemed. Then they investigate.'

Lonsdale regarded him for a moment. Yes, he would tell the police what he knew, but he would also meet Cath Walker tomorrow night. There might be credence to her claims after all.

Lonsdale was woken the next morning by the customary tap on his door, which preceded the entry of Hillary, the older, primmer of the household's two maids, with tea and toast. She placed the tray beside the bed and opened the curtains. Lonsdale pulled the sheet over his head to avoid the daylight.

While Lonsdale groaned and muttered his way into wakefulness, Hillary bustled about, brushing ash from the fireplace and lighting a fire. She then went to draw his bath, knowing that, although he invariably grumbled immediately upon awakening, soon he was bursting with energy. Thus, before long, Lonsdale had bathed, dressed, breakfasted, and was striding towards the offices of *The PMG*.

He had intended to spend the day investigating the Donovan case, but life as a reporter was never predictable, and he arrived to learn that one of the sub-editors was ill – and as the first liner through the door that morning, he was assigned to replace him. Lonsdale considered objecting, but not for long – he would not win the contest for a permanent post if he questioned orders. Then followed a day that was so hectic that he had scant time to even think of the man in the mortuary with the mangled head – other

51

than when he took ten minutes to talk to the policeman who came to take his statement at noon.

Late in the day, Stead called to Lonsdale, who stepped into the assistant editor's office.

'You have fifteen minutes,' said Stead, while standing with his back to the door, warming a glass of stout on some exposed hot-water pipes.

Lonsdale regarded him blankly. 'For what?'

'To be at the Garrick Club, where Harris will be waiting. So go – Voules can finish here.'

Lonsdale did not need to be told twice, as he would need to shift if he did not want to be late. 'You spoke to him?' he asked, brushing off his coat and grabbing his hat.

Stead nodded. 'He is expecting you. Can I assume that you will be meeting Miss Walker afterwards?'

'Most definitely,' said Lonsdale, nodding in a gesture of farewell and making for the door.

The Garrick Club occupied a handsome, twenty-year-old Italianate building near Leicester Square. The area was not the usual venue for such establishments – most were located near Pall Mall and St James's Street – but gentlemen's clubs were becoming increasingly popular, and more were being founded every few years. The Garrick was known for a membership that included actors, journalists, and barristers.

When Lonsdale arrived, Harris was waiting at the porter's lodge. 'You're late,' he said irritably, as he wrote their names on the thick cream paper of the visitors' book.

Harris was a stocky American, who possessed a wide jaw filled with a set of vast gleaming teeth that Lonsdale was certain were false. He had a long-standing bet on the matter with Hulda, who maintained that no one would spend good money on a set of dentures that looked so patently unreal. Several attempts by both had been made to find out the true status of the teeth, but Harris had so far eluded their efforts to solve the mystery.

'I appreciate your invitation,' said Lonsdale pleasantly. 'It's good of you.'

'It is,' agreed Harris gracelessly. 'And you can expect me to call on you for a return favour some day. You *and* Stead.'

Lonsdale raised his eyebrows. Reciprocation went without saying, so it was in poor taste to mention it. He fought down his dislike of the man, although something Hulda had said came unbidden into his mind – that Harris had a reputation for getting young, gullible reporters drunk, then stealing their ideas. Such behaviour – as well as his lack of subtlety and his natural tendency to boorishness – was part of why the American was unpopular among London's press fraternity. But the dislike went deeper than his personal qualities or the natural rivalry between reporters. Harris was seen as the embodiment of *The New York Herald*, a paper with a huge circulation and power in the United States – and that could even be purchased in London. But it was also a newspaper that most of the members of the English press considered to be, as one of Morley's friends wrote, 'cheap, filthy, false, and extravagant . . . appealing to the basest of instincts, with sensational stories about romance, rape, murder, suicide, and improbable tales from exotic lands.'

Despite his reservations about the man, Lonsdale followed Harris inside. The Garrick boasted the same elements as most clubs: a sizeable drawing room lit by tall windows; a more formal, panelled morning room; and a variety of other facilities, including a library and a billiards hall. On the walls of its impressive staircase was a magnificent collection of artwork, said to be the finest of any club in London. On the first floor there was a reading room, a coffee lounge, and a dining hall to cater for men who chose not to return home for an evening meal.

'Wilson will be in the reading room,' said Harris, pointing to a door. 'I've got better things to do than spend an evening in the company of *that* crusty old buzzard, so I'm off to eat. You can sign yourself out.'

'Very well,' said Lonsdale, thinking he would never let Harris loose in *his* club. Moreover, as Lonsdale was about to pester Wilson in the one place normally considered a haven from such encounters, Harris leaving him to his own devices was rather rash, as there were likely to be repercussions for the man who had let him in.

Lonsdale entered the reading room and immediately saw Wilson dozing near the fireplace, chest covered by a copy of that morning's *Standard*. He sat for a moment on a leather chair across from Wilson, to study his prey. The director of the Zoological Gardens possessed an ample belly, wild black eyebrows that looked as though they were trying to escape from him in any direction possible, and a bald crown circled by unruly tufts that had been rumpled into miniature horns. In the midst of his thick-featured face, blubbery lips quivered each time he breathed.

The reading room was almost empty. An elderly gentleman with mutton-chop whiskers muttered to himself next to the window, disturbing a thin gentleman who was trying to read a newspaper, while a third sat and gazed blankly into space. He sat so still that Lonsdale began to wonder if he was dead. Then a waiter arrived with a large glass of brandy and a box of cigars, and the man stirred to avail himself of them. Almost immediately, the pungent stench of the cigar filled the room; Lonsdale had seldom smelled anything quite so rank, even at the mortuary, and wondered why the fellow elected to choose such a brand.

Wilson awoke from his nap choking. 'Good God, man!' he gasped, flapping at the air in front of him. 'What are you burning this time? Nettles soaked in lion urine?'

'An interesting notion,' called his colleague cheerfully. 'Nettles are easy to come by, although the lion urine might prove a challenge. I don't suppose you could procure me a drop?'

Wilson glared at him, then produced his own case of cigars. After a moment's hesitation, he offered one to Lonsdale, who declined.

'These will help cover up the smell of Deacon's foul concoctions,' he said, before stopping and studying Lonsdale with a hard stare. 'I haven't

55

seen you here before, although you do have a familiar look. Are you a new member?'

'A guest of Ambrose Harris,' replied Lonsdale. He proffered a hand. 'Alec Lonsdale of *The Pall Mall Gazette*.'

Wilson's handshake was firm enough to hurt. 'Scurrilous Liberal rag! I have argued not to take it at the Garrick. Much better to have an honest, Conservative evening paper like *The St James's Gazette*.'

'I beg to differ,' said Lonsdale, more calmly than he felt was warranted after such an insult. 'Few newspapers offer more insightful political reviews than *The PMG*.'

'Rubbish,' retorted Wilson. '"Liberal" and "insightful" are mutually exclusive concepts. By the way, I'm Dr Oliver Wilson, secretary of the Royal Zoological Society and director of the Zoological Gardens. No doubt you've heard of me?'

'I've visited the zoo a number of times recently,' replied Lonsdale carefully. 'You've done an admirable job with the great apes.'

'We expect a renewed interest in apes over the next few weeks,' said Wilson, paring off the end of his cigar with a silver pocketknife. 'Darwin's death will resurrect the fascination with them that we had in the sixties.'

'People looking for their great-grandfather?' mused Lonsdale.

Wilson leaned back in his chair and eyed Lonsdale through a pall of smoke that was every bit as foul as Deacon's. 'Not a believer in natural selection? That's unusual in a man of your generation. They usually leap to defend modern science against us older, wiser fellows.'

'I accept most of Darwin's theories,' said Lonsdale. 'But only in nature. I can't agree with Herbert Spencer and those who apply Darwin's ideas to humans. If natural selection is operating in us, then why are there so many poor and sick?'

'Because our society has transcended the principles that apply to nature,' replied Wilson with unexpected vigour. 'We are godlike compared to the rest of the beasts, and we have used our powers to bypass natural selection. Now we need to use that knowledge to force natural selection to operate once again, for the benefit of our species as a whole.'

'How?' asked Lonsdale, not at all sure what Wilson was telling him.

'By not allowing the lower classes to breed indiscriminately, like animals – because we are *not* animals. We must decide who produces offspring, and who does not.'

'An *un*natural selection, you mean?' said Lonsdale coolly. He had heard such arguments before, and considered them unethical and impractical.

'On the contrary, what could be more natural than man using his intellect to improve his race? The greatest minds of all time have supported the notion. Plato's *Republic* idealized a society with constant selection for the improvement of human stock. And the Old Testament makes positive references to such concepts.'

'I'm not sure most experts on the Bible would

57

agree,' countered Lonsdale. 'And those examples don't speak to the reality of today.'

Wilson was becoming angry. 'In savage societies, the weak in body or mind soon die, so the ones that survive are stronger, healthier, more vigorous. But we, the "civilized" society, interfere with this process. We build hospitals for the sick, asylums for the imbeciles, and homes for the maimed. We try to extend life for every moment possible, which means the weak have been allowed to propagate. Anyone who has bred animals will tell you that this is highly injurious to the race of man.'

Lonsdale wanted to ask who, in Wilson's scheme, would decide which individuals were allowed to reproduce, but as he could not use such a frightening interpretation of evolutionary theory in his article, he decided he had better steer the conversation to something less controversial.

'Do you think—?'

'It's obvious,' Wilson interrupted, leaning forward with the gleam of the fanatic in his eyes, 'that the high birth rate among the poor is a threat to our very civilization. You see, morals and criminal behaviour are linked to specific physiological types. If a person possesses these physical features – which are much more common in the lower classes – then it's likely that his behaviour will soon degenerate into the criminal or the immoral. Because both behaviour and physiological types are inherited, these people *must* be prevented from producing offspring. Then we'll have what we all want – a world with no crime and no sin.'

'I don't think it's as simple as that,' Lonsdale objected.

'I've applied such methods in the zoo. I isolate the weak and ugly animals, and only allow the strong and attractive to breed. You must have noticed that all my monkeys are powerful, handsome beasts?'

'But people don't live in monkey houses,' Lonsdale pointed out. 'How do you propose to prevent human beings from breeding – short of putting them in our already overflowing prisons?'

'Something must be done, and it *will* be done,' replied the director. 'You'll see, soon enough.' He raised his paper to indicate that the discussion was over. It most certainly was *not* closed for Lonsdale, however.

'What do you mean?' he demanded, clenching his fists to prevent himself from hauling the newspaper away from Wilson's face.

The paper was lowered impatiently. 'Exactly what I say. We can't go on as we are. Our cities can't provide for a population that continues to increase, and the lower classes – which breed at such a ghastly pace – won't sit idly by and accept the division between rich and poor forever. Disraeli gave them a vote. Gladstone and his cronies gave them education. So now they have aspirations, and if we don't control them, they'll revolt. Now, if you'll excuse me, I must bid you goodnight.'

He tossed his newspaper to one side, and stalked out. Watching him leave, Lonsdale realized that the encounter had left him with nothing he could possibly use in his article.

* * *

59

The visit to the Garrick Club had not only been unproductive, it had made Lonsdale late for his meeting with Cath Walker. The bells had long since finished chiming eight and the light had almost faded when he reached the Gloucester Gate entrance to Regent's Park. He headed toward the huge drinking fountain on the Broad Walk – the wide but poorly lit road that traversed the park from north to south.

As Lonsdale neared the fountain, which was illuminated by its own lamp, he slowed and became more cautious. The path that led to the bandstand, a short distance west, appeared to be deserted. He peered into the darkness, and could just see the outline of the bandstand, eerie in the deepening shadows. He had not realized how few lights there were and how dark the park could be; a lone, unarmed man was an easy target. But he told himself that his experiences in Africa – which had taught him more than a modicum of self-defence – combined with having boxed at Cambridge, made him capable of defending himself reasonably respectably.

He approached the bandstand warily. It had a conical roof supported by wrought-iron pillars and was surrounded by waist-high railings. The chairs on which the band sat were piled in the middle and covered with a tarpaulin. There was no one to be seen.

He was reaching for the railing when a rustle brought him to a standstill. Away to the right was a row of bushes and trees, a pleasant, shady area for those who did not want to sit in the sun to listen to music. Had the noise come from there? He took several steps towards it.

'Miss Walker?' he called softly. For several moments, nothing happened, then there was a dull thud behind him. He had spun round before realizing with disgust that he had fallen for an old trick: someone had thrown a stone behind him to make him turn, so he could be attacked from behind.

He had barely started to whip back around when he was knocked from his feet. He went sprawling onto the wet ground, feeling sodden grass against his face. He rolled, aware that his attacker was already bearing down on him. Against the dark grey sky, he saw something glint before it plunged down.

He squirmed sideways and kicked out, catching his assailant across the backs of his legs. There was a grunt as the man tumbled to the ground, but as Lonsdale struggled to his knees, someone else grabbed him from behind. A detached part of his mind acknowledged that Jack had been right – Cath *had* enticed him to an isolated spot where he could be robbed. Anger at his own gullibility spurred him into action.

He jabbed his elbow backwards into the groin of the man behind him, putting every last ounce of his strength into it. There was a satisfying howl of pain, and the man doubled over. The man with the knife circled, a dim silhouette in the dark. Lonsdale feinted to his left, and then followed with a right cross that connected with the man's jaw with a loud crack. The man went down as though poleaxed and lay still.

Lonsdale swung round quickly, sensing that the knifeman's accomplice had recovered and was preparing another attack, but a well-aimed rock hit him squarely on the eyebrow, making bright lights explode inside his head. He struck out blindly to deter the man from coming too close, but when his vision cleared, he did not see his assailant advancing on him but disappearing into the night. He had fled.

Lonsdale knew that the most sensible course of action would be to leave, but he surmised that if Cath's friends were there, so was she. And he was going to find her. He ignored the still-prostrate attacker and strode to the bushes, listening intently. There was a soft sound, like a moan, then all was silent. He pushed aside an overhanging branch, but could see nothing. He grabbed a stick and began prodding in the undergrowth, aiming to flush her out.

'Cath! I know you're—'

He stopped as his foot encountered something soft. He knelt and reached out. His fingers encountered something warm and sticky, and he withdrew them with a sharp intake of breath. Blood! He struggled to light a match. It had barely flared into life before he dropped it in shock, plunging him into darkness once more. Cursing his unsteady hands, he lit another. Lying on her side in the long grass was Cath Walker. He reached out and touched her cheek with the back of his hand. It was still warm, although the gaping wound in her throat and the glassy-eyed stare confirmed she was dead.

He sat back on his heels in bewilderment. Then

the flame burned his fingers and brought him to his senses. He stood and hurried back towards the place he had been attacked, aiming to lay hold of the second assailant. But the place was deserted.

Hoping to find a constable, Lonsdale ran back to the Broad Walk, as he knew the police patrolled it at night. As he skidded to a halt on the muddy gravel, a man wearing a top hat shot him a nervous look and hurried on. Lonsdale looked around wildly, then spotted the distinctive domed hat of a policeman in the distance. He tore towards him.

'There's a dead woman in the bushes near the bandstand,' he gasped, seizing the constable's arm. 'I think she's been murdered.'

The constable was young, and excitement suffused his face at the prospect of a vicious crime to explore. He whipped out his rattle and whirled it furiously to attract colleagues within hearing distance. Then he raced off towards the bandstand. Not knowing what else to do, Lonsdale followed, although his thoughts reeled and his head ached. He raised one hand to his head and felt a tender spot where the stone had hit him.

'She's dead!' yelled the policeman, when Lonsdale had directed him to the spot where the body of Cath Walker lay.

'Yes,' said Lonsdale tiredly. 'She was a—'

'Murder!' bellowed the policeman, accompanying a frantic and ineffective search of the bushes with more violent shaking of his rattle. Eventually, his colleagues began to arrive. A sergeant took control, while the youngster was posted to the

Broad Walk to search for witnesses. Suddenly exhausted, Lonsdale sank down, his back against the metal railing and his chin on his knees.

'What happened, sir?' called the sergeant, swiping through the undergrowth with vigorous sweeps of his truncheon. 'A lovers' tiff that ended in violence?'

'It most certainly was not,' replied Lonsdale indignantly. 'The woman was a prostitute.'

'I didn't mean between you and her, sir,' said the sergeant placidly. 'I meant between her and him.' He pushed back a bush to reveal a second crumpled figure lying in the wet leaves. 'There are two corpses here, sir, not just one.'

Within the hour, one Inspector George Peters – a lean, spare man whose droopy moustache served to enhance his resemblance to an elderly spaniel – appeared. He ordered the area cordoned off and the search of the bushes abandoned until daylight. Then he turned to questioning Lonsdale.

Unfortunately, the attack had happened fast and a long way from the nearest light, so Lonsdale was unable to furnish much of a description of his assailants. All he could say was they were smaller than him, and had worn dark clothes.

'Really?' asked Peters coolly. 'It may have escaped your notice, Mr Lonsdale, but most men wear dark clothes. Unless they are performing in music halls.'

'I'm sorry.' Lonsdale rubbed his eyes. 'It all happened so fast. One minute I was calling the prostitute's name, and the next they were all over me.'

'They had knives, you say?'

'One had a knife. The other threw a stone.'

'And where is this stone now?' asked Peters.

Lonsdale stared at him incredulously. 'I don't know. On the ground, I imagine. Why?'

Peters shrugged, and with a shock Lonsdale realized that the inspector did not believe a word he was saying. He wondered how to convince the man. He had no desire for a sojourn in police custody until he could contact Jack. But even as he fretted, salvation came in the unlikely form of Robert Bradwell, summoned to inspect the bodies *in situ*.

'We meet again,' Bradwell said, shaking Lonsdale's hand warmly. 'Which is more than I can say about my wife. I haven't been home since I saw you and I'm due at the hospital tonight. I'll have to wait until tomorrow to face her wrath.' Without further ado, he headed for the bodies. Peters resumed his discussion with Lonsdale, who was feeling wet, cold, and miserable.

'So, let me summarize,' said Peters, after Lonsdale had related his story yet again. 'You came to meet this unfortunate – Cath Walker – in an attempt to discover more about the murder of Patrick Donovan?'

Lonsdale nodded. 'She said she'd bring someone to answer questions, so we could publish the story in *The Pall Mall Gazette* and put a stop to it.'

'I see,' said Peters. 'Put a stop to what, exactly?'

'I don't know.' Lonsdale sensed that the more he said, the less convincing he sounded.

65

'She claimed Donovan was at least the sixth to have died, although the only one in a fire.'

'Although remember that Donovan didn't die in the fire,' put in Bradwell helpfully, having finished his duties in the bushes. 'He died because he was strangled.'

'What?' blurted Lonsdale. 'You didn't mention this yesterday.'

'I didn't know it then. After you left, I re-examined the body, and found that Donovan's hyoid was broken, although the other neck bones were intact. That's a classic sign of strangulation – as were faint ligature marks in the charred flesh. So, Donovan was strangled, his cerebrum removed, and his skull smashed and his house burned to make his death appear accidental.'

'Wait,' said Peters, raising his hand. He turned to Lonsdale, and fixed him with stern eyes. 'I hope you're not thinking of printing this in your newspaper?'

'We never publish details of police investigations without consent,' said Lonsdale indignantly. 'We're not *The Echo*, you know.'

'Good,' said Peters. 'You may report that there's been a double murder in the park, but keep this other business to yourself. In fact, I'll make you an offer – stay silent until I have this matter in hand, and I'll give you the details twenty-four hours before I release them to any other papers.'

'Fair enough,' said Lonsdale, thinking that all he really wanted was to go home and soak away the horrors of the night in a hot bath. 'I'll let my editor know.'

'However, do not take this as permission to begin your own investigation,' said Peters. 'That would be most inadvisable.'

'Why would someone go to such lengths over a person like Donovan?' asked Bradwell. 'I can see someone making an effort to disguise the murder of an aristocrat or a politician. But Donovan was a shop assistant.'

'You're asking the wrong question,' said Lonsdale, watching two constables carry Cath away on a stretcher. 'Instead, consider why someone was so determined to have his cerebrum.'

'Good point,' agreed Bradwell, nodding. 'The fire seems to have been arranged specifically to ensure that no one noticed it had been taken.'

Peters looked from one to the other, his expression deeply sceptical. 'But who would have a penchant for . . . a cerebrum did you call it? Whoever it might be, if we believe Walker's claim that Donovan was at least the sixth victim, then he has done rather well for himself. But she was an unfortunate, and, in my experience, such women are not reliable witnesses.'

'Yet it would be rash to dismiss her, just because others in her profession have lied,' argued Bradwell. 'Donovan's death is odd, and she clearly knew something about it.'

'Perhaps,' said Peters, in the bland tone that Lonsdale began to realize was his normal manner of speaking. 'But it occurs to me that Mr Lonsdale has a very good reason for wanting us to believe someone *else* might've killed this potentially valuable witness.'

Bradwell raised his hand to silence Lonsdale's

67

immediate protestations. 'But Lonsdale discussed her claim with me at the mortuary yesterday. He'd hardly have told me he was planning to meet her if he intended to dispatch the woman, would he?'

'Maybe not,' hedged Peters, cautiously.

'I'm telling you the truth,' Lonsdale said quietly. 'She said she'd bring proof. Have you searched her body? Perhaps she has something in her pockets that'll answer your questions.'

'Of course we searched her body – and that of her friend,' said Peters, the edge to his voice suggesting that he did not need Lonsdale to tell him how to do his work. 'There was nothing on either.' He turned to Bradwell. 'She claimed another six victims, but surely you would have noticed the absence of a cerebrum in any of your bodies, yes?'

'I would, of course. However, there is always a possibility that they went to another mortuary. Or were buried secretly. The lack of cerebra in—'

'The lack of what?' came a sharply disapproving voice from behind. 'What in the devil are you talking about?'

'It seems we may have an overlap between cases, sir,' said Peters, turning to nod a greeting; Bradwell promptly made himself scarce. 'Mr Lonsdale, may I introduce Superintendent Ramsey and his assistant, Chief Inspector Leonard.'

Ramsey nodded at Lonsdale but made no attempt to shake hands, although his assistant smiled pleasantly enough. The two officers could not have been more different. The superintendent was tall, aloof and self-important, with a thick, white moustache; his lofty demeanour and elegant dress made him appear more like a member of the House of Lords than a policeman. His assistant was short, thin, and cheerful, and wore a Norfolk jacket and the kind of old-fashioned knickerbockers that Lonsdale was surprised could still be purchased.

'Mr Lonsdale is assisting us with our enquiries,' Peters said. 'Or would you care to take charge of the case?'

'Hardly, George!' laughed Leonard. 'The super-intendent has more important—'

'Every murder is important,' Ramsey interrupted pompously. 'It doesn't matter if the victim is a Member of Parliament or an unfortunate. I'll main-tain a watch on it, but the case is yours, Peters. Now tell us what happened.'

Both officers listened as Peters gave them a summary. Leonard shook his head in silent compas-sion, while Ramsey's sallow face remained expressionless. When Peters mentioned the mutilation of Donovan, Ramsey gave a shudder of disgust.

'These damned perverts! You put one behind bars, and another appears. London is a veritable breeding ground for them. We need to nip this one in the bud, Peters. I don't want head-stealing lunatics frightening every decent soul in the city.'

And with that, he turned and strode away, not deigning to acknowledge the salutes of his constables. Leonard shot Peters an apologetic smile and made a hurried offer of help before hurrying after him.

69

'You may be reading too much into this, Bradwell,' said Peters when Bradwell reappeared, continuing the discussion as though the two officers had not interrupted. He pulled a pipe from his pocket and began to tamp it with tobacco. 'You're trying to intellectualize what might be a simple, brutish crime.'

'Simple?' echoed Bradwell. 'Someone went to a good deal of trouble to try to make me miss the fact that Donovan had been strangled and mutilated. It wasn't simple, Inspector, although I concur it was brutal.'

Peters was thoughtful. 'How about this for an explanation,' he began, puffing billows of white smoke into the still night air. 'Donovan was strangled over some private grudge, and his body mutilated as a bizarre form of revenge. When Walker saw Mr Lonsdale making notes at the scene of his death, she saw an opportunity to lure him here to rob him. But her accomplices decided a four-way division of spoils was less attractive than a two-way split, and killed her and her friend. Mr Lonsdale then fought off the remaining two.'

It was a plausible scenario, and Lonsdale could not deny that he had questioned her motives himself. He did not reply, so Peters began to issue orders to his men, instructing them to find out where she had lived and the identity of her companion. While respectable London would soon be retiring to bed, another side of the city would just be waking. It was among them that Peters would concentrate his search.

'You can give your formal statement tomorrow,

Mr Lonsdale,' he said. 'Tonight, I'd rather have my men out on the streets looking for the killers.'

'One of the policemen who attended the fire at Donovan's house knew Cath Walker,' said Lonsdale helpfully. 'He might know where she lived.'

'There are hundreds of police officers in London,' said Peters dryly. 'I don't suppose you could furnish me with a name?'

'No, but I can tell you the number he wore on his collar.'

'Yes?' Peters looked marginally impressed.

'Six-nine-six-D.'

Peters stared at him. 'Are you sure?' he asked eventually.

'Yes, of course,' said Lonsdale, puzzled. 'Why?'

'Police Constable Cyril Iverson, number six-nine-six-D, is no longer with the force,' replied Peters. 'He disappeared six months ago, while on duty, and hasn't been seen since. Well, not by us at least. His antics have certainly been reported by a number of other people, however.'

Three

The background buzz of conversation in the Queen's Arms and the warm, slightly humid feel of too many people crammed into one room were making Lonsdale drowsy. He leaned back and gazed up at the ceiling, noting it was stained from decades of smoke. The floor was not much better. What had been a handsome red and gold carpet was dulled where booted feet had tracked the muck of the streets across it. The walls, on the other hand, were a rich brown pine boarding, which looked new. Cigar and pipe smoke enveloped all in a thick, hazy pall.

He had already drunk more than was wise, and it proved difficult to bring his attention back to the discussion. It had been Bradwell's suggestion to continue their conversation in the nearby tavern. Peters had readily agreed, although Lonsdale suspected it was only in the hope of gaining more information. Of course, Lonsdale's motive was the same – he wanted the opportunity to quiz Peters. And Bradwell? Lonsdale had a suspicion that he was eager to avoid his wife.

All the private bars – the screened-off booths in which patrons had some seclusion – had been full, so the three men had taken a table in a corner of the public bar, surrounded by omnibus drivers, shopkeepers, and labourers.

'I told you Iverson was ill months ago,' said Bradwell, as Lonsdale mentally re-entered the conversation. 'I spoke to his wife, and she told me he often talked about suicide. The poor man is deranged.'

Lonsdale took another sip of the bad port that Bradwell had bought him. 'So, you think Iverson may have killed Donovan – then dispatched Cath Walker and her companion?'

'There's no evidence to say so,' replied Peters, although it was clear he considered it a possibility.

'He definitely knew her,' said Lonsdale. 'He addressed her by name and asked if she was soliciting. She ran away; I assumed from a prostitute's natural fear of the police.'

'Fear?' snorted Peters. 'If that were true, our job would be a damned sight easier! These women don't fear us, Mr Lonsdale. Distrust, perhaps. Loathe, certainly. But fear – no. What can a policeman do other than lock a prostitute up for a few nights in a place where she'll be warm and fed?'

'And that's more than most can expect on the streets,' put in Bradwell. 'A policeman's lot might not be a happy one, but a whore's is worse.'

'Cath was afraid,' said Lonsdale firmly. 'She almost fell over in her haste to escape.'

'So describe Iverson,' ordered Peters. 'We need to be sure the man you saw was not just someone wearing a uniform bought cheap in a tavern.

Lonsdale considered carefully before replying. 'He was forty to forty-five years old, and had a large blackish-grey moustache that needed trimming. He had a beer-drinker's paunch and the mottled skin of a man who likes spirits. He had dark eyes that were watery, and a scar that ran into one eyebrow.'

'You're observant,' remarked Peters. 'And you've a good memory for details.'

'I met a good many people of low integrity while I was in the Colonial Service,' said Lonsdale, 'many of them diplomats. It was as important for me to remember their faces as it is for you to know those of thieves and robbers.'

Peters gave what was almost a smile. His moustache twitched and some teeth made a fleeting appearance beneath it.

'Iverson's appearance is very distinctive with that scar,' said Bradwell, snapping his fingers to attract the attention of a tap-boy and order more drinks. 'That's why I'm surprised he hasn't been caught yet. Would you be offended if I suggested that some of your men might be protecting him, Inspector?'

Peters looked at Lonsdale. 'Iverson's scar was earned when he saved another officer from a partially collapsed railway tunnel. Policemen are a loyal breed, and it goes against the grain to betray each other, but Iverson's case is different. We all know he's ill, and I don't think anyone would help him stay free when he should be in a hospital.'

'What do you mean by "ill" exactly?' asked Lonsdale.

Peters answered quickly, as though he did not want Bradwell revealing too much. 'Policemen see some dreadful sights, and he isn't the first to crack under the strain.'

'But Iverson's case is more than just cracking under the strain, isn't it?' fished Lonsdale. 'Earlier, you didn't seem surprised when I told you he'd spoken to Cath, or that he was at the scene of Donovan's murder.'

'His presence in Wyndham Street doesn't mean he killed Donovan,' said Peters.

'Well, I can tell you that he didn't have a cerebrum with him when we spoke,' said Lonsdale, then reconsidered. 'Unless it was in his pocket.'

'The cerebrum is fragile,' said Bradwell. 'Ramming it into a pocket would ruin it.'

74

'Would that matter?' asked Lonsdale. 'Perhaps he didn't intend to keep it, and the excitement lay in its removal.'

Peters toyed with his glass of four-ale, then raised it to his lips and drained the remainder, standing to leave as he did so.

'I must return to the station,' he said. He nodded his thanks to Bradwell for the drinks, and then fixed Lonsdale with a stern eye. 'You'll remember our agreement? No word of this until I say?'

Lonsdale nodded.

Peters sighed. 'You'd think there was more than enough crime and tragedy in this city to satisfy the press, but they always want more. Take a walk in Whitechapel or Spitalfields, Mr Lonsdale. You'll see enough to keep your newspaper in tales of scandal, vice, and wickedness for a decade.'

'He's a cheery soul,' remarked Lonsdale, watching the inspector thread his way through the crowded bar.

'But a fine detective,' said Bradwell. 'Don't be fooled by that plodding façade. Had he thought you were lying, you'd be in his cells now. I doubt it'll be too long before your audience will be reading this story; if anyone can get to the bottom of it, Peters can.'

'I assume Cath died from the wound to her throat?' asked Lonsdale, deciding he had better collect some facts if Peters was as good as Bradwell claimed.

'There was a single slash to her neck, severing the jugular vein and carotid artery on the left side, and slicing through the trachea,' said Bradwell.

'Is that a common way to kill?'

'Fairly,' said the surgeon. 'Cutting a throat is easy and takes very little power. All too often the police assume a killer is male because of its violent nature, but I'm sure a good many are women.'

'What about a theft of a cerebrum?' asked Lonsdale. 'Was that committed by a man or woman? I suppose it requires no great strength either.'

'On the contrary, the brain is surrounded by a protective layer of bone, and sawing through it is hard work.'

'Did Cath's companion die from knife wounds as well?' asked Lonsdale as they made their way outside, to stand with their hands in their pockets in the cold night.

'No,' said Bradwell. 'He was probably poisoned with arsenic.'

Lonsdale stared at him in astonishment. A crowd of drunken dockers staggered past, cheering and laughing. Behind them were three women with hard, calculating eyes, doggedly keeping pace with men who would soon be in no position to decline an offer of their services. One gave Lonsdale and Bradwell a speculative glance, but evidently decided the pickings would be better with the rowdy wharfmen.

'Arsenic? But that makes no sense!'

'Yet it's true, because the body displayed all the characteristic signs of arsenic poisoning, and I recognized the smell of it in his mouth.'

'But how, for God's sake?'

Bradwell shrugged. 'As I told you before, I present the facts to the police and leave them to do the speculating.' He glanced at his watch. 'I'm taking a hansom to Bart's Hospital. I'd offer you a lift, but I doubt you live Clerkenwell way.'

'Other direction.' Lonsdale held out his hand to the doctor. 'Let's hope that the next time we meet will be in more pleasant circumstances.'

'I doubt it,' sighed Bradwell. 'I seldom meet anyone in pleasant circumstances.'

The next morning, Lonsdale woke with a bruise over one eye and a stiff shoulder to remind him of the previous night's events. He left before Jack could see it, and took a cab to Marylebone Lane police station, where he dictated his statement to a sergeant with the largest handlebar moustache he had ever seen. He then walked briskly to *The PMG*'s offices, ascending the rickety wooden staircase to the first floor in the hope of finding Stead. There was a thick cloud of dust outside the reporters' office, and voices were raised in protest. Intrigued, Lonsdale poked his head around the door.

The formidable Hulda Friederichs stood on a stool in the centre of the room armed with a rag tied to a long stick. She was flailing at the ribbons of cobwebs that hung like stalactites from the ceiling, bringing down flakes of ancient brown paint as she did so. Her colleagues cried their objections, but Hulda was not a woman to be deterred by mere words. And it would be a brave man who attempted to use force.

Watching from a safe distance, arms folded and eyes flashing with amusement, was Stead. He saw Lonsdale, and his merriment faded. Leaving the chaos, he took Lonsdale by the elbow and led him to his own office, closing the door behind them.

'What happened to your eye?' he asked.

'My meeting with Cath Walker,' explained Lonsdale, and quickly described what had happened.

Stead tugged at his bushy beard. 'I had a visit this morning from a Chief Inspector Leonard. Nice fellow. He told me that you had stumbled across more murders. Three in two days, Lonsdale! That's remarkable by anyone's standards.'

'I think Cath and her companion were dispatched to prevent them telling me about Donovan's death,' said Lonsdale, and began to outline his theories. Stead listened, his vivid blue eyes never leaving his reporter's face. When Lonsdale finished, the assistant editor scrubbed at his luxurious beard, and then sprang to his feet, to pace back and forth in front of the mantelpiece.

'*The PMG* always complies with the wishes of the police in the interests of justice,' he said, tossing an egg from hand to hand. 'I told Leonard that we'll go no further than a simple statement saying two people were murdered in Regent's Park last night. He assures me that the park murders and the death by fire are unrelated.'

'But they—'

Stead raised a finger to quell Lonsdale's objections, but the reporter started again.

'But Cath said—'

Seeing the authoritative finger was not going to work, Stead threw Lonsdale the egg, forcing him to scramble to catch it before it smashed on the carpet. It was, Lonsdale supposed as he juggled with it, a novel way to shut someone up.

'It matters not one iota what you think, as nothing will be printed until the case is closed. Leonard promised to pass us all the details a day before releasing them to the rest of the press. Now, a day might be an eternity in journalism, but it isn't long to write a decently researched article containing interviews with the people involved.'

Lonsdale saw immediately what Stead was suggesting. He opened his mouth to speak, but Stead had another egg and it was already sailing towards the grimy glass cupboard on Lonsdale's left. Lonsdale's hand shot out, and the brown missile slapped into his palm.

'Talk to Donovan's neighbours,' ordered Stead. 'Find out what kind of man he was, and discover why anyone should want to kill him. Then go south of the river, and see about this murdered girl.'

'Girl?' asked Lonsdale. 'You mean Cath, the prostitute?'

Stead fixed him with a hard stare. 'She was a girl – twenty-three years old, forced to sell the one commodity that someone is always willing to buy, just to have a four-pence bed for the night.'

'How do you know how old she was?' asked Lonsdale, recalling that Stead had an unwavering compassion for prostitutes, and often used *The*

PMG to highlight their miseries to the newspaper's readers. 'Because she looked a lot more than twenty-three.'

'If so, that's more a reflection on our society than on her,' said Stead. 'But we're wasting time. I managed to squeeze from a friend in Scotland Yard that she lived in Bermondsey. Go there – find out about her and the man who died with her. Learning his name would be a start.'

'So you believe me – that Donovan's death and the murders in the park are connected?' asked Lonsdale, astonished that Stead was prepared to let him investigate when the police had asked for discretion.

'I do,' said Stead. 'Poor Miss Walker and her friend died trying to tell you about Donovan, so you are under a moral obligation to ensure that they didn't die in vain. Moreover, it is significant that this missing policeman, Iverson, was at the scene of the fire, and that she was terrified of him. He might be at the heart of the whole affair.'

'He might.'

'Then off you go,' said Stead, selecting a third egg from a box on his desk and tossing it so high in the air that it almost hit the ceiling. He turned and caught the egg behind his back. 'Take Hulda with you.'

'Friederichs?' blurted Lonsdale. 'But she's—'

'A woman?' asked Stead, raising quixotic eyebrows. 'Exactly! You can't let it be known that you're a reporter, or you'll have people selling you all kinds of lies for the price of a beer. Hulda will make a splendid foil. After all, who'd imagine that we'd send a female journalist into the roughest areas of London? Besides, she needs the experience.'

'Very well,' said Lonsdale reluctantly.

'But before you go, I want the zoo story. Go, go! You have not a moment to lose!'

In reply, Lonsdale lobbed both eggs he was holding at Stead, who, as he had anticipated, made no attempt to catch them.

'Hard-boiled,' grinned Stead.

Completing the article on the Zoological Gardens was not easy when the Prussian Governess leaned over his shoulder every five minutes to see if he had finished. When she was not demanding to know if he was writing a novel, she was swiping at those cobwebs she had missed earlier. Sensibly, the other reporters had made themselves scarce, Voules trailing an especially repellent, dust-enriched cobweb that everyone noticed, but no one mentioned. Eventually, the article was written, approved, and sent to the compositors on the top floor.

'At last!' exclaimed Hulda, wiping her hands on a manly handkerchief. 'Are you ready now, or do you want to write about the decline of the barter system in rural Bechuanaland? Stead told me you know it well.'

'What an excellent idea!' exclaimed Lonsdale, sitting down again and reaching for his pen. 'It will only take an hour or two.'

She gaped in dismay until Lonsdale flung his pen down and made for the door, laughing at her for being so gullible.

He led the way out of the building and walked

towards the Strand, suddenly struck by the dismal greyness of London compared to the vivid wonders of Africa. In what, when he was assigned there, had been known as the West African Settlements, he had seen mounds of red, green, and orange fruits piled on brightly coloured rugs and sold by women in clothes the colours of rainbows. By contrast, the apples and potatoes on the street barrows of London had a tired, wizened look, and the vendors' faces were pinched grey with cold above their filthy aprons.

'I suggest we visit Donovan's neighbours first,' he said. 'We can walk there in forty minutes. Or take a hansom – you choose.'

Hulda put her hands on her hips. 'We could never manage that distance in forty minutes! Unless we ran, which is not something I feel inclined to do. Of course we shall take a cab.'

'A cab it is then,' muttered Lonsdale, flagging one down.

Appointing Hulda had not been a popular decision among the staff of *The PMG* – not because she was a woman, but because she was Hulda. She was aggressive, spoke her mind without considering the consequences, and was of the opinion that she was a better journalist than most of her associates. She was not someone Lonsdale would have chosen to work with, but no one went against Stead's specific instructions.

He glanced at her out of the corner of his eye. She was pretty, but severe looking. Her thick fair hair was scraped austerely back from her face in a neat, no-nonsense bun. Her blue eyes were icy, but her complexion was fresh and clear.

She held herself so erect that she looked down her nose at people, even those taller than her, and her clothes were immaculate. She had not been nicknamed 'the Prussian Governess' for nothing.

The cab was cramped once Hulda had her floor-length skirt, pelisse, and gable bonnet wedged in, leaving Lonsdale barely enough room to sit. Even so, he received a withering look as she freed her skirt from underneath him with an irritable tug.

'Why are we going to Wyndham Street first?' she asked. 'Why not go straight to Bermondsey? That is where the real answers lie.'

'Because of the time,' explained Lonsdale, cramped and uncomfortable in the small space she had allotted him. 'No self-respecting prostitute will be up at eleven o'clock on a Saturday morning.'

'Why are *you* familiar with the daily routines of whores?' asked Hulda, regarding him with a disconcertingly candid gaze. 'Are you a customer?'

It was not a question a decent lady would ask, and for a moment Lonsdale was at a loss as to how to respond. He was saved from a reply – and he suspected that a denial or an affirmation would meet with equal disapproval – by the horse stumbling in a pothole.

'Watch where you're going!' yelled Hulda in stentorian tones to the driver. 'We are not at Ascot, you know!'

Lonsdale cringed, hoping the driver would not be rash enough to answer back, sure that if he did an altercation would follow. Hurriedly, he resumed the conversation.

'But Wyndham Street is solidly respectable. Its residents will be up and awake.'

'Yes, but out working,' Hulda pointed out. 'Not lounging about at home.'

'The men perhaps, but we want to speak to their wives – people who were at home when Donovan's house caught on fire.'

Hulda nodded. 'So, how shall we approach them? Honestly, making it clear we're reporters?'

'Stead said we'd have more luck if we didn't. I noticed that there was a house for rent in Wyndham Street. Across the street and down a bit from Donovan's. We could pose as a married couple considering a move to the area.'

'You mean pretend we're married to *each other*?' asked Hulda, aghast. 'Me to you?'

'I doubt we'd get far if we pretended to be married to other people,' said Lonsdale dryly. 'It would offend their morals if I claimed to be a married man intending to move in with someone else's wife.'

'All right then,' conceded Hulda reluctantly. 'What occupation will you claim? You're too untidy to be a clerk, and your clothes are too good for you to be a menial. How about a glass-blower?'

'We should stick to what we know,' said Lonsdale, wondering how she had come up with such a bizarre choice. 'How about an accountant at the zoo? And you can be a ticket vendor at the Haymarket Theatre.'

'Very well,' agreed Hulda. 'Are you sure they won't remember you?'

'They probably will, but why shouldn't I have

84

been looking for a suitable house alone, before bringing my wife to see it?'

'You'll have to remember to call me Hulda, though. Do you have a match, by any chance?'

'Why?'

'Why do you think?' She took a La Jurista cigar from her bag, waggled her fingers for the matches, and lit up. Acrid smoke began to billow round Lonsdale. He leaned forward, pretending to look at houses, in the vain hope of escaping the stench.

'Please don't ask for a light or a glass of brandy if any witnesses invite us into their homes,' he warned. 'I don't want to miss out on information because you like to smoke and drink.'

'Don't be so fastidious!' she said testily. 'Many women smoke and drink these days.'

'Not the ones who live in Wyndham Street. While we're there, just pretend to be a normal person.'

'But I'm not a normal person,' objected Hulda. 'I'm a very superior person.'

'Your name,' said Lonsdale curiously. 'Is it really Prussian?'

'It is,' replied Hulda proudly. 'I was born in Ronsdorf in Rhenish Prussia. My grandfather once told my mother that unless all of her children were christened with Prussian names, he would exclude her from his will.'

'And did "Hulda" satisfy him?'

'You mean did he leave her an inheritance? Yes, he did, although what was left once his debts had been paid was not a great deal. My family's financial position was one reason I

85

sought a profession in which I could rise to the top, as I am currently doing.'

Lonsdale was spared from having to reply because they were travelling down Crawford Street. He banged on the roof to tell the driver to stop. Hulda regarded him askance.

'We're not there yet. What are you doing?'

'A ticket vendor and an accountant are hardly likely to arrive in a hansom when there's a perfectly good omnibus service,' he said. 'We don't want people to be suspicious before we begin. Come on. It's not far.'

They walked to the blackened ruins of Donovan's house. Most of its roof had collapsed, exposing the timbers beneath. The tiny garden at the front was full of broken glass and soggy, burnt wood. The door was charred, but still firmly closed.

'I want to look at the back of the house,' said Lonsdale, leading the way to the alley. He considered taking Hulda's arm, as a man might do with his wife, but was afraid she would bludgeon him with the hefty bag she carried.

The rear door lay in the back garden, the freshly splintered wood showing where the firemen had smashed it with their axes to enter. Lonsdale crouched next to it and inspected the lock. It was still intact, with the metal bar protruding from it, while the doorframe hosted an impressive gash where the bar had torn through the wood. So, he thought, it had been locked when the firemen had forced their way in.

Glass and cinders crunched under his feet as he walked inside. The walls were expanses of scorched wood and hanging timbers, while the stairs had been burned away completely, and the upstairs rooms had collapsed downwards in heaps of blackened rubble. Dark grey clouds were visible between the remaining roof joists. Lonsdale's foot went clear through a floorboard in the hall, forcing him to grab at the remains of a banister to prevent him from plunging to the cellar below.

'There's nothing to see,' said Hulda, surveying the damage from the door. 'Come out; it isn't safe. The roof will go at any minute.'

'I need to examine the front door,' said Lonsdale, extricating his foot and resuming his journey. 'Stay there.'

When he reached the door, he was not surprised that Donovan's neighbours had been unable to break through, as a heavy chest had been placed across it. The box had been opened by looters, but the unburned floor underneath when he tugged it away suggested he was the first to move it since the fire.

So either Donovan had put it there after raising the alarm, or someone else had done so with the intention of preventing anyone from trying to rescue him. The first solution made no sense. The second, along with the rear door being secured, fitted Lonsdale's suspicion that someone had gone to a good deal of trouble to hide the fact that Donovan's death was no accident.

'Lonsdale!' yelled Hulda suddenly as there was a groan of tearing wood. 'Look out!'

* * *

Lonsdale could only cringe against the wall with his arms over his head as several roof tiles slipped from one of the sagging rafters and hit the ground with ear-shattering explosions. Then the beam itself fell, thumping down next to him in a cloud of choking, black dust. Before anything else came down, he scrambled over the beam and aimed for the back door. There was another creak, directly above. Instinctively, he glanced up, and then fell heavily as his foot caught in the hole he had made on his way inside.

The creak grew louder, and Lonsdale struggled to stand, but his foot had snagged on the jagged wood and he could not pull it free. Then strong hands grabbed his collar, the charred floorboards flew away from his foot, and he was hauled forward. There was an almighty crash as more of the roof collapsed, right where he had been lying, and for a few moments he could see nothing but swirling ash and cinders. The hand tightened on his collar, and he was assisted, none too gently, into the garden. He bent, hands on knees, as he struggled to clear his lungs of the suffocating dust.

'I warned you,' said Hulda tartly, relinquishing her hold and brushing herself down. 'I told you it wasn't safe, and you put me in danger by forcing me to come to your rescue.'

'Not so!' he wheezed. 'I told you to stay outside.'

'Ungrateful wretch! Next time, I'll just stand and watch! You could at least say thank you.'

'Thank you,' said Lonsdale, realizing he had been ungracious. 'I mean it.'

She sniffed to acknowledge his capitulation,

and tried to brush some of the ash from his clothes. She was still dusty herself, but to reciprocate was more than his life was worth. When she deemed him presentable, they made their way to the front of the house.

'You do realize we are being watched,' she whispered.

'Where?'

'Number twenty-seven,' said Hulda. 'And now she's coming out.'

'What are you doing?' demanded a harsh female voice. 'There's nothing left to steal. This is a respectable neighbourhood, so why don't you leave us alone? Oh, it's you.'

It was the wife of the railway guard whom Lonsdale had met on the day of the fire. He recalled her name was Mrs North. He smiled and tipped his hat, while she continued to regard him suspiciously.

'We haven't come to loot,' he explained. 'My wife and I are thinking of moving into number thirty-five. I came the day before yesterday to look around the area. I'm an accountant you see – and I need to be near my work at the zoo.'

The woman's manner softened somewhat, although her eyes remained wary. 'I remember – I suppose you saw more than you bargained for, then?'

'You could say that,' agreed Lonsdale. 'And my wife is anxious. Was it an accident, do you think, this poor gentleman's death?'

'Of course it was an accident!' exclaimed Mrs North. 'What else could it have been? This is a respectable . . .'

89

She stopped abruptly when Hulda astonished her and Lonsdale alike by giving a groan and pressing her hand to her stomach.

'It's the baby,' she whispered, in a remarkable change to the local accent, while giving Mrs North a weak little smile.

Horrified, Lonsdale took a step away.

'For heaven's sake!' exclaimed Mrs North, rushing to Hulda's side. 'Don't duck away from her like a cornered rat! Help her into my house.'

'I couldn't possibly impose . . .' said Hulda weakly.

'Nonsense,' declared Mrs North. 'I'll put the kettle on. Everyone feels better after a cup of tea.'

'Yes,' whispered Hulda with pathetic gratitude. 'I think you're right.'

'Bring her inside,' instructed Mrs North, treating Lonsdale to an admonishing glower. 'You should be ashamed of yourself, dragging her here when she should be at home with her feet up.'

Lonsdale slipped a cautious hand under Hulda's elbow, and escorted her into Mrs North's best room, a cluttered parlour at the front of the house. The wallpaper had a dark red floral design on a chocolate background, and the floorboards were polished to a treacherous shine. An enormous pair of brass candlesticks dominated the fireplace, and every available inch of space was crammed with knick-knacks and silver-framed sepia photographs.

Once Hulda had been settled on a lumpy horsehair sofa, and furnished with a plate of Bath Oliver biscuits and a cup of tea, Lonsdale tried to restart the conversation.

'You said the other day that Mr Donovan raised the alarm about the fire, then ran back inside his house,' he began, intending to ask whether she had noticed any visitors before his final appearance.

Mrs North's lips pursed in annoyance. 'I've already told you all I know about poor Mr Donovan. It isn't seemly to dwell on it, and I strongly disapprove—'

Again, the intended tirade was interrupted by a timely groan from Hulda.

'Men!' snapped Mrs North, pouring her more tea and glowering at Lonsdale. 'Your poor wife is carrying your child, and you're more concerned with gossip than in her well-being. You don't deserve her.'

'That's certainly true,' muttered Lonsdale.

'I'm much better now, Mrs North,' said Hulda, with the smile of a martyr. 'And my husband doesn't mean to be callous – he's just concerned that we choose the right house, so our child can grow up with respectable, God-fearing folk.'

'Well, you couldn't choose better than Wyndham Street,' averred Mrs North. 'Bert Evans next door is a clerk for the Board of Works, and earns thirty-five shillings a week, while his daughter brings home another twelve as a waitress in the Royal Hotel. And then there's my Harry. He makes almost thirty-three shillings, while my oldest boy earns ten as an apprentice railwayman, even though he's only fifteen.'

She paused to acknowledge the murmured approvals of her two guests, then continued.

'Mr Donovan worked in Salmon and Eden, the gentleman's outfitters, and must have been earning at least forty shillings a week. More, probably.' Her voice dropped reverently, and Lonsdale could see she was deeply impressed by such heady finances.

'Was he a drinking man?' asked Lonsdale.

Mrs North's eyes widened in shock. 'No! What gave you that idea?'

'You did,' replied Lonsdale, unruffled. 'Two days ago, when you said he seemed intoxicated when he ran into the street shouting.'

'Did I?' she asked, frowning. 'Perhaps I did. He sounded different, you see.'

'Different in what way?'

She gave a shrug. 'Hoarse – although I suppose that could have been the smoke. I don't know why I said he'd been drinking. He'd never done it before.'

'Was he married?' asked Hulda, sipping her tea.

'No,' said Mrs North. 'He wasn't the type. Don't get me wrong – there were few gentlemen as respectable – but he was shy.'

At that moment, there was a tap on the door, and the sound of someone entering the house.

'That's Molly Evans from next door, come to find out who I'm entertaining,' said Mrs North. 'We're all good friends here – always in and out of each other's houses. In a neighbourly way, of course.'

'Except Mr Donovan,' said Hulda, regarding Mrs North with wide, innocent eyes. 'Because he was shy.'

92

'Front parlour, Molly,' called Mrs North, not happy at being caught in an inconsistency.

Lonsdale glimpsed Molly Evans smoothing her hair down in front of the hall mirror, before entering Mrs North's parlour.

'This nice couple are thinking of moving into number thirty-five,' explained Mrs North. 'So I've been telling them all about us.'

'Are they?' asked Molly, surprised. 'The agent told my Bert just yesterday that it's been let to a family from Wales – a Mr and Mrs Rhys.'

Mrs North's eyes narrowed in suspicion, and Lonsdale wondered whether she would demand recompense for all the biscuits Hulda had scoffed.

'Yes, but the agent prefers us,' said Hulda with remarkable aplomb, reaching for another Bath Oliver. 'Because of our references – from the vicar of St Alfrege's and Sir William Stead, my husband's employer.'

'A vicar, and a knight of the realm!' breathed Mrs North.

Hulda nodded. 'Whereas Mr Rhys is a rag-and-bone collector, and only earns fifteen shillings a week. The agent said he was afraid he'd get behind with the rent.'

'A rag-and-bone man?' echoed Molly aghast. She exchanged a look of horror with Mrs North.

'He plans to run his business from behind the house,' continued Hulda relentlessly. 'He has three ponies, two carts, and three of his four sons work for him. All want to move here with him.'

'Four sons?'

'And five daughters, two of whom are unmarried with children. Moreover, one of the sons has a police record. What was his crime, Alec? Was it robbery with violence or arson?'

'Is there any more tea?' asked Lonsdale, to stem Hulda's flow of lies. The two women ignored him and gaped at Hulda. Molly was positively white.

'You must tell the agent the people on the street favour you,' gulped Mrs North. 'You won't find a better neighbourhood in London. And with the exception of this dreadful business with Mr Donovan, the police have never been here.'

'Poor Mr Donovan,' said Molly. 'He was such an upstanding gentleman. He polished the church brass every Saturday afternoon.'

'He was too set in his ways to marry,' said Mrs North, to ensure that her guests read nothing untoward in the fact that Donovan was a bachelor. 'But then, he looked after his father until the old man passed away last year.'

'Did he have no other relations?' asked Hulda.

'None,' replied Mrs North. 'After his father died, he was quite alone. I said he could come over for tea any time he felt lonely. Of course, he never did.'

'He loved his work,' put in Molly. 'He left every morning at seven-thirty, and was never back before nine. Other than church, his only pastimes were books and walks in the park.'

'It seems a terrible thing to happen to such an upright, Christian man,' went on Mrs North. 'I'd give anything to live Thursday over again, and prevent him from running back into his house.'

'I doubt you could have stopped him,' said

94

Lonsdale kindly. 'But we mustn't keep you. You've been very kind.'

'Please consider number thirty-five,' begged Mrs North, reluctant to let them go without some assurance that they would deliver her neighbourhood from the sinister presence of the ominous Rhys family. 'I can't stress enough how respectable we are.'

'You can't let Mr Donovan's accident put you off,' added Molly. 'It was the chimney sweep's fault, after all.'

'The sweep?' asked Hulda, while Lonsdale recalled that Mrs North had mentioned the chimney being cleaned before.

'The firemen said the flue was blocked, and that's how the blaze started,' explained Mrs North. 'Kendal's getting too old. He left a brush up the chimney, and that was that.'

'I shan't have him again,' said Molly firmly.

'Nor will I,' declared Mrs North.

'That poor woman,' said Lonsdale as they walked away, Hulda remembering to take his arm as a pregnant wife might do. 'She's appalled at the prospect of having your rag-and-bone man in her street.'

'Serves her right for being such a self-righteous bigot,' said Hulda, chin in the air and regular accent firmly back in place. 'What makes her think she's better than a man who earns only fifteen shillings?'

'But now she'll race off to the agent, and learn you've spun her all manner of lies. And we won't be able to question her again. How could you prey on someone's kindness like that, pretending to be pregnant and eating all her biscuits?'

'Because if I hadn't, she wouldn't have given us the time of day,' replied Hulda, snatching her arm back as they rounded the corner. 'Your questioning was clumsy, and she had taken a dislike to you before we'd even started.'

'But surely you didn't have to be quite so inventive?'

'Molly was about to reveal us as a pair of frauds,' said Hulda unrepentantly. 'I saved the day *and* inveigled all the information we needed. And the disguise was *your* idea, so don't get at me for embellishing the theme. You'd better lose those scruples if you want to succeed at *The PMG*. You won't do it by being prissy and squeamish.'

'We can bicker later,' said Lonsdale, aware that people were looking at them, 'but if we want to speak to anyone else, we must do it now, before Mrs North finds out we're imposters. Can you bring yourself to act the part of a respectable woman again?'

Seldom had Lonsdale been treated to a look of greater malevolence than that with which Hulda favoured him. He was grateful she was not armed, or there might have been another murder in Wyndham Street.

With Hulda coldly rigid at his side, they spoke to several other neighbours, but none had anything more to add. All said kind things about Donovan, but no one had really known him. Furthermore, there was nothing in his life that warranted being singled out for such a brutal attack. If he had been fond of the taverns, or had gambled, Lonsdale would have known how to proceed, but there was nothing.

'I can only see one curious thing in what we've been told,' he said to Hulda later, as they sat in a dingy chophouse at the Great Western Railway Terminus. She was the only woman present and was attracting the interested gazes of several men. Lonsdale was considerably more uneasy about it than Hulda, who treated the admiring glances with contemptuous indifference, concentrating instead on cleaning the greasy cutlery with a scrupulously white lace handkerchief.

'Me, too,' she said. 'Salmon and Eden must have closed by eight o'clock, so why did Donovan never reach home until after nine?'

'No,' said Lonsdale, who had not thought of this. 'I mean, yes. He lived alone, so perhaps he ate out before going home so he wouldn't have to cook. But, I was thinking about something else. Everybody has told us that he left for work every morning at half-past seven. But he died mid-morning on a Thursday. Why was he at home when he should have been at Salmon and Eden?'

'By God, you're right!' exclaimed Hulda, slamming her hand on the table. 'That *is* good thinking, Lonsdale. How could I have missed something so obvious?'

'We should visit his shop,' said Lonsdale, choosing to ignore her condescension. 'We can ask his colleagues why he stayed at home – if he took a day off or was ill.'

'Right,' said Hulda, downing half a glass of

stout at an impressive rate, and leaping to her feet. 'Off we go, then. Do you know where it is?'

'Near Oxford Street. But we should go to the office first to tell Stead what we're doing. And can we finish the chops?'

'No,' said Hulda briskly. 'I suppose we should see Stead, but there is another lesson you should learn – you will never make a good reporter if you stop to eat.'

Had Hulda known what was awaiting them at Northumberland Street, she would have been less willing to return there. The moment they looked through Stead's doorway it was apparent that all was not well.

'Ah, my happily married couple,' he said in subdued tones. 'I hope you've solved your crime, because you may not have another opportunity.'

Lonsdale raised his eyebrows questioningly, while Hulda glowered in a way that would have been intimidating to most people.

'We're on our way to conduct more interviews,' she said firmly. 'Shall we tell you what we learned at Wyndham Street?'

'Yes, and Mr Morley will be interested, too,' said Stead. 'He returned today, rather earlier than expected. You know he's been at home, writing a biography of Richard Cobden—'

'Who?' demanded Hulda.

Lonsdale and Stead regarded each other uncertainly. 'The economist and politician who helped found the Anti-Corn Law League,' said Lonsdale. 'One of the most influential figures of his age.'

'He sounds tedious in the extreme,' declared Hulda. 'I'm not surprised Morley has given up.'

'Well the issue of the moment is not his book, but this,' said Stead, handing Lonsdale a piece of stationery, which, in Morley's firm hand, read:

My dear Stead,
Your editorial of last night turned my hair grey. In fact, the entire first six pages were crammed with stories that strike me as downright unseemly, and smack of – dare I say – sensationalism. I find that I must return to once again put a chilly frost on your exuberance.

Hulda glowered anew. 'But sensational stories sell newspapers. Unlike biographies of economists.'

'I know,' said Stead soberly. 'But Mr Morley is the editor, and if he doesn't like our work, we must change what we do. And I'm afraid that he doesn't want you to look into the Donovan case. Unfortunately, no power on Earth will interest him in such matters – he says they "only excite the British tomfool". He told me to take you to him the moment you arrived.'

He led the way to Morley's office, which was lit by a six-paned window on each side of his writing table. In front of a fireplace were three chairs on what had once been a fine Oriental carpet, before ages of coal cinders had leached it of colour. The austere, stern editor signalled for them to sit, while he remained at his desk, dressed in a single-breasted, navy-blue suit with a crisp white shirt and spotted necktie, his thinning grey hair combed neatly backwards. His expression, as always, was grave and dignified.

'Mr Stead told me what you've been doing,' he began coolly. 'I don't believe such matters should occupy you when there are major issues requiring analysis and discussion.'

Lonsdale heard Hulda stifle a sigh. For Morley, 'major issues' meant the Irish situation, for which he owned a deep and abiding fascination.

'Superintendent Ramsey contacted me,' Morley continued. 'He says the Donovan business is too sensitive to be released, and has asked us to withhold publication.'

'I've already assured the police of our discretion,' said Lonsdale, irked that his word as a gentleman seemed to be in question.

'Ramsey gave two reasons for his request, both reasonable,' Morley went on. 'First, he wishes to avoid alarming the public. Do not forget the garrotting murders of 1862, which caused widespread panic.'

'There are few who will forget those,' sighed Stead. 'It was later claimed that the press and police created such a sense of unease that it discouraged people from coming forward with evidence, helping the murderer escape justice.'

'Second, he feels that publishing details will hinder the course of justice. The police can determine guilt or innocence on the basis of what the suspect knows about the crime, but if everything is public, there's a danger that the wrong man might be convicted.'

'So we forget about the murder?' asked Lonsdale, thinking about Stead's contention that

The PMG was under a moral obligation to investigate because Cath had died for it.

'We do,' nodded Morley. 'We leave it to the police. Superintendent Ramsey has promised to keep us informed of progress, although whether we will ever cover such a sordid affair is debatable.'

'But what happens if the police fail?' demanded Hulda, standing and putting her hands on her hips. 'Do we forget about justice for Walker? And what if the police take months to solve it? No one will be interested in a crime that happened in the dim and distant past.'

The question she did not ask, but that was clear in the way her eyes flashed with righteous indignation was: is that what you want – for the matter to be so ancient that details about it will never sully the pages of *The PMG*?

Thunderclouds gathered across Morley's craggy features. 'The news with which *you* should be concerned, Miss Friederichs,' he snapped icily, 'is that which deals with great affairs – Ireland or the new reform bill to increase the electorate. *These* are the type of topics we should be writing about in order to help our readership understand them.'

'But will they sell papers?' demanded Hulda, while Lonsdale and Stead regarded her askance, astonished that she should challenge the man who had broken convention by hiring her in the first place.

Lonsdale braced himself for an explosion, but Morley only stood and went to the window, standing with his hands behind his back so

101

they would not see his face. Lonsdale sensed he was struggling to control his temper. 'They will if they are well written,' he said. 'So we shall know where the blame lies if circulation falls. Meanwhile, leave crime to the sensational weeklies.'

'But—' began Hulda.

'I will *not* be gainsaid,' he snapped, turning so quickly that Hulda took an involuntary step backwards. Then, to Lonsdale's surprise, Morley's voice became gentler, and he saw the crusty editor had a soft spot for his passionately outspoken assistant. 'Yet Mr Stead believes that the crime is more important than an unsavoury fallout between robbers and unfortunates, and I trust his judgement. Perhaps we will publish a short account of it later – although not until the police say we may.'

Hulda was glaring. 'So what would you like us to write about today?' she asked, her tone only just avoiding insolence.

Morley smiled briefly. 'There's a performance of Gilbert and Sullivan's *Patience* at the Savoy Theatre tonight. I want a review, because there is a new female lead. Now, if there's nothing else . . .'

On leaving Morley's office, Stead disappeared to the compositors' office without a word. Lonsdale went to the reporters' room, Hulda, fuming silently, at his heels. There was only one person there when they arrived – Alfred Milner, a thin-faced Oxford graduate who had abandoned a career in law for journalism. Lonsdale sensed that the mild-mannered Milner was destined for great things, and *The PMG* would not contain his budding genius for long.

'I assume you have just seen Mr Morley,' he said drily. 'You have a look on your face that would curdle new cream, Friederichs.'

'That man—' Hulda began hotly.

'Is one of the greatest intellects of our time,' interrupted Milner. 'A deep-thinker who has turned *The PMG* into a great bastion of political analysis.'

'But there's more to the news than that,' said Lonsdale, finally voicing his own disappointment at Morley's decision.

'How can he not see how important this story might be?' spat Hulda.

'I doubt it will be *important*,' said Milner, gently reproachful. 'Grisly, certainly. Fascinating, perhaps. But not important.'

'I disagree,' said Lonsdale, while Hulda sat at the desk and slammed a few drawers to vent her ire. 'Donovan's murder was superbly planned, and so was Cath's. This isn't the work of some deranged madman; it shows considerable resourcefulness and a highly organized mind.'

Hulda fumbled for a cigar, although she did not light it. 'I'm not surprised to hear *you* speak on his behalf, Milner,' she said sullenly. 'You being a regular guest at his dull Sunday afternoon tea parties. Thank God we have Stead to balance the man.'

'They do complement each other,' agreed Milner. 'But I can assure you that Mr Morley's parties are far from dull – he entertains some of

103

the greatest thinkers in the country. But on a more immediate note, will you read this, Alec? It's about whether Britain should send warships to Egypt, to quell the anarchy brought about by Colonel Arabi's coup.'

With the deadline approaching for the final issue of the week, Lonsdale spent thirty frantic minutes helping Milner finish his article. When it was done, the pressure turned onto the compositors, and Lonsdale gave a sigh of relief as he heard the clatter of the printing machines start up. Within minutes, the papers would be packed in bales and handed to armies of paperboys.

Milner took a handkerchief from his pocket and dabbed at his forehead. He was not physically robust, and rarely came to work before ten o'clock. He screwed the lid back on the ink bottle and leaned back in his chair.

'Thank you, Alec,' he said, running a hand lightly over his slicked hair. 'I'll do the same for you – if you survive another week.' He cast a meaningful glance at Lonsdale's bruised eye. 'I heard what happened. You shouldn't have gone there alone; you should've taken one of us.'

'Me,' said Hulda, looking Milner up and down disparagingly. 'He should have taken *me*. If you had escorted him, there would have been two of you with bruised faces. I, on the other hand, can look after myself.'

Before Milner could respond, the door to the office opened. It was Stead, the customary twinkle back in his eye, and his irritation at Morley's intervention already a thing of the past. 'I've assignments for you two,' he said, looking at Lonsdale and Hulda, 'and you'll be pleased to know they *don't* involve an evening at the Savoy. Cook will handle that. Hulda, I want you to look into an art exhibit that opens in the East End on Monday.'

'Monday?' asked Hulda, brightening. 'Then in the meantime I can explore—'

'No,' interrupted Stead. 'You heard Mr Morley. It is too late to do more today, so I suggest you go home and read anything you might need in preparation for the art exhibit. But not tomorrow, of course. It's a sin to labour on the Sabbath.'

Hulda opened her mouth to argue, then thought better of it. Clamping her cigar between her teeth, she grabbed her coat and stalked out. They heard her heavy steps going down the stairs.

Stead turned to Lonsdale. 'She has the simpler of the assignments,' he said. 'What I have in mind for you is far more difficult, and may even involve a little danger.'

Four

That Sunday, after attending church with Jack, Lonsdale began preparing for the assignment that had been allocated by Stead. Then, the following morning, he slept as late as he could, before starting what he imagined actors went through prior to every performance: he readied himself to play a role. At about nine o'clock on Monday night, an unshaven and deliberately

105

grubby Lonsdale was dropped off by a brougham carriage near the insalubrious Fox and Hounds tavern on a rough backstreet of Lambeth. The first step in the assignment allocated by Stead had been taken.

Stead's idea had developed from a brief report in Saturday's final edition – a snippet of news that had been taken from one of the morning newspapers by a sub-editor and included only because there had been unused space on page five. To Stead, however, it represented the tip of an iceberg in an appalling case of neglect and cruelty:

> *A coroner's jury yesterday returned a verdict of manslaughter against the master of the Holbeach Union Workhouse in Lincolnshire, for causing the death of a pauper named Bingham. The man had been suffering from a skin disease, and was placed in a fumigating box used to disinfect persons, and apparently forgotten. His cries at length attracted attention, and he was released, but not until he had been so terribly burned that skin and flesh fell from different parts of his body. He died a few hours afterwards.*

'We *must* find out what the conditions in a work-house are really like,' Stead had said. 'How are these men lodged and fed? What goes on when night comes, and the misfits and outcasts crowd around workhouse doors? How can a man be left in a box to die? Bingham deserves such questions to be answered!'

'The New Poor Law is behind it,' Milner had stated. 'The law that says able-bodied persons unable to support themselves should only receive relief in workhouses.'

'Workhouses!' spat Stead. 'Wicked places where the standard of living is obliged by law to be inferior to that of the lowest-paid worker, in order to serve as a deterrent to shirkers and drive them back to honest toil. But such centres repress, not help, the poor.'

Stead's plan was for Lonsdale to spend a night in a workhouse to see what it was like to be treated as a 'casual pauper'. The reporter now shuffled away from the carriage in his filthy boots, dressed in what had once been a snuff-brown coat, but was faded to the colour of imperfectly baked bricks. The coat was too small, and his arms projected beyond the sleeves, with his hands thrust deep in his pockets against the chill of a clear, cold night.

Lambeth Workhouse loomed gloomy and squat over Princes Road. Its thick front door was caked in a greasy patina of soot and grime, and Lonsdale could smell the rankness of unwashed bodies from outside, although it was not nearly as powerful as the reek of despair and hopelessness. It unnerved him, and it took considerable courage to knock and ask for a bed.

Once allowed inside, he was interviewed and taken to a room with three large baths, each containing a liquid that looked so much like mutton broth that he baulked at going near them, let alone immersing himself. But the clerk was waiting expectantly, so Lonsdale gave the man his clothes tied in a bundle and plunged into the water. It was icy cold, with a thin layer of scum across the top, and the bottom was full of grit, perhaps an inch deep in places. Lonsdale made a show of splashing about, and scrambled out as soon as he was sure he would not be ordered back in. It was, he thought, one of the most disgusting things he had ever done.

After drying off with a cloth as coarse as sand, he was given a lump of stale bread and was issued a blue sleeping shirt, a rug to cover himself, and a numbered tag so that he could retrieve his clothes in the morning. He was then sent across an open court to a large shed, one side of which was comprised only of a canvas sheet with a gap of some four feet at the bottom. The floor was flagstone, but so thickly encrusted with slime it could barely be seen, and it was sticky under his naked feet.

Inside were, he estimated, at least a hundred and twenty hay-stuffed bags, almost all occupied by men streaked with filth, despite the baths. In a number of places men had moved the bags close to each other – 'clubbing' they called it in self-denigrating sarcasm – as a feeble measure against the cold. Most were asleep, although a few ruffians squatted on their beds, singing ribald songs or telling obscene jokes, their eyes gleaming in the embers of their foul pipes. The place stank of acrid, fetid bodies, rotting bed-straw, and the foul pools on the floor where men, declining to make the chilly trip to the latrines, had created lavatories of their own.

Lonsdale found a free bag and, despite it having a bloodstain bigger than his hand, lay down, knowing that to baulk would show a degree of fastidiousness likely to make the other lodgers take notice of him. He looked at the bread, thinking he would have to eat at least some of it if he did not want to stand out.

'Not hungry, old pal?' asked one of three lads watching him keenly – a short, thin boy of fifteen or so, with large blue eyes and close-cropped hair. 'Chuck it here, then.' Obligingly, Lonsdale tore the bread in two and threw the larger piece to the lad, who devoured it quickly as his friends tried to grab it from him.

'Aw, Jamie,' grumbled one when it was gone. 'You could've shared.'

Determined to learn all he could, Lonsdale propped himself against a post and pretended to doze, watching as Jamie and his friends lit their pipes. He listened in growing horror as the youth began to relate tales of stealing, sex, and fights. Eventually, they slept, and the noise in the shed subsided, so that by the time the bells from nearby St Mary's Church tolled twelve, all was still. It was not quiet, though, with the flapping of the canvas curtain in the wind, snoring, the sounds of drinkers at the communal water pail, and the scuttle of those who got up to relieve themselves at the latrine or against the wall inside.

For hour after hour Lonsdale sat there, counting the time until seven o'clock – when he thought

109

he would be able to leave. Four o'clock came and went, then five, by which time he was so cold that he doubted he would ever be warm again. At six, factory bells called working men to their jobs, but no one stirred in the workhouse, and the snoring continued unabated. Then it chimed seven. Lonsdale jumped up, relieved that the ordeal was almost over, before realizing he was the only one who had moved. Eventually, two men appeared and began bawling out numbers, so that the bundles of clothes turned in the night before could be exchanged for the borrowed shirts.

When everyone was up and dressed, the boys took the rugs, and the men made a heap of the bags against the wall, turning the shed from bedroom to breakfast room. There followed three-quarters of an hour of waiting for a paltry breakfast – a slice of bread and a pint basin of gruel, which had an unpleasant taste but warmed his numb hands. To Lonsdale, frozen, uncomfortable, and thinking longingly of home, it seemed an eternity. Hardly had he finished – having again given half of the bread to Jamie – before a rough-looking man known as the 'taskmaster' said in a loud voice, 'Now then, you lot belong to me!'

The sun shone brightly as Lonsdale, his ordeal finally over, walked through the busy streets to where the same carriage that had dropped him off the night before was waiting. His friend Milner, whom Stead had assigned to collect him, was lounging comfortably inside, reading *The Daily Telegraph*.

'You look a sight,' said Milner in distaste. 'I'm not sure I want you in here with me.'

Ignoring the comment, Lonsdale flopped back against the plush upholstery and accepted a gulp of brandy from Milner's hipflask. He relished the warmth as it settled in his stomach.

'I've been waiting two hours,' Milner grumbled, as the carriage moved away. 'It's well past eleven o'clock, you know.'

Lonsdale shuddered. 'There are duties to be performed before the inmates are allowed out. I had no idea they'd take so long.'

'What were they?'

'Today's was turning cranks that work a flour mill. Turning the crank is like turning a windlass. It shouldn't have been too laborious, because only four measures of corn have to be ground each day. The problem was that the taskmaster set us to work, then left. At least half the men immediately stopped working. The miller came in once or twice, and suddenly everyone was at work, but when he left, all was as before. It shouldn't have taken more than an hour, but it took three.'

'The poor laws at work,' mused Milner. 'What do . . .'

He trailed off when he saw Lonsdale had fallen asleep, and they rode in silence until the carriage clattered to a halt outside the tall, elegant Georgian façade of Jack's house. Lonsdale woke when the driver jumped down to tend his horses.

'Do you own this?' asked Milner.

'My brother does,' replied Lonsdale. 'But he'll marry soon, and then I'll be looking for rooms. I don't suppose you—?' His question was interrupted by a thump from behind them. 'What was that?'

'It sounded like someone jumping off the back of the carriage,' said Milner peering out of the window. 'I have a feeling we might just have given someone a free ride.'

Wednesday, 26 April
My dear Lonsdale,
I write to congratulate you on your coming of age, not just as a journalist, but as a crusader in the cause of right-eousness. I enclose a copy of today's early edition of The PMG, *which includes the first instalment of your account of a night in a workhouse. Milner told me that he had never seen so great a change in appearance wrought in a single night. He felt that when you went in, you were well disguised, but that after spending fifteen hours in the cold and squalor, you had absolutely become confirmed in the visage of a tramp. The experiences that wrought these changes show in your account. You have written with passion of the filth, immorality, and hopelessness, and you have written so that things might be done, not merely discussed.*

It appears from early comments that your work is creating quite a stir. Represent-atives from several dailies have asked about carrying extracts of the second and third instalments tomorrow and the following day.

Inspector Peters came to find you. You are required to appear tomorrow morning at nine o'clock at the County Court, Great Portland Street, for the inquest into the death of Miss Walker. Although you'll undoubtedly testify early in the proceedings, you may, if you wish, remain there to see if any new facts have arisen.
Yours cordially,
Stead

The County Court dated from the previous century, but it had none of the attractiveness of most Georgian architecture. It was a grim, ineloquent building and everything about it screamed functionality. Lonsdale was directed to a dirty wood-panelled room on the ground floor, where the coroner sat in a high-backed, tatty red-velvet chair, almost hidden by the pile of papers in front of him. Dr Danford Thomas was a small, grey-haired man, with brown eyes hidden behind thick glasses and nicotine-stained teeth.

To Thomas's left, at right angles to his desk, were twelve uncomfortable wooden chairs, on which sat the members of the jury, while to his right were benches for witnesses. A large Bible marked with greasy fingerprints sat in imposing isolation on its own table so that witnesses might swear on it to tell the truth.

Before Lonsdale could sit down, Inspector Peters approached.

'I have to take the jury to see the body before witness testimony can be heard. While we're gone, Leonard would like to speak to you.'

113

He nodded to where the chief inspector was waiting by the door. Lonsdale went to join him, and they walked outside for privacy.

'Superintendent Ramsey wants you to understand several things before testifying,' Leonard began after a brief exchange of pleasantries. 'You must, of course, explain how you came to find Walker in Regent's Park, but you cannot mention her connection with Donovan.'

'But that's why I was there!' objected Lonsdale. 'If I'm asked—'

'You won't be,' interrupted Leonard. 'Ramsey has already spoken to the coroner, and . . . arrangements are in place.'

Lonsdale regarded him askance. 'You're asking me to withhold information from a legal inquiry?'

Leonard nodded rucfully. 'There are usually reporters at inquests, and if the issue of Donovan's disfiguring comes up, it'll be in the papers. Ramsey has good reasons for keeping it quiet for now, and Thomas has agreed both to avoid the subject and to postpone Donovan's inquest. I can't tell you more yet, but I can assure you that we have the interests of justice at heart.' He saw Lonsdale's doubtful expression. 'You're being asked to co-operate by a very high-ranking police officer.'

'In my experience, that might mean he has something to hide.' He pondered for a moment. 'Very well, I shall do as you ask,' he said, albeit reluctantly.

Leonard patted his shoulder. 'Good man! Now, when Thomas asks what you were doing in the park, you may say that you were meeting Walker . . .'

'No,' said Lonsdale firmly, not about to give some of his less scrupulous colleagues an opportunity to say he had arranged an assignation with a prostitute in a deserted park at night. 'I shall say that she offered me a story, but that I never learned the details. That's true.'

Leonard reflected, then nodded. 'That should be enough. When this is over, I'll give you the whole story. Then you'll see how important your cooperation was.' He reached out to shake Lonsdale's hand. 'Now I must bid you good day.'

Lonsdale watched him walk away, thinking about Milner's belief that the story would not be important, just sensational. Yet senior police officers were prepared to control how the press handled it. Was there more to the tale than a grisly murder and the slaughter of a prostitute and her accomplice? Did the police know of similar cases? He was inclined to conclude they did, as Ramsey would not be concerned with the random killing of a few friendless Londoners. But how could he find out? And could he disobey Morley's order to leave it well alone?

As he turned to go back into the courthouse, he saw a figure dodge into the nearby Portland Hotel. He frowned, then told himself that it had nothing to do with him, and headed back inside the courthouse.

Shortly after ten o'clock, the jury shuffled into their seats, and the inquest began. The initial witness was young Constable Lamb – the first policeman on the scene – who wore a freshly pressed jacket with buttons that gleamed

115

like mirrors. He described how Lonsdale had approached him and what happened in the ensuing minutes. His testimony was followed by that of his colleagues.

Inspector Peters was the last policeman to testify. He rattled off the oath, then turned his lugubrious gaze on the coroner, waiting with all the cheer of a calf sent for slaughter. Thomas led him through his testimony, then asked why the search for clues – which had initially been postponed until daylight – had not yet taken place. Lonsdale leaned forward – he had assumed it had been completed.

'Inspector Beck of Scotland Yard volunteered the use of bloodhounds,' explained Peters. 'But Chief Inspector Leonard informed me that Superintendent Ramsey had countermanded that order. By the time the matter was resolved – it was an unfortunate misunderstanding apparently – a search of the area would have been futile because of the public nature of the place.'

Lonsdale stared at him. A misunderstanding? Or a deliberate attempt to prevent Cath's death from being properly explored? He listened as Peters recounted what he had learned about the victim.

'She was born Catherine Mitchell, was a Primitive Methodist, and had worked briefly as a calico weaver. She could read. Her arrest record included charges of vagrancy, drunkenness, wilful damage, and prostitution.'

'Has your investigation so far shed any further light that would be helpful to this inquiry?' asked Thomas.

116

'No, sir,' said Peters. 'But the investigation is ongoing.'

Lonsdale was next, and recounted his meeting with Cath at the fire and her offer of information for a story. He then told of being attacked by two men he assumed were her friends.

'She stipulated the bandstand,' said Thomas in a gentle Welsh lilt, 'but you looked for her near the trees and bushes when she failed to appear. Why?'

'Because I heard a noise in that area when I first arrived, then the two assailants came from that vicinity. I just assumed that Miss Walker might be there.'

'Thank you, Mr Lonsdale. That will be all.'

'He must like you,' whispered Hulda, as Lonsdale sat at the back of the courtroom. He was surprised to see her. 'He could have asked a lot more questions.'

Next on the stand was a large woman of about thirty, who said her name was Mary Lawrence. She wore a jacket and skirt of stiff green material and had clearly gone to some trouble to look her best. She identified the body as that of her sister.

'When did you last see her alive?' the coroner asked.

'A quarter to seven last Thursday evening. She came to Red Lion Street, where I work – I'm a seamstress. She was frightened, but wouldn't say why, and stayed less than an hour.'

'Did you know what she did for a living?' asked Thomas quietly.

'She'd been before the police court magistrates

117

once or twice for . . . selling her personal wares.'
Her lips compressed in a disapproving line.

'Do you know why she seemed frightened at
your final meeting?'

'No, sir. But I can tell you she wasn't one to
scare easily.'

Hulda leaned over to whisper to Lonsdale,
disapproval in every word. 'He's making it sound
as if she was killed because she was a whore
– nothing to do with Donovan.'

'Ramsey's orders,' Lonsdale whispered back.
'Leonard told me I had to be careful with what
I said, too.'

'So we're wasting our time here? Then let's
leave.'

But Lonsdale was determined to see it through.
He stayed, a reluctant Hulda at his side, and heard
the testimony of a thin, frail-looking woman named
Margaret Tanner, a widow who ran the lodging
house where the dead woman often stayed.

'When did you last see her alive?' asked Thomas.

'About six thirty on the night she died. She
was in the Dog and Bone public house, on Minto
Street. She was a lively soul usually, but she
seemed out of sorts that night.'

Thomas pressed her for details, but the woman
spoke very cagily, obviously determined to ignore
any implications that her lodging house might be
of dubious reputation. Finally, Thomas dismissed
her with a wave of his hand.

Lonsdale felt hungry, so when Thomas announced
a thirty-minute lunch break before the afternoon
session, he crossed the road and bought a pie

from a street vendor. After making some disparaging remarks about it, Hulda followed suit, seduced by the light yellow pastry and the sweet scent of meat and onions. They sat on a grimy bench in a little park to eat, and had barely started when they were hailed.

'I thought you'd be gone,' said Bradwell. His smiled broadened. 'And of course, it's always a pleasure to see you, Miss Friederichs.'

'Dr Bradwell,' beamed Hulda, offering a hand to the pathologist. 'Would you like some of my pie?'

'No, they're made from cat,' replied Bradwell. 'I dislike eating carnivore.' He turned to Lonsdale. 'I've heard you've been ordered not to investigate Donovan's death. Is it true?'

Lonsdale nodded as he threw the remainder of his pie to the pigeons. Hulda finished hers with enthusiasm. 'Which is a pity, because I'm sure something significant is happening – something deeper than a lunatic with a penchant for cerebra.'

'I agree, which is why I hoped to catch you. Can you meet me after the inquest is over?'

'We shall look forward to it,' said Hulda, clearly assuming she was included in the invitation. She dabbed her lips with a piece of lace and glanced at the pie-seller, as if considering a second piece.

They took their places in the court and listened while Bradwell gave his evidence in a concise, professional tone that suggested he had done it many times before. After describing the scene, the placement of the body, and the details of the long and fatal incision in her throat, he noted

119

that the injuries were beyond the possibility of self-infliction.

'Was any anatomical knowledge displayed by the incision?' asked Thomas.

'I believe so,' said Bradwell. 'There seems to have been some knowledge as to where to cut the throat in order to cause a fatal and quick result.'

Bradwell's testimony was followed by that of several of Cath's acquaintances. When Thomas had dismissed the last of these, he looked at the jury. 'Your task now is to decide whether you have been presented with sufficient evidence to decide the cause of Catherine Walker's death.'

Within a matter of moments, having conferred with other jury members, the foreman returned a verdict of 'wilful murder by person or persons unknown.' Thomas added nothing more, but the way his questions had been asked left the distinct impression that Cath was just another unfortunate killed in the course of her occupation.

'Inspector Peters is adjourning to a coffee house,' Bradwell said to Lonsdale following the inquest. 'Shall we join him there? It would be another opportunity to quiz him.'

Lonsdale was not sure he wanted another encounter with the law, particularly as it went contrary to Morley's instructions. However, Hulda accepted the offer with alacrity, so he trailed after them to a seedy establishment on the other side of the park.

'Will Lonsdale have to attend the inquest on Walker's dead friend?' asked Hulda when they were settled around a grimy table. 'What was his name?'

'We don't know it,' replied Peters. 'Not yet.'

'Really?' asked Hulda, voicing Lonsdale's surprise. 'You've had days!'

'Yes,' acknowledged Peters, reaching into his pocket for a briar pipe and Virginia tobacco. 'But he's not my only active case, and these matters are never easy – this is a city of millions of people, and the Metropolitan Police District is huge. Since Walker is from south of the river, it is likely the man is as well, and that means in theory I should be liaising with my colleagues in Southwark Division. But due to professional jealousies, many officers decline to share information with those in different divisions.'

'Is there no way you can obtain this evidence yourself?' asked Hulda, sounding sceptical.

'It's difficult – one has to be careful not to be seen subverting official channels. I did quietly send a detective to Walker's lodging house and then to trawl several local pubs to ask after her friend. Unfortunately, the police are regarded with suspicion in that area.'

'Can *we* help you?' asked Hulda in her most innocent manner.

'No thank you,' responded Peters, a smile twitching his moustache as he knocked the bowl of his pipe on the table and rubbed a bit of burnt tobacco out with a stubby index finger. 'We may move slowly, but we get there in the end.'

'So tell us what's happening with the Donovan case,' said Bradwell. 'I've been informed that I won't be needed for the inquest, which is odd.'

121

'That's correct,' said Peters flatly. 'Superintendent Ramsey believes that there's no link between Walker and Donovan, and I've been told to wait until I receive further instructions.'

'How can he say they aren't linked?' demanded Lonsdale. 'Cath met me at the fire and *told* me she knew something about the killing of Donovan.'

'So I understand,' said Peters. He rose, putting his pipe and tobacco in his pocket. 'It is all very curious. However, although Dr Bradwell clearly thinks we should all work together on the case – that *is* why you brought them here, is it not, Bradwell? – it *is* a police matter, and I strongly advise you to leave well enough alone.'

'It *is* curious,' said Hulda. 'And perhaps Dr Bradwell is right.' She smiled at the pathologist, who blushed.

'No,' said Inspector Peters, 'he is not. Come, Bradwell. You should return to your house of the dead and I have work to do.'

Hulda allowed Bradwell to keep her hand rather longer than was strictly necessary as the pathologist took his leave, and then the two men were gone, leaving her and Lonsdale alone.

'One has to try to obtain information however one can,' she said in answer to Lonsdale's questioning gaze regarding her coquettishness. 'Now, tell me why the coroner protected you from any serious questioning.'

Lonsdale obliged, and Hulda sat still, thinking.

'Peters is right: this *is* curious,' she said eventually. 'First, Superintendent Ramsey and Chief Inspector Leonard tell our editors that they don't want us investigating. Then Ramsey has Donovan's inquest suppressed and sees to it that you aren't asked why you were meeting Walker, not to mention the "misunderstanding" that saw the scene of the crime left unsearched. Peters pretends not to mind, but he does – terribly. All this points to one thing: Ramsey is covering something up, possibly to protect the missing policeman, Iverson. Maybe Peters has been told to keep quiet, too. If he has, he'd never say.'

Lonsdale agreed. 'But there's nothing we can do.'

'Oh, yes, there is – we can explore these deaths ourselves.'

'But we've been told to leave it alone – by the police, and more importantly by Morley, who is, after all, the editor of *The PMG*.'

Her blue eyes gleamed. 'He also said we might publish a short account when the murders were resolved – which they won't be unless someone actually investigates. The police are willing to forget about it, but I'm not. How can they object when they've already given up?'

'I cannot see Morley being impressed by that argument,' said Lonsdale.

'This is more important than him,' determined Hulda. 'So first thing tomorrow we shall go to Donovan's place of work, and we will inform Morley what we're doing when we have proof of something odd. Then he'll have to agree to let us continue.'

'Morley would certainly rather we consulted him *before* we go to Donovan's workplace,' said Lonsdale. 'But I agree we need a carrot to dangle in front of him. So I will go with you tomorrow, but only if we agree we won't do anything else until he gives us his permission.'

'Of course,' said Hulda, a triumphant smile playing on the edges of her mouth. 'Would I ever do anything without official approval?'

Salmon and Eden Gentleman's Outfitters was a discreet establishment located at the corner of Oxford and Bird streets. Its windows were spotlessly clean – a remarkable feat in London – and in each there was a tasteful display of suits and coats and hats. Inside, the atmosphere was reverently hushed.

The shop had been open no more than ten minutes when Lonsdale arrived with Hulda. They were barely inside before an assistant came to offer a seat for the lady and his services for the gentleman. While Hulda sat, Lonsdale inspected shirts and trays of collars.

'Are you new?' the reporter asked nonchalantly of the assistant, a neat, dapper little Welshman with thinning hair, a huge moustache, and the name of Rhys. 'The last time I was here, I was attended by Donovan.'

Rhys's face became sombre. 'Mr Donovan is no longer with us, sir.'

'Really?' asked Lonsdale, inspecting a collar. 'I suppose he left because of his father? He told me the old man was ill, but of course this was over a year ago.'

'The old man died, sir,' explained Rhys. 'And, it grieves me to say, so did Mr Donovan. Just last week, in a tragic accident.'

'How dreadful,' Lonsdale exclaimed. 'How?'

'I don't know the details.' Rhys lowered his voice as one of his colleagues darted forward to greet a tall gentleman in a grey double-breasted reefer, who strolled in asking for collar studs. The newcomer glanced around the shop imperiously, allowing his gaze to settle on Lonsdale briefly, before giving his attention to the proffered box.

'What *do* you know?' asked Lonsdale.

'It was Mr Donovan's half-day,' began Rhys, 'Wednesday a week ago, and he said he was going to Hyde Park to watch the model boats. I told him he'd catch a chill in the rain, but he didn't listen. Model boats were his passion, you see. Then, the next day, he didn't arrive for work, which was unusual.'

'I see.'

'Most unusual,' continued Rhys, shaking his head mournfully. 'Regular as clockwork was Mr Donovan. I assumed he'd got a cold from being out in the wet, and planned to stop off to see him on my way home. But the police came and said there'd been an accident. A fire.'

'How terrible!'

'He must have become chilled watching the boats, and then set his house ablaze accidentally when he lit a fire to warm himself. Dreadful business!'

'Did he go boating alone?' asked Lonsdale.

Rhys looked at him curiously, but answered politely enough. 'I believe so, although he didn't boat himself – he just liked to watch. He was a quiet man, not given to chatter. He must have taken a shine to you, if he told you about his father. None of us knew about that until he asked for an hour off to attend the funeral last year.'

'Poor Donovan,' said Lonsdale, genuinely sorry for a man who should be quite so without friends. 'Was he ill Wednesday? Is that why you advised him against boating in the rain?'

'Never had a day's sickness in his life, and never missed a day of work! He was looking forward to his afternoon in the park, humming and singing under his breath as he always did when boating was planned.'

'Is there a wife or dependants whom I might help with a small donation?'

Rhys shook his head. 'It's a kind thought, sir, but Mr Donovan had no family. He was a very private man, and, even though we worked side by side for almost a year, he only invited me to his house once – just a few days before he died.'

'Gracious,' said Lonsdale. 'Did he have a reason for inviting you then?'

'I saw an advertisement for a house to rent in his road,' said Rhys. 'Number thirty-five. When I mentioned it to him, he invited me to pop by when I'd finished viewing it. I did, but I could tell he was uncomfortable, so I stayed only briefly. In fact, it had been so long since he'd had company, that he had to hunt about for a spare cup and saucer.'

'Number thirty-five?' asked Lonsdale, realizing that this was the Welshman about whom Hulda had spun her tales of rag-and-bone men. He felt a surge of guilt.

Rhys nodded. 'My wife and son liked the look of the place. Affordable homes in decent neighbourhoods are harder to find than you'd imagine, so we wanted to take it. But there seems to be a problem, which the agent says is of an "undefined" nature.' He frowned, his pleasant, earnest face puckering in consternation.

'We will be late for our appointment, dear,' said Hulda, standing abruptly and indicating that she and Lonsdale should leave. 'We must go.'

'I'll take three of these,' said Lonsdale, feeling obliged to buy something, so pointing to the first items he saw. He needed new shirts anyway, and disliked shopping. He jotted down his address. 'And half-a-dozen collars.'

Rhys saw them to the door, and Lonsdale took Hulda's arm until they were out of sight, when she promptly tugged it away.

'And you accuse *me* of leading people astray with lies!' she exclaimed. 'Hypocrite! You even offered to give money to a family you knew perfectly well doesn't exist.'

'To be frank, I seriously considered giving it to poor Rhys, given that you ruined his chances of moving into the house of his dreams.'

She had the grace to look guilty, but still retorted, 'Well, for all I know, *you* gave him a false address to which to send the shirts.'

'I most certainly did not,' objected Lonsdale indignantly. 'I—'

'You barely noticed what you were buying,' she interrupted, clearly spoiling for an argument. 'That obviously comes from having more money than sense.'

'I beg your pardon?' said Lonsdale, startled at her effrontery.

'You are independently wealthy, aren't you?

Voules told me that one reason he believes he should get the upcoming job at *The PMG* is that whereas he is not financially independent, your father left you a quarter of his not inconsiderable estate when he died. He said it was a fortune that was divided between you, two brothers, and a sister, and that you want for nothing.' She tipped her head back and regarded him defiantly.

'And how is Voules so familiar with my personal affairs?'

'He has contacts in important places.'

'Well, his contacts are wrong,' said Lonsdale coolly. 'My parents are both alive, and my father is the rector of Raunds in Northamptonshire – a country parson, living in a rectory he does not own. And I have a sister and *three* brothers: Jack, one who is the rector in Withersfield in Suffolk, and one who is a lieutenant in the Royal Navy. The reason I live with Jack is that I don't have independent means, and when Jack marries and I move out, I shall probably be all but destitute.'

'Then let's hope you get the position at *The PMG*,' said Hulda, in what Lonsdale supposed was intended to be a placatory manner. 'I'd rather have you than Voules.'

'Thank you,' said Lonsdale, thinking it was not much of a compliment. 'But we should be discussing Donovan, not my personal finances.'

Hulda nodded. 'He was chilled from the rain, so he lit a fire when he got home from the park. The chimney caught fire, and he rushed into the street to raise the alarm. He went back inside, where the killer strangled him, removed his cerebrum, crushed his head to hide the mutilation, left the fire to destroy any other clues, and escaped unseen.'

'Would a killer just happen to be there when the chimney caught fire?' asked Lonsdale doubtfully. 'And, more importantly, why did he want Donovan's cerebrum—'

'Don't look now, but I believe we're being followed,' interrupted Hulda.

She sighed irritably when Lonsdale glanced behind him, just in time to see the tall man who had been in Salmon and Eden duck through a door. Lonsdale frowned. The man had looked respectable, so why was he heading into the jug-and-bottle room of a pub, where drink was normally fetched for home consumption? He shrugged mentally, realizing that his imagination must be spiralling out of control – and so was Hulda's – if they were beginning to question the antics of complete strangers.

'Are you sure he was after us?' he asked. 'He looked a respectable gentleman.'

Hulda glared at him. 'Not him, Lonsdale – the boy.' The one who . . . damn it! He's gone. You would make a hopeless spy. You should have pretended not to notice him, while I doubled back and nabbed him.'

'A boy?'

'A scruffy one. But never mind him now. You and I are going to Morley, and we shall convince him that Donovan's death *must* be investigated. Well, don't just stand there with your mouth hanging open – flag down a hansom.'

* * *

When Hulda and Lonsdale reached the reporters'
office at *The PMG*, they were greeted by Voules,
his chubby face split by a lascivious leer. The
only other person there was young Edward Cook,
who was looking angry, as people often did when
obliged to spend any time with Voules.

'Coming to work in the same hansom, are we?'
Voules asked, rubbing his hands together. 'A
romance! How delicious! It is—'

Hulda instantly advanced so menacingly on
him that he stepped back in alarm, the grin wiped
from his face as though she had used a flannel.

'If I were having a romance, it would not
be with Lonsdale, and it would certainly not be
any business of yours,' she hissed dangerously.
'So keep your slanderous opinions to yourself.
You lied about Lonsdale and his fabled wealth,
and now you dare to gossip about me. You're
walking directly towards disaster, and it is a very
short path.'

Voules opened his mouth to defend himself, but
she turned on her heel and stormed away, leaving
him standing spluttering at empty air.

'You're playing with fire, Voules,' warned
Cook, who was dressed as smartly as Voules
was untidily, his thick hair perfectly groomed.
'No one insults The Friederichs and lives to
tell the tale.'

'Why, what will she do?' sniggered Voules,
vibrating with unpleasant laughter now his
intimidator was gone. 'Call me out? Pistols at
dawn?' He turned toward Lonsdale. 'Will you be
her second?'

Lonsdale ignored him, thinking such remarks

beneath his dignity to acknowledge. Cook was not so sanguine, and flushed with anger.

'Friederichs wouldn't need a second,' he said hotly. 'And if it *were* pistols, you would be wise to stay away. She's said to be handy with guns – rifles, shotguns, *and* pistols.'

'Does she fence, too? Or box?' smirked Voules acidly. He sat at his desk and pulled out his pipe. 'Nothing would surprise me about her. She probably doesn't swoon at the mention of knickers, either, as any well-bred woman should.'

'And any well-bred *man* would not speculate on a lady's personal life,' snapped Cook. 'By such comments, you reveal that you are no gentleman.'

Voules's flabby cheeks burned crimson with anger at the insult, but before he could reply, Cook stood and stamped out. Lonsdale followed, gratified to see Voules seething with indignation. As he passed Stead's office, he was startled to hear Alfred Milner calling him.

He retraced his steps and saw Milner kneeling on the floor, sifting through a pile of morning papers.

'What are you doing?' he asked. 'And where is Stead?'

'At the House, Alec. The budget is to be announced today.' He smiled. 'Your workhouse experiences have created quite a sensation! We had to print extra copies yesterday because of the demand for the second part of the story, and the print run will be higher yet for the final instalment today.'

'If you have time to chat, Milner, I assume you've found what I asked you to retrieve,' came Morley's icy voice from behind Lonsdale.

Lonsdale knew immediately the editor was in a bad mood, as he never criticized Milner as he did the rest of his staff – Morley liked him, because he not only understood the Irish Question, but was interested in it. He decided to make himself scarce, but Hulda arrived at just that moment, still irked by her encounter with Voules.

'Mr Morley,' she began brusquely. 'I'd like a word with you, please.'

'And I with you,' replied Morley coolly. 'Indeed, I was about to send for you. Lonsdale, too.'

They followed him into his office, where he held out an imperious hand, and Milner hurried forward to place a selection of articles in it; all, Lonsdale read upside down, related to Ireland. Milner backed away quickly, as Morley regarded first Hulda and then Lonsdale with a chilly glare.

'Neither of you produced a review of *Patience* as I ordered – Cook did it. I require my reporters to complete the assignments *I* give them, not ones they choose to do themselves. Do I make myself clear?'

'Yes, sir,' said Lonsdale, although Hulda remained silent.

'Good. And now you will redeem yourselves. There is a performance of *The Parvenu* at the Court Theatre tonight, and one of you *will* write a review. That means *going*, Miss Friederichs, not reading what *The Times* has to say and copying it.'

'I would never—' Hulda began indignantly.

132

Morley overrode her. 'Meanwhile, Miss Friederichs will work on our Occasional Notes section, remembering that they are supposed to give life and smartness to the page. Lonsdale, I want a piece on the miners' riots in Camborne. Plus, there's an intriguing story about a charging sperm whale sinking a ship. Whoever escapes the theatre tonight will investigate that.'

'A sperm whale?' echoed Hulda doubtfully.

'Find the truth and write it,' replied Morley, turning to the first of his articles. They both knew they had been dismissed.

'Do you want the theatre or the whale?' Lonsdale asked as they walked into the reporters' room.

'The whale,' replied Hulda at once. 'I can't abide the theatre.'

'Professor Seeley, my old tutor from Caius, is dining at our club tomorrow night,' Lonsdale told Milner later, as several reporters wrapped up their day after the edition had gone to the press. 'Jack and I will join him, and I was wondering if you would, too.'

'John Seeley was your tutor?' asked Milner, eagerly. 'The greatest thinker on historical issues of Christian doctrine? I had no idea you were so well connected!'

Lonsdale smiled fondly at the thought of his mentor. 'So will you come?'

'I can't,' said Milner with a grimace. 'Stead made me promise to take Harris to the club tomorrow, to thank him for taking you to the Garrick. Damn! I don't see how I can escape now that the invitation has been issued.'

'I suppose he could come, too,' said Lonsdale, although the prospect of introducing the erudite Seeley to a boor like Harris was alarming.

'Don't do it!' warned Cook, laughing. 'Not if you have an iota of affection for your old mentor. Harris is a pig and I cannot imagine why the Garrick let him in.'

'No indeed,' agreed Milner. 'Of course, it could be worse. We could drop into our clubs one day and find The Friederichs there, hogging the best papers and smoking her revolting cigars.'

'Hulda doesn't smoke cigars,' said Cook, ever the gentleman.

Lonsdale said nothing.

'She keeps some on her desk, but perhaps they're just for show,' said Milner. 'Well, why not? There's nothing so healthy or as satisfying as a fat cigar.' He went to Hulda's desk and picked up a La Jurista before grimacing and dropping it in distaste. 'Not one of these! But an El Diamante is one of the great pleasures in life. I always smoke during interviews, as it puts the people being questioned at ease.'

'I can't see Friederichs smoking a cigar, though,' said Cook loyally. 'It would be unbecoming in a woman.'

'True,' conceded Milner. 'In this day of women gaining new legal rights and being allowed to receive a superior education, a cigar is still one of the great benefits of being a man.'

Lonsdale continued to remain silent.

By the time Lonsdale had eaten a quick supper at home, changed into his evening suit, and caught a hansom to the Court Theatre, the performance was about to begin. The theatre was full, at least in part because the Prince of Wales was there, exuding his customary melange of gentility and debauchery. Lonsdale quickly lost interest in the play, and found himself thinking about Donovan, Cath, and the mysterious Constable Iverson. He reviewed his encounter with the prostitute again, in the hope of uncovering some previously overlooked clue.

Did she have a tale to tell him, or had her intention been to rob him? She had promised to bring a witness to prove her claims, and then she and the unidentified man were killed – her with a slit throat and him by poison. Why two such different modes of execution? It all seemed unnecessarily complex.

More to the point, who had killed them? The two men who had attacked him? He pondered the question and decided not, on the grounds that they had been such inept fighters, and the killer of Cath, her accomplice, and Donovan – he no longer doubted that the deaths of Donovan and Cath were related – had been ruthlessly efficient.

Applause from the audience brought him out of his reverie, and he stood for intermission. The theatre stank of perfume, hair lacquer, eau-de-Cologne, and other beautifying potions, all vying with the reek of smoke from cigars, cigarettes, and pipes. The latter grew worse as people collected their refreshments from the foyer. Eventually, it proved more than Lonsdale could bear, and he walked outside for some fresh air.

Or, rather, some cooler air. Smoke from thousands upon thousands of chimneys poured into London's sky. Lonsdale took a deep breath and felt grit between his teeth. He was about to go back inside again, when there was a low rumble followed by the sound of smashing glass and a blast of hot air. For a moment, nothing happened, then people began to scream, and dust billowed through the doors.

Lonsdale's first thought was that it was an attempt by Irish Fenians on the life of the Prince of Wales. He covered his mouth and nose with his handkerchief and raced inside.

In the foyer, a huge chandelier hung by a thread from the ceiling, threatening to drop at any moment. Broken glass was everywhere. A woman shrieked in terror, and another was sobbing. Lonsdale saw that someone had organized a line of people with water buckets to douse the flames. Indeed, most people were leaving in a surprisingly calm fashion, gentlemen even pausing to assist older ladies. Several stewards had manned the cloakroom and were returning hats, cloaks, and capes.

He knelt next to a young doorman, who lay on the floor, clutching his knee. It was messy but not serious, caused when the lad had fallen on some glass. He staunched the flow of blood with his handkerchief and made a crude bandage with his tie.

Above the clatter of heels on the marble floor, whispers told Lonsdale that the Prince of Wales had taken charge, and was overseeing the evacuation. Lonsdale lifted the lad in his arms, and joined the flow of people outside.

'Was it one of those Irish mobs, do you think?' one man asked as they went. 'They certainly wouldn't hesitate to inflict such an outrage.'

'We were damned lucky,' said another. 'The bell had rung to announce the second act, so people were on the move. Had the explosion occurred five minutes earlier, there would have been a massacre.'

Two firemen informed the white-faced manager that they would not be able to tell whether the explosion was caused by gas or something more sinister until the following morning. Seeing there was no more to learn, Lonsdale decided to go home.

He relinquished the lad into the care of a steward, retrieved his overcoat and gibus hat, and began searching for a hansom. He was about to hail one when he saw a nicely dressed young lad watching him from the kerbside on the opposite side of the road. He was familiar, but it took Lonsdale a moment to remember where he had seen him before.

'Hello, Jamie,' Lonsdale said, approaching the boy he had seen at the workhouse. 'Not your normal area, is it?'

'I get around,' shrugged Jamie. 'Same as you.'

'How did you . . .?' began Lonsdale curiously, but then understanding came in a flash. 'You rode on the back of the carriage when I was collected from the workhouse. You jumped off when I reached home – I heard you.'

Jamie grinned. 'I saw you getting into a big carriage, so I thought to myself, "why don't we see who this feller is?" So I went along for the

137

ride, all the way to Bayswater. The houses kept getting bigger and bigger, and yours was one of the biggest.'

'And you were on Oxford Street this morning . . .'

'Your lady friend spotted me, I suppose. But, yeah, I've been watching you since, seeing if I could figger what you really are. One thing you ain't, is a man that needs to doss at a workhouse.'

'Nor are you, judging by your clothes,' said Lonsdale wryly.

'Just did a bit of snow-droppin', didn't I?'

'You mean you stole them from a line while they were drying?'

Jamie grinned again. 'So now I look like a right little gen'leman.'

'Well then, little gentleman, what do you want from me?'

'It's what *you* want from me, old pal – I can tell you things for your newspaper.' He smirked when Lonsdale's eyebrows rose. 'Yeah, I know you're a reporter. I ain't stupid – you stay at home for a couple of days after you leave the workhouse, and then all of a sudden everyone's talking about what happens there. I guessed right away what you done.'

'But what makes you think I need more information? I learned more than enough the other night.'

'You'll want to hear what I got to say, old pal. But speaking the Lord's truth is hungry work.' He looked at Lonsdale meaningfully.

'All right,' said Lonsdale, laughing. 'There's

138

a café nearby. I'll buy you a meal in exchange for your gossip.'

The Aerated Bread Company cafés were small, respectable, and known for their quick service, clean cutlery, and inexpensive food. The one on Sloane Street was filled with clerks and white-collar workers who had been working late, and the air was heavy with the smell of hot lard from the skillets. Feeling conspicuous in his finery, Lonsdale selected a table at the back.

'So, what can you tell me?' he asked, after Jamie had ordered enough food to fill someone twice his size. The lad had been gawking at the displays of food in walnut cases along the wall, but when he looked back at Lonsdale, his bravado seemed to wilt. He grew sombre.

'You seem a nice man,' he said. 'Maybe you can do sommat to help me. And you got reason to, because the same men who've taken me mates are looking for you.'

'What do you mean?' asked Lonsdale, bemused. 'Who's looking for me? And what happened to your friends?'

'I know lots of people from the workhouses. You stay there long enough, you get to know most. And I've been there for years – since me dad did a runner. Lately, some've disappeared, including two of me mates.' He paused and looked around furtively. 'I see things, but I don't get seen, if you know what I mean. I've seen a number of people being taken away – and they ain't never come back.'

'Taken away?' asked Lonsdale.

'Loo-ered,' said the lad, giving a particularly sinister tone to a word he obviously did not use often. 'Talked into going off with women.'

'Lured away by prostitutes?'

'No. I know dollies, whether they're the fanciest flash-tails, the common dress-lodgers, or the wrens that hang about the military barracks. None of them. These were women that were hired to get men away from the workhouse.'

'Perhaps they're just wives or girlfriends.'

'They ain't, I tell you,' insisted Jamie. He paused as the waiter brought his food, and did not speak again until he had scoffed his first cake. 'The men go away with the women, and they don't come back. It's because of the men who're watching.'

'What men?' asked Lonsdale, bewildered by the flood of information.

'Four or five of 'em, usually a couple at a time.' Jamie spoke from around a massive bite of beef pie. 'The one I've seen the most is older'n you – short, but with big arms, like a blacksmith. He's got thinnish hair and a long beard. And he's got a real swagger, like some lord.'

Lonsdale took out his pocket book and began to write. 'And the others?'

'Another's small, not much bigger'n me. I've seen him walking into a pub once, over in Stepney, and he was cursing to himself sommat vile. He's got a funny moustache – half dark, half grey. And one of those top hats that the killer wore – the cove that was hanged.'

'A Müller cut-down?' Lonsdale asked, giving

140

a name popularly used for a hat that resembled a top hat trimmed to half its height. It was named for a murderer whose penchant for them had led to his eventual identification and arrest.

'That's it. And then there's an older feller. He's big too, but fat. Hands shaking with excitement all the time and a great scar through his eyebrow—'

Lonsdale sat bolt upright. 'What?'

'I said you'd be interested,' said Jamie smugly. 'Saw him following you the other day. You and your lady friend.'

'Where?' demanded Lonsdale.

'Great Portland Street. He was just there, watching. Didn't know I was watching him – like I said, I see but I don't get seen. And he ain't the only one. There's a gent, too. Dark grey suit, top hat, and nice shoes. Not nearly so good at staying out of sight as Eyebrow is.'

'I've seen him, too,' mused Lonsdale. 'Although I hadn't given him much thought. Do they know each other?'

'Dunno.' Jamie gave him a conspiratorial glance. 'Seems you've been up to more than just going to a workhouse.'

'I think it's the ones following me who have been up to something,' muttered Lonsdale. 'Murder – I think they've murdered people.'

Jamie stopped chewing. 'Then me mates is done for?'

'I don't know yet. Tell me more about what you've seen.'

So Jamie did.

141

Five

Lonsdale was at Northumberland Street early the following morning to write an eyewitness account of the explosion at the Court Theatre. That done, he went to see Stead, whose bright eyes and cheerful smile were due to the continued success of the workhouse story and the subsequent questions that were being asked by influential individuals about urban poverty. Lonsdale poured out all he had learned from Jamie, while the assistant editor listened without interruption. Leaving Lonsdale sitting on a stack of newspapers, Stead went to request an appointment with Morley. Moments later, he poked his head back in. 'Mr Morley will see us now.'

'Us?' queried Lonsdale.

'This requires a united front, Lonsdale. We besiege him together. Come.'

Lonsdale followed him along the hall to Morley's office, where the editor sat at his desk, fingers steepled. He nodded for them to sit, and his sombre gaze settled unflinchingly on his reporter.

'Mr Stead tells me that you wish to continue your investigation into these murders,' he said. 'Pray tell me why, when the police asked us to desist.'

'More information has come to light since we last spoke,' Lonsdale began. 'And to be frank, sir, there's something odd about the police investigation – almost as if they want to deny that Donovan's death is suspicious, and hope that if they obfuscate long enough, all will be forgotten.'

'Go on,' said Morley.'

'There are questions that *should* be asked, but that the police – or rather Superintendent Ramsey – seem unwilling to pose,' Lonsdale continued. 'Such as why Donovan, who never missed work, was at home when he was killed? Why did he run back inside his house and lock his doors after raising the alarm? Did the chimney sweep leave a brush that caused the fire? Who was the man killed with Cath and why was he poisoned?'

Lonsdale then outlined all Jamie had told him about the men being lured away by women and never seen again.

'Tell him about you being followed, too,' ordered Stead when Lonsdale had finished. He glanced at Morley. 'Followed by men involved in the luring, one of whom matches the description of a missing and very dangerous policeman – one Constable Iverson.'

'Miss Friederichs told me yesterday that you were being stalked by a child – not a deadly ex-officer of the law,' said Morley.

'It was both – and more,' said Lonsdale. 'I was not the only one who saw the tall man in the suit – Jamie did, too.'

Lonsdale could see that, although Stead was convinced that something was badly amiss, Morley remained sceptical. He realized he needed to present a stronger case. The inspiration hit him in

143

the form of an article Milner had written, and as Morley admired Milner . . .

'Do you recall Milner's two-part article entitled "British Nomads", sir?' he asked, going to where Morley kept a copy of the back issues and riffling through them to find the one he wanted.

'Of course,' said Morley, pointedly consulting his fob watch.

'There was a bit about marriage, and how some women select husbands.' Lonsdale found what he was looking for and began to read:

We will suppose that a female hawker of small wares is in want of a partner. She has ways of making money, and can maintain herself and a partner in comfortable style, but she would rather not join fortunes with one of her own sort, as such a one would arrogate supremacy in the partnership, and insist on keeping the purse. In short, she would be little better than a drudge. She therefore prefers to pick a man who will allow her to play the leading part – a fellow considerably younger than herself, whom she may rule and regulate according to her liking.

Failing to meet the right sort on her travels, she looks elsewhere – the casual ward. Ere many evenings pass she is sure to meet just the sort of person she wants, beckons him aside, and makes a proposal that he can hardly refuse. She wants somebody to carry her baskets; she offers in return food, lodging, drink, and a little

money. The work is light, and a shiftless
tramp is not likely to refuse such an offer
– and the woman carries off her prey.

'What are you saying?' asked Morley, incredulously. 'That your urchin's friends are being
whisked away to become kept men?'

'No – I'm saying that someone is using the
technique Milner described to ensnare them,'
explained Lonsdale. 'Jamie said his friends
were "picked up" by women – definitely not
prostitutes – near the workhouses. These aren't
men with money for prostitutes, and he's seen
the same women at workhouses in different
parts of the city. And once the men go, they
never come back.'

'How do you know they have not been recruited
to earn an honest wage elsewhere?' asked Morley,
still sceptical. 'Labouring, perhaps? I see no
reason to think these "disappearances" are related
to your murders.'

With the editor seemingly intractable, Lonsdale
decided to play his last desperate hand to
convince him.

'There's one other vital piece of information,'
he said. 'Jamie's friends who disappeared from
the workhouse are named Joseph Killian, Sean
MacDermott, and Eamon O'Sullivan. Add Patrick
Donovan to that, and what do you have?'

Lonsdale held his breath, hoping that four
Irish names would snag Morley's interest, as
there was little about that country that did not
fascinate him.

'How can you be sure it's not coincidence?'

asked Morley, although Lonsdale saw a glimmer of curiosity flare in his cool, grey eyes.

Lonsdale handed him page five of that morning's *Daily Telegraph*. Circled near the bottom was a small note that read:

> *Yesterday morning the body of John Keefe, a small farmer from Kingwilliamstown, County Cork, was found in a ditch, under circumstances that left no doubt as to his being murdered. A multitude of wounds showed that the unfortunate man had been subjected to shocking violence, and his head had been fractured and crushed to the point that the only way he was recognized was by his clothes.*

'With a head crushed like that, do you think he still had a cerebrum inside?' asked Lonsdale, seeing with satisfaction that Morley's reservations were crumbling at last.

The editor sat in silence for a long time before speaking. 'Lonsdale, you've known me long enough to appreciate that I dislike tales that appeal to the readers of police gazettes and exploitative weeklies. That said, I see you may have stumbled across a crime that might have deeper and wider-ranging consequences. We don't know if there's a connection between Keefe and your murders, but if there is, exposing it is our moral duty. After all, disruption in Ireland is one of the greatest threats our society faces today.'

'I quite agree,' said Stead. 'It is the only ethical decision to make.'

'However,' continued Morley, 'I do not want Miss Friederichs to investigate with you, given the obvious danger of the quest.'

Lonsdale sincerely hoped he would not be the one assigned to tell her, but Stead waved an airy hand. 'We need all our staff to be available for this, but I promise to keep her away from anything risky. Come, Lonsdale – there is not a moment to lose.'

'Stay,' ordered Morley as Lonsdale aimed for the door. 'You cannot explore a case with Irish implications without a clear understanding of the nuances of the Irish situation, and much changed in the years that you were out of the country. It would be dangerous if you proved to be dealing with individuals involved in the armed struggle. So sit. I shall apprise you of the important issues and details now.'

Stead winked at Lonsdale as he left, amused that he should use the editor's obsession to get his way. Lonsdale floundered for an excuse to escape, too, but he saw Morley's determined expression and realized there was none.

Forty minutes later, Lonsdale emerged with his head spinning. He left the building quickly, unwilling to risk being waylaid by colleagues, and eager to begin his investigation in earnest now he had the editor's approval. He decided his first task was to visit the sweep to find out if the man really had left one of his brushes up Donovan's chimney. He remembered from the comments made by Donovan's neighbour, Mrs North, that his name was Kendal.

He walked to the Victoria Embankment and stopped near Cleopatra's Needle, resting his elbows on the low wall and gazing across the greasy, grey-brown swirl of the Thames as he thought about his next move. The river stank, despite the sewer system and its elaborate pumping stations that had been built at great expense two decades before.

While he listened to ships' horns and the scream of gulls, he pondered how he might find the sweep. Then he recalled that Jack had recently employed one. He took a hansom home, and rifled through his brother's desk until he found a card that read:

J. Hanker, Chimney Sweep, respectfully begs to inform the Gentry and Inhabitants of Bayswater Road and its Vicinity that he hopes, by his unremitting Attention, to merit liberal Support.

At the bottom was an assurance that Hanker always used clean cloths.

The card gave an address on Woodchester Street, near the Great Western Railway, so Lonsdale set off on foot, aiming to ask Hanker for Kendal's address – as there was bound to be some form of fraternity among fellow workers. As he walked, the houses changed from spacious mansions to middle-class semis, to working-class terraces, and finally to grimy hovels. All were located within close proximity of each other, something that upset many of the wealthier inhabitants of the city on those occasions when they let themselves think about it.

Eventually, Lonsdale found Woodchester Street, a road with houses built from dull, charcoal-grey bricks that seemed to leach every speck of colour from their surroundings. An occasional pot of flowers had been placed in brave defiance of the monochrome. Lonsdale's progress was monitored closely by men and boys slouching outside their houses, smoking clay pipes or cheap Early Bird cigarettes. Painfully aware of the less-than-inviting looks, he knocked on Hanker's door until it was answered by a woman holding a screaming baby.

'Mr Kendal!' yelled Lonsdale, above the ear-splitting screeches. 'Where does he live?'

'Why?' demanded the woman. 'My husband John does chimneys better than old Kendal. When do you want him to come?'

'He's already been,' shouted Lonsdale, then added hastily, seeing the woman's lips harden into a thin line, 'and a splendid job he did. We'll most definitely ask him again. But I need to speak to Kendal about something else.'

'I know, you think Kendal can do better,' said the woman bitterly, jigging the baby up and down vigorously enough to make it sick. 'Well, there isn't a finer sweep in London than John. And his cloths are always clean. I wash 'em myself.'

'Then tell him to come to Number Seventeen Cleveland Square next Thursday at nine o'clock,' yelled Lonsdale, to convince her he was not

149

taking his custom to Kendal. 'Now, where can I find Mr Kendal?'

The woman nodded her satisfaction. 'All right, then. He lives on Hatton Street, the other side of Edgware Road. But if I hear you employed him over John, I'll be round to your house – and not with clean cloths!'

Lonsdale believed it. He escaped from her and her shrieking offspring with relief.

Hatton Street was even more downtrodden, and equally populated with sullen, resentful men who watched him with open suspicion. Lonsdale asked one where Kendal lived. The fellow nodded at a house with planks of wood nailed over the glassless windows.

A young woman with a white face and a tubercular cough answered Lonsdale's knock and conducted him to a small room at the back. The sweep sat in the only chair, huddled next to a miserable fire that produced a pall of choking smoke. Lonsdale felt like recommending he have his chimney swept. A broken-down iron bed stood near the window, strewn with covers that had been coal sacks in a previous incarnation. A wooden table with a broken leg was pushed against the wall to keep it standing. The sweep himself was elderly, with red-rimmed and runny eyes. Gnarled, soot-impregnated hands clutched a dirty bottle filled with a colourless liquid. He raised it to his lips when Lonsdale entered and drank deeply.

'Please forgive the intrusion,' said Lonsdale. 'I wondered whether you might be able to help me.'

Kendal looked him up and down. 'Of course,' he said bitterly. 'I'm sure there's all manner of things the likes of me could do for the likes of you.'

Lonsdale took a shilling from his pocket and laid it on the mantelpiece.

'It's about the fire in Wyndham Street—'

'I see!' snarled the sweep, coming unsteadily to his feet. 'You've come to accuse me of killing Mr Donovan!'

'No,' said Lonsdale, standing his ground as Kendal staggered towards him. 'I just wanted to ask—'

'That fire ruined me,' said the sweep, turning from anger to self-pity in the way that drunks often did. 'I should be out there now, working. I had a full week booked. Then Donovan sets himself alight, and who gets the blame? Everyone's cancelled me, even the vicarage – and I've been doing them chimneys for thirty years.'

'I'm sorry,' said Lonsdale quietly.

'The Fire Brigade accused me of leaving a brush up there!' Kendal gestured to a shadowy corner, where there was a collection of black-headed brooms and poles. 'But you tell me what you see there. All my brushes, that's what. They're expensive! How do they think I can afford to leave them up chimneys?'

'I see your point.'

'I went back to Donovan's house, you know,' said Kendal, slumping back down in his chair. 'On Friday – the night after the fire. I looked up the chimney.'

151

'What did you see?'

'Nothing,' said Kendal mournfully. He slumped further down in his chair and studied the reporter blearily. 'You don't get it, do you?'

Lonsdale struggled to understand. 'Nothing? You mean you couldn't see up the chimney? It was blocked?'

The sweep nodded. 'But I could see right up it when I finished cleaning. I got down on my hands and knees, like I always do, and saw a ring of sky like a bright, round penny. I take pride in my work, and if that penny hadn't been round, I'd have had the brushes up again.'

'Yet it was blocked after the fire?' asked Lonsdale.

Kendall nodded. 'I poked about with a stick, and a ball of burned rags came down. I looked up the chimney again, and there was the penny of sky.'

'So, someone deliberately stuffed them up it, so that the fire would be deemed an accident?'

'Why would someone do such a thing to me?' wailed Kendal. 'I've been honest all my life. I've had plenty of opportunities to slip a silver spoon or a few coins in my pocket, or to filch a bit of crockery. But I never did it, not once. Now I wish I had. There's so many sweeps that it's not easy to get work, but I've done all right, because everyone knows I'm honest. But some folks are struggling something cruel.'

Lonsdale glanced around Kendal's grimy, sparsely furnished home, and wondered how those 'struggling something cruel' were forced to live.

'I believe you're innocent of any wrong-doing, Mr Kendal,' said Lonsdale. 'And I'm going to prove it, but I need your help. Will you tell me – with all your knowledge of chimneys and fires – how the blaze started in Donovan's house?'

Hope lit the old man's eyes. 'I think the rags were shoved up the chimney and set alight. Of course, they'd need to have been soaked in something to make them burn. Oil perhaps. Then the chimney would catch fire, because the flames would be fed by the air coming down it. Once a chimney is going, it's a devil to put out. More often than not the whole house goes. I told the police all this, but I could tell they thought I was just trying to save my own skin.'

'Did you catch the names of the officers?'

'No, but I can tell you that the first one I spoke to was older, with a scar over his eye, while the second had ginger hair and looked young enough to be my grandson.'

Lonsdale felt his heartbeat quicken. 'Was the first one a large man, with black hair?'

'I suppose,' said the old man, frowning as he tried to recall. 'Of course, they don't know their arses from their elbows – the ginger lad told me that the scarred one had never been here.'

Kendal could tell him no more, so Lonsdale took his leave, promising again to clear his name.

The Oxford and Cambridge Club was a grand building at 71–77 Pall Mall, with a pillared porch and an imposing façade. Its only requirement for membership was matriculation at – not

153

necessarily graduation from – one of the two universities. It had been founded in the 1830s, after the waiting list for the United University Club had become too long to be tolerated.

Gentlemen's clubs tended to be understated on the outside, but the Oxford and Cambridge was unique in having a smartly uniformed porter on the *outside*, and by the time Lonsdale and Milner reached him, the door was open. They nodded their thanks and entered the spacious hall. They gave their hats and overcoats to another porter, and Milner also handed over an umbrella topped with a finely carved eagle's head with very conspicuous eyes. He dreaded the possibility of getting wet in a sudden shower.

'Stead got hold of that today,' said Milner, nodding to it. 'He came to the reporters' room to hold forth. Suddenly, it was in his hands, whirling around as if he were leading a cavalry charge.'

'Did you manage to ditch Harris?' asked Lonsdale. The American was nowhere to be seen.

Milner grimaced. 'He has promised to grace me with his presence later. I'm hoping that it will be late enough that everyone I know will have gone home.'

They headed up the stairs to the drawing room, a sumptuous wood-panelled chamber packed with comfortable chairs, sofas, and low tables scattered with newspapers. Jack was there, sitting with John Seeley, Regius Professor of History at Cambridge, and the man who had convinced Lonsdale to join the Colonial Service. Lonsdale introduced him and Milner.

'Are you a Cambridge man?' asked Seeley, shaking Milner's hand. 'Or are you from the Other Place?'

'Alfred is too modest to boast,' said Lonsdale, 'but he not only took a double first at Balliol, but won no fewer than four of Oxford's major scholarships.'

Milner blushed, and Lonsdale was amused to see him at a loss for words. Seeley motioned for them to sit down.

'Jack has been regaling me with the most alarming news, Alec,' he said. 'That you've decided to turn your unfortunate interest in journalism into a full-time profession. You were one of my best students . . . and to be telling stories for a newspaper! There must be something we can do to make you return to the Colonial Service.'

'There isn't,' said Lonsdale, shortly. 'This is what I want to do.' He was very fond of Seeley, so had not wanted to respond too forcefully. But before he could change the subject, Seeley turned to Milner.

'Can *you* persuade him to abandon this reckless course of action?' A man of your scholarly background must deplore a squandering of such talents. Alec could someday be a foreign ambassador. Urge him to follow this path.'

'That would be beyond my capabilities,' Milner responded, 'not to mention rather hypocritical if I attempted it, under the circumstances. Besides, journalists *are* ambassadors, are they not? They interpret events and opinions, which they then present to a large body of people.'

155

'That's an intriguing notion,' said Seeley, contemplating Milner's argument.

'I understand that you have written another book, Professor,' Lonsdale said quickly, hoping to avoid any awkward differences in opinion. 'One to be published next year?'

'Indeed I have,' said Seeley. A discussion of the theories that his new work would propound ensued, and both the professor and Milner were pleased with the challenge of the other's intellect. Finally, there was a pause, and Seeley looked around gloomily.

'The club isn't what it once was. I hardly know a soul here. I recognize Francis Galton, but no one else.'

'Galton?' asked Jack, sitting up abruptly. 'I'd like to meet *him*! His theories relating to natural history . . . well, they are astounding to say the least.'

Seeley gave a sly smile. 'Perhaps I *should* introduce you to him, Alec. He was in Africa, so he might be able to talk some sense into you about the Colonial Service.'

Francis Galton, one of the country's most eminent gentleman-scientists, an expert on travel, and author of several much-acclaimed books on heredity, looked up with rude disinterest when Seeley introduced the Lonsdale brothers and Milner. Galton was a stocky man with thick eyebrows, bald except for a fringe of long, dangling grey hair around the back, and a pair of colossal mutton-chop sideburns. A gentleman in a charcoal grey lounge suit was engrossed in

156

his paper in the chair opposite; he vacated his seat politely when he saw that Galton had visitors, so that they all might sit down together. Something about him was familiar, but Seeley was making introductions, so there was no time for Lonsdale to ponder about him.

'I was hoping you might persuade Alec to rejoin the Colonial Service,' said Seeley amiably once introductions had been made, 'instead of wasting his great talents on newspapers.'

'You're a reporter?' asked Galton, in much the same way that he might have spoken to a dung collector; clearly, there was no difference between the two in his eyes. 'I hope you don't think I shall speak to you about my cousin Charles Darwin. I've had the press pestering me day and night, wanting a eulogy. Well, you shall not have it!'

'I see,' said Lonsdale, taken aback by his vehemence and exchanging an uncomfortable glance with Milner. 'But we didn't—'

'Your work on heredity and intelligence can only be described as brilliant, Mr Galton,' said Jack enthusiastically, breaking into what could have become an embarrassing discussion. 'I can't tell you how much I enjoy your writing.'

Galton's pale eyes immediately softened. 'Of course you do. Any man of breeding and intellect will appreciate the significance of my work.'

Milner caught Lonsdale's eye and raised an amused eyebrow. Lonsdale looked away quickly, not wanting to laugh, although Galton was far too engrossed in himself to notice.

'I'm working on another book entitled *Inquiries into Human Faculty and Its Development*,' he

157

continued pompously. 'It will be a seminal work, admired and consulted by scholars for many generations to come.'

'What's its central thesis?' asked Jack keenly.

Galton preened. 'It builds on my previous work, including *Hereditary Genius* and *English Men of Science*, and it presents the results of several experiments. It begins with an analysis of physical characteristics – such as facial features and physical build. Then it considers energy and sensitivity, both of which are shown to be greater in the intellectually gifted – like me – than in the less able of our species.'

'Goodness!' blurted Jack, showing that even he was taken aback by Galton's boastful manner.

'I have investigated the subject of *character*, perhaps best illustrated in the traits that distinguish the sexes,' Galton went on. 'You see, characteristics found in mankind can also be discovered in lesser species – such as directness in men and a caprice in women.'

'Caprice?' echoed Lonsdale, thinking of Hulda and unable to imagine her ever having a 'capricious' moment in her life.

Galton nodded impatiently. 'Yes. The willy-nilly disposition of the human female in matters of love is also apparent in the butterfly, so it must have been continuously favoured from the earliest stages of animal evolution. Capriciousness has thus become a heritage of ladies, together with a cohort of allied weaknesses that men have come to think admirable in their wives and lovers, but that they would never tolerate among themselves.'

'I would hardly—' Seeley began, but Galton droned on mercilessly.

'The *next* section of my book investigates such matters as fear, revulsion, conscience, and gregariousness. And the last part draws it all together by showing how selective breeding would control these characteristics and benefit our race as a whole.'

'How intriguing,' said Jack nervously.

'Breeding,' announced Galton in a loud voice, 'is the heart of the problem. It should never be done without thought or reason.'

Lonsdale regarded the scientist in genuine horror, thinking his comments were every bit as distasteful as those made by Wilson.

'To no nation is a high human breed more necessary than our own,' Galton brayed on. 'We plant our stock around the world, laying the foundation for future millions of the human race. Yet you've only to walk in Whitechapel to see how the weak are numerically supplanting the strong – and the appalling poverty that accompanies this. It cannot be allowed to continue, and, by denying criminals, the idle, and other undesirables the opportunity to breed, we would abolish much suffering and misery.'

There was a stunned silence before Seeley, with a stricken, apologetic glance at the three younger men, hastened to change the subject. Lonsdale was relieved, having never expected to hear such offensive sentiments in his own club. 'Lonsdale was in southern Africa for a spell,' Seeley said, a little desperately. 'You were there, weren't you, Galton?'

'A spell?' drawled Galton, in distaste. 'And what was your "spell", young man? A couple of weeks? It is my contention that one cannot understand a continent in less than a month.'

'Nine years,' replied Lonsdale, gratified to see the great man's surprise. But good manners got the better of him, obliging him to add, 'I hear you were there in the forties, sir. Your experiences must have been fascinating—'

'I can tell you about them now,' said Galton, glancing at his watch. 'I have a few hours to spare.'

And without further ado, he began a detailed monologue describing every moment of what sounded to be a remarkably dull expedition. His audience listened politely, but all attempts to change the subject or escape were ruthlessly quashed. After an hour, a steward came to say that Harris had arrived, and it was a testament to Galton's tediousness that Lonsdale actually envied Milner for being able to go and greet the obnoxious American. Galton droned on, and Lonsdale looked at Milner with pleading eyes when he returned with his guest a few moments later. Milner took a deep breath and returned to the fray.

'I'm afraid I must take my friends away, Mr Galton,' he began. 'They—'

'Nonsense,' said Galton and continued his story. 'I found the daughter of the king of Ovampoland installed in my tent in her finery – she was covered with red ochre and butter, and as capable of leaving a mark on anything she touched as a well-inked printer's roller.

Meanwhile, I was dressed in my one well-preserved suit of white linen—'

But Galton had reckoned without Harris, who, on recognizing him, homed in on him like a bluebottle on rotting meat. He thrust his outstretched hand into Galton's face. 'Ambrose Harris of *The New York Herald*. I wonder if I might ask you a few questions about Mr Darwin for the overseas audience.'

'Young man,' said Galton, brushing the proffered hand away contemptuously, 'a gentlemen's club is for *gentlemen*. It is not somewhere to demonstrate distasteful forwardness.' He stood and addressed Seeley. 'If you ever needed an instrument of persuasion against journalism, that man is it. He has quite put me off my dinner. I shall go home instead.'

'Thank God,' muttered Jack as the scientist gathered up his belongings. 'And thank Milner!'

'You seem a decent enough fellow,' said Galton, turning to Lonsdale before he left. 'I've enjoyed discussing Africa with you. Call on me at home next Friday afternoon, and I shall finish my story, although I appreciate you will find it hard to wait for the denouement. And then I shall show you something you will never forget – my collection of dried grasses from the Trans-Orange region!'

'I can think of little I'd enjoy more,' lied Lonsdale.

'I do enjoy the Reverend Carpenter's sermons,' said Jack the following morning – Sunday – as he and his brother strolled through Kensington Gardens. 'He makes his case about the teachings

161

of the Church with the intellect of a barrister, the precision of an engineer, and the force of an Evangelical.'

'I'm not sure that he would appreciate being called an Evangelical,' said Lonsdale. 'Or worse yet, a barrister.'

'Do not try to vex me – not today of all days,' said Jack mildly. He tipped his hat to a couple strolling the other way. The gentleman tipped back.

'Don't worry. I'll behave when your fiancée and her sister come to dine today.' Lonsdale glanced at him. 'This custom of constantly raising the hat is very odd. Before I left for Africa, it was thought to be foreign and in bad taste. Now everyone is doing it.'

'Emelia likes the respect it affords,' said Jack, tipping to another couple. 'And I aim to please. Shall we go home now to make sure Mrs Webster and the servants have returned from church and are preparing the meal? If it is not ready by two, Emelia will be irked.'

Lonsdale disliked the way Jack was constantly changing himself to please Emelia. The couple had first been introduced a year before at a meeting in support of the Married Women's Property Act, and had become engaged at Christmas. He had dined with her family three of every four Sundays since, and, despite him being twelve years older than her, both families had been supportive of the proposed union.

Jack had hosted Emelia and her family before, but never when Lonsdale had been there. Lonsdale had thus never met any of the

162

clan other than Emelia. Jack was anxious that they – and especially Emelia's sister Anne – should like his brother, and evidently was terrified that Lonsdale might do something to make them think twice about having given him permission to marry their younger daughter. Lonsdale was mildly offended that Jack did not have more confidence in him, and could only suppose that the decision to become a journalist had given his brother a deeper shock than he had realized.

'Don't worry, Jack,' said Lonsdale kindly. 'You have a gem of a housekeeper in Mrs Webster. No one realizes better than she does that this is the first time you have entertained Emelia with only her sister and me as chaperones. Moreover, I am sure Anne will like me and will sing my praises to your fiancée.'

'You sound like Galton,' muttered Jack, eyeing him suspiciously and very nervously.

Shortly after one o'clock, Emilia and Anne arrived by private carriage. They were clearly sisters: tall, dark eyed, slim, and with naturally curly hair brushed back into a bun at the nape of the neck in the popular fashion of the day. Emelia's was dark brown; Anne's was lighter, almost blond. Lonsdale found Anne, the elder by just over two years, not only much prettier but far more charming.

Emelia was also nervous of the first meeting between Anne and Lonsdale, although he could not imagine why, as Anne seemed a rational, intelligent woman, not at all the prim, dull spinster he had feared. Knowing that the affianced couple were more concerned that Anne might not like him rather than the other way around, he went out of his way to be as courteous and pleasing as possible.

Most of the conversation at the meal revolved around the changes that Emelia would make to Jack's house when she became mistress of it. Bored, Lonsdale asked Emelia to describe how she and Jack had met, knowing she loved to recount the tale. However, in the presence of Anne, he learned two things Emelia and Jack had not told him before – that Emelia had only attended the meeting to support the Married Women's Property Act because Anne had begged her to, and that Jack had only been there because a colleague had done the same to him. Lonsdale wondered why Jack had persisted in his courtship, given that he and Emelia had little in common, but saw from Jack's besotted expression that no amount of reasoning or logic would convince him that he could do better.

Even when Emelia rose from the table and began to walk around the room pointing out items that would have to be removed or changed when she was in charge, Jack watched her dotingly, and Lonsdale saw that there was nothing he would not do for her. Yet how dull she was! He glanced at Anne and saw that she had been studying him. Embarrassed to be caught, she quickly looked away.

After the meal, Emelia suggested a stroll around the square onto which Jack's house backed. The engaged couple walked leisurely arm-in-arm, while the chaperones followed behind, Lonsdale with his hands clasped behind his back, and Anne clutching her pelisse.

'Do *you* think my brother's house needs complete renovation?' Lonsdale asked, as he heard Emelia's high-pitched assurance that dark-blue flock wallpaper would look charming in the morning room.

'I wouldn't presume to judge. At the risk of sounding radical, I believe people should decorate the inside of their homes as suits them, rather than as convention dictates.'

'I agree,' said Lonsdale, pleasantly surprised. 'In Africa, houses are designed for comfort, and fashion is a very distant second.'

Anne transpired to be an easy, pleasant conversationalist once away from her silly younger sister, and they soon advanced from Mr Lonsdale and Miss Humbage to Alec and Anne. She and Emelia had spent their early years in India – the daughters of a former brigadier – and she talked intelligently and astutely about it. She listened with fascination as Lonsdale spoke of Africa – the lands, peoples, and wildlife. He was surprised to find he was enjoying himself.

'Your descriptions make me wish to visit Africa,' said Anne. 'It's obvious you care about it, so why did you leave?'

'Because of the actions and attitudes of some of those in charge,' said Lonsdale. 'I was a Colonial Service administrator, first under Bartle Frere in Zanzibar and then General Wolseley in the Gold Coast and Ashanti. I served under both again in southern Africa. But for every gem like

Sir Henry or Sir Garnet, there were other governors or commissioners who were morally bankrupt. Eventually, Owen Lanyon's treatment of the Boers and the other Africans became so oppressive and bigoted that I resigned.'

'But I thought Jack said you were at Whitehall after you returned home.'

'When I reached London, I found my resignation had been treated as a reassignment to the Colonial Office itself. I suspect Wolseley was behind that, because by that time he was back in England, but he's never admitted it. However, it still wasn't what I wanted, so after eight months I resigned again.'

'And now you're a reporter.'

'Yes,' he said, not mentioning that he would not be a real one unless he earned the full-time post. He glanced at her. 'How do you spend *your* days?'

'Wishing I had what you do: the freedom to live my life as I want, without being hindered by social constraints. I want to wear *comfortable* clothes, not silly dresses that are so tight I feel hobbled like a horse. And I want to study at the university, to read philosophy and politics as I please, and to vote for the government that runs my country.'

'That's not unreasonable,' said Lonsdale.

'I'm glad to hear you think so,' said Anne, and smiled.

Lonsdale's stomach did a curious little flip, and he felt not a little irritated that Jack and Emelia should have conspired to keep this pretty, intelligent woman away from him for so long.

Six

As Lonsdale had been told that he would not be needed until Monday afternoon, he decided to see if the pathologist Bradwell had any new information to share. He pushed open the mortuary door and was startled to see a number of policemen gathered in the hallway. Inspector Peters was there, fiddling with his pipe, while Bradwell leaned nonchalantly against a wall next to him, oblivious to the black mould that stained his coat.

'Lonsdale,' drawled the inspector. 'Ever a man at the scene of a crime, I see. Well, I want a word with you.'

'That sounds ominous,' said Lonsdale. 'Why?'

'You went to see the sweep, Kendal,' said Peters. 'Even though my superiors ordered you to leave Donovan's death for the police to explore.'

'Yes, I did,' said Lonsdale, unrepentant. 'It was an enlightening conversation, and has convinced me even more that something is badly amiss.'

He outlined the sweep's discovery of the rags in the chimney and what they might have meant. When he had finished, Peters was scowling.

'So why did he say nothing of this to us?' he demanded.

'He did, sir,' said a young policeman with a mop of ginger hair, overhearing. He hastened to explain himself. 'But he was drunk – he said he'd already

167

spoken to the police, but that was a lie because *I* was the first sent to interview him. I assumed he was trying to worm his way out of being blamed.'

'I see,' said Peters, turning his lugubrious stare on the young officer, who blushed and began a detailed study of the mud on his boots.

'The "policeman" Kendal referred to had a scar through his eyebrow,' announced Lonsdale, unable to resist a touch of the dramatic.

'No!' gulped the lad in alarm. 'I meant . . . I didn't ask for a description, but why would I? He was drunk, so I thought he was making it all up. As I said, I was the only one sent . . .'

Peters pursed his lips. 'Then you'd better go and talk to him again, lad. Determine for certain if it was Iverson who quizzed him.'

Eager to make amends, the constable hurried out. 'So someone deliberately started the fire to hide that Donovan had been mutilated,' said Bradwell. He glanced at Peters. 'I think you should take Lonsdale into your confidence, because we need all the help we can get, and you cannot rely on your superiors to supply it.'

'No, I can't,' acknowledged Peters, tiredly.

Lonsdale looked from one to the other. 'Has something happened? Why are all these officers here?'

'Because our killer has just acquired himself another cerebrum,' said Bradwell, 'from here, right under our noses.'

Lonsdale stared down at the body on the dissecting table. The injury looked like the one Bradwell had

168

shown him on his first visit, although this victim was older and fitter. There was a gaping wound in the neck, although the head seemed to be intact.

'I don't understand,' he said. 'Donovan's head was crushed, but this one seems normal enough.'

'Look closer,' instructed Bradwell. Seeing Lonsdale's bemusement, he sighed impatiently. 'No, closer! You won't see anything from back there, and it won't bite.'

Lonsdale was disinclined to pore over corpses just to satisfy Bradwell. 'Just point out what I'm missing,' he suggested. 'It will be quicker.'

Bradwell slipped his hand under the fringe of hair that dropped across the body's forehead and lifted it. Underneath, there was a thin, but distinct incision.

'I take it you didn't do that,' said Lonsdale.

'Why would I look at the head of a body with a slashed throat?' asked Bradwell. 'I don't have time. In cases like this, where the cause of death is obvious, I perform the briefest of examinations and move on. If I performed a complete, extensive examination on every one, we would be drowning in them.'

'Do so many people suffer violent deaths, then?' asked Lonsdale.

'Fortunately not,' replied Bradwell. 'Most die from dysentery, phthisis, children's fevers, or diseases of the heart and lungs – such as heart attacks, pneumonia, and bronchitis – not to mention accidents.'

Lonsdale indicated the corpse on the table. 'So how can you be sure that this cut wasn't made by his killer?'

Bradwell looked indignant. 'I may be forced to work fast, but I always follow specific procedures. I look for stab marks on the torso, look in the mouth for blistering or discoloration from poison, look at the hands and forearms for any evidence of self-defence, and check the skull for dents and bumps.'

Lonsdale raised his eyebrows. 'Even when it's obvious that the person died of a disease or an accident?'

Bradwell nodded. 'I've seen many cases where a family has hastened the end of an ill relative.'

Lonsdale stared down at the body. 'So when was he . . .'

'Some time between when I finished his post mortem on Thursday night and about two hours ago, when the body was due to be released for burial. But I imagine it happened last night, after O'Connor and I had gone home. Sundays are always quiet here.'

'And the cerebrum is gone?'

Bradwell peeled back the scalp to reveal a circular groove in the bone, where the uppermost part had been sliced through, like taking the top off a hard-boiled egg. He eased the detached cap away, and Lonsdale saw a dark cavity coated with a yellowish-grey matter and clots of blood.

'What do you think, Lonsdale?' asked Peters, calmly puffing at his pipe, which, mixed with the smell of death and disinfectant, made Lonsdale slightly queasy.

'That whoever did this must have lost control of his wits. Have any of the other bodies been . . .?' He hesitated. The words savaged, despoiled,

170

or mutilated seemed too brutal for such a clinical procedure.

'No,' said Bradwell. 'I've been uneasy since I was almost fooled over Donovan's death, so I've inspected every corpse as it arrives, then again when it's released. Thank God I did!'

'How did the culprit get in?' asked Lonsdale.

'Through the small window at the back. It's not the first time we've been burgled that way, despite it being seven feet off the ground. Thieves think we keep the personal effects of the deceased here, but few people we house have much worth stealing.'

'That depends on your standards,' said Lonsdale, thinking about the workhouse. 'Have you asked around for potential witnesses?'

'Around here?' asked Peters archly. 'The rule of the folk in this area is "see nothing, hear nothing, know nothing", especially if it's the police who ask.'

'But surely they'd only keep quiet if the culprit was someone they knew,' persisted Lonsdale. 'They wouldn't lie to protect a stranger, would they?'

'Even a criminal has a greater claim on their allegiance than a police officer,' said Peters. 'They—'

Suddenly there was a loud knock at the door to the post-mortem theatre, followed by an irate demand to open up at once. Peters turned quickly to Lonsdale and pointed towards a large closet. With a shock, Lonsdale saw he expected him to hide there.

'Superintendent Ramsey might not be as

171

understanding about your meddling as I've been,' said Peters, when Lonsdale hesitated. 'Hurry, man! He might order you arrested.'

Reluctantly, Lonsdale did as he was told, entering a tiny room containing stacks of reports on shelves. He did not close the door completely, but held it open a crack so that he could watch and listen.

Ramsey strode in like a Shakespearian actor, Leonard at his heels like a faithful dog. The superintendent immediately began a furious diatribe, although Leonard smiled genially and nodded friendly greetings to his colleagues. Lonsdale was wondering how two such completely different individuals could work together, when a vision of Hulda sprang to mind. Leonard probably had no more control over whom he worked with than did Lonsdale.

'This is an outrage!' stormed Ramsey. 'Is nowhere safe? What are you doing about it, Bradwell?'

'There's not much I *can* do,' responded the surgeon with a shrug. 'O'Connor has boarded up the broken window. I'd board up the others, too, but my budget won't allow it. As it was, O'Connor had to use wood taken from a pile near a railway line.'

'You stole wood to mend police property?' breathed the superintendent, aghast. 'What do you think the newspapers would make of that?'

Bradwell's patience was wearing thin. 'I imagine they'd suggest giving me more money,' he snapped. 'The Metropolitan Police pay nothing towards the upkeep of the building. Look in the hall. If you wondered why it's so dark, it's

172

because the gas pipes have been stolen, and your finance department has ignored my requests for replacements for eighteen months.'

'There's no need for light in the hall,' said Ramsey defensively. 'It's not as if the occupants need to see their way out.' He gestured at the gleaming tray of instruments. 'Moreover, you can't possibly need all those knives. One is sufficient, surely? Learn to manage your budget properly, man.'

Seeing the surgeon's face turn white with anger, Leonard stepped forward to intervene. Lonsdale imagined that he probably had a good deal of experience in calming waters troubled by his pompous, acerbic senior officer.

'Perhaps you could tell us what happened,' he suggested gently. He nodded to the body. 'How came it to lose—'

'I haven't finished my examination yet,' said Bradwell, his temper barely under control. 'You'll have to wait.'

He selected the largest knife from his arsenal of weapons and waved it in a way that was vaguely threatening. Hastily, Ramsey suggested he and his officers wait elsewhere, so Bradwell would not be distracted. Before Peters could object, Ramsey strode towards Lonsdale's hiding place.

Alarmed, Lonsdale looked around for a place to hide, and saw that the only possibility was behind a short cabinet at the back. He shot towards it and crouched down just as the door flew open and Ramsey marched in.

'This place is a disgrace,' the superintendent

muttered. With horror, Lonsdale saw Ramsey's feet come closer, and realized that he intended to perch on the pile of papers directly in front of him.

'Here is a chair, sir,' Peters said, quickly grabbing one from next to the door and placing it so Ramsey's back was towards Lonsdale.

'I'm not sure Bradwell's appointment was wise,' said Ramsey, once Leonard had closed the door and all three – four including Lonsdale – were crowded inside. Lonsdale was tempted to laugh at the ridiculousness of the situation. 'The man's a fool. We never had problems like this with old Dr Robbins.'

'But Bradwell's reports don't make me want to request second opinions,' said Peters. 'We're lucky to have a man of his calibre. Don't forget that he covers the entire district north of the Thames, and we only pay him for twenty hours a week, regardless of how much time he works.'

'But this place is a disgrace,' Ramsey growled again, kicking at a stain on the floor.

'Very true,' agreed Peters. 'But that's hardly his fault.'

'So what do you plan to do about this stolen brain business?' Ramsey snapped. 'House enquiries around here will be useless. Have you checked the lunatic asylums for escapees? God knows, only a lunatic can be responsible for this outrage.'

'I've two men making enquiries as we speak. Yet I wonder if this may be the work not of random madmen but someone with a desire for specific human organs.'

Ramsey groaned. 'Lord help us! What depths

some folk will sink to! Are there any links between the fellow in the fire and the chap whose body's just been violated?'

'I cannot tell you that, sir. You took me off the Donovan case, if you recall.'

'Besides, there is the matter of jurisdiction,' put in Leonard. 'Peters is in Division D, but the most recent mutilation—'

'Philip Yeats,' put in Peters, causing Lonsdale to blink at yet another Irish name.

'—is in Division M,' finished Leonard. 'Southwark.'

'To hell with that administrative nonsense,' barked Ramsey. 'I want Peters investigating both these corpses – sort it out, Leonard. It's obvious there's a connection between Donovan and Yeats. Forget the other two – the whore and her accomplice.'

'But they're—' began Peters.

'We need to be *seen* on the Yeats murder,' interrupted Ramsey. 'When news that two desecrations have occurred seeps out, the press will be demanding an arrest.'

'Yeats died five days ago,' said Peters placatingly. 'His murder is old news, so there's no reason why this should leak out.'

'Then for God's sake, let's keep it that way. This *must* be kept from reporters. The last thing we want is headlines declaring that we have organ-stealing murderers on the rampage – especially ones who strike at men like Yeats. I'd lose my position for certain.'

'Men like Yeats?' asked Peters, bemused. 'What do you mean, sir?'

175

'He was a music-hall entertainer,' explained Leonard. 'He's famous in his way.'

'Bastards,' Ramsey snarled. 'We should hang them all.'

'Entertainers?' asked Peters, startled.

'Reporters!' snarled Ramsey. 'I mean the damn reporters! They encourage the lower classes to expect better than they deserve. They disclose secrets they've no business knowing in the first place. And they constantly get in the way of investigations and then tell us how to do our jobs! If this brain-thief was putting reporters in here, I wouldn't lift a finger to stop him.'

'Steady on, sir,' said Leonard, shocked. 'I find them irritating, too, but they're only doing their jobs.'

'And I have occasionally found them very helpful,' said Peters. 'They can offer a fresh perspective and have the advantage of gaining access to people and places denied to us.'

'You are a fool if you trust them,' declared Ramsey, breathing hard. He made an effort to bring his temper under control. 'Now listen, Peters, because I have an avenue I want you to explore. I'm giving you a pointer here.'

'Yes, sir?'

'I was in India for some years, so I am acquainted with the methods of Eastern criminals. I believe these murders might have been committed by a Malay or some other low-class Asiatic, of whom there are many in London. Mutilations are *Eastern* habits intended to express insult, hatred, and contempt. But there has never been an instance of murder and mutilation of

176

this kind by an Englishman. So I think that some Asiatic man has taken the lives of those he holds guilty of injuring him in some way.'

'There's no evidence—' began Leonard, but Ramsey forged on.

'Thousands of them live in London, speak English, and dress in normal clothes. Such a man would be quite safe in the haunts of his fellow countrymen. Unless caught red-handed, being polite and even obsequious, he would be the last to be suspected. But when the villain is primed with opium or gin, and lustful for slaughter, he'll destroy his victim with the ferocity and cunning of a tiger. And past successes will render him even more daring. So we might face the terrors of this wily Asian again and again, unless he has joined a crew of Lascars on a steamer leaving the country.'

'I'll bear this insightful observation in mind, sir,' Peters said flatly.

'Good man. But don't dither, as there are more important matters to take up our time. For example, the Prince of Wales was almost blown up at the Court Theatre on Friday night, and there are rumours that the Fenians did it.'

'Those rumours are false,' said Leonard. 'The report from the Fire Brigade said that faulty gas pipes were responsible.'

'Gas!' spat Ramsey. 'The new miracle fuel! It won't last. You mark my words. No one wants a substance in his home that'll kill him just as easily as light his rooms.'

Before Ramsey could rant further, Bradwell walked in, to report what he had already told Peters and Lonsdale: that someone had removed

Yeats's skullcap, sliced out the cerebrum, and concealed his work by carefully arranging the victim's hair. Ramsey responded with an interrogation, quizzing the pathologist about his methods, and even going so far as to intimate that Bradwell might have mutilated Yeats's corpse himself, as a ploy to increase his budget. When Bradwell's expression became murderous, Leonard suggested that he and Ramsey should leave so as not to be late for their next appointment. Ramsey glanced at his watch, his eyebrows shot up, and he hurried from the room without another word.

'I'm sorry, Peters,' Leonard said before he followed. 'But he's right – Yeats and Donovan must take priority. Forget about the prostitute.'

'Walker also deserves justice,' said Peters.

'And she'll have it – as soon as you've caught the maniac who steals brains,' said Leonard, and hurried after Ramsey.

'Bastard!' muttered Bradwell, as Lonsdale stood and emerged from his hiding place. 'Did you hear him accuse me of being the murderer? How dare he!'

'It was no more bizarre than his suggestion that the culprits are thuggees from India,' said Lonsdale.

'I'd be careful, if I were you, Lonsdale,' said Peters. 'When there's pressure to solve a crime, Ramsey usually responds by arresting someone, regardless of guilt or innocence. It could be you.'

'I admire your fortitude, Alec,' said Milner, as he and Lonsdale entered the Victorian Embankment Gardens for a moment's peace late that afternoon.

They sat on a wooden bench that was soft with rot, and watched a flurry of pigeons squabbling over a bag of crumbs emptied out by a man in a bowler hat. Dark clouds massed overhead, promising rain, and the wind that sliced up from the river had a keen edge to it. 'To *choose* Hulda to help you, when Stead offered you the choice of all of us.'

'She's meticulous and perceptive. If anyone can find links between past murders and these current ones, it will be her.'

'How will you do that?'

'By looking in *The PMG* archive. Stead has given us his blessing to spend as much time there as need be, so now I'm just waiting for him to give us the key.'

'An interesting approach,' said Milner. 'And if that's what's been dominating your thoughts, then I needn't ask about Emilia's sister. If you meet a woman and all you can think about is murder . . .'

'Oh, I don't know,' said Lonsdale, recalling the fair, pretty features of Anne. 'We got on rather well.'

They walked back towards Northumberland Street, where Hulda was waiting. She brandished a key. 'You're late,' she said, although Lonsdale did not recall setting any particular time. 'I suppose you were talking about sport.'

'Sport?' he echoed, bewildered. 'Why would we be talking of sport?'

'All men do,' she replied authoritatively. 'They can't help themselves. It is a male obsession – whether they would rather shoot birds or mammals;

whether they want a shotgun or a rifle; whether foreign animals are as enjoyable to kill as home-grown ones. The scope is endless.'

'Don't take a gun of any description into the archive with you, Alec,' warned Milner as Lonsdale prepared to follow her down the stairs. 'You might be tempted to use it on The Friederichs, confined as you will be.'

The Pall Mall Gazette archive was a claustro-phobic basement room with a low ceiling, stone floors, and walls lined with metal cabinets holding copies of most London dailies. The filing was performed irregularly, which, in combin-ation with reporters casually borrowing copies and tossing them back without regard for organ-ization, meant that many were misfiled or lost altogether. It was also exceedingly noisy, as the two Marinoni presses turning out *The PMG* were located only a thin door away.

After only a few minutes on Tuesday morning – his first full day in the archive – Lonsdale felt filthy. Clouds of dust swirled when he shifted the piles of papers to get at those further back. The lighting was from a single hanging lamp that was inadequate, so Hulda was obliged to fetch a storm lantern from the reporters' room. The dry mustiness of the air and the oil fumes combined to make Lonsdale's head pound. It was a depressing place, and he could not rid himself of the notion that he was incarcerated in an Egyptian tomb.

By late afternoon, they were obliged to drink multiple cups of tea to stay awake. He had not

180

realized what a daunting task he had given them – ploughing through each of six London morning dailies, five major evening papers, five quality Sunday publications, and numerous weeklies, including sensational gazettes that specialized in crime. Even with Hulda's help, he realized that he was going to have to spend days there.

However, he did feel they were making some progress. The more he read, the more he became sure that he had led Morley astray regarding the so-called Irish connection. It was true that Jamie's friends, along with Donovan and Yeats, had Irish names, but that was not to say they were Irish themselves. It was coincidence, although he and Hulda agreed to keep that to themselves, lest Morley took them off the case again.

'It's almost seven, and you've been down here all day,' came a voice from the door. 'Come to the club for dinner.'

'Thank you,' said Hulda, standing from where she had been kneeling on the floor. 'I should be delighted.'

'Hulda!' gulped Cook, *The PMG*'s youngest reporter. 'I did not realize you . . . I thought you'd gone home.'

'We'll go to the Oyster Bar,' said Lonsdale, and because he did not want Hulda to begin a rant on the injustice of women being barred from gentlemen's clubs, added, 'We won't be allowed in unless we change – we're filthy.'

Hulda nodded acceptance of the offer and they abandoned the dungeon with relief. Milner joined them, too, and they aimed for Fleet Street together.

Its convenience to the offices of numerous newspapers meant that Craig's Oyster Bar was always packed with reporters. It was open from midday to midnight, and the bustling, deadline-driven nature of its customers gave it a hectic, noisy atmosphere. Most newspapermen were well dressed, wearing clothes that were as suited to the Houses of Parliament or research in the British Library, as to visiting the scenes of accidents or conducting interviews. One man was different, however – a burly fellow wearing a dirty cloth cap. Lonsdale supposed he was an informant, instructed to meet a reporter there.

Hulda, Lonsdale, Milner and Cook ordered oysters for a shilling a dozen, washed down with warm, sweet stout. They talked about Prime Minister Gladstone's announcement that day of the release of Irish nationalist leader Charles Stewart Parnell from gaol, speaking loudly over the ear-shattering yells of other patrons and the crash of crockery and glasses from inside the bar.

When Hulda went to powder her nose, two reporters from *The Standard* joined them, changing the discussion to the explosion at the Court Theatre. They were openly jealous that Lonsdale had been on hand to see the Prince of Wales taking charge. They pestered him for details. Then one of them suddenly leapt to his feet, dragging his colleague with him, and headed for the door. Before Lonsdale knew what was happening, he felt a hand drop on his shoulder with considerable force.

'Glad I've found you lot,' boomed Harris, and sat uninvited. He grabbed a beer that one of *The Standard* men had abandoned, drained it in a single swallow, and wiped his sleeve over his lips. 'I received an official reprimand from the Garrick because of you, Lonsdale.'

'Have you?' asked Lonsdale, not surprised, given his unpleasant interaction with Dr Wilson in the Garrick's reading room.

'They won't say why,' said Harris, 'but a number of people have suddenly taken against me. All I can think is that you misbehaved when you were my guest.'

'You don't think you've done anything yourself, then?' Cook asked mildly. 'Clubs do like a certain air of gentility and elegance.'

'Of course they do,' replied Harris unabashed. 'Which is why I can only think Lonsdale must have done something wrong.'

'We need to be at the House of Commons in half an hour to hear the Opposition's responses to Parnell's release,' lied Lonsdale, aiming to escape, although he was aware that would leave Hulda with the man when she returned. 'Are you two ready?'

'Yes,' said Milner with relief, despite having only eaten half his food.

'You don't want these then?' asked Harris, nodding to the oysters Milner had left on his plate.

'No, but neither do you,' said Milner. 'I think there's something wrong with them. They taste off.'

'Nonsense,' declared Harris, hauling the plate over to where he was sitting. 'Waste not, want not, as they say.'

'We should go,' said Lonsdale, starting to stand.

'Not yet,' said Harris, as he forked an oyster into his mouth. 'Mr Northcote, the Conservative leader, won't speak for at least another hour. You've plenty of time to enjoy more of this warm beer you English love. And I want to talk to you anyway.' Butter dripped down his chin.

'About what?' said Milner, gaping in astonishment as Harris leaned across the table and helped himself to Hulda's stout.

'Wilson – the zoo director,' replied Harris, pushing his hat onto the back of his head and taking another crustacean. 'He told me not to let you near him ever again. I want to know why. Is there a story I should know about?'

'There is,' said Hulda, who had returned unnoticed. She reclaimed her stout, but did not drink it. 'However, it's a secret. Can we trust you not to run with it first?'

'Of course,' said Harris, eyes gleaming. 'What is it?'

'Apes,' replied Hulda. 'Several hundred have escaped recently, and have been hired to work in Shoreditch by the East London Waterworks Company, which likes them because they accept lower wages. Obviously, Dr Wilson doesn't want to be accused of flouting employment laws, so he's keen to keep a low profile.'

Harris gazed at her. 'You're serious?'

'Completely,' said Hulda without the flicker of a smile. 'Go and check for yourself. However,

184

please promise not to report it before *The PMG*. We don't want to lose such a scoop.'

'I promise,' said Harris, scrambling to his feet. 'Good evening to you, ma'am.'

'What?' asked Hulda when he had gone, aware of the others' raised eyebrows. Then she allowed herself a small smile. 'Well, he's been asking for it for a long time.'

'Men like Harris make me worry about what is in store for the press in the future,' said Milner, as he and Lonsdale strolled at a leisurely pace along the Strand together. Cook and Hulda had gone to their homes in different directions. Gas lamps threw insipid pools of light onto the pavements, and there was a damp, chill feeling that suggested more drizzle was in the offing.

'In what way?' asked Lonsdale.

'That, before long, we'll all be ordered to climb up drainpipes to spy on public figures and their illicit loves, or fight each other for statements from the bereaved at the scenes of accidents.'

'The press will never sink so low,' said Lonsdale firmly.

'It will,' insisted Milner. 'Reporters will become jackals, feeding off the famous and the infamous, grubbing about in the gutters for ever more vile and filthy tales.'

'Lord!' breathed Lonsdale. 'You're in a melancholy mood tonight.'

'Your current story is a case in point,' Milner went on. 'Stolen body parts and murdered prostitutes. It's all too horrible. It will create an

185

appetite for ever more sordid stories, and we will descend into the pit of sensationalism.'

The two men walked in silence for several moments.

'Are you interested in what Hulda and I found in our search today?' Lonsdale asked. 'Or will it be too horrible?'

Milner sighed. 'Probably – but proceed anyway.'

'She found several items in the February papers,' said Lonsdale, pulling his notebook from his pocket. He strained to read aloud in the poor light:

> *An inquest was held yesterday concerning the deaths of Frederick Kempster, aged twenty-eight, and Edmund Corlett, aged twenty-six, who were burned to death on Tuesday morning at a fire that occurred in Southampton Row, Holborn, on the premises of Messrs Morson and Sons, manufacturing chemists. Mr Kempster was the manager of the retail department, and Mr Corlett the first assistant.*

'Surely you're not suggesting that every fire in London has a sinister motive?'

'Just listen.' Lonsdale read on:

> *The evidence indicated that the only explosive upon the premises was benzo-line, of which not more than ten gallons were kept at a time, and that was stored in a vault. All the fires were put out the previous night, a gas jet being the only*

light left on the premises. When the fire was discovered it had full command of the premises. No explanation could be given for its origin. Both men were badly crushed by the collapse of parts of the building, obliging the bodies to be identified by the keys in their possession.

Milner stopped walking and looked at Lonsdale. 'You think they are victims, too?'

'There's more. According to *The Daily Telegraph*, a similar fire occurred a week later at the Thornycroft shipyard in Chiswick, where one person's head was mutilated beyond recognition. And shortly after that, several papers carried accounts of how the entire upper body of a workman disappeared in a violent explosion at a vinegar works in Peckham.'

'*Four* other cases?' breathed Milner.

'*Possible* cases,' corrected Lonsdale. 'But those are only the ones we've found so far. There may be others. Many others.'

'Then you are right to pursue it,' said Milner grimly. 'Vile it may be, but if you can catch the perpetrators and save lives . . .'

Before they had walked much further, both Lonsdale and Milner were assailed with a great feeling of weariness. A hansom drove near, and Lonsdale hailed it. 'Pimlico,' he told the driver, pushing Milner into it. 'Fifty-four Claverton Street.'

He waved at the disappearing cab and looked for another. But most hansoms were engaged, because the theatres were just letting out. After several unsuccessful attempts, he decided to walk towards Oxford Street in the hope that the area away from Trafalgar Square might have fewer customers for the cabs. As soon as he turned from the colourful bustle of the Strand and its amber gaslights, everything seemed colder and less friendly. Despite being used to traipsing around the city at night, Lonsdale felt that St Martin's Lane seemed black and sinister, and he could not shake off the sense that he was not alone. But each time he glanced behind him, he saw nothing amiss. The gradual lessening of the traffic noise as he moved away from the main thoroughfare made his footsteps echo, and once or twice he thought he heard a second set behind him. He began to doubt the wisdom of his decision to leave the main streets.

He glanced behind him again, abruptly. There! A shadow flickered briefly at the periphery of his vision before fading into the darkness of a doorway. There was indeed someone on his heels. He walked faster and, when he came to a particularly dark section, ducked to one side. Then he waited, heart thudding, to see what his pursuer would do. He was not disappointed. Seconds later, a shadow slipped past, and he heard a litany of ripe curses as his stalker saw he had been given the slip. Lonsdale's arm shot out of the gloom and grabbed him by the scruff of the neck.

'Still following me, Jamie?' he asked softly, gratified to see the alarm on the boy's face.

'Steady, old pal,' gasped Jamie, wriggling free.

'You fair set me old ticker racing like a pigeon's. Why're you leaping out on me like that?'

'Why are you still following me?' retorted Lonsdale coolly.

'Because I was worried,' explained the boy. 'You said you'd find out about me pals, and I'm just making sure you do it – and that I can warn you if them other coves are about.'

'Have you seen any of them since?'

'Ol' Big Arms,' replied Jamie. 'He followed you to that oyster bar, but he likes a drink, and by the time you left he was three sheets to the wind. He's still there. You can go back and see for yourself, if you don't believe me.'

'I do,' said Lonsdale, recalling the burly man in a cloth cap. Not an informant waiting for a reporter after all.

He walked to the nearest gas lamp and studied the lad in the light. He was shabbier than when they had last met, and his stolen clothes looked as though he had lived in them every second since. The cuffs of his trousers had been trodden into the muck of the streets, and his hat looked ready for the rag-and-bone men. Jamie sniffed, and ran the back of his hand over his nose, and Lonsdale saw the dirt deeply ingrained in his skin. The boy sneezed, then sniffed again, wetly.

'A cold?' asked Lonsdale sympathetically, holding out his handkerchief.

'New-moan-yer, I 'spect,' said Jamie, taking the proffered linen and dabbing his nose very carefully before offering it back. 'Comes of following folks around in the cold and wet.' He

189

regarded Lonsdale challengingly, and the reporter laughed, thinking he had some gall to blame him for his sniffles.

'So, what do you want from me this time?' he asked, waving the handkerchief away. Jamie secreted it carefully in his pocket, and ran his sleeve across his nose instead.

'You to give me a job.'

Lonsdale stared at him. 'A job? You mean at the paper?'

'I could do it,' Jamie assured him. 'I can go places where you can't and blend in. Like I'll find out about that Walker tart for you.'

'No,' said Lonsdale immediately. 'That's too dangerous. However, there *is* something you could do. Did you hear about a fire in the chemical factory in Holborn? Two men – Frederick Kempster and Edmund Corlett – were killed back in February. I want to know what kind of people they were.'

'What kind of people?' asked Jamie, confused. 'You mean whether they liked doxies or boys?'

'Nothing so colourful. Find out if they had families, and, if so, where they live. I want to know if they were quiet or loud, rough or respectable. Ask their neighbours.'

'Why?' asked Jamie doubtfully. 'It doesn't sound like much of a job.'

'It is,' said Lonsdale. 'It's very important. And when you've finished in Holborn, there may be work for you in Chiswick and Peckham.'

Jamie listened avidly while Lonsdale explained what he wanted him to do, and his eyes gleamed. 'Really, so I'll be a reporter?' he asked.

'An investigator,' said Lonsdale, wondering what information the boy would bring back. *Would* there be a connection between the death of quiet, shy, decent Donovan and the two men in Holborn? Or was he grabbing at straws that weren't there? Regardless, Jamie's enquiries would save him time if it was a wild-goose chase, and if it was not, well, he could always go back and ask the same questions himself.

'All right then,' said Jamie, and held out a grimy hand. 'But I need money for expenses.'

Lonsdale handed him a florin and some pennies. 'Start tomorrow. You know how to find me. And there will more when you tell me what you've discovered – whatever you find out. You'll be paid regardless. Just be careful.'

'I'm always careful, old pal,' declared Jamie.

Seven

Wednesday began poorly for Lonsdale. He had slept uneasily and was woken well before six, roused by the raucous shouting of a coalman outside. An early breakfast in the kitchen, under the disapproving eye of Mrs Webster – who did not believe it was proper for a gentleman to eat at the table used by the servants – ended in disaster when Lonsdale accidentally knocked a bowl of porridge from the hands of the younger of the two maids. It splattered across the floor and the lower half of her uniform.

On arriving in Northumberland Street, he went straight to the archive, where Hulda joined him not long after. But her presence proved more tiresome than helpful, and he began to wish he had chosen one of the others to help him – quiet, clever Milner or shy young Cook, neither of whom would have interrupted him ten times an hour with irritable sighs and grumbles.

'I'm going to Bermondsey tonight,' he said eventually. 'To see what I can find out about Cath Walker – her friends, her life, her dreams. It'll make the story more real, should we ever get to write it.'

'Oh, we'll write it,' said Hulda confidently. 'And if you're going to Bermondsey, I'll be with you.' She raised a hand to quell his immediate objections. 'It's not negotiable, Lonsdale. I'm coming.'

Lonsdale could tell from the determined jut of her chin that she meant it. They returned to their work, and he was pleased that the notion of an escapade to some of the city's most notorious slums had given her food for thought, because she was quiet for a long time. In the end, it was he who broke the silence.

'Hah!' he exclaimed in the mid-afternoon, by which time his shoulders and neck were cramped from his labours. He held up a paper. 'I think this might help me.'

'Don't you mean "help us"?' Hulda asked archly, 'or are you trying to pre-empt my part of this investigation?' He bit back a brusque reply and noticed that despite the dust and cobwebs that covered her usually pristine clothes, there was something attractive about Hulda. Lonsdale found himself staring at her, almost as if for the first time. He could not help but think that she was unusually pretty and would be enticing if only . . .

'Don't just sit there gaping like a fish, man. Tell me what you've found, so *I* can assess if it's relevant.'

The spell had been shattered, not for the first time, by her opening her mouth, and he felt his customary reservations about her flood back. But, he told himself after reflecting for a moment about the advantages of working with Milner on the investigation, his and Hulda's disguise as a couple had been successful in Wyndham Street, and he would probably be better served with Hulda in Bermondsey for the same reason. Annoyed nevertheless, he turned his chair back to the table.

'Well?' she said, looming over him. 'What is it?'

'A letter to the editor in *The Times*,' he replied. 'Back in February, a man wrote about what he considered an inadequate investigation into the death of his son.'

Hulda leaned over Lonsdale's shoulder to read what was on the table:

Sir – In the absence of the precise nature of William Willoughby's demise on the railway line, the French authorities have issued a verdict of accidental death, although they acknowledged in private correspondence the possibility of suicide. The English police, rather than pressing

193

for answers, have stated that the case is out of their jurisdiction.

In response, I make an appeal for help, to beg that a more thorough investigation is carried out on behalf of a young man so horribly and prematurely taken from those who loved him. The close relationship of a father with his only son allows me to state with certainty that he did not end his own life. Nor would he engage in 'larks' that would see him accidentally killed on a railway line.

Moreover, the manner in which his poor body was found and the high degree of anatomical knowledge shown by the crime speak clearly of his life being taken by others. The initial French investigator speculated that my son was attempting to avoid individuals who had followed him. I believe that a full investigation would reveal the complicity of such individuals, and I pray that the authorities will pursue this topic with vigour.

I am, Sir, your obedient servant,
Edward St John Willoughby.

'This is very sad,' said Hulda, looking up. 'But I don't see—'

'Now read this,' interrupted Lonsdale, handing over a second paper. 'It's from the week before, and is a brief report on the son's body being discovered in France.'

194

Scotland Yard has received a communication from the French police respecting a death on a railway near Boulogne. It is stated that on the morning of 17th January the body of a young Englishman, about twenty-two years of age, was found on the railway line between Nesles and Camiers. The remains were somewhat disfigured, and had the appearance of having been run over by two trains. The top of the head was cut clean away . . .

Hulda looked up at Lonsdale. 'Is this . . .' Then she bent her head without waiting for his reply and continued to read:

One item of underclothing was marked 'W. J. Willoughby'. The medical evidence does not show whether the young man met his death by murder, accident, or suicide, but the guard of the train states that the victim was accompanied by two other Englishmen. One spoke French well, and was about forty years of age, with a thin brown moustache. The other was large, between forty-five and fifty, and had a long beard tinged with grey. The trio appeared to be friendly, and were seen laughing. The guard last saw the party together shortly before Étaples. Anyone knowing any of these men is requested to contact Scotland Yard.

'Here's the final piece about it,' said Lonsdale. 'Dated five days after the initial report and two days before the letter to the editor.'

Hulda read:

> *The French authorities are now satisfied that Mr Willoughby died accidentally. The door of his carriage was not properly fastened, and it has been suggested that he opened the window to lean out, and fell to his death. It has now been shown that he was the only occupant of the carriage at the time, his companions having alighted at Étaples. His watch and chain remain missing, but vagrants have been spotted in the vicinity, so it is concluded that the items were stolen after the victim's death. The deceased's father has contested the verdict, on the basis that the injuries sustained are inconsistent with being hit by a train, particularly pertaining to the head. The French authorities have expressed their deepest sympathy for his loss, but remain convinced that further investigation will serve no purpose.*

'The French police are worse than ours,' she said, looking up at last. 'He was with friends, he was on his own. He jumped, he was pushed, he fell. They have no idea. And if there is a question about the injury to his head – it is similar to that inflicted on Donovan – well, all I can say is that trains do not remove cerebra. Not surgically, at least.'

196

'We don't know that's what happened to him,' said Lonsdale. 'But we're going to find out. I'll contact a friend at *The Times* and ask for the father's address. His letter suggests he'll be willing to tell us everything he knows.'

'When shall we go?' asked Hulda yet again, as they sat in the reporters' office. 'It's almost six. Surely the layabouts of Bermondsey and their whores will be awake by now?'

Cook blushed at her coarseness, but Lonsdale ignored her. He had already told her several times that there was little point in going before ten, as people would be more willing to divulge information in the cosy camaraderie of a pub in the late hours than they would when they were alert and sober. He tried to concentrate on the letter he was writing to Willoughby, and couldn't help but think he was already reaching the depths Milner had predicted: requesting an interview with a bereaved parent. But it wasn't like that, he told himself – he was doing the right thing.

After a while, Hulda grew restless, and began to poke around in Voules's belongings, moving his pens, ink and pencils so he would be unable to find them. She fidgeted with boredom, then tried to start a conversation with Cook, and finally became exasperated and went home to change.

Returning to the archive, Lonsdale laboured on until well past nine o'clock, after which he changed into some grubby clothes he had brought with him and joined Cook for a snack in the reporters' office.

'You're filthy,' the younger man said. 'Perfect for going to rough taverns in Bermondsey. But are you sure you don't want me to come? I know The Friederichs is a veritable gorgon, but I don't see her being much use in a fight.'

Lonsdale was not so sure about that. 'There won't be any fighting,' he said. 'But I'd better go. If I'm late, she might decide to trawl the taverns on her own.'

'She might,' agreed Cook. 'But be careful, Alec – for her as well as yourself. She might be the Prussian Governess, but she's *our* Prussian Governess, and I'm fond of her.'

Outside, a blanket of yellow-grey fog hung over the city. It had been thickening all day, so that by mid-afternoon it had been necessary to turn on the gaslights, and the street traffic had become very snarled. The air reeked of soot and smoke, and carried a sharp chill that was unusual for the spring.

As Lonsdale pulled shut the office door in the dim light of the overhead lamp, a woman swayed towards him, swinging her purse. She was clearly drunk, and Lonsdale thought she needed to take herself in hand unless she wanted to be arrested for prostitution. She stopped next to him, closer than was decent.

'Can I call you a hansom, madam?' he asked, edging away.

'It's me, you idiot!' snapped Hulda in a hoarse whisper. 'Who did you think I was? A whore?'

Lonsdale was at a loss for words. She had exchanged her usual skirts and stays for a dress that fell in thick folds to the floor. Her fair hair

198

was bundled up into a peculiar turban-like hat, and a bright neckerchief was knotted around her throat. To keep warm, she wore a shawl that was fastened at the front with a cheap brooch. It was not so much her clothes that had led him to jump to the conclusion that she was touting for business, but the undulating walk she had adopted.

'It occurred to me it would look odd if a well-dressed lady was seen in company with a ruffian like you,' she added, when Lonsdale had nothing to say. 'So, I thought I'd wear the clothes I use for cycling.'

'You cycle?' asked Lonsdale, glad he had not congratulated her on her disguise if this was an outfit she liked to wear in public.

'Of course! How else would I get to archery on Saturday afternoons? Hansoms can't be had for love or money at that time, and walking is such a waste of time. Do you cycle?'

'Not unless my life depends on it. Metal wheels on cobbles . . . they don't make for a comfortable journey.'

'That's why I like horse manure on the streets,' confided Hulda. 'There's nothing like it for softening the surface.'

As no suitable response came to Lonsdale's mind, he changed the subject. 'I recommend we take a hansom to Great Dover Street, and walk the rest of the way.'

'Walk?' objected Hulda. 'Why?'

'Because the kind of people we need to meet tonight can't afford hansoms, and if we arrive in one, we'll stand out like a bishop in a brothel from the start.'

199

Hulda peered at him in the gloom. 'You seem very sure about the way the seedier areas of London work. Have you done this many times before?'

'That, Friederichs, is none of your business,' said Lonsdale loftily. In fact, his first commission with *The PMG* had been to write a series of articles on the Billingsgate Fish Market, which had led him to frequent some of the less salubrious areas of London. He was surprised she did not recall the pieces, since they had caused a vigorous debate between Morley, who maintained that Lonsdale's descriptions of poverty were exaggerated, and Stead, who stoutly asserted they were not.

They flagged down a hansom and gave the driver directions. Hulda's outfit and Lonsdale's dirty clothes were evidently convincing, because the driver demanded to see their money before he would accept their custom.

In the cab, both covered their mouths and noses with their sleeves, to avoid inhaling the moist, sulphurous fog. The gas lamps hardly penetrated the fug, and it was only on Blackfriars Bridge, where new electric lights had been installed, that they could see more than two or three feet ahead. The black sludge of the Thames could just be seen sliding fast and sleek through the arches below.

Eventually, they reached Great Dover Street; as soon as his fares alighted, the driver beat a hasty retreat to the more affluent areas of the city. Lonsdale and Hulda continued deeper into the slums, walking down roads that were foul with dirt and refuse. Hulda adopted a curious hopping gait as she struggled not to step in anything vile.

Eventually they reached Westcott Street, where Cath had rented a room. It was narrow, with tall houses on either side, reducing the road to little more than a dingy tunnel. There was a lamp at each end, but it was mostly the domain of darkness and fog. Hulda and Lonsdale walked along its entire seedy length to get a feel for the place. At the far end, a lamp lit a sign that read, 'Board School'.

'A school? Here?' asked Hulda.

'Like the one in *Nicholas Nickleby*. A home for orphans, probably,' said Lonsdale. 'Here we are, in the great capital of Victoria's Empire, and this is how we look after our wards of state. Hardly makes you proud, does it?'

'Walker lived at number twenty-nine,' said Hulda, looking away in disgust. 'It's over there.'

Lonsdale approached the house, but there was no reply to his knock. He stepped back and peered up, noting that the eaves were rotting and most of the windows were boarded over. The place looked abandoned. Something fluttered on the ground at his feet, and when he bent to retrieve it, he saw it was a notice of eviction – the building had been condemned as structurally unsound.

'Mrs Tanner gave this as her permanent address at the inquest,' objected Hulda when he showed it to her, 'and that was only a few days ago. Did she lie?'

'Not necessarily. The notice is dated yesterday,

so she was doubtless in business here until the very last minute . . .'

As he spoke, the door opened, and a boy darted out, loaded down with lead pipes. He gave Lonsdale and Hulda a friendly nod as he passed.

'Ain't much left now,' he said helpfully. 'Better hurry.'

'Where's the nearest alehouse?' Lonsdale called after him.

The boy nodded to a spot past the Board School. 'Just down there – the Jolly Tar.'

'I can't imagine why he'd be jolly around here,' muttered Hulda. 'Still, I see why you want to go – it would have been Walker's local, and we know from the inquest that she plied her trade in taverns.'

The Jolly Tar was crammed to bursting, but exclusively with men. As Lonsdale and Hulda entered, all conversation stopped, and every eye in the room turned to them in what Lonsdale could only describe as naked hostility. To persist would be reckless, so he left abruptly, pulling Hulda with him. As the door closed behind them, the buzz of conversation resumed.

'Are they all going to be like that?' asked Hulda uneasily.

'I hope not,' said Lonsdale. He thought for a moment. 'At the inquest, Mrs Tanner said that she last saw Cath at the Dog and Bone on Minto Street. Let's try there. I think I can find it – I looked at a map before we left.'

Lonsdale had been in areas of chronic privation before, but few were as mean, poor, and hopeless as the area between Westcott and Minto streets. They traversed alleys into which even the police seldom ventured, lined with lodging-houses of the worst type, catering to costermongers, mudlarks, robbers, pickpockets and prostitutes. They were teetering, half-ruinous buildings that looked less safe than Mrs Tanner's lodgings – but were still in use.

They turned into a passage about twenty-yards long and three-feet wide. At the end of it was a rectangular court, illuminated only by the light from upper-storey windows. Slimy wet mould grew on the few paving stones that had not been prised up and spirited away, and on the rubbish that littered the yard like bizarrely shaped gravestones. It stank of urine and decay, and rats scurried in the shadows, brazenly feeding on a dead dog.

'Here?' asked Hulda, gripping Lonsdale's arm tightly. 'Are you sure?'

Lonsdale struck a match, and in its momentary flare he saw an old horse trough filled with all manner of putrid rubbish. To his right were three latrines, open to the elements, the pit below them overflowing and topped by a layer of scum. A bucket of filthy water was set for those individuals inclined to rinse their hands. Lonsdale was not surprised that cholera and typhoid regularly ravaged the population.

The match went out, so Lonsdale groped his way forward, right arm extended to feel his way ahead and left hand holding Hulda's. He moved gingerly until he felt a clammy, dirt-encrusted wall. A small arch halfway along gave access to

203

a tiny, stinking alley that led into Minto Street. Evidently it was an important watering hole, as it was heaving with beer houses, gin palaces and taverns of every description. Despite it being eleven o'clock, the road was busy with people walking in pairs or alone, some weaving, some strolling, a few moving purposefully.

'Why are all these children out?' asked Hulda, retrieving her hand now they were in a better-lit place. 'Why don't they go home?'

'Some people make money by letting out their rooms for immoral purposes at night,' explained Lonsdale. 'Or the mothers are prostitutes who need somewhere to take their clients. The children will go home in the morning.'

Before he could add more, Hulda pointed to a decaying sign of a rather wicked-looking dog holding what looked unpleasantly like a human femur. She strode purposefully towards it, ignoring Lonsdale's suggestion that they look through the windows first, to avoid a repetition of their first experience. She put her hand on the door handle, and glanced back at him.

'I'll do the talking,' she said. 'You just stand and listen.'

The Dog and Bone was tightly packed, with men, women, and even children collectively exuding a breathtaking stench of sweat, unwashed clothes and cheap tobacco. Underlying all was the warm aroma of horse manure, brought in on the patrons' shoes. A fire popped and hissed in one corner, adding its own pollution but doing little to provide warmth. The walls were brown and splattered with stains, and the sawdust on the floor had not been changed in months.

A woman wearing a black wig reeled into Lonsdale, wafting gin-laden breath into his face as, simultaneously, he felt her hand slide into his coat pocket. He had taken the precaution of hiding the small amount of money he had brought in the lining of his jacket, so he was not unduly concerned about theft. He could not deny, however, that being frisked so brazenly was disconcerting. He eased away, then almost tripped over a child so small that she had to use both hands to hold her jug.

'Watch it!' she snarled, as the mild stout known as 'entire' slopped over the rim. 'This costs money!'

She raised the jug to her lips and quaffed a good part of it with all the ease of the experienced drinker. Then she wiped her lips on her sleeve before joining two other children under a table.

Hulda reached the bar and perched on a stool, where she was immediately surrounded by men, several of whom offered to light the cigar she pulled out and clamped between her teeth. Lonsdale's heart sank, and he wondered whether she had considered the fact that it cost more than these men would earn in a day. Thankfully, none of them seemed to notice, and he watched in growing alarm as she affected an appallingly bad cockney accent and began to hold forth. Whether because they were interested in what she had to say, or because she was by far the most attractive woman in the room, she soon had quite a following.

Lonsdale edged as close as he dared and watched as she artfully steered the conversation around to Cath. To his astonishment, her admirers vied frantically with each other to answer her questions. All the while, Hulda looked from one to the next, giving each the impression that she had never met anyone more interesting in her life.

'It was a shame about Cath,' said a short, stocky fellow with scarred hands that suggested he worked in a steel foundry; his friends called him Frank. 'We all liked her, if you know what I mean.' He treated Hulda to a leering wink.

'She was a good friend,' agreed Hulda in her terrible accent. 'More like a sister, really.'

'And old Joe,' said another, raising his frothing tankard of four-ale in tribute. 'I'll miss him, too.'

'Joe?' asked Hulda guilelessly. 'You mean Joe Johnson? Was she still knocking around with him?'

'I don't know any Joe Johnson,' said the tankard man doubtfully. 'Who's he?'

'Must have been before your time, Bob,' suggested Frank. He beamed at Hulda, keen to win her favour. 'Was he a skinny fellow, lived in Long Walk and died of the consumption?'

'Maybe,' hedged Hulda, too clever to agree to something that might trip her up later.

'You must be older than you look, if you remember Cath with him,' said Frank, giving Hulda a dig in the ribs with his elbow; if Lonsdale had taken such a liberty, he was certain Hulda would have responded with violence. As it was, she simply listened. 'We're

206

talking about Joe Greaves, who she walked out with more recent-like.'

'Oh, Joe *Greaves*,' exclaimed Hulda. 'The one who worked on the railway?'

'No,' said Bob. 'That's Joe Hayes. He died about five years ago, hit by a train.'

Lonsdale resisted the urge to point out that being named Joe was dangerous in Bermondsey.

'Joe Greaves worked on the coal barges,' said a short, bald man. 'Up London Pool way. Good job, too. It's a wicked shame that someone did away with him. He had a wife and children.'

'Poor things,' sighed Hulda. 'Perhaps I should visit them, seeing as me and Cath were close.'

'She'd like that,' said Baldy, although Lonsdale could not imagine why the widow could possibly want to see a friend of the woman her husband 'walked out with'. 'She still lives in the same place.'

'The workhouse?' asked Hulda, sipping her second gin from a thick, greasy glass.

'Don't talk daft!' Frank said, while Lonsdale cringed – there were only so many mistakes Hulda could make before even the most drunken of admirers would suspect something amiss. But he was underestimating Hulda's charm. 'Mrs Greaves wouldn't be at the workhouse with what her Joe was making on the barges. She lives in Mermaid Court, over by the Zion Chapel; number ten.' Frank smacked his hand on the bar to gain the attention of the landlord, then gestured for Hulda's glass to be refilled, while Hulda beamed at him and blew a thin stream of cigar smoke up at the ceiling.

'Makes you sick, don't it?' came a low voice at Lonsdale's side. He turned to see a sad-eyed woman sitting next to him. She wore a cheap sateen dress, which had faded from black to brown. She had a pale, thin face, and greasy hair with nits nestling at the roots.

'It does,' agreed Lonsdale, and turned to watch Hulda again.

'See? Even you're at it,' said the woman spitefully. 'As long as she's here, no one else will get a look in. I been working here for six years, and now some north bank tart comes swanning in and takes all my regulars. And Frank's been buying her quarterns of gin like they're free. It ain't right.'

So, thought Lonsdale, Hulda might be able to wrap men around her little finger, but she had only made enemies among the women. He decided to leave her to it and work on the ladies instead.

'She's only here because Cath died,' he said reassuringly. 'She'll leave soon.'

'She'll be back,' predicted the woman, eyeing Hulda with raw jealousy. 'The likes of her knows a good thing when she sees it.'

Lonsdale was sure she did, but he was equally certain that she would not consider it to be the clientele of the Dog and Bone.

'Drink?' he asked.

'Well, yes,' said the woman, pleased. 'And to show I got more taste than she does, I'll have a Scotch.' She spoke the last word at quite a volume, sliding her glass across the bar for the landlord to fill. 'Come on, Bill. The gentleman here is buying.'

'Right you are, Tilly,' said the landlord. 'Large one, is it?'

'Of course,' said Tilly, regarding him askance. 'What else?'

When the glass had been filled so high that there was a meniscus across the top, Tilly put both hands on the bar for balance and lowered her lips towards it. Lonsdale watched entranced as, with a soundless slurp, her lips made contact: not a drop was spilled, although he suspected that if one had, she would just have licked it off the counter.

'Did you know Cath?' asked Lonsdale when the glass had been drained and the whole process repeated. 'I met her a couple of times.'

Of course, he thought, once was when she was dead, but there was no need to mention that.

'Of course I knew her! Poor lass – throat slit like an animal to slaughter. It happened up in Regent's Park, although God knows what she was doing there. Always did have ideas above herself, Cath. Ain't so grand now, is she?'

'What ideas?' asked Lonsdale.

'What are you, a peeler?' asked Tilly, loud and suspicious.

Several heads turned in his direction, and Lonsdale realized that he was asking too many questions, instead of steering the conversation subtly like Hulda.

'Do *I* look like a peeler?' he asked with as much indignation as he could muster.

'Yeah, you could pass for one, actually,' said Tilly. 'But if you say you're not . . .'

'I do,' said Lonsdale firmly.

Tilly grimaced. 'They were in here last week asking about Cath. Of course, they don't care about her now, not when they got the music-hall man's killer to catch.' She smiled suddenly. 'Did you ever see him? He had this wonderful turn with a bicycle, an umbrella and an accordion. His place was at the Wilton Music Hall, over on Sayer Street.'

'He was good?'

'The best – folks came all the way from Hampstead to see him. And that explains why Cath and Joe are getting ignored.'

'Did the three of them know each other?'

Tilly laughed at the notion. 'The likes of Philip Yeats doesn't mix with the likes of us, no matter how grand Joe and Cath thought they was with their flash money and smart clothes.'

'I thought Joe was a bargeman. What flash money?'

'Lord, sir! A woman could die of thirst in here.'

Lonsdale put two shillings on the counter for the remainder of the bottle. Tilly hooked dirty fingers around it and held it close to her chest. She tipped forward on her stool, and Lonsdale was not sure whether she was going to kiss him or pass out in his lap. Neither would have been welcome, but all she did was lower her voice and start to talk.

'Joe had a good wage from the barges – sometimes ten shillings a week! But lately he had extra. A lot extra. So did Cath.'

'Where did this extra come from?'

'I wish I knew,' said Tilly resentfully. 'Because

210

neither of them could do anything I can't, and I'd like some cash myself. All I can tell you is that they had meetings in different parts of the city – and when they came back, they always had money.'

'Do you know where?'

'No, but if you find out, will you tell me? If you do, I'll share what I get with you.'

'Thank you,' said Lonsdale politely, suspecting that Tilly would be wiser to stay away from the whole affair.

Leaving the Dog and Bone was more difficult than arriving, because Hulda's throng of admirers had grown while Lonsdale had been entertaining Tilly. He eased his way through them and nodded to indicate that it was time to go. Hulda, however, had been an interesting diversion with her stories and wit, and the men who encircled her were enjoying themselves. When she tried to take Lonsdale's arm, he became the object of some venomous looks, while she was propelled back onto her stool and ordered to tell them another tale, like the one about the bishop's daughter and the jar of Macassar oil.

Fortunately, Lonsdale was not the only one who wanted Hulda out of there. So did Tilly, who was more than happy to help oust the pretty rival from her domain.

'When you hear me holler, grab the doxy and run,' she ordered. 'Some might follow you, so nip into the doorway around the corner. They won't bother looking for long. It's a rotten night, and it's nice in here.'

Idly, Lonsdale wondered what her home was like if she considered the Dog and Bone 'nice'.

Tilly took one more gulp from her bottle, then tottered towards a table, which she climbed onto unsteadily. She almost fell, but was steadied by eager hands. Whatever she was about to do, Lonsdale had the sense that she had done it to good effect before, as Hulda was already losing her admirers. Suspecting the diversion would not last long, Lonsdale edged towards Hulda.

When it came, Tilly's yell created a sensation. Heads whipped around, and men began to cheer. Lonsdale darted forward, grabbed Hulda, and steered her towards the door.

'What's she doing?' demanded Hulda, trying to pull away. 'I want to see.'

'I don't think you will,' predicted Lonsdale. 'Now, move – unless you want to be here all night.'

Not everyone was diverted by Tilly, however, and a couple of men cried their indignation when they saw what Lonsdale was doing. He barged outside, hauling Hulda unceremoniously down the alley and into the doorway Tilly had mentioned. Several men followed, but Tilly was right – they did not linger long before returning to the shabby tavern. Lonsdale heaved a sigh of relief, while Hulda regarded him furiously.

'That was unnecessary,' she whispered curtly. 'I was enjoying myself – and so was my audience.'

'Perhaps so, but I suspect it wouldn't have been long before they lost interest in your stories and demanded a different kind of entertainment.'

Hulda's eyes narrowed. 'What do you mean?'

Lonsdale stared at her, not sure whether she genuinely wanted an answer or was merely trying to embarrass him. He realized he did not understand her at all. She swore, was more outspoken than was seemly, and she smoked. Yet there was a curious, contradictory innocence in her.

'Things might have become unpleasant,' he hedged.

'It was unpleasant the moment we stepped inside,' sneered Hulda, then sighed. 'But it was worth it – we have a name for Walker's dead friend. Shall we go and see the widow now?'

But Lonsdale demurred. They had escaped from the Jolly Tar and the Dog and Bone, but their luck would not last forever. 'Tomorrow, at a more decent hour.'

'But you've been saying all day that *this* is the time to deal with whores and ruffians.'

'Mrs Greaves is – or was – a wife and mother. We've no reason to believe that – although poor – she has anything but the best character. So, we should call on her in the evening, not late at night. If we want information from her, we shouldn't start by treating her with disrespect.'

Hulda pulled her shawl more tightly around her shoulders. 'I wish I had seen what your woman was going to do, though. I might have learned something.'

'I doubt it was anything you'd want to try yourself,' said Lonsdale. 'Incidentally, she told me that at times Greaves and Cath had extra money that had nothing to do with their regular work.'

213

Hulda nodded. 'Frank said the same. Greaves would swagger into the tavern and buy drinks all around, even though it wasn't payday. People asked him how he could afford it, but he wouldn't say. Walker didn't share her windfalls – instead, she bought herself new clothes and drank whisky rather than gin.'

'When we learn who paid them and why, we may know why they died.'

Hulda nodded. 'Let's hope that Widow Greaves will know, so that tomorrow will see us with answers at last.'

Lonsdale peered into the shadows to ensure none of Hulda's suitors were still there. The alleys seemed safe, so he led the way to Minto Street, aware that while the road had been crowded when they arrived, it was now virtually deserted. Before he could step into the street, Hulda grabbed his arm.

'Someone's over there,' she whispered. 'In the shadows by the Fountain and Grapes.'

'I don't see anyone . . .' said Lonsdale. But, even as he spoke, he saw a flash of silver in the dim yellow light that spilled through the thick glass of the window. Hulda was right.

'Oh, it's a policeman,' he said in relief. 'I can see his buttons and the striping of his cuffs. He . . . My God! It's Iverson!'

'How can you tell?' breathed Hulda. 'Can you see his face? I can't.'

'No, but I recognize his posture and shape. It's him, Hulda, I'm sure of it.'

'So what are we going to do? Can we take him into custody? With this, perhaps?'

She produced a handgun with a long barrel. Lonsdale gaped at it, stunned not only that she should have armed herself so, but that she had kept such a massive thing concealed all evening. It was too large to have been in her handbag.

'Where'd you get that?' he asked.

'It's a family heirloom.' All Hulda's attention was on Iverson. 'Damn! He's too far inside the doorway for me to get a clear shot.'

'You can't just kill him,' gulped Lonsdale, horrified.

Hulda glared at him. 'Of course I won't *kill* him – just give him a fright, so he surrenders without a struggle.'

Instinctively Lonsdale knew it was a very bad idea. 'We should let the police deal with him.'

'But they've been hunting him for months with no success. Come on, Lonsdale, we can't just walk away. Imagine what your friend Peters will say if he learns you had Iverson in your sights and let him go.'

'What do you have in mind?' asked Lonsdale reluctantly.

'We trap him in a pincer-like movement,' she said firmly. 'I'll stay here – you get on his other side. Then we pounce. What could go wrong?'

A lot, thought Lonsdale, but nodded agreement. 'But for God's sake don't tackle him until I'm ready.'

Hulda pulled a face that indicated she would do what she liked. 'Well, go on, then,' she hissed when he still hesitated.

He set off at a run, terrified that if he took too long, she would do something rash. He skidded on mud, and when he reached out to steady himself, he felt a wall, moist and sticky with filth. Wiping his hand on his trousers, he hurried on. Eventually, he reached a point where the Fountain and Grapes was between him and Hulda, its yellow lights spilling through the fog like phosphorus eyes. He peered out carefully and saw the mist had thickened in the few moments he had been gone. He could see Iverson's doorway, but not him. Was the fugitive still there? Lonsdale could not tell. He began to inch forward, his hands balled into fists, ready for action. He froze as he trod on broken glass and it cracked under his foot. He tensed, expecting Iverson to come out of the shadows, but nothing happened. He took another step towards the doorway, and then another, then jumped to the doorway ready to lay hold of his quarry. But Iverson had gone.

Lonsdale glanced around wildly. He still could not see Hulda's hiding place through the fog. He groped in his pocket for his Alpine Vesuvians, and lit one with unsteady fingers. He held it up, half expecting Iverson to be crouching in the shadows at the back, but the doorway was empty. He experienced a gamut of emotions – relief, frustration, but strongest of all disappointment, and a sudden pang of concern for Hulda.

What happened next was a blur. There was a sharp crack as more broken glass snapped under a heavy boot, and something struck him hard across the shoulders. He fell forwards and out of the corner of his eye saw Iverson holding a truncheon in one hand and a knife in the other.

As Lonsdale put out his hands to scramble to his feet, he felt a sack of rubbish. He grabbed it and swung it hard at Iverson's knees. It exploded, sending foul-smelling kitchen waste and a cloud of cold ashes scattering across the alley. Iverson staggered, then charged, slashing wildly with his knife. Lonsdale raised an arm to protect himself, and felt the knife nick him as it sliced through his coat. He scrambled upright and his left fist shot out at Iverson's chin. Iverson staggered backwards two steps, then circled to his right.

Lonsdale dived at him and managed another punch, this time to Iverson's chest. But Iverson fought back like a wild animal, flailing with the dagger with one hand, while the other tried to grab Lonsdale's throat. As they grappled, Iverson's face was briefly illuminated by the tavern's lights, and Lonsdale saw his eyes burning like coals, dark and filled with rage.

Lonsdale twisted away, and landed a third punch, but Iverson grabbed his coat, pulling so hard that both men lost their balance on the slimy, rotting vegetables from the sack. Despite his bulk, Iverson was fast, and while Lonsdale twisted away from the knife, he lashed out with his foot, catching the reporter on the side of the head. Lonsdale fell again, and a meaty hand hit him twice in quick succession. He was dimly aware of a knife beginning to descend.

The gunshot sounded like a cannon in the enclosed space of the doorway. Lonsdale blinked to clear his vision and was aware that Iverson had gone. He heard receding footsteps, and then a clamour of voices – among them, Hulda's strident tones. He sat up, disconcerted to find himself surrounded by people.

'Drink this, mate,' said a voice, which turned out to be that of Barman Bill from the Dog and Bone. He crouched next to Lonsdale, offering something dark brown in a glass. 'It'll see you right, and it only costs a penny.'

Dimly Lonsdale realized Hulda had very wisely returned to the scene of her recent triumph and asked them for help – Frank and Bob were there, as well as Tilly and half a dozen others. Hulda appeared over the barman's shoulder and gave him the required coin.

'Drink it, Lonsdale,' she ordered. 'You're as white as a sheet. Fright, I imagine.'

She patted his shoulder condescendingly, then looked with disgust at the muck that stained her fingers, while Lonsdale sipped what might have been brandy. Whatever it was, it burned his bleeding mouth. He climbed to his feet, assisted by several helpful hands, and allowed himself to be guided back to the Dog and Bone, where Hulda ordered him a pint of 'best'. He grimaced his revulsion at the taste, but Tilly was there to help.

'Put a drop of this in it, to take away the taste,' she suggested kindly, giving him a very small tot from the bottle he had bought her.

'Why were the police after you?' asked Frank, taking the stool next to him. The hostility he had experienced earlier, Lonsdale noted, had gone now he had been engaged in fisticuffs with a uniformed policeman.

'He's wanted for a burglary in Mayfair,' explained Hulda proudly. 'The peelers have been after him for weeks.'

Lonsdale listened in mute horror while she fabricated an elaborate tale about a highly implausible crime, which had her audience agog. She then confided that he had another equally impressive crime planned in Knightsbridge, but that, unless he wanted to lose his opportunity to carry it out, they should be on their way.

'Although we'll pay our respects to Mrs Greaves before we get down to serious business,' she said.

'Hulda, no,' whispered Lonsdale. 'Not tonight.'

She ignored him, and they left the Dog and Bone amid nods of approval. Several men shook Lonsdale's hand, and Bob slapped him on the shoulder in a congratulatory fashion. Frank offered to escort them to the Greaves's house, and Lonsdale found it easier to accept the offer than to argue. He and Hulda were proudly introduced to everyone they met – an astonishing number, considering it was past midnight – as the woman who shot at the police, and the man wanted for a burglary in Mayfair.

'That'll teach the peelers,' said Frank gleefully. 'They must want you bad, because they know they're not welcome around here. We only ever see them if there's a murder.'

He stopped outside a tall, filthy building with boarded-over windows and a front door that hung loose on its hinges, and told them that the widow lived on the top floor. Hulda thanked him.

Frank gave her a leering smile, then addressed

Lonsdale. 'If you ever want to do the steelworks, I know where the cash is kept.'

'That might be useful,' said Lonsdale vaguely.

Frank scowled. 'They're laying me off in a couple of weeks – they got a machine to pour the metal now. I wouldn't mind paying them back for tossing me out on my ear after twenty years.'

'He'll be in touch,' promised Hulda. 'Good night.'

'No,' said Lonsdale firmly, as Hulda aimed for the stairs. 'Not tonight – it's too late. We're going home.'

He expected her to argue, but she only began to walk to where the hansom had dropped them what felt like ages before. Her acquiescence told him that, for all her bravado, he was not the only one who had been unsettled by the events of the evening.

Eight

The next morning saw Lonsdale emerge from his bed stiff, bruised, and dull-witted from lack of sleep. Ignoring the maids' horror at the filthy bathwater and ruined clothes, he snatched a hard-boiled egg from the kitchen table and ate it as he walked to Northumberland Street for another day in the archive. Tired and sore he might be, but there was no time for lounging at home.

'Hulda tells me you're going back to Bermondsey this evening,' said Milner that afternoon. Aware that Lonsdale had not left the basement since he had arrived, he had come to bring him a cake baked by Cook's mother. Hulda had stayed for most of the morning, then had left at Stead's request to produce a story about the eruption of Mount Etna. She had asked how he was, awkwardly and formally, then had busied herself without another word.

'We're going to see Greaves's widow,' said Lonsdale, barely looking up to acknowledge Milner's kind thought.

'Are you sure that's wise?' asked Milner soberly. 'Hulda says you were almost killed there yesterday. Moreover, the killer's still free, and he may try again.'

Lonsdale disagreed. 'We fought because I was trying to lay hold of him. It was a chance encounter, and not one that will be repeated.

'I'm not so sure,' said Milner quietly. 'Doesn't it strike you as odd that, with the entire police force looking for Iverson, he hasn't been caught? And isn't it peculiar that you and Hulda are the only ones bothered about linking these odd deaths? And didn't Superintendent Ramsey tell the coroner, the police surgeon and Inspector Peters not to bother about Walker and Greaves?'

Lonsdale looked up at him, feeling his eyes gritty from tiredness and dust. 'I'm not sure what you're trying to tell me.'

'That Iverson – said to be insane by some – might not be mad at all, but following orders from a senior officer.'

Lonsdale frowned. 'You think someone in authority is involved in a business that involves Greaves being poisoned, Cath's cut throat, mysterious meetings, and missing cerebra?'

Milner shrugged. 'I cannot answer, but the whole affair is very odd.'

Lonsdale continued to stare at him. 'What made you come up with this? You said not long ago that it was not going to be important. Now you say there's a conspiracy.'

Milner was sombre. 'You've been down here all day, so you haven't seen the latest reports from the news services. There was a report from the Exchange Telegraph that caught my attention. Here.'

Harry Cannon, aged fourteen, mysteriously disappeared in the fog last night. While walking along the river to his home in Limehouse, accompanied by his brother and sister, he sat down near the Shadwell Dock Stairs, promising to catch up with them. He was last seen speaking to a man described as being short, strongly built, with thin hair and a long, uneven beard. A search has been made along the river, but nothing has been seen or heard of him.

'Your workhouse lad described a man like that waiting in the background while his friends were enticed away,' said Milner when Lonsdale had finished. 'And now read the addendum to the report, which was released an hour ago.'

Cannon's brother and sister were not concerned at the time, as when their brother sat down, the man in question was speaking to a police constable. They did not see the policeman's number, but stated that he was a large man with a scar above one eye.

Lonsdale decided that six o'clock was the best time to call on Mrs Greaves – a time when most of her daily chores would be done, but before she had settled down for the evening. The city was busy, as people finished work and travelled home, but it was a pretty evening, with a clear blue sky and the sun casting long shadows. They alighted from the hansom and Lonsdale set a brisk pace to Mermaid Court. It was even less attractive in the cold light of day – windows broken and patched, and the roof pitted with holes. The walls bulged precariously and the whole place was in such terrible condition that Lonsdale wondered if it should be condemned as unfit for human habitation.

Inside, the odour of urine, mildew and dirt made Lonsdale want to gag. Even Hulda's brazen confidence wavered when they stepped inside. Moisture oozed down the walls in a fine green film, and the floorboards were dark with filth. A dead kitten lay on one step, its bedraggled fur matted with blood. Rats skittered in the shadows; the little corpse would not remain there for long.

'Come on,' muttered Hulda. 'Let's get this over with.'

Her jaw jutted purposefully as she made her way towards the stairs, hand on the gun in her bag, acting not so differently, Lonsdale thought, to some desperado in the American West.

It was not easy to reach the top floor. The banister had been stolen and the stairs were rotten – some were missing altogether, revealing a drop to the floor below. As they rose, the stench became increasingly foul, as overflowing chamber pots stood on each floor, presumably to save the residents the trouble of going down to the communal latrines.

Each floor boasted six rooms. Lonsdale peered into one and saw a filthy floor and walls with mould. There were at least five people asleep there. From another came the sound of heavy breathing, as a couple snatched some desperate pleasure. Hulda faltered, and Lonsdale pushed her gently, to urge her to continue.

'Close your eyes and think of England,' he whispered.

'If I close my eyes, I'll fall and break my neck,' she muttered, then gave a sigh of relief when they reached the top-floor landing. 'Here we are at last. Now where?'

The rooms in the attic had no doors, but some privacy was granted to the tenants by filthy blankets, which were pinned over the frames. Lonsdale pushed one aside and glanced in. It was occupied by an elderly crone who crouched by a dead hearth, her toothless jaws muttering indecipherable words. The next one was uninhabited, and the third belonged to the Greaves family.

The room was almost bare. The fireplace housed a pile of smouldering embers, and a log lay in front of them to act as a fender. There was a chair against one wall, along with a shelf that held a battered saucepan, a piece of dry bread, and what appeared to be horse bones, almost certainly salvaged from the glue factory. Against the opposite wall was a pile of sacks, greasy and evil-smelling, which served as a bed. On them, ragged, begrimed and bare-legged, perched a girl of about four.

A woman sat on the chair, rocking a second child who was painfully thin and was missing several front teeth. Something about her reminded Lonsdale of a weasel. A pink scalp shone palely through wisps of fair hair, and her clothes were stiff with engrained grime.

Lonsdale knocked on the doorframe. 'Mrs Greaves?'

'I'll pay you tomorrow,' said the woman tiredly. 'I'd be out working tonight, but my little one's sick.'

'We haven't come for the rent,' said Lonsdale gently. 'We're here to say how sorry we were to hear about your husband.'

Fear and confusion flared in her eyes. 'Who are you? What do you want?'

Hulda pushed her way inside. 'I'm a friend of Cath's,' she declared. 'A couple of weeks ago, she said that if anything happened to her, I was to see you got this.'

She held out her hand to reveal a plain silver ring. Mrs Greaves's eyes opened wide with astonishment.

225

'She gave you that for me? But why? She'd never done nothing like that before.'

She reached out slowly and took the ring, as if afraid a sudden movement might make it disappear. She bit it between yellow molars, and then walked to the window to inspect it in the light.

'It's silver,' said Hulda, 'so don't let anyone give you less than thirty shillings for it.'

'Thirty shillings!' breathed Mrs Greaves. 'Then I'll get my furniture back! They took it two days ago for the rent, as I ain't been able to pay nothing since . . .' Her voice tailed off.

'It'll buy medicine for the baby, too,' added Hulda comfortingly.

'So what do you want?' asked Mrs Greaves, gripping the ring hard, as if she were afraid Hulda might demand it back. 'People don't give stuff away unless they want something.'

'Information,' Hulda replied briskly. 'People have been saying that Joe often had lots of extra cash. Where did he get it from?'

The woman's eyes narrowed suspiciously. 'Go away! I don't want to talk to you!'

Lonsdale stepped forward, poking Hulda in the back to warn her to be quiet. 'Don't be frightened,' he said gently. 'All we want is for whoever killed Cath and Joe to be brought to justice. Can you tell us anything to help?'

'Why should I?' demanded Mrs Greaves, suddenly tearful. 'Especially for Cath. It was her what got Joe killed.'

'How?' asked Lonsdale.

'She was always in the Dog and Bone, wearing

new clothes and drinking her whisky. She took a shine to Joe and said she'd take him to people who'd give *him* money, too.'

'And did she?' asked Lonsdale.

She nodded. 'Every so often he'd come home with a sovereign or a guinea. He'd give me a shilling, but that was all. His friends at the Dog and Bone did better – it was drinks all round for them.' Her voice was bitter.

'Where did this money come from?' persisted Lonsdale.

The younger child began to cry, so Mrs Greaves sat back down, bouncing it up and down on her knee.

'From somewhere he went after work,' she said. 'He wouldn't tell me where. He usually came back in the small hours, mad drunk.'

The child gave up screaming, and grew still. Mrs Greaves regarded it suspiciously, then poked it to see whether it moved. Satisfied when it did, she looked up at Lonsdale.

'Did anyone else earn sudden, inexplicable amounts of money?' he asked.

'Oh, yes, but they all came to bad ends. I told Joe he'd go the same way, but he wouldn't listen. Now look at him.'

'Do you know their names?' asked Lonsdale, hopes rising.

'First was Len Baycroft – he disappeared last summer. Mind you, none of us miss *him* – he was a nasty piece of work. Then there were the Johnson sisters, Long Lil and Bill Byers, but I ain't seen none of them for a while.'

'Did Joe – or any of them – ever say anything

to make you think whatever they were doing was dangerous or illegal?'

She gave a sharp bark of laughter. 'No, but no one would hire the likes of Joe, Cath or Len if they wanted angels. Of course what they were doing was against the law, although none of them would tell me about it, so I don't know what they did for their money.'

'Were any of them worried or afraid at any point?'

Mrs Greaves thought carefully. 'I think Cath was. She had a blazing row with Joe the day they were killed.'

The baby drew breath for another howl, so she stood up quickly, to allow more room for bouncing.

'What about?' he asked.

'It was something about telling someone something. She said they should, he said they shouldn't. They were still arguing the last time I saw them.'

The baby vomited suddenly and spectacularly, and Hulda only just leapt out of the way.

'Now look what you done,' said Mrs Greaves. 'That's enough. I want you out.'

Almost immediately, a thickset man with a large black beard appeared.

'Are they bothering you, Helen?' he asked. 'Do you want me to throw them out?'

'We're just leaving,' said Lonsdale, before the man could oblige.

Mrs Greaves's burly protector shadowed them down the stairs, and watched as Hulda set a rapid pace down Mermaid Court.

'You're going the wrong way,' said Lonsdale, as she turned a corner.

'I know,' muttered Hulda. 'But I want to get away from that place as quickly as possible. It was worse than Hades!'

Lonsdale took her arm and guided her back towards London's more civilized face, glancing back every so often to ensure Mrs Greaves's friend was not following them. Because he was looking for a man with a beard, he failed to spot the small, clean-shaven man who pulled his Müller cut-down low against the gathering chill of a clear evening, and began to dog their footsteps. Behind him, in a silent procession, were five others.

'So, we make progress at last,' said Hulda as they walked along Great Maze Pond, a road along the side of Guy's Hospital. The daylight had almost gone, and the gas lamps were lit, but a thick fog had rolled in from the river while they had been with Mrs Greaves. Lonsdale pulled the collar of his top frock up around his neck to keep out the gathering chill.

He nodded. 'Cath told me that at least six people had died, and Mrs Greaves gave us names of five who are missing. They are doubtless the same.'

'So, when Donovan was killed, Walker decided she'd put a stop to whatever was going on, and worked on Greaves to support her. But both were killed before they could talk.'

'The five people Mrs Greaves mentioned seemed to have one thing in common,' mused Lonsdale. 'None of them was missed. Her comments suggest that she just woke up one day and realized she hadn't seen them for a while. The same is true of Jamie's friends – he's the only one who cares about them disappearing. And Donovan lived alone, with no friends or family.'

'I see where you're going with this, Lonsdale. You think someone is targeting the unwanted and unloved, and that Walker and Greaves were involved in it until she decided she had had enough – although her conscience took a while to prick, if she was paid as much as Widow Greaves seems to think.'

Lonsdale took a detour around a deep puddle. 'It was kind of you to give Mrs Greaves that ring,' he said.

'I assumed she wouldn't tell us anything unless we won her over. And I felt sorry for her in that disgusting place.'

'At least she'll put it to good use, getting her furniture back. Her husband would have . . .' Lonsdale stopped suddenly. 'What was that?' He peered back into the darkness of the swirling fog.

'I didn't hear anything,' said Hulda.

They stood silently, but all they could hear were sounds from the nearby Barclay Perkins Brewery. The business of producing ale was a round-the-clock concern, and clanks, hisses and the restless whinnies of drays could all be heard emanating from behind a glass-shard-topped wall.

They had just started to walk again when Hulda exclaimed, 'I know the answer!' She slapped her forehead dramatically. 'And it's obvious!'

Before Lonsdale could respond, he heard

230

running footsteps behind them. He whipped around to see six scruffy men hurtle out of the gloom. Hulda scrabbled for her gun, but two of the men were already on her, grabbing her arms before she could reach it. She kicked out furiously, and one attacker doubled over. But the other four advanced on Lonsdale, one of them brandishing a broken bottle.

Unlike in his other recent encounters, this time Lonsdale was prepared to fight. The man with the bottle lunged, so Lonsdale stepped neatly to one side, seized him by the collar, and used his momentum to bowl him into one of his comrades. Both went sprawling, and while the others' eyes were fixed on their fallen colleagues, Lonsdale landed a right cross directly in the face of one of them, breaking his nose and dropping him as if he were poleaxed. The other he felled with a sly kick to the groin. Meanwhile, the man with the bottle picked himself up and advanced again. Lonsdale feinted to one side, then launched an attack of his own, landing three short right jabs that left him reeling.

He glanced over to see how Hulda was faring. It was a mistake. The man he had kicked used his inattention to grab him around the knees. When the other two moved in, Lonsdale ducked the first punch, then lost his balance, falling backwards over the man who clung to his legs. As he landed, his scrabbling fingers encountered a spoke from a broken cartwheel. He rolled away, jumped up, and swung it at the man who was trying to grab his legs again. There was a

231

sickening crack as wood met head, and the man collapsed into a puddle.

The remaining two assailants both drew knives. One, more confident than his crony, feinted to his left and then lunged at Lonsdale, who flinched backwards as the blade whipped past his face. The fellow grinned, tossing the weapon from hand to hand in a display of careless dexterity. He lunged left, narrowly missing skewering Lonsdale, who jerked hard to the other side. Thinking the reporter was still off balance, he lunged again, but Lonsdale landed a heavy blow with his makeshift cudgel, making the knifeman howl in pain. Lonsdale advanced on him, but before he could strike again, the man hurled his knife in a last-ditch attempt to kill and fled. The remaining man followed suit.

When Lonsdale looked over to Hulda, it was to see her brandishing her revolver with a menace that any eighteenth-century highwayman would have envied, while her two assailants also took to their heels.

'Are you all right?' Lonsdale asked her.

She nodded. 'Although I would feel better still if this damned thing had not jammed and I could have disabled one. Then we could have questioned him before taking him to hospital.'

'Right,' said Lonsdale, not sure whether he should be relieved or disappointed.

'Their leader was the one who threw the knife,' Hulda went on. 'The fool thought I would be easy prey and decided to lend his own talents to dispatch you. It was a serious mistake on his part. I heard one of them call him "Pauly" when they ran off, although I'm not sure if that was from "Paul" or was a last name.'

'Regardless, let's leave before they return,' said Lonsdale, uncomfortable with the way Hulda was shaking and prodding at her pistol. 'We should be able to catch a hansom from the front of the hospital.

He led the way quickly, although his one attempt to remove the firearm from her irritable attentions earned him such a glare that he did not try it again. He was glad to see a hansom outside the hospital and glad also that the entrance was so brightly lit and busy. No one would attack them there. Then he remembered what she had been saying before they were attacked.

'You were about to tell me the answer to all our questions,' he said, waving to the cab, then opening the door to help her in.

'I was,' she said, closing the door and calling her address to the driver. 'But it'll have to wait until tomorrow, because I need to think about it.'

'No!' cried Lonsdale. 'You cannot make me wait. Besides, this is the only cab, and who knows where I might find another. Can't we share?'

'We live in different directions, Lonsdale, and I'm too tired for messing about with detours. I shall see you tomorrow.'

With wordless disbelief, Lonsdale watched the hansom disappear into the fog.

It was some time before Lonsdale found another hansom, by which point he was seriously considering visiting Hulda's home and making a scene in front of her parents, landlord, or whatever other unfortunate individuals were forced to endure her company. He thought about her claim to have solved the mystery, and wondered what her explanation could possibly be.

He did not reach home until midnight. Going straight upstairs, he threw his dirty clothes in the linen basket and washed quickly, and not very carefully, in some cold water in the long, narrow bathroom that had been installed on the same floor as his bedroom. Then he threw on an old, comfortable dressing gown and went downstairs. The sitting room smelled of expensive cigars, and Lonsdale recalled with a pang that Jack had invited Emelia's family to dinner, and had asked him to join them. It had seemed like a good idea at the time, and the prospect of seeing Anne was delightful. But, with everything that had happened in the last two days, it had completely slipped his mind.

Blocking out the prospect of a tirade from Jack, he meandered into the drawing room. There was still a red glow in the embers of the fire, so he poked them about and added another log. He then poured himself a large brandy and sat in Jack's favourite armchair. Running all the new information through his mind, he heard the clock of Trinity Church on Bishops Road chime one, but he had fallen asleep long before it tolled again.

There was a brief moment of bewilderment when Lonsdale woke the next morning, and he opened his eyes to something other than his bedroom ceiling. Then he heard the servants chatting on the floor below, so supposed he had better be up and about, too. He stood and stretched, stiff from a night in the chair and aware that his bruised knuckles throbbed painfully. He supposed 'Pauly' and his friends would also be sporting some impressive bruises that day.

He was hungry, so he made for the kitchen, drawn there by the warm aroma of fresh bread. The kitchen was steamy from the clean clothes hanging from frames on pulleys that were hoisted high up to the ceiling. Every Thursday was laundry day in Jack's household, so all had been washed, beaten, boiled and wrung the previous day. Lonsdale thought with disgust of the filthy items in his bedroom, which would now wait nigh on a week to be cleaned.

The housekeeper was sitting near the fire, reading *The Daily Telegraph* – one of three newspapers Jack had delivered – before it was ironed and sent upstairs for his breakfast. She jumped guiltily to her feet when Lonsdale arrived.

'Sorry to disturb you, Mrs Webster,' he said, taking a seat at the large, scrubbed wooden table in the centre of the room. 'Do you mind?' He thought she well might, as the kitchen was chaotic. Dirty pans were everywhere, while the daily battle with 'blacks' – the small pieces of soot that blew inside the house from every door and window – had obviously not yet been initiated. Hillary was chatting at the door with the milkman, and, judging from her giggles, the topic was not of matters dairy.

Lonsdale felt a surge of irritation that they

235

should take advantage of his brother's benign nature. Jack's staff had a relatively easy existence – as long as meals were on time and the house superficially clean, Jack tended to leave them to their own devices. However, their days of idleness were numbered, as things would change when Jack married Emelia.

'May I help you, sir?' asked Mrs Webster, regarding him oddly.

'Is there anything to eat?' he asked, and then chastised himself for such a foolish question. Of course there was something to eat: it was a kitchen. 'Something that's ready now?'

'You should've said if you needed to be up early, sir,' she said, hastily scrambling to oblige.

'Not much in the paper,' said Lonsdale, lingering only because he knew they wanted him gone – the atmosphere was rather frosty. 'Other than Ireland, of course. Hah! This is interesting! Lord Frederick Cavendish has been named Chief Secretary. I expected it to be Joseph Chamberlain.'

Mrs Webster looked at him out of the corner of her eye. 'Were you expecting to see something particular, sir?'

Lonsdale thought it an odd question. He treated her to as searching a glance as the ones she was shooting at him. Then she handed him a plate of fried potatoes and what looked to be curry.

'That was left over from Mr Jack's meal with two legal associates yesterday,' she said. 'I don't like foreign food myself – all them hot spices lead to violent tempers. Shall I carry that upstairs for you, sir?'

'I'll eat it here,' said Lonsdale, sitting at the

table and smiling after she made a show of chopping some onions. At least she would earn her keep for a few minutes that morning. 'Crikey!'

He had taken his first bite of curry and could well believe that her cooking could lead men to do violent things. Seldom in his life had he tasted anything quite so powerful, which was a considerable achievement, given some of the places he had visited.

'Tasty, is it, sir?' she asked.

'Very,' said Lonsdale. His mouth and lips burned, and he had the feeling that if he spilled any on the table, it would sear a hole and drop through onto the floor. 'How much chilli powder did you put in it?'

'About a pound, sir. It's what gives it that lovely red colour.'

'I see,' said Lonsdale, wondering whether Jack had managed to eat any of it, and if it had later interfered with his evening entertaining Emelia's family. 'Is there any bread?'

She quickly cut him some, although she did not change knives, so the slice she gave him tasted of onions.

'Lamson, who poisoned his nephew with aconite, is in the news again,' she said chattily. '*The Telegraph* has letters he wrote to those relatives he didn't have time to kill. Fancy a doctor poisoning his crippled nephew just for – oh! Sir!'

Lonsdale followed Mrs Webster's surprised gaze to where Jack stood at the door.

'Good God, Alec,' he exclaimed. 'I shall send for a doctor forthwith!'

* * *

237

A short while later, Lonsdale and Jack sat in the morning room, where, over a more appropriate breakfast, Lonsdale told his brother what had happened the previous night. The services of a medical man had not been required, as a glance in a mirror had revealed to Lonsdale that he had been less than assiduous with his ablutions the previous night and that one side of his face remained a dark blue-black. He supposed it explained why the staff had behaved so oddly towards him, and why Mrs Webster had asked what he was expecting to see in the papers – clearly she thought one might carry word of a brutal assault.

As Lonsdale told a horrified Jack of his experiences, he took an antimacassar from one of the armchairs, dipped the end in a vase of flowers, and washed his face.

'Well, thank the Lord for that!' exclaimed Jack, seeing his brother's sinister-looking injury vanish. 'However, this affair has gone quite far enough. I never approved of you entering the news trade, and nor did Father. But we accepted your decision, and I think we've been more than patient. We were wrong.'

'But it was only—'

Jack silenced him with an imperious hand. 'While you might care nothing for your own reputation, you should at least consider ours. A scandal could damage my practice, and it could ruin the reputations of your father and brother in the Church. They might find themselves ousted from their current livings to some vile backwater.'

'The Church would never do such a thing!' objected Lonsdale. 'And—'

'Being attacked twice in two nights *proves* that what you are doing is dangerous and sordid. And worse yet, to allow a woman to accompany you . . .'

Lonsdale could see how that might appear to an outsider. He thought about the other women he knew – not least Emelia and Anne – and could not imagine embarking on such an adventure with them. To hide his chagrin, he wiped his face again with the antimacassar, then realized with a guilty start that he had ruined the thing, and that it was one lovingly crafted by Emelia. Reasoning that she had already given Jack enough of the things to furnish Buckingham Palace, and one would not be missed, he set it furtively on the mantelpiece, from whence he assumed one of the staff would dispose of it later.

'It is hard to believe that you are risking your life for a story,' Jack went on, pretending not to notice what was happening to Emelia's lacework.

'It isn't *just* a story,' Lonsdale said softly. 'Cath Walker was murdered while she was trying to right a wrong. She deserves justice.'

Unexpectedly, Jack softened. 'I can see that's important. But if you want my blessing with this wretched career, you *must* promise to be more careful. In other words, try to emulate the dignified Mr Morley, who manages to be a journalist *and* maintain his respectability and his reputation as a scholar and a gentleman. I shall be married

239

soon, and can you imagine what Em would have said if she had come downstairs and seen you looking like some Bermondsey bully-boy?'

'Nothing,' replied Lonsdale shortly. 'Because when you're married, I won't be living here. I'll need to find rooms of my own – which is another reason I must make a success of this story. I need *The PMG* to hire me full time.'

'Nonsense,' said Jack. 'You know that you can stay here for as long as you like.'

'Emelia will have something to say about that,' said Lonsdale ruefully. 'She and I disagree on so many things that you'd never have a moment of peace.'

'That, unfortunately, is true,' said Jack. 'Speaking of which, Em was vexed when you failed to appear last night. So was I, while Anne was openly disappointed.'

'Was she?' asked Lonsdale keenly. 'Then perhaps I'll call on her to apologize.'

'Please don't,' said Jack sternly. 'I suspect you'd receive a chilly reception from my future father-in-law, and I should be on hand to mediate. Sir Gervais is a difficult man, and I won't have you upsetting the apple cart.' He grinned suddenly. 'He spent most of last night complaining that my house smelled of India.'

'I'm not surprised,' said Lonsdale, grinning back, glad the momentary spat was over. 'Mrs Webster gave me some of her curry this morning. It was . . . powerful.'

Jack nodded. 'She blamed you when I told her it was inedible. She claimed the recipe was one that you'd brought back from Afghanistan.'

240

'But I've never been to Afghanistan, and none of my recipes call for a *pound* of chilli powder, I assure you.'

Before Jack could answer, the front doorbell rang, and a moment later Hulda was shown in.

'What do you want?' Lonsdale asked coolly, having neither forgotten nor forgiven her selfishness over the hansom the previous night.

'Alec!' breathed Jack, and turned quickly to Hulda. 'Forgive our poor manners, madam. We're unused to visitors at such an early hour.'

'Friederichs,' Lonsdale said with ill-disguised hostility, 'may I introduce my brother, Mr Jack Lonsdale of the Inner Temple. Jack, this is Miss Hulda Friederichs, reporter from *The PMG* and dangerous company.'

She did not rise to the bait, but stared down at her hands, folded demurely in her stole. Lonsdale's suspicions rose – Hulda was never demure unless she had an ulterior motive. All sweet charm, she accepted Jack's offer of tea, and then made a series of polite remarks on the house's décor.

Lonsdale felt his temper rise at her flagrantly transparent attempts to appear the upright, well-behaved lady. 'What do you want, Friederichs?' he asked curtly.

'It's . . . personal,' replied Hulda, blushing shyly. Her lower lip trembled, and, with horror, he saw she was about to cry.

Immediately, Jack was at her side to present her with a clean handkerchief. 'Calm yourself, madam, and tell us how we might help.'

241

'I need to speak to your brother,' said Hulda, and gave a brave little smile. 'Alone.'

'Impossible! Leave you unaccompanied with a single man? Your reputation—'

'It's quite all right, dear Mr Lonsdale,' said Hulda, closing her eyes and touching her forehead with the back of her hand in a dramatic gesture Lonsdale had only ever seen used in bad comedies at the theatre. 'I trust your brother with my honour.'

'Very well,' said Jack, standing reluctantly. 'I'll be across the hall if you need anything.'

'Never mind *her* calls for help,' hissed Lonsdale. 'You're more likely to have one from me!'

As soon as Jack closed the door, Hulda's façade of timid vulnerability disappeared. She abandoned her chair and went to the table, where she began to help herself to the remains of their breakfast.

'What a stuffed shirt, Lonsdale! I wouldn't tell him too much about our work if I were you. He might faint.'

'He's a good man,' said Lonsdale stiffly. 'And if you came here to insult my family, you can—'

'No, no,' interrupted Hulda quickly. 'I'm sure he meant well. Do you have any preserves?'

She began removing the lids of various pots and dishes to see what was inside.

Lonsdale's patience began to wear thin. 'What do you want, Friederichs? I'm going to cover an exhibition at the British Museum in a minute, so tell me what you need and go.'

'You're an ungracious beast, Lonsdale,' said

242

Hulda, unperturbed. 'I came to apologize, if you must know.'

'Apologize?' asked Lonsdale suspiciously.

'I should have let you share the cab, especially since you put up such a splendid fight against those ruffians. And I should have told you what I'd reasoned. But the truth is, once I'd started thinking about it, my solution didn't work, but I was loath to admit it.'

For several seconds, the only sound was the chiming of the grandfather clock in the hall.

'You confess you were wrong?' asked Lonsdale.

'You're not making this very easy,' grumbled Hulda reproachfully. 'Yes. I was wrong, although if you tell anyone else, I shall deny it. I was wrong to abandon you last night, and I have not solved the case.'

'So where does that leave us?'

'With Bradwell,' said Hulda, taking a large bite of toast.

'Bradwell?' echoed Lonsdale warily.

Hulda waved the toast at him. 'Would *you* know how to remove a cerebrum? I wouldn't. But he would – maybe he's conducting some kind of macabre experiment on corpses. Superintendent Ramsey is suspicious of him – you told me that he thought Bradwell might have taken Yeats's cerebrum, as it went missing while in his care.'

'But it was Bradwell who started our investigation by pointing out that Donovan was missing a cerebrum. If he was the thief, why draw attention to the crime?'

Hulda waved an airy hand. 'Yes, there are

243

problems with my theory, so it needs further investigation. I suppose it's what the Americans would crudely call "a hunch".'

Lonsdale was bemused. 'But I thought you liked him. He is certainly enthralled by you.'

'He is, but that could be a ploy to confuse us – all gushing admiration for *The PMG*'s most astute reporter.'

Lonsdale ignored her hubris. 'So your suspicions are based on the fact that he works in a mortuary and has access to corpses.'

'And that he has a family to support, but his post at Bart's is poorly paid. He *needs* a second income, yet he chooses to work for the pittance offered by the Metropolitan Police – he could earn a fortune in private practice. Why?'

'Perhaps he isn't very good with living patients.'

'I checked,' said Hulda. 'He's excellent, according to his colleagues. It is my contention that Bradwell chooses to be a police surgeon because it allows him to use corpses as subjects for some dark and sinister research. Moreover, a couple of months ago, I visited the City of London Police mortuary – the one on Golden Lane. It was well staffed and brightly lit.'

'So?'

'I learned that Bradwell was offered a post there, but that he declined it. I'm no connoisseur of such places, but Golden Lane is a lot nicer than the mortuary he runs. Why opt for dirty, old, under-funded, when he could have new, bright and clear? It makes no sense – unless he happens to like working with a single assistant, rather than a team, and in a place where visitors rarely tread.'

Lonsdale could not believe that the man who had been so helpful would transpire to be the culprit, but supposed there was no harm in humouring her.

'Then shall we pay him a visit and see what he has to say for himself?'

'Unfortunately, he's taken his family to Brighton, and won't return until next week.'

'Brighton? Why would he go there? Especially now, when we need his expertise?'

'Exactly,' said Hulda, with satisfaction. 'The plot thickens, eh, Lonsdale?'

Shortly after Hulda had left, jaws still working on the toast she had filched, Lonsdale received a letter from the father of William Willoughby, the young man who had been killed in France. Willoughby Senior was elderly and unable to travel to London, so Lonsdale was asked to meet him in Brookwood, the closest village with a train station to Willoughby's home in Bisley.

To expedite matters, the envelope also contained a first-class ticket for the ten thirty a.m. train the following day, a Saturday. Willoughby also promised a longer letter would arrive before Lonsdale left the next morning. Lonsdale was pleased, hoping that the interview would provide information that would allow him to develop an alternative solution to the one Hulda had proposed. He disliked – and was generally scep- tical of – the notion of Bradwell being involved in anything untoward.

Nine

Lonsdale left the house and went directly to the British Museum, where he spent much of the morning at the 'Religions of the Empire' exhibition. Afterwards, feeling he would make better progress alone than in the reporters' room, he went to the Museum Tavern across Great Russell Street. He ordered shepherd's pie, which he ate while he wrote a review of the exhibition.

When he had finished, Lonsdale hurried to Northumberland Street and handed the article to Stead. The assistant editor read it quickly, the fingers of one hand drumming his desk, while the other hand dipped into a dish of sultanas. His jaws worked rhythmically and he nodded approval of the piece at the same time. Idly, Lonsdale wondered how he managed to carry out so many completely independent movements and read at the same time.

Stead finished, then assumed his customary position – feet on the desk and chair tilted back at a precarious angle. Sultanas sailed through the air towards his mouth, but before he could say anything, there was a perfunctory knock at the door and Hulda entered. Without so much as a nod or greeting, she launched into her suspicions regarding Bradwell.

'No!' snapped Stead, slapping a hand on the table,

246

sending sultanas cartwheeling across the room. 'This accusation is absurd! I know Bradwell.'

'But the evidence,' began Hulda.

Stead raised one arm, closed his eyes, and tipped his face towards the ceiling. Not even Hulda could ignore such a peculiar posture, and she faltered into silence.

'You're grasping for solutions willy-nilly,' he said, standing and beginning to pace. Lonsdale leaned down to retrieve some of the sultanas before Stead ground them into the carpet, dropping them back into the bowl. Eventually, Stead sat again and began to eat the fruit that Lonsdale had picked up. 'The notion of Bradwell using corpses to conduct unsavoury experiments is too ridiculous to entertain.'

'So what should we do now?' asked Hulda. 'Write up the facts that we've uncovered so far, and leave our readers to form their own conclusions?'

'Facts?' demanded Stead. 'You have no facts – just gross speculation or downright slander.'

'Not so,' objected Hulda indignantly. 'We know that Walker *did* have information about missing people, and we have learned some of their names. We also know that Donovan is connected to them, and that Iverson is involved.'

'Yes, yes,' said Stead impatiently. 'But you don't know *why*! What you can report at the moment isn't the essence of a great story. We need to know *why* they went missing, and *why* someone killed Donovan and desecrated his body.'

He tipped the last of the sultanas into his hand

247

from the bowl. He gazed at it, slightly puzzled. 'How curious! I thought I had more of these. Have you two been eating them?'

'There are few things more repellent than a sultana,' replied Lonsdale in distaste.

'In that case,' said Hulda, 'I recommend we travel to Brighton and—'

'No!' snapped Stead crossly. 'Leave Bradwell alone. What happens now is that Lonsdale will continue trawling the archive, while you, Miss Friederichs, will write about the Americans' disastrous North Pole expedition.'

'Which one?' asked Hulda sulkily.

'The one where the ship sank, two-thirds of the crew are either dead or missing, and reporters from *The New York Herald* are racing all over Siberia interfering with the search for survivors,' said Stead. 'So off you go.'

While Hulda went to the reporters' office, Lonsdale – knowing she would be down in the archive within minutes to rant about Stead's inter-ference – left the building and hurried to Scotland Yard, hoping for a word with Peters. But the inspector was out, so he turned to retrace his steps, hoping enough time had lapsed to spare him a tirade from Hulda.

Had he not been so preoccupied, he would have noticed the tall, well-dressed gentleman gaping at him as their paths crossed, Lonsdale leaving the building and the man on his way in.

The man watched Lonsdale hurry away with a combination of disbelief, anger and frustra-tion. How could the reporter still be alive, given

248

that he had been assured that no fewer than six men would make certain he could not continue any investigation? Yet he was, and moreover he was clearly still actively pressing his enquiries – given that there could be no other reason for his presence at the Yard. *The PMG* knew little so far that could prove awkward, but it was only a matter of time before that changed. And once that happened, there would be serious repercussions.

But the man had no intention of letting matters go that far. Full of resolve, he entered the building for his meeting.

Lonsdale spent much of the afternoon conducting his search through recent newspapers, uninterrupted until Milner walked in shaking his head.

'The Prussian Governess won't stop grumbling about Stead,' Milner said, leaning against a filing cabinet, then inspecting the dust on his sleeve with annoyance. 'Even though he gave her the North Pole story.'

'Would you have liked it?' asked Lonsdale, glad of the interruption, as his hours among old papers that day had yielded nothing new and he was bored, tired and disheartened.

'My goodness, yes!' said Milner. 'A rival paper sends its own expedition to the Arctic, and it ends up an unmitigated disaster? Who wouldn't want to write about that? Even the relief expedition was a catastrophe, needing yet another relief expedition to save *it*! It certainly has a great deal of drama and, if nothing else, it's a chance to snipe at Harris.'

Lonsdale carried a pile of copies of *The Daily Telegraph* to the table, then wiped his hands on his trousers. 'It does sound more appealing than grubbing around in this lot.'

'Don't give up,' said Milner, perching on the table. 'I've been mulling over what you told me, and I think I was wrong to say the matter would be horrible, but not important.'

'You do? What changed your mind?' asked Lonsdale hopefully.

Milner gave a self-deprecating shrug. 'Just a feeling. It seems to me that you may have not just a single killer, but a group of them with a common purpose.'

'What common purpose?'

'Now that I cannot tell you – not yet. But I'll keep pondering and perhaps something will occur to me. Incidentally, a message from Francis Galton arrived a few minutes ago. He wrote that five o'clock will be a good time for you to arrive at his house today, and he has invited you to stay for dinner afterwards.

Lonsdale grimaced. He had forgotten about Galton's invitation, and was not in the mood for more tedious stories or admiring a collection of dried grasses, in which he had no interest whatsoever.

'A reporter should be interested in everything,' said Milner, reading his mind. 'Cheer up, Alec. Perhaps he will tell you something about his cousin Darwin. Then you can write it up, and Morley will have to give you a permanent job here. But meanwhile, you'd better go home and change soon. You can't arrive at his house dressed like a ragamuffin.'

Lonsdale dressed carefully for his meeting with Galton, selecting a black lounge coat and matching evening trousers of doeskin, offset with a light grey waistcoat. Galton lived in a handsome house at a corner of Rutland Gate, just south of Hyde Park. The door was white with shiny brass fitments, and Lonsdale had hardly taken his hand off the knocker before it was answered by a haughty butler with an amply bejowled face. Lonsdale was shown into Galton's study, a large first-floor room with an enormous table in the window. The overflowing bookcases reached the ceiling; the desk was piled high with notes, letters and manuscripts; and even the parquet floor was cluttered with teetering columns of papers and pamphlets. The walls boasted portraits – photographs or sketches – of Galton's famous friends: men like Darwin, Thomas Henry Huxley and Herbert Spencer.

'Lonsdale,' said Galton, with a movement that dismissed the butler and reached for Lonsdale's outstretched hand in one motion. 'We shall talk here, because Mrs G is in the drawing room, having tea with her ladies.'

Lonsdale sat and glanced around. On a table near his elbow were sheets of paper covered with curious diagrams, comprising arches in-filled with complex patterns. Galton saw him looking at them and came to sit next to him.

'Those are fingerprints,' he explained. 'Well, thumbprints to be precise.'

'Really,' said Lonsdale, trying to think of an intelligent response to something so manifestly peculiar. 'What are they for?'

'They will be the most powerful weapon the police have ever possessed,' declared Galton. 'Sir William Herschel has been collecting these in Bengal for almost two decades, and he has thousands of them. They do not change with age, and they are unique to an individual – so if you pick up that glass and leave your fingerprints behind, they'll prove you touched it just as surely as if you wrote your name.'

'But they all look the same,' said Lonsdale, studying the sheets.

'Not to the trained eye,' said Galton grandly. 'There are arches, loops, whorls and compounds, as well as an almost endless possibility of differences, with circles, spirals, ellipses, plaits and twists – each one different to any other. There are no external bodily characteristics comparable to these markings, Lonsdale. The limbs and body alter in the course of growth and decay. The colour, quantity and quality of hair, the number of teeth, even eye colour, change. There is no persistence in any visible parts of the body, *except* these minute ridges.'

'I've never heard of this before,' said Lonsdale. 'How do you collect them?'

'A light coating of ink on the thumb,' replied Galton. 'Then this is pressed on a piece of paper. I aim to index them, so they can be consulted and used to catch malefactors. But you didn't

252

come here to discuss my detective work, fascinating though it is. You came to look at African grasses.'

On the contrary, Lonsdale thought fingerprints were far more interesting than decades-old plants. He tried to think of a way to avoid them, but Galton went to a bureau and began to remove a number of shallow trays. Lonsdale's heart sank. There were dozens of specimens, and he was sure Galton planned to provide him with the life history of every one.

Galton had just opened his mouth to commence, when the door opened and the butler arrived with a silver tray bearing fine porcelain cups. Galton muttered under his breath while the man served them, then drained his in a single swallow. He indicated that Lonsdale should do likewise, so they could give their full attention to the grasses.

'I met a colonel in the Gold Coast who had cups just like these,' Lonsdale said, in a last-ditch attempt to delay the inevitable. 'He was later committed to a lunatic asylum.'

Galton chuckled. 'Not as a consequence of making your acquaintance, I hope. Of course, there's a very narrow margin between sanity and insanity. Did you happen to notice the size of his head?'

Lonsdale blinked. 'I beg your pardon?'

'You should read my books, like your charming brother. Men with large heads, like me, have greater intelligence than those with small ones. We are also less likely to go insane.'

'But surely, the size of a man's head must relate to the size of the rest of his body,' said Lonsdale.

253

'I've measured more heads than you can imagine,' said Galton sternly, 'and I can tell you that many small people have large heads, and many large people have small heads. The correlation isn't to the size of the body, but to the *intellect*. Have you never noticed that our Prime Minister, Mr Gladstone, is amusingly insistent about the size of *his* head?'

'No,' said Lonsdale noncommittally. 'I can't say I have.'

'He asked me once if I'd ever seen such a large head, to which I replied that he must be very unobservant, as it was in no way remarkable – well shaped but of average circumference. He was devastated until I admitted that I was jesting with him. He does indeed have a large head, although not as large as my own, of course.'

'Hmm,' said Lonsdale, wondering if the two of them had been drinking at the time, as it sounded altogether a peculiar conversation. 'Is there anything that you can tell from the *shape* of a head as opposed to its size?'

'I've seen nothing to suggest that head *shape* relates to specific abilities,' Galton went on enthusiastically, 'but things can certainly be learned from variation in the *size* of body parts, the skull included. My current work is on anthropometry – you know, relating body size and shape to certain types of moral and social behaviours.'

'Really?' asked Lonsdale, beginning to wonder if Galton was wrong about men with big heads being immune from insanity. 'And yet we all know that appearances can be deceptive.'

'My conclusions go well beyond anything as simple as *appearances*,' said Galton with rank disdain. 'I include not just analysis of specific body parts, but weight, height, strength, breathing capacity, reaction times, sight, hearing and quantitative judgements. And I correlate all these with tests and interviews for intelligence and morality.'

'How do you test for morality?' asked Lonsdale, as Galton lifted a tray of grass lovingly from its drawer.

'By posing questions that assess a person's ethical, religious and social character.'

Lonsdale was sceptical, but decided not to say so. 'I see.'

'Perhaps you do,' said Galton. 'But I should have to measure your head to be sure. Measurement will tell us everything we need to know about the human species. Measurement and scientific assessment. Have you heard of my "beauty map" of the British Isles?'

'No,' said Lonsdale warily, wondering what was coming next.

'Whenever I travel, I carry a cross of paper and a pin with which to prick it. Every beautiful girl, I record by pricking a hole in the upper end of the cross; the average ones are recorded on the cross arms; and the ugly ones on the long lower arm. Ergo, I can tell you that the incidence of pretty girls is highest in London and lowest in Aberdeen.'

'According to *your* concept of beauty,' Lonsdale pointed out. 'Aberdonians might have a different one.'

'Then they would be wrong,' said Galton shortly.

Deciding that dried grasses might prove less contentious, Lonsdale asked about them with as much ardour as he could muster.

Galton was delighted in the sudden interest in his collection, and, in repayment for his feigned enthusiasm, Lonsdale saw dinner moved back half an hour so that Galton could finish his lecture. Before long, Lonsdale was looking forward to meeting Louisa Galton as if she were his saviour.

However, dining with the Galtons transpired to be a peculiar experience. The dining room was long and thin, with photographs on all the walls. A large black sideboard held tiny blue and white Japanese dishes, and a Zulu bead pot was used as a receptacle for the fire tongs and poker. The table was set for three.

Louisa was a small, sickly lady who ate little and complained a lot, while Galton chatted about population statistics and African flora, neither subject of which required any input other than occasional eye contact. After a few moments, Lonsdale realized he was holding two conversations simultaneously, although neither Galton nor his wife seemed to resent the other's interference. Had he not been there, Lonsdale suspected the discussion would have been much the same.

'The kitchen maid is with child,' confided Louisa in a hoarse whisper during the consommé Desclignac. 'I'm sure the butler is responsible.'

Service being in the fashionable *à la Russe* style, the butler was standing near the door, and Lonsdale was certain he must have heard the accusation, although his impassive features revealed nothing.

'There are more species of grass than any other type of plant,' announced Galton in a voice more suited to the lecture hall than the dinner table. 'Barley, wheat and rice are grasses, you know.'

'I'll never be able to replace Potter, if I let her go,' continued Louisa. 'I don't know what I'll do. It's most inconsiderate of her.'

'Maize is a grass, too,' said Galton sagely. 'It's been cultivated for thousands of years.' He picked up a piece of bread and waved it. 'People were eating food like this when they were still living in caves and hunting mammoths.'

'Are any of your servants in the family way, Mr Lonsdale?' asked Louisa. She stole a venomous glance at the butler. 'I couldn't find my silver hairbrush this morning, and one can't help but wonder *what* one would find if one searched the servants' rooms.'

The butler stepped forward to manoeuvre a fillet of salmon à la Belle-Ile onto her plate. He seemed competent, but Lonsdale could not but help notice that he left a trail of sauce drops down her back. The master of the house was subjected to no such indignity, and Lonsdale suspected that the servants disliked Louisa every bit as much as she disdained them.

'All populations – animal and plant – share a normal distribution,' droned Galton. 'Like humans, most individuals are normal, while

257

others are so far removed from the usual that you wonder whether they're the same species.'

'Servants are a different species,' declared Louisa confidentially, when the remains of the fish had been removed and replaced by fricandeau de Duc de Cambridge. Lonsdale noticed that her veal was considerably more singed than his or her husband's.

'When I was in southern Africa, I ate maize meal in a village once,' said Galton. 'It comes in a paste. You roll it into a ball, push a dent in one side with your thumb, and use it to scoop up meat grease. After the meal, the natives allowed me to measure their heads.'

'I came across an interesting case recently,' said Lonsdale, during a rare lull in the conversation, when both Galtons were concentrating on sawing through their leathery lamb. This was mostly concealed by a rather oily gravy that spilled across the tablecloth when anyone tried to ply a knife. 'A man was murdered, after which the killer removed his cerebrum.'

He glanced up nervously, suddenly aware that such a statement was hardly the kind of topic enjoyed by the average household over dinner. The Galtons, however, were far from average, and neither seemed disconcerted by his choice of subjects.

'Oh, yes,' said Galton, waving his knife. 'The cerebrum is a fine organ. It's what separates us from the monkeys, you know. Have you ever seen a monkey's cerebrum, Lonsdale?'

'Not that I recall,' replied Lonsdale, wishing he had kept quiet.

'That Potter has no brain of any kind,' said Louisa, giving the butler a glare. 'If she had, then she wouldn't have allowed herself to fall pregnant.'

'A scientist can learn a great deal from a cerebrum,' said Galton, slicing a potato in two with the neat precision of a surgeon, and eating one half so quickly that Lonsdale thought it might not have touched the inside of his mouth before it was swallowed.

'The butler doesn't have a brain, either,' whispered Louisa. 'He has a good position here, and he'd never secure himself another if I dismissed him for tampering with the maids.'

'The cerebrum is the seat of the soul,' announced Galton. 'It was once thought to be the heart, but we now know that the heart is merely a muscle, and does nothing but pump blood around the body. The cerebrum, however, holds the very essence of our humanity.'

Lonsdale was relieved when Galton turned to the subject of his cousin Darwin, whom he had previously refused to mention. His wife, meanwhile, began a tirade on their coachman's gambling habits.

'It reflects badly on us, his employers,' she said bitterly. 'What if he gets into debt, and undesirables come knocking on our door? The scandal would be almost as grave as if news of Potter's pregnancy leaked out.'

'But if Potter is with child,' said Lonsdale, speaking for only the third time since the meal had started, 'then people *will* find out. It will show.'

Galton went into a fit of coughing, but as soon

as his wife and guest gave him their full attention, he miraculously recovered, and began to
hold forth on the different methods used for
drying peas.

'Do you like peas, Mr Lonsdale?' asked Louisa,
then forged on before he could answer. 'The
servants do, which is why they are such a rascally
horde. No good can come of eating peas.'

'Chickens eat peas, but then a chicken's crop
is a remarkable organ,' interposed Galton. 'Have
you ever looked at one under the microscope,
Lonsdale? But of course you have! You are a
Cambridge man, are you not?'

The time passed slowly, despite the fact that
the butler served the roast quail and its accompanying salad, and then the Boodle's gentleman's
pudding, at impressive speed. The moment the
port had been removed, Louisa retired, leaving
the butler to serve coffee to Galton and Lonsdale.

'Don't smoke?' said Galton, as Lonsdale
declined a cigar. 'My constitution wasn't made
for smoking or London fogs. I've had to go to
Switzerland to get away from them. But, speaking
of Switzerland, I made some intriguing scientific
measurements there. Fill up your glass – you'll
be interested in this.'

It was almost eleven o'clock before Lonsdale
was able to escape. He did so armed with a
baboon skull Galton thought might remind him
of Africa. He walked through Kensington
Gardens, feeling the meal settle in his stomach
like molten lead, while the teeth of the ape
formed an uncomfortable lump in his coat pocket.

260

When he arrived home, the first thing he heard was Emelia's nasal voice emanating from the drawing room, despite the late hour. He tried to sneak past without being seen, but she heard him and came out to demand that he play the piano. He opened his mouth to refuse, but closed it when he saw Anne was there, along with a pair of elderly aunts who had accompanied the young ladies for decency's sake. As it was late, both were sound asleep.

'A sonata,' demanded Emelia imperiously, and then named the fiendishly difficult 'Grande Sonate' by Alkan, which was well beyond Lonsdale's modest abilities. He thought he saw gleeful spite gleam in her eyes when he started to demur.

'No, play Haydn's "Sonata in C Major",' said Anne. 'Alkan is too taxing for the listener at this time of night. Come, Alec, I'll turn the pages.'

Lonsdale did as he was told, enjoying her easy company. She looked particularly lovely that night, in a long, silky dress of pale blue that drew attention to her long neck and fine skin. Emelia he was quite happy to ignore.

'Em and Annie will come dine on Sunday after church,' said Jack, speaking too loudly, as he usually did when he had had too much to drink. 'Join us, Alec.'

Anne smiled. 'Please do.' Lonsdale inclined his head to accept, pleased when Anne smiled with what appeared to be genuine delight.

'Excellent!' cried Jack. 'I'll ask Mrs Webster to make something special.'

He drained the brandy in his glass and Lonsdale

261

saw Emelia's dark brows draw downwards, leading him to suspect that it would not be long before after-dinner drinking was forbidden. He could not imagine why his sensible, rational brother had chosen such a gorgon, but supposed it was love. He hoped it would last, or both of them were going to be unhappy.

'Why don't we visit the botanical gardens at Kew afterwards,' suggested Anne. 'There's an exhibition of African grasses.'

She smiled sweetly at Lonsdale, who wondered if Jack had put her up to it.

'How about the British Museum instead?' asked Lonsdale. 'A new wing has just opened and there is a copy of the Magna Carta, letters written by Queen Elizabeth, and some of Darwin's original manuscripts.'

'Who's Darwin?' asked Emelia.

Lonsdale regarded her doubtfully, not sure whether she was teasing. Her puzzled expression told him that she was serious. He was amazed at her astounding ignorance: it could not be easy to be so unaware.

'The chap who described the evolution of life-forms,' explained Jack. 'He was very controversial – particularly with clerics.'

'Oh, he's the one who claimed to be descended from a monkey,' said Emelia in distaste. 'We don't want to see his nasty scribblings, do we, Annie? That sort of thing belongs in a Penny Dreadful.'

'*On the Origin of Species* is a great scientific work,' said Jack, startled.

'It is tedious in the extreme,' proclaimed Emelia firmly. 'And I want to do something *fun* anyway. How about a Punch and Judy show?'

'You choose Punch and Judy over Darwin?' asked Lonsdale, unable to disguise the disdain in his voice. Emelia's expression turned ugly.

'Punch is a subversive maverick, and his political opinions are an interesting commentary on modern society,' put in Anne quickly, thus saving her sister from further embarrassing herself, and Lonsdale from saying anything he might later regret.

'How was your evening with Galton?' asked Jack, also eager to change the subject. 'Did he tell you anything about his new book?'

'Boring,' muttered Emelia under her breath.

'He mentioned that—' began Lonsdale, but stopped when Emelia gave a small scream.

'He has a skull in his pocket!' she shrieked, pointing at Lonsdale's coat.

Lonsdale regarded her in astonishment before realizing that the baboon skull from Galton could be seen poking out of his pocket. He pulled it out, to show her it was a baboon, but she backed away in alarm.

'Ugh! Disgusting!' she cried. 'Keep it away from me.'

'It's interesting, Em,' said Anne, taking it from Lonsdale and turning it over in her hands. 'Look at these teeth.'

'I shan't,' snapped Emelia, folding her arms with a pout.

'Damn funny thing to keep in your pocket,

Alec,' muttered Jack, while Lonsdale thought that Emelia might well possess less inside her skull than the baboon had.

'I never realized how massive their canines are,' said Anne, handing it back to Lonsdale, 'or how tiny the brain case. I wish we had a human skull, so we could compare.'

Lonsdale was half tempted to promise to find one, but had no wish to provide Emelia with more reasons to dislike him. It was a pity, he thought, that the two women were sisters, as any attempt to further a friendship with Anne would necessarily throw him into company with Emelia, and he would have to endure her quite enough when she married Jack.

'Shall we say the Chelsea Physic Garden for Sunday, then?' asked Anne, and Lonsdale was pleased she seemed to want the outing to go ahead. He smiled at her, and she blushed and looked away.

'As long as it's not raining,' said Emelia. She rested her hand on Jack's arm and smiled coquettishly; Lonsdale saw his brother melt. 'Alec and Anne can discuss skulls, and we can talk about our wedding.'

'I'm sure we can find something more interesting than skulls,' said Lonsdale, noting with pleasure that Anne seemed to regard the prospect with as much delight as he did.

The next morning, the train from Waterloo rumbled through the Surrey countryside and toward Brookwood station, where Lonsdale was to meet Willoughby Senior. It had been a

264

scramble to make the train, as he had overslept after his late night. The promised letter from Willoughby had arrived, but it was only when the train was moving that Lonsdale was able to read it. What he learned caused his heart to beat faster. At last! He was about to get the answers he needed!

The Manor House, Bisley, Surrey

Dear Mr Lonsdale,
I am grateful for your letter and for your understanding of the distress and pain caused when my only son, the beloved child of my old age, was taken from me in so brutal a fashion.

You kindly offered to visit me to discuss my son's fate and the subsequent lack of interest in it by the French and our own police. The train ticket I have already sent you will give you passage from Waterloo to Brookwood, and I will have a coach awaiting you on your arrival. For your convenience, the driver will take you to a local establishment, The Volunteer in Brookwood. I will be awaiting you there, and we will have some four hours together before you must catch your train to London.

In your letter, you asked about certain specifics of William's death. I shall provide you with a detailed account when we meet, although I can answer two of your questions briefly here.

First, I can tell you few details about my son's recent activities. He completed his degree at Oxford last June, then returned home for the summer. I had expected him to follow me into law, and with the foolish indulgence of a doting parent, allowed him a summer of idleness and leisure. Thus, imagine my surprise when, in September, he announced an intention to accept a post as a predoctoral researcher in London, and that he would be moving there directly. I was naturally concerned by the haste with which he jumped to an alternative career to the one I had envisioned, and my concerns grew when he declined to provide me with details. My insistence appears to have driven a wedge between us; nothing of the kind had ever entered our relationship before.

From that time, we grew more distant. I was not inclined to visit him without an invitation, which I never received. The mystery of my son's altered character was also of interest to Inspector Peloubet, the officer in charge of the investigation into his death.

Your second query related to the manner of William's death. I sent Dr Quayle, the family's physician throughout the entire twenty-two years of my son's life, to make such examination as would be permitted by the French authorities. He reported that my son was found lying next to a railway track, the top of his head cut off. The French authorities concluded that a train ran over his head, his body being flung to one side by the impact.

This raises several questions. Would not the wheels of a train crush a head, rather than slice off the top? How could William jump or fall from a train, yet land with his head on the track? Does this not indicate that my son's head was mutilated by other means, and his body placed near the tracks as if by 'accident'? Moreover, if one were to fall from a moving train, would there not be other injuries? No such injuries were observed by Dr Quayle.

Now I come to the most horrifying element of the tale: one section of my son's brain had been removed. The French authorities believe this to be consistent with injuries caused by the train. Dr Quayle disagreed, and is of the opinion that someone killed William, cut off the top of his head with a long, sharp knife to remove part of his brain, and left him on a railway track to disguise the fact.

I hope these facts will convince, rather than dissuade you from exploring the matter further. I enclose a family photograph of William, taken in happier times, in the hope that you will see the hopeful promise in his sweet face and feel my concerns about his death should also become your own.

*I wish to express my fervent thanks for
your offer of help.
I am, Sir, your obedient servant,
Edward St John Willoughby*

The photograph had been cut from a larger
picture, and showed a youth of twenty or so,
with light hair and a smooth face. There was
indeed something hopeful and endearing about
the youthful features, and Willoughby Senior
was right in that his son did truly make a jump
from faceless victim to a person in Lonsdale's
eyes.

Lonsdale returned to the letter and read it again,
and then a third time. By the time the train rattled
into Brookwood, he was beside himself, not just
with anticipation of answers about to come, but
also with a resolve to see justice for William.

He alighted on a platform at a pretty place,
with painted pots bursting with spring flowers
and a cluster of attractive little brown and white
cottages where the stationmaster and his staff
lived. After the clanking, hissing train had gone,
Lonsdale stood for a moment to savour the peace
and collect himself. A pheasant issued its croaking
call, and Lonsdale could see it strutting around
a field, resplendent in its russet-bronze feathers.

He went outside and was pleased to find a trap
waiting for him. The driver opened the door for
him, then climbed into his own seat, and encouraged the horse to a lively pace. Within minutes,
after little more than a mile, the driver drew up
outside a nondescript tavern.

Lonsdale stepped into the main taproom to find

268

two workmen standing at a long bar, talking to someone on the other side of a door behind it. As Lonsdale approached, he realized that they were addressing the publican, who was heating mutton chops for their midday meal. There had been a time when it had been common for workmen to bring in a cut of meat in a cabbage leaf for the publican to cook, in return for the men buying a quart of porter or four-ale. Lonsdale felt a momentary sadness that such a pleasant custom was disappearing.

'Harry,' called one of the men at the bar. 'You've a gentleman out here.'

The publican stepped into the doorframe and looked enquiringly at Lonsdale, who said he was looking for Edward Willoughby.

'You'll be wanting the saloon bar, then,' said Harry. 'Take the staircase to the first floor, go down the hall, and it'll be on your right.'

Lonsdale followed his instructions, and entered a room with attractive dark wood walls, plush carpeting, and two comfortable leather chairs, one of which was occupied by a tall man, impeccably dressed. His hair was neither long nor short, and his sideboards and thin moustache were neatly trimmed. He had a pleasant but unremarkable face. He rose as Lonsdale entered.

'Thank you for coming.' He extended his hand. 'Francis Willoughby.'

'You seem familiar,' said Lonsdale, frowning.

Willoughby smiled. 'Yes – you might not remember, but we met a year ago at the Oxford and Cambridge Club.'

Lonsdale had the sense that they had met more

269

recently than twelve months before, yet poor Francis was so undistinguished that Lonsdale knew he might have passed him a dozen times in the street and not noticed. Then something occurred to him. 'Francis Willoughby? My appointment was with *Edward* Willoughby.'

'He's my father. Please take a seat – I'll explain everything.'

With a knock, the landlord entered with two glasses of beer and a tray of food. Lonsdale wondered if he had been waiting outside, listening.

'Well?' asked Lonsdale when Harry had gone. He did not touch the proffered meal or drinks, and had the sinking sense that answers that had seemed so near his grasp were about to be snatched away.

'My father is not a well man,' began Willoughby. 'He has a weak heart, and my brother's death has been a terrible shock. Those of us who care about him decided that it would be best if I met you in his place, to prevent him from becoming overexcited.'

'Surely that should be his decision – not yours?' said Lonsdale.

Willoughby gave a tight smile. 'I'm a doctor, Mr Lonsdale, and I consulted both my father's regular physician – Dr Quayle – and the heart specialist who treats him. It was a decision made by all of us in his best interests.'

'Your father agreed to this?'

'He doesn't know,' said Willoughby, gently apologetic. 'When you fail to arrive, he'll assume you've been delayed or have decided against listening to the ramblings of an old man broken

270

by grief. He'll go home, where I shall continue my efforts to help him let poor William go.'

Lonsdale looked around him. 'So this isn't The Volunteer? The man in the trap outside the station effectively kidnapped me to bring me here, while your father waits elsewhere?' He did not try to conceal his frustration.

'Please forgive the dramatics, but I hope you can appreciate that I won't endanger my father's health,' said Willoughby politely but firmly. 'It might be a story to you, but it's my father's future at stake.'

'I understand,' said Lonsdale, trying to be as agreeable as possible, since he was not going to see the man's father regardless. 'But I have reason to believe his concerns about your brother are justified. Certain injuries . . .'

'Then share your suppositions with me, and I will try to answer any questions you have.'

Lonsdale disliked the situation he was in and was full of suspicion. 'How do I know you are who you claim to be? Your father's letters – both to me and *The Times* – said that William was his only son. He did not mention you.'

Willoughby sighed sadly that Lonsdale should doubt him. 'I can show you documents bearing my name, I suppose. And I have a family photograph . . .'

He removed it from his wallet, much folded and fingered, showing two men sitting side by side. Lonsdale recognized them at once: one was William, the other the man who sat opposite.

Lonsdale handed it back. 'So why did your father say William was his only son?'

271

'He and I had a falling out some years ago,' said Willoughby, re-folding the photograph and putting it away. 'It was what one might call a mutual disinheritance. My recent re-entry into his life was brought about by the death of my brother – my half-brother, actually.'

'So you and he are reconciled?'

Willoughby grimaced. 'Let us say we are working to that end. Unfortunately, the hurt we inflicted on each other will take time to mend. But I love him and will do all I can to comfort and protect him.'

'I see.' Lonsdale was uncomfortable hearing such intimate details. It felt like the prurient prying that Milner feared reporters would soon have to undertake for their stories.

'The cause of our disagreement was his shameful treatment of my mother,' Willoughby went on. 'They had been married for more than twenty years when he divorced her for a younger woman – William's mother. He hurt her and ruined her reputation, simply for selfishness. William was born seven weeks later.'

'Hmm,' mumbled Lonsdale, beginning to be embarrassed by the confidences.

'I was seventeen at the time,' Willoughby went on, oblivious. 'And I sided with my mother – the innocent party. But although my disgust at my father and my dislike of his new wife intensified, I was fond of my new half-brother. When my mother died, I washed my hands of my father and his woman, but remained in touch with William. Then, when William went up to Oxford, away from my stepmother's poisonous interference, he and I were able to become friends.'

'Your father didn't know?'

Willoughby shook his head. 'William and I both decided it would be easier for all concerned if he didn't. I had no wish for William to lose his father, as I had done. However, in the last four years of his life, I knew William better than his parents did.'

Lonsdale took a sip of beer. 'Your father mentioned a falling off of his relationship with his son. Was that why?'

William smiled. 'Of course not. What happened was that Oxford turned William from a cosseted, smothered boy into a man. He grew up, Mr Lonsdale – outgrew the need to tell his papa every little thing. I had nothing to do with it.'

'Is his mother still alive?'

An expression of pain crossed Willoughby's face. 'She decided against spending her life nursing an elderly husband, and left for greener pastures when William went to Oxford.'

Lonsdale wanted to ask his questions and leave. The Willoughby family troubles were not relevant to how William had died in France. He eased the discussion to more practical matters. 'How did you know your father planned to meet me?'

'He mentioned it to Dr Quayle, who told me.'

'Are you familiar with your father's investigation into William's death? That he believes William was followed to France and murdered?'

'Yes, of course, but there's no evidence to support his claims.'

273

'On the contrary – he has the evidence of Dr Quayle, who travelled to France at his request and examined your brother's body.'

'Dr Quayle did not go to France alone. Do you think I would sit back and do nothing if I thought someone had deliberately hurt William? I went with him, and I saw the same things that he did.'

'Which was that William's cerebrum had been removed?'

Willoughby made an impatient sound at the back of his throat. '*That* did not happen. First, William's poor head was far too badly damaged to allow any such assessment to be made. And second, Dr Quayle would never have reported such a ghoulish detail to my father. I can only assume that this has come about due to the strain. Hearing it makes me wonder if he's lucid enough to understand what Dr Quayle said at all.'

'So Dr Quayle said nothing about a knife being used on William?'

'The only knives involved were the scalpels employed by the pathologist at the mortuary,' said Willoughby firmly. 'The top of William's head was severed, and parts of his brain were missing, but to say it had been surgically removed . . . it is a nonsense!'

Lonsdale was not sure what to think. 'There have been other cases of missing cerebra recently . . .'

Willoughby initially looked sceptical, but seeing how serious Lonsdale was, his face showed actual relief. 'Thank God! That explains where my father got the idea. I was afraid it might have derived from some sickness of his own mind. He must have read about it in one of the less responsible papers, and thought that as William's brain was also damaged . . .'

Lonsdale shook his head. 'That's impossible, because several of us at *The Pall Mall Gazette* are the only ones other than the police who are aware of the details of those cases.'

'Then all I can imagine is that my father misunderstood what Dr Quayle told him. Perhaps Dr Quayle indicated that part of the brain was gone, and my father made the leap to assuming that meant it had been taken.'

Lonsdale supposed that made sense, and with bitter frustration saw answers slipping further away. And yet the picture of William's youthful face drove him to ask his last questions.

'Was William's death an accident then?'

'It was not suicide. He had no reason to terminate his life. It was, I believe, a tragic accident. And let me add that my father's criticisms of the French police are unreasonable. They assessed the situation carefully and minutely, and I believe their conclusions: that William was killed by a train, his body being thrown aside by the impact.'

'Is it possible to fall from one moving train, be hit by another, and sustain no injuries other than to a head?'

'But William *did* suffer other injuries. Dr Quayle and I found significant bruising to his chest, legs, and back.'

'So what do you think happened?'

Willoughby looked away; the subject was painful. 'That William fell out of the train because he leaned on an insecurely fastened door, that he suffered serious bruising in that fall, that perhaps he staggered back to the tracks before passing out with his head on or next to the tracks, and that he was killed when another train hit his head as it passed later. And that, Mr Lonsdale, is a much more plausible explanation than my father's.'

'I guess it is,' acknowledged Lonsdale reluctantly.

'Are you free to share with me any of the details of these other cases that you thought my father might know about?' asked Willoughby. 'I'm just wondering if I might be able to see a connection.'

And because he did not want his journey to Brookwood to have been a total waste of time – and as Willoughby was a medical man – Lonsdale told him about the other deaths he had been investigating. Willoughby was a good listener, and Lonsdale outlined every detail of the cases, including his suspicions that incidents in Holborn, Peckham and Chiswick might also be related.

'I see now why my father's letter brought you running,' said Willoughby when he had finished. 'But to answer your earlier question, I have no idea why anyone should want to steal a fellow's cerebrum. However, I seriously doubt the business has anything to do with the medical profession. You would do better to look among the criminal fraternity for your culprits.'

'Probably,' admitted Lonsdale. 'Just one more question: do you know what "research post" William took in London?'

Again, Willoughby winced. 'None, as far as I know. I strongly suspect he was in the city enjoying its delights, and the claim of employment was to avoid our father's censure. He deplores idleness.'

The two men sat in silence. After several moments, Lonsdale stood to leave. 'Thank you for your candour. My condolences on the loss of your brother.'

The trap was waiting, so he climbed in and nodded to the driver to take him back to the station. Willoughby watched him go and, had Lonsdale glanced back, he would have seen the mask of poised suffering slip to reveal something else altogether.

On Sunday night, Anne lay in bed and stared at the ceiling, but all she could think about was Lonsdale, and the time they had spent at the Physic Garden. He had not returned from Surrey early enough to join Jack, Emelia and her on Saturday, but after church on Sunday the four of them dined together and had a lovely afternoon. She and Lonsdale were officially acting as chaperones for the betrothed couple, but she remembered nothing at all of what they had said or done. All she remembered was Alec – his slightly awry hair, his laughing eyes, and his bright, intelligent conversation.

They had sauntered lazily around the garden and, at one point, when Jack and Emelia had followed a bend in the path before she and Lonsdale reached it, he had taken her hand and held it gently. She remembered the warmth of his hand, and the light, affectionate squeeze he had given hers before he had let go.

Then, when he had helped her to the carriage – at the end of the most glorious evening she could remember – he had turned towards her. Their lips had been scant inches apart, and she had desperately wanted to kiss him. Smiling, she slipped into a contented slumber.

Ten

Lonsdale arrived so early at Northumberland Street on Monday morning that he was there before anyone else. Eager to speak to Stead, and knowing the assistant editor crossed the Hungerford Bridge each day from his house at Wimbledon Common, Lonsdale went to meet him. He headed towards a cavern that led to Villiers Street under the South Eastern Railway Terminus – lit by a single lamp at each end, and wet with mineral-rich moisture dripping from stalactites in between. Just as he was entering it, Stead appeared, trudging with a slouching step and bent shoulders, and a large leather satchel swinging from his right hand. Next to him was Milner.

'Wonder of wonders,' said Stead. 'First Milner calls at my house at six. Now you meet me before seven.'

Without waiting to hear what had drawn Milner – never an early riser – from his bed at such an hour, Lonsdale told them both about his foray to Surrey. Stead barely listened.

278

'I appreciate you have the bit between your teeth with this cerebrum business, Lonsdale, but it will have to wait, I'm afraid. All our attention must focus on the tragic events of Saturday.'

'What events?' asked Lonsdale.

But they had reached the office, and Stead sprang up the stairs without answering. Lonsdale looked at Milner for an explanation.

'On Saturday, Lord Frederick Cavendish, the new Chief Secretary for Ireland, arrived in Dublin,' Milner explained. 'That evening, he and Under-Secretary Burke were walking in Phoenix Park when they were set upon by four men armed with knives and murdered within sight of the Viceregal Lodge.'

'Members of the Irish Republican Brotherhood?' asked Lonsdale, hating the thought of what such an outrage would mean for the continued troubles in Ireland.

'Probably, although no one has yet claimed responsibility. Because yesterday was Sunday, almost nothing's known, but the public will soon be clamouring for information, and we'll be expected to provide it. Morley has already set up a meeting with Gladstone, his close personal friend. We'd better go upstairs.'

In all his time at *The PMG*, Lonsdale had never seen everyone so intent on a single story. Milner was sent to Dublin, and every other member of staff was allocated a different aspect of the crime. Nothing else seemed to matter.

Thus it was not until Wednesday, when the furious activity had abated, that Lonsdale had time to return to the archive. The first thing he did was to address an issue that had been niggling at the back of his mind ever since he had boarded the train from Brookwood. Willoughby Senior claiming that William's brain had been taken was just too much of a coincidence at a time when similar incidents were occurring, and Willoughby's explanation for the 'confusion', although possible, simply did not feel right. Lonsdale suspected that a second attempt to see the father would be no more successful than the first, so he decided to approach Dr Quayle – to ask for a detailed account about William's body and *exactly* what he had told Willoughby Senior.

It took a while for Lonsdale to compose the missive, as he needed to mention his correspondence with the father and his meeting with the son, without betraying his doubts about what the younger Willoughby had told him. But at last it was done, and he took it upstairs to be posted, before returning to the drudgery in the archive.

He had been working steadily for several hours when Hulda arrived with a visitor. She looked tired after the frenzy of the Phoenix Park murders, but her eyes had not lost their customary gleam. Lonsdale was somewhat startled to see Jamie in her wake. The boy's once-fine clothes were even more rumpled and stained, but he was grinning in triumph.

'I found what you asked,' he said proudly, 'and I'm here to make me report.'

'Very well,' said Lonsdale, indicating the archive's

only other chair. 'Take a seat and tell us what you've discovered.'

'No,' said Jamie, turning to Hulda with a clumsy but sincere bow. '*Ladies* sits. Gentlemen stands.' Hiding her amusement, Hulda inclined her head in gracious thanks and perched on the edge of the seat.

'Are you hungry, Jamie?' Lonsdale asked.

'She bought me a pie, didn't she?' he said, nodding toward Hulda. 'She ain't nearly so stiff as she looks.'

'You won't get another if you don't watch your tongue,' Hulda snapped brusquely, although a smile twitched at the corners of her mouth.

'Right,' said Lonsdale. 'Frederick Kempster and Edmund Corlett. What have you learned?'

'Neither had any family or friends,' Jamie replied, 'except each other. They shared rooms, and kept to themselves. Their neighbour says they was dolly boys.'

'Homosexuals,' translated Lonsdale for Hulda's benefit. 'And probably ostracized by their families so, like Donovan, they were alone.'

Jamie nodded. 'No one went to their funerals, and no one collected their belongings – those are still at the police station. I asked to see them, but the peelers wouldn't let me.'

'Right,' said Lonsdale, thinking the boy had some gall to try.

'No one could say how the fire started,' Jamie continued. 'But I think it was deliberate, like the one that did for Donovan. I gave a penny to the mortuary guard, and he let me see them. Neither had no head – it was like they'd been squashed right off.'

'You inspected the bodies?' asked Lonsdale, aghast.

'I'm a thorough reporter, me,' said Jamie with haughty pride. 'But there's more, old pal. While I was visiting me mates at the workhouse, they told me that *he's* been seen again, doing his stuff.'

'Who?' asked Lonsdale. 'Iverson – the big man with the scar?'

'No, the blacksmith-like feller. His appearance has changed because he shaved off his beard. But he's got the same snake tattoo on one of those big old arms.'

'What did he do, exactly?'

'Me mate – Roger – he said Big Arms went off with a woman called Agnes over in Hackney after they'd been making eyes at each other all night. It's been a week now, and she ain't been seen since. I figure she thought she was catching herself sommat good, but got caught instead. And she's as dead as me mates.'

'Has her disappearance been reported to the police?' asked Lonsdale.

'Sure, but they said they couldn't do nothing.'

'And you're absolutely certain?' asked Lonsdale. 'Big Arms is the same man we talked about earlier?'

Jamie nodded firmly. 'Roger said they all calls him Captain, because he has the same name as the pirate.'

'What pirate?' asked Lonsdale. 'Drake? Bluebeard?'

'No, the one from Bristol. Morgan. Henry Morgan. That's Big Arms' name.' Jamie grinned, delighted with his success. 'So now I'm ready for the next job. Chiswick, you said.'

Lonsdale explained what he wanted, and urged Jamie to be careful. He then gave him two shillings, one for the job just completed and one for the next. Jamie tossed them in the air, caught them, and raced up the stairs to begin at once. Hulda regarded Lonsdale sceptically.

'He's a child. Are you sure you should use him like this?'

'No,' admitted Lonsdale, 'but from what he told us, I think he'll be safer in Chiswick than anywhere frequented by Big Arms Morgan.'

'So have you discovered anything yourself, or have you left it all to your helpmeet?'

'I've found out that a milkman – John Poole – who's due to attend court tomorrow, has disappeared. He's accused of stealing canisters put out by other milkmen, and was supposed to report to the police each evening. He hasn't for several days.'

'You're clutching at straws,' said Hulda. 'Maybe he just absconded.'

'Well, it's a minor charge, but if he runs away, he could end up behind bars. His barrister insists that he was keeping to the terms of his bond because he was so frightened of prison. He and the police are baffled. Have you found anything?'

Hulda fumbled in her handbag and pulled out a newspaper. 'I asked a friend in Brighton to keep an eye out for any murder or disappearance that might occur in the area after Bradwell went down there. Here is yesterday's *Brighton Herald*.'

The body of Teresa Godley, aged fourteen, was discovered yesterday after a fire at a beach arcade. She had gone missing a week ago after being released until trial following her arrest with her brother for stealing a gold chain and watch and two pounds from a man named Frank Wood. Her body was burned beyond recognition, but she was identified by the chain taken from Mr Wood.

'Are you ready to investigate Bradwell now?' Hulda asked.

When Lonsdale arrived at Northumberland Street on Thursday morning, he headed to the reporters' room to collect Hulda, so they could investigate her contention that Bradwell's 'holiday' was connected to the death of Teresa Godley. But before he had reached the top of the stairs, Stead called out. Lonsdale stuck his head into the assistant editor's office, and saw him sitting on a stack of newspapers. His back was to the door, his feet were on the mantelpiece, and he was rhythmically beating the sides of his trousers with a long-handled clothes brush.

'Ah, Lonsdale,' he said, leaning back until his head was almost upside-down, and regarding the reporter in a most unorthodox fashion, 'I understand you had plans with Hulda today, regarding poor Bradwell. It's therefore with some pleasure that I destroy your nefarious intentions by telling you what I told her fifteen minutes ago: the two of you will be needed here all day, because Mr

284

Morley, Milner and I shall be attending the funeral of Lord Frederick Cavendish.'

Stead spun around, looked his reporter up and down, and held out the clothes brush. 'You need this more than I do.' He scratched his thick beard. 'I'd like you to write a note on last night's storm. There's been damage throughout the south.'

When Lonsdale reached the reporters' office, the most serious storm appeared to be in Hulda's face. She was furious, and Lonsdale could tell from the flushed, angry features of Voules that he had experienced the sharpness of her tongue. He glanced at Lonsdale as he entered, and resumed reading the morning papers. Wisely, Cook had retreated to the furthest corner.

'Stead can be most irritating,' she said angrily. 'Rather than investigating Bradwell, we're forced to remain here. I should *never* have told him what we were planning.'

'A mistake I wouldn't have expected from you,' said Cook, rashly joining the discussion.

'Easy for you to say,' she hissed. 'All you do is gallivant around speculating about assassination. But just exactly what have you learned about the Phoenix Park murders, eh?'

'Not much,' agreed Cook, in a manner that indicated he was not going to give her the satisfaction of an argument. 'It'll be a long investigation.'

'But no more difficult than ours,' said Hulda grumpily. 'And at least the Phoenix Park murders don't have Stead slowing down the investigation.'

Lonsdale arrived home at Cleveland Square that evening to find Jack just bidding farewell to

285

Emelia and Anne, who had joined him for late-afternoon tea. Anne's face lit up when she saw Lonsdale, which was not lost on Jack, who gave his brother a meaningful wink. Emelia saw the wink, but did not understand it, and looked from one to the other in confusion. 'Surely you don't have to go just yet?' asked Lonsdale, sorry that he had taken a leisurely walk through the parks instead of the more direct route. 'Do you have plans for this evening?'

'We're expected home – Mother and Father are hosting a dinner party,' said Anne. 'We need time to dress.'

'And we're dining at the United Service Club tonight, Alec,' Jack added. 'We were invited by Taylor, who is in London on leave. He's moved up the ranks since he and I were young together, and you can't have seen him for years.'

Lonsdale sighed ungraciously.

'It's gratifying to see you disappointed to miss my company, Alexander,' said Emelia blithely. 'I've been labouring under the impression that you didn't like me, but now I see I was wrong.'

'Yes,' said Lonsdale hesitantly, not sure how to respond.

'What would you like to do this coming Sunday?' asked Anne, addressing Jack, but glancing at Lonsdale. 'A picnic in Greenwich Park?'

'Oh, no,' said Emelia with a shudder. 'There would be too many ants.'

'Hampton Court might be nice,' suggested Lonsdale, speaking to Anne.

'Rather than making a major outing of it, we could dine here,' Jack said. 'And then we could

286

stroll to Hyde Park to watch the boating. The Serpentine is famous for its model yachts.'

'That sounds dull,' said Emelia. 'Toy boats are for children.'

'Not necessarily,' said Lonsdale, thinking about Donovan's love of watching them during his half-days off. Suddenly, Jack's idea seemed very attractive. 'It might be interesting.'

'I suppose Annie and I can find something to amuse ourselves while you grown men play,' said Emelia sulkily.

'Don't worry, Em, I'm certain we'll all have an enjoyable time,' said Anne, and smiled happily.

Lonsdale had not been home long when he received a message from Stead. Due to public and legal pressures, it had recently been decided that the Hampstead Smallpox Hospital would cease admitting smallpox patients and would concentrate instead on treating scarlet fever and diphtheria. Stead wanted Lonsdale to ascertain whether this change was due to the wealthy residents of Hampstead using their political influence to override public health concerns. Stead also had a new assignment for Hulda, and Lonsdale was just as glad he would not be there when she found out that her goal of looking into Bradwell had been delayed again.

When Lonsdale awoke on Friday morning, he felt as though he had not slept at all. For much of the night, he had been plagued by unsettling dreams, and, although he could not remember them, he still had a lingering sense of unease. But he felt considerably better after three cups of tea and a large plate of bacon and coddled eggs, and, despite a light rain, he was soon walking to the Midland Railway Station to take the 10.05 a.m. to Hampstead.

Late that afternoon, having interviewed administrators at the hospital as well as the locals who were among its greatest adversaries, Lonsdale took the train back to London. He dozed fitfully throughout the journey, sleep alternating with wondering if a response had arrived from Dr Quayle. Reaching the Midland Station, he began to move along the platform with a wave of humanity from another train that had arrived simultaneously. Someone behind bumped him hard with a large bag, and he turned his head around in annoyance.

A glimpse of a figure further back, however, drove all other thoughts from his mind. Iverson was not wearing his police uniform, but a dirty black jacket of the kind favoured by dockers. His eyes met Lonsdale's. Turning quickly, Lonsdale knocked into a hurrying businessman. By the time he looked up again, Iverson had gone.

Once outside the station, Lonsdale decided that rather than heading to Northumberland Street, he would go straight home, in the hope of finding Anne and Emelia there again. He was disappointed to discover the house empty except for the servants. He retired early to his rooms and sat near a fire, reading and dozing.

He woke Saturday morning pleasantly refreshed and found Jack had already left. Lonsdale wandered down to the drawing room, where he read *The Morning Post* and *The Daily Telegraph*. He was just perusing more speculation about the Phoenix Park killings when Dillon, the butler, opened the door to admit Hulda.

'Are you all right?' asked Hulda without preamble. 'You didn't come to work yesterday, and there was no sign of you today. Are you ill?'

Lonsdale poured her some tea. 'It's good to know you care, Friederichs.'

'I wouldn't want anything to happen to you in the middle of our investigation,' she said stiffly. 'Have you made any progress, or have you just been lounging about?'

He told her about his dull day in Hampstead, finishing with, 'but I saw Iverson at the Midland Railway Terminus, although he disappeared before I could reach him.'

Her eyes widened. 'He seems to be everywhere. I have news also: Peters sent a message yesterday saying that O'Connor has apparently absconded with an unspecified sum of money.'

'O'Connor the mortuary assistant? Perhaps we should see what Bradwell can tell us about it. He must be back from Brighton by now.'

'Great minds, Lonsdale. I've heard that he *is* back, and I want to know if he had a role in the murder of Teresa Godley. Shall we go?'

They arrived at the mortuary to find its windows boarded over with fresh wood and its door secured with a strong, new lock.

'Have the Metropolitan Police finally provided sufficient funds for Bradwell to make his building safe?' asked Hulda, rattling the door. 'He *will* be pleased! But quick – stop that hansom before it gets away. He's not here, so we need to locate him at the hospital.'

St Bartholomew's Hospital was a substantial complex, comprising a number of large brick and stone edifices and a mass of outbuildings. Lonsdale and Hulda were directed on a complicated route along corridors, across patches of scrubby grass, and up and down stairs. Hulda was beginning to become frustrated when they finally found the surgical section, with its brightly lit operating theatres. Bradwell, just leaving a recovery room, was not pleased to see them.

'How may I help you?' he asked stiffly, leading them into a grimy corridor away from his colleagues. 'Much as meeting you is a pleasure, Miss Friederichs, I am busy today.'

Lonsdale noticed that his face was paler than it had been and his hands were unsteady – his sojourn in Brighton had evidently not been the restorative jaunt he had hoped.

'We wanted to ask you about O'Connor,' said Hulda. 'Where is he?'

'I don't know,' said Bradwell. 'I haven't been to the mortuary in days, so I can't answer questions about what the staff do without me. Is there anything else? I have patients waiting.'

'But you must know,' insisted Hulda. 'You worked with him for . . . how long was it?'

Bradwell shook his head quickly, glanced up and down the hall, and then looked her squarely in the eyes. 'Please, Miss Friederichs, I'd love to help you, but I've an operation to perform in ten minutes. Now, if you will—'

'Have the police asked you about O'Connor's disappearance?' persisted Hulda.

'Of course, but I'll tell you what I told them: I haven't seen him in days. I've been in Brighton, you know, with my family.'

'So what did you do there?' asked Hulda. 'Meet any local young girls?'

Bradwell blinked. 'Pardon?'

'One was murdered,' said Hulda. 'Teresa Godley.'

Bradwell raised his eyebrows. 'Yes, I read about it in the newspapers.'

'She was found dead after a beach arcade was set ablaze.' Hulda forged on. 'Sounds rather like what happened to Donovan, don't you think?'

Bradwell gaped at her in horror. 'You can't think that *I'm*—'

'Is it a coincidence that you leave for Brighton and a similar murder occurs there?' she pressed relentlessly. 'We don't know if Godley had her cerebrum taken out, but we *will* find out.'

'Good,' said Bradwell unsteadily. 'I hope you do. But remember who first mentioned the excised cerebrum to Lonsdale. What possible motive would I have to do so if I were involved?'

'That's a good point,' said Lonsdale to Hulda.

'But I'm afraid I can no longer help you on this case or any other,' Bradwell said. 'I've resigned my post with the Metropolitan Police.' He shrugged. 'I'm tired of long hours for little pay in a broken-down building. Bart's offered me an appointment that'll suit me much better, and I'll be able to spend more time with my family. Now, please excuse me. My patient—'

'Has someone threatened you?' asked Lonsdale, moving to block the surgeon's way as he turned to leave. 'Is that why you're so frightened?'

'I'm not frightened.' Bradwell glanced around uneasily again. 'But I do have a wife and children to think about.'

'So someone *has* threatened you?' pounced Hulda.

'Please stop,' begged Bradwell, the fear now obvious in his face. 'Leave me alone!'

He turned from them and strode down the corridor.

'Well,' said Lonsdale thoughtfully. 'That's not the ebullient, friendly man I met a few weeks ago.'

'No,' Hulda agreed. 'Something's terrified him.'

'I wonder if Iverson reached him,' said Lonsdale.

There was no more to be done, so while Hulda returned to *The PMG*, Lonsdale went to see Inspector Peters. The policeman's willingness to talk to Lonsdale – without chastising him about interference – indicated his own investigation was not going well.

'I had another encounter with Iverson,' Lonsdale told him. 'Yesterday at the Midland Railway Station.'

'Really?' asked Peters, raising his eyebrows. 'Are you certain it was him?'

'Oh yes. Positive.'

'Then we have a most peculiar problem,' said Peters, puffing clouds of blue-grey smoke. 'Because I saw Iverson, too, the day *before* you did. He was floating face down in the Thames. He was very dead, and had been for some time.'

Nothing Lonsdale could say would induce the

policeman to believe he had seen Iverson. The inspector simply pointed out that a large moustache and a scar often made quite different men appear similar, especially when only a fleeting glance was possible. The two parted on friendly but sceptical terms.

Upon arriving home, Lonsdale was initially disappointed not to find a response from Dr Quayle, but then he heard Jack talking to the sisters in the sitting room. He felt a surge of pleasure when Anne looked as delighted as he felt when he joined them.

'What happened to you?' demanded Emelia. 'We came to invite you to Pagani's, only to find that you had left with another woman.'

'Not another woman,' Lonsdale said. 'Just Friederichs. She's a colleague.'

'A pretty one, though,' remarked Jack, watching Anne mischievously.

'If you like that sort of thing,' responded Lonsdale stiffly, disliking his brother's teasing.

Emelia had watched the exchange with a puzzled frown. 'Do you have many female colleagues?'

'Just the one,' replied Lonsdale. He turned to Anne. 'Let's not talk about Friederichs. I'm sorry I wasn't here. Did you enjoy Pagani's?'

'It would have been better with you there,' said Jack bluntly.

'No,' contradicted Emelia. 'It was better *without* him. The three of us never argue when we're alone, but we often do when he's here.'

'I like a lively debate,' countered Anne.

'I had planned to stay home today,' Lonsdale

said, 'but Friederichs suggested that we locate a certain doctor at St Bartholomew's, and—'

'You went off the moment another woman beckoned?' snapped Emelia. 'Without leaving a message to say where you had gone?'

'Why would I leave a message, when I was out for an undetermined period following up on my investigation?' Lonsdale asked reasonably.

'So you didn't want anyone to know where you had gone?' Emelia looked him up and down in some disgust. 'How often do you disappear with that kind of woman?'

'Steady on, Emelia,' said Jack, startled by her venomous tone. 'There's no need to react like that.'

'Please, Em,' said Anne softly, mortified by her sister's outburst and trying to make peace. 'Tomorrow's the day that we're all to go to the park together, and as there's a red sky outside, the weather should be fine. I think we should have a picnic there, rather than eating here.'

'I don't want to go,' said Emelia waspishly. 'Not with him.' She eyed Lonsdale malevolently.

'Why not?' demanded Lonsdale. He had had enough of Emelia and her unpleasantness. 'I've done nothing wrong by having a female colleague, and I don't know why you would have so unfairly taken against her.'

'I see,' said Emilia stiffly.

'She's a perfect lady,' he stormed on. 'And would never stoop to besmirch the reputations of those she doesn't know.'

'Well,' said Anne in the awkward silence that followed, 'I've heard there are lots of ducklings on the Serpentine this year.'

294

'I shan't go,' said Emelia sulkily. 'I don't like ducks.'

'Don't be silly,' said Jack, rather sternly. 'It'll be pleasant to spend an afternoon in the sunshine, and I will have Mrs Webster prepare us the picnic Anne has suggested.'

'Or you can stay here, and we'll tell you about it when we come back,' suggested Lonsdale.

'Very well, I'll come,' said Emelia, yielding when she saw that Jack and Anne were ready to go along with Lonsdale's suggestion. 'But Alexander had better not decide to run off—'

'How about a little music before we go,' interrupted Anne.

The four trooped into the drawing room, where Anne selected a lieder by Brahms. Lonsdale was ordered to play the piano, while Anne and Emelia sang. Lonsdale did not like Brahms, but was prepared to suffer as long as Anne was happy. Emelia, he decided, could go to the Devil, and he brazenly risked more censure by attacking Jack's brandy. Emelia watched sullenly, but said nothing.

Lonsdale woke the following morning when his brother burst into his room and threw open the curtains, letting in a stream of golden sunlight.

'Don't you know it's Sunday?' groaned Lonsdale, trying to pull the covers over his head. There was a brief tussle when Jack tried to haul them off him. 'It is the one day we can sleep in. Why are you up so early?'

'Because it *is* Sunday,' said Jack, beaming happily. 'We're going to church, then we're going to have a pleasant afternoon in the park.'

The prospect of a day with Anne pleased Lonsdale. He promised himself not to give the murders a moment of thought, but to enjoy the glorious spring day. He dressed with more than his usual care, and Jack had to drag him away from the mirror.

After enduring an unusually long and complex sermon, and five fervently patriotic hymns, the brothers strolled back through Kensington Gardens. They had just arrived home when they were hailed by a familiar voice – Hulda. Lonsdale regarded her in astonishment. She was sitting astride a bicycle, wearing a skirt short enough to reveal a full four inches of leg above the ankle.

'You're looking unusually smart today, Lonsdale,' she said, dismounting and wheeling the contraption towards him. 'Are you going out?'

'To Hyde Park, with my fiancée Emelia and her sister Anne,' said Jack cheerfully, oblivious to her provocative apparel. 'It's an excellent day for a picnic.'

'I was going to ask if you wanted to come cycling,' said Hulda, crestfallen. 'I'm sure you know cycling is good for the constitution.'

'I don't think my constitution would survive long on that thing,' said Lonsdale, eyeing the bicycle doubtfully.

'Well, don't exert yourself, then.' Hulda gave her bicycle a shove, and flung her leg over it to mount in much the same way that Lonsdale had seen men do. She was around the corner at a furious speed before Lonsdale could tell her about Peters claiming Iverson was dead.

'She's quite a lady,' said Jack ambiguously, watching her disappear.

When Emelia and Anne arrived, the four of them walked to Hyde Park's Italian Water Garden, and picnicked near the statue of Jenner.

'Emelia and I have been discussing taking her parents to Raunds, so they can meet Mother and Father,' Jack told Lonsdale as they ate. 'We were thinking of August. Would that appeal to you, Alec?'

'Certainly,' he replied. 'I've not seen Mother and Father nearly as much as I expected when I returned to England, and I'm sure they'd enjoy meeting the Humbage family.' He was certain they would be hospitable and kindly, although – based on Jack's descriptions – he suspected his gentle, intellectual father would be disappointed in his future in-laws.

'Good, it's settled then,' said Jack. 'But look – the sun's going behind a cloud. Shall we go for a walk before it turns cooler?'

But it was already too late: as soon as they began to stroll along the Serpentine, a chill breeze picked up. Some of the clouds drifting towards them were heavy and dark; despite Anne's prediction of fine weather, a downpour was in the offing.

Jack and Emelia walked ahead, arm in arm like a married couple, while Lonsdale and Anne dawdled behind. Anne talked about her childhood in India, then, seeing several women in three-quarter-length dolmans, switched to a commentary on fashion. After a moment, she stopped suddenly and turned towards him.

'I can't believe that I'm blathering about fashion! I'm sorry. I'm not usually so silly.'

Lonsdale smiled and reached for her hand. 'I don't think you are silly, and if we were somewhere on our own, I'd kiss you, Annie.'

'And if we were somewhere on our own, I'd let you.'

He smiled at her, and they continued walking, hand in hand. Ahead, Lonsdale could hear Emelia's strident voice as she held forth about the price of satin. He wondered how Jack – or Anne – could bear to spend so much time with her.

Anne, on the other hand, was such easy company – unlike Hulda, whom he found himself also thinking about, to his surprise. He compared them: Hulda was strong, flaxen-headed and driven, like some Viking, whose sole aim was conquest, while Anne was slim, also light-haired and eager, although just as serious and intelligent. But, despite his growing attraction to Anne, Lonsdale could not but help notice that she was not as challenging as Hulda – in both the positive and negative senses.

They had reached the part of the Serpentine that was used as a boating lake. There was a wooden pier on which sat a number of men and boys, many proudly displaying tiny craft and happily criticizing those of others. It was here that Donovan came on his days off. Lonsdale gazed at the boat owners, wondering if any had known him.

'Come on,' he said, springing up the steps that led to the pier, and forgetting his intention to put Donovan's death from his mind for the day.

Anne hesitated. 'You want me to go with you? With all those men?'

It had not occurred to Lonsdale that Anne – independent and curious – would hesitate, or that she would be alarmed at the prospect of people discussing model boats.

Stemming his impatience, he offered her his arm. 'I'd like to see the boats more closely.'

'No.' Anne was firm. 'You go, and I'll wait here. I don't feel comfortable clambering out there.'

Lonsdale hesitated. It was ungentlemanly to abandon a woman, even in as public a place as Hyde Park. But it was only for a moment, and the pier was only a few yards from the shore.

One of the men saw him looking, and beckoned him over in a friendly fashion. Lonsdale's mind was made up. He walked briskly onto the jetty, and stood facing the bank so that he could still see Anne. She was well away from the water, and Lonsdale wondered if she were frightened of it. But his attention was not on her for long, as several men were more than pleased to show him their boats.

'An acquaintance – a chap named Donovan – recommended I come here,' he said after he had admired and complimented their vessels. 'He often told me how splendid your boats were.'

'Donovan,' sighed one, shaking his head sadly. 'Poor codger died in a fire. He was a lovely fellow, too. He came here without fail every Sunday and Wednesday, although he never had a boat himself. Said he didn't have the talent to make one, but I think he'd have done all right, if he'd tried.'

299

'He came twice a week?' asked Lonsdale, watching carefully to make sure that Anne was not being disturbed by an elderly man with a cane, who was strolling past her.

'Usually, but he was less regular just before he died,' said a young man with a peculiarly shaped felt cap. 'He was taking part in some survey or other.'

'Was he?' queried the first man. 'I didn't know that.'

'Well, you know Donovan,' said Felt Cap. 'He wouldn't tell anyone anything. I asked him where he'd been, but he just said something about business. I said it must be pretty important to keep him away from the boats, but he wouldn't tell me anything else.'

'Quite right, too,' said the first man. 'You'd no right asking him questions. He was a private man, was Donovan.'

'He was a bit *too* private, if you ask me,' said Felt Cap. 'It wasn't normal. And I only asked so I could look out for him, like friends do. I thought I ought to find out what was keeping him away from the boats.'

The first man shook his head again. 'It must've been sommat important, that's all I can say. And you're right – friends *do* look out for each other, and he had no friends except us. The snobs at Salmon and Eden never cared about him.'

'Did you find out what kept him from coming here?' asked Lonsdale, all his attention on them, Anne forgotten.

'I did,' said Felt Cap, unable to disguise his pride.

'You see, Harold's boat sank, and Donovan took off his jacket to help him get it back.'

'He did,' acknowledged Harold sadly. 'I wouldn't have got *Endeavour* back if he hadn't helped me. What did you do, Fred? Look in his jacket pockets?'

Fred looked offended. 'What do you think I am? I don't rummage through people's things. But I did notice a piece of paper sticking *out* of one pocket. Because he was a friend – and I look out for friends – I looked to see what was on it.'

'What did it say?' asked Harold, keenly interested.

'There was a date,' said Fred. 'It was in his fancy handwriting – Wednesday the nineteenth of April at three o'clock.'

Lonsdale's interest quickened. That was when Donovan had told his colleague at Salmon and Eden that he was going to watch the boats. He had died the following morning.

'So did Donovan come boating that day?' he asked. Harold shook his head. 'The last time we saw him was the Sunday before. What else did this piece of paper say, Fred?'

'After the date and time, it said, "survey at the Imperial sommat or other Institute, Brunswick Gardens." That's where he went instead of coming here.'

'The Imperial Statistical Institute?' asked Lonsdale, recalling reading about a grand opening of such a place in the distant past.

'That's the one!' exclaimed Fred.

Lonsdale was disappointed. He could not imagine that an appointment at some obscure academic department could have anything to do with Donovan's death.

'Did he say what he was going to do there?'

'No, but he was furious when he saw me with the paper in my hand. He snatched it away and said it was none of my business, and that I shouldn't tell anyone, or I'd put him in an embarrassing situation.'

'And have you told anyone else?' asked Lonsdale.

'Not until now – you can't embarrass the dead, can you? Anyway, I didn't see why it should be cause for embarrassment, but then it struck me. It probably wasn't this statistical institute he was visiting, but a hospital. Men's diseases – you know. He must have had a tart somewhere.' Lonsdale was glad Anne was not with him.

'You think he had the clap?' asked Harold in wonderment. 'Never! Not him.'

'Can you think of a better explanation?' demanded Fred. 'Can you see old Donovan missing an afternoon here to talk about numbers or some such thing?'

'Maybe he was having money problems,' said Harold. 'He lived in a fancy house on Wyndham Street, but when his father died, he didn't inherit as much as he thought he would, and his windows needed replacing. He told me his neighbours are the type to complain about a bit of shabbiness, and that he'd have to fork out for them to be replaced.'

'So he may have taken paid work at the Institute,' mused Lonsdale, 'to pay for house repairs?'

Yes,' said Harold firmly.

302

'No,' said Fred at the same time. 'He had the clap. And if he *was* short of money, it was because he needed it for his fancy piece.'

Lonsdale left them debating and turned to hurry back to Anne. But she was not there.

Lonsdale looked around quickly, trying to see where she could have gone, but she was nowhere to be seen. He ran to the end of the pier and was about to start asking passers-by if they had seen her, when he spied both sisters with Jack on a bench.

Emelia gave Lonsdale a nasty look when he rejoined them, but Anne just laughed and did not seem to mind that she had been abandoned.

'Really, Alec,' muttered Jack crossly as they began to walk home, Emelia and Anne lagging behind when they stopped to admire some bluebells. 'How could you leave Anne alone?'

'Hardly alone! I could see her the whole time.'

'Not the *whole* time, or you would have noticed her coming to sit with us,' said Jack pointedly. 'You should be more thoughtful. They had a brother who drowned when they were young, so neither of them likes water.'

'How was I supposed to know that, for Heaven's sake?' Lonsdale asked, although he felt mildly ashamed of his neglect.

'These are two *ladies*, not the frontier women you met in Africa. Or Hulda Friederichs, for that matter, who, if you don't watch out, will have you riding bicycles and chaining yourself to railings in favour of women's votes.'

'What's wrong with letting women vote? They do comprise half the population.'

'A year ago, I would have agreed,' said Jack. 'But do you really want the likes of Emelia deciding the future of our country? She doesn't read the newspapers, and has no idea what's happening in the world.'

'I'm sure the same is true of a lot of men, but they're allowed to do it. Besides, some women are extremely well informed. Look at Friederichs, who knows more about British politics than virtually any man I know – including you. And Anne is no dullard.'

'No, she's not.' Jack gave Lonsdale a playful jab in the ribs. 'Pretty girl, Anne. Good family, too. You could do a lot worse than her.'

Lonsdale was not about to confess his regard for her, because he knew he'd never hear the end of it. He changed the subject back to Emelia.

'If you think Emelia can't be trusted to vote, why in God's name are you marrying her?' There. It was out, and there was no turning back. Lonsdale realized he was holding his breath.

'A man needs a woman, and she has everything I require,' said Jack simply. 'And I love her.'

Lonsdale was spared from responding, as several penny-sized spots appeared on the path and Emelia screeched her horror.

'Rain!' she shrieked, as if it were acid dropping from the sky rather than water.

'Dash it all!' exclaimed Jack. 'I was hoping to reach home first. Can we make it to those trees, do you think?'

They trotted across the grass to a small copse,

considerably hampered by Anne's uncontrol-
lable giggles. The sky was now a solid mass
of grey, and the rain that fell was the kind of
downpour that might set in for the rest of the
day. Lonsdale offered to fetch a hansom, more
to escape Emelia's grumbles than from any
sense of chivalry.

'I'll bring it down Carriage Drive, so you can
just come over when you see me arrive.'

'Don't forget us then,' said Anne, as the drips
came through the branches onto her hair.

Lonsdale began to hurry across the grass to
where there were always hansoms for hire. Other
strollers were thinking along identical lines, but
he was faster than most, as ladies in fashionable
sheath and tie-back dresses moved slowly.

He reached his destination ahead of the crowds
and hailed a carriage. But they had gone no more
than a hundred yards when he heard a loud crack.
The horse screamed at the same time that the
carriage lurched forward, throwing Lonsdale
headfirst against its interior wall. His mind
reeling, all he could think was that someone was
shooting at him.

Eleven

'You all right, mister?' the driver asked.
Lonsdale tried to clear his wits. 'The axle
snapped when we went over a pothole. Sorry
if you was thrown about. If it makes you feel

any better, the underside of me carriage looks worse than you do.'

Lonsdale climbed out and inspected the damage. Rain drummed on the umbrellas of the people who clustered around watching. A policeman hurried over and asked him to wait while he helped the driver to disengage the horses. Several people asked if they could help, and one gentleman invited Lonsdale to share his umbrella.

Eventually, after shuffling impatiently while the policeman made ponderous notes about the accident in his pocket book, Lonsdale told him that he had to go. Then it took a while for him to find a replacement carriage. He directed the driver to the trees under which Jack and the sisters had sheltered, but they were no longer there.

Grimly, knowing he was in for lectures from both Jack and Emelia, he told the driver to take him home. When he reached Cleveland Square, Dillon the butler informed him that the others had not returned. For a reason he couldn't put his finger on, Lonsdale began to feel uneasy.

Using the same cab, he gave the driver the Humbages' address – Gordon Square in Bloomsbury – and told him to hurry. Progress was agonizingly slow, as the traffic was heavy because of the rain. After what felt like an age, Lonsdale was deposited at the door of the handsome, five-storey affair with window boxes, yellow shutters, and twin marble columns leading to a front door. He flung a handful of coins at the driver, and ran up the steps. His knock was answered by a maid, who gasped as he thrust past her into the hall.

'Are Jack and Anne here?' he demanded, darting down the corridor and looking through open doors as he went. In one, an elderly woman regarded him with obvious interest. 'And Emelia?' he added as an afterthought.

'Alexander!' came Emelia's shocked voice from behind him. 'Whatever's the matter with you? You're frightening our grandmother.'

He turned to see Emelia and Anne coming down the stairs, from where they had evidently been changing into dry clothes. He sighed in relief.

'Thank goodness you're safe,' he said. 'I wasn't sure where you'd gone.'

'Where *we'd* gone?' demanded Emelia, glaring at him. 'You were gone for an age, but our neighbour, Sir Henry Hartley, saw us and offered us a ride in his own carriage. Jack insisted that we accept.'

'So where's Jack?' asked Lonsdale. 'Did you leave him behind?'

'Who might you be, sir?' interrupted an imperious voice from the top of the stairs. 'Anne? Emelia? Who is this ill-dressed fellow? What is the meaning of this unseemly commotion on the Lord's Day?'

'It's Jack's brother, Father,' said Emelia, giving Lonsdale a warning look. 'Here to ensure we arrived home safely.'

'Is he now?' asked Sir Gervais, in a voice that dripped hostility. He was a tall man, with stern features, vast mutton-chop whiskers, and a manner that indicated he was used to having his own way. He wore a silk smoking jacket and had *The Pilgrim's Progress* tucked under his arm, a tome that Lonsdale considered one of the dullest ever written. Evidently, Sir Gervais had been reading it aloud to his household, as a bevy of servants emerged to stand at his heels.

With them was a large, squat woman whom Lonsdale took to be the lady of the house. Lady Humbage wore a heavy, uncomfortable outfit that would not have improved her enjoyment of the afternoon, as it looked hot, stiff and restrictive. No wonder Emelia was such an ignoramus, thought Lonsdale: her parents had turned literature and education into an ordeal. He wondered how Anne had survived.

'He looks drunk to me,' said Lady Humbage, coming to take the arm of the old lady, who had emerged from her room to watch. 'Go and sit down, Mother.'

'*Are* you drunk, sir?' asked Sir Gervais, reverently placing the Bunyan on a small table before descending the stairs with a majesty of which the Old Queen would have been proud.

'He's always like this,' said Emelia petulantly. 'And, this afternoon, he abandoned Annie to the attentions of crude men on the banks of the Serpentine and then ran off alone, leaving us without a carriage.'

'He did *what?*' exploded her father, glowering at Lonsdale as if he wished to thrash him there and then.

'Em is teasing,' said Anne, giving her sister a sharp glare. 'We had a most pleasurable walk

308

together, and then – with my blessing – Alec went to interview some men for a story he's writing.'

'You abandoned my daughter? And what do you mean, "for a story"?' His voice oozed contempt.

'Look at him,' said Lady Humbage, before Lonsdale could defend himself. 'His hair is uncombed and he's dripping on the Persian rug.'

'It's raining,' said the old lady tartly, speaking in a voice that was unexpectedly strong. 'Of course he's dishevelled. But he's not drunk. I know a drunk when I see one.' She smiled enigmatically, leaving Lonsdale to wonder whether the family's roots were as respectable as Emelia and her stiff, pompous parents would have everyone believe.

'You're right, Grandmother – he isn't drunk,' said Emelia, trying to bundle Lonsdale towards the door. 'But he *is* leaving.'

'Stay,' countered the old lady, extending Lonsdale a warm smile and holding out a gnarled hand. 'A visitor kind enough to brave a wet Sunday must not be allowed to escape so easily.'

'I agree,' said Anne quickly. 'He should stay.'

'He's busy,' said Emelia. 'He has work to do.'

'On the Sabbath?' asked Sir Gervais coldly. 'The day the Lord instructed us to rest? What kind of heathen are you, man?'

'No kind, indeed, sir,' responded Lonsdale shortly. 'As a matter of fact—'

'Alec's father is a rector,' interrupted Anne, trying to salvage a degenerating situation.

'Well, obviously,' said the old lady dryly, 'if he's Jack's brother.' She chuckled softly.

'A rector who failed to teach his son that

cleanliness lies next to Godliness,' intoned Sir Gervais. 'It's hard to believe he's related to Jack.'

'Yes,' agreed Lady Humbage. 'Breeding is important, and one can tell a good deal from families.'

Emelia blanched, as she realized doubts were being cast on Jack because of her unwarranted hostility to Lonsdale. He felt a twinge of malicious satisfaction.

'How can you account for your actions towards my daughter, and then for bursting in on us during our devotions?' demanded Sir Gervais.

Lonsdale adopted a pompous voice of his own, speaking loudly enough to ensure he would not be interrupted. 'I regret the weather has made it difficult for me to appear my best. I have the utmost regard for your daughters, and I would never intentionally put them in the way of verbal unpleasantness or physical harm. My arrival here was based on concern for them and my brother, who left the park before I could bring them the transport I had secured.'

'Don't take that tone with me, sir,' blustered Sir Gervais. 'By God, if there weren't ladies present—'

'Oh, go and sit down, Gervais,' ordered the old lady crossly. 'You'll give yourself a seizure. You, too, Agatha.'

'Where's Jack?' Lonsdale asked of Anne.

'Jack's a charming fellow,' said the old lady, before Anne could answer. 'One brother a rector, another in the Royal Navy.' She smiled at Lonsdale. 'And now I meet the baby of the family.'

'Alexander was in the Colonial Service,' said Emelia, to repair any damage she might have caused. 'Weren't you?' There was desperation in her eyes.

Lonsdale nodded his head obediently. 'Jack?' he asked.

'Walking home,' replied Anne gently. 'Don't worry. He'll be wet, but a drenching will do him no harm.'

'Stay for some rum punch,' ordered the old lady. 'I have a recipe that will put some colour back in your cheeks.'

'Go back to the sitting room, Mother-in-law!' snapped Sir Gervais unpleasantly. 'He is not here to listen to the prattle of elderly women. Or to imbibe sinful substances.'

'Pity,' sighed the old lady, genuinely disappointed.

'Perhaps another time,' said Lonsdale gallantly.

'Good day, sir,' said Emelia's father and, without another word, he turned and stalked back upstairs, his wife and servants in his wake.

'Goodbye,' called the old lady wistfully, as Lonsdale aimed for the door. 'Do call again.'

'Hopefully we'll see each other soon,' put in Anne.

'I'm not pleased with your treatment of that antimacassar, Alexander,' hissed Emelia, anger erupting again now her parents were no longer present.

'What antimacassar?' asked Lonsdale, bewildered by the sudden change of topics.

'You obviously wiped your dirty hands on it,' continued Emelia. 'It was ruined, and it was one of a set that took me a month to make.'

'It fell out under the trees while Jack was looking for his handkerchief to wipe spots of rain

311

off Em's face,' said Anne, laughing at Lonsdale's guilty look. 'At first, we couldn't imagine why he had such a filthy rag, but then she recognized the stitches.'

'Jack said he had put it in his pocket because he thought he'd have a replacement made,' said Emelia. 'As if I wouldn't notice the difference between my lacework and someone else's! You men must think us stupid.'

'He told you *I'd* ruined it?' asked Lonsdale, thinking it unlike his brother to land him in trouble quite so shamelessly.

'Of course not,' said Emelia, scornfully. 'When I demanded to know what had happened to it, he said he had found it on the mantelpiece and that one of the servants must have damaged it. But from the way he blustered, I knew he was protecting *you*. Now go. I don't want Father to have second thoughts about what kind of family he's letting me marry into.'

Lonsdale walked down the steps to find the driver of the carriage still looking for coins in the mud.

'You don't know how much there was, do you?' he asked unhappily. 'Only I'm not sure I've got it all, see. People don't usually lob money at me.'

'Sorry, I don't,' said Lonsdale. 'I hope it was enough.'

'It'll suffice,' said the driver smugly. 'In fact, I'll take you back to Bayswater for free if you like.'

He had a final prod in the mud with the whip, and then they were off, travelling sedately along the tree-lined streets.

Lonsdale rubbed his head. Was he mad, tearing all over London and making bad impressions on Jack's intended in-laws? He decided he had better be careful, or it would be Jack he would have to worry about, not some crazed killer.

When Lonsdale arrived home, he was surprised when the door was opened before he reached it – the servants were not usually so assiduous. He was even more surprised to see Hulda in the hall.

'Your butler told me that you'd shot in and out again with no explanation,' she said. 'I was concerned.'

'I went to see Emelia and Anne,' said Lonsdale vaguely, and turned to Dillon. 'Is Jack home?'

'Not yet, sir.'

Lonsdale went to the drawing room. Hulda followed and sat opposite him.

'Jack should be home by now. Where could he be?'

'His club?' suggested Hulda. 'The place where men go to do things mere women are not permitted to witness?'

Lonsdale ignored the barb. 'Anne said he planned to come home.'

'Well, he would say that, Lonsdale,' said Hulda. 'He'd hardly confess that he aimed to spend his evening drinking and playing cards. Why are you so worried? Has something happened?'

'No,' admitted Lonsdale, not sure how to explain the irrational fear that had been with him ever since he had come home to find the place empty.

Hulda fumbled in her bag for an Esmonda cigar. 'A hansom knocked me from my bicycle just after noon,' she said quietly. 'It would have run me over had I not rolled out of the way.'

'Hulda!' exclaimed Lonsdale, appalled to think he had been so engrossed in his own concerns that he had failed to notice her. He looked her over quickly, noting that her hands were scraped and that there was mud on her skirt. For a woman of her impeccable appearance, this was unusual indeed. 'Are you hurt? Can I fetch you anything?'

She shook her head, but her voice was unsteady. 'I was on my way to a special Sunday archery session when the attack came. I'm damned if I'll allow a maniac to interfere with something I enjoy, so I picked myself up and continued. I was a little alarmed, but once at the butts, I could protect myself by treating any comers to an arrow in the heart. After practice, I came here.'

She seemed subdued, and he sensed she was still in shock.

'Did you see the driver? Was it Iverson?'

'No, but someone just as interesting.' She blew out a large ring of smoke. 'I believe it was the man who attacked us near the hospital – the one we think is named "Pauly".'

'But he didn't harm you?' he asked again, thinking that for Hulda to admit to being 'a little alarmed' probably meant that she was terrified.

'Just my pride. I had to submit to the indignity of being helped to my feet and fussed over by a group of men. But there is more important news.'

314

'What could be more important?' he asked uneasily.

'I met Wheatley, *The PMG*'s business reporter, just before I was knocked over. He told me that the police had sent a note to Stead saying that a body had been found in Shepherd's Bush.'

Lonsdale waited while Hulda blew a stream of smoke towards the hearth.

'It was Poole, your missing milkman,' she said. 'He was *sans* cerebrum.'

While rain splattered against the window, Hulda and Lonsdale sat by the fire. The flames sent a comfortable orange glow around the room, and snapped and popped in a way that always made Lonsdale think of toasting teacakes when he was a child. He might have enjoyed sitting there, talking quietly while the storm fussed outside, were they not discussing a series of brutal murders, and had he not been worried about Jack.

'Poole wasn't killed where he was found – in an alley – because there wasn't enough blood, apparently,' said Hulda, sipping her tea. 'And because a number of people saw the corpse and that its cerebrum was missing, the police have not tried to conceal it.'

'Leaving him in an alley,' said Lonsdale. 'The killer is getting audacious.'

'And perhaps selective. Greaves's and Walker's cerebra were left intact when they were killed in Regent's Park, but Donovan and Yeats, the music-hall entertainer, were despoiled.'

'There's no pattern, is there? Some victims

315

he mutilates, and others he doesn't.' Lonsdale felt dispirited, unable to see a way forward.

'Let's think this through,' said Hulda. 'Iverson – I think we can safely name *him* as our culprit, given he had been seen, and his past record – has been killing people and taking their cerebra. Obviously, there's a limited number of times he can do this and escape, as there would be a public outcry, and the police would mount a major hunt. So, he concealed what he did in his early victims.'

'And Iverson is *not* dead, as Peters claims,' said Lonsdale. 'I know what I saw at the train station. He's alive and he has help – men like Morgan, whom Jamie mentioned.'

'I believe you,' said Hulda. 'I'm also sure he's the man we want. So, he's been killing people and removing parts of their brains . . .'

'The five people Cath Walker claimed are dead are so well hidden that their bodies have yet to be discovered,' said Lonsdale. 'And the removal of Donovan's and Yeats's cerebra was also cunningly concealed.'

'It was only because Bradwell was observant that it was discovered,' said Hulda. 'Which brings up the question of him – Bradwell.'

'Well, he was so thoroughly rattled that he disappeared on an impromptu holiday with his family and resigned his position as police surgeon. I don't think he's involved, but I do think he's been warned not to help us any more.'

'Spineless!' sneered Hulda contemptuously.

'Better spineless than brainless,' said Lonsdale. 'Perhaps we shouldn't be looking at Bradwell, but at his assistant, O'Connor,' suggested Hulda. 'He went missing during the time that Bradwell took his holiday.'

'He may have disappeared because he was also intimidated,' said Lonsdale. 'And he fled to save his life. There's nothing to say he's involved. But speculating is taking us nowhere. Let's go back to facts.'

'Well, we know Walker decided to put an end to it – not by telling the police, because if Iverson was involved, so might other officers have been. I have not forgotten that high-ranking officers came to warn us against investigating, and when we did it anyway, we were attacked.'

'So her only other option was the press,' said Lonsdale, 'hoping that the resulting furore would see Iverson and any cronies arrested. But she was murdered herself before she could do more than pique our interest. The killer poisoned Greaves first, then he cut Cath's throat. But that's odd, isn't it? Why poison one victim and slit the throat of another?'

'It *is* odd,' agreed Hulda. 'Everything about the case is odd. Indeed, at the risk of sounding defeated, I wonder if we shall ever have any answers.'

When the drizzle brought an early dusk, Hulda went home, having refused to let Lonsdale accompany her. A few minutes later, Inspector Peters was shown into the drawing room.

'You've heard the news, I take it?' Peters asked. 'Another victim relieved of his cerebrum?'

'Yes,' said Lonsdale, noticing the rings of

317

tiredness around the inspector's eyes. 'Iverson strikes again.'

'Iverson's dead,' stated Peters firmly. 'I've known the man for twenty years, and I can assure you it was *his* body we dredged from the Thames.'

'But I saw him on Friday,' insisted Lonsdale. 'And it *was* him – the same man I saw at Donovan's house fire, and who attacked me in Bermondsey. Unless you think a different man happened to have a scar through his eyebrow and be wearing the uniform of PC six-nine-six-D.'

'Regardless,' said Peters, in a way that showed he clearly thought Lonsdale was mistaken, 'he seems not to like you much.' He pulled his pipe from his pocket and began to tamp down the tobacco. 'I wonder whether we might put that dislike to use.'

'Meaning?'

'I'll be blunt. These murders are random – there's no pattern in location, time, choice of victim, or anything else. Ergo, it'll be almost impossible to catch the culprit. You don't need me to tell you that the milkman's fate will hit tomorrow's headlines like a mortar shell. We must lay hold of this maniac before we have mass panic.'

Lonsdale nodded. 'But what do you want from me?'

'Our evidence suggests that the same man or group of men are responsible for these deaths, and I'm inclined to think that he or they have also made attempts on your life.'

'Oh Lord!' gulped Lonsdale. 'You want me to wander about the city in the hope that he'll come after me?'

'Exactly,' said Peters, without the trace of a smile. 'Of course, you'll be closely followed by my best officers, and I'll be on hand to make sure nothing goes wrong.'

'But what can you do if he shoots at me from a distance?' asked Lonsdale. 'He might still escape.'

'He might,' agreed Peters. 'And he might kill you. But I'll make damn sure he doesn't get your cerebrum.' He could tell his last statement was not much comfort. 'I know I have no right to ask, Lonsdale, but you won't be safe until he's under lock and key anyway.'

'True,' said Lonsdale, 'but even so . . .'

'Of course, there have also been attempts on the life of Miss Friederichs,' said Peters slyly. 'Perhaps she'll—'

'*No!*' Lonsdale was horrified at that notion, sure she'd volunteer in an instant. He took a deep breath and looked into Peters's gloomy features. 'Keep her safe and I'll do what you ask.'

'Thanks,' said Peters. 'I know there's little I can say that'll be of comfort, but please believe that my men *will* give all they have. And I'll send a message to Superintendent Ramsey, who will get someone to go to Miss Friederichs' home to watch over her.'

Lonsdale recalled seeing natives in Bechuanaland leaving tethered goats as bait for lions. Now he would be put in the same position.

'What do you want me to do?' he asked grimly.

Peters studied the backs of his hands, and Lonsdale sensed he was not happy either. 'You'll need to act normally – it's no good me suggesting a walk down the Strand if you never usually set foot there. Our man would know something was amiss, and he might not go for the bait . . . for you. What do you normally do on a Sunday evening?'

Lonsdale swallowed hard. 'You mean we start *now*? Tonight?'

'Unless you'd rather wait for him to come to you.'

It was a fair point.

'I was about to go to the Oxford and Cambridge Club to see if my brother's there. He should have been home by now, but . . .'

'Would you take a hansom?'

'If I can find one. It's usually relatively easy at Westbourne Terrace. What will you do? Follow in another?'

'In another two or three. We could arrange to have a man in one with you, although I suspect that would reduce the chances of the killer showing himself.'

'I'll go alone,' said Lonsdale. 'If Jack's not at the club, I'll go to his chambers at the Inner Temple – Number Three Paper Buildings.'

Peters stood. 'It's ten minutes before eight now. Give me half an hour to organize my men, then leave the house and go about your business. Walk normally.'

'What do you mean?'

'Not too slowly and not too quickly. Don't

look around for him, but at the same time, be vigilant. When you reach Westbourne Terrace, approach the hansom with a driver wearing a flower in his buttonhole. He'll be one of ours. Go directly to your club, not stopping for any reason. Is that clear?'

'Perfectly,' said Lonsdale. 'If I find Jack, I'll stay for a while and come home with him. No, I won't! I don't want him involved. If he's there, I'll go to Northumberland Street. If he isn't there, I'll take the same hansom to the Inner Temple.'

'Very well. I won't wish you luck, because that simply implies an element of good fortune. But I'll warn you to take care. And no deviating from the plan.'

Lonsdale nodded understanding. 'But what if he's watching the house now? He'll see you leave and his suspicions will be raised.'

Peters gave a grim little chuckle. 'Credit us with *some* sense, man. I entered by the back door, and I'll leave the same way. No one will see me.'

Lonsdale glanced at the clock in the hall as Peters took his leave, and wondered how he would pass the next thirty minutes. His clothes were still damp, and hardly suitable for the club, so he went upstairs to change. He opened a trunk in a spare bedroom that he had turned into a rather messy storage area. There, wrapped carefully in a well-oiled cloth, was the revolver he had carried in Africa.

He studied the weapon for a moment. It had been given to him by an officer who had been killed in Wolseley's campaign against the Ashanti. Lonsdale had learned to shoot well but, even a decade later, he could not look at it without thinking of his friend. He loaded it, put it in his pocket and headed downstairs.

Finally, it was time to go. He left the house and walked as purposefully as he could towards Westbourne Terrace. His heart pounded when a drunk staggered across the street, but he forced himself to breathe normally again when he recognized one of Peters's men. He reached the line of hansoms, and looked for a driver wearing a flower in his buttonhole. With horror, he saw there were two: one sporting a bunch of daisies, another a drooping daffodil. One fingered the daisies and winked.

Lonsdale gripped his revolver in his pocket and climbed into the cab. Then they were away, the horse trotting briskly. At one point, another hansom pulled level with theirs, and, for a horrifying instant, Lonsdale thought Iverson would lean out and shoot him. He clutched his own weapon harder, but the driver slowed and the other carriage rattled past.

After what seemed an eternity, they arrived at the club, where the doorman told Lonsdale that Jack hadn't been there that day. Lonsdale returned to the hansom.

From a window of the smoking room, a tall, slim man watched Lonsdale arrive and leave. He sighed irritably and threw down his newspaper in disgust, causing another member to glance up in annoyance at the disturbance. The man at the window fixed him with such a cold, harsh look that the fellow blanched. By the time the tall man looked out of the window again, Lonsdale's driver was awaiting his instructions.

'Where to, sir?' asked the driver, when Lonsdale gave him none.

How stupid, thought Lonsdale. If he were acting normally, he would be expected to give directions to the driver, even though they both knew where the next stop would be.

'Inner Temple,' he called, sitting back and trying to relax. The hansom headed for the Strand. It was late enough that the streets were clear, and they made good time. They turned into the pleasant courtyard outside the library. Lonsdale glanced both ways before alighting and then headed for Jack's chambers. A sharp yelp made him spin round.

There was nothing to see. The driver slouched in his seat with his head down against the drizzle, and the horse stamped restlessly. Then Lonsdale looked more closely. The driver was sitting very still. As the horse jolted the vehicle, the driver slowly tipped forward and pitched out of his seat to the ground.

Lonsdale did not wait to see more. He turned and raced to the nearest building, which was the library. It was locked, although he could see lights at the windows, so he knew there were people inside. He pounded on the door, but his yell to attract attention was choked off as a strong arm snaked around his neck so tightly he could barely breathe, followed immediately by the touch of cold steel against his throat.

* * *

'Now, then, sir,' came a calm, reasonable voice that Lonsdale recognized instantly from the scene of the fire at Donovan's house. 'We don't want to be making a racket and disturbing these good folk reading, do we?'

It was Iverson. Lonsdale tried to struggle, but could not remember having ever been in such a powerful grip. Then he felt his captor tense in anticipation of the sharp stroke that would slice through his neck.

'Wait!' he croaked, trying to gain some time. 'Was it you? Did you kill them all?'

'Now who might you be meaning, sir?' asked Iverson, with unseemly interest.

'Poole,' said Lonsdale, feeling the grip ease very slightly. Where was Peters?

'Certainly, I killed the milkman,' said Iverson, sounding chillingly pleasant. 'He was quite a challenge. I went to see him in uniform, but he wouldn't speak to a policeman. So I went back in my civilian clothes, and the problem was solved.'

'But there was no problem with Donovan, was there?' said Lonsdale, playing for time. 'That was flawless.'

'Practice makes perfect, they say, and that was definitely one that filled me with pride,' said Iverson, as if claiming to have helped a lady across the road, rather than confessing to a murder.

'And Yeats – the entertainer who was murdered?'

'Murder is such an unpleasant word,' said Iverson, his voice becoming harsher. 'I think 'sacrificed" might be a better way of putting it.'

'Sacrificed?' gasped Lonsdale, visions of a Satanist coven flashing through his mind. 'Sacrificed to what? To whom?'

'So many questions! I can hardly keep up with them. Sacrificed to the cause, of course. Just as you are about to be. That *will* happen tonight – it's been made quite clear.'

'By whom?' asked Lonsdale, wondering if Iverson really was receiving instructions from someone else, or if he was one of those who 'heard' mysterious voices. 'Who's making you do these things?'

'Depends what things you're referring to,' he replied enigmatically. 'But it doesn't really matter, does it? Not to you. Not now.'

Lonsdale tried to jerk away, but Iverson held him too tightly. Suddenly the door to the library opened and a short, balding barrister with thick glasses stepped out.

'Is someone knocking?' he asked. His jaw dropped in horror when he saw the knife.

The interruption made Iverson loosen his grip fractionally, which was enough for Lonsdale to lift one leg and stamp down as hard as he could on the policeman's foot. Iverson gave a sharp hiss of pain, and his arm flinched upwards, scoring a shallow nick in Lonsdale's neck. But his wrist ended up near the reporter's face, so Lonsdale sank his teeth into it. The knife fell to the ground, and Lonsdale twisted and drove his elbow into his attacker's chest. Iverson let go entirely, and Lonsdale slithered away from him, fumbling for his revolver.

But before Lonsdale could take aim, Iverson produced a truncheon and struck out with it, cracking it down on Lonsdale's forearm, making him drop the gun. It skittered into the bushes. He swung again, and Lonsdale jerked back to avoid the blow, then ducked behind one of the Corinthian pillars.

'Stop this at once!' blustered the barrister.

Drawing attention to himself was a mistake. In an instant, Iverson scooped up his knife and grabbed him by his coat, pulling him close to his chest.

'Let him go,' shouted Lonsdale, as Iverson put his knife at the little lawyer's throat. 'He has nothing to do with this, and they haven't told you to sacrifice *him*, have they?'

The policeman looked at Lonsdale with a mixture of hatred and wonder. 'In some ways, it's a shame you have to die, Mr Lonsdale. You *do* appreciate what we do. Most people would still be talking about "killing", when we both know they're "sacrifices". But as to your question, I don't think it appropriate that a civilian should be asking such things of a member of the force.'

'My apologies,' said Lonsdale, at a loss as to how to deal with someone so patently insane, but hoping to keep the terrified barrister alive until Peters came. 'It was clever, the way you killed Greaves and Cath. How did you manage it?'

'That wasn't me,' said Iverson, 'although I *would* have done it. She was going to tell you about me. They wanted her killed quickly, but I was busy collecting another sample.'

'Who?'

'Someone who is hidden in a place you won't find, no matter how hard you look. Anyway, one of my colleagues did it.'

'Who? Pauly or . . .' Lonsdale broke off, trying to remember the name Jamie had given him. 'Morgan. Was it Morgan?'

'You know Morgan? That *is* a surprise. But then, if you know us all, shouldn't you be able to tell our work apart? Certainly, you don't think my sacrifices are like those of the others?'

'Others? How many of you are there?'

'Now, Mr Lonsdale, I know you journalists like numbers, but it wouldn't be polite to tell other people's secrets, would it?'

'What are you doing with the cerebra?'

'I give them to the people I work for, of course. That's why the sacrifices were made, after all. They told me to strangle or slit the throat, but never to poison. It might pollute, you understand.'

'I see,' said Lonsdale, speaking loudly to mask the sound of the police rattle in the distance. 'And did they tell you what they were doing with them?'

'I wouldn't want to know,' said Iverson with a shudder. 'It's a disgusting business, if you ask me. I think they're quite mad, personally. Morgan is mad, and so is that nasty little tyke in the Müller cut-down—'

'Pauly?' interrupted Lonsdale.

Iverson nodded. 'Even the people in the hospital thought *he* was mad.'

Desperately trying to keep Iverson talking, Lonsdale thought about the people whom Mrs Greaves had said had disappeared. 'Did these mad people tell you to sacrifice the Johnson sisters and Leonard Baycroft?'

'Baycroft?' snapped Iverson, his manner suddenly changing and a hint of real menace in his voice. 'What do you know about him?'

The knife jerked up, and Lonsdale saw that he had made a mistake. He moved out from behind the pillar, but before he could come any closer, Iverson drew his blade with great force across the neck of the barrister, and let the dying man drop to the ground. Without pausing, he leapt at Lonsdale.

Twelve

Shocked by the casual brutality of the attack, Lonsdale darted back behind the pillar, trying to keep it between him and Iverson, who lunged at him, knife in one hand, truncheon in the other. He wondered how long he would be able to duck and weave, when the penalty for failure would be his life. Then another police rattle sounded nearby. The police were nearly there!

'Peters!' Lonsdale yelled. 'Here!'

Iverson's face twisted with hatred and he swung his truncheon. Lonsdale ducked away from the blow aimed at his head, and heard the wood splinter as it struck the pillar. Iverson grunted in pain as the shock of the blow travelled up his arm.

'You tricked me,' Iverson hissed. 'You kept me talking, so Baycroft would get me.'

He saw the police racing towards them and, abandoning his prey, turned to flee. Lonsdale tore after him, and managed to snag a corner of the rough serge uniform jacket, but Iverson whipped around, lashing out with a punch that sent Lonsdale sprawling, while the killer disappeared towards the Temple Gardens.

'Are you all right?' Peters yelled, as he ran up.

'Where were you?' demanded Lonsdale, climbing to his feet and hurrying to retrieve his gun from the bushes.

'He killed my men!' Peters's customary poise was gone, and he looked almost as insane as Iverson, hair in disarray and blood on his hands. 'He crashed his hansom into ours, killing Evans, then came here and stabbed poor Kemp to death.'

'But why—'

'To distract us so he could get to you!' snarled Peters. 'He played us like fools! Where in God's name is the bastard?'

'This way!' Lonsdale set off in the direction Iverson had taken, Peters and half a dozen constables at his heels.

Peters put on an immense burst of speed when he saw their quarry in the distance, and Lonsdale was hard-pressed to keep up. Iverson was little more than a dark blur, running with a speed that belied his heavy physique. A helmet was flung away, followed by a cloak; unencumbered, Iverson began to pull away from them.

'Cut him off!' screamed Peters frantically. 'He's heading for the river! Cut him off.'

Obediently, the men peeled away to either side. There was only so far Iverson could run before the river stopped him, at which point he would either have to turn left or right. Policemen were already fanning out to both sides, while Lonsdale and Peters were directly behind.

Iverson scaled the wall at the end of Temple Gardens and disappeared from sight on the Victoria Embankment. Two policemen were already scrambling over it, Peters screaming at them to hurry.

Lonsdale reached the wall and vaulted to the top, kneeling there for a moment to use its height as a vantage point. Policemen were everywhere, heads turning this way and that as they hunted for Iverson among the shadows of the trees. Carriages clattered past, obscuring Lonsdale's view.

'We've lost him,' he gasped as Peters struggled up beside him.

'No!' yelled Peters, pointing. 'Look! He's heading for the river, like a rat returning home!'

A flicker of movement behind one of the trees betrayed the burly form scrambling over the wall that separated the Victoria Embankment from the river. Lonsdale tore after him, causing a hansom driver to swerve. Oblivious to the driver's curses, he reached the wall and leaned over it. The river was at low tide, revealing a thin ribbon of silty beach. Iverson was stumbling along it, slowed by slippery debris and sucking mud.

'Hah!' muttered Lonsdale grimly. 'He makes a mistake at last.'

330

He raced along the road until he was ahead of Iverson, making better time than the killer on the flat, paved surface, then climbed the wall. As Iverson pounded past below, Lonsdale dropped on top of him, allowing his full weight to land on his quarry.

But Iverson seemed invincible. With a roar of rage, he flung Lonsdale off as though he was made of feathers. Then he swung round with his broken truncheon, catching Lonsdale a blow that knocked him clean from his feet and into the stinking waters of the Thames. By the time Lonsdale had struggled back to the beach, Iverson was some distance away.

'He can't escape,' he gasped as Peters staggered past. 'Where can he go?'

'The sewers,' Peters cried in desperation. 'There's an entrance ahead. Once he gets in there, we'll never catch him.'

Lonsdale stumbled on after him, wet clothes dragging him down and the foulness of the Thames in his mouth. He tugged the gun from his pocket.

'Stop, or I'll shoot,' he yelled, aiming to loose a couple of rounds to let Iverson know he meant it. He thought the threat made Iverson falter, then realized the killer was actually wresting with a heavy metal grille. Lonsdale aimed skyward and pulled the trigger, but there was only a sharp click. He tried it again with the same response, cursing himself for not having checked it before he went out. He had not used it in years, so why would it work now? He shoved it back in his pocket and began running again, each breath rasping painfully in his chest. The mud made him feel as though he were running in treacle.

Ahead, Peters was straining every fibre in his body to reach Iverson before he got the grille open. Lonsdale heard a distant screech of protesting metal, and Iverson looked back at his pursuers before disappearing from sight. It was dark, but Lonsdale could have sworn he saw him smirk.

'No!' yelled Peters, his voice cracking in despair.

Inside the sewer, Iverson felt he was free and safe. He knew the tunnels like the back of his hand, and needed no lamp to guide him. He took a convoluted route that he was sure his pursuers would never follow, then stopped to listen. In the distance, he could hear Peters organizing his troops, but Iverson was not bothered. They wouldn't catch him now. He reached a cavernous tunnel and groped in an alcove for the lantern he had left there for just such an occasion. He lit it and splashed on through a stinking soup of sewage and rainwater.

Suddenly, there was a sharp sound ahead. Iverson stopped in alarm. Then there was an agonizing pain in his chest. A second bang followed, and a second centre of pain. Slowly, disbelievingly, Iverson set his light on a nearby ledge and looked down at himself. Blood was pouring from his chest. He tried to straighten up, but the wounds were draining his energy as well as his blood.

Suddenly, hands wrapped round his throat. He had no strength to fight, and was pushed against the wall and then down to the bottom of the passage. Water filled his shrieking mouth.

Peters watched as his men carefully pulled the body out of the water and laid it on a ledge, next to the lamp that someone had left there so conveniently. It illuminated the dead man's face. Now the chase was over, Peters had lost the wild look that had so transformed him, and was once more his impassive self.

'Do you recognize him, Lonsdale?' he asked.

'It's Iverson,' replied Lonsdale. 'You can see the number on his collar – six-nine-six-D.'

'He's wearing Iverson's uniform,' acknowledged Peters. 'But, as I told you, we fished Iverson out of the Thames days ago. This is Leonard Baycroft from Bermondsey, whose speciality was robbery with violence. He liked to break into houses, and if the residents put up a defence, he liked it even more. He was a vicious brute, and London will be a safer place without him.'

'Baycroft,' echoed Lonsdale. 'He was one of the people who Mrs Greaves said had disappeared. I mentioned his name when I was trying to keep Iverson – I mean this man – talking until you arrived. He accused me of trying to keep him talking until Baycroft came to get him.'

'But he *was* Baycroft,' said one of the constables in puzzlement. 'What was he on about?'

'The ramblings of a deranged mind,' said Peters. 'His crimes had been growing more violent for some years, and the most recent time we arrested him – last summer – we asked Dr Bradwell to assess him. Bradwell said Baycroft was no longer sane and recommended he be sent to an asylum before he killed someone. The judge ignored the advice, and, based on the one charge we could prove at the time – although we knew he had perpetrated a lot more crimes – sentenced him to six months in Newgate instead.'

'He was released in December,' said a constable. 'We knew it was only a matter of time before we came across him again.'

'December was when people started to disappear,' mused Lonsdale. He recalled the other names that Mrs Greaves had mentioned. 'The Johnson sisters, Long Lil, Bill Byers and Baycroft.'

'And we don't know if Baycroft killed them, or whether there is some other reason for their disappearance,' said Peters. 'Did he say anything else?'

'He mentioned other murders – said we wouldn't find the bodies,' replied Lonsdale. 'And he said he had "colleagues" who killed Cath and Greaves – Pauly and Morgan, I suppose. He also claimed the stolen cerebra were for "them", but he didn't want to know what "they" did with them.'

'In other words,' said Peters, 'he was not responsible for his own actions – any wrong-doing was someone else's fault. It's not the first time I've heard criminals claim this.'

'You think he was making "them" up?' asked Lonsdale. 'He was actually acting alone?'

'Yes and no. I don't believe there's some grand enterprise in operation, with arch-criminals delivering orders to minions. However, I am sure Baycroft had help. Our search is far from over.'

'And you are sure this isn't Iverson?' Lonsdale felt he had lived with the spectre of the man for so long that it was somehow unsatisfactory that he should transpire to be someone else.

'Quite sure. Iverson had a scar on his forehead, but it looked nothing like this.' Peters pointed to the jagged cut on Baycroft's eyebrow. 'I suspect this was self-inflicted, probably when he decided to assume Iverson's identity.'

'But why would a robber impersonate a policeman?' asked Lonsdale.

'For the authority it gave him, and for access to people and places that would otherwise have been closed to him. It worked – you believed he was one of us.'

'But why Iverson?'

'Almost certainly because he was ill and easy prey. Not to mention that Iverson would have needed money – I imagine he sold Baycroft the uniform.'

'Or Baycroft murdered him for it.'

'Poor Iverson killed himself. There were no marks of violence, although Bradwell says he was poorly nourished. He was ill, poor, and clothed in little more than rags. We failed him miserably. If Baycroft was alive, we'd be able to confirm all this. But now it's just speculation.'

'Which brings us to the question of who shot him, down here in the sewers,' said Lonsdale.

'Someone who knows his way around. We

heard the shots, but it took us how long to find the body? Twenty minutes? The killer could have gone anywhere.'

'Can you tell anything from the body?' asked Lonsdale. 'I confess the gunshots meant nothing to me – whether large bore or small.'

'Definitely large,' said Peters. 'Whereas the blood smears on the wall suggest there was a bit of a struggle between Baycroft and his assailant.'

He began to organize a makeshift stretcher, using his men's cloaks, carefully knotted together. Lonsdale watched, alert for another attack, but the sewers were eerily silent, the peace broken only by the soft gurgle of water and solids oozing towards the pumping station by Chelsea Bridge.

'Tell me about these other men,' ordered Peters, as four officers each grabbed a corner of the stretcher to carry Baycroft's body outside.

'Morgan is short, powerfully built, and has a tattoo of a snake on one arm. Pauly led a group that attacked Friederichs and me. He's slight, with dark brown hair and a moustache that's half brown, half grey. He swears almost constantly. Baycroft said he had spent time in a hospital or an asylum.'

Peters started. 'That's Thomas *Pawley*! P-A-W-L-E-Y. He's a murderous fiend, and he *has* been in a number of asylums, most recently Bethlem, from which he escaped. You say he's the man who attacked you?'

'Twice.'

Peters groaned. 'What a mess! Just when you

think you might be getting near a solution, it all slips away.'

Peters had sent for Bradwell to examine Baycroft's body. When Lonsdale expressed surprise that the surgeon was still on the payroll, Peters said he was serving two weeks' notice. They waited for him on the narrow beach, Baycroft's body lying on the mud at their feet. It was not long before he arrived, and Lonsdale immediately noticed the change in him. Gone was the nervous pallor; he was back to his ebullient self. He greeted Lonsdale and Peters enthusiastically.

'You got him, then? Thank God! I told you Baycroft was dangerous, Inspector.'

'Especially to you,' said Lonsdale. Both Peters and Bradwell regarded him uncertainly.

'I know why you went on your sudden trip to Brighton. And why you resigned your post so abruptly.'

Peters looked perplexed, but Bradwell sighed and gazed up at the sky. When he looked back down again, his face was sombre.

'I made a grave error in judgement,' he said to Peters. 'And I overstepped my duties as a police surgeon. It cost me dear . . .'

'Explain,' ordered Peters and, when Bradwell hesitated, added, 'Or do you want Lonsdale to do it, given that he seems to know already?'

Bradwell took a deep breath and began. 'I started to think about the nature of the murders, and I made a list of suspects – criminals I'd examined in the past with certain mental abnormalities.

337

In the medical trade, we call it *dementia praecox*. Baycroft was on it.'

Peters frowned. 'That doesn't sound like over-stepping the mark to me. It sounds like initiative.'

Bradwell winced. 'Yes, but then I did something stupid. I decided to speak to them before passing the list to you. I thought my medical training would make me better equipped for it. I was right!' He gave a bitter laugh. 'I managed to trace Baycroft, and saw immediately that he had lost touch with reality. He had delusions, hallucinations, and his cognitions were accompanied by severe emotional disturbances.'

'So what did you do about it?' asked Peters.

'I made an appointment for him to come and see me at the hospital the following day.' Bradwell shrugged apologetically.

'Did he come?'

An anguished expression crossed Bradwell's face. 'He visited my wife instead, and said that if I attempted to contact him or mentioned him to the police, he'd kill our children.'

Peters made an exasperated sound at the back of his throat. 'We could have taken your family somewhere safe. Why didn't you ask us for help?'

'I had every intention of doing so. But first, I escorted my wife and children to Brighton. My plan was to see them safely installed in a hotel, then take the next train back. But I had no sooner left the hotel when there he was – Baycroft.'

'He had followed you to Brighton?'

Bradwell nodded miserably. 'He was leaning

338

against the seawall, smirking. I'd been so careful to ensure we hadn't been followed, yet there he was. I realized there was nothing I could do without endangering my family. I *had* to do what he demanded.'

'And what was that?' asked Peters.

'To have nothing more to do with these murders, and give up my post as police surgeon.' Bradwell shrugged. 'So I did.'

'And what's happened *since* you resigned?' asked Peters, pulling out his pipe.

The surgeon sighed. 'I put my family in an isolation ward at Bart's, claiming they had diphtheria. My wife and I agreed I should tell you everything, because neither of us thought we should put our own safety over the lives of others any longer. I was on my way when I heard you'd got him.'

'What about O'Connor?' asked Lonsdale. 'Was he was aware of any of this?'

'Of course not,' said Bradwell. 'I was told he'd absconded with money from the mortuary – although I find that difficult to believe.'

'*What* do you find difficult to believe?' asked Lonsdale. 'That there was money to abscond with, or that O'Connor would take it?'

'Both. There's nothing to steal, and once, when I left ten shillings sitting out on my desk, O'Connor put it safely in a drawer and reminded me to take it the following day. He was odd, but no thief.'

'Odd in what way?'

'Well, wanting to be a mortuary assistant for a start,' said Bradwell. 'It's hardly a rewarding

339

occupation – low pay, dismal surroundings, frequently harrowing duties. He just happened to turn up when I needed an assistant, and now he's moved on.'

Peters gaped at him. 'Are you telling me that you hired him without checking his credentials? The mortuary is a police facility, man! We must observe certain security precautions.'

'He had written references,' objected Bradwell. 'And I was having trouble finding someone to do it. He was basically an itinerant who wanted a job for a few months. Come August, I expect he'll be in Kent, picking hops.'

'I suppose such people do exist,' acknowledged Peters. 'And I can see why men aren't exactly queuing for that post. By the way, a further review shows that nothing was actually taken from the mortuary. As you say, he appears to have been an honest man.'

By the time Lonsdale finished giving his official statement, it was the early hours of the morning. He trudged home wearily, and lay down on his bed, intending to rest for a moment before undressing and sluicing the muck from his skin, but he fell asleep almost at once. He awoke after eight to the sound of the servants moving about downstairs.

Rubbing sleep from his eyes, he walked down the stairs and knocked at his brother's room. When there was no reply, he opened the door and saw the bed had not been slept in.

'Where is Jack?' he asked Dillon, who had appeared at the top of the stairs.

'He failed to come home last night, sir. But I knew not to expect him for dinner, as he had an appointment at six o'clock.'

'An appointment at six on a Sunday?' asked Lonsdale in surprise. 'With whom?'

'I don't know, sir. Might I suggest you check his diary? Perhaps after your bath?'

Lonsdale glared at him. If his own days were numbered in the house, then so were the butler's, because Emelia would not appreciate his smug condescension. Nevertheless, the idea was a good one, so Lonsdale found Jack's diary and flicked through it.

'Sunday,' he muttered. 'Six o'clock, Regent's Club re Imp Dem Ins with O.'

What was Imp Dem Ins, and who was O? And why would Jack be going to the Regent's Club? It was one of the newer establishments, located on Regent Street, away from the exclusive atmosphere of the St James's area known as 'Clubland'. He was sure Jack had never been there before. Moreover, six o'clock on a Sunday was a peculiar time to meet anyone, and dinner was unlikely to last until morning, although it would not be the first time Jack had drunk too much and accepted an offer of a room for the night.

Lonsdale went upstairs to wash away the stench of the Thames. He threw his clothes in the linen basket, on top of the last ones he had ruined. Perhaps Louisa Galton had been right to complain about the difficulty of finding good help, he thought, and if he ever dined with her again, he could match her stories of lazy servants.

He sat on the edge of the bathtub as a thought struck him. Galton! Had part of the solution to the murders been staring him in the face all along? The scientist had spoken at length about fingerprinting, and only hours before, Peters had commented on Baycroft's blood being smeared on the sewer wall. Could Galton glean anything from it? Were there prints that could lead to Baycroft's killer?

As he considered, Lonsdale realized that Galton might have answers to other aspects of the case as well – he certainly knew about the human brain. He not only had sophisticated theories about its development, but had conducted studies. To Lonsdale, the cerebrum seemed an odd organ to take, but perhaps Galton could explain why someone might want one.

Then again, Baycroft had been insane. For all Lonsdale knew, the man might have believed that by taking cerebra he would be able to absorb intelligence. Maybe he was even eating them. Still, Galton might be able to help him understand even that. Lonsdale decided that he would put everything else aside and try to see the scientist.

After a hurried bath and dressing in clean clothes, he penned a quick note to Stead and Morley, outlining what had happened and telling them he was going to see Galton. He gave it to Jack's valet with the order it be taken straight to *The PMG*. He then left the house at a run, waved down a hansom, and promised the driver double if he took him to Rutland Gate as fast as he could. Determined to have the money, the man whipped his horse into a gallop, and there followed a frantic journey full of jolts, angry yells from other road users, and urgently clattering hooves. They arrived, Lonsdale shoved money at the man, hoping he would spend some of it on extra oats for his lathered horse, and hammered on Galton's door.

The great man was shuffling papers into a series of boxes when his guest was shown into his study. Lonsdale reached out to shake his hand, but his host's limp appendage returned little pressure, and the reporter quickly withdrew his own.

'I'm just filing my notes for *Human Faculty*,' said Galton grandly. 'Material of this importance can't be treated with too great a care.'

'I quite agree,' said Lonsdale. 'But I wanted—'

'Louisa is away,' interrupted Galton. 'She will be sorry to have missed you. She told me your conversation was a delight.'

As Lonsdale could not recall her having listened to a single word, he could only suppose that she preferred the kind of discussion where she was the only participant.

'I need your help, sir,' he said urgently. 'Lives depend on it.'

Galton looked pleased. 'Then sit down. We'll have tea while I save the day. And not just out of one of those asinine thimbles of Louisa's. We'll have man-sized receptacles.'

In the next hour and a half, while drinking tea served in what appeared to be plant pots, Galton gave the reporter a penetrating assessment of the structure and functioning of the human brain.

'I can think of no one who has conducted

343

more research into cerebral functions than I have,' Galton declared. 'And I certainly can't see any benefit in collecting them. But you say this man Baycroft was mad. Perhaps that is your answer – he was possessed of the lunatic belief that owning the part of the brain that controls sensory processing allowed him to absorb its power. Similar beliefs have been shown to exist among some of the cannibals along the Congo River.'

Lonsdale felt that information led him nowhere, and he was further disappointed to learn that, unless Baycroft's murderer had placed his fingertips on the sewer wall, there was unlikely to be evidence that could be interpreted by the scientist. Moreover, even if he had, if the prints were smudged – and the entire area had been one large smear – they would be useless. Lonsdale sighed. He was faced with more dead ends.

'You are hungry,' declared Galton. 'We shall dine.'

Lonsdale was not hungry at all, and itched to leave, to visit the Regent's Club and ask after Jack, but he still had questions for Galton, as the very faintest glimmer of a solution was beginning to grow at the back of his mind. He realized he needed to stay, as he could not be sure of a welcome if he declined the invitation and tried to resume the conversation later.

'You'll observe that no grace was said prior to this meal, unlike the last time you were here,' said Galton between mouthfuls of radish soup. 'Louisa insists on prayers before meals, but I avoid them. Unless I am analyzing them.'

344

'You analyze prayers?' asked Lonsdale warily.

'To determine whether they are answered. The scriptures, of course, express the view that blessings, both of long life and a spiritual nature, should be requested in prayer. I have compiled a table of the mean age of death for males of various occupations. It shows that the clergy and missionaries, who should be good at prayer, have lifespans less than that of doctors, who do not have time for them. Meanwhile, lawyers, who are a godless horde, live the longest of all. Ergo, prayers are futile.' He beamed proudly.

Lonsdale could see a lot wrong with that thesis.

'But doesn't your assessment ignore the fact that some pray for others, not just petition the Almighty for a longer life?'

Galton's eyes fixed on Lonsdale. 'If such prayers had any influence, don't you think that insurance companies would make allowance for them? But they ask no questions about their customers' religious habits, nor do they take into account the risk to ships and buildings owned by pious individuals. Members of the civilized world must give up this childish belief in the efficacy of prayer, and be guided by an understanding of demographics and statistics.'

The last sentence grabbed Lonsdale's attention. 'Demographics and statistics,' he echoed. 'Are they the same?'

'Of course not. Demographics is a new field of science and refers to studies of the life conditions of people as shown by the statistics of their births, deaths and diseases.'

'There is an Imperial Statistical Institute,' said

Lonsdale, recalling what the boaters had seen on the paper in Donovan's pocket.

'It closed last year,' replied Galton. 'But there is an Imperial Demographic Institute. It's fairly new, and is located at the end of Kensington Gardens, on Brunswick Gardens.'

Lonsdale's mind was in a whirl. Jack's diary had read 'Imp Dem Inst'. It had to be the same place. Moreover, Donovan's appointment had been the day before he died, so the chances were that he had gone to the Demographic Institute, and the boaters, unfamiliar with the term, had misremembered. His stomach churned. Was Jack in danger? He wanted to dash to the place immediately, but forced himself to wait. First, he had to find out as much as he could.

'What is its remit?' he demanded.

Galton looked up in surprise at the urgency in his voice.

'I haven't had extensive dealings with the place, as I consider its director an egotistical dogmatist, but I imagine data are being compiled that will become relevant to my studies on eugenics—'

'Eugenics?' interrupted Lonsdale curtly, wishing the man would speak plain English.

'A term I've coined in *Human Faculty*. If I tell you what it means, it will spoil the surprise when it's published.'

'Please,' begged Lonsdale. 'Believe me, I wouldn't ask if it wasn't a matter of life and death.'

'Life and death,' mused Galton. 'Very well, then. Eugenics is the science that deals with improving the human race. Its aim is to further the ends of evolution more rapidly than if events

346

were left to their own course. First, we identify the characters we want to propagate, then we see about promoting them and eliminating useless rivals.'

'But sir,' cut in Lonsdale, 'how can you reconcile a desire to expedite evolution by directing it to a predetermined end? It contradicts the notion of natural selection.'

'Eugenics won't *control* natural selection, but will assist it. Helping the weak and preventing suffering is all very well, but eugenics will improve the life of our entire community. We must, for example, breed *out* feeble constitutions and immoral instincts, and breed *in* those that are vigorous and noble. Eugenics cooperates with natural selection by ensuring that humanity is represented by the fittest individuals. What Nature does blindly, slowly and ruthlessly, we may continue providently, quickly and kindly.'

'From what I've observed,' remarked Lonsdale dryly, 'humanity is already doing an admirable job of continuing itself.'

'That's not the purpose of eugenics,' responded Galton. 'Quite the reverse, in fact. Improving a race depends on increasing the *best* stock. That is far more important than repressing the worst. Eugenics encourages the best characteristics to be passed on to future generations.'

'But how will you dissuade your "lesser stock" from reproducing?' demanded Lonsdale, not realizing he was sounding exasperated. Eugenics was as mad a theory as anything Baycroft had believed, and here he was listening to Galton go on about it while he should be finding out

347

what had happened to Jack. 'Besides, other than the occasional extraordinary men, aren't people rather similar?'

'Such a lack of understanding!' spat Galton, annoyed in turn. 'Those who believe in natural equality are deluding themselves. I've no patience with the hypothesis that all babies are born alike – they aren't. Furthermore, the British man *is* superior to any others. It's a fact.'

Lonsdale was shocked by the imperial arrogance. 'I hardly think—' he began.

'So we must control breeding,' interrupted Galton, 'or the intelligent, thoughtful and prudent members of society will be outnumbered by the ignorant and non-thinking, and therefore bring utter ruin upon our country. It may seem monstrous that the weak should be crowded out by the strong, but it's still more monstrous that the strong should be crowded out by the incompetent and unfit.'

'And this is what the Imperial Demographic Institute is exploring?' asked Lonsdale. 'How to manipulate some ideal devised by an elite few? Eugenics?'

Galton looked at him as if he were an unruly school child. 'Consider the gain to our nation if the practice of eugenics were applied. Our race would be less foolish, less frivolous, and politically more provident. We should be better fitted to fulfil our vast imperial opportunities. And able men would thrive.'

Lonsdale had had enough, and also felt an urgent need to find Jack. 'I am sorry, sir, but I simply must go to an appointment at *The PMG*,' he lied, standing abruptly. 'But thank you for sharing your fascinating theories, and I shall look forward to reading *Human Faculty* when it's published.' Mind whirling, he left Galton.

As Lonsdale walked out of Galton's front door, he decided to go straight to the Regent's Club to ask about Jack. He hurried up Rutland Gate towards Kensington Road.

Questions and answers poured into his mind in equal measure with every step. The relevance of eugenics to the murders had been apparent the moment Galton explained it. Could it be that a group of scientists was conducting investigations not unlike Galton's, but going a step further and looking at their subjects' cerebra? What if Baycroft's 'them' was not a delusion? What if someone really had ordered him to steal cerebra – someone who had already collected other data from his subjects, and who had paid them for their time, so they were able to make house repairs or buy whisky?

What if that same someone hoped to match his results to the part of the brain where the answers originated? Baycroft had confided that he had been ordered not to poison his victims lest he pollute the organs. Is that why Baycroft had been shot? Because he had not managed his 'takings' properly?

But certainly legitimate scientists would never condone such an unethical study, and the results could hardly be published. Any such information would be worthless, for who could ever admit how he had come by it? And yet, did the results

349

need to be published? Could they not be given to those able to act on them? There were genuine fears that the rising numbers of poor would rebel against the wealthier classes. Wilson from the zoo had talked about it, for example. But whereas Galton proposed a fairly sedate rate of change, Wilson had wanted something done fast. Would other, like-minded, people try to put such a plan into practice now?

Or were strain and tiredness causing his imagination to run riot? No one would seriously consider implementing such a scheme. Yet someone *was* killing people for their cerebra. He decided to go to the Imperial Demographic Institute to see what he could discover the moment he had assured himself that Jack was safe and well.

'Lonsdale! Lonsdale, here!' A voice cut through his thoughts as he turned onto Kensington Road, and he looked around wildly. It was Hulda, sitting in a carriage and motioning to him. He found himself wondering if Peters had been true to his word and had had her watched over for the night. 'I've been waiting for you here, because I didn't want Galton to see me sitting outside his home,' she said. 'Get in.'

'I must go to the Regent's Club to try to find Jack,' he replied.

'Morley sent me to collect you,' she said. 'You've been summoned to his office – Superintendent Ramsey was sending Inspector Peters over to speak to you. I have some other news as well.'

'After I find Jack. I need—'

'No, *now*,' she interrupted. 'Besides, *The PMG*

350

is not that far from the Regent's Club, and it will be quicker for you to get in now, even with the stop there, than to walk the whole way.

Knowing she was right, Lonsdale acceded to her demand, and the hansom shot off. As it raced along Knightsbridge Road, he began to tell her what he had learned from Galton and how it helped explain the pattern of events. But after several minutes, she suddenly interrupted him again.

'A gentleman was killed around one or two o'clock this morning,' she blurted, 'and his cerebrum taken.'

'But Baycroft was dead by then.'

'Nevertheless,' said Hulda, 'it has happened again.' Lonsdale felt his stomach churn, but didn't have time to speak before Hulda added: 'We're there. Now come upstairs.'

The first floor was in its usual controlled chaos. Morley's door was closed, a murmur of voices emanating from within. Stead was distributing fresh orange peel into various containers – which he insisted counteracted the smell of the printing presses – while simultaneously dictating an article for the final edition. Lonsdale slipped into the reporters' office behind Hulda but, before he could close the door, Morley emerged from his office, looking grave. 'Do you have a moment, Lonsdale?'

Lonsdale followed him inside, with Hulda at his heels. Peters was there, looking grey from lack of sleep. Morley gestured for Lonsdale and Hulda to sit, but Lonsdale refused. He had

351

a very bad feeling about the look on Peters' face.

'There's been another murder,' said Peters. 'It happened while you were at the station giving your statement. The victim was a barrister, judging from the papers with the body. We don't yet know his name, but you told me last night that your brother was missing. Have you seen him this morning?'

'No,' whispered Lonsdale. He felt sick. 'He didn't come home last night.'

'We found this with the body.' Peters held out a dirty rag that Lonsdale saw with horror was Emelia's spoiled antimacassar. He did not need to tell Peters he recognized it: the answer was clear on his shocked face.

'I'm sorry,' said Peters gently. 'That was all the killer left, other than some miscellaneous court papers.'

'The Imperial Demographic Institute,' said Lonsdale numbly. He gazed at the antimacassar but could not bring himself to touch it. 'Jack wrote it in his appointment book. He went to discuss it with someone at the Regent's Club at six o'clock yesterday evening.'

'The Regent's Club?' asked Peters. 'That's a strange place for a gentleman of your brother's standing to go. But what is this Institute? Where is it?'

Lonsdale tried to force his stunned brain to work. What had Galton said? 'Brunswick Street. No – Brunswick Gardens.'

'Right,' said Peters. 'Now go home, Lonsdale. Can I have your assurance that you won't go to

352

this Institute or the Regent's Club? We can't risk losing our culprit because you storm into these places and start demanding information.'

Lonsdale nodded, barely hearing. Peters patted his shoulder, then was gone, leaving Lonsdale with the antimacassar.

The journey to Cleveland Square was a blur. Lonsdale was dimly aware of Hulda sitting next to him, but he heard nothing of what she said. He looked at the familiar streets in a daze, feeling as though he were in the grip of some terrible dream.

Once home, the butler took Hulda's umbrella and cloak, then reached out to remove Lonsdale's hat, seeing he was not going to do it. Dully, Lonsdale aimed for the morning room.

'There you are,' said Jack, looking up from the remains of a meal. 'I do hope you two haven't been doing dangerous things again.'

'God's blood!' breathed Hulda, gazing at him. 'What are *you* doing here?'

'I live here,' said Jack curtly. 'Where else would I be?'

Lonsdale lurched over and enveloped Jack in a hug, bewilderment, relief and shock vying for attention in his mind. He wanted to yell at his brother for giving him such a fright. Instead, he pulled the antimacassar from his pocket and held it out to him.

'Where in God's name did you get that?' demanded Jack. 'I thought it was lost.'

'It was found with . . .' began Lonsdale, but could not bring himself to say it had been retrieved from a corpse.

353

'If you have any sense, you'll keep your dirty fingers away from Emelia's lacework from now on,' advised Jack. 'She's not as stupid as you think – she knows you had something to do with it.'

'You lost it?' pounced Hulda. 'When? Please think. This is important.'

Jack frowned. 'It fell out of my pocket at the park – which is when Emelia saw it – but I put it back in my coat. But the coat – and the anti-macassar with it – disappeared last night.'

'Where did it disappear?' demanded Lonsdale, finally regaining some of his composure.

Jack was becoming irked. 'Can't a man spend a night away without being the subject of all this commotion? What's wrong with you?' He glowered in a way that, along with the dark circles under his eyes, told Lonsdale he had a headache, almost certainly from having had too much to drink.

'We should tell Peters,' said Hulda briskly and, without further ado, sat and penned a note informing the inspector that he now had an unidentified body. Once the butler had gone to deliver it, Hulda stood with her hands on her hips.

'Right,' she said, all business. 'Lonsdale needs to eat. He's white as a ghost. Tell your people to prepare devilled kidneys, curried potatoes, and scrambled eggs with a healthy shake of black pepper. Tasteless food is no good for a man recovering from a shock. Besides, I cannot bear it, and I'm hungry, too.'

Jack hastened to relay the 'request' to the

kitchen. 'Now tell me what's going on,' he said.

Lonsdale did, falteringly at first, but with more conviction as his shock receded. The food helped – Hulda was right about that.

'And now you,' he said to Jack when he had finished. 'Where have you been since you vanished from the park without leaving any hint about where you might be.'

'I wasn't aware that I was under any obligation to do so,' said Jack stiffly, but then relented. 'I was with John Otherington at his club – the Regent's. It's a grim old place, with lazy and incompetent staff. Anyway, the upshot is that they gave someone else my coat, leaving me with some shabby thing.' He shuddered. 'I think Otherington has mine, and I shall demand it back later.'

'The "O" in your diary referred to Otherington?' asked Lonsdale.

'You looked in my diary?' Jack was outraged. 'A chap's diary is his own personal business!'

'It was an emergency,' said Lonsdale, unrepentant.

'Well, I don't see why you were worried,' said Jack, miffed. 'I sent a message to tell you I might be very late back. There was a lot to drink, you see.'

'Then you should choose your messengers more carefully – it never arrived.'

Jack grimaced. 'I hired a lad from the Regent's. I told you it wasn't a decent place.'

'So why did you go?'

'Because Otherington – a clerk from work

– invited me. He's a lonely sort of fellow and I felt sorry for him, so I accepted. He's damned hospitable – one drink led to another, and . . . well, you know how it is.'

'So you've been drinking all night?' asked Hulda in distaste.

'Not at all!' said Jack defensively. 'I spent a good part asleep in the reading room. Naturally, I assumed Otherington would stay with me, as it's considered poor manners to leave a chap slumbering in a club that isn't his own. But he didn't.'

'He abandoned you to go home?'

Jack nodded. 'But he drank even more than I did, so that explains the lapse in manners. Regardless, I suspect he donned my coat in a drunken stupor, leaving me with his ratty old thing.'

'Then poor, drunk Otherington is probably the man the police found dead,' said Hulda.

Jack turned white. 'Otherington is *dead?* No! We were getting along like a house on fire last night! I was beginning to like the man. Please don't say it was for my coat . . . a better one than most members of that place owned!'

'No, the coat was irrelevant,' said Lonsdale. 'Did Otherington tell you about the Imperial Demographic Institute?'

Jack gaped at him. 'How did you know that? Yes, he blathered on about some survey he was participating in there.'

Jack listened with growing horror as Lonsdale explained his theory: 'I think someone there has embarked on a two-tiered study. The first is

356

a battery of tests to ascertain the religion, morals, intelligence, etc., of the subject. The second compares these results to the subject's cerebrum.'

'A cerebrum?' echoed Jack. 'How? Those are inside their heads.'

'Not once the likes of Baycroft, Morgan and Pawley have been issued with orders to collect them.'

'Then Otherington got it badly wrong,' said Jack soberly. 'He said the work there is sensitive, and the government wants it kept quiet. He said it's noble stuff, of paramount importance to the future of the Empire. I was on the verge of volunteering when he'd finished waxing lyrical.'

'What did he tell you exactly?'

'That there are tests for solving mathematical and logical problems, and interviews about religious and ethical matters. There's also a physical examination, where they measure your height, weight, hat-size, and so on. Otherington swore me to secrecy – the scientists running the programme say that if people know what they'll be asked, it'll ruin the objectivity. Gentlemen and ladies are trusted to be discreet, but there's a deferred payment for the rest to stop them from talking. If they blab, they don't get paid.'

'Perhaps they should have made a deferred payment to Otherington, then,' said Lonsdale dryly.

'We should go to this Imperial Demographic Institute,' determined Hulda. 'It sounds more sinister than anything I've ever encountered, and *The PMG* should tell people what it's up to.'

357

'But I promised Peters—' Lonsdale began. He stopped when there was a knock at the front door.

Moments later, the butler delivered a message addressed to Jack, who opened it, then frowned in mystification before handing it to Lonsdale.

It was a pleasure to interview you and find out what was inside your head. Thank you for visiting the Imperial Demographic Institute.

'But I never went anywhere near the place,' said Jack, shaking his head. 'And nor will I now.'

'It isn't meant for you,' said Lonsdale, knowing exactly what was going on. 'It's for me. And it's not a thank you, either. It's an invitation.'

'Explain, Lonsdale,' ordered Hulda.

'Whoever wrote this thinks Jack is dead,' said Lonsdale. 'They're goading me, hoping I'll storm over in a rage, so they can finish what Baycroft failed to do.'

'Lord!' breathed Jack.

'And I was wrong when I said that that the coat was irrelevant. I've no doubt that they would have claimed Otherington eventually – you said he was a lonely sort of chap, and they have a preference for such folks. However, this note tells me that you *were* the one they wanted – Otherington was killed because he was wearing your coat. Now they are daring me to go there in order to do something about it. Doubtless they hope Friederichs will accompany me, so they can be rid of both of us.'

'But once they killed him, they would have

realized Jack wasn't the victim if they knew Otherington,' objected Hulda.

'But it doesn't matter if it was me or not,' said Jack, suddenly understanding. 'All that matters is that Alec *thinks* it was me.'

'But how would they know what he's thinking?' asked Hulda, unconvinced.

'There's only one way,' said Lonsdale. 'Someone knows that Peters told me of Jack's murder. So it must be Peters or Ramsey who is working with them. I'd like to say I trust Peters, but he *was* agonizingly slow last night.'

'Ramsey is a pompous, upper-class ass who cares nothing for the victims,' said Hulda. 'He interfered with Walker's inquest so that some basic questions wouldn't be asked. He delayed Greaves's inquest indefinitely. And he ordered Peters not to investigate their murders. He's done nothing but sidetrack and obstruct the investigation from the start. *He's* the snake in the cradle.'

'So, what are you going to do?' asked Jack.

'Go to the Demographic Institute—' began Hulda.

'No,' said Lonsdale decisively. 'That's what they're expecting. We'll go tomorrow – our delaying will confuse them. For now, we'll drive by in a hansom to get a feel for it, which will make our trip tomorrow safer. If Peters is there, we can stop and tell him what we've reasoned.'

'But surely not everything – in case he's involved!' Hulda was horrified.

'Of course, not everything. Enough so he'll be able to help if we need him, but not so much that he knows we suspect him or Ramsey.'

359

Hulda grinned and gave him a rather painful thump on the arm. 'We're very near the end of this. And then we'll have a story to rock London!'

Thirteen

Brunswick Gardens, just west of Kensington Palace, was a shady street dominated by a medieval church and large, graceful Georgian terraces with pillared entrances, wrought-iron railings and shuttered windows.

The driver had been ordered to traverse the street as slowly as possible without attracting the attention of the police. Well before they reached the Institute, Lonsdale and Hulda could see these were out in number. Peters was talking to three, while others were conducting house-to-house enquiries and swarming in and out of the building in the middle of the street.

The Demographic Institute was more modern than its neighbours, and boasted an elegant edifice of carved white marble, blind arcading and a splendid portico. There were tall windows on all three floors, and the building was entered through an impressive arched doorway at the head of a flight of wide stairs.

Before Lonsdale could stop her, Hulda had jumped from the still-moving carriage and was striding towards Peters, arms swinging purposefully.

'Did you receive my message?' she demanded.

'The body you found wasn't Jack Lonsdale. Indeed, it wasn't even a barrister – it was a clerk.'

Peters regarded her lugubriously. 'Do you know his identity?'

'John Otherington,' replied Lonsdale, who had just caught up with her. 'I don't know his address, but the Regent's Club will.'

'I doubt it,' muttered Peters dryly. 'I've rarely met a less-competent group of individuals.'

Nevertheless, he nodded to one of his men, who clambered into the carriage that had brought Lonsdale and Hulda and clattered away.

'Aren't you going to ask us how we know?' demanded Hulda, regarding him through eyes that were narrowed with suspicion.

'I assume because Jack Lonsdale returned home and answered some questions,' said Peters, maddeningly unflustered. 'But we agreed you were to stay away. You've been a great help, but we can take matters from here. Go home, Lonsdale, and take Miss Friederichs with you. I promise to keep you informed of any developments.'

'We can prove the people here are involved in these murders,' said Lonsdale. 'If you'll let us.'

'Not now, thank you. When it's over I shall listen all you like. Now please go home.'

'Is there a reason we can't stand here and watch?' demanded Hulda, growing more indignant by the minute.

'There's nothing *to* watch,' said Peters. 'There's nothing untoward happening in there, and Superintendent Ramsey has instructed me to

361

pester the scientists no further. He informs me that his orders come from the highest possible authority.'

'From God?' asked Hulda archly. 'Ramsey must be powerful indeed!'

The ends of Peters' moustache quivered in amusement. Lonsdale recalled that Otherington had told Jack that the government wanted the Institute's work kept secret, but Lonsdale found Ramsey closing the investigation sinister – particularly as Peters could not have had time to conduct a thorough search.

At that moment, Ramsey emerged from the building, his assistant Chief Inspector Leonard at his heels. Ramsey glanced briefly at Lonsdale and Hulda, snapped something to Leonard, and strode off in the other direction.

'We've just heard that the "highest authority" has deemed this place off limits,' said Hulda accusingly, turning the full force of her personality on Leonard as he approached. 'Who is it? The Home Secretary? The Prime Minister? The Queen?'

'I understand it was more of a corporate decision, madam,' replied Leonard, not at all discomfited by her temper. 'The Institute has been conducting important research for several years, and no one wants to see its findings harmed by unwarranted publicity.'

'Poppycock!' snapped Hulda. 'Something very odd is going on here, and I mean to find out what.'

She began to flounce towards the entrance, but

Leonard caught her arm in a grip that was gentle but firm and stopped her.

'Please,' he said. 'I must insist you leave now. If Superintendent Ramsey sees you interfering, he'll have you arrested.'

Lonsdale hastily offered his arm to Hulda, and was surprised when she accepted it and allowed herself to be led away. Leonard followed them down the road until he could flag down a hansom.

'I'm sorry,' he said, offering his hand to help Hulda climb inside. 'But we have our orders.' He turned to the driver. 'Take the young lady home, please. Longridge Road. And no stopping.'

Hulda sat rigidly in the carriage until it had turned several corners.

'Driver!' she called imperiously. 'Pull over.'

'The gentleman said not to,' objected the driver. 'And he gave me a shilling.'

'I'm about to be sick,' said Hulda icily. 'You have ten seconds before the inside of your hackney will never be the same again.'

The hansom immediately halted, and Hulda scrambled out. She straightened her skirts, patted her hair into place and looked around haughtily. It was obvious to anyone that she was the picture of robust good health, and vomiting was not on her immediate agenda. Lonsdale climbed out more slowly.

'You needn't bother to wait,' she said loftily. 'I might be some time.'

The driver cracked his whip and the carriage moved away. Apparently, there were limits to what he would do for a shilling, and taking on Hulda was well beyond them.

'Now what?' asked Lonsdale. 'We can't go back there. Peters is—'

'Peters is powerless!' snapped Hulda. 'Ramsey *is* behind all this! How did Leonard know where I live? I don't give my address to just anybody. He knew it because *Ramsey* told him, and Ramsey doesn't want us investigating.'

Lonsdale sensed she was right. 'So we'll visit the Institute ourselves, but I stand by what I said earlier. We go tomorrow when they won't be expecting us.'

'Very well.' She began to walk away, then stopped. 'I want you to promise me one thing, however.'

'What?'

'I shall have my gun. Bring yours as well.'

That night three people thought seriously about how Lonsdale and Hulda would slip into the Imperial Demographic Institute. On Longridge Road, Hulda carefully cleaned and loaded her pistol, and laid out the clothes that would serve most effectively in helping her to conceal it.

At Cleveland Square, Lonsdale cleaned the muck of the Thames from his pistol, and pondered ways to invade a place he imagined was fairly secure. Would they have to smash locks or break windows? Slowly, he began to gather a range of tools that might be needed.

Not far away, in Chesham Place, a third man wondered what the reporters would do. He had

364

no doubt that Lonsdale would come to the Institute, and was equally certain that Hulda would accompany him, especially after the note he had sent to Cleveland Square. It was a shame they had to die the next day: they were obviously intelligent and resourceful, and, despite being a nuisance, had earned his grudging respect. Moreover, Lonsdale had seemed quite a gentleman when they had met. Under different circumstances, the forces that brought them together might have made them friends.

The man jotted down some private thoughts in his diary, as he did each evening. He recalled how, more than a dozen years before, with the aid of one short letter, he had conceived the plan now nearing fruition. He wondered what destiny had brought Lonsdale into his otherwise well-ordered world. It was interesting how destiny had brought the two of them together: one soon to be world-famous, the other – like so many – to have his cerebrum in a jar.

'We need to know as much as we can about this place,' said Hulda, surveying the Demographic Institute from a discreet distance the following day. 'If we sit under the trees in the churchyard, we can observe comings and goings and make sure it's safe to go in.'

The plan sounded suitably cautious to Lonsdale, although it obliged them to push their way into the middle of some thick bushes for an unobstructed view of the Institute entrance. It would not be comfortable to stand there for long, thought Lonsdale, and it became less so when Hulda wedged herself next to him.

Their surveillance began around nine in the morning. Dozens of people from all walks of life came and went, but there was only one policeman in sight: a lone constable at the front door. As slipping past him was out of the question, Lonsdale suggested looking at the back. This was reached via an alley behind the Kensington Dispensary, a narrow lane flanked by tall walls pierced by locked gates through which rear gardens could be glimpsed. The Institute's had a door banded with steel, above which glinted broken glass. The wall, too, was topped with sharp, protective wire.

'For a research facility, these people seem remarkably conscious of their security,' mused Hulda.

'I could throw my coat over the barbs to climb over it,' suggested Lonsdale, eyeing the precautions uneasily, and wondering what had led him to be pondering how to burgle a government-approved research foundation.

'That never works when I try it,' said Hulda, drawing a surprised look. 'What about through a neighbour's garden?' Lonsdale went to the nearest gate, but it was locked, and looked sturdy. The one on the other side was also locked, but the bolt snapped under his hefty kick. He ushered Hulda inside, and closed it quickly behind them.

The wall that divided the neighbouring garden from the Institute's was tall, but a well-placed compost heap allowed them to hoist themselves

366

up to peer over the top. They looked into a rectangular yard, mostly paved, but with a tree and a bench that would be pleasant in summer. It appeared to be deserted. Lonsdale jumped down, and helped Hulda do the same. Carefully, they crept towards the back door.

'Do you think we should come back at night, when the building's empty?' whispered Lonsdale.

'I doubt it's ever empty. We've seen a huge number of people enter. But that works to our advantage. We shall claim we're participants in a study if anyone challenges us.'

The back door was locked, but a window was open. They climbed into a small room with a low ceiling and untidily stacked shelves. Lonsdale inched open the door and listened. Voices came from a room at one end of a corridor, while a flight of steps stood at the other. They headed for the stairs.

At the top was a hall that led to the front door. When someone opened it, they saw the policeman outside. To their left was a large room that looked like a lecture theatre, while to the right were a series of doors. Lonsdale ducked back as one opened and a young couple walked by, the man twisting his hat nervously in his hands.

'They look like subjects for the study,' breathed Hulda. 'Come on.'

She and Lonsdale trailed the couple to a large room, well appointed with chairs and tables. Others were already there, drinking tea or reading the newspapers provided. Hulda sat and pulled Lonsdale down next to her, snatching up a paper and using it to hide their faces. He

367

peered over the top. There were about fifteen people present, comprising a curious cross-section of society. He ducked behind the paper as a man in a white laboratory coat entered the room. He spoke to an elderly man, who nodded and followed him out.

'We can't stay here,' he said uncomfortably. 'If someone asks who we are, it'll be obvious we don't belong.'

'But we haven't seen anything incriminating yet. Let's try some more doors.'

She linked her arm in his and marched back into the hallway, head held high. Her confidence was convincing, as no one asked where they were going. They reached the end of the hall and selected a door that led to a narrow corridor. Hulda tried one of the doors that led off it, but it was locked, as was the next one, and the next. Lonsdale took the opposite side, and they worked their way down. Then Lonsdale lurched suddenly into an office when a handle unexpectedly turned.

Hulda pushed past him and tried the desk drawers before turning her attention to the cupboards.

'They're locked,' she hissed in frustration. 'Can you break into them?'

'Are you mad? It'd be too noisy. We need to come back later. Let's go before someone catches us.'

'You've left it a little late for that,' came a voice from behind them. Lonsdale and Hulda spun around to face a tall man, who smiled at them from the doorway, although there was neither amusement nor friendliness in the expression.

He stepped into the room, followed closely by three hefty louts, who wore white laboratory coats that looked odd on their beefy frames. One held a lead tied to a growling Alsatian with yellow fangs and a mean look.

'I have been expecting you, Lonsdale,' he said. 'I knew you'd understand when I sent the note to your brother's house. And I knew you'd come. I assumed you'd be here too, Miss Friederichs. You do realize that you've put me in a most awkward position.'

'We apologize,' said Hulda, smiling ingratiatingly. 'And now we'll be on our way.'

One of the thugs closed the door, while another stepped in front of her, and the dog obligingly growled.

'I'm afraid not,' said the man. 'You'll have to stay for a while – quite a while.'

'Is that so?' snarled Hulda. 'And who are you, anyway?'

'We dined together in Surrey,' said Lonsdale. 'His name is Francis Willoughby.'

The tall man contrived to smile, although it was an expression that chilled Lonsdale, and reminded him of a crocodile he had once seen in Africa. He heartily wished he'd listened to Peters and left the Imperial Demographic Institute to the police, as he was sure of one thing: he and Hulda would not escape the place alive. And who would ever know what had happened to them? They had told no one what they planned to do, on the grounds that the police had ordered them to stay away. How reckless they had been!

369

'Yes, when you met me, it was as Francis Willoughby,' he said. 'Although my name is Weeks: Professor Nathaniel Weeks. You won't know of me yet, as my research is so far unavailable to the general public.'

'Your research?' said Hulda scathingly. 'Is that what you call it?'

'Work of vast importance, Miss Friederichs.' Weeks looked back at Lonsdale. 'As you've reasoned, I am investigating what the famous Mr Huxley has recently called "the struggle for existence in human society". I prefer to think of it as "human Darwinism" – that is, man's relation to Darwinian principles.'

'Why have you been following us around?' demanded Hulda, not at all worried by the situation in which she found herself. Lonsdale admired her audacity and courage. 'I remember you buying collar studs at Salmon and Eden.'

'An excellent memory, although "following us around" is overstating matters. I watched you once or twice, but not for long – I am a busy man. But I *am* impressed with your memory, Miss Friederichs – when I met Lonsdale in Surrey, he couldn't place me at all. But to return to your question: you are of interest because you've presented problems for my work.'

'What work?' asked Lonsdale. 'You mean . . . murdering people for their brains?'

'I needed them,' replied Weeks simply. 'My team and I have tested and studied hundreds of people for intelligence, decision-making, moral and social behaviour, emotions, and more. We've studied lawyers, dockers, physicians, Members of

Parliament, beggars, vicars, clerks, railwaymen, scientists, shopkeepers, naval officers and ratings, even reporters. But it didn't go far enough.'

'So you decided you needed their cerebra as well,' surmised Lonsdale.

'Quite,' said Weeks. 'I have seventy representative samples in jars downstairs, if you'd care to see?'

Seventy! Lonsdale was appalled.

'No, thank you,' he said quickly, lest Hulda accepted. 'You claim the government supports your research, but it would never condone murder.'

Weeks smirked like a mischievous child. 'Obviously, we don't tell them *everything* about the project. But there's nothing more terrifying to a politician than civil unrest, which is what they fear we'll have if our population continues to expand at its present rate. They grasped my promise of a solution with desperate hands.'

'You told them you could solve overpopulation and inherent civil unrest?'

Weeks nodded. 'Galton's reputation is such that when I claimed *he* was collaborating with me, I gained instant credibility. But I have more genius in my little finger than he has ever had in that great thick skull of his. I would *never* work with that boring, pompous old man.'

'So you lied to the government about him?'

'I massaged the truth a little, but the ends justify the means. Galton's not only unable to see a practical way forward, he's inexplicably squeamish. I've developed the pragmatic solution that was beyond him. I'm providing valuable information

371

on human behaviour and thought, not at an individual level, but on an entire population. In order to control demographic growth, we first need to understand it. How can you hope to comprehend such a complex organ as the cerebrum without matching test results with physiology?'

'But—' began Hulda.

Weeks overrode her. 'It's obvious that a lawyer and a flower girl think differently, yet no one knows why. I will.'

'But the nature of your work means you can never tell anyone,' argued Lonsdale. 'What's the point of it?'

'Oh, I shall tell them,' said Weeks. 'And then I will be hailed as the greatest scientist who ever lived. Greater even than Darwin. I have many supporters; men who realize that the laws of evolution have been the laws of the jungle – cunning, brutishness, ruthlessness – and they have rewarded the wicked and punished the righteous. There are many who feel this is horrifying, and that something must be done.'

'Men like Wilson of the Zoological Gardens?' asked Lonsdale.

'Why, yes – Wilson is with us.'

'And Superintendent Ramsey?'

Weeks threw his head back and laughed. 'He'd be the last man I'd include in my coterie. He lacks intelligence, courage, or freedom of thought.'

Lonsdale was about to ask more, but there was a knock on the door. A man in a white coat entered.

'Inspector Peters is here. Dr Sorenson feels you should be the one to talk to him.'

'Thank you, Dr Hancock,' said Weeks. 'I'll go and meet him now. My guests will have to wait in my office until I've finished.'

Lonsdale and Hulda were bundled out into the hall, but any hopes of escape were quickly quashed by the three louts, who took their arms and marched them upstairs.

Weeks's office was a beautiful, wood-panelled room. One wall was filled to the ceiling with books; another was dominated by three large, well-spaced windows, which Lonsdale noted were nailed shut. On the wall behind the fine walnut desk were certificates of Weeks's various degrees and qualifications, as well as a letter, all in specially constructed frames. Their guards left them there and shut the door behind them. Lonsdale dropped to his knees and looked through the keyhole. They were outside with the dog, and he sensed there was nothing they would like more than the chance to pummel him if he tried to escape. But he and Hulda had one advantage: they still had their guns. Hulda read his mind.

'See what we can find out, Lonsdale,' she whispered. 'Then we'll shove the evidence in our pockets and shoot our way out. Now *hurry*! I don't think Weeks will be long.'

Lonsdale quickly began to browse through the papers on Weeks's desk. After only a few moments, he gestured to Hulda.

'This looks like a master ledger,' he said. 'There are hundreds of pages of statistics and test results. Some tables note where the subject lives, whether he has completed his tests, and there are other columns that I don't understand.'

Hulda scanned the entries. 'Norma Johnson, Adele Johnson, Frederick Kempster, Edmund Corlett, William Byers, Teresa Godley, John Poole, Patrick Donovan . . .'

'And a lot more we've never heard of,' said Lonsdale. 'What's this column – "Collected"? There's just one letter for each entry: B, C, M, P or T . . .'

'There's a B next to the Johnson sisters and one next to Poole. Don't you see, Lonsdale? B is for Baycroft. Next to Kempster there is a P – Pawley. It records who collected the cerebra – which means there are far more people taking them than we ever imagined.'

'There probably *are* seventy entries with letters in that column,' said Lonsdale. 'But what about the rest? I assume they're still alive, but for how long?'

'We don't need cerebra from *everyone*,' said Weeks sourly from the door, making them jump with the stealth of his entry. 'But I must say that you are behaving more like a reporter and less like a gentleman, Lonsdale – going through the papers on a fellow's desk.'

Lonsdale did not bother to point out that his antics were a lot more gentlemanly than murder.

'As long as we're discussing what we've found, why is "Francis Willoughby" on the diploma from Oxford?'

'Isn't it obvious? I was born Francis Nathaniel Willoughby, but I later adopted my mother's maiden name – Weeks. These days, my father knows no more about me than he does the Mountains of the Moon. But I've kept a close watch on *him*, because I'll inherit his fortune when he dies.'

'So you didn't meet me out of concern for his health?'

'I would never have any concern for that vile old bastard. His valet is secretly in my employ, so I was familiar with your correspondence, and he was given a note expressing your regrets that you couldn't accept his invitation, as your research had shown that William died in a foolish accident. He might come to believe it in time, although he's right to be suspicious, of course. Meanwhile, I was able to persuade you that the business in France had no bearing on your cases.'

'But it actually did? You mean William *was* murdered?'

'Of course. His cerebrum is downstairs with the others. You see? I have fooled you every step of the way. You have been so out of your depth – I could even tell that you would come back from our meeting and write to Dr Quayle to see if he would support my version of events or my father's. I couldn't allow him to tell you the truth, so I had his butler bribed to forward the letter to me when it arrived – Quayle never saw it.'

'But he would have confirmed your father's story?'

'Certainly – but he never had the opportunity, because I am prepared for every eventuality. You need the cool, calculating mind of a scientist to carry out an audacious plan like mine.'

'So it's true that you stole your brother's brain!' breathed Hulda, appalled.

'My *half*-brother,' corrected Weeks. 'And I wouldn't say stole, Miss Friederichs. After all, I *was* next of kin, and he *was* dead. Morgan had seen to that. A little too enthusiastic about that kind of thing is Morgan, but he *is* conscientious.'

'Why kill William?' asked Lonsdale.

'Well, if you must know, he was a problem. I gave him a job here, but he wasn't really suitable – not enough courage in his convictions. He wanted to leave, but that was impossible. He knew we'd never let him go – not with the secrets he was familiar with – so he tried to run.'

'And he's just one of the people you've had butchered?' asked Hulda coldly.

'Not "butchered", Miss Friederichs. All our subjects are treated with surgical care. Baycroft worked in the kitchens at Newgate, where he became proficient with the heads of sheep and pigs. That expertise first drew my attention to him while I was gathering data there. My other collectors, I trained myself. All are skilled in the delicate processes required.'

'If Baycroft was useful to you, then why did you have him killed?' asked Lonsdale.

'Because he was becoming mentally unstable,' explained Weeks. 'He dreamed *you* were going to drown him – rather like Morgan ultimately did. His irrational fears led him to engage in progressively riskier behaviour. For example, he tried to have you killed – telling Pawley that I wanted him to do it. I didn't mind the concept, but I hadn't approved the action. So he had to go.'

'I don't understand how you could have taken seventy cerebra with no one noticing,' said Hulda. 'It would be impossible.'

Weeks looked smug. 'We conceal our work in a variety of ways: fires, explosions, a quarry landslide, and of course train accidents.'

Lonsdale looked at Weeks and thought he and Baycroft had a lot in common – both were happy to discuss their monstrous acts and expected to be congratulated on their efficiency.

'You took a lot of trouble over Donovan,' he said. 'It was almost impossible to tell he had been strangled. One of your collectors killed him, took his brain, then ran into the street yelling that the house was on fire. Then he ran back inside, sealed off the front door with the chest, and locked the back door on the way out to ensure the body was incinerated, leading to the assumption that the fire was caused by a blocked chimney.'

'That was me, actually,' said Weeks. 'I couldn't trust Baycroft to imitate Donovan well enough. I was extremely convincing, despite being much taller than my subject.'

'You weren't as good as you think. One of Donovan's neighbours heard the difference in your voice – she thought it meant Donovan was drunk. And your cool, calculating scientific mind missed the detail that his chimney had been swept the previous week.'

'I wondered why you visited his sweep,' said Weeks. 'He'll be one of my subjects, by the way. He's perfect – an old man slipping ever more deeply into debt. It'll be assumed he couldn't pay the rent and fled his creditors.'

'Why kill the music-hall entertainer, Yeats?' asked Lonsdale. 'He seems a little high-profile.'

'And so he was. He was killed in a street robbery – nothing to do with us. But as he'd been part of the study, it seemed a shame to waste a good cerebrum.'

'Where does Cath Walker fit in?' asked Lonsdale.

'Her job was to entice subjects to come here.'

'You mean poor people, so desperate for money that they'd do anything for a bed for the night?' asked Hulda. 'Or men, thinking of sex? And, in so doing, signing their death warrants?'

'Let's not be emotive, Miss Friederichs. You can't allow the scientific process to be hampered by sentimentality. Walker was a whore. She just whored for me in a different way. Then she brought me Greaves, and he was *very* useful.'

'What did he do?' asked Lonsdale. 'Dispose of bodies in the river?'

'Exactly! He was a bargeman, who knew where to drop corpses. But then he asked for more money, and said Walker was trying to persuade him to go to the press with the "whole story". As if *they* understood the whole story.'

'She must've realized she wouldn't be allowed to live once the study ended,' said Lonsdale. 'She probably thought telling me was her last hope. If her story were to be publicized, you'd be arrested, and she might escape. But I imagine when Greaves betrayed her to you, you thanked him for his loyalty, and then slipped arsenic into whatever you gave him to drink.'

'Finest French brandy,' said Weeks. 'I reckoned he'd be dead before you arrived at Regent's Park, and my timing was, as usual, impeccable.'

Lonsdale could see through the window that Leonard and Peters were bickering on the street below. He glanced at the three thugs outside the office, and noticed the fingers of one of them twitching in anticipation of violence. It was time for him and Hulda to pull out their guns and put an end to the horrible affair. But there was one thing more that he wanted to know, and he was certain this would be his only chance to ask it.

'Why did you try to kill my brother?'

'Try? If I'd wanted Jack dead, he would be dead. It was Otherington's cerebrum that I wanted, so I sent one of my collectors for it. It was only later that I realized he had been wearing Jack's coat and that such a misunderstanding would lead you a merry dance. Which it did! I also knew how you would respond to my note. You *are* predictable.'

'And you,' retorted Lonsdale, 'are insane.'

'Hardly,' said Weeks, annoyance creeping into his voice. 'You just lack the intellect to understand my work, which will be admired for centuries to come. The world's greatest mind tells me that my research will cause just as

379

great a watershed in scientific thought as *On the Origin of Species* did when it was published twenty-three years ago.'

'The world's greatest mind?' sneered Lonsdale in disgust. 'No reputable scientist would endorse you.'

'Darwin would!' Weeks shouted, his voice quivering with agitation. He strode over to where the framed letter had pride of place on the wall and took it down. 'Look, Lonsdale! Darwin himself – *blessing* my work!'

Lonsdale and Hulda looked at the letter in its thick gilt frame, dated 3 December 1869.

My dear Galton,
I have been reading your book Hereditary Genius, *and I do not think I ever in all my life read anything more interesting and original. You have made a convert of an opponent, for I have always maintained that, excepting fools, men did not differ much in intellect, only in zeal and hard work. I see now that education and environment produce only a small effect on the mind and that a man's natural mental abilities are derived by inheritance. Your contention that human intellect and talent are therefore subject to natural selection and can be improved – whether by nature or by our own concerted efforts – is compelling. I congratulate you.*
Yours most sincerely,
Charles Darwin

380

'But this wasn't written to *you*,' said Hulda, bewildered. 'It was to Galton! How did you get it?'

'I took it from Darwin's home before he sent it. It was just sitting there for me to find. When I read it, everything became clear! Even then, Galton was expounding the theories that have led to what he calls eugenics. The letter proves Darwin *knew* that was the way forward. All I had to do was to carry it out!'

'But it is unethical!' cried Lonsdale.

'Just the opposite!' said Weeks. 'Darwin realized that progress depends on the survival of the fittest. But as modern medicine helps the sick, and governments support the weak, there's nothing to check the inferior stock. But *I'm* attaining an understanding of the true differences among individuals and the determining features of natural selection. Through *my* work, humanity will secure ultimate perfection. The shouldering aside of the weak by the strong, and the dominance of the superior races – these are the decrees of natural selection, and these are what *my* work will guarantee.'

Lonsdale saw that Weeks had done nothing but twist Darwin's and Galton's theories into pathetic, evil visions. 'You're not a scientist,' he said in disgust, 'just a self-righteous, murdering lunatic.'

Weeks glared. 'It's been interesting talking to you, but now you begin to bore me. Your efforts to interfere with my work have failed, but you can be assured that your cerebra will be added to my collection today – to advance my great and noble theories.'

'Wait,' said Lonsdale. 'Who's been protecting you, other than Wilson. Who?'

'Enough,' said Weeks, and gestured for his thugs to enter. 'Remember that a squashed organ is no good to me.'

He strode off, slamming the door behind him.

Lonsdale glanced at the three louts, as wicked, mirthless grins crept across their faces. He stuck his hand inside his coat, but the biggest jumped at him, knocking him backwards before he could reach his gun. He followed with a swing, but Lonsdale ducked and came back with a right cross that sent him reeling. Meanwhile, as another grabbed Hulda, she sank her teeth into his arm. The dog began to bark frantically, snapping the air with its dripping fangs. Its owner let it go, and chaos ensued.

The dog was poorly trained, and entered the melee little caring whom it bit. It delivered a sharp nip to its owner's ankle, then sank its teeth into the calf of the man Hulda had already bitten. The man yelled and kicked out, catching it on the nose. The dog yelped, and retreated under Weeks's desk. With the owner's attention briefly diverted, Lonsdale landed a hefty blow to his stomach, driving the air from his lungs so he dropped to his knees. He followed it with an uppercut to the jaw, which dropped him senseless. Meanwhile, there was a thump as Hulda's attacker slumped to the ground. Out of the corner of his eye, Lonsdale saw her holding a heavy paperweight that had been on the desk.

Having recovered sufficiently to determine he

382

wanted no more, the first man made for the door. Lonsdale leapt at him, pushing him hard against the wall, and proceeded to deliver a series of short jabbing punches to his head until he, too, slid to the ground.

'We're becoming quite proficient at this,' said Hulda coolly. 'Now, let's find Weeks!'

Lonsdale pulled out his gun, then paused. 'No, we fetch Peters and Leonard,' he said, dropping it into the outside right pocket of his coat. 'We've done enough.'

They left Weeks's office and ran down a flight of stairs.

'That way,' shouted Lonsdale, and they went through a set of doors leading to the front.

'Leonard!' gasped Hulda, spotting the policeman standing in the hallway talking to a man in a white coat.

Leonard looked up in astonishment, while the other man turned round slowly.

'O'Connor!' exclaimed Lonsdale.

'*Dr* O'Connor *Sorenson*, actually,' said the mortuary assistant. The Irish brogue was gone, and in its place was a drawling upper-class accent. 'But not at your service.'

'Chief Inspector, arrest this man!' ordered Hulda imperiously.

'I don't think so,' said Leonard, pulling out a revolver. 'Much as I'd like to oblige a lady of the press.'

Hulda gaped as Leonard pointed his gun unwaveringly at her.

'Professor Weeks said he'd taken care of you,'

383

said Leonard, 'but he spoke too soon. That comes of having others do your dirty work.'

'You?' breathed Lonsdale. He glanced at the door – could he run out to reach Peters?

Leonard shook his head.

'I wouldn't, Lonsdale. I'll shoot you and Miss Friederichs. And then shoot the constable outside. It will be easy to explain away – you are trespassing in direct contravention of police orders.'

Lonsdale sensed that Leonard was a far more dangerous adversary than Weeks, and that he and Hulda would not escape a second time. After all, Leonard had more to lose if *The PMG* exposed what was happening at the Institute – Weeks would use influential friends to escape justice, but Leonard had no such connections.

'Now,' said Leonard, 'I doubt Weeks will be overjoyed to see you again, but go through that door.'

Lonsdale glanced at Hulda; both were still armed, but attempting to reach their weapons was too dangerous. Leonard would kill at least one of them before they could stop him.

'I told you to go through that door,' said Leonard when neither moved. The look on his face indicated there was no alternative. O'Connor led, and Leonard brought up the rear. They went through a lecture theatre and beyond to a series of offices, in one of which was Weeks. His eyes became hard and cold, and he looked at Leonard for an answer.

'You might be a great scientist, Weeks,' said

Leonard, 'but you don't know anything about hiring the right men for this kind of job.'

He stood to one side of Lonsdale, the gun in his left hand. Lonsdale eased closer to him, wondering what the chances were of jumping him before he could fire. Slim, he decided. He glanced out of the window, and saw Peters talking to several constables.

'Don't expect help from that quarter,' Leonard said, watching him. 'All the windows in the front of the building are specially made, and you won't attract attention by breaking one. You could hit one with a rock and it wouldn't shatter. Besides, *I* don't make mistakes.' He waved with his gun towards a cabinet that stood next to a desk on the other side of the room. 'Stand over there and keep your hands where I can see them.'

'So it was you all the time,' said Lonsdale. 'Not Peters or Ramsey.'

'Neither has the vision to understand what Professor Weeks is doing,' responded Leonard shortly. 'His research will make a great step forward for our society.'

'But you're a policeman,' objected Lonsdale. 'You should want to help those who can't protect themselves.'

Leonard sneered. 'We'll help them into a better world all right – the next one.'

'So, you protect Weeks and his project?'

'Working with that idiot Ramsey makes it easy. He listens to all my suggestions and follows them slavishly, because he knows I'm cleverer than he is. I only have to say he wants something, and it happens. I can act as though I'm trying to be helpful, while subverting anything that threatens us.'

'He's been invaluable,' said Weeks smugly.

Leonard glanced at O'Connor on his left and Weeks on his right. 'Can you keep them here if I give you the gun? I need to get rid of Peters – he's almost as much of a menace as they are.'

'We'll keep them quiet,' said Weeks confidently, as O'Connor pulled a long, thin knife out of a cabinet. 'Hand me the gun.'

As Leonard reached over to pass Weeks the pistol, Lonsdale groped for his own revolver. Without taking it out of his pocket, he pulled the trigger. The bullet shattered the strengthened glass of the window and everybody in the room froze.

'Down,' yelled Lonsdale to Hulda, dropping behind a desk and pulling out the gun. But before she could react, O'Connor grabbed her hair and thrust the knife against her throat.

'She'll be dead within seconds,' he hissed.

'So will you,' said Lonsdale, levelling the gun at him from behind the desk.

'Which makes three,' said Leonard, aiming at Lonsdale. He spoke urgently. 'Kill her now, Sorenson, and they'll both be dead before Peters gets here. I'll clear everything.'

'I'll do it,' said Weeks. 'I have an MP visiting tomorrow, and I don't want a mess on the Turkish rug he gave us.' He stepped in front of Leonard to reach O'Connor, and in that instant Lonsdale fired again. The bullet hit O'Connor's right shoulder and he dropped both the knife and his hold on Hulda.

Leonard shoved Weeks, sending him sprawling to the floor, and then leapt at Lonsdale over the desk. Lonsdale tried to re-aim, but Leonard landed on him, knocking the pistol away. In a moment, Leonard had jammed his knee onto Lonsdale's chest and grabbed his throat with a two-handed grip. They struggled for a moment before Leonard's vice-like clamp began to suffocate Lonsdale. Disobeying the instinct to pull the hands away, Lonsdale let go of Leonard's wrists, and swung with all his remaining strength up into his groin. The policeman screeched, released Lonsdale, and fell on top of him.

'What's going on?' Peters shouted, as he raced into the room, brushing by Weeks at the door and looking around wildly. The first thing he saw was Hulda, skirt awry and pointing a huge revolver at O'Connor, who was groaning and bleeding profusely. The second was Lonsdale, who pushed out from underneath Leonard, grabbed the chief inspector's left arm, and brought it up behind his back. Two constables who had momentarily detained Weeks let him go as they came to help their superior.

'Leonard is one of them, Peters,' shouted Hulda. 'Weeks is escaping! Get him!'

'Now, Miss Friederichs,' said Peters, infuriatingly slow on the uptake, 'put down that gun. Constable, see to the chief inspector.'

'It's true, Peters,' Lonsdale said, breathing heavily. 'Leonard *is* one of them.'

'Arrest them, George,' Leonard gasped. 'They shot Sorenson, then tried to kill me.' He began to reach for his gun.

'Don't move, Leonard,' said Hulda, pointing her gun at him.

'Miss Friederichs!' shouted Peters. 'Disarm! Let me sort this out.'

'No,' she shouted frantically. 'Lonsdale! Don't let Weeks escape!'

Lonsdale tore from the room. An open door at the far end of the corridor told him which way Weeks had gone. He leapt down the narrow spiral stairs beyond, three at a time. At the bottom was another door. He burst through it and found himself in a long, cold room lined with shelves. He didn't pause to look at the dozens and dozens of glass jars, but plunged forward, and into what was apparently a dissecting area. A man sat at a bench, chopping something up on a piece of white polished marble; he did not look up as Lonsdale raced past.

Then Lonsdale was outside, exiting through the now unlocked door they had seen earlier at the rear of the building. Weeks was nowhere to be seen. Lonsdale dashed to the gate, but it was locked. There was no other way out, so he could only assume that Weeks was doing what he himself had already done – climbing through someone else's garden. He pulled himself up onto the wall he had scaled earlier, just in time to see Weeks disappearing over the one beyond it.

He leapt off the wall, and ran across the neighbouring garden. The next wall was high, but his running start helped him reach the top and haul himself over. What he saw from the top filled him with horror.

The 'garden' surrounded a gaping hole with silvery lines at the bottom, and the house to which it was attached was just an empty façade. It was the Metropolitan Line's vent, through which underground trains ridded themselves of excess steam. There was a maintenance ladder attached to the side, down which Weeks was climbing.

Lonsdale heard a yell from behind and saw Peters and his men were running after him. He could not wait for them to catch up. Weeks had boasted about his supporters, and if he was not caught now, pressure would be brought on the police to abandon the search. He jumped off the wall and raced to the ladder. Weeks was almost at the bottom, and Lonsdale saw him drop the last few feet and disappear into the tunnel. Placing one hand on the rusty metal, Lonsdale swung down.

The ladder groaned, and he felt it ease away from the wall. Frantically, he grabbed at the rim of the pit, but then it steadied, and, knowing it had held Weeks, he began to climb down. One rung disintegrated under his feet, so that, for a moment, he was suspended by his hands. His feet scrabbled for the next rung down.

He knew that the longer he took to climb down, the greater the distance Weeks would be able to put between them, so he struggled to move faster. He was almost at the bottom when he discovered the last part of the ladder had rusted away completely. Weeks had evidently known it, indicating it was not the first time he had used the thing, but Lonsdale was unprepared. With a screech of tearing metal, he plunged into empty space, still clutching a rusty bar.

Lonsdale landed with a crash, the stench of engine oil and steam rising about him. From above, he could hear Peters shouting, but the echoes made it impossible to decipher what the inspector was saying. He climbed to his feet, and stared at the black tunnel down which Weeks had vanished. A long way in the distance was a tiny pinprick of light marking Kensington Station. He listened intently for the rumbling of a train, but the tunnel was silent. As he looked down the line, he saw a flicker of light. Weeks had struck a match to illuminate his way – he had been groping his way in the dark, and was not as far ahead as Lonsdale had feared. Now the professor had decided to abandon stealth for speed.

Lonsdale shot off down the tunnel after him. He could hear the tap of Weeks's feet and the rasp of his breath. Lonsdale increased his speed, then fell over an uneven tie, bruising his knees and scraping his hands. He lit a match of his own and started to trot, the glow from his tiny light making eerie shadows on the walls.

'Weeks!' he yelled. 'You can't escape!'

He heard the scientist laugh in derision. Lonsdale continued running, concentrating on the pinprick of light that marked Kensington Station. His breath came in ragged gasps as the foul, stale air of the tunnel choked him. He felt himself grow dizzy, and he stumbled again.

He forced himself to move on, each step becoming more of an effort. He felt a blast of cooler air on his cheek. He blinked, and saw the lights from the station were a good deal closer now, and that Weeks was not very far ahead of him. He staggered on. And then he noticed the rails beneath his feet beginning to tremble. Glancing back, he saw a great round light. A train! He ran faster, feeling the shaking increasing beneath his feet, and hearing the dull rumble of metal on metal, growing louder and louder.

Lonsdale ran harder, knowing that to fall now would mean death. The train was lighting the entire tunnel, and there was a shrill whistle from the engine as the driver saw him. It screamed in his ears like a creature from hell. Then he saw one of the alcoves that had been built into the wall for workmen to use when trains went past. As the brakes were applied in a screech that Lonsdale thought would split his skull, he dived into the niche, and the train hurtled past in a shower of sparks.

He thought he was going to be sick. His lungs were burning, and he fought for breath, clutching at the sooty wall of the alcove as the train thundered past. Then it was gone and, glancing out, he saw a figure emerge from another alcove ahead, and make its way towards the back of the train, which was pulling into the station. Weeks was going to escape after all!

Lonsdale forced himself forward. Weeks had reached the train, and was climbing up the back. With a shock, Lonsdale saw he planned to lie on the top, and wait until he reached a place where there were no police, when he would calmly climb down. Then he would be free.

Lonsdale forced himself forward. He was almost there! He reached the back of the train and stretched up, snagging a handful of trouser leg. Weeks kicked backwards, and Lonsdale struggled to hold on. From behind him, he could hear running footsteps. Peters and his men were coming. Then, very slowly, the train began to move. Lonsdale knew that if he did not hold onto Weeks now, he would escape. The police were too far away to help.

He reached up with his other hand, hanging onto Weeks's ankle with all his strength as the train began to gather speed. Weeks kicked again and, this time, Lonsdale was unable to maintain his grip. He felt his hand sliding, and then he was down, tumbling onto the track.

Peters arrived just as the engine began to disappear into the tunnel at the other end of the station, breathing hard, his face streaked with sweat and soot.

'Damn!' he yelled, all exasperated fury.

Weeks was looking back at them with a gloating smile. He was kneeling on the top of the train, swaying slightly as it gathered speed. He raised his hand in a triumphant farewell.

Lonsdale closed his eyes tightly as the last carriage entered the tunnel. From the platform, he heard a woman scream. Weeks had misjudged the height of the hole.

Peters's men rushed towards the crumpled body, while Lonsdale pulled himself up onto the platform, away from the rails. Peters followed Lonsdale, watching his constables mill about the body that sprawled across the tracks in a bloody heap.

Lonsdale slumped on the platform and tried to catch his breath.

'I hope it dashed the bastard's brains out,' he said in a hoarse whisper.

Peters sat next to him. 'Oh, it did,' he said grimly. 'It did.'

Epilogue

'I find it utterly reprehensible that you won't let us tell the entire story,' raged Hulda. 'We exposed the plot at great personal risk, and now all we can publish is a watered-down version. We can't even use the perpetrators' real names.'

'Don't blame me, Miss Friederichs,' said Peters, pulling out his pipe and tobacco. 'It came from one of those "higher sources" you dislike so much.'

'Small wonder she's vexed, then,' put in Bradwell. 'If that's what higher sources do, perhaps they shouldn't be in higher places.'

It was Monday afternoon, six days after the fateful encounter at the Imperial Demographic Institute. For the first time since then, Lonsdale, Hulda, Peters and Bradwell were together, enjoying a meal at the restaurant in Derry & Toms.

'It was Morley who agreed not to print everything,' Peters said mildly. 'So some of your irritation should be directed *his* way. Not mine.'

'Morley has his reasons,' said Lonsdale. 'But it would be different if Stead were editor.'

'Something we may see before too long,' said Hulda enigmatically.

Lonsdale raised his eyebrows. 'Do you know something I don't, Friederichs?'

'A great deal,' replied Hulda. 'But as regards

The PMG, I just sense a change in the offing. There'll be a seat in the Commons open soon, and Morley will be Gladstone's choice to fill it.' She smiled in anticipation. 'Then, with Stead in charge, we'll have some excitement!'

There was silence at the table for several moments, before Lonsdale spoke again.

'So, we all know that the Imperial Demographic Institute has been closed down and a number of individuals arrested, Inspector. What else can you tell us?'

'That Weeks kept most of the important documents elsewhere, and we haven't been able to locate them, and the ledger you mentioned had disappeared by the time we searched his office. That leaves us struggling to hunt down many of those involved. We found seventy-six cerebra in the basement, but we don't know if that was the total number of victims.'

'Has Leonard told you anything?'

'Not much – he feels I helped destroy his dreams. He says Ramsey and I are two of a kind – neither with the vision to understand the greatness of Weeks's plan. Sorensen has been more helpful, and answered some of the questions you wanted us to ask. For example, one of their colleagues was supposed to follow you home after the Walker inquest, so that Weeks would know where you lived. But he followed Miss Friederichs' hansom instead, so Weeks went to her house in the morning, hoping she would lead him to your residence. Instead, of course, he followed her to Salmon and Eden.

'Sorensen has also identified some of the

low-level participants. We've caught two men who were involved in murders, although Morgan has disappeared. You heard about Pawley, didn't you?'

'No,' said Lonsdale.

'He was found on a Great Western train travelling without a ticket. He refused to pay so was taken into custody, where his identity was ascertained. He's been incarcerated in an asylum. He denies any involvement with Weeks, and says he'll break out at his first opportunity.'

'So, do you think,' asked Bradwell, 'that there are individuals who'll try to continue the scheme?'

'We seem to have the most important *active* participants,' said Peters. 'There are people like Wilson who believe in the concept, but didn't play a role that we know of – they're still free. But, without Weeks, I think we're safe from more of this madness.'

'And hopefully, we always will be,' sighed Lonsdale.

Lonsdale sat comfortably in the morning room at Cleveland Square and opened *The Observer*. He had three-quarters of an hour to spare before he and Jack were to meet Emelia and Anne. He was looking forward to the afternoon considerably more than to dinner that night with Emelia's family. But he had found in recent weeks that he was prepared to put up with a great deal to please Anne.

Idly, he scanned through the news. The world seemed to be holding on for one more day. But the smile left his face when he read:

397

A gunpowder explosion resulted in a double fatality yesterday morning at 94 Old Bath Road in Bristol. After a fire in the upper rooms was extinguished, the lodgers, Mr and Mrs Hicks, were found on the floor with the upper portion of their heads blown off. An examination revealed a large number of canisters containing gunpowder and loaded cartridges. It was apparent that Hicks was filling cartridges when the explosion occurred. The police say there is no need for further investigation, and that the case is closed.

Lonsdale felt himself shaking. 'The case may be closed,' he muttered. 'But it certainly hasn't ended.'

Historical Note

The account of the gunpowder explosion that killed Mr and Mrs Hicks in Bristol was true, as were all the news articles and many of the events described in *Mind of a Killer*. The quotations were taken directly from *The Pall Mall Gazette*, *The Times*, or other London newspapers. This is just one interpretation of what might have happened when this strange series of seemingly unrelated events took place.

In 1882, *The PMG* was a small but very influential London newspaper. Founded in 1865, it had been on the verge of financial collapse when Frederick Greenwood, the first editor, convinced his brother James to spend a night in the Lambeth workhouse and to write a series of sensational articles about the experience. The four instalments not only exposed the horrific conditions in workhouses, but also helped guarantee the paper's success by doubling its circulation in three days.

In 1880, the newspaper's ownership and political orientation changed, and John Morley (1838–1923), a much-respected intellectual and political commentator – called 'the last of the great nineteenth-century Liberals' – became editor. Morley left *The PMG* in 1883 after being elected to Parliament. He later twice served in the Cabinet as Chief Secretary for Ireland, having told Prime Minister Gladstone that if he could manage Stead, he could manage Ireland. He was also twice Secretary of State for India, and was created Viscount Morley in 1908, after which he became Lord President of the Council.

One of Morley's first moves as editor was to hire the Liberal firebrand W. T. Stead (1849–1912), from the *Northern Echo* of Darlington, to serve as assistant editor. Stead succeeded Morley as editor, and in the next seven years his 'New Journalism' introduced many innovations, brought American-style sensationalism to the British press, and demonstrated how the press could be used positively to influence government policy in the creation of child welfare and social legislation – what Stead called 'Government by Journalism'. In 1890, Stead founded and became editor of the non-partisan monthly *Review of Reviews*, a position he held until his death in 1912 on *Titanic*.

Under Morley and Stead, the staff of *The PMG* was one of the most remarkable in the history of the press. Alfred Milner (1854–1925) served as a reporter and then Stead's assistant editor, before abandoning journalism for a career as a politician and colonial administrator. He was High Commissioner for South Africa and Governor of the Cape Colony, a member of the War Cabinet during World War I, Secretary of State for War, and Secretary of State for the Colonies. He was knighted in 1895 and created Viscount Milner in 1902.

Edward Tyas Cook (1857–1919) ultimately succeeded Stead as editor, and in 1893, after new

400

ownership had changed *The PMG* to a Tory newspaper, he founded a new Liberal evening paper, *The Westminster Gazette*. He later became editor of *The Daily News*, and was renowned as the world's leading authority on John Ruskin – editing his writings, which were published in thirty-nine volumes. He was knighted in 1912.

Hulda Friederichs (1856–1927) initially joined *The PMG* as Stead's personal assistant, and thereafter became the first woman journalist in London engaged on exactly the same terms, with regard to work and pay, as the male members of staff. In 1893, she went to *The Westminster Gazette* with Cook and, three years later, became editor of the *Westminster Budget*. She wrote biographies of several important British figures of the time.

Clustered in the months around the death of Charles Darwin on 19 April 1882 were numerous incidents appearing in this book. For example, W. J. Willoughby was found dead on a train track in France, after two companions with whom he was travelling disappeared; the murderer Dr George Lamson confessed his crimes to his gaoler; the pauper Bingham died after being placed in a fumigating box; and Frederick Kempster and Edmund Corlett were burned to death at their factory.

The PMG also featured coverage of the death of Jesse James; the explosion at the Court Theatre, during a performance that the Prince of Wales was attending; an attack on a ship by a sperm whale; the riots in Camborne; the eruption of Mount Etna; and Milner's two-part story on 'nomads', explaining the way vagabond women selected men at workhouses. Other pieces of news included milkman John Poole being arrested for stealing milk, Teresa Godley being killed in a beach fire after being part of a group that robbed Frank Wood, and Thomas Pawley – an escapee from a lunatic asylum – being found on a Great Western Train travelling without a ticket.

Perhaps the most intensely covered news event of the time was the double-murder of Lord Frederick Cavendish and Thomas Henry Burke in Dublin's Phoenix Park. The resolution to these murders did not come until the next year, after the members of the 'Invincibles', a small, violent faction of Irish rebels, had been arrested. Ultimately, five were hanged and three given penal servitude for life, while James Carey, who turned Queen's evidence against them, was murdered while being smuggled by the government to Natal.

The other newspapers mentioned in the book all existed. At the time, *The Daily Telegraph* and *The Standard* had the largest daily circulations in the world. *The New York Herald* – which was widely disliked by the British press for its use of sensationalism – at times had the largest circulation in the United States and full-time staffs for both its Paris and London editions. The restaurants mentioned – including Craig's Oyster Bar, Pagani's and the Aerated Bread Company – were all successful at the time, as was Derry & Toms, the London department store. The homes that Lonsdale, Milner and Galton lived in can still be seen in London, although Galton's is much changed after being damaged by a bomb in World War II.

Galton was one of the great gentleman-scientists of his generation. He had travelled in Africa and then returned to Britain, where he achieved prominence for his investigations into numerous aspects of heredity and genetics. The originator of the concept of eugenics, he received the letter from his cousin Charles Darwin in December 1869. His book *Inquiries into Human Faculty and Its Development* was published to critical acclaim in 1883, and his later achievements included the founding of the anthropometric laboratory and being one of the fathers of finger-printing. At this time, several of Lonsdale's other acquaintances – including Sir Garnet Wolseley (1833–1913), who was raised to the peerage as Baron Wolseley later in 1882, and Professor John Robert Seeley (1834–1895) – were also at the height of their powers and influence.

PUFFIN BOOKS

First Prize for the Worst Witch

Jill Murphy started putting books together (literally with a stapler) when she was six. Her Worst Witch series, the first book of which was published in 1974, is hugely successful. She has also written and illustrated several award-winning picture books for younger children.

Books by Jill Murphy

THE WORST WITCH

THE WORST WITCH STRIKES AGAIN

A BAD SPELL FOR THE WORST WITCH

THE WORST WITCH ALL AT SEA

THE WORST WITCH SAVES THE DAY

THE WORST WITCH TO THE RESCUE

THE WORST WITCH AND THE WISHING STAR

FIRST PRIZE FOR THE WORST WITCH

DEAR HOUND

This book belongs to

For Pamela Todd
with tons of love

'What Larks eh?'

FIRST PRIZE
FOR
THE WORST WITCH

JILL MURPHY

PUFFIN

PUFFIN BOOKS

UK | USA | Canada | Ireland | Australia
India | New Zealand | South Africa

Puffin Books is part of the Penguin Random House group of companies
whose addresses can be found at global.penguinrandomhouse.com.

www.penguin.co.uk
www.puffin.co.uk
www.ladybird.co.uk

First published 2018

001

Copyright © Jill Murphy, 2018

The moral right of the author/illustrator has been asserted

Typeset in Baskerville MT Std
Printed in Great Britain by Clays Ltd, Elcograf S.p.A.

A CIP catalogue record for this book is available from the British Library

ISBN: 978–0–141–35509–2

All correspondence to:
Puffin Books
Penguin Random House Children's
80 Strand, London WC2R ORL

CHAPTER ONE

Mildred Hubble was cruising above the trees and villages, on her way to Miss Cackle's Academy for the start of Summer Term. Like all her classmates, she was longing to get this last term over with and go up to the very top class next year, when they would be the proud wearers of the Year Five uniform to set them apart from the lower school. In fact, there was not much difference to the usual uniform, only a multi-striped tie and braid sewn round their cloaks, but Year Four couldn't wait to be wearing it.

There seemed to be more luggage with each passing term, especially *this* one, Mildred reflected, as she peered down through the treetops, looking out for the usual landmarks. Apart from her bags of clothes and books, and her cat, Tabby, and tortoise, Einstein (both tucked up safely in the cat basket), there was also Star, the stray dog she had found last term. Star had proved to be such a natural acrobat that he and Mildred had won the national swimming-pool competition for Miss Cackle's Academy. After such a triumph Mildred had been allowed to keep him as her broom-companion.

2

Star was perched behind Mildred, on top of a box of books, as if it was the most natural place in the world for him to sit, and every now and then he let out a volley of barks, which made Mildred feel as if he was talking to her.

'Come on, Star!' Mildred called back to him. 'You can sit at the front with me if you like. We'll be flying for at least another hour – we've only just passed over the watermill at Greater Bustling.'

Star leapt over her shoulder in an instant, landing neatly in her lap.

'*Woof!*' he barked, giving her a joyful slurp under the chin.

'Oh, look!' exclaimed Mildred. 'There's a big striped tent down there at the edge of the village – it must be a circus! What a shame it's so far from the school or we could have pleaded with Miss Cackle to take us there for an outing.'

As she said this, Star took a flying leap back over her shoulder and dived between the book box and the cat basket.

'Hey!' said Mildred. 'What's the matter, boy? Is it a bit too windy for you up this high? Come on – let's fly a bit lower down.'

A blustery wind had sprung up, and the broomstick was swaying from side to side and making sudden lurches, hindered by the luggage piled on top and hanging from the back of it.

Mildred dropped down six metres, hovering evenly like a helicopter.

'There you are,' she said to Star. 'That's *much* better – hardly any wind at all. You can jump back if you like.'

However, to Mildred's surprise, he didn't move from his hideaway and no amount of cajoling, even the offer of a treat, could tempt him out.

Twenty minutes passed by and Mildred still hadn't seen anyone from the academy. She was just beginning to wonder if she'd got the wrong day, when, to her great relief, she saw Maud flying along steadily in front of her.

'Maud! Maudie!' she yelled, delighted
to see her best friend. 'What a fantastic bit
of luck! You're the first Cackle-ite I've seen
this morning.'

'Millie!' squealed Maud, equally thrilled.

They tried to fling their arms round each
other but gave up, laughing as they clashed
broomsticks and narrowly avoided falling
off.

'*Concentrate, girls!*' bellowed Mildred
sternly, doing an excellent impression of

Miss Hardbroom, the strictest teacher in the school. *'I don't expect to see such silly nonsense from fourth-years!'*

'Gosh, Mildred,' said Maud, 'you sound scarily like her. I wonder what ghastly projects she's lined up for us this term.'

'Well, one thing's for sure,' said Mildred. 'There's going to be a lot of swimming!'

'Oh yes, of course! I'd forgotten about the swimming pool,' said Maud. 'Do you think they've actually built it yet?'

'I don't know,' said Mildred, 'but I had a crash course of swimming lessons during the hols, just in case.'

'I didn't know you couldn't swim,' said Maud. 'You managed all right when we went on holiday to Grim Cove.'

Mildred smiled. 'I just pretended,' she confessed. 'I hopped along on one foot and did swimming movements – I didn't want Ethel sneering!'

Over the years Ethel had somehow become an implacable enemy of Mildred, and never missed an opportunity to make her look small.

'Well, no one noticed,' said Maud.

'And now they never will!' said Mildred. 'I can do ten lengths of our local pool, which is huge. The school pool will be a quarter of that size, so it should be fine.'

'It's going to be brilliant,' said Maud happily. 'Lovely, warm clear water, with sparkly blue tiles – and all thanks to Mildred Hubble and Star! Where is he, by the way? He's too big to go in the cat basket.'

'He's hiding in between the luggage,' said Mildred. 'I don't think he's feeling too well. He was fine when we started out – I probably shouldn't have given him any breakfast.'

CHAPTER TWO

On the last day of Summer Term there was a ceremony called Fourth Year Firsts, when prizes were awarded to pupils who had proved themselves best in certain subjects over the past four years. It was also the occasion when the witch chosen to be Head Girl for the coming year would be solemnly announced. This event was actually more important to the girls than the final year itself, when there would be no time for distractions, as everyone would be working madly to pass the Witches' Higher Certificate.

'Have you got any hopes for Fourth Year Firsts?' asked Maud, passing Mildred a chocolate biscuit as they coasted along smoothly, cloaks and hair streaming behind them in the wind.

'Not *exactly*,' replied Mildred. 'What about you? Tell me yours and then I'll tell you mine.'

'Well,' said Maud, 'I'm sort of average at everything, but there *is* a First Prize for Team Spirit, so I'm going to work on that one – you know, being extra helpful and so on. What about you?'

'If I tell you what I'd like to get,' confided Mildred, smiling shyly at her friend, 'you have to promise not to laugh.'

'Cross my heart!' promised Maud.

'OK then,' said Mildred. 'It isn't *exactly* a first prize, more of an honour, but it would be the only first prize that I would want.'

'Go on!' urged Maud, intrigued. 'Tell me!'

'You mustn't laugh!' Mildred reminded her.

'My word is my bond,' said Maud, looking at Mildred with a very serious face.

'Right,' announced Mildred. 'I'd like to be chosen as Head Girl for next year.'

Maud really did try to keep her serious face on, but almost immediately she erupted into such peals of laughter that she nearly fell off her broom.

'You promised not to laugh!' exclaimed Mildred indignantly. However, within

12

seconds she was drawn into Maud's infectious and unstoppable fit of giggles, and soon the two of them were doubled over on their broomsticks, desperately trying to steer and keep their balance.

'It isn't *that* funny!' snorted Mildred. 'I have done quite a few good things for the school, in between disasters!'

Maud was now laughing so much that tears streamed down her cheeks and blew away in the wind. 'Sorry, Mil!' she howled. 'It's just so incredibly un*likely.*'

'Understatement of the year!' Mildred laughed, beginning to wonder why she had ever mentioned it in the first place.

'And anyway,' continued Maud, between fits of mirth, 'if there's a Hallow in the school, it always goes to them and we've got Ethel Hallow –'

'*Un*fortunately!' commented Mildred.

For some reason, this observation struck them both as so utterly hilarious that they could hardly see – what with their screwed-up faces and their tears of laughter and the buffeting wind – and they suddenly realized that the treetops were alarmingly close.

'Come on, Mil!' said Maud, trying hard to calm down. 'Let's land in that nice big field down there and take a ten-minute break before we have a crash landing.'

'Good idea, Maudie,' agreed Mildred, explosions of laughter still erupting every few seconds. 'I must say, there really is *nothing* quite like a good fit of the giggles!'

CHAPTER THREE

Ethel Hallow, an hour ahead of Mildred and Maud, was flying very fast at a high altitude, baggage jolting behind her; even her perfect cat, Nightstar, was having difficulty holding on. Ethel's best friend, Drusilla, who was not such an accomplished flier as Ethel, was frantically trying to keep up. Ethel was in a *very* bad

mood, remembering how Mildred Hubble
had somehow managed to drag herself up
from total hopelessness to become quite an
exceptional pilot, with that scruffy little
rescue dog as her broom-companion.

'*Please* slow down, Ethel!' yelled Drusilla,
doing her best to keep the annoyance out of
her voice, as it always made things worse if
you tried to stand up to Ethel. 'I'm going to
fall off in a minute! We aren't all brilliant

16

fliers like you,' she added, hoping that flattery might improve things.

It did. Ethel slowed to a calmer speed and they both turned round to check that their luggage was secure and to reassure their ruffled cats. Nightstar, who had a rather touchy temperament like his owner, turned his back on Ethel, stuck one leg in the air and began washing. He wasn't the sort of cat to let on that he had been scared.

'What is it, Eth?' asked Drusilla. 'You were OK five minutes ago.'

'I was just thinking about Mildred Hubble,' replied Ethel grumpily. 'I mean, how on earth has she actually got through four years at Cackle's? Every time she messes something up, I think, "Bingo! That's got rid of her!" Then she somehow manages to make things better for herself, and now she has that ridiculous dog on her broomstick she's actually turned into a really decent flier. If she was still with that awful cat, she'd be back to square one just like that –' She clicked her fingers. 'It *so* isn't fair. I mean, she might even win First Prize for Best Pilot at this rate, especially now that they've won the swimming-pool competition together and everyone thinks they're *so* perfect.'

18

'Don't get in a state about it, Ethel,' said Drusilla soothingly. 'You'll definitely win First Prize for Chanting *and* for Potions. Mildred's hopeless at both.'

'I'm not *in* a state, thank you very much, Drusilla,' snarled Ethel dangerously. 'And she *isn't* actually hopeless at potions any more, thanks to that animal-speaking spell she invented last year that got me into so much trouble.'

'Ethel!' exclaimed Drusilla before she could stop herself. 'You really can't blame Mildred for what happened! You *did* steal her spell and pretend it was yours.'

'Look, Drusilla,' snapped Ethel, 'whose side are you on? Why don't you go and team up with Mildred's little gang of friends if you think they're so hard done by?'

'Sorry, Ethel,' mumbled Drusilla miserably. 'Of course I'm on your side – always, whatever happens. Anyway, one thing you can be sure of, you'll definitely be announced as Head Girl for next year! If there's a Hallow in the running, they always get elected – there have been at least thirty-five Hallow Head Girls over the centuries.'

'Yes, at least that's a dead cert,' agreed Ethel moodily.

In the distance, they could see the shadowy shape of Miss Cackle's Academy for Witches, perched on top of a mountain, half hidden among dense pine trees. Already, other pupils were visible on the horizon, struggling with their baggage and cat baskets.

'Come on, Druse,' said Ethel, feeling a little better at the thought of the gold Head Girl medal, pinned weightily to her multicoloured Year Five tie. 'We'd better get a move on if we're going to arrive before anyone else – First Prize for Perfect Punctuality as well as everything else!'

'We hope!' Drusilla laughed, relieved that they were friends again.

Ethel suddenly took off with such a whoosh of air that Drusilla's hat flew off

20

and spiralled into the trees below.

'Hang on a mo!' called Drusilla, but Ethel was already too far ahead to hear her. It was a very pleasant morning, Ethel reflected, as the school grew closer, turrets glinting in the early-morning sun, and the vast beech forest beginning to mingle with the dark pines that surrounded the school.

'Nearly there, Druse,' she shouted over her shoulder. 'Druse?'

She turned and saw her friend far behind her, desperately trying to catch up. Ethel could just make out her voice in between gusts of wind.

'Ethel, wait!' she was calling. '*Please* wait! I've found something really interesting!'

Ethel hovered impatiently.

'Come on, Drusilla,' she snapped. 'What have you been *doing* back there? We're going to be *last* at this rate.'

'Sorry, Ethel,' said Drusilla, juddering to an untidy halt. 'I dropped my hat – but while I was down in the forest looking for it I found this, pinned to a tree. Take a look!' She handed Ethel a small, faded poster.

Ethel smoothed out the poster on her lap. 'I don't believe it!' she exclaimed when she saw what was on it. 'Gosh, Druse, what an amazing bit of luck on the first day of term – espccially after what we were talking about!'

'What shall we do with it?' asked Drusilla.

'I think we'd better take it to Miss Cackle,' said Ethel, a horrible smile creeping across her face. 'I mean, it's our *duty* really, isn't it?'

CHAPTER FOUR

I n the playground there was the usual mixture of teachers keeping a beady eye on the arrivals: new pupils anxiously trying to land successfully and old friends joyously reuniting.

'Look, Maud,' said Mildred. 'There's Enid!'

'Hey, you two!' shouted their friend, leaving her broomstick hovering and rushing to greet them with a delighted hug.

'Quick,' said Maud. 'We'd better line up – they're here!'

Miss Hardbroom and Miss Cackle had suddenly appeared, quite literally, in the middle of the playground.

Miss Hardbroom clapped her hands. 'Line up now, girls,' she commanded, already sounding slightly irritated, even though no one had done anything wrong. 'Hurry along. You all know the drill.'

Everyone hastened into line, arranging their assortment of luggage and broomsticks in neat rows beside them.

'Excellent, girls!' Miss Cackle smiled with all the warmth that her terrifying deputy lacked. 'Wonderful to see you all looking so cheerful and rested after your nice long holiday.'

24

'Brains fully re-charged and ready for lots of hard work, I hope!' Miss Hardbroom cut in grimly.

'But of course, Miss Hardbroom,' twittered Miss Cackle. 'Now then, girls, I expect you all want to know about the swimming pool! Well, it was finished just in time for the start of term and is up and running. So I thought, as Mildred's form won the pool for us, that they could have first dip, as it were!'

Mildred's class let out cries of joy, and Mildred and Enid actually jumped up and down, but only for a few seconds as Miss Hardbroom shot them a glance that quenched any high spirits like a water-cannon.

Miss Drill, who was Form Four's teacher, also flashed a look at the girls, but hers was full of pride and happiness.

After everyone had parked their broomsticks in the broom shed, Miss Drill announced that Form Four could collect their swimming costumes and towels, as soon as they'd unpacked, and meet at the new pool in the old Small Playground, a yard that had originally been used for individual broomstick lessons.

'This is just brilliant!' exclaimed Maud as she joined the bustling throng of excited pupils making their way through the maze of corridors.

'It's along here,' said Mildred cheerfully. 'I've had lots of extra lessons there over the years so I remember exactly where it is!'

'I expect you do,' came Ethel's sneering tones. 'Of course, *I've* never been there in my life as I could already fly like a professional by the time I was three years old!'

'You get younger every time you mention your early flying skills,' Maud replied witheringly over her shoulder. 'Sure it wasn't three months?'

'Anyway,' said Enid loyally, 'Mildred's one of our best fliers now, so all those extra lessons must have paid off.'

'True,' agreed Ethel with a wink at Drusilla, 'but only because she found that stupid dog.'

'Oh, do lay off,' said Maud. 'Can't you just be nice for five minutes, Ethel? We've got swimming as our first lesson of term, thanks to Mildred.'

'Yes – and she's as good a pilot as anyone now,' said Enid, '*and* Miss Cackle said she can keep the dog forever so nothing's going to change.'

'I wouldn't be quite so sure of that,' mumbled Ethel to Drusilla, so quietly that no one else heard.

'Here it is!' yelled Mildred from the front of the line. They all stopped to look at the new door with SWIMMING POOL emblazoned across it. Apart from the gold lettering, it was the usual type of sturdy wooden door and, for a brief moment, Mildred wondered if there really was a swimming pool on the other side.

CHAPTER FIVE

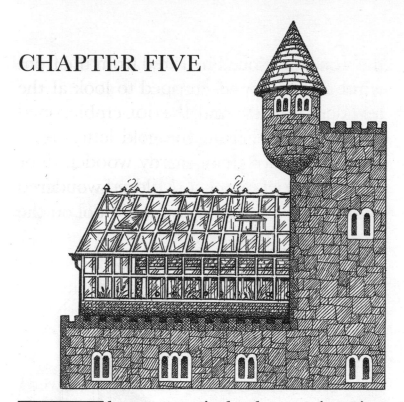

There was indeed a swimming
pool – but it was not quite what
the girls had been expecting.
True, it was a large rectangle
full of water, but the structure surrounding
it was like an enormous old-fashioned
greenhouse, with a huge pitched roof made
entirely of steel struts and glass. Several of
the skylights were propped open to let out

the condensation, but they also let in the wind that whipped constantly around the high castle walls, and the girls shivered as they imagined getting into their costumes.

Neat rows of changing rooms ran along one side of the pool, but there were huge gaps at the top and bottom of the doors, so there would be no escape from the cold. To make matters worse, the water was so crammed with bulrushes and plants that no one could quite imagine how they would actually get in and attempt any sort of swimming. Far from the turquoise tiles of Maud's imagination, the water was dark and sinister; you couldn't see the bottom and it looked as though *things* might be lurking.

Miss Hardbroom and Miss Drill stood at the far end of the pool, watching as Form Four shuffled through the door, keeping close together like a huddle of penguins contemplating a snowstorm.

'This is an ecological pool,' explained Miss Hardbroom. 'Self-cleaning, with

carefully chosen plants, so no need for chlorine or any polluting chemicals, which means it's full of fascinating pondlife – perfect for your natural history studies, which you can get on with while you're taking exercise. There you are, girls, two lessons together – an excellent use of time management and brain power! Any questions before you all get "stuck in", as they say nowadays?'

The girls saw the flicker of amusement flitting momentarily across Miss Hardbroom's stern features as she noted the appalled expressions on their faces.

'What *sort* of pondlife is in the pool, Miss Hardbroom?' asked Mildred nervously.

'Many wonderful creatures,' replied Miss Hardbroom. 'There are water snails to assist with the cleaning process; all sorts of flying insects, which will find their way in and out of the skylights; frogs, of course; and dragonflies. Their underwater larvae have an extraordinary hinged lower lip,

which they use to *grab* their prey and deliver
it into their crushing mandibles –'

'What are mandibles?' whispered Enid
to Mildred.

'Look it up later, Enid,' Miss Hardbroom
interjected seamlessly. 'Plus lots of healthy
silt at the bottom to assist with frogspawn
and other developing larvae and eggs.'

The girls remained in their huddle, transfixed with horror at the thought of plunging into the uninviting brown cloudy water. They were also wondering how Miss Hardbroom had managed to hear Enid's whisper from ten metres away. Although they had been at the school for four years now, it never failed to surprise them when Miss Hardbroom seemed to pick up everything they said, even if she wasn't actually in the room. Sometimes she seemed to know what they were thinking, which made life extremely nerve-racking for Mildred, who was often hatching a plan that she would rather keep secret.

CHAPTER SIX

The next morning, Mildred and Maud were perched on chairs outside Miss Cackle's study. During breakfast one of the first-years had been sent to find Mildred with a message that Miss Cackle wanted to see her. Mildred was convinced that she must be in some sort of trouble, so Maud was waiting with her until she went in.

'Don't worry, Mil,' soothed Maud, patting her friend's arm. 'You know that you haven't put a foot wrong –'

'Yet,' added Mildred gloomily.

'We only arrived yesterday!' laughed Maud. 'She's probably just going to ask you to run some errand, or maybe she's going to give you a special award for winning the pool in the first place.'

'Or perhaps she's going to ask me to be Head Girl next year!' said Mildred with a smile. 'We could always look on the bright side!'

'ENTER!' called Miss Cackle's voice.

Mildred and Maud leapt to their feet.

'I'll be here when you come out,' said Maud, grabbing Mildred for one last hug.

Mildred found herself sitting across the desk from Miss Cackle and Miss Hardbroom.

'Good morning, Mildred, my dear,' said Miss Cackle in a kind voice.

'Good morning, Miss Cackle,' answered Mildred. 'Good morning, Miss Hardbroom.'

'And good morning to you too, Mildred,' replied Miss Hardbroom, sounding slightly friendly.

Mildred relaxed. It was going to be all right after all.

'Well now,' continued Miss Cackle, 'I expect you must be wondering why I sent for you.'

'I *was*, rather,' replied Mildred humbly.

'Let's not beat about the bush, Miss Cackle,' said Miss Hardbroom.

'Quite right, Miss Hardbroom,' agreed

Miss Cackle. 'Here, Mildred – we think you should take a look at this.'

She pushed a tattered piece of paper across the desk, and Mildred could see at once that it was a LOST DOG poster. The poster was faded, but clear enough to show a ringmaster in a top hat, a lady on a trapeze, a seal and a Shetland pony. Sitting on the back of the pony was a small dog.

'It's Star!' gasped Mildred.

'Yes,' said Miss Cackle. 'I'm afraid it is. Drusilla found this poster in the forest yesterday and Ethel thought I ought to see it. Well, we always did wonder where he'd come from, didn't we?'

'And now we know,' said Miss Hardbroom.

'But it's a circus,' said Mildred, 'so it must have moved on by now. Look, the poster is really faded so it's been there for ages. They're probably hundreds of miles away –' She stopped abruptly, remembering the circus tent she had flown over at Greater Bustling, which was only twenty miles from the school. 'He's so happy with me now,' she blurted out, '*and* he helps me to fly. I can't give him back – *please*, Miss Cackle, can we just not tell anyone? They've probably got another dog by now anyway, *please!*'

She began to cry, huge tears sliding down her face, while trying hard to control herself, as she could see from Miss Hardbroom's pursed lips that getting hysterical wouldn't help.

'This *is* a very difficult situation, Mildred,' said Miss Hardbroom, sounding faintly sympathetic, which gave Mildred a glimmer of hope, 'and we *can* see your point of view, but if the dog actually belongs to –' she glanced at the poster with distaste before continuing – '*Brilliantine's Amazing Travelling Circus*, we ought at least to find out if they want him back. No wonder he had such a fine sense of balance – just look at him on the back of that pony.'

Mildred gazed at both teachers, utter desperation written across her face, hoping she could will them into changing their minds.

'That's everything we know so far,' said Miss Cackle. 'Don't look so tragic, my dear. Perhaps we won't be able to find the circus after all – then you'll be able to keep the little acrobat, and at least we will know that we've tried to do the right thing.'

'That will be all for the present, Mildred,' said Miss Hardbroom, sensing that the kindly headmistress could prattle on for another ten minutes, eating into her potions time with the Year Threes.

Mildred dragged herself out of the room, feeling as if a lead-lined cloak had been dropped over her shoulders.

'What on earth has happened, Millie?' asked Maud as Mildred fell sobbing into her arms.

'It's Star,' said Mildred. 'He was lost from a circus and they're trying to find it and give him back – and it's all Ethel's fault! Why does she always have to ruin everything for me?'

CHAPTER SEVEN

Mildred sat hunched on her bed, wearing Tabby round her neck and clasping Star tightly in her arms. He was so delighted to have Mildred's company mid-morning that he didn't notice her tears falling on to his fur. It was break-time and the three friends had sneaked up to Mildred's room to make a plan to keep him.

'It's probably all going to be a storm in a teacup,' said Maud. 'I'm sure they'll never be able to find the circus anyway.'

'Oh, yes they will,' muttered Mildred. 'Ethel's probably hiring a detective right now.'

'Well, I think Maud's right,' said Enid. 'H.B. and Miss Cackle are *far* too busy bossing us all around to waste time zooming up and down the country looking for a travelling circus.'

'The thing is,' said Mildred, 'it *hasn't* travelled that far. I saw the tent on the edge of Greater Bustling as I flew into school yesterday, and that's only twenty miles away.'

'Are you sure it's the same one?' asked Enid hopefully. 'Perhaps it was just a marquee – you know, like the ones people use for parties?'

Mildred shook her head. 'No,' she replied gloomily. 'It was definitely a big striped circus tent and, now I come to think of it,

Star hid behind me when he saw it as we were flying over. You see, he doesn't want to go back, and it would be cruel to make him.'

'I think we'd do best to keep quiet about it,' said Maud, 'and, whatever you do, don't say anything to Ethel.'

'Why not?' asked Mildred. 'I was going to tell her exactly what I think of her.'

'Well,' said Maud wisely, 'if Miss Cackle and H.B. *don't* make a huge effort to find the circus, enough time might pass so that they genuinely give up and Star will be safe with you. If you start a row with Ethel, it will fire her up to find the circus, just to make things worse for you.'

'Thanks, Maudie,' said Mildred, smiling gratefully at her friend. 'You always know what to do.'

CHAPTER EIGHT

There were so many things to occupy every waking moment that Year Four were often falling asleep over their dinner by the end of each day. Mildred actually began to forget about the circus for most of the time, as they concentrated on swimming sessions twice a week, double lessons of chanting and broomstick aerobatics, while grappling with several complicated new spells.

One of their favourites was a spell to turn any sort of brush into a flying object. This was a Privilege Spell given to the Form Four pupils in preparation for their final year. Until now, the pupils had used broomsticks, which were already primed to fly, so it was most exciting to enchant flying objects of their choice.

It took two days of learning chants and working out sizing, similar to the animal-speaking spell that Mildred had invented, for which you had to get the measurements correct before the spell would work.

Once they'd finally mastered the spell, Mildred, Maud and Enid had great fun in Mildred's room during break-time, enchanting a motley selection of anything with bristles attached, just for fun. Maud persuaded a snail to perch on a toothbrush and kept the brush very steady while it flew sedately across the room. The snail didn't seem to mind at all and carried on gliding up the plastic handle without a care in the world.

Enid had chosen a dustpan and brush, and she was delighted when they both took off together, as she had cast the spell when the brush was resting inside the dustpan. The brush chased the pan around the room, skimming the ceiling, and even tried to sweep the bats off the picture rail, causing great upset as they were trying to have their daytime sleep. The brush seemed to have a life of its own, and in the end Enid had to rugby-tackle it, while Maud grabbed the dustpan and held on to it tightly until it had calmed down.

Mildred chose a hairbrush, with Enid's hamster Nibbles (Enid had been hiding him in her room) balanced on top. She did her best to keep the hairbrush level, but the hamster hated it and clung on with his eyes shut, looking as if he had taken lessons from Tabby.

'Take him off, Millie!' said Enid, laughing. 'He really hates it. Give him to me and I'll put him back in my room.'

Mildred and Maud tidied away their flying implements and curled up on the bed for a chat. There were no chairs in their cramped rooms, so it was either the bed or the floor.

'It's gone very quiet on the circus-finding front,' confided Mildred. 'Nobody's mentioned it again so maybe they've given up . . .'

'Given up what?' asked Enid, returning from her room, where she had put the traumatized Nibbles back under her bed.

'Mildred was just saying maybe H.B. and Miss Cackle have given up trying to find the circus,' said Maud, 'so it's looking hopeful for Star.'

'It *does* seem hopeful,' agreed Enid. 'The poster was found in the beech forest just below our mountain, so the circus must have been near here and then moved on in the opposite direction until it got to Greater Bustling. Mildred saw it there on her way to school, so let's just hope it's gone on another twenty miles by now.'

'Or maybe sixty!' said Maud.

Mildred laughed. 'Why stop at sixty?

Let's make it three hundred miles and falling into the sea!'

Unfortunately, Drusilla was outside the door to Mildred's room, listening to this conversation. She had been feeling guilty about finding the poster and giving it to Ethel, especially as everyone now knew that Mildred was upset, which had made Drusilla unpopular with the rest of the class. As usual, Ethel had somehow managed to hide the fact that she was the one who had taken the poster to Miss Cackle.

Ethel was such a difficult person to be best friends with, reflected Drusilla, and she was very grumpy at the moment, as nothing had come of her attempt to sabotage Mildred's flying skills by getting rid of Star.

Drusilla had been on the verge of apologizing to Mildred for giving the poster to Ethel in the first place, but, as she pressed her ear to the door and heard the vital piece

50

of information about the whereabouts of the circus, the weak side of her nature overrode the impulse to do the right thing.

She knew that it would please Ethel to get rid of Mildred's dog, and Drusilla found herself imagining how nice her difficult friend would be – at least, for a day or two.

She couldn't resist it and, turning away from the door, she went to find Ethel.

CHAPTER NINE

Year Four were out in the playground having a flying lesson with Miss Drill. They had been allowed to try out their brush-enchantment spells, and everyone (even Mildred) had got their calculations spot on.

The playground was full of gleeful girls casting spells and trundling along on an assortment of normal household brooms and yard-brooms. Enid had managed to find a feather duster with a long handle and was hunched over with her feet almost touching the ground. Her cat was hanging on while trying to catch the feathers, and the girls were helpless with laughter, watching as they bobbed along. Even Miss Drill couldn't resist smiling.

'*Very* funny, Enid,' she said, trying (and failing) to look stern. 'But I think a feather duster isn't *quite* the thing, is it? Off you hop and find something else. There are still a few household brooms in the corner to choose from.'

The door from the school opened and an anxious-looking First Year came out and handed a note to Miss Drill. The girl was so nervous that she actually curtsied, and the pupils all burst out laughing.

'Thank you, Dulcie,' said Miss Drill. 'No need to curtsy, dear – I'm not the queen. That will be all now. Off you go.'

Dulcie couldn't stop herself curtsying again, amid gales of laughter.

Miss Drill read the contents of the note. 'Now then,' she said, 'I need Mildred Hubble for a moment. Miss Cackle and Miss Hardbroom want to see you in the headmistress's study immediately. Don't forget to de-activate your yard-broom before you go, otherwise anyone could make it fly – Oh, and it's all right to take Star with you. It says so in the note.'

'Thank you, Miss Drill,' replied Mildred, jumping off the broom and de-activating it before putting it back on the pile.

'I wonder what they want,' whispered Maud to Enid.

'No idea,' said Enid, who was measuring Mildred's yard-broom to try to work out the size part of the spell. 'But I'm sure we'll soon find out.'

CHAPTER TEN

As they approached Miss Cackle's study, Star had begun sniffing the ground like a Bloodhound until he arrived at the gap beneath the door. He took one last sniff, jerked the lead out of Mildred's hand and trotted off determinedly down the corridor.

'Star!' called Mildred. 'Come back here!' But, to her great surprise, he took no notice at all and disappeared round the corner.

'ENTER!' called Miss Hardbroom's voice, sounding as sharp and unwelcoming as ever, leaving Mildred no choice but to go in without him.

There, inside the headmistress's study, was Mildred's worst nightmare come true. Miss Cackle was busy handing cups of tea to a man and a woman who were dressed in rather gaudy clothes – although most people looked gaudy compared to the staff and girls at Miss Cackle's Academy.

The woman was wearing a pink hat with a flower on it and a striped poncho, and the man had a bushy moustache and a bright red jacket. Even without the ringmaster's outfit and the woman's trapeze costume from the poster, Mildred knew exactly who they were.

'Ah, Mildred,' said Miss Cackle. 'Come and sit down. Mr and Mrs Brilliantine, this is Mildred Hubble, who found your lost dog and has been taking excellent care of him for you. Mildred, this is Mr and Mrs Brilliantine, owners of the circus that we've been attempting to find, as you know.'

'Where *is* the dog, Mildred?' asked Miss Hardbroom.

'He ran off down the corridor,' replied Mildred. 'Shall I go and find him?'

'In a moment, my dear,' said Miss Cackle in her warmest voice. 'I'm sure he won't have gone far – would you like a macaroon?'

'No thank you, Miss Cackle,' said Mildred in a very small voice.

'While you all chat,' said Miss Hardbroom, 'I'll go and check the corridor to Mildred's room; he's probably up there somewhere.'

Mr and Mrs Brilliantine were surprisingly nice and thoughtful. Miss Cackle had already explained to them how attached Mildred and the dog had become – Mildred had perked up on hearing this – but her hopes were dashed when Miss Cackle told them that Mildred had always known he would have to go back to the circus if it was found.

Mrs Brilliantine leaned forward and patted Mildred's hand.

'I can see how upset you must feel about

this, my dear,' she said kindly, 'but we have so missed him at our little circus. It really is very small and he was always the best thing in it. He fell out of the back of his crate while we were on the move and got hopelessly lost.'

'I'm not going to lie to you,' said Mr Brilliantine. 'It wasn't an easy life for him in the circus. Between shows, he was in his crate most of the time, but he got plenty of food and the audience loved him.'

'Audiences are hard to come by these days,' said Mrs Brilliantine, 'so we really would like him back, if you could bear to part with him.'

Hope flared in Mildred's heart.

'Well, I'd rather *not* –' she began.

'Of course she can,' said Miss Cackle. 'He wasn't hers in the first place – was he, Mildred? Just on loan – Ah, there he is now.'

They heard Star before the door opened, and Miss Hardbroom came in holding him in a vice-like grip as he yelped and struggled.

'BINKY!' exclaimed Mrs Brilliantine. 'Come to Mummy!'

'That's him all right!' agreed Mr Brilliantine. 'Full of beans, as ever. Come here, old chap.'

Miss Hardbroom put the dog down on the floor and dragged him, all four feet splayed, past Mildred to his rightful owners. He gave a despairing glance at Mildred, who realized that there was nothing she could do to stop it. He would have to be returned to these people whether she liked it or not.

Mildred stood up and took his lead. 'Come on now Star – I mean Binky,' she said, kneeling down and trying to keep the quaver out of her voice. 'It's time to go home. We've had such fun, haven't we? I won't forget you.'

She looked up at Miss Cackle. 'Can I visit sometimes, once he's settled back in?'

'I *don't* think so, Mildred,' said Miss Hardbroom before the Brilliantines could respond. 'That would just confuse him – and you. Best to make a clean break, don't you agree, Miss Cackle?'

'I rather think Miss Hardbroom is right, Mildred,' said the headmistress.

As Mildred handed the lead to Mrs Brilliantine, Star sat down suddenly and drooped, as if he had completely given up. He wouldn't look at Mildred and kept his head lowered, still as a mouse with an owl hovering overhead.

Mildred thought she might explode trying to keep the tears at bay.

Meanwhile, Mr Brilliantine had been peering around the room, taking in the strange outfits worn by Miss Cackle and Miss Hardbroom.

'What sort of school *is* this?' he asked rather suddenly.

'Difficult to describe really,' replied Miss Cackle with a smile.

'It's very old-fashioned,' said Miss Hardbroom crisply. 'Old-style values and extremely hard-working.'

'But lots of fun too,' added Miss Cackle. 'A *magic* sort of school, you might say! Off you go now, Mildred – you've done very well. I'm sure the dog will be fine once he's settled back into his old home.'

'Yes, Miss Cackle; thank you, Miss Cackle,' said Mildred, and she left the room without looking back even once, as she was kind enough not to make things worse for the little dog when there really was nothing she could do to stop them taking him away.

Mildred went straight to her room, and that's where Maud and Enid found her, under the covers with Tabby, sobbing her heart out.

'What is it, Mil?' exclaimed Maud, perching on the edge of the bed, trying to get an arm round her.

'It's Star,' wept Mildred, sitting up with Tabby still clutched tightly to her chest. 'He's gone. The circus people came to take him away and there was nothing I could do to stop them. I couldn't even try, so I just had to give him back.'

She dissolved into huge, shuddering tears, and Maud and Enid cuddled up on either side of her, like bookends.

'What were they like?' asked Enid. 'Were they horrible? Do you think that's why he ran away?'

'He didn't run away,' said Mildred between sobs. 'He fell out of his crate while they were travelling – and he's not called Star; his real name is Binky. I saw the picture of him on the circus poster. He was sitting on a pony, and there was a seal in the background. It was definitely him – he really *is* their dog. I just wish they weren't going to keep him in a crate, now that he's got used to being with me all the time. I'm going to miss him so much.'

'Well,' said Enid, 'there's no use getting in a state about it if there's nothing to be done.'

'I suppose that's true,' said Maud, 'and it's lunch-break now and we've got double chanting afterwards, and Miss Bat's got a test ready, so you'll just have to get up and get on with it, Millie.'

'I know you're right,' said Mildred, climbing out of bed, wiping her eyes and gently putting Tabby on the pillow, 'and I *know* I can't, but I *so* wish I could do something to get him back.'

CHAPTER ELEVEN

After double chanting, which had an extremely complicated rhythm that was virtually impossible to get right, Mildred sneaked into the playground with Tabby to reintroduce him to flying on a broomstick. Poor Tabby thought that Mildred was taking him for a little carry around the school, and nearly fainted with shock when she commanded the broomstick to hover and proceeded to put him on the back. As ever, he sat frozen in terror, then suddenly took a flying leap on to the wall. Mildred held out her arms to him, but he skittered along the top as fast as he could and jumped through a window, disappearing out of sight.

'*Oh* dear, Mildred,' said a voice behind her. 'Having cat trouble again?'

It was Ethel, with Drusilla beside her as usual. 'So where's the circus dog?' she continued. 'How come poor old Stripey's back on the broom – or *not*, as the case may be?'

'You *know* about this, don't you?' said Mildred, glaring at Ethel. 'That's why you've come to gloat!'

Ethel was wearing her you'll-never-find-out expression, but Drusilla couldn't look Mildred in the eye and was actually blushing.

'*You* know about it too, don't you, Drusilla?' challenged Mildred, her voice rising with anger and tears. 'Well, I hope you're both really pleased with yourselves.'

'Poor old Mildred,' sneered Ethel as Mildred grabbed her broomstick and marched out of the playground.

'Well, at least we'll see how good she really is at flying, now that she's back with her stupid cat,' said Drusilla.

'Yes,' agreed Ethel. 'Anyway, she was cheating, having a circus dog as her broom-companion. Everything's back to normal now: Mildred Hubble the worst witch in the school, just as it should be.'

CHAPTER TWELVE

Things had been going so smoothly for Mildred, who had been really enjoying herself, confident at last that she could hold her head up among her classmates. Without Star she had taken an instant nosedive and found herself right back at square one.

'It was just like surfing,' she explained to Maud and Enid when they were sitting in the broom shed, taking shelter during a rainy lunch-break. 'You know, zipping along on the top of a wave, having a brilliant time, taking everything for granted, and then – BANG! – you hit a rock and everything just falls to pieces.'

'Not *everything*,' said Enid.

'Well, it *feels* like everything,' said Mildred gloomily. 'I can't tell you how nice it was to finally be good at flying – and the more praise I got from the teachers, the better I got at everything else. It encouraged me to try harder – but it wasn't really *me*, was it? It was Star who was brilliant at flying, and he sort of admired me – you know what dogs are like – so *I* had to keep up with *him*, not the other way round. Now that I'm back with Tabby, everyone can see I'm like a beginner, as Ethel never stops pointing out. She's right really. I *am* a hopeless case – everything

I do always *does* go wrong in the end.'

'Well, it *sort* of does,' said Maud, 'but then it sort of doesn't, because usually, when it's gone disastrously wrong, something happens to save the day – like when you won the swimming-pool competition –'

'And rescuing Mr Rowan Webb,' said Enid.

'*And* finding the treasure on our school holiday after Miss Hardbroom was knocked out in the boat,' said Maud. 'That looked fairly hopeless at the time, didn't it? Do you know what I think, Millie?' she continued cheerfully. 'I think you've got a magic pixie keeping an eye on you. Something will *happen* to get things back on an even keel for you. It always has done before, so I don't see why it won't this time.'

'It's logical, my dear,' said Enid kindly, doing a very good impersonation of Miss Cackle. 'We just have to wait patiently and everything will turn out fine – meanwhile, let's all have a biscuit!'

Mildred couldn't help smiling at her friends, who were always on hand to cheer her up.

'I don't know what I'd do without you two,' she said as they all huddled up and leaned against each other affectionately. 'Although I honestly can't see how I can get myself out of this particular nosedive.'

'I just *told* you,' said Maud. 'You don't have to do anything at all except wait and see.'

CHAPTER THIRTEEN

Mildred *did* try to heed Maud's advice and wait patiently for things to start looking up, but in reality they seemed to be going from bad to worse.

For a start, after several months off from flying, Tabby couldn't cope at all. Mildred spent most of her time hauling him out from under her bed or pursuing him down the corridors, which was most embarrassing, especially when Ethel was watching. Sadly, it didn't take long before Mildred found it impossible to concentrate on anything, and she was soon back at the bottom of the class in all subjects.

One night she had a horrible dream about Star. He often featured in her dreams (usually happy ones, although these made her sad when she woke up and found they weren't true), but this one was a nightmare. In the dream, Star was locked up in a crate, with a thunderstorm raging outside, and she was flying around, dodging lightning bolts while trying to get him out.

Mildred woke with a jolt. She was partly glad that it had only been a dream, but she also had an unsettled feeling that the little dog might have been trying to send her a telepathic message. The dream had seemed so *real*.

It was just getting light. Outside the window a cloudless, windless day was beckoning. Someone had mentioned to Mildred that the circus was now pitched at Queen's Warren – a large market town fifteen miles on from Greater Bustling. She could easily get there and back in time for the rising bell – just to make sure that Star had settled into his old routine and was reasonably happy.

However, she hadn't thought about what she would actually *do* if he wasn't.

'Where on earth are you going, Mildred?' whispered Maud, who had opened her door to let her cat in and found Mildred creeping down the shadowy corridor. 'You're not running away, are you?' she asked. 'Just as well I got up early to revise for H.B.'s ultra-important potions' test. You do realize it's our first lesson, don't you?'

Another door creaked open and Enid peered out, blinking at Maud and Mildred, who had stopped in her doorway.

'What's going on?' she asked in a just-woken-up, croaky voice.

'Mildred's obviously *up* to something,' whispered Maud.

'Well, you'd better both come in here,' whispered Enid, 'or we'll wake the whole corridor.'

Mildred and Maud stepped into Enid's room and closed the door.

'Look,' said Mildred. 'I can't stop. I'm just nipping to Queen's Warren to make sure Star's all right. I had a horrible dream about him and I want to check that he's OK. I'm not going to steal him or anything – and I'll be back before the rising bell.'

'You're just *nipping* to Queen's Warren!' exclaimed Maud. 'You've never even been there, Mildred! You'll get lost, and H.B. will go bonkers when she finds out.'

Enid grabbed her cardigan and started putting it on over her pyjamas.

'Come on, Maud,' she said as she pulled on her cloak. 'We'll have to go with her. I've got a bat-nav so we won't get lost *and* we'll get there much, much faster.'

'What's a *bat-nav*?' asked Mildred and Maud, intrigued.

'It's a specially trained long-eared bat,' explained Enid. 'You say the name of a town or village into a special device clipped to its ear, which translates it into sonar squeaks, and the bat just takes you there like magic.'

'Wow!' exclaimed Maud. 'Are they actually allowed?'

'Course they aren't,' said Enid, 'but *I* won't tell if *you* won't.'

'Are you coming then, Maud?' asked Mildred.

Maud hesitated. She most definitely *didn't* want to set out on such a perilous journey, abandoning her early-morning revision. On the other hand she didn't want to abandon her best friend either, especially now that Enid was definitely going with her.

'Hang on,' said Maud. 'I'll get my cloak and hat and meet you at the broom shed.'

The bat-nav halved the journey time. Maud and Mildred were fascinated as the little brown bat danced along ahead of them, leading the way.

'Won't he want to go to sleep soon?' asked Mildred. 'The sun's getting bright.'

'Nope,' said Enid. 'They're specially trained to fly whenever you give them instructions, whatever hour of the day. Brilliant, isn't it? Look, there's the circus!'

The clock tower in the town square at Queen's Warren showed six o'clock as they glided past it to the outskirts of the town, where they could clearly see the red-and-white-striped Big Top, plus a large caravan, several cage-like metal crates and containers, and two flatbed trucks.

A small, fat pony with an overgrown mane and tail was tethered in the field next to the crates. He shook the hair from his eyes and looked up curiously as the three witches skimmed silently over him, landing out of sight behind the Big Top.

The girls parked their broomsticks with their hats perched on top, and Enid settled the bat-nav with a stick wedged under the brim of her hat so that he could hang upside down and have a rest.

Star was in one of the crates and he began barking wildly when he saw Mildred creeping past.

'He's in here,' gasped Mildred, thrilled to find him so easily. 'Stop it, boy. Shh! It's all right; it's all right.'

But it clearly wasn't all right. The crate was cramped and dark with its heavy canvas cover, and it was more than Mildred could bear, seeing him imprisoned, frenziedly barking and trying to lick her hands through the bars.

'I *knew* this wasn't a good idea,' muttered Maud.

'OK,' said Enid, trying to sound jaunty. 'It's not the Ritz, but you knew he was going to be kept in a crate between shows. He's fine. Come on – let's go before he wakes everyone up.'

But it was too late. The caravan door crashed open, and there was Mr Brilliantine, wrapped in a maroon silk dressing gown.

'What are you up to?' he thundered. 'Hilda!' he called behind him. 'We seem to have visitors.'

CHAPTER FOURTEEN

Ever the peacemaker, Maud rushed forward.

'We're so sorry to have woken you,' she said politely. 'We've come from Miss Cackle's Academy. It's just that Mildred's been so unhappy without Star – I mean, Binky – that she wanted a quick cuddle before school! We really didn't mean to wake you – so we'll be off now. Come on, Mildred!' she said, grabbing Mildred by the arm.

Enid grabbed her other arm and they yanked her away from the crate. Mrs Brilliantine had now come out on to the

caravan doorstep, wearing a green satin dressing gown with an orange feather collar, covered in bright pink embroidered flamingos.

'I recognize you,' she said, peering at Mildred. 'You're the girl who looked after our Binky when he was lost. How did you *get* here?' she asked, suddenly noticing their assortment of cloaks and pyjamas.

'Well – um – er . . .' said Mildred. 'We –'

'Got a lift,' announced Enid.

'From my aunt!' added Maud. 'She was just passing so she said she'd drop us here.'

'At six o'clock in the morning?' queried Mr Brilliantine. 'Where on earth was she going at such a time?'

84

'To – um – er – the hairdresser's!'
announced Mildred desperately.

'She works from home – the hairdresser, that is,' continued Enid, noting
the astonished look on Mr and Mrs
Brilliantine's faces.

'She starts at the crack of dawn,'
explained Mildred, 'so she can fit everyone
in – she's very popular. People have to make
appointments months ahead.'

'Well, your aunt obviously isn't back yet,'
said Mrs Brilliantine.

'That's because she's having a perm,'
Mildred announced wildly. 'They take
hours, so she'll be ages yet.'

'Well, you'd better join us for breakfast
then,' said Mrs Brilliantine in a kindly voice.

'She's got very long hair!' Mildred burbled on, beginning to believe that Maud really did have a long-haired aunt who was taking ages at a real hairdresser's.

'I'm sure she does,' said Mr Brilliantine distractedly. 'Hilda, could you let Binky out of his crate before he does himself an injury? I'll go and put the kettle on.'

The three witches couldn't believe their luck when Mr Brilliantine went off to make them tea and toast, while Mrs Brilliantine unlocked Binky/Star's crate. He hurtled out, straight into Mildred's arms, knocking her over on to the grass. Maud and Enid joined in, rolling about and patting him while he tried to wash all three of them at once.

CHAPTER FIFTEEN

While they were waiting for their breakfast, Mrs Brilliantine took them to look round the Big Top. It was small and old-fashioned, exactly like a circus you might see in a picture book, with a trapeze hanging from the centre, and three rows of benches surrounding a ring with a sawdust floor.

'Would you like to meet Spotty, our seal?' asked Mrs Brilliantine, who was being so friendly that the girls were beginning to enjoy themselves.

The seal was in a large crate with a tiny

pool at one end. She was sitting in the murky
water, looking sad, and the girls were upset
to see her in such an unappealing space.

'She doesn't look very happy,' ventured
Mildred, trying not to sound disapproving
in case Mrs Brilliantine stopped being nice
to them.

'She's *never* very happy,' said Mrs
Brilliantine. 'I don't know why we keep
her, really. We found her on a beach and
have tried everything to train her, but she's
useless – can't even balance a ball on her
nose.'

'The pony's not much better,' complained Mr Brilliantine, as he came to find them, bringing an inviting breakfast tray and setting it down on an upturned packing case. 'He trots around the ring, and that's *it* as far as he's concerned! It's our Binky who is the star of the show with all his jumping and twirling, and of course the kids love him because he's so cute.'

'They like your clown act too,' said Mrs Brilliantine encouragingly.

'And you too, my dear,' said Mr Brilliantine fondly. 'So graceful on the flying trapeze.'

Gloom settled on the three friends as they sat around the packing case munching their toast. Time was getting on, and any minute now Star would have to go back into his crate with a broken heart, and Mildred would have to brace herself to say goodbye all over again.

Miss Hardbroom had been right. Mildred had only made things worse for both of them. And now that she knew about Spotty the sad seal, Mildred would worry about her too. She found herself wishing that she had never come.

'Well, girls,' said Mrs Brilliantine as they made their way back to the caravan, 'will you be all right waiting for your aunt out here while we get ourselves ready for the day?'

She picked up Star in a firm hold and carried him, yelping, back to his crate.

'Thank you for our breakfast,' said Mildred, managing not to cry. 'It was very kind of you to let me see him again.'

'That's all right,' said Mrs Brilliantine. 'I can tell that you and Binky have a real bond. To be honest, you could take all three animals home with you if there was something to replace them, but there isn't, so our little star attraction will have to stay.'

As soon as the caravan door closed, Enid and Maud grabbed Mildred and frog-marched her round the back of the

Big Top to their broomsticks and hats. The bat-nav was so deeply asleep that he had to be prodded awake before Enid could re-program him.

'Are you feeling all right, Mildred?' asked Maud, noting her miserable expression as they rose vertically and sped away.

'Not really,' said Mildred. 'I just *hate* to see unhappy animals, that's all. It's such a waste of Star, leaving him in a crate all day, and Spotty wasn't having a great time either – even the pony looked fed up.'

Mildred glanced back wistfully at the striped tent, which was already a tiny speck behind them. 'I so wish there was something we could do,' she said.

'Well, there isn't,' said Maud firmly. 'And right now we'd better follow that bat and get home before the rising bell.'

CHAPTER SIXTEEN

'If only I could *ask* the animals if they were all right,' said Mildred fretfully to Maud a few days later when they were sitting in the playground. 'I mean, it looks awful to *us*, the way they live, but *they* might not mind as much as we would.'

'Actually,' said Maud, 'you *could* ask them, if you use that speaking spell you invented last year – then they could tell you what it's really like, being in the circus day in, day out.'

'What a brilliant idea, Maudie!' said Mildred. 'I'll borrow Enid's bat-nav and sneak back tomorrow morning before the circus moves on. I know where Star's crate is now, so I'll tell him to be quiet as soon as I arrive. He's really good at keeping quiet after hiding in my room when I found him. And even if he does wake the Brilliantines up, I'll just say I'm visiting again – they didn't seem to mind last time!'

Maud was only too happy that Mildred wanted to go on her own as she was still hoping for the First Prize in Team Spirit and did not want to spoil her chances.

'Well, if you're sure,' she said. 'Just be careful to leave early – Enid and I will think up an excuse if you're late coming back.'

'Thank goodness it's summer,' thought Mildred as she hovered over the school gates the next morning. The sun was just rising into another perfect day, and Mildred

could see for miles ahead. She had borrowed
Enid's bat-nav, who was flittering along in
front of her.

When she was up early on her broom,
Mildred often noticed unusual wildlife, and
on this particular morning she suddenly
found herself in the middle of a cloud of
skylarks. She watched entranced as they

twirled up and down like tiny helicopters,
singing their exquisite 'Good morning' to
the world. No need for a speaking spell
to understand what these exuberant little

birds were telling her: 'Hello, world! Such a beautiful day – so nice to be up and about before anyone else!'

She touched down beside the Big Top in record time. It was only five thirty and the blinds were still tightly drawn in the caravan. She parked her broomstick and the bat-nav, and crept silently through the damp grass to the front of Star's crate. Mercifully, he was fast asleep, so she sat and watched him fondly for a minute or two.

'Star,' she whispered. 'Wake up, and no barking.'

He had been dreaming that he was curled up under Mildred's bed with Tabby, so he was overjoyed to find that she was really

there. He managed to restrain himself from barking, and Mildred unbolted the crate and let him out for a silent cuddle that went on for ages. At last she put him down, with a finger to her lips, then she untethered the pony and led him round to the seal's crate.

Mildred had brought a tape measure with her so that she could measure the animals to work out the precise formula for the speaking spell. The measurements had to be perfect or the spell wouldn't work.

'Right then, Star,' she said. 'You first.'

CHAPTER SEVENTEEN

'**D**id I get it right?' asked Mildred. 'Can you speak?'

'You did!' woofed Star. 'I can.'

'Quietly,' she whispered. 'Not a word – don't say anything just for one moment while I magic the others.'

The pony was very good about being measured, as he often had a saddle and reins put on and was used to standing still, but the seal was more tricky. She wasn't keen at all and flumped off into the pool the minute the door was unbolted. Mildred had to crawl in to get the tape measure around her. The crate was slimy and smelled of old fish, so it was not very nice for Mildred, inching her way along on her hands and knees to the pool, where the nervous seal was pressed against the bars. Then she had to wriggle out backwards, feeling slightly sick, so that she could work out the sizes for each animal's spell.

Both spells worked, and all three animals began talking excitedly at once – Mildred could barely hear what they were saying!

'Shh!' she commanded in a loud whisper. 'One at a time, please, and keep your voices down – Spotty,' she said, pointing at the seal, 'you first.'

The seal shuffled forward importantly.

'My name isn't Spotty,' she said in a soft, gentle voice, almost as if she was singing. 'It's really Selkie, after the creature in the myth – you know, the one that's half seal, half human – and I'm not a performing seal at all. I was lost on the beach and the Brilliantines found me at a place called Grim Cove. There's a colony of us there, and I so want to go back and join my family. Common Seals don't *do* tricks – well, we can do one: it's pretending to be a banana. Look, I'll do it now if you like – all Common Seals can do it naturally,' she said proudly.

Mildred had to stop herself laughing as Selkie curved her body and flippers into a perfect banana shape.

'That's truly wonderful,' said Mildred

with a smile. 'And I *know* Grim Cove – a friend of mine owns a castle there.'

'You *know* where it is?' gasped Selkie. 'Can you take me back there? I hate it here – I'm just no good at *anything*, and I can never seem to please them, whatever I do.'

'I know how you feel about *that*,' agreed Mildred earnestly. Next, she turned to the pony. 'What about you?' she asked. 'Do you like being here?'

'Not much,' he replied in a voice with a whinny, as if he was clearing his throat. 'It's not *that* bad. I mean, I get food and lots of rest, and I don't mind trotting around the ring with Binky on my back –'

'I'm not Binky,' muttered Star crossly. 'My real name is Star. Mildred gave it to me, and I belong to her, not the Brilliantines.' He gave Mildred an adoring look that melted her heart.

'Sorry, Bink– I mean Star –' continued the pony. *I've* got the wrong name too. I was renamed Mr Smartie, but my real name is Merlin, and I used to belong to a darling little girl. Then her parents had to sell me so she could go to boarding school, and the Brilliantines bought me. She was a really nice little girl and she took such care of me – I'd give anything to see her again. Do you think you could help me get out of here? I get so lonely standing in a field all day –'

'And we *all* hate the travelling,' continued Selkie. 'It's really horrible being stuck in a crate, jolting along on the back of a truck.'

Mildred turned to Star. 'How about you?' she asked. 'How do *you* feel about living here?'

'To be truthful,' he said, 'I came here as a puppy, so I didn't mind it too much because I didn't know any other way of life. I quite enjoyed doing my acrobatic acts each evening, though it did get a bit boring being left outside and sleeping so much. Then I fell out of the crate when we were on the move, and you found me, and that was wonderful. But when the Brilliantines took me back, I hated every minute here because I knew what I was missing – it was you! Can I come home with you? *Please?*'

'Can I come too?' asked Merlin. 'I'd work for you. I wouldn't be any trouble!'

'Me too,' said Selkie. 'Don't leave me here. If you could just get me back to Grim Cove, I could sit on the rocks with my family, and go diving into the deep cold water – mmmm!'

'*PLEEEEEEASE!*' they all pleaded at once.

Mildred gazed at the three earnest creatures, staring at her with eyes full of hope and trust, and wondered what on earth she was going to do now.

'You won't just leave us here, will you?' asked Star. 'You won't just fly off and never come back?'

'Of course I won't,' said Mildred firmly, trying to sound like a person in charge. 'I *will* have to go back to school for a week or so while I think up a plan, but I'll definitely be back to collect all of you.'

The three pairs of eyes stared into her very soul.

'I promise on my honour,' she continued. 'Meanwhile, don't say a human-word in front of the Brilliantines. Speaking animals in a circus – just imagine it – they'd *never* let you go! So you must take great care. Quickly now, back into your crates and the field, and I'll get you locked in and tethered. Not for much longer, though – I'll be back. All you have to do is trust me and wait – and no talking!'

CHAPTER EIGHTEEN

Now came the difficult part. Mildred had promised on her honour that she would rescue all three circus animals – but she hadn't the faintest idea how she could possibly achieve that.

'Whatever made you promise to rescue *all* of them?' asked Maud crossly, while she and Enid were helping Mildred with an extra flying lesson for Tabby. 'You won't even be able to rescue *Star* unless the Brilliantines agree. You can't just go charging in there and steal them.' At this point Maud tried (and failed) to grab Tabby, who had suddenly leapt straight up and over the wall, as agile as a squirrel.

Mildred sat down on her hovering broom.

'I don't know why you're sounding so cross,' she muttered. '*You're* not the one who promised. *I'm* the one who has to think up a plan and put it into practice!'

'That's not strictly true,' said Enid. 'If you come up with a workable plan, you're going to need some help transporting three large animals, especially the seal. *I'm* not too worried about getting into trouble, as I'm not trying for an award, but Maudie's set her heart on First Prize for Team Spirit.'

'Well, it *would* be team spirit, helping your friends,' said Mildred.

'It wouldn't be the right *sort* of team spirit, though,' said Maud. 'Leaving school premises without permission, probably using unauthorized spells – we'd all be lucky not to get expelled, let alone win a first prize for anything.'

'Anyway,' said Enid as Tabby reappeared on top of the wall several metres away, yowling miserably. 'You've got to come up with a good plan first.'

'The annoying thing is,' said Mildred, 'the Brilliantines *said* that they'd give us all three animals if someone could come up with a crowd-pulling replacement act. They actually said it to us – don't you remember?' She held her arms out to Tabby, who looked the other way and didn't budge.

'So, we have to think up two plans,' said Enid brightly. 'Plan one: we have to find a great replacement act to offer the Brilliantines. And plan two: what to do with Selkie and Merlin if the Brilliantines let us have them all.'

Mildred had been inching her way along the playground wall and suddenly made a grab for Tabby, who leapt into the air, landed neatly a metre away and disappeared through a convenient window.

'That will be two virtually impossible plans then,' said Maud flatly. 'We'll never manage it.'

'Don't say that,' said Mildred. 'I promised, on my honour, to rescue all three of them, so I have to come up with something. There must be a solution – there *has* to be.'

CHAPTER NINETEEN

Mildred was shaken awake the very next morning by an excited Enid. It was hours before the rising bell, and Mildred had been deeply asleep, dreaming that she was trying to hold on to a slippery and upset Selkie, who was sliding off her broomstick.

'Gosh, Enid,' said Mildred, moving Tabby, who had been draped on top of her, and propping herself up on one elbow. 'I was having such an awful dream – thanks for waking me. Why *did* you wake me? It's really early . . .'

'I've cracked it!' exclaimed Enid. 'Well, I've cracked the first part of the plan so it's a start. I've thought up an act that we can offer the Brilliantines in exchange for the animals.'

'Oh, wow!' said Mildred. 'Go on, tell me!'

'Easy-peasy,' said Enid. 'Don't know why we didn't think of it straight away. It's our Privilege Spell – you know, the one where we can enchant any sort of brush. We could do a flying dustpan and brush for Mr Brilliantine when he's being a clown, and a big yard-broom for them to do acrobatics on. *And* a whole load of toothbrushes in different colours – they'd be really cute even without the snails, and they could fly through the audience. Do you remember that Miss Drill said you had to de-activate the brushes or anyone could use them? Well, we just won't take the spell off, then the Brilliantines could use them forever.'

'Wow, Enid!' said Mildred, impressed.

'That's such a brilliant idea!'

Enid smiled. 'It is, isn't it? A brilliant idea for the Brilliantines! Let's go and tell Maud.'

'Hmmm,' said Mildred. 'She's not going to be too happy about this.'

'Shall we just not tell her?' asked Enid. 'Then she won't feel that she has to come, so she'll be safe if anything goes wrong? I really would hate it if she lost out on First Prize for Team Spirit.'

'Tricky,' said Mildred. 'She might be hurt if we sneaked off without her. I think it's best if we *tell* her but insist that she doesn't come.'

The brush-exchange idea was actually an excellent plan, and soon Maud was up to her neck in it with the other two. Although it was a bit risky, she knew it might just work and she couldn't bear to be left out.

'You don't *have* to come, Maudie,' said Mildred, stuffing twenty-five brightly coloured toothbrushes into her satchel. 'Just in case there are a few awkward things to explain later.'

'Like these toothbrushes!' exclaimed Maud. 'Where did you get them?'

'From the bathroom supplies cupboard,' said Mildred. 'There are stacks of them behind the toilet rolls. No one's going to check, and we can replace them later.'

'And I've got one of the yard-brooms under my bed,' said Enid. 'It's the spare one from the Big Playground. They'll never notice. I've got that nice green dustpan and brush from the cloakroom too. It's always stuffed at the back of the boot locker, so it won't be missed.'

'Well, I suppose we'd better set off soon and get on with it,' said Maud.

'The sooner, the better,' agreed Mildred. 'We've been dithering about for nearly two weeks since I last saw them and they'll be wondering if we're ever going to come and rescue them. Let's go at first light tomorrow,' she said to Enid. 'We can come to your room and help you with the yard-broom and the dustpan.'

'OK,' said Enid. 'I'll program the bat-nav.'

'Right,' said Maud reluctantly.

'That settles it then,' said Mildred. 'Tomorrow morning it is!'

CHAPTER TWENTY

They didn't really need the bat-nav. Now that Mildred had flown to Queen's Warren twice, it was easy to recognize landmark villages and towns on the way. On the other hand, it was nice just to follow the bat so that they could chat to each other without having to concentrate on the route.

The weather was perfect again, with only a light breeze, which made balancing easy. Enid had already enchanted the yard-broom because it was too cumbersome to carry, and had tethered it to her broomstick to keep it going in the right direction.

Maud had stuffed the dustpan and
brush into her backpack, ready to be
enchanted when they arrived, along with
the toothbrushes crammed into Mildred's
satchel.

'If they *do* agree to our swap,' said Maud,
'what are we actually going to do with the
seal and the pony?'

'Not absolutely sure about that,' mumbled
Mildred.

'One thing we *must* do,' said Enid, 'if they
actually agree to the swap, is get a letter

116

from the Brilliantines to show Miss Cackle, otherwise it will look as if we've stolen all their animals.'

'Good thinking, Eenie-meeny,' said Maud, 'but what *are* we doing to do with them all?'

'I'm sure Miss Cackle would let me have Star back anyway,' said Mildred, 'and perhaps they could keep the pony for riding lessons! Pentangle's has two ponies – it might attract more pupils to our school. Miss Cackle would love that.'

'And the seal?' asked Maud.

'Let's cross that bridge when we come to it,' said Mildred. 'Look, we've arrived!'

They parked their broomsticks and the bat-nav in the usual place, and set about enchanting the dustpan and brush, which immediately began capering about, the brush chasing the pan. Maud grabbed the brush in one hand and the dustpan in the other and hung on tightly.

Mildred shook the toothbrushes out of her satchel on to the grass.

'Could you enchant all these individually?' she asked Enid. 'You'll have to trap them back in the satchel, ready to show the Brilliantines, or they might go bobbing off and get lost. I'll go and wake everyone up.'

Waking everyone up had already happened. Star was barking his head off, Selkie was honking, and Merlin was whinnying and neighing. Mildred counted the days on her fingers and realized that exactly two weeks had passed, so the spell had worn off and they could no longer speak. She knelt down to scratch Star's head through the bars and he blinked his eyes and gazed at her.

'We don't have to speak to each other anyway,' she said tenderly. 'Just a look will do.'

'*Arrff,*' woofed Star. '*Woof, WOOF!*'

The caravan door crashed open, and Mr and Mrs Brilliantine emerged in their dressing gowns, looking half asleep and annoyed.

'Not you again!' said Mr Brilliantine. 'Why do you always have to come at such an unearthly hour?'

'Actually,' said Mildred, 'we've brought some things with us, to give you in exchange for the animals. That's if you think they're a good idea, of course. They're sort of magical props for a show-stopping act to bring in huge audiences. You'll probably have to buy a bigger Big Top!'

Mr and Mrs Brilliantine exchanged unimpressed glances.

'It's a really *good* idea,' said Mildred enthusiastically. 'I just know you're going to love it.'

'All right then,' said Mr Brilliantine. 'You might as well show us what you've brought, now that you're here.'

CHAPTER TWENTY-ONE

Everything went like clockwork in the Big Top. The Brilliantines were simply astonished by the display put on by Mildred and her two best friends.

Mildred and Enid sat on the bristle end of the yard-broom and flew it up to the trapeze, then took it sedately around the top of the tent. Maud allowed herself to be chased by the dustpan and brush, both of which got

slightly out of hand and had to be stuffed into Maud's backpack. But it was the twenty-five pretty toothbrushes that clinched the deal.

They were utterly charming, swooping and diving in an orderly line wherever Mildred sent them, and flying back politely into her satchel as soon as she asked them to.

'How does it all work?' asked Mr Brilliantine, picking up a toothbrush, which lay motionless in his hand. 'How do you switch them on? Do they run on batteries? How long will they last?'

'They'll last forever,' said Mildred. 'With no maintenance – you just have to speak to them in a particular way. I'll show you how in a moment. And you have to be very firm with the dustpan and brush. The yard-broom is fine, and the toothbrushes are a dream, but for some reason the dustpan and brush have a bit of a wild streak so you have to show them who's boss! Shall we give you some lessons?'

The Brilliantines spent the next hour flying up to the trapeze on the yard-broom, launching the toothbrushes around the empty benches, and being chased by the extremely naughty dustpan and brush. Mr Brilliantine could see how much fun this would be during his clown performance, and Mrs Brilliantine could certainly see how much more fun it would be to fly up to the trapeze before she did her routine. Within minutes they were completely hooked on their new magic equipment.

'We could leave you the backpack like a sort of kennel for the dustpan and brush,' said Maud helpfully.

'And you can have my satchel for the toothbrushes,' said Mildred. 'They settle down really quickly in there.'

'The yard-broom's fine anywhere,' said Enid. 'It's very laid-back and no trouble at all.'

'*Will* you swap with us then?' said Mildred. 'Our magic brushes in exchange for the seal, the pony and the dog?'

Mr and Mrs Brilliantine twinkled at each other.

'Done!' they said in unison, laughing.

CHAPTER TWENTY-TWO

As soon as the Brilliantines had written their letter of new owner-ship for Mildred to present to Miss Cackle, they disappeared inside the caravan to change into their costumes so that they could start practising their routine, and the girls rushed over to the animals to tell them the good news.

'So,' said Maud, 'what *are* we going to do with the seal?'

'It's OK,' said Mildred. 'I thought this out in bed last night. I already know where she wants to go – back to her colony at Grim Cove – so all we have to do is a transference spell and – *hey presto!* – she'll be back with her family, telling them all about what happened. Won't you, Selkie? Is that where you'd like to go? If you can understand me, do a banana for me.'

Immediately Selkie curved herself into the banana shape, waving one flipper and honking happily.

'That's sorted then,' Mildred responded, laughing. 'And I've written out the transference spell, so we can do it right now.'

Mildred smoothed Selkie's damp head.

'I must admit, being transferred does feel a bit weird,' she told her. 'H.B. did it to me once and you feel sort of squashed and pulled at the same time, but don't worry, because it's all over in a few seconds and then you suddenly arrive where you've been sent. Just think of splashing down in Grim Cove, and don't forget to keep your eyes shut as there are lots of bright lights and stars.'

'Gosh, Millie,' said Enid admiringly. 'You've really planned this perfectly.'

'Can you get a move on?' asked Maud nervously. 'We can't possibly get back before the rising bell and they're bound to see us flying in.'

'But we've got our ownership letter to show Miss Cackle,' said Mildred. 'And Selkie will be safely back in the sea by the time we get home, so there's nothing to worry about.'

'Relax, Maud,' said Enid. 'Nothing can go wrong now.'

CHAPTER TWENTY-THREE

There was still half an hour before morning assembly, and Miss Cackle was sitting in the staffroom with Miss Hardbroom, beginning their assessment of all the Year Four pupils in order to pick the worthiest recipients for the various prizes at the end of Summer Term.

'I was wondering if we could have a First Prize for Art this year?' suggested Miss Cackle.

'I thought we'd decided this already,' replied Miss Hardbroom wearily. 'We were both in *complete* agreement that prizes would be awarded for serious subjects relating to the ethos of the school.'

'Yes, I do know that,' said Miss Cackle. 'It's just that, well, Mildred Hubble is so very talented at art and it seems a shame that there is no award for it.'

'I'm sorry, Miss Cackle, but I really think that a prize for "Art" would be the thin end of the wedge in a fine academic school like this,' continued Miss Hardbroom, somehow managing to make the word 'art' sound unsavoury. 'I seem to remember that you have already sneaked in a prize for the tidiest room, as a sop to less academic pupils – which, incidentally, most certainly won't be won by Mildred Hubble! Have you seen her room lately?'

At this point, to their great astonishment, the door suddenly crashed open and an irate Miss Bat barged into the room, wearing her swimming costume, with a towel wrapped round her shoulders.

'*Really!*' she exclaimed. 'As if frogs and

water snails aren't bad enough, but to swim straight into a *seal* when one is taking an early-morning dip is the last straw – one just doesn't *expect* it!'

'Did you say a *seal*, Miss Bat?' asked Miss Cackle in disbelieving tones.

'I most certainly did,' quavered Miss Bat. 'I know what a seal looks like! It appeared out of nowhere and splashed down in the deep end. Then it plunged under the water and surfaced right in front of me, making a sort of honking sound – that is the only way to describe it! Well, I got out smartish, I can tell you!'

'There, there, Miss Bat,' soothed Miss Cackle, placing an arm round Miss Bat's towel-clad shoulders and leading her to the door. 'Why don't you go and get into some nice dry clothes and come back here for some lovely tea and biscuits? I'll speak to Miss Drill and she can sort it out as soon as possible.'

She gently nudged Miss Bat out of the staffroom and closed the door.

'I really do think it might be time for Miss Bat to retire,' she continued sadly, suddenly noticing that Miss Hardbroom was staring out of the window.

'Come and take a look at this, Miss Cackle,' said Miss Hardbroom, her voice harsh with annoyance. 'It's Mildred Hubble and Co. down there by the gate – and it looks as if she's decided to rescue her magical mutt from the circus. It also looks as if she's stolen a pony at the same time – and she's got Enid Nightshade and Maud Spellbody assisting her in this folly. I really thought Maud would have had more sense.'

'Oh *dear*,' said Miss Cackle. 'Such a very silly thing to do. They *must* realize that they'll have to take them straight back again.'

'They certainly will,' said Miss Hardbroom briskly. 'We'd better go down and nip this in the bud before it goes any further.'

The journey back to school had taken longer than expected, with Merlin trotting along beneath them and Star on his back. The three young witches had been flying overhead as low as possible, taking care

not to crash into the treetops, calling out Merlin's name to keep him going in the right direction. They also had to slow down and wait every now and then, so that he could have a rest. Merlin was exhausted when they finally arrived at the school gates, but Star couldn't contain his joy and started barking and twirling.

'Shh,' said Mildred, glancing around nervously. 'We've got some explaining to do before H.B. finds out about this.'

'You most certainly have,' agreed Miss Hardbroom, materializing right next to the petrified pony, who could sense that she was not friendly. 'Perhaps you could start by telling me precisely what you think you are doing – *all* of you.'

The three friends stood frozen with fear, as it suddenly dawned on them that this might not be as simple as they had thought. Pupils at Miss Cackle's were never encouraged to take matters into their own hands, and their behaviour would be met with disapproval, however worthy their motives.

Miss Cackle came out into the playground and bustled across to the gates. Unlike Miss Hardbroom, she preferred to use normal methods of arrival, such as walking upstairs and opening doors, only using magic on very special occasions.

Maud and Enid both had their arms around Merlin's neck, and Mildred was clutching Star. All three of them looked exceptionally guilty.

'Perhaps *you'd* better explain, Mildred,' coaxed Miss Cackle. 'Surely you must know that you can't just take back something that isn't yours – and where did this pony come from?'

Mildred couldn't think how to begin. She opened her mouth to start and then closed it again.

'Well,' said Miss Cackle, 'it looks as if you've had a very long journey, so I think you'd better all come up to my study and have a cup of tea while we get to the bottom of this. What shall we do with the pony, Miss Hardbroom?' she continued, stroking Merlin's soft nose.

'Just leave him here,' said Miss Hardbroom harshly. 'He'll be going back where he came from in a very short while.'

'But he'll need a rest after coming all that way,' said Miss Cackle. 'And a drink. We can find a first-year to fetch a bucket of water. Come along now, girls – I'm sure we can sort this out in no time.'

On their way to Miss Cackle's study, they passed Dulcie.

136

'Ah, Dulcie', said Miss Cackle. 'Just the person to run a little errand for me.'

'Of course, Miss Cackle,' said Dulcie politely.

'There's a pony in the playground, tethered to the gate,' explained Miss Cackle. 'Could you take him a bucket of water? He's had rather a long journey, and I seem to remember that you are especially fond of horses.'

CHAPTER TWENTY-FOUR

Everyone had just sat down in Miss Cackle's study with a cup of tea when there was a loud knocking at the door.

'What *now*?' snapped Miss Hardbroom.

'Well, it sounds quite urgent,' said Miss Cackle, 'so I think we'd better find out. Come in!'

The heavy door creaked open and Dulcie tumbled into the room, her eyes shining.

'What is it, Dulcie?' asked Miss Cackle. 'Is everything all right?'

'Oh, it's so much *more* than all right, Miss Cackle!' exclaimed Dulcie. 'That pony, the one tied to the gate, it's Merlin! He was my pony before my parents sold him! If he's going to be here as our school pony, can I be the one to look after him? Please, Miss Cackle – I would look after him so well. He was just thrilled to see me again – Oh, Miss Cackle, I just can't believe that he's come to live at the school!'

'Calm down now,' said Miss Cackle, looking fondly at the delighted first-year. 'Nothing is settled yet, but if we *do* keep the pony, then you will certainly be at the top of my list of helpers. Off you go now – mustn't be late for lessons.

'Now then, Mildred,' she continued as the door closed behind her, 'may we have an explanation about the recent additions to your ever-growing menagerie?'

Mildred took out the letter signed by the Brilliantines and handed it to the headmistress.

'I think it would be simplest if you just read this, Miss Cackle,' she said. 'It's a document transferring ownership to me, signed by the Brilliantines, so it's perfectly legal. They've given us Star and Merlin – we thought you might like to keep a pony here for riding lessons. There was a seal too, but we couldn't think what to do with her so we transferred her back to the sea at Grim Cove – I saw a colony of Common Seals there once,' she added, not wanting to admit that she had cast a speaking spell to find out where the seal had come from.

Miss Cackle and Miss Hardbroom exchanged knowing glances.

'When you cast the spell, Mildred,' said

140

Miss Hardbroom, 'did you make sure that you pictured Grim Cove in your mind, clearing your thoughts of *everything* else?'

'I *think* so,' said Mildred, feeling a little unnerved.

'Are you sure that the school swimming pool wasn't in your thoughts at all?' asked Miss Cackle. 'You do realize that your mind must be totally focused on the place of transfer when casting a transference spell? I was just wondering if you hadn't read the small paragraph at the end when you were looking up the spell.'

Mildred began to feel uneasy. 'Um,' she murmured, suddenly remembering that she *had* been feeling a bit sad about saying goodbye to Selkie and had wondered for a mad moment if they could keep her in the swimming pool.

'Well, I did, sort of, *slightly* think of the swimming pool,' she admitted, 'but only round the *edges* of my mind. I was very much concentrating on Grim Cove in the *middle* of my mind – and much more than anything else!'

'That explains it,' said Miss Hardbroom. 'I have to tell you, Mildred, that there is, at this precise moment, a seal in the school swimming pool – don't you find that a rather odd coincidence? It frightened Miss Bat out of her wits this morning, and we'll have to re-transfer it immediately before anything else untoward happens. Indeed, I rather think we should transfer it right now.'

'Yes, yes,' agreed Miss Cackle. 'Miss Hardbroom, could you take the girls with you? I think we should make absolutely sure that it *is* the seal from the circus.'

Miss Hardbroom led the way through the maze of corridors to the swimming pool, with the girls trooping along behind, suddenly feeling exhausted after their busy morning.

The pool seemed to be empty, the water dark and still.

'Shall I call her, Miss Hardbroom?' asked Mildred. 'I could sit on the side and see if I can get her to come out. She's probably feeling a bit confused and scared.'

Miss Hardbroom nodded, and Mildred crouched down by the water's edge.

'Selkie,' she called softly. 'It's me, Mildred.

143

I got the spell wrong – please come out. It's going to be all right now.'

The bulrushes quivered, then stopped, and a few moments later, with bubbles and snorting, Selkie surfaced directly in front of Mildred.

'It's definitely our seal, Miss Hardbroom,' she said. 'Please could I just explain to her what happened?'

'Why on earth would you want to do that, Mildred?' asked Miss Hardbroom tetchily. 'It's a seal – it won't know what you're talking about. Move aside now and let me do a *proper* transference spell. I really *don't* have all day to sort this out.'

Mildred leaned forward and put her hand on Selkie's head.

'I know you can understand,' she whispered. 'H.B. might *seem* a bit cross, but she knows how to get you back to Grim Cove at once – she's the very best at spells! Shut your eyes and think of home.'

Then Mildred looked up and said, 'OK, Miss Hardbroom. You can do the transference spell now. She's ready.'

'Take your hand off her head, Mildred,' said Miss Hardbroom, 'unless you want to go with her!'

'Sorry, Miss Hardbroom,' said Mildred, hastily removing her hand. 'Can you make sure she gets to Grim Cove this time? That's definitely where she wants to go.'

'Grim Cove it is,' said Miss Hardbroom.

After Selkie had been safely sent on her way, Miss Cackle summoned Miss Bat to

her study, and the girls apologized profusely about the failed transference spell and for ruining her morning swim.

'Not to worry, my dears,' said Miss Bat cheerfully. 'I'm just *so* glad that I wasn't imagining things.'

'May I take Star with me?' asked Mildred, as Miss Cackle sent them to hang up their cloaks and hats, and to ask the kitchen staff for some late breakfast.

'You might as well,' said Miss Cackle. 'I'll talk to all three of you later when we've decided on our long-term plans for both the animals.'

With relief, the three friends hurried out of the headmistress's study.

146

'I hope I haven't messed up my chances of First Prize for Team Spirit,' said Maud anxiously.

'I can't see why,' said Enid. 'All three of us have displayed *brilliant* team spirit, if you ask me.'

'What do you think they'll decide?' asked Maud. 'I mean about Merlin and Star.'

'No idea,' said Mildred. 'We'll just have to wait and see.'

CHAPTER TWENTY-FIVE

In Miss Cackle's study, Miss Hardbroom was pondering the same question.

'What do you think we should do, Headmistress?' she asked, reading through the Brilliantines' document for the third time. 'Do you think this note is genuine?'

'Yes, I do,' said Miss Cackle. 'Mildred Hubble is an honest pupil, and so is Maud. Enid might have been a little scatterbrained and attention-seeking when she first came here, but she's a different girl these days.'

'But how did Mildred get them to change their minds?' Miss Hardbroom persisted.

'*And* to give up a pony *and* their performing seal? Mildred must have made some sort of bargain with them – it doesn't make sense otherwise. Shouldn't we press all three of them for more information?'

Miss Cackle smiled. 'I don't think that will be necessary, Miss Hardbroom,' she replied. 'You and I both agree that this letter of ownership *is* genuine, so it would seem most logical to retire Mildred's poor unfortunate cat *again*, let Mildred have fun with Star, and advertise riding lessons in our coming year's prospectus – and it's *such* a pleasant coincidence that Merlin was Dulcie's pony in the first place. So there you are – everyone's happy and no harm done. No need to ask any awkward questions, wouldn't you agree, Miss Hardbroom?'

149

'Whatever you say, Miss Cackle,' muttered Miss Hardbroom reluctantly. 'You are the headmistress.'

Mildred, Maud and Enid were overjoyed when Miss Cackle sent for them the very next day and informed them that they could keep both Star and Merlin at the academy.

'You see, Maudie,' said Mildred, smiling, 'I *told* you it would all be fine.'

'As long as they don't find out about the magic-brush exchange,' said Maud.

'Oh, stop being such a worrywart,' said Enid. 'They won't find out – how could they?'

CHAPTER TWENTY-SIX

Ethel and Drusilla were resting on their broomsticks, getting their breath back after a nosediving session in the playground. Through the gates, they could see Dulcie leading Merlin, with a delighted friend on his back, and several other pupils queuing for a ride.

'I don't know how she does it every time,' grumbled Ethel.

'Dulcie?' asked Drusilla. 'Well, she must be quite good with ponies, as Merlin used to belong to her.'

'Not *Dulcie*,' snarled Ethel scornfully. 'I mean Mildred Hubble. How on earth did she get those circus people to give up all their animals – for nothing, as far as I can make out. If she didn't have the letter to prove it, I'd think she'd just stolen them. She *must* have given them something or they would never have let them go – especially the dog. He's excellent at acrobatics, even if he does look absolutely ridiculous on the back of a witch's broom.'

'Miss Cackle didn't seem to think so,' mused Drusilla, straying into dangerous waters; 'neither did the judges of the swimming-pool competition. Everyone agreed that Mildred could keep him as her broom-companion in the end – even Miss Hardbroom.'

Ethel narrowed her eyes and glared at Drusilla.

'Do you know, Drusilla,' she said unpleasantly, 'I really wonder why I'm friends with you sometimes. We don't think alike on anything and –'

'Oh, but we do,' said Drusilla hastily. 'Perhaps the letter *was* a forgery and Mildred just stole the animals. *I* know! Why don't we fly out to the circus tomorrow evening and do some detective work before it moves on somewhere else?'

'That's a really good idea, Druse,' said Ethel, sounding friendly again. 'But you'll have to go on your own and report back to me. I'm taking some of the first-years for a picnic tomorrow afternoon.'

'A picnic!' exclaimed Drusilla. 'With a whole lot of first-years?'

'I just thought I'd do a few things to prove how popular I am with the whole school,' said Ethel. 'You know, just to make sure I'll be chosen as next year's Head Girl.'

'*You* don't have to worry about that,' said Drusilla admiringly. 'You don't have to do anything at all except be a Hallow.'

'True.' Ethel smiled smugly. 'But it won't hurt to do a few extra bits and pieces. Being nice to the first-years will help towards First Prize for Team Spirit, and I've had

the highest grades in everything for the last four years so I'll definitely get First Prize for Highest Grades, and probably First Prize for Best Pilot now that Mildred's had an awful Summer Term with Tabby.

154

So I'm bound to win everything, plus the nomination for next year's Head Girl – I don't know why the rest of the school is bothering to turn up!' She laughed merrily at her own joke – though Drusilla suspected that Ethel wasn't joking at all.

'I can't think of any prize *I* might get,' said Drusilla.

'Cheer up,' said Ethel. 'There's a prize for keeping your room tidy. You might get that.'

'I don't know why they even have a prize for that,' mumbled Drusilla. 'We've only got a bed and a wardrobe.'

A tiny flicker of sympathy flared in Ethel. 'Come on, Druse,' she said. 'We *do* have a good time together – well, *mostly* – don't we? And I just know you'll get some key piece of information about Mildred and those animals tomorrow. I can't wait to find out.'

Drusilla's news was better than anything Ethel could have imagined. She had arrived at the circus in time for the evening show, and saw with increasing astonishment that all the Brilliantines' new acts consisted of an assortment of enchanted brushes, which could only have come from Miss Cackle's Academy – all of which she recounted in great detail to Ethel the moment she arrived back at school.

'This is totally perfect, Druse!' cackled Ethel, grabbing Drusilla and jumping up and down. 'Trivial use of magic! Stealing school property! Leaving school without permission! You are an absolutely ace detective! I'd better go and tell Miss Cackle right now before things get any worse.'

CHAPTER TWENTY-SEVEN

When Ethel arrived with her news, Miss Cackle and Miss Hardbroom had been in the process of making a final list of candidates for next year's Head Girl.

'Well, that explains everything,' said Miss Cackle with a sigh, closing the door behind Ethel. 'I wondered how Mildred had managed it.'

'Ethel's right, of course,' said Miss Hardbroom. 'You can't get more trivial than using magic for a circus act.'

'And yet,' said Miss Cackle, 'it *isn't* exactly

trivial when you consider that Mildred was doing her very best to get her broom-companion back again. It must have been hard for her, sending him away when he really didn't want to go. I can't help feeling that, if the circus owners are happy with their new display and Mildred can regain her place as one of our best fliers, it does seem that everyone's happy, arcn't they? Even little Dulcie.'

'Whatever you say, Headmistress,' muttered Miss Hardbroom unenthusiastically.

'I must admit,' continued Miss Cackle, 'Mildred does have a quite extraordinary knack of sorting things out, doesn't she?'

'I suppose that is *one* way of looking at it,' sniffed Miss Hardbroom.

'Sometimes I think it is the *only* way of looking at it as far as Mildred is concerned,' said Miss Cackle. 'I mean, here we are, making lists of all the qualities needed for our Head Girl and, when you *really* think about it, Mildred has the lot.'

Miss Hardbroom glanced sharply at Miss Cackle, as she could suddenly see which way this conversation was heading.

'But I thought we had agreed that Ethel was our candidate for Head Girl,' she said firmly. 'Her marks are always one hundred per cent, and of course she is a Hallow and they are always Head Girl – if there is a Hallow available. A Hallow has been Head Girl for the last two hundred years – it's a proud family tradition. Five minutes ago Mildred Hubble wasn't in the running at all!'

'I'm not so sure about Ethel,' pondered Miss Cackle. 'She can be a real sneak sometimes, which, if you think about it, is not exactly a sterling quality – and on one occasion she even stole Mildred's spell and tried to pass it off as her own. You wouldn't

160

catch Mildred Hubble doing something like that, *and* Mildred saved the entire school from my appalling twin sister not once but twice!'

'Both times by accident,' said Miss Hardbroom. 'That first time, she was actually running away and only stumbled across your sister's coven by chance.'

'A happy chance, though,' parried Miss Cackle. 'If she hadn't been there, we would have all been turned into snails. Then the dear girl saved Mr Rowan Webb from a lifetime of frogdom in the school pond, and he was so grateful to her that he invited us to stay in his castle for our summer holiday – surely you remember all this, Miss Hardbroom? And, while we were there, Mildred found the lost treasure chest, which paid for all the school roofs to be mended. And that spell I mentioned, the one that Ethel stole, happens to be the best spell ever invented by a pupil in all the time I have been headmistress here.

'And only last term Mildred teamed up with that dear little dog and won the swimming-pool competition – no wonder she wanted him back at any cost! She may have a very exasperating way of doing things, but she does get there in the end – and in the most spectacular way, you must admit, Miss Hardbroom.'

'What exactly are you suggesting?' asked Miss Hardbroom.

'I think I'm suggesting,' said Miss Cackle, 'that it's time for a change.'

CHAPTER TWENTY-EIGHT

The ceremony of Fourth Year Firsts had finally arrived, and the Great Hall echoed with the joyful notes of Miss Bat's piano, playing the customary tune of 'In an English Country Garden'.

The girls entered the hall, one class at a time, very tightly controlled, as if they might all run amok if Miss Hardbroom's beady eye was taken off them for one second – which was ridiculous really, as they were all wearing their best robes and were on their very best behaviour to match. They shuffled along the rows of chairs, arranging themselves as neatly as possible, with Year One at the front, followed by Year Two behind them, and so on, with Year Four at the back. Year Five sat on the stage, behind the teachers.

There would be countless awards, cups, medals, prizes and certificates given out, plus lengthy speeches and accolades to the Year Fives, who would be leaving the school on that very day, and Miss Cackle would be droning on for hours. Mildred had little hope for a Fourth Year First in anything, so she had brought a mini book of crosswords and a pencil, to surreptitiously pass the time. It was helpful that they were in the back row, with several rows of pupils blocking the view from the stage.

'Let's wait and see if Maud gets First Prize for Team Spirit,' said Mildred to Enid, 'then we can get stuck into these crosswords. I can do one, then pass the book to you, and we can see who finishes the most. It's going to be a bit boring otherwise, just sitting here

for hours, watching Ethel get every prize in the universe.'

'Hey!' said Enid. 'I might actually win something.'

'Like what?' asked Mildred as they both dissolved into giggles.

'You never know,' said Enid. 'They might invent a new category just for me!'

'Quieten down in the back row!' barked Miss Hardbroom. 'Things are getting a little raucous!'

Mildred and Enid stopped whispering and immediately sat bolt upright.

At last, the entire school was crammed into the Great Hall, the final notes of the piano died away and the speeches began. Miss Hardbroom was first, congratulating the departing Year Fives on all their hard work and wishing them luck with the results of their Witches' Higher Certificate exams, which they would not receive for several months. Mildred had always thought that this was an excellent system, as no one would know if she had failed until they had all left the school.

Maud had laughed when Mildred pointed this out. 'You're such a pessimist, Millie,' she'd said. 'I mean, you might do really well, then you'll miss out on all the praise *and* Ethel seething. It's always seemed odd to me that we'll all leave without knowing if we passed or not.'

'And now,' continued Miss Cackle, taking over cheerfully from Miss Hardbroom, 'to our first award of this most important day. The First Prize for Highest Grades over the last four years goes to . . . Ethel Hallow! No surprise there!'

She smiled, beckoning to Ethel, who barged along the row of seated pupils, sending cats flying as she hurried to claim her trophy, a huge wooden and silver shield with Ethel's name neatly inscribed beneath last year's winner.

No sooner had Ethel sat down than she was called up again, this time to take First Prize for Best Pilot: a beautiful cup with handles shaped like broomsticks. Drusilla clapped loudly, and the rest of the school clapped too, but without the burst of spontaneous delight that sometimes erupts at such a prize-giving.

'Of course there have been other excellent fliers recently,' said Miss Cackle, 'and many pupils who have improved considerably, but these Firsts are for consistent work since day one, so another big "Well done" to Ethel Hallow.'

Ethel beamed from ear to ear, looking unbearably smug.

'This is going to be a wipeout,' muttered Enid.

CHAPTER TWENTY-NINE

I n fact, it wasn't a total wipeout. To everyone's delight, Maud won First Prize for Team Spirit.

This prize was voted for by the girls themselves, so Maud won hands down, as she was genuinely helpful, always spending time with the younger pupils, and on the lookout for team-spirited activities, such as tidying the broom shed and gathering up litter. The first-years had seen through Ethel's last-minute efforts, and everyone in the school (except Drusilla and Sybil, Ethel's younger sister) had voted for Maud.

A huge cheer burst out when Maud clumped up to the stage, beaming from ear to ear, to collect her prize, a gigantic silver urn, which was almost as big as herself.

The cheers died away and Maud struggled back to her seat and re-arranged herself, almost hidden by the trophy on her lap.

'Oh, Maudie!' said Mildred, who was immensely proud of her friend. 'I'm so glad

you won it. Now we can all go home happy.'

'Congrats, Maud,' agreed Enid. 'That's *some* trophy! You'll need an extra room to keep it in!'

'Settle down back there!' said Miss Hardbroom, rising ominously from her chair and peering in their direction. Everyone dropped their eyes obediently.

Next, Miss Cackle began her tribute to the Year Fives, saying, amid much waffling, how much they would all be missed and wishing them luck for the future. As usual, most of the leavers were in floods of tears.

'Why on earth do they always cry?' whispered Mildred, ducking conveniently behind Maud's trophy.

'It's weird, isn't it?' replied Maud. 'The Year Fives always cry on the last day. I suppose we will too.'

'I won't!' whispered Enid.

Maud put a finger to her lips, anxious not to draw attention to herself, now that

171

the much-wanted Team Spirit trophy was in her clutches.

The ceremony dragged on. Speeches were made to the departing pupils by all the teachers, including Miss Bat, who kept forgetting what she was saying, so it took twice as long. More first prizes were awarded to the Year Fours, mainly won by Ethel, who was now sitting at the end of the row, so that she could pile up the cups and shields.

Mildred and Enid had given up hoping for a prize. The only ones in their range were non-academic ones such as First Prize for the Tidiest Room or First Prize for the Best-Trained Cat. Unfortunately, the whole school knew about Mildred's troubles with Tabby, as well as Enid's monkey episode, and they were both renowned for their inability to keep their belongings tidy.

Mildred had already opened the book of crosswords, keeping it out of sight on her lap. The first one had been easy; she'd finished it in ten minutes, then passed it sideways to Enid. Twenty minutes later, Enid completed the second one and passed it back, taking great care not to be seen.

At first, Mildred kept glancing up at the stage while she was trying to solve the clues, in case anyone noticed that she wasn't paying attention, but the third crossword was much more difficult than the first. This one was full of references to books or plays containing magic objects, and Mildred became so engrossed in it that the background noises of speeches and applause faded away, until she was no longer aware of them.

She had only managed to answer three clues before she got completely stuck on Four Down: *To whom did the Lady of the Lake give the Ring of Dispel? (Two words: 3,8.)*

'This is really hard,' Mildred thought to herself, racking her brains. '*I* know! The Lady of the Lake gave Excalibur to King Arthur – *that's* two words! Maybe she gave him the ring too! No, hang on – the first word has only three letters, and there are four letters in "King". I wonder if –'

'Stand up, Mildred Hubble!' Miss Hardroom's voice rang out across the rows of silent pupils.

CHAPTER THIRTY

Horrified, Mildred leapt to her feet.

'I – er – um – I'm . . . ' she spluttered.

'Surprised?' said Miss Cackle, smiling warmly. 'You were miles away, weren't you, my dear?'

175

Confused, Mildred realized that Meredith Frost, the outgoing Head Girl, was standing between Miss Cackle and Miss Hardbroom, unpinning the Head Girl medal from the front of her robe.

'Come along, Mildred,' said Miss Cackle encouragingly. 'Up you come. We're all waiting for you!'

Mildred glanced at Maud, still half hidden behind her Team Spirit trophy, then at Enid. Her two friends looked astounded, and at the end of the next row Ethel had turned to glare at her.

'Perhaps you didn't hear at the back there!' said Miss Cackle, now beckoning to Mildred with both arms. 'Mildred Hubble, you have been chosen to take over from Meredith as next year's Head Girl!'

Mildred looked around in shock as the whole school erupted in cheers of delight – well, *almost* the whole school. Ethel was also in shock, her mouth open in astonishment as she realized that she would be the first Hallow in two hundred years not to be Head Girl. Mildred couldn't help feeling sorry for her arch-enemy as she made her

177

way through the joyful throng and bounded up the steps to receive the medal, swept up on a wave of total happiness.

Miss Cackle put an arm around Meredith and Mildred. 'You can't wear it yet!' she laughed as she saw that Mildred was attempting to attach the medal to her robe.

'Sorry, Miss Cackle,' gasped Mildred. 'I got a bit carried away!'

'Just keep it safely,' said Miss Cackle. 'Ready for next year.'

'Or we could keep it for you here, Mildred,' suggested Miss Hardbroom. 'In case you lose it.'

'I don't think that will be necessary, Miss Hardbroom,' said Miss Cackle. 'One of the reasons why we chose Mildred as Head Girl, if you remember, is her ability to learn from her mistakes over the last four years, and to become stronger and more reliable as a result – an excellent role model for the younger girls, don't you think?'

'Hmmmm,' muttered Miss Hardbroom. 'Simmer down now, girls!' she continued waspishly. 'We can see that you're all *overjoyed* with our choice of Head Girl, but that's quite enough silly nonsense for now.'

Gradually, the noise died down. Meredith returned to her seat with a kindly squeeze of Mildred's shoulder, and Mildred slipped the treasured medal into her pocket and turned to the steps.

'Wait a moment, my dear,' said Miss Cackle. 'Don't forget. You must choose your deputy – Head Girl's privilege!'

'May I choose anybody?' asked Mildred.

'Of course,' said Miss Cackle. 'It's absolutely your choice.'

'So choose wisely, Mildred,' sniped Miss Hardbroom.

Mildred looked around the sea of pupils – Ethel buzzing with rage, and various friends looking up at her hopefully, giving little waves or pointing at themselves, mouthing, *Pleease!*

Mildred's gaze came to rest on Enid, who was smiling madly, eyes like saucers, and Maud, who was craning her head above the Team Spirit trophy, pointing at Enid and nodding.

'I'd like Enid as my deputy, Miss Cackle,' said Mildred solemnly. 'Would that be all right?'

CHAPTER THIRTY-ONE

The three friends were on the way back to their rooms, which was taking forever, as Mildred and Enid were stopped by friends every five minutes to show off their medals, and Maud had to keep putting down the heavy Team Spirit trophy to rest her arms.

'I don't know how I'm going to get it on the broom,' she said. 'I've got too much luggage already.'

'Don't worry,' said Mildred helpfully. 'You can tie it on. I've got a big laundry-bag that I could lend you – you can pack clothes round it so it won't get scratched.'

'That's our new Head Girl,' said Enid, 'sorting out all our problems. Thanks for choosing me as your deputy, Millie. I wasn't expecting anything at all.'

'Isn't it brilliant?' Maud laughed, picking up her trophy and tottering up the corridor. 'All three of us covered in glory! Who would have thought it?'

'Certainly not me!' said Miss Hardbroom's chilly voice as she appeared, literally, in a dark doorway ahead of them. The girls stopped in their tracks. 'Quite the little game-changer, aren't you, Mildred Hubble? Dogs on broomsticks and a non-Hallow as Head Girl – whatever next? I only hope that you will work hard next year and live up to this challenge.'

'Oh, I *will*, Miss Hardbroom,' said Mildred sincerely. 'I'll do my very best to set an example to the lower school. I won't let you down – I promise on my honour.'

Miss Hardbroom peered at them silently for a few moments, noting how petrified they all looked – even Star, now cowering behind Enid's ankles; and she found herself wishing that the girls weren't *quite* so terrified of her *all* the time.

'Now, girls,' she said suddenly, a tiny smile flickering for a brief second. 'I forgot to say a resounding "Well done!" to all three of you!'

'Thank you, Miss Hardbroom,' chorused the girls, not quite sure what to do next.

'Well, off you go then,' said Miss Hardbroom, whose kindly mood had lasted precisely thirty seconds. 'Oh, just one more thing, Mildred.'

Mildred froze.

'The answer to Four Down in your crossword puzzle,' continued Miss Hardbroom. 'It's "Sir Lancelot" – I thought you might like to know.'

'Thank you, Miss Hardbroom,' mumbled Mildred.

'Well, you'd better collect your belongings and get down to the playground for end-of-term take-off!' announced Miss Hardbroom. 'Happy holidays, girls – and take care of that medal, Mildred!' – so saying, she vanished abruptly.

184

The three friends waited in silence for several minutes, as she sometimes lurked, invisible, to catch them out.

'That's it!' said Mildred. 'The air's warmed up – she's gone! Come on, let's get out of here –'

'– before anything goes wrong!' said Enid.

'I'm sure it won't,' declared Maud. 'Anyway I'm just pleased we all got what we wanted –'

'Even me!' announced Mildred happily. '*Just* what I wanted – First Prize for the Worst Witch!'

Agatha Raisin

DISHING THE DIRT

M.C. Beaton

Agatha Raisin

DISHING THE DIRT

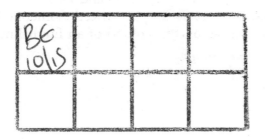

Constable • London

CONSTABLE

First published in the US in 2015 by Minotaur Books,
an imprint of St Martin's Press

This edition published in Great Britain in 2015 by Constable

1 3 5 7 9 10 8 6 4 2

A CIP catalogue record for this book
is available from the British Library.

ISBN 978-1-47211-720-5 (hardback)

Printed and bound in Great Britain by CPI Group (UK) Ltd,
Croydon CR0 4YY

Papers used by Constable are from well-managed forests and
other responsible sources

MIX
Paper from
responsible sources
FSC
www.fsc.org FSC® C104740

Constable
is an imprint of
Little, Brown Book Group
Carmelite House
50 Victoria Embankment
London EC4Y 0DZ

An Hachette UK Company
www.hachette.co.uk

www.littlebrown.co.uk

This book is dedicated to Martin Palmer
with many thanks for all his hard work
on my behalf

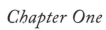

Chapter One

After a dismal grey winter, spring came to the village of Carsely in the Cotswolds, bringing blossoms, blue skies and warm breezes.

But somewhere, in the heart of one private detective, Agatha Raisin, storms were brewing.

When Agatha had been a member of the now defunct Ladies Society, she had got to know all the incomers to the village. But as most of her time was taken up away from the village, she did not recognise the thin woman who hailed her one Sunday when she was putting out the trash, ready for collection.

"It is Mrs. Raisin, is it not?" she called out in a reedy voice.

Agatha came to the fence of her thatched cottage. "I am Victoria Bannister," said the woman. "I do so admire you."

Victoria was somewhere in her eighties with a long face and a long thin nose and large pale eyes.

"Oh, I just do my job," said Agatha.

"But you have come such a long way from your poor beginnings," said Victoria.

"What poor beginnings?" snarled Agatha. She had been brought up in a Birmingham slum and somehow always dreaded that somewhere, someone would penetrate her lacquer of sophistication and posh accent.

"I heard you came from such a bad start with drunken parents. I do so admire you," Victoria said again, her pale eyes scrutinising Agatha's face.

"Piss off!" said Agatha furiously and went into her cottage and slammed the door.

Victoria walked off down Lilac Lane feeling happy. She enjoyed goading people.

Inside her cottage, Agatha stared bleakly at her reflection in the hall mirror. She had glossy brown hair and small bearlike eyes, a generous mouth, and although quite small in stature, had long well-shaped legs. Over

2

the years, she had laminated herself with the right clothes, and the right accent. But deep down, she felt vulnerable. She was in her early fifties, which she reminded herself daily was now considered today's forties.

She knew her ex-husband, James Lacey, a travel writer, had just returned from abroad. He was aware of her background as was her friend, Sir Charles Fraith. Surely neither of them would have gossiped. She had challenged James before and he had denied it. But she had to be sure. That therapist, Jill Davent, who had moved to the village had somehow known of her background. James had sworn then he had never told her anything, but how else would the woman have known?

Agatha had visited Jill, prompted by jealousy because James had been seen squiring her around. She had told Jill a highly romanticised story of her youth, but Agatha had left in a fury when Jill accused her of lying.

"Any odd and sod can call themselves a therapist these days," she said to her cats. "Charlatans, the lot of them!"

She went next door to his cottage and rang the bell. James answered and smiled in welcome. "Come in, Agatha. I've got coffee ready. If you must smoke, we'll have it in the garden."

Agatha agreed to go into the garden, not because she particularly wanted to smoke, but because the inside of James's cottage with its bachelor surroundings always reminded her how little impact she had made on his life when they were married.

Blackbirds pecked at the shabby lawn. A magnolia tree at the bottom of the garden was about to burst into bloom, raising pink buds up to the pale blue sky.

James came out with two mugs of coffee and an ashtray.

"Someone's been gossiping about me," said Agatha. "It must be Jill Davent. Someone's found out about my background."

"I could never understand why you are so ashamed of your upbringing," said James. "What does it matter?"

"It matters to me," said Agatha. "The Gloucestershire middle classes are very snobby."

"Only the ones not worth knowing," said James.

"Like some of your friends? Did you tell anyone?"

"Of course not. I told you before. I do not discuss you with anyone."

But Agatha saw a little flash of uneasiness in his blue eyes. "You did say something about me and recently, too."

He ran his fingers through his thick black hair, hair that only showed a little grey at the temples. He cursed Agatha's intuition.

"I didn't say anything about your background but I took Jill out for dinner and she asked a lot of questions about you, but I only talked about your cases."

"She's counselling Gwen Simple. She knows I was on that case where I nearly ended up in one of her son's meat pies."

Agatha's last case had concerned a Sweeny Todd of a murderer over at Winter Parva. Although she suspected his mother, Gwen, of having helped in the murders, no proof was found against the woman.

"Actually, it was more or less on your behalf that I took not only Jill out for dinner, but Gwen as well."

Agatha stared at him, noticing that James with his tall, athletic body was as handsome as ever. Jill looked like a constipated otter, but there was something about Gwen Simple that made men go weak at the knees.

"So what did creepy, slimy Gwen have to say for herself?" she asked.

"Agatha! The poor woman is still very traumatised. Jill did most of the talking."

Gwen probably sat there with a mediaeval-type gown on to suit her mediaeval-type features, thought Agatha bitterly. That one doesn't even have to open her mouth. She just sits there and draws men in.

"So did Jill have anything to say about the case?" she asked. "And I thought Gwen had sold the bakery and moved."

"Jill naturally will not tell me what a client says," remarked James. "And Gwen has moved to Ancombe."

"I would have thought she would want to get as far away from Winter Parva as possible," said Agatha. "I mean, a lot of the villagers must think she's guilty."

"On the contrary, they have been most sympathetic."

"Tcha!" said Agatha Raisin.

Agatha decided to call on her friend, Mrs. Bloxby. She suddenly wondered why on earth this therapist should have gone to such lengths as to ferret out her background. As usual, the vicar's wife was pleased to see her although, as usual, her husband was not. He slammed into his study.

As Mrs. Bloxby led the way into the garden, Agatha poured out her worries. "I'll get you a glass of sherry," said Mrs. Bloxby soothingly.

As she waited for her friend to come back, Agatha felt herself beginning to relax. Over in the churchyard, daffodils were swaying in the breeze amongst the old gravestones. In front of her, a blackbird pecked for worms on the lawn.

Mrs. Bloxby returned with a decanter of sherry and two glasses. After she had finished pouring out the drinks, she said, "I find it most odd that Miss Davent should obviously have gone to such lengths to dig up your background. She must see you as a threat. And if she sees you as a threat, what has she got to hide?"

"I should have thought of that," said Agatha. "I'm slipping. And why bring her business to Carsely? Surely she would get more clients in town."

"I think she *makes* clients," said the vicar's wife.

"What do you mean?"

"For example, she called on me. She said it must be awful for me not to have had any children. That, you see, is a vulnerable spot. She was trying to draw me in so that I would decide to use her services. I told her I was very busy and showed her the door. Everyone has some weakness, some frailty. I do not want to spread gossip, but she has built up quite a client base. They come from villages round about as well as here. She is a very clever woman. You have been so outraged about her finding out about your background that you did not stop to wonder why she had targeted you in this way."

On Monday morning, Agatha's small staff gathered for a briefing. There was Toni Gilmour, blond, young and beautiful; Simon Black with his jester's face; ex-policeman Patrick Mulligan; Phil Marshall, gentle and white-haired; and her secretary, Mrs. Freedman.

Agatha had decided she had given up caring about her lousy background and so she told them that somehow

Jill had gone out to target her and she wondered why. "We've got other work to do," she said, "but if you have any spare time, see what you can find out about her. Anyone these days can claim to be a therapist without qualifications. I can't remember if she had any sort of certificates on her walls."

"Why don't I just visit her and ask her why she is targeting you?" said Phil. "She'll deny it, but I could have a look around."

"Good idea," said Agatha.

"I'll phone now and see if I can get an appointment for this evening," said Phil.

"You'd better take sixty pounds with you," said Agatha. "I'm sure that one will look on any visit as a consultation."

Phil made his way to Jill's cottage that evening, having secured an appointment for eight o'clock. The cottage was on the road leading out of Carsely. It had formerly been an agricultural labourer's cottage and was built of red brick, two storied, and rather dingy looking. Phil, who lived in Carsely, knew it had lain empty for some time. There was a small, unkempt garden in the front with a square of mossy grass and two laurel bushes.

The curtains were drawn but he could see that lights were on in the house. He rang the bell and waited.

Jill answered the door and looked him up and down from his mild face and white hair to his highly polished shoes.

"Come in," she said. There was a dark little hall. She opened a door to the left of it and ushered him into her consulting room. Phil looked at the walls. He noticed there were several framed diplomas. The walls were painted dark green and the floor was covered in a dark green carpet. The room had a mahogany desk which held a Victorian crystal inkwell, a phone and nothing else on its gleaming surface. There was a comfortable leather chair facing her and a standard lamp with a fringed shade in one corner, shedding a soft light.

Jill sat behind her desk and waved a hand to indicate he should take the seat opposite.

"How can I help you?" she asked. She had a deep, husky voice.

"I work for Agatha Raisin," said Phil, "and it is well known in the village that you have been spreading tales about her poor upbringing. Why?"

"Because she wasted my time. Any more questions?"

"You are supposed to help people," said Phil in his gentle voice. "You are not supposed to go around trying to wreck their reputation. Your behaviour was not that of a caring therapist."

"Get the hell out of here!" screamed Jill with sudden and startling violence.

Phil rose to his feet, clutched his heart, grabbed the desk for support, and then collapsed on the floor.

"Stupid old fart," said Jill. "Too damn old for the job. I'd better get an ambulance." She picked up the phone from her desk and left the room.

Phil got quickly to his feet, took out a miniature camera and photographed the certificates on the wall before sinking back down to the floor and closing his eyes.

She returned and stared down at him. "With any luck, you're dead," she said viciously, and then left the room again. She had not even bothered to search for a pulse or even loosen his collar.

Phil got to his feet again and moved quietly into the hall. He could hear Jill's voice in the other room, but could not make out what she was saying.

He opened the front door and walked back down the hill. He would print the photos and e-mail them to Agatha's computer.

Later that evening, Agatha decided to walk up to the local pub for a drink. As she left, she saw James welcoming Jill and felt a sour stab of jealousy.

In a corner of the pub were three blond women the locals had dubbed "the trophy wives." They were each married to rich men and were rumoured to be third or even fourth wives. They were left in the country during the week, each looking as if she were pining for London. They were remarkably alike with their trout-pout mouths, salon tans, expensive clothes and figures maintained by strict diet and personal trainers.

Do women have trophy husbands? wondered Agatha. Perhaps, she thought ruefully, that now she had no longings for James, she wanted him to be kept single so that she could bask in his handsome company, a sort of "see what I've got" type of thing.

The pub door opened and Sir Charles Fraith strolled in, tailored and barbered, and almost catlike with his smooth blond hair and neat features. He saw Agatha, got a drink from the bar and went to join her.

"How's things?" he asked.

"Awful." Agatha told him all about Jill Davent.

"So she sees you as a threat," said Charles. "What's she got to be scared of?"

"That's what I'm trying to find out," said Agatha. "I'm furious. Phil went there this evening and got some pics of her certificates. He's sending them over."

"I bet you've been playing into her hands by raging all over the place," said Charles. "You're an old-fashioned snob, Aggie. This is an age when people who have risen from unfortunate beginnings brag about it all over the place."

"I am not a snob," howled Agatha, and the trophy wives giggled.

"Oh, don't laugh too hard," snarled Agatha. "Your Botox is cracking."

"You're a walking embarrassment," said Charles. "Let's get back to your computer and look at those pictures."

Agatha saw Charles's travel bag parked in her hall and scowled. She often resented the way he walked in and out of her life, and sometimes, on rare occasions, in and out of her bed.

They both sat in front of the computer. "Here we are," said Agatha. "Good old Phil. Let's see. An MA from the University of Maliumba. Where's that?"

"Africa. You can pay up and get a degree in anything. It was on the Internet at one time."

"A diploma in aromatherapy from Alternative Health in Bristol. A diploma in tai chi."

"Where's that from?"

"Taiwan."

"The woman's a phony, Agatha. Forget her."

"I can't, Charles. She's counselling Gwen Simple and I swear that woman helped in those murders. I'd like to see her records."

"Oh, let's forget the dratted woman," said Charles, stifling a yawn. "I'm going to bed. Coming?"

"Later. And to my *own* bed."

Agatha would not admit that she was sometimes lonely, but she felt a little pang when Charles announced breezily at breakfast that he was going home.

For the rest of the week, she and her staff were very busy and had to forget about Jill.

But by the week-end, what the locals called "blackthorn winter" arrived, bringing squally showers of rain and sleet.

Agatha decided to motor to Oxford and treat herself to a decent lunch. Her cats, Boswell and Hodge, twisted around her ankles, and she wished she could take them with her.

She parked in Gloucester Green car park, wincing at the steep price and began to walk up to Cornmarket. This was Oxford's main shopping street and one ignored in the Morse series, the producers correctly guessing that viewers wanted dreaming spires and colleges and not crowds of shoppers and chain stores.

Agatha had initially planned to treat herself to lunch at the Randolph Hotel, but instead she walked into McDonald's, ignoring the cry from a wild-eyed woman of, "Capitalist swine." Agatha ordered a burger, fries and a black coffee and secured a table by looming over two students and driving them away. She wished she had gone to the Randolph instead. It was all the fault of the politically correct and people like that woman who had shouted at her, she reflected. It was the sort of thing that made you want to buy a mink coat, smoke twenty a day and eat in McDonald's out of sheer bloody-mindedness.

She became aware that she was being studied by a small, grey-haired man on the other side of the restaurant. When he saw Agatha looking at him, he gave a half smile and raised a hand in greeting.

Agatha finished her meal, and, on her road out, stopped at his table. "Do I know you?" she asked.

"No, but we're in the same profession," he said. "I'm Clive Tremund. I'd like to compare notes. Would you like to get out of here and go for a drink? What about the Randolph? I could do with a bit of posh."

Along Cornmarket, he talked about how he had recently moved to Oxford from Bristol to set up his agency.

In the bar of the Randolph, Agatha, who had taken note of his cheap suit, said, "I'll get the drinks."

"I'll be able to get you on my expenses," he said.

Agatha waited until the waiter had taken their order and come back with their drinks, and asked him what he had meant. "Never tell me I am one of your cases!"

"The only reason I am breaking the confidentiality of a client," said Clive, "is because the bitch hasn't paid anything so far and it looks as if she isn't going to."

"Would that bitch be a therapist called Jill Davent?"

"The same. I was supposed to ferret out everything I could about you. Got your birth certificate and took it from there."

"I'll kill her! Did she give a reason?"

"She said she was about to be married to a James Lacey, your ex. Said if you had got him to marry you, she might learn something by knowing all about you."

"I think it's because she's hiding something and wants to keep me away," said Agatha.

"Don't tell her I told you," said Clive. "She may yet pay me, although I'll probably have to take her to the Small Claims Court. She was one of my first clients."

"Why did you leave Bristol?"

"Got a divorce. Didn't want to see her with her new bloke. It hurts. Then I had to get my private detective's licence."

"I've just got one of those," said Agatha. "How's business?"

"Picking up. Missing students, students on drugs, anxious parents, that sort of thing."

"What did you make of the Davent woman?"

"She seemed pretty straightforward, until I gave her the report on you, and then she was sort of gleeful in a spiteful way. I asked for my fee and she demanded more. She told me your first husband had been murdered and maybe the police had got it wrong and you did it yourself. I haven't done anything about it. I sent her an e-mail, saying until she paid something, I couldn't go on. She had an office in Mircester before she moved to Carsely."

"I'll pay you instead," said Agatha. "Send me a written statement about the reasons she gave for employing you." Agatha took out her cheque book. "I will pay you now." She scribbled a cheque and handed it over.

"This is generous," said Clive. "I'll be glad not to see her again, except maybe in court. She gave me the creeps."

As Agatha drove back to Carsely, she could feel her anger mounting. As she turned down into the road leading to the village and to Jill's cottage, an elderly Ford was driving in the middle of the road. She honked her horn furiously, but the car in front continued on in the middle of the road at twenty miles an hour.

Victoria Bannister was the driver. She finally saw Agatha pull up outside Jill's cottage, and stopped as well a little way down the road. Her long nose twitching with curiosity, Victoria decided to see if she could hear what Agatha was up to.

The window of Jill's consulting room was open and Agatha's voice sounded out, loud and clear.

"How dare you hire a detective to probe into my life. Leave me alone or I'll kill you. But before I murder you, you useless piece of garbage, I am going to sue you for intrusion of privacy."

Said Jill, "And that will be a joke coming from a woman who earns her money doing just that."

Agatha stormed out as Victoria scampered down the road to her car and this time, drove off at sixty miles an hour.

Chapter Two

Mrs. Bloxby had been worried ever since Agatha had told her all about Jill having paid a private detective to look into her background. The vicar's wife felt that Mrs. Raisin should simply have asked Miss Davent *why* she had gone to such lengths.

Two days after Agatha's confrontation with the therapist was clear and quite cold. The waxy blossoms of the magnolia tree in the vicarage garden shone against the night sky where that peculiar blue moon was rising, a blue moon everyone had been told was because of forest fire in Canada.

Mrs. Bloxby came to a sudden decision. She would visit this therapist and ask her herself.

Mrs. Bloxby put on her old serviceable tweed coat and set out to walk through the village and up the hill to Jill's cottage.

She rang the bell and waited. A light was on in the consulting room. Perhaps, thought Mrs. Bloxby, a consultation was in progress and the therapist had decided not to answer the door. But having come this far, she was reluctant to leave. She banged on the door and shouted, "Anyone there!"

Silence.

Mrs. Bloxby walked to the window of the consulting room and peered through a gap in the curtains. She let out a startled gasp. She could see a pair of feet on the floor but the rest was masked by a desk.

She went back to the door and tried the handle. The door was unlocked.

Mrs. Bloxby went straight to the consulting room and walked round the desk. The ghastly distorted face of Jill Davent stared up at her. A coloured scarf had been wound tightly round her neck.

The vicar's wife backed slowly away, as if before royalty. Her legs felt weak and she was beginning to tremble.

She made it outside and, fishing in her old battered

leather handbag, took out her mobile phone and dialled 999.

It seemed to take ages for the police to arrive and as she stood there the pitiless blue moon rose higher in the sky.

Mrs. Bloxby let out a gulp of relief when she at last heard the approaching sirens.

It was only when she was back at the vicarage, having given her preliminary statement and been hugged by her worried husband, that she realised she should really phone Agatha Raisin.

Agatha was on her road home when Mrs. Bloxby phoned. Her first reaction was, "Oh, God! I threatened to kill her!"

"Did anyone hear you?" asked Mrs. Bloxby.

"No. I bet it was Gwen Simple. I swear that woman's a murderer."

As Agatha drove down into the village, she could see the police cars and ambulance and a little knot of villagers standing behind the police tape.

Her friend, Detective Sergeant Bill Wong, and Inspector Wilkes could be seen waiting outside the cottage for the forensic team to do their work. Agatha parked her car up the road and walked forward to join the crowd.

Victoria Bannister saw her approach and called out loudly, "There's the murderer. I heard her threatening to kill her."

Wilkes swung round, saw the contorted accusing face of Victoria and that she was pointing at Agatha.

"Wong," he said to Bill, "get that Raisin woman here and whoever that woman is who's accusing her."

How many weary hours have I spent in this interviewing room, having questions fired at me? thought Agatha dismally. She had been taken to police headquarters and Wilkes was interrogating her.

Over and over again, Agatha explained that she had found out that Jill had hired a private detective to ferret into her background and that had enraged her.

"I like my unfortunate upbringing to be kept quiet," she explained.

"You're a snob," said Wilkes nastily. "My father was a porter on the railroad and my mother worked in a factory. I'm proud of them."

"I am sure they were sterling people," said Agatha wearily, "but did *they* force you to work in a factory and then take your wages to buy booze? And did it ever cross your mind that she wanted to get me off her case? She was counselling Gwen Simple, for a start. And why did she leave Mircester?"

"That's for us to find out and for you to keep your nose out of police business," snapped Wilkes.

Agatha explained she had not left the office until eight o'clock in the evening. She had stopped for petrol outside Mircester. Yes, she had the receipt.

Agatha looked to Bill for sympathy but his face was blank.

By the time she was allowed to go and told not to leave the country, Agatha was in a rage.

Mrs. Bloxby, who had driven her to police headquarters, got the full blast of Agatha's tirade on the road back to Carsely. At last, when Agatha had paused for breath, Mrs. Bloxby said mildly, "But what a great incentive to find out who murdered her. I am sure it would be a wonderful idea to get revenge on Mr. Wilkes."

"Yes," said Agatha slowly. "There must be something fishy in Jill's background. I've asked that private detective of hers to detect for me."

Mrs. Bloxby looked surprised. "Why did you do that? You have detectives of your own."

"True," said Agatha. "I did it on the spur of the minute, but I will need all the help I can get. You see, there suddenly seems to be a great amount of adultery going on, and much as I hate divorce cases, they pay well and we are all stretched to the limit. Now I know you don't like to gossip, but I have to start somewhere. Who in Carsely has been consulting Jill?"

"I suppose there's no harm in telling you. There is your cleaner, Mrs. Simpson."

"What! Doris? She's the sanest person I know. Anyone else?"

"I believe Miss Bannister went to see her."

"That old cow. I could murder *her*."

"Mrs. Raisin!"

"Well, she's the reason I have been stuck in the police station half the night. Who else?"

"Old Mrs. Tweedy."

"You mean the old girl who lives round the corner from the vicarage. What's up with her?"

"Nothing more than loneliness, I should think," said Mrs. Bloxby. Then she added reluctantly, "Mr. Lacey spent a great deal of time with Miss Davent. Of course, there were women from the other villages but I don't know who they are."

As Mrs. Bloxby turned the corner into Lilac Lane where Agatha lived, they saw a car parked outside James's cottage. Bill Wong and detective Alice Peterson were just getting out of it. Bill saw Agatha and signalled to the vicar's wife to stop. "Don't go to bed yet," he said to Agatha. "I want to ask you a few more questions. Mrs. Bloxby, a minute of your time."

"Do you want me to come in with you?" asked Mrs. Bloxby as Agatha got out of the car at her cottage.

"No, you've done enough and thank you," said

Agatha. She had a sudden impulse to hug Mrs. Bloxby, but resisted. Agatha Raisin, somehow, could not hug anyone—handsome men excepted.

Once inside her cottage, she slumped down on her sofa. The cats prowled around her hopefully. Agatha often forgot that she had fed them and would feed them again, but this time, she felt too tired to move.

Her eyes were just closing when she heard the imperative summons of her doorbell. She struggled to her feet, went to open it and stared bleakly at the two detectives.

Agatha led the way to the kitchen. "Have a seat and make it quick," she said.

"We've got to go over it again," said Bill soothingly. "You should know better than to go around threatening to kill people."

"I was exasperated," said Agatha. "How dare she hire a private detective to dig up my background?"

"We will be interviewing Clive Tremund," said Bill. "Begin at the beginning."

Agatha did not want to say again that she had initially lied to Jill about her upbringing. Tell a detective that you've lied about one thing and they might assume you're lying about everything else. She detailed the previous day. She had been working on a divorce case and had been out on it with Phil. He had the pictures to prove it. They then had both met with the client's lawyer and handed over the evidence. Agatha worked late, typing up notes on other outstanding cases, and, as she was heading home, that was when Mrs. Bloxby had called her.

"Why do you call Mrs. Bloxby by her surname?" asked Alice, when the interview was over.

"There was a society for women in this village when I arrived here," explained Agatha. "We all addressed each other by surnames and somehow it stuck. I know it's strange these days when every odd and sod calls you by your first name. But I rather like being Mrs. Raisin. I hate when in hospital nurses call me Agatha. Seems overfamiliar, somehow. And, yes, it's ageing, as if they think I'm in my second childhood." She stifled a yawn.

"We'll let you get some sleep," said Bill.

When they had left, Agatha noticed that a red dawn was flooding the kitchen with light. She opened the garden door and let her cats out. The morning was fresh and beautiful. She went into the kitchen and got a wad of paper towel and wiped the dew off a garden lounger and then sank into it, sleepily enjoying the feel of the rising sun on her face and the smell of spring flowers.

She closed her eyes and drifted off to sleep. Two hours later she was in the grip of a nightmare where she had fallen overboard a ship, and as she struggled in the icy water, above her, Jill Davent leaned over the rail and laughed.

She awoke with a start to find the rain was drumming down and she was soaked to the skin. Agatha fled indoors and upstairs, where she stripped off her wet clothes, had a hot shower, pulled on a nightdress and climbed into bed.

Agatha awoke again in the early afternoon and reconnected her phone, which she had switched off before falling asleep. She checked her messages. There were worried ones from her staff and several from the press.

She dressed and went wearily downstairs. Looking through a small opening in the drawn curtains in her front room, she saw the press massed outside her cottage. Agatha went upstairs and changed into an old T-shirt, jacket, loose trousers and running shoes.

Down again and out into the back garden, where she seized a ladder and propped it against the fence. She had somehow planned to heave the ladder up when she was straddled on the top of the fence but could not manage it. She was just about to give up and retreat when James appeared below in the narrow path which separated her cottage from his.

"I'll get my ladder," he called up to her.

If this were a film, thought Agatha grumpily, I would leap down into his strong arms. A watery sunlight was gilding the new leaves of the large lilac tree at the front of her cottage, which mercifully screened her off from the press, which might otherwise have spotted her at the end of the passage.

James came through a side gate from his garden carrying a ladder which he propped against the fence.

Agatha climbed down. She smiled up at James and then ducked her head as she realised she wasn't wearing make-up.

"Come in and have a coffee," said James. "But I really think you should have a word with the press, even if it's 'no comment' or they'll be here all day."

"In these clothes!"

"Agatha! Oh, all right. We'll climb back over, sort yourself out, and then go out to face them."

James waited impatiently in Agatha's kitchen for half an hour until she descended the stairs, fully made-up and teetering on a pair of high heels.

Agatha went out to face the press. She competently fielded questions while television cameras whirred and flashes went off in her face. Yes, she had spent a long time at police headquarters. Why? Because she was a private detective who lived in the village where the woman was murdered.

And then to her horror, Victoria Bannister pushed

her way to the front. "You threatened to kill her!" she shrieked.

"Jill Davent hired a private detective to find out all about me," said Agatha. "I was annoyed with her. That is all. The question that arises is, why was she afraid of me? What had she got to hide?"

"You're a murderer," shouted Victoria.

"And you," said Agatha, "will be hearing from my lawyers. I am going to sue you for slander."

Victoria's wrinkled face showed shock and alarm. "I'm sorry," she babbled. "I made a mistake." She turned to escape, shouting at the press to let her through.

Agatha's voice followed her, "There's one in every village."

And in that moment, Victoria could have killed Agatha. As she fled up to her cottage, she vowed to find out the identity of the murderer herself. She knew all the gossip of the village. Once inside, she poured herself a stiff sherry and went off into a rosy dream where *she* was facing an admiring press and telling them how she had solved the case.

"All done?" asked James as Agatha teetered back into the kitchen, sat down and kicked off her shoes.

"I think they've gone off to the vicarage to persecute Mrs. Bloxby."

"Will she be able to handle it?"

"Oh, yes. A vicar's wife has to be tough. In the past, she's had to confront several women who developed a crush on her husband. It's a lousy existence and she's welcome to it. Half her time is acting as an unpaid therapist. A lot of people take their troubles to her."

"Including you?"

"I'm her friend. That's different. I'll phone Toni to take over tomorrow. I think I'll go into Oxford and talk to Clive."

Clive Tremund's office was in a narrow lane off Walton Street in the Jericho area of Oxford. It was situated in the ground floor of a thin two-storied building. Agatha tried the handle and found the door was unlocked.

There was a little square vestibule with a frosted glass door on the left bearing the legend TREMUND INVESTIGATIONS. She pushed open the door and went in.

Agatha let out a gasp. It was a scene of chaos. Papers were scattered everywhere. Drawers hung open at crazy angles. A filing cabinet had been knocked over onto the floor. She backed slowly out, took out her phone and called the police. Then she went outside to wait.

The cobbled lane was very quiet.

After only five minutes, a police car rolled to a stop

and two policemen got out. Agatha quickly told them who she was, why she had called and what she had found. The police called it in. Another wait while two detectives arrived. Agatha had to make her statement again and was told to wait until a forensic team arrived.

The day was becoming darker and a damp gusty wind promised rain. Agatha retreated to her car and lit a cigarette, noticing that her fingers were shaking. Where was Clive? What had happened to him? She felt in need of support. Agatha noticed that neighbours were emerging from the surrounding houses. She phoned Toni and asked her to join her, saying, "Pretend to be a curious onlooker and question the neighbours before you come and talk to me."

A forensic team arrived and suited up before going into the office. The morning dragged on. At last Toni arrived and Agatha could see her questioning the neighbours. Then Toni finally walked off and disappeared around the corner into Walton Street while Agatha fretted. Where on earth was she going?

After ten minutes, Toni returned, carrying a large brown paper bag. She slid into the passenger seat of Agatha's car.

"Coffee and sticky buns," said Toni, opening the bag.

"You're an angel. What did you get from the neighbours?"

"Not much. He lived upstairs."

"Oh, snakes and bastards!" howled Agatha. "I didn't even think to have a look. He could be lying dead up there."

"Don't think so. No ambulance. Have a bun."

"Ta. So what else?"

"Didn't speak to the neighbours. His clients mostly called in the evenings. Yesterday evening, one young woman, blond, slim, that's all the description."

"Could be you," said Agatha gloomily.

"Two men at different intervals, both looking like middle-aged businessmen, one tall and thin and the other small and tubby. Not much to go on."

"I should have looked for a client list," mourned Agatha, "instead of rushing out to phone the police. But you know how it is, one fingerprint and they'd haul me in for breaking and entering. I'll come back when things have quietened down and try the next-door neighbours. The police are already knocking at doors."

"That's why I couldn't try them myself," said Toni. "All I could do was to pretend to be one of the crowd. Have another bun. They're very comforting."

"Oh, well, why not?"

There came a rapping on Agatha's window. The detective who had interviewed her earlier said, "You are to come with me to Thames Valley Police to be interviewed. Leave your car here. An officer will drive you back. Who is this young lady?"

Oh, to be young and beautiful, thought Agatha grumpily. The man's practically leering.

"Miss Toni Gilmour," said Agatha. "One of my detectives."

"She'd better come with you. I don't want anyone messing up this crime scene."

Agatha made her statement again to a refreshingly young and efficient female detective. She was just about to leave when the ax fell. She was told that she had to recover her car and then drive to Mircester police headquarters and make another statement, and Agatha knew that Wilkes's idea of an interview could run into hours.

There was no sign of Toni. Agatha got into her car and phoned her.

"I got chased away," said Toni. "I'll come back this evening, if you like."

"Let me think about that. Do you know if they've found Clive?"

"Not a sign of him. A friendly policeman told me his flat was empty before he got reprimanded."

"I hope to God he's all right," said Agatha. "I've got to go to Mircester to make another statement. I'll call you tomorrow."

Agatha knew the rush-hour traffic would be building

up and so she decided to drive to the Botley road and exit Oxford by the ring road.

But as she got to the bottom of Beaufort Street, the traffic slowed to a stop and she could see police erecting a barrier.

She swung off into the Gloucester Green car park and then made her way on foot to the barrier. "I must get past," she said to a policeman on duty. "My train's about to leave," she lied, quickly thinking of an excuse to find out what had happened.

"All right. But keep clear of the police activity on the canal bridge. There are enough rubberneckers there already."

Agatha hurried down Worcester Street to Hythe Bridge Street. "What's up?" Agatha asked a man.

"Body in the canal," he said.

With a feeling of dread, Agatha elbowed her way to the front, ignoring angry protests. A weak sun was gilding the black waters of the canal. As Agatha watched, the sun shone down on the dead face of Clive Tremund as his body was dragged from the water.

She realised that if she was spotted by any detectives who had been at Clive's house, then there would be more questions, and so she shoved her way back through the crowd.

———

Agatha felt miserable as she drove to Mircester. Clive had been her one hope of getting a break in the case. Once she got to Mircester and before she went into police headquarters, she phoned Patrick Mulligan and briefed him on what had been happening. "See if your old police contacts can tell you anything," said Agatha.

As the long interview progressed, Agatha realised to her horror that Wilkes was beginning to regard her as the number-one suspect. He seemed to believe that Agatha had searched Tremund's offices herself, because there was something in her past she did not want anyone to know.

After fifteen minutes, Agatha lost her temper. "I want a lawyer," she shouted.

She was escorted to a waiting room where she phoned criminal lawyer Sir David Herythe. She had met David at a party on one of her brief visits to London the year before. Agatha had found him very attractive, so, she thought, why not kill two birds with one stone. She knew he commuted to London from Oxford.

He listened patiently to her furious tirade and then to her relief, he said he was actually in Oxford and would be right over. David knew that Agatha had a knack of getting into situations which drew in a lot of publicity and David loved to see his own photograph in the newspapers.

He arrived half an hour later and walked with

Agatha to the interview room. He was a tall man with silver hair and a high-bridged nose. He was famous for his waspish remarks in court.

He quickly established that Agatha had not been charged with anything, that she had already made a full statement to the Oxford police, suggested they read the report and stop wasting his client's time, smiled all round and ushered Agatha out.

"Let's have dinner," he said. "The George?" And without waiting for a reply, he set off with long rangy strides. Agatha raced to keep up with him.

As the evening was fine and warm, the earlier miserable weather having cleared, they found a table on the terrace overlooking the hotel gardens.

Agatha lit a cigarette and studied her companion's face. He was examining the menu as if reading a brief. His face was lightly tanned.

"Been on holiday?" asked Agatha.

"Yes, Monaco, at a friend's place. Be with you in a minute. Food is a serious business. I'm going to be very conventional. I'll have the lobster salad followed by tournedos Rossini. Oh, how grand. They have a bottle of Chateau Montelena Sauvignon 2010."

Agatha blinked rapidly, recognising the wine as the most expensive on the menu.

Not another cheapskate, she thought. He's going to stiff me with the bill. She realised she was very tired and that her make-up needed repair. But what did it all matter, she grumbled to herself, with dead bodies following me around like wasps?

"I'll have the same," she said.

He waved an imperious hand to summon the waiter and gave the order.

Agatha could only be thankful that he had not ordered another bottle of wine to accompany the first course.

"Now," he said, "tell me all about it."

Agatha gave him a succinct report without her usual exaggerations.

When she had finished, he said, "So we have a therapist with dicey credentials, who, nonetheless, must have had a strong personality to draw in quite a few clients. Can you think of anyone in the village amongst the people who consulted her who might be a murderer?"

"It can't be my cleaner, Mrs. Simpson. Too decent and honourable. I would like it to be Victoria Bannister because she's a malicious old cow. Mrs. Tweedy, I don't know, but she is elderly. But my money's on Gwen Simple. Remember her? Son put people in meat pies?"

The first course arrived and they both concentrated on eating it, Agatha finding that she was very hungry.

Then he surprised her by saying, "I could be of help to you. I have seen so many criminals. I have not yet finished my holiday. If you like, I could visit the four clients that you know of and see what conclusions I come to."

Agatha hesitated. "I would not charge you a fee," he said. "It would be a sort of busman's holiday."

Looking at him with new eyes, Agatha realised he was an attractive man. Was he married?

When the main course arrived, he turned all his attention to the food and wine, leaving Agatha to eat her dinner automatically and dream of being married to him. And wouldn't that put Charles's nose out of joint!

By the end of the meal, he had taken a note of the names and addresses of the three women who had consulted Jill. He had a good contact in the police in Oxford and felt sure he could find out a lot about Clive Tremund.

More than that, he paid the bill!

He escorted Agatha back to her car in the square and said he would call on her in her office on the following afternoon.

When she arrived home, Agatha patted her cats, fed them, and then rushed to her computer to look up Sir David Herythe. He had been married to a glamorous model but the marriage had ended in an amicable divorce.

Rats, thought Agatha, dismally looking at a photograph of the ex-wife. She was blond and beautiful. If his taste ran to arm candy, there wasn't much hope for one middle-aged detective.

Mind you, there weren't any children and that—

"How's it going?" asked Charles from behind her. Agatha leapt up in alarm. "What are you doing here?" she demanded.

"Heard about Tremund's murder and came to hold your hand. Why are you looking up Sir David Herythe?"

"I employed him," said Agatha, "to get me out of the clutches of Wilkes, who seems to think I go around murdering people."

"He's wickedly expensive," said Charles.

Agatha switched off her computer and moved to the drinks table.

"If you're having a nightcap," said Charles, "get me a brandy."

Agatha poured two goblets of brandy and handed one to Charles. She sat down beside him on the sofa.

"Listen to this, my miserly friend," she said. "He not only paid for a very expensive dinner at the George, but he has a week's holiday left and is going to detect for me. For nothing!"

"Oh, do be careful, Aggie. He tears people apart."

"That's his job. He prosecutes people."

"I'm not talking about his behaviour in court. I've met him before at several parties. He befriends someone, usually a woman, and when his interest dies, he mocks her in public."

Agatha felt a qualm of unease. Then she rallied. "Look, I need all the help I can get."

The next morning, Agatha, who had gone up to bed telling Charles to lock up on his way out, was irritated to find him sitting at the breakfast table. What if David should drop by?

"I thought you had left," she said grumpily.

"I'm bored," said Charles, lifting Hodge off his knee. "I thought I'd join you in a bit of detecting."

Agatha hesitated. Then she remembered the magic of Charles's title had been the means before of gaining good interviews. "But buy your own cigarettes," she added as she tried to move her packet of Bensons out of his reach. She wasn't quick enough and he extracted one and lit it.

Producing an electronic cigarette from her handbag, Agatha fiercely inhaled.

"Oh, have a real one," urged Charles. "You may not

get cancer but you'll give yourself a hernia trying to get a hit from one of those."

"I must give up," fretted Agatha. "It's so yesterday to smoke. Not to mention the smell."

Charles blew a smoke ring and smiled lazily at her. He rose to his feet and let the cats out into the garden. "No need for the pets to suffer."

"I thought of trying Mrs. Tweedy first. She's reported to be very old but she may be able to tell us something about Jill. I'll have a coffee and then we'll take a walk up there."

Mrs. Tweedy lived in a cul-de-sac at the back of the vicarage in a row of Georgian cottages. There was no bell. Agatha seized a brass knocker in the shape of a lion's head and hammered with it.

The door opened and an elderly woman surveyed her. Agatha introduced herself and Charles and they were invited in. Mrs. Tweedy led them through a small dining area to her living room. The room was very dark because of the ivy which covered the windows. Flickering sunlight, shining through the ivy leaves, danced about the room, which was sparsely furnished with a three-piece suite covered in chintz and a small television set. Mrs. Tweedy was a thickset woman with grey hair and a pugnacious face. She was wearing a dress with a chintz pattern, like the furniture. Her long, gnarled fingers were covered in diamond rings. Her thick black-stockinged legs ended in a pair of tartan slippers. Her eyes were small and shrewd.

"We want to ask you for your impression of Jill Davent," Agatha began.

"People are saying you killed her," said Mrs. Tweedy.

"Well, I didn't," said Agatha. "What did you make of her?"

"Good listener. No one listens to the old these days. In fact, nobody listens to anyone these days. While you're talking to them, all they do is wait for you to finish so they can talk about themselves."

"Is that the only reason you went to her?" asked Charles. "To get someone to listen to you?"

"And what's up with that, may I ask?"

"Not a thing," said Charles. "What did you make of her?"

"Silly bitch!" said Mrs. Tweedy venomously.

"What? Why do you say that?" asked Agatha.

"Last session, I was talking about my life. I miss my brother, who died in an accident. I was living in Oxford and decided to move to the country because cities can be lonely places. Well, I was talking and her phone rang. She took it out into the hall and shut the door. I went to the door and listened. She must have been talking to a fellow because it was 'darling this' and 'darling that.' Then she came back in and said the session was over and tried to charge me. I told her to get stuffed. Never went back. I wish I had never come here. This village is creepy and you, Agatha Raisin, are one of the creepiest things about it—entertaining your fancy man here at nights." She glared at Charles.

"You ought to make an honest woman of her."

Before Agatha could say anything, Charles smiled and said, "You are one truly horrible woman."

Mrs. Tweedy let out a cackle of laughter. "I like a man who speaks his mind."

"And I hate old frumps who speak theirs!" yelled Agatha. "I'm getting out of this dump!"

As they left, they were followed by roars of laughter from the old lady.

"Ah, the dignity and grace of old age," said Charles as they walked through the village. "Let's visit Mrs. Bloxby and see if she's picked up some gossip. Also, you should let Bill know about that 'darling' phone call. Pity we haven't the means to trace it. I mean, if she carried the phone out it must have been on her mobile and that'll be in the evidence locker."

"Not necessarily," said Agatha. "It could be one of those hands-free phones and it might still be there. If only we could break in and have a look. You can find out recent phone calls. I wonder who inherits? Wait a moment and I'll phone Patrick and see if he's found out anything."

Charles wandered up to the road. People were coming and going from the village shop. It all looked like a rural idyll. In the old days, he thought, Agatha would be blamed for attracting murder and burnt at the stake.

"That's interesting," said Agatha, coming to join him. "Her brother inherits. He's called Adrian Sommerville and he lives in Mircester. He's an interior decorator and I've got the address."

"Oh, well, bang goes tea and sympathy at the vicarage," said Charles. "We'll take your car."

"Meaning, you'll take my petrol, cheapskate."

"You're slipping, Aggie," commented Charles as they approached Mircester. "You should have looked up Sommerville in the phone book."

"Don't tell me how to do my job," said Agatha huffily. "I've got the address. I don't need to phone. Let's see. He's got a business address in The Loans. That's the lane by the abbey. We'll park in the main square and walk."

There was a brass plaque outside the door with the legend SOMERVILLE INTERIORS. A small sign said, PRESS BELL AND ENTER.

44

Inside, a blonde was sitting behind a reception desk. She put down a copy of *House & Garden*, smiled at them and asked how she could be of assistance.

Agatha performed the introductions, wishing not for the first time that she was in the police force and could just flash a warrant card.

The secretary disappeared into an interior office. They waited.

Agatha was just saying, "Do you think he's escaped out the back?" when the blonde returned.

"Mr. Sommerville can spare you a few moments," she said grandly, radiating disapproval from every thread of her tailored power suit.

Adrian Sommerville came as a surprise. Agatha was expecting some sort of willowy stereotype, but the man who rose to shake hands with them was dark and squat, wearing a sober grey suit, silk shirt and tie. He had a thick thatch of black hair, thick lips and designer stubble. He was seated behind an antique desk. Agatha and Charles sat down on chairs facing him. The walls of the office were decorated with photos of expensive-looking rooms.

His first question surprised Agatha. "Who is paying you?"

"No one," said Agatha. "The murder took place in my village and I want to know who did it."

"I hear the police suspect you."

"Well, I didn't murder anyone," retorted Agatha crossly. "I wouldn't be wasting my time otherwise."

"Unless to throw them off the scent."

Agatha half rose to her feet but Charles pulled her down.

"Stop being so aggressive," he said. "Don't you want to find out who murdered your Jill?"

"Of course I do. But it's better to leave it to the police."

"We're sorry for your loss," said Charles. "But it's a loss you don't seem to be grieving over. What do you plan to do with her house?"

"Sell it. Why?"

"I might like to buy it," said Charles. "I collect properties. Hobby of mine. How much?"

"Five hundred thousand or so."

"Rubbish," said Charles. "A nasty little cottage where a murder has taken place? Three hundred thousand?"

"It's not on the market yet." Adrian's eyes held a mercenary gleam.

"I might like to have a look at it," said Charles.

"You own that big place in Warwickshire, don't you?"

"Yes."

"Give me your card. I'll phone you when the police have finished with it. Don't want to bother with blood-sucking estate agents, now do we?"

"Of course not."

"So, goodbye."

Charles could feel the volcano that was Agatha simmering beside him.

He handed Adrian his card and heaved Agatha out of her chair. "Let's go, darling."

Chapter Three

Outside, Agatha raged, "Horrible man!"

"Oh, calm down," said Charles. "We want a look inside her cottage, don't we? You nearly spoiled things."

"I am sorry," said Agatha in a suddenly mild voice. Charles looked at her suspiciously. Agatha had just remembered that David Herythe was due to call at her office and she didn't want Charles around. "Why don't we split up? I can't interview Victoria because she'll just curse me. But you could and we could meet up later."

"All right," said Charles reluctantly. "What are you going to do?"

"I've got to get to the office and see how the others are getting on. I do have a business to run, Charles, and no one is paying me for all this effort."

"But we came in your car, or have you forgotten? How am I to get to Carsely?"

Agatha whipped out her mobile phone. "Toni," she said, "could you be an angel and run Charles back to Carsely? Great. We'll meet you in the car park."

Now, why doesn't Agatha want me in her office? wondered Charles. "We haven't had anything to eat," he said. "Why don't we all go for a late lunch?" he asked as Toni came hurrying towards them.

"I'm not hungry," lied Agatha. "Why don't you and Toni go for a bite first?"

"I've already had lunch," said Toni.

"You can watch me eat," said Charles.

They were about to walk off, when Toni called, "My wits are wandering. Herythe is waiting for you in the office, Agatha."

Charles gave a malicious smile. "I haven't seen David in ages. Must say hullo," and to Agatha's horror, he set off for her office without waiting for her.

Toni and Agatha hurried after him.

<hr>

To Agatha's further irritation, when she got to the office it was to find David Herythe seated behind her desk and going through the contents of her computer.

"Charles Fraith!" cried David. "What are you doing here?"

While Charles explained that he was a close friend of Agatha's and the conversation turned to the sort of do-you-know about people Agatha had never met, she leaned over and switched off her computer. Still talking, David vacated her desk and walked round to join Charles.

"Why don't we go for a drink?" said Charles.

"Great idea." Both men headed for the door.

"Stop!" shouted Agatha.

They both turned around. Charles smiled at her sweetly and David raised his eyebrows.

"I mean," said Agatha desperately, "you were supposed to find out something for me, David."

"Oh, that. I've got as far as finding out how Tremund was murdered. He wasn't strangled. He was struck on the head with some blunt instrument. A bag of stones was slung round his neck and he was tipped into the canal. The divers found it when they brought him up."

"How did they know he was in the canal?" asked Agatha. "And when was he shoved in?"

"They haven't done the pathology thoroughly yet, but some students have finally come forward. They said it was about three in the morning and they were coming back from a party when they heard a splash from the canal. One girl said she thought she saw a man's head above the water and then it disappeared."

"Why didn't they come forward sooner?" asked Agatha.

"The police guess they had been on drugs and didn't want to get involved, but one of them, a girl called Hayley Martin, got a fit of conscience and called in at the police station and reported what they had seen."

"Did she see anyone else around?" asked Toni.

"She saw a dark figure on the towpath but couldn't see if it was a man or a woman. Her friends told her to forget it, that it was just someone fly tipping.

"I went to see this Hayley Martin. I told her that anything she told me would not be reported to the police. She said the others were drunk and had been smoking pot. She said she didn't take drugs and hadn't had all that much to drink. I could see why the police took her story seriously. She's a very pretty girl and very honest.

"Now, to Tremund's office. His computer has been taken and as you saw, Agatha, papers and correspondence were scattered all over the place."

"Did the police say whether Jill Davent kept tapes of her sessions?"

"Evidently she didn't. That's all I've got. Come along,

Charles. All this talking has given me a thirst. I'll be in touch, Agatha."

Over drinks in the George, David said, "Are you in a relationship with that Raisin woman?"

"We are very close friends."

"Didn't think it could be anything else," said David. "Why?"

"Men like us can have a pick of the young ones," said David. "Though I must admit Agatha is sexy. Might have a fling there."

Charles rose to his feet. His light voice carried around the bar.

"Don't you dare!"

"Why?"

"Because I'll kill you," said Charles and strode out of the hotel bar.

David Herythe was furious. People treated him with respect. He would bed Agatha and make sure Fraith heard about it.

He finished his drink and decided to return to his home in Summertown in Oxford.

He lived in a Victorian villa, one of the ones that had been built for the Oxford dons in the nineteenth century when the decision was made to allow them to live out of college and marry. It is the most expensive part of

Oxford. He also had an apartment in the Inner Temple in London, one of the Inns of Court.

He parked his car in the short drive under a laburnum tree and got out, savouring the peace of the evening. He let himself in, reset the burglar alarm, went to the kitchen and poured himself a glass of Chardonnay and carried it through to his desk in the office.

He started to make out a bill for his services at police headquarters to send to Agatha. That being done he opened the window wide, for the evening was warm, listening to the blackbirds singing and the hiss of traffic going down the Banbury road.

His phone rang. A gruff, sexless voice said, "If you want to know who done those murders, meet me at the Hythe Bridge canal in half an hour." Then whoever it was rang off.

Now this is either some nutter or the real murderer, thought David. He phoned the police and told them about the call. They said they would send plainclothes detectives to keep watch.

As he got into his car and set off, he felt the thrill of the chase. He parked in the Worcester Road car park and walked round to Hythe Bridge. He could not recognise the detectives, but the road was busy with young people coming and going. As the time dragged past, he realised the call must have been a hoax. He phoned the police and said he had been the victim of a silly trick and he was going home.

As he parked, he noticed to his irritation that he had left his office window open in his excitement. He let himself in, reset the burglar alarm and decided to make himself an omelette before going to bed.

After he had eaten, he undressed, showered and went to bed. But he felt restless, tossing and turning until he decided to take two of his prescribed sleeping pills, the ones he had been trying so hard to do without.

With a sigh of relief, he settled back against the pillows. Soon his eyes closed and he was fast asleep.

He slept naked. A gloved hand came out of the darkness and gently pulled the covers down. Leaves were pressed against his chest. The figure moved silently away.

David jerked awake as palpitations racked his body. His body arched in convulsions, he writhed in agony and then fell into a coma.

The dark figure came back and picked the leaves from his body and then disappeared.

David Herythe's cleaning woman, Mrs. Danby, let herself in the following morning. She reset the burglar alarm and went into the kitchen, hoping to be able to have a cup of tea before Mr. Herythe, whom she knew to be an early riser, descended the stairs.

She was not only able to have a cup of tea in peace but a cigarette as well. Then she began to clean the downstairs. When, by midmorning, her employer did not appear, she began to become worried. His car was in the drive. Heaving the old vacuum up the stairs and cursing her employer for being too mean to buy one of the newer, lighter ones, she left the machine on the landing and pushed open David's bedroom door.

A shaft of sunlight shining in between a gap in the heavy curtains shone full on the twisted rictus of agony that was David's face.

Mrs. Danby backed slowly away. She knew she should check for a pulse but she was too frightened to go any-where near that awful death mask. She retreated to the landing and slammed the door, scrabbled in the pocket of her old trousers for her phone and called the police before going downstairs on shaky legs to cut off the burglar alarm and leave the door open.

Two police cars arrived, then three detectives and then the pathologist, followed closely by a forensic team, whose job it was to go over the whole house, while Mrs. Danby sat on a kitchen chair in the front garden, shivering despite the warmth of the day.

56

Agatha allowed a small television in the corner of her office to play the BBC's twenty-four-hour news service, so long as the volume was turned low. She was just saying to Phil, "Get your cameras and we'll try that adultery case again," when Phil said, "Listen!" He went over and turned up the sound on the television. David Herythe's face came up on the screen, dressed in wig and gown. "His body was found at his home in Oxford by his cleaner, Mrs. Danby," the announcer was saying, "but the police do not suspect foul play. Preliminary reports suggest that the eminent barrister died of a massive heart attack."

"Don't believe it," said Agatha. "Where's Patrick?"

"At the supermarket, checking out the staff to see who's been nicking the electric goods."

Agatha phoned him and told him about Herythe. "Have you any contacts in the Thames Valley Police?" she asked.

"I've got one. I'll see what I can find out."

Agatha rang off and turned to Simon. "Find out this Mrs. Danby's address and get over there. It must be murder."

It was evening before Simon was able to track down the cleaner who lived in tower block on the Blackbird Leys council estate. The door was opened by a young woman with an improbable colour of aubergine hair, two nose rings, and holding a screaming baby.

"Mrs. Danby?" asked Simon.

"Naw, she ain't speaking to no press, so get lost."

"I'm not press. I'm a detective," said Simon.

"Oh, well, that's different. Hey, Beryl," she called, "another of them police."

Simon knew he should reveal his proper identity but he decided to do that as he was leaving.

He was ushered into a filthy living room, showing that some cleaners can't be bothered with their own homes after they've finished cleaning someone else's. Empty pizza boxes littered the floor, empty beer cans spilled over out of a plastic bin in the corner and old newspapers and magazines were piled up everywhere.

The woman with the baby said, "I'm off home, Mum, to get Frank's tea. I'll be round in the morning."

When she had gone, Simon said, "Just a few questions, Mrs. Danby."

"Could you give me a minute to change?" said Mrs. Danby. She raised one powerful freckled arm and sniffed her armpit. "I stink something awful."

"Go ahead," said Simon. When she had gone, he opened a window wide because it wasn't only Mrs. Danby's armpits that stank.

Mrs. Danby went into her bedroom and stripped off her blouse and trousers. Her trousers were too long for her and she had rolled up the bottoms. She took the trousers and threw them on top of a pile of clothes in the laundry basket. A large leaf which had been stuck to the bottom of the trousers fell at her feet. She automatically picked it up and rolled it between her fingers while she wondered if she had anything clean to wear.

She suddenly clutched her heart as she was seized by a violent allergic reaction. "Help!" she shrieked.

Simon came running in, looked at her contorted face and wondered why the matronly Mrs. Danby was wearing a scarlet thong. He phoned for an ambulance.

Desperate to do something, he went into the kitchen, filled a glass of water, poured a pile of salt into it, mixed it up and took it to her. "Drink!" he shouted. He got her to take a large gulp and then she vomited all over the floor. "Did you eat or drink something bad?" he asked.

"Leaf," she said weakly. "That there leaf."

Simon heard the wail of a siren. He took out a little plastic back and put on gloves. He lifted the leaf carefully into the bag.

"What's your daughter's phone number?" he asked.

"On the wall. Above the kitchen phone. Josie Maller."

The ambulance men arrived, closely followed by two policemen and a detective. The woman was Detective Sergeant Ruby Carson. She had blond hair and deep blue eyes. Simon forgot all about Toni and fell in love on the spot. He rapidly told Ruby and the paramedics about the leaf. She said she would take his statement while waiting for the pathologist and a forensic team to arrive, while they sat in her car.

Said Ruby, after Simon had reverently handed her the little plastic bag with the leaf inside, "I'll phone the hospital in a few minutes to make sure she's still alive. I'll give this leaf to the forensic lab." She took his statement down, printed it off on her mobile printer and got him to sign it.

"It all seems to have started in that village where your boss lives," said Ruby. "What's the connection?"

"David Herythe was on holiday and keen to do a bit of detecting," said Simon. "He dies. His cleaning woman picks up this discarded leaf and has a seizure. Jill Davent, that therapist, I am sure, found out something about someone, and whatever it was panicked a murderer."

"I'll just phone the hospital." Simon waited while

Ruby phoned, studying her attractive profile. How old was she? Maybe a good bit older than he was. He wondered whether to ask her out.

She finally rang off and said that Mrs. Danby was still alive.

Simon took the plunge. "What do you do in your spare time?" he asked.

Ruby flashed him an amused look. "Are you chatting me up?"

"Trying to," said Simon.

There was a rap at the car window. "Detective Inspector Briggs, Mr. Black," said a man, leaning in the passenger window. "Have you made a statement?"

"Yes."

"Well, you are to go directly to Mircester police headquarters and tell them what you've been up to." Off with you."

When he had left, Simon groaned. "They'll probably keep me up all night. Do you have a card?"

Ruby smiled and handed one over.

"Thanks," said Simon. "I'll be in touch."

She isn't wearing any rings, he thought happily, as he drove off to Mircester.

Unaware of what was going on, Agatha sat in her own cleaner's cosy parlour and asked, "Why did you consult

Jill Davent? I would have thought you were the last person to need a therapist."

"I met her in the village shop," said Doris Simpson. Her cat, Scrabble, jumped on her capacious lap and settled down to sleep. "I had been suffering with pains in my shoulders. She said it was tension and she could take the pain away. Well, the doctor couldn't find nothing wrong so I thought I'd give it a try. She massaged my shoulders and said she was taking all my tension away. Then she not only made me cough up sixty pounds but charged me twenty for the massage oil."

"If you are suffering from tension, you're worried. Out with it."

"I'm right ashamed. We decided to buy this council house, but I was overambitious, like. I'm behind with the payments and the bank is threatening to repossess."

Agatha thought rapidly. The council houses were good solid property.

"Who would you have left it to, if you had succeeded in buying it?"

"We haven't even made a will, Agatha. We couldn't have children and there's no one close."

"Well, here's what we'll do," said Agatha. "I'll buy it, but you live in it till the end of your days. I'll put a codicil in my will to that effect. We'll see the lawyers and bank tomorrow."

"But your job is dangerous! What if me and hubby outlive you? You won't get any benefit."

Agatha hadn't thought of that. On the other hand, Doris was a superb cleaner and she looked after Agatha's cats when Agatha was away.

She shrugged. "Oh, let's go for it. Deal?"

"Oh, Agatha! You're a saint. May you live forever."

But out in the nighttime darkness of the Cotswolds, someone was already planning to send Agatha Raisin to an early grave.

Chapter Four

E verything seemed to grind to a halt. Spring moved into summer. Agatha could not find out the results of Mrs. Danby's illness, except that somehow it was because she had picked up a leaf. But what type of leaf? Agatha could not understand why it was taking them so long to identify it.

The fact was, as Patrick Mulligan was at last able to find out, that the leaf had somehow become lost in the forensic lab. How?

A young forensic scientist who had gone on holiday was eventually tracked down to one of the Greek islands. At first she claimed to know nothing about it, but under the grilling of two Thames Valley detectives, who were determined not to find out that their journey had been unnecessary, burst into tears and confessed she had opened the lab window to call down to her boy-friend and several bits and pieces had blown out.

A hurried and frantic search of all the debris below that window at last revealed the little envelope blown up against a wire fence.

This Simon was also able to tell Agatha because he was in constant touch with Ruby, although, so far, he had not persuaded her to come out on a date with him.

The leaf was at last identified as coming from monks-hood, a deadly killer of a plant. It was once used to kill wolves and mad dogs and was then called wolfsbane. All parts of the plant are poisonous and it doesn't even need to be taken by mouth; the poison can be absorbed through the skin. It looks like a delphinium and the most common colour is purple.

"So are they going to exhume Herythe's body?" asked Agatha one morning as he staff were gathered in the office.

"No point," said Patrick. "It's the perfect killer and the poison doesn't stay in the body. But the police are regarding it as murder and Charles has been pulled in for questioning."

"Why Charles, of all people?"

"Someone tipped off the police that he was heard threatening to kill Herythe in the bar of the George."

"I'd better get round there and see if there's anything I can do," said Agatha.

She was about to leave when there came a tentative knock on the door. Agatha opened it and found herself faced with a small boy carrying a bouquet of flowers. "Are you Mrs. Raisin?" he asked.

"That's me."

"These are for you."

Agatha was just reaching for the bouquet when Toni shrieked, "Don't touch it. You, boy, drop it on the floor."

Startled, the boy did as he was told.

"Look at the flowers," said Toni. "That looks like monkshood."

"Who gave you those flowers?" asked Agatha.

The boy was small and fair-haired. "It was a big chap. He gave me ten pounds to deliver them."

The flowers were wrapped in gold paper. "Did you touch the flowers anywhere?" Patrick asked the boy.

"N-no."

"The stems are wrapped up so he should be all right," said Patrick. "I'll call the police."

"What's your name?" Agatha asked the boy.

"Jimmy Martin, miss."

"Look, Jimmy, go into the toilet over there and wash your hands thoroughly. That bouquet may be poisonous.

You'll need to wait here. The police will want to interview you."

"Like in the fillums?"

"Just like that."

"Wicked!"

There was a long delay, waiting for the boy's mother to arrive before he could be interviewed. His description of the big man who had given him the flowers was vague. But it had taken place at the corner of market square, which was covered by a video camera. Not for the first time, Agatha fretted at not having the powers of the police. She would dearly have loved to have a look at the videotape.

When it was all over, and the boy had been taken home by his mother, Charles strolled in.

Agatha told him about the latest development. The usually urbane and unflappable Charles looked worried. "So you're the killer's new target. You'd better take a holiday, Agatha."

"Not me," said Agatha. "Patrick, take money out of the petty cash and stand drinks for your old police buddies and find out what's on that video."

"Too soon," said Patrick. "Give it a few hours. I'll get on with that divorce case and then I'll let you know if I find out anything."

"So, Charles," said Agatha, "how did you get on?"

"Wilkes was really nasty," said Charles. "The press are breathing down his neck. He all but accused me out-right. Come on, Aggie. I could do with a drink."

"Too early."

"The sun is over the poop deck or whatever."

"Wait until I arrange things here. What have we got, Toni?"

"Simon and I have that missing girl. Patrick's got his divorce case and Phil is going with him to take pictures. And you forgot about yourself. So you have some free time."

"All right, Charles," said Agatha. "One drink and then I'll get back here and go through my notes."

In the pub, Agatha surveyed Charles over the rim of her glass. There he sat, impeccably tailored and barbered, as if they had never known a few nights of passion. Agatha's hands began to shake and she carefully put her glass down on the table. "Take a deep breath," said Charles. "It's not every day someone tries to kill you, although it sometimes begins to look like that. Be sensible. Go away for a long holiday. Leave it to the police for once."

"It would haunt me," said Agatha. She carefully lifted her glass again and took a swig of gin and tonic.

"There must be something in Jill Davent's past. I find my mind has been blocked by Gwen Simple. I want her to be guilty. I feel she got away with murder. So who else have I got? There are the ones in the village who consulted Jill. Bannister's a vicious old bitch but I can't see her as a murderer. Doris wouldn't harm a fly and Mrs. Tweedy's too old. I took a note of Jill's old address in Mircester. I think I'll go there and ferret around. There must be some reason she moved to Carsely. Why leave a big town where she could have found many more clients? She paused. "Why were the police questioning you?"

"I threatened to kill Herythe and was overheard."

"Why?"

Charles didn't want to tell her that he had lost his temper when Herythe had threatened to seduce her. "Oh, he got on my nerves. I had forgotten how waspish he could be. Take someone with you to Mircester," urged Charles. "I've got to go home. Got a meeting with the land agent."

"I'll be all right," said Agatha. "I think I'll be safe now."

"But for how long?" asked Charles. "What about your cats?"

"What about them?"

"You get your milk delivered, don't you? Little bit of poison injected into the bottle."

"All right. I'll take them to Doris. I swear they like her better than me. I forgot to ask you. How did you get on with the Bannister woman?"

"Nothing but spite and malice. Two sandwiches short of a picnic."

Outside the pub, Charles paused for a moment and watched Agatha as she walked to her car. She was wearing a short linen skirt, which showed her excellent legs to advantage. He had begged Wilkes to give her police protection, but Wilkes had said brutally that he had no intention of wasting manpower on a woman who had chosen a dangerous job. Charles decided to call on her that evening, although he rationed his visits to Agatha. It was, he told himself, no use becoming overfond of a woman who was a walking obsession constantly searching for a host. Agatha's habit of falling in love with highly unsuitable men had irritated him in the past. He wondered gloomily who the next one would be.

What had once been Jill's consulting rooms was now a handbag shop. A man with a thick moustache and an even thicker Eastern European accent approached her and asked if she would like to see any of the bags.

"No," said Agatha. She handed over her card. "I'm interested in the therapist who used to have an office here. Did you buy the premises from her?"

"No, I rent, see. Don't know no therapist."

"Who do you rent from?"

"Harcourt and Gentle."

"Where can I find them?"

"In the shopping arcade."

Mircester's shopping arcade was an uninspiring place, half full of closed shops. The other half boasted chain stores and the estate agent.

Agatha pushed open the door and went in. A tall woman was sitting at a desk. She had grey hair and was wearing old-fashioned harlequin glasses. Agatha thought she looked remarkably like Dame Edna Everidge.

"Take a seat, dear," said the woman. "You can call me Jenny. What can I do you for? That's my little joke. We like to put our customers at ease. Some poor souls are forced to downsize and Jenny's here to hold their poor hands. Why I remember, just the other day—"

"Stop!" commanded Agatha. "I am a private detective and would like some information about one of your previous clients."

"Naughty, naughty! Jenny does not give out information about clients."

"And Agatha would like to point out to Jenny that this client was brutally murdered."

"Oh, Jill Davent! Such a tragedy. I wept buckets. I'm ever so sensitive."

The door opened and a tubby, balding man bustled in. "It's all right, Mother," he said. "Thanks for minding the shop. You can go home now. Ah, here's your nurse."

A muscular woman came in and led Jenny away. "I'm James Harcourt," said the man, sitting down in the chair his mother had vacated. "I don't know how Mother got the key to this place or how she got out of the home. I locked up and went out for only ten minutes."

"Which home is your mother in?" asked Agatha.

"Sunnydale. So what are you looking for?"

Agatha handed over her card and explained the reason for her visit.

"I really can't tell you anything," he said. "She took a short lease for only six months."

"Where was she before that?"

"Some address in Evesham."

"Would you please let me have it?"

"I gave all the documents to the police. You'll need to ask them."

"Snakes and bastards!" muttered Agatha outside the estate agent's. "Fat chance of the police letting me see anything."

A mother walking past pulled her child away. "I've told you. Don't stare at crazy people."

That's it, thought Agatha. I'm sure Jenny Harcourt is only eccentric. Sunnydale. I'll give it a try.

She checked on her iPad. Sunnydale was situated a few miles outside Mircester. Agatha got into her car and drove there. As she stopped in the car park, she wondered how to introduce herself. She doubted very much whether they would let a detective interview a mentally disabled patient.

At the reception desk, she said she was Mrs. Harcourt's cousin. A male nurse behind the desk looked at her doubtfully. "Mrs. Harcourt went wandering off today. She has her good days and bad days. Wait here."

Agatha took a seat and looked sadly around. We all live so long these days, she thought, that unless you're very lucky, you can lose all your marbles. What would I do? Would I even know I was dotty?

The nurse came back. "I think it's all right. Mrs. Harcourt will be pleased to see you."

This is not bad, thought Agatha. Mrs. Harcourt had a sunny room with a view of lawns and trees. There were a few pieces of antique furniture she had been allowed to bring with her.

"How nice to see you again so soon," said Jenny Harcourt. "Jenny was talking about Jill Davent."

"Why are you not allowed to leave the home?" asked Agatha

"I have a little problem, but we won't talk about it. Ah, poor Jill. She came here, you know. My son sent her. We had lovely chats. She wanted me to leave her that little desk over there in my will. But it's George II and I told her she couldn't have it because I am leaving everything to my son and she never came back. Sad."

"Did she tell you anything about herself?" asked Agatha.

"Oh, yes. She was married when she was living in Evesham. But she said he was a brute and threatened to kill her."

"Have you told the police this?"

"They didn't ask Jenny."

Agatha leaned forward. "Have you any idea where in Evesham she used to live and was her married name Davent?"

"She said the cinema was at the end of the street. Wait a bit. A tree. She was married to a tree. No, the house was called after a tree."

"Something like The Firs?" said Agatha, beginning to feel she had wandered into Looking-Glass country.

"What was it?" Jenny stared at the ceiling for inspiration. "Sycamore? Oak? Douglas, that's it. Like the Douglas fir."

A nurse appeared in the doorway. "Time for your exercises," she said. The nurse smiled at Agatha. "We like to keep our clients mobile."

"Will you come again?" asked Jenny.

"Certainly," said Agatha.

As they moved together out of the room, the nurse whispered to Agatha, "Check your belongings and make sure she hasn't taken anything." Agatha looked in her handbag.

"My wallet's missing!"

"Wait there. I know where she hides things."

The nurse returned with Agatha's wallet. Jenny was walking ahead down the corridor.

"I've got to catch her," said the nurse. "If I don't, she'll be back to the shops in Mircester, pinching things. See yourself out."

Agatha stopped at the reception desk. "I gather that Mrs. Harcourt is a kleptomaniac," she said to the male nurse.

"Fortunately, not all the time," he said. "She can go months until something excites her and then she raids the shops. But you're her relative. You must have known that."

"It's been kept very quiet," said Agatha. She was heading for the door when she stopped still. What if Jenny had stolen something from Jill and it was still in her room?

She turned around. The nurse had left the reception desk and was hurrying into the back regions. Agatha ran lightly up the stairs and located Jenny's room. When that nurse had gone back to get her wallet, she had gone to the desk. In the drawers of the desk were old photographs, scarves, and cheap jewellery. Grateful for all the programmes on antiques on television which showed where secret drawers were located in old desks, Agatha found one. Inside was a small black book. She snatched it up as she heard footsteps in the corridor outside. The footsteps went on past the door. Agatha ran down the stairs and out to her car and drove away as quickly as possible.

She stopped a little way from Sunnydale, parking in a space by a farm gate.

Agatha opened the book. Jill's name was on the inside front page. It was a sort of small ledger with lists of payments. The entries ranged from twenty to five hundred pounds. Beside each sum of money was only one initial and the dates of the payments. Agatha sighed. If, by a very long shot, this book belonged to Jill and was evidence of blackmail, then it followed that she should turn it over to the police so that they could match it with any files they had taken from Jill's office or with anything on her computer.

But she could imagine the questions. "You *stole* this book, Mrs. Raisin. Did you inform Sunnydale you had taken it without a patient's knowledge?" And on and on it would go.

It must be Jill's, surely. It had her name on it. The payments stopped one day before her murder.

Were these single initials from first or last names? The twenty-pound payment was marked with the initial *V.* Could that be Victoria Bannister?

Agatha thirsted for revenge on Victoria. She decided to go to Carsely and confront the woman. Then she would decide what to do about the book.

Victoria was weeding in her front garden when Agatha opened the gate.

"What do you want?" Victoria demanded harshly.

"I wondered why you were paying Jill Davent blackmail to the sum of twenty pounds a month," said Agatha.

Victoria's face turned a muddy colour. "Nonsense!"

Agatha shrugged and held up the little book. "Just thought I'd give you a chance to explain before I turn this record over to the police."

Victoria slumped down onto the grass and buried her face in her hands.

"If you tell me and it's nothing really awful, I won't tell the police," said Agatha.

Victoria slowly got to her feet. "Do you mean that?"

"Depends what you did."

"Come inside. Someone might hear us."

The kitchen into which Victoria led Agatha was surprisingly welcoming and cheerful to belong to such an acidulous woman. There was a handsome Welsh dresser with Crown Derby plates and geraniums in tubs at the open window.

They both sat down at an oak table. "It's like this," said Victoria. "Do you remember Mrs. Cooper's dog?"

"The nasty little thing that yapped all the time?"

"She lives next door. I couldn't bear the noise anymore. I crushed up a lot of my sleeping pills and put them in a bowl of chopped steak. When the beast fell unconscious, I put it in a sack and drowned it in the rain barrel. Then I buried it."

"And how did Jill find out?"

"She seemed ever such a good listener, and no one ever listens to me. So I paid for a consultation. The death of that dog was on my conscience. So I told her. The next thing I know she was demanding regular payments for my silence. I had to pay up."

"You've confirmed for me that this was Jill's," said Agatha. "I won't tell the police. But why did Jill tell you about my background?"

"That was before I actually consulted her. We were having a drink and she told me."

"So why spread it around?"

She hung her head. "I don't know. I told the police about you threatening to kill her because I didn't want them to start looking at me."

"Just keep clear of me in the future," said Agatha. "You are a sickening woman."

As Agatha was about to enter her cottage, she was hailed by James Lacey, who hurried to join her. "Toni's just called me," he said. "She told me to look out for you as someone just tried to kill you."

"Come in and I'll tell you all about it. I haven't had lunch and I must eat something."

Agatha told him, between bites of a cheese sandwich, everything that had happened, ending up with, "So I think I'll have to throw myself on Bill's mercy, but first, I'd like to track down the husband."

"I'd better come with you."

Agatha looked at him. There he was, as handsome as ever from his lightly tanned face and bright blue eyes to his tall muscular figure. Why did she no longer feel a thing?

"Right," said Agatha. "Let's go. I'll drive."

As they turned into the road that led up the side of the Regal Cinema, Agatha said, "I'm glad they restored that old cinema. Must go one day. Now, I'll put the car in the parking place and we can start knocking on doors."

When Agatha parked the car and got a parking ticket, she returned to find James searching his iPad. "I'm just checking if there are any Davents in this street. Did she keep her married name?"

"Oh, Lord, I don't know," said Agatha crossly, cross because she had been caught out at missing a basic piece of detection.

"Oh, here we are," said James. "There's a T. Davent at number 905A. That must be right along at the end. The *A* probably means it's a basement flat, or what the estate agents call a garden flat."

"So it's not called Douglas. I wonder what she was talking about?"

"Who?

"Tell you later."

They started to walk. The day had turned hot and humid. Agatha felt uneasily that her make-up was melting and running down her neck.

"Don't take such long strides," she complained.

"You shouldn't wear such high heels the whole time," commented James. But he slowed his pace. He looked down at the top of Agatha's glossy hair and felt an odd pang of loss. But surely it was Agatha's fault that their marriage had not worked out. She would go on smoking and insisted on carrying on working. But what he missed was her old, unquestioning adoration of him.

"Here we are at last," said Agatha. "Of course, with my bloody luck, he'll be out working. Let's try the basement. Yes, the name on the door is Davent." She rang the bell.

The door was opened by a small, blond woman with a discontented face. Agatha guessed she was in her late thirties.

"I don't want encyclopaedias, I've got double glazing and I don't believe in God," she said harshly.

Agatha rapidly introduced herself. "I was hoping to talk to Mr. Davent."

"I'm his sister, Freda. If you want to ask him about the bitch from hell, you'll find him at his shop, Computing Plus, on the Four Pools estate."

"Did you know Jill Davent?" asked James.

"I don't want to talk about that cow. The day I heard about her murder was like Christmas. Now shove off."

The door slammed.

"Back to the car," said James, "and let's see exactly where we can find Computing Plus."

After circling around the Four Pools business estate, they found the shop, parked the car and walked in. The shop was full of expensive-looking equipment. One young man was serving a couple, while another leaned on the desk, reading a newspaper. Agatha approached the newspaper reader. "Is Mr. Davent available?"

"If it's a complaint, I can maybe deal with it," he said in a strong Eastern European accent. Probably Polish, thought Agatha. Evesham was rapidly becoming Little Poland.

Agatha handed him her card. "Tell him I would like to ask him a few questions."

The young man disappeared into a back office with a frosted-glass door. "Stop eyeing his bottom, Agatha," admonished James.

"It's those skintight black jeans," said Agatha ruefully. "They just scream, 'look at my bum.'"

"Be your age."

"No wonder our marriage didn't work out," snarled Agatha. "Always nitpicking and complaining. Furthermore . . ."

The office door opened. "You're to go in," said the assistant.

They walked in. Davent stood up to meet them. Agatha introduced herself and James.

"I don't know how I can help you," he said. "I have had so many grillings from the police."

"Just a few questions, Mr. Davent."

"Call me Tris. It's short for Tristram."

He was a good-looking man in possibly his early forties. He was of moderate height with a thick head of hair with auburn highlights. He was wearing a charcoal grey suit with a striped shirt and blue silk tie. He had neat regular features and a square chin with a dimple in it.

"Please sit down," he said. Tris sat behind his desk and Agatha and James took chairs in front of it.

"It's like this," said Agatha. "In order to find out who murdered your late wife, we have to know more about her background. Was she a therapist when you met her?"

"No, she was a tart."

"Why did you marry her?" asked James curiously.

He sighed. "I'll begin at the beginning. I went to a computer conference in Chicago, ten years ago. Jill was blond then. She just seemed to be one of the computer crowd. My wife had died of cancer the year before. Jill was a good listener. She was English and I was lonely. We ended up in bed together. In the morning, she said she had an important appointment and had to rush. We arranged to meet in the hotel bar that evening. That's when I found my wallet was missing."

"Did you tell the police?"

"I felt I had been conned. I was too ashamed. I still turned up in the bar that evening at the appointed time and wasn't much surprised when she didn't turn up. I put it down to experience. Two months later, she turned up at my address in Evesham in tears, saying she was pregnant. I accused her of stealing my wallet and she looked horrified. She denied the whole thing and said someone must have picked my pocket when we were in the bar. She said she was a qualified therapist. My late wife could not have children and I wanted to believe her. So we got married.

Then after four months, she said she'd had a miscarriage. I had begun to get suspicious of her. She was somehow so . . . how can I describe it? . . . glib.

One day when she was out, I searched her things. I found my wallet. No money, but the cards were there. I taxed her with it and she said that she had been unable to keep her appointment in the bar but had been so worried about the missing wallet that she had got hold of the hotel detective. The wallet had been found in the hotel trash. When I was in my shop, I phoned the hotel and asked to speak to the detective. He said no one had asked him to look for any wallet. He asked for Jill's name. I told him her maiden name was Jill Sommerville. He told me to phone him the following day, which I did. He said Jill had been working for a high-class escort agency and I had been well and truly conned. I confronted Jill again and said unless she agreed to an immediate and uncontested divorce, I would take her to court. She agreed. She moved out immediately. She was as cold as ice. She jeered at me and called me a boring fool. She said she had been tired of the life."

Agatha supressed a groan. Prostitution, however classy, often came with a package of drugs, crime and pimps. Someone could have followed her from America. It could even be some other man she had cheated. Agatha felt deflated and at a complete loss. She could not bring herself to believe that this ex-husband might be a murderer.

"Are you two an item?" asked Tris.

"We were married but it didn't work out," said Agatha.

Tris grinned. "Join the club."

Outraged, James got to his feet. "I will wait for you outside," he said coldly to Agatha, and stalked out.

"I shouldn't have said that. Should I go after him?" asked Tris.

"It's all right. He's miffed because it was a bit rude to compare your awful marriage to ours."

"Let me make it up to you?" said Tris. "What about dinner one night?"

"All right," said Agatha. Inside, a little Agatha was jumping around, yelling, "Yipee! I've still got pulling power."

"What about tomorrow night?" asked Tris.

"Where and when?" asked Agatha.

"Would you like to try Polish food? There's a good restaurant round the corner from where I live called Warsaw Home."

"Won't it be dumplings and red cabbage?"

"No, the menu's varied."

"I'll meet you there," said Agatha. What time?"

"Eight o'clock."

"You're on. I better go and soothe James down."

"I wouldn't trust that one as far as I could throw him," raged James. "Cheeky sod."

"He apologised very nicely," said Agatha.

"Has it crossed your tiny mind that he might be the murderer?"

"I don't think so," said Agatha. "We've forgotten about wolfsbane or monkshood. The Carsely gardens are open to the public on Saturday. Let's go round as many as we can and see if anyone is growing the stuff."

"You go," said James, folding his arms and staring out of the windscreen. "I have work to do. Are you seeing that chap again?"

"I shouldn't think so," lied Agatha. "I think he's told us the lot. I wish someone would pay me to find out the identity of the murderer because a trip to Chicago would be expensive."

Agatha dropped James and went to search out the soothing presence of her friend Mrs. Bloxby.

When she had finished telling Mrs. Bloxby all the latest news, the vicar's wife looked worried.

"I would almost feel relieved if the murderer were someone from Chicago," she said.

"Why?" demanded Agatha.

"I feel it must be someone Miss Davent was blackmailing."

"She's Mrs."

"Oh, well. Her. They are slimy sorts of murders. Someone from Chicago would not necessarily know about you. Are you going to take that blackmailing ledger to Detective Wong?"

"I suppose I must," said Agatha. "But I can't say I stole it from Jenny Harcourt's desk. I can't lie and say she gave it to me or they'll question her and she's not that daft. Certainly, she wouldn't have known it was there. For some reason, Jill picked on that as a good hiding place. She must have begun to feel threatened. I know, I'll say it was shoved through my letter box. Now, to try to get Bill on his own. But first, I'd better go home and copy out what's written in that book."

Chapter Five

Through Patrick Mulligan's contacts, Agatha found that Bill was due to finish his shift at seven that evening. Realising she was still very hungry, she stopped in at an all-day breakfast restaurant and demolished a plate of sausage, eggs, bacon and chips, all washed down with coffee. Then she managed to secure an appointment for a facial at a beauty parlour and feeling refreshed and newly made-up, she called in at the George Hotel bar for a double gin and tonic before finally taking up a position in the car park opposite police headquarters, where she could watch for Bill coming out.

At last she saw him emerging and called to him. "Get in the car," ordered Agatha. "I've got something to show you."

"What have you been up to now?" asked Bill.

"This came through my letter box," said Agatha. She had carefully wiped the book free of prints other than her own, because she thought that they might have Jenny Harcourt's fingerprints on file, as the woman was a kleptomaniac. Agatha suddenly wondered if Jill had hidden the book in that desk or if Jenny had stolen it.

"What do you think it is?" asked Bill.

"It looks to me of a record of blackmailing payments," said Agatha. "There is only one initial at each payment."

Bill had that sixth sense that a few good detectives are blessed with and he was suddenly sure that Agatha had not just received the book through her letter box.

"You'd better come back to the station with me and make a statement," he said. "Are you telling me the truth? This really did come through your letter box?"

"Would I lie to you?"

"Yes."

"Oh, Bill. Wilkes will get in on the act and he'll bully me."

"He's off duty. Come along."

As Bill carefully took down Agatha's statement, he seemed to turn from friend to efficient detective. When exactly had she found the book? Why had she taken so long to contact the police? She should have phoned right away.

Exasperated, Agatha complained, "I wanted to tell you! Right! I did not want Wilkes accusing me of murder or interfering in a police investigation." At last the ledger was bagged up and she was free to leave. "Coming for a drink?" she asked.

"No," said Bill. "I'll need to get onto this right away, and, sorry, but I'll need to contact Wilkes at home."

"Did you find out who sent me that poisonous bouquet?"

"Yes. One of the market traders said he found the flowers on his stall with a letter and a fifty-pound note asking him to deliver it to you. He didn't want to leave his stall, so he gave that little boy the bouquet to take to your office. Just think, Agatha. If he hadn't been so honest, he could have pocketed the money and taken the flowers home to his wife."

When Agatha parked outside her cottage, James came hurrying to meet her. "There's something you should know," he said.

"What?"

"I think Davent gets highlights put in his hair and that dimple on his chin, I'll bet, was put there by a cosmetic surgeon."

"So what?" demanded Agatha. "I've just had a facial."

"It's different for men. He's probably gay."

"If he's gay, why has he asked me out on a date?"

"Probably to bump you off, you silly woman."

"Oh, go and take a running jump, you tiresome bore."

James swung round and stomped off.

Agatha was just about to unlock her door, when a car bearing Wilkes and Bill drove up, followed by a forensic unit. Agatha groaned. Of course, they would want to check her door for fingerprints.

"Get in the car," ordered Wilkes. "We've got to let the forensic boys do their stuff."

"No," said Agatha. "I don't want to sit in a stuffy car. You can interview me in the pub."

It was a warm, humid evening. They sat at a table in the pub garden, away from the other drinkers.

To Agatha's relief, Wilkes was less suspicious than Bill. But while she talked, Agatha was aware of Bill's almond-shaped eyes fastened on her face, those beautiful eyes he had inherited from his Chinese father. Bill Wong had been her first friend after she had moved to the Cotswolds. Agatha was very fond of the young detective and hated lying to him. The tape recorder on the table recorded everything Agatha said.

Victoria Bannister watched the group through the pub window. From her vantage point, it looked to her as if Agatha were being treated with great respect. She felt a sudden surge of jealousy. The fact that Agatha had promised to keep her name from the police did not seem to count. She was bitterly jealous. She had staked out Jill's consulting room, watching her clients, trying and failing to summon up courage to plead with Jill to stop blackmailing her. Surely, she had not been the only one blackmailed. But she did not want to find herself in the clutches of a murderer. She did not trust Agatha to keep her name from the police. Victoria suddenly decided that she needed company in her misery. Perhaps if she followed the last likely person she had seen visiting Jill and had followed them home, she might get help.

Although Agatha kept busy the following day and looked forward to her date with Tris, she found she was nervous. Somewhere out there was a murderer trying to kill her. The first attempt had failed but surely the murderer would try again. Usually, she would have fretted about what to wear for her date, but fear of a lurking murderer made her concentrate on her work to try to banish fear.

She got into her car after work and reversed into a lamppost. Cursing, she got out. There wasn't much damage. Taking a deep breath, she drove carefully to Evesham, looking all the while in the rearview mirror in case she was being followed. A man driving a BMW appeared to be tailing her closely. Agatha swung into a lay-by and waited but the BMW drove on. She suddenly wanted to forget about her date and get home to the security of her cottage, well protected by burglar alarms. She missed her cats. Although they often seemed indifferent to her, there had been occasions when, sensing her distress, they had followed her up to bed and snuggled down beside her. And where was faithless Charles?

At that moment, Charles, who had called on Agatha, and, finding her not at home, knocked on James's door and asked if he knew where Agatha had gone.

James let off a diatribe about Agatha's morals. He ended with, "And I don't believe her when she says it isn't a date. Just detecting."

"Might check it out," said Charles. "Where does this Davent live?"

"You'd better order for me," said Agatha after a look at the menu. "All this is new to me."

He signalled the waitress and ordered two vodkas. "This'll be my limit," said Agatha. "I don't want to be charged with drink driving."

"By the time you've got through this meal," said Tris, "you'll be as sober as anything. The food really mops the alcohol up."

He ordered a thick mushroom soup to start and then to follow, bigos, a "hunter" stew full of various types of meat and sausages, cooked in sauerkraut, and a pile of potato pancakes. He wanted to order beer, but Agatha said she detested the stuff so he ordered more vodka. They talked idly of this and that, about the decline of the centre of Evesham and what had caused the death of the high streets of Britain, Agatha being lulled by the heavy food and the vodka. When he ordered yet more vodka, she didn't protest. Agatha was tired of feeling frightened. And he was an attractive man. He couldn't be gay. He'd been married. She fought down the voice in her head reminding her of gays she had known who were married. And did it matter a damn anyway? It was not as if she was going to spend the night with him. She began to talk about the murders and how an attempt had been made on her life.

Over the dessert of huge slices of cheesecake, he leaned across the table and took her hand. "You're a very attractive woman, Agatha. I wish you would drop this case."

"Why?"

"It's too dangerous. Just drop it."

He was staring into her eyes and his grip on her hand tightened. His voice had held a note of command.

Agatha could feel the euphoria induced by vodka and heavy food fading away. She tried to pull her hand away, but he held on to it.

"Promise me," he said. "I am sure if you go on with this investigation, something really nasty could happen to you. He's already tried to kill you with wolfsbane."

Agatha jerked her hand savagely away with such force that a glass went flying. "How did you know it was wolfsbane?" she asked. "That wasn't in the newspapers."

"It stands to reason. Herythe was killed with wolfsbane."

"But Jill was strangled and Clive Tremund was clubbed and drowned."

"Don't get mad at me," pleaded Tris. "It was an educated guess. It was—"

"Hullo, darling. Not watching your waistline again?"

"Oh, Charles," said Agatha weakly. "What are you doing here?"

"Came to find you. The police want to talk to you again, so I thought I'd come and hold your hand. Maybe I'd better drive you. Been swilling the vodka, have you?"

Agatha made the introductions. "I'd better go," she said to Tris.

"When will I see you again?" he asked.

"I'll phone you," said Agatha.

"How on earth did you find me?" asked Agatha, as they walked to Charles's car.

"James told me about your interviewing Tristram Davent and knowing your predilection for unsuitable men, I went to the address James gave me and his sister told me where you were. Leave your car. I'll take you to pick it up in the morning."

When Agatha was seated in the passenger seat, Charles turned to her and asked curiously, "Why aren't you livid with me for breaking up your date with fancy pants back there?"

"Drive on. He has to pass the car park to get to his home. I don't want to see him again."

"Okay." Charles left the car park and swung round onto Port Street.

"It's like this," said Agatha. She told him what had happened in the restaurant. "It wasn't just what he said," she explained. "I've been a bag of nerves since the attempt on my life and he actually scared me."

"Why on earth did you agree to a date with him?"

"I'm a detective! Remember!" howled Agatha. "I thought he might come up with some more interesting information on Jill."

"Be honest, Aggie. He asked you for a date and you jumped at it. Raise your standards. A man with highlights in his hair."

"It could be natural."

"Rubbish."

A tear ran down Agatha's cheek. "J-just take me home and b-bugger off," she sobbed.

Charles swung into a lay-by and switched off the engine.

"I didn't mean to be so rude. Don't cry. I've never seen you so rattled before. Cheer up. We'll go to your cottage, have a drink and watch something silly on television. I know you won't give up. So what's your next move?"

Agatha dried her eyes and sniffed loudly. "I'm going round the Carsely gardens tomorrow. They're open to the public. I want to see if anyone's got wolfsbane."

"If they had the stuff, they've probably uprooted it by now. Don't worry. I'll come with you. Do you know how to recognise it?"

"I've Googled lots of photos. It's sometimes called monkshood and the poison is aconite."

"Right. We're on for tomorrow. But I do think you should tell Bill about your dinner. I mean, the man was threatening."

"Maybe," said Agatha, but feeling she could not bear another questioning as to why she had agreed to have dinner with Davent. She was only in her early fifties. But had she fallen so low, she wondered, that she would consider any man who asked her out attractive?

The following day, when they set out to tour the gardens, was sunny. Great fleecy clouds were tugged like galleons across a large blue Cotswold sky by a light breeze. "Not all the gardens are open to the public, surely," said Charles.

"We'll pretend we don't know. I hope this isn't a complete waste of time. Someone Jill got on the wrong side of in America could have followed her over."

"Then," said Charles, "one would think that person, having murdered her, would clear off back to the States. Okay. There's Tremund. But whoever our murderer is, he might have thought Tremund had dug up something. But what about Herythe and the attempt on your life? That suggests someone closer to home."

"Let's try Victoria Bannister first," said Agatha. "Now, she *is* deranged."

"Is her garden open?"

"Don't know. We'll pretend it is."

They made their way along the cobbled streets of the village, up past the vicarage to where Victoria lived.

"Not many people about," commented Charles. "Is it always this quiet when it is open gardens day?"

"Probably," said Agatha. "Mrs. Bloxby once said that they are so jealous in the village that at the beginning of the day they often don't want to visit anyone else's garden. Then they all turn out."

"Aren't you worried that Victoria will start screaming insults at you?" asked Charles.

"No, she got a shock when I threatened to sue her for libel."

"She hasn't got a 'Garden's Open' sign up on her gate," Charles pointed out.

"So what?" demanded Agatha, pushing the gate open.

The little front garden of the thatched cottage was crammed with flowers. Tall hollyhocks raised their blossoms to the summer sky. White rambling roses tumbled round the low front door.

Agatha stopped suddenly on the path and Charles bumped into her. "Look!" whispered Agatha. "Wolfsbane!"

"You need to study those photos," said Charles. "That's a delphinium."

"Rats! I should have known it would be too easy."

Agatha rang the bell. "She must be out," she said, after they had waited a few minutes. "I know, let's go round to the garden at the back. If she comes home and catches us, we can lie and say we thought hers was one of the open gardens."

But when they arrived in the back garden, it showed that the flower display was all at the front. There was a shaggy lawn dominated by a clothesline. At the end of the garden was a shed. Along the back fence were two crab apple trees.

"Let's have a look in the shed," said Agatha.

"She might catch us."

"Don't be a wimp. Come on."

"No," said Charles firmly. "You see that garden chair up by the house? I'm going to sit on that until you are finished. If I hear her coming, I'm running away."

"Boneless creep!" Agatha made her way down the garden. Three large crows that had been pecking at something flew up at her approach.

Outside the shed, what at first looked like a bundle of clothes lay on the ground. Curious, Agatha moved forward. Then she let out a high-pitched scream that brought Charles running to her side.

The dead eyeless face of Victoria Bannister stared up at them. "The crows," babbled Agatha. "They've pecked her eyes out!"

Charles put an arm round her. "Come away. We'll call the police. Come on, Aggie. Back away carefully or we'll be charged with mucking up the crime scene."

The police arrived. Agatha and Charles were taken outside the house to wait in a police car while the pathologist and Scenes of Crimes Operatives got to work.

Wilkes turned up and rapped on the window of the car in which Agatha and Charles were sitting. "We'll move down to your cottage, Mrs. Raisin," he said, "and take your statements there."

Why is it so sunny? wondered Agatha bleakly. It ought to be dark and gloomy. The village looks so normal. Unaware yet of the drama, some villagers had started to trot in and out of the gardens.

At her cottage, Agatha insisted they move into the garden, where she could smoke. Wilkes was accompanied by Bill Wong, Alice Peterson and a policewoman.

"I'm amazed you are still indulging in that filthy habit," commented Wilkes.

"A woman has been found dead with her eyes pecked out by crows and all you can do is bitch about my smoking," said Agatha. "Get on with it."

They crowded round Agatha's garden table and the questioning began. When the grilling came to an end, Agatha told them about her dinner with Tris Davent, saying, "He scared me. I'll bet he did it."

"Wait a minute," said Wilkes. "I've got to make a phone call."

He moved off into the kitchen. "Are you all right, Agatha?" asked Bill. "You look quite white."

"I'm shaky," said Agatha. "It was really nasty."

Wilkes came back. "The first estimate of the time of death from the liver temperature is yesterday evening, maybe between seven and midnight. The coroner will have a better idea when he checks the content of her stomach. It can't be Davent. You're his alibi, Mrs. Raisin."

"Not necessarily," said Agatha stubbornly. "I left the restaurant at nine-thirty. He would have time to get to Carsely and bump her off."

"Highly unlikely," said Wilkes sourly. "Now, you, Sir Charles Fraith. We'll now have your version of events."

Agatha envied the calm way Charles talked. He looked just as if finding a gruesome murdered body was a normal event. She had nearly gone to his bed the night before, stopping herself just in time, reminding herself that casual sex was out. But she had longed to be held and comforted. Neither James nor Charles were exactly affectionate, she thought. James was more of the "wham, bam, thank you, ma'am" type of lover. Charles was expert and yet when it was all over, he remained as much of an enigma as ever, never betraying what he really thought of her. She closed her eyes against the glare of the sun and went off into a dream of a steady, dependable man. He would have a rugged face and wear tweeds. He would potter about the garden and in the winter's evenings, they would sit by the fire. He would be passionate and loving in bed. He—

"You've gone quite red, Aggie," said Charles.

"It's the sun," said Agatha, opening her eyes and looking at the beautifully dressed and barbered figure that was Charles.

The doorbell rang. "I'll get it," said Alice.

She returned, followed by Toni, Simon and James.

"James phoned us," said Toni. "How awful, Agatha. Are you all right?"

"Surviving," said Agatha. "We'd better move indoors. There isn't enough room here."

"We're off," said Wilkes. "Report to headquarters later today and sign your statements. And don't speak to the press!"

James, Simon and Toni settled themselves in the garden chairs vacated by the police and demanded to know what on earth had been happening. James said the news of Victoria's death had gone round the village, thanks to a policeman on duty who had been found gossiping.

Agatha wearily went over the whole thing again, including her dinner with Davent. She had just finished when there came a furious ringing at the doorbell.

"I'll go," said Toni.

"Look through the spy hole and if it's the press, don't open the door."

When Toni came back, she said ruefully, "If you wonder why the ringing has stopped, Agatha, your friend Roy Silver is on your doorstep, holding forth."

Agatha groaned. "James, be a darling and go and open the door and jerk him inside."

Roy Silver had once worked for Agatha when she had run her public relations business.

James returned with a sheepish-looking Roy. To Agatha's horror, the young man seemed to be covered in tattoos. "What a mess you've made of yourself," she said. "Do you know that when that fad dies, you'll be left with a large bill for cosmetic surgery to get all that removed?"

They all stared at the spider decorating his neck and the swirling multicoloured tattoos of snakes up his arms. "It washes off," said Roy sulkily. "It's the thing. I'm doing PR for this boy band, Hell on Earth. They're going to be big."

"What did you say to the press?" demanded Agatha. "I've been warned not to talk to them."

"I simply told them the truth," said Roy moodily. "I said I had helped you with cases before and I was helping you with this one."

"How did you know about this one?" asked Toni.

"I didn't. But the reporters told me there had been a murder in the village, so I winged it."

Agatha looked sourly at his weak face and gelled hair, and at his jeans carefully torn at the knees, and said, "You look as if you've crawled out of a young offenders' institute. Go upstairs and wash that muck off, or you're not staying!"

"That's the trouble with you burying yourself in Peasantville," said Roy. "You're no longer trendy. Oh, I'm going."

"I think," said Toni, "that now we are here, Simon and I should do a tour of the gardens and see if we can find that wretched flower anywhere. We can split up and—"

"Go together," said Agatha. "I don't want either of you getting killed."

Chapter Six

"Are you sure we shouldn't split up?" asked Toni uneasily. Simon had been relentlessly pursuing her for a long time.

Simon's jester's face crinkled up in a smile. "Relax. I'm spoken for."

"Who? What's happened?"

"I'm engaged," said Simon triumphantly.

"Who is she?"

"Detective Sergeant Ruby Carson."

"The one from Oxford?"

"That's her. I can't believe my luck. I finally got her

out on a date last night. I said, joking, you know, 'Marry me!' And she said, 'Yes.'"

"Was she serious?"

"Yes. I'm going to meet her children tonight."

"Children? Is she divorced?"

"Yes, she's got two kids, Pearl, who's five, and Jonathan, nine."

Toni looked at him uneasily. "How old is she?"

"Early forties."

"You're early twenties, Simon. Oh, please don't rush into things."

"I'm in love," said Simon stubbornly. "If you're going to be nasty about it, I don't want to talk about it anymore. Let's look for this damned plant."

"You know," said Toni slowly, "before we start here, what about running over to Ancombe and having a look at Gwen Simple's garden? I think, because Agatha can't ever get anywhere with her, she's forgotten that she should really be our prime suspect."

As Toni drove the short distance to Ancombe, she worried about Simon. Agatha was bad enough, falling into obsession with one man or another, but surely Simon was just as bad. He had claimed to love her more than anyone in the world before he joined the army and left for Afghanistan, only to return engaged to a female sergeant, whom he then ditched at the altar, and then had begun to pursue her again. Like Agatha, there was something not quite emotionally grown up about Simon.

She could not imagine Simon as a stepfather. She remembered Ruby Carson to be, yes, beautiful, but highly efficient and, Toni was sure, highly ambitious.

At that very moment, Chief Superintendent Alistair White was admiring Ruby's naked curves as she climbed out of bed. "I'd better collect the children from Mum," she said. "Oh, I won't be seeing you for a while."

"Why? Nobody knows about us."

"I know. But I'm engaged."

"You're what! Who to?"

"A young fellow called Simon Black who works for Agatha Raisin."

"Why on earth . . . ?"

Ruby came back and sat on the edge of the bed. "He works for that Raisin agency and that bloody woman has solved more cases than I've had hot dinners. Young Simon will keep me in the loop as to what she's found out. Then goodbye. But in the meantime, we'll cool it. Anyway, God forbid your missus should find out."

"You're a hard woman, Sergeant."

Ruby grinned. "Now, inspector sounds so much nicer, doesn't it?"

Gwen Simple lived in a bungalow in the shadow of the church in Ancombe.

"Oh, good," said Toni, as they got out of the car. "She's got a 'Gardens Open' sticker on her gate. They must be having an open day as well."

"She'll think we're still chasing her," said Simon.

"Too bad," said Toni. "There are a good few people in her garden. Can't see her. Come along." Toni gave him a coloured photograph of wolfsbane.

"Is it wolfsbane or monkshood?" asked Simon.

"Two names for the same plant," said Toni. "I prefer wolfsbane. Sounds more murderous." Her phone rang. She pulled it out of the pocket of her shorts. Simon heard her say, "Hullo, Agatha. What? Are you sure? Do you believe that?"

When she had rung off, she said, "It seems as if Victoria Bannister is the murderer, or so the police believe."

"Why on earth do they think that?"

"When they pried open her dead hands, she was clutching wolfsbane. And she left a note, saying the death had been on her conscience. They found two plants in her shed with a lot of the leaves torn off."

"I don't believe it," said Simon. "It's a nasty death."

"Agatha says she confessed to killing her neighbour's

dog. What if someone knew about that?" said Toni. "A village lady such as Victoria would not be able to face the shame. And she said 'murder,' not 'murders.' Can you imagine Victoria even killing Tremund and dumping him in the river? It's ridiculous. But, believe me, the police have been under a lot of pressure from the media. They won't want any other solution. Oh, there's Gwen in the doorway. Let's look at her garden anyway."

Gwen still looked as if she had stepped down from a mediaeval painting from her dead-white face, long nose and thick eyelids shielding brown eyes. She was wearing a long silk summer gown in a swirling pattern of green and gold.

She stood very still, watching them as they entered the garden and made their way from plant to plant to bush to flower.

"Gwen gives me the creeps," whispered Simon, "but she wouldn't have the strength, say, to murder Tremund."

"That one could charm a man into doing it for her," said Toni.

Gwen had moved into the garden and was speaking to a large muscular man.

He approached Toni and Simon and growled, "Get lost. Mrs. Simple has had enough of you detectives making her life a misery. Get out or I'll throw you out!"

"See what I mean?" said Toni when they had beaten a retreat.

As Roy Silver sat in Agatha's living room that evening, desperately switching from news channel to news channel in the hope of seeing himself talking to the press and failing to find anything, Simon was arriving at Ruby's house in Oxford.

He had an engagement ring in his pocket and was clutching a large bouquet of roses.

Ruby answered the door but turned her face away to avoid a kiss. "I've heard the news," she said curtly. "Case solved. This is not a good evening, Simon. I've had a hard day and I'm pretty tired. Can we take a rain check?"

"The case isn't solved by a long shot," said Simon, looking hurt and disappointed. Two children appeared behind Ruby and stared at him with flat eyes.

"What? Come in, sit down," said Ruby, suddenly smiling. "What do you mean it's not solved?"

She led him into the kitchen. Simon, although she had originally invited him for dinner, noticed gloomily that there were no signs of cooking.

The boy, Jonathan, said, "Have you brought us presents?"

"Sorry," said Simon.

"Go and watch television," ordered Ruby. "You can have half an hour before bed."

They trailed off. "Now," said Ruby eagerly. "What's all this?"

Simon told her about Victoria killing the neighbour's dog and said that Agatha was sure someone had threatened to expose her, left her the wolfsbane, and Victoria had committed suicide or that she had been forced into leaving the note.

Ruby rose from the kitchen table and came back with a notebook and began to write busily. Simon felt he was back in the interrogation room as she asked question after question. At last she leaned back in her chair and smiled. "Is Agatha Raisin really clever?"

"Well, sometimes you wouldn't think so. But she blunders about, never giving up and she's got the most marvellous intuition."

"We've still got the outstanding murders of Tremund and Herythe," said Ruby. "Any chance of an introduction to your boss?"

"Yes, of course."

"What about now?"

"What about our dinner?"

"That can wait." She leaned forward and gave Simon a lingering kiss on the lips. "Phone her."

Agatha said she would like to meet Ruby. Charles had left and Roy was moaning about his lack of publicity.

Ruby took her children round to her mother's, but before they set off in Ruby's car, Simon said awkwardly, "I wouldn't mention anything to Agatha about us being an item. She can be controlling."

"Don't worry. Won't say a word."

"We met before," said Agatha to Ruby. "Simon tells me you are still interested in the murders. Come in. This is a friend of mine, Roy Silver. Roy, Detective Sergeant Ruby Carson."

"Any press in the village?" asked Roy.

"Couldn't see any," said Ruby. "If there are any, they'll be hanging around the Bannister woman's cottage."

"I think I'll get some fresh air," said Roy, heading for the door.

After he had gone, Agatha suggested they should sit in the garden because the evening was fine.

Over drinks, Ruby began to question Agatha. And when Agatha answered her questions, her curious bear-like eyes moved from Ruby's face to Simon's adoring one. Oh, dear, thought Agatha, I do believe she's using him and now me as well. Still, information works both ways. She could come in handy. But what's with young Simon? He looks well and truly smitten.

"There is the matter of Gwen Simple," said Agatha. "I could never believe she was innocent of the murders her son committed. For some reason, men go weak at the knees when they come across her. I think she uses people, and if there is one thing I cannot bear, it is women who use sex to further their own ends. Don't you feel the same?"

"Of course," said Ruby, suddenly taking an intense dislike to Agatha.

"Are you married?" asked Agatha.

"Divorced."

"Children?"

"Two. Look, thank you for a most interesting talk but I'd better be getting back. Come along, Simon."

Simon was silent on the road back to Oxford. He was also hungry and bewildered. Agatha and Ruby had somehow made him feel like a small boy caught between two domineering aunts. The ring was in his pocket. But he was damned if he would give it to Ruby until there was a more romantic time.

Outside her house, Ruby looked at his worried face and said, "My darling, I am treating you horribly. Let Ruby make it up to you."

Simon could only be glad that because of the humidity of the evening and the sexual athletics in the front seat, the windows soon became steamed up.

After it was over and Ruby gave him a final kiss

goodnight, he got into his own car, wondering why he felt like a small boy who had failed his exams and had been given an apple by a sympathetic teacher.

Agatha sleepily answered the door, after peering through the spy hole, to survey a miserable-looking Simon. In the light of the lamp over the door, her sharp eyes took in his rumpled hair, swollen lips and love-bitten neck.

"Need a drink?" she asked, leading the way to the kitchen.

"I need food," said Simon.

"I'm not the world's greatest cook," said Agatha.

"Have you eggs?"

"Yes. Loads."

"Give me a pan and some butter and I'll make an omelette."

With rare forbearance, Agatha waited until he was fed. Then she said cautiously, "You look used."

"That's it," said Simon. He told her what had happened, ending up with, "I feel awful. In her car, in front of her house! What if the children had looked out of the window? What if Granny had brought them back? I've got a ring, Agatha. I meant to ask her to marry me."

"Take it back to the shop," said Agatha, stifling a yawn.

"Maybe she really does love me," said Simon plaintively. "Maybe I'm being too uptight about it all."

"The woman invites you for dinner," said Agatha patiently. "Instead, she uses you to come and grill me. She then gives you a quickie to keep you on the leash. That one is walking, talking ambition. Why don't you use her? We need good police contacts. Did they contact any of the people going into Tremund's office? Is there CCTV in that street?"

"Okay." Simon visibly brightened. He had been feeling hunted. Now he could play the role of the hunter.

"What do you feel about her now?" asked Agatha.

"I'm still in shock."

"Couldn't you just have held her off and suggested a bed would be a better place?"

"She was all over me. I thought we would move out of the car and into the house. I didn't expect to be dismissed."

"Did you use any protection?"

"Ruby had it with her."

"Cheer up," said Agatha. "She's got what she wants for now. But she'll be back."

"Another subject," said Simon. "Toni and I went over to Gwen's. We felt you had forgotten about her for the moment. We tried to look round her garden but a man chased us off."

The doorbell rang. "That'll be Roy back from a publicity hunt," said Agatha.

As she opened the door to him, she saw, over his shoulder, Charles arriving.

"Does nobody want to go to sleep?" complained Agatha.

"I'm off to London," said Roy sulkily. "I'll get my bag."

"What brings you?" Agatha asked Charles.

"I got a call from Adrian Sommerville. He says I can pick up the keys tomorrow and have a look at Jill's house. After we've had a look, we should call on him again, Agatha. I mean, did he know his sister was hooking in Chicago? What's her background? What does he think of her ex?"

"I'm tired," said Agatha. "I'll see you in the morning."

The day was humid and overcast. They collected the keys from an estate agent in Mircester, saying they did not need anyone to show them over, and then went back to Jill's cottage in Carsely.

The front garden looked even more neglected than the last time Agatha had seen it. Bits of yellow police tape fluttered amongst the bushes. Down in the village, the church bells rang out. Then came the tenor bell, and then the silence of a country Sunday.

"Here goes," said Charles, unlocking the door.

"You'd think that brother would have cleaned the place up," complained Agatha. "I'm surprised the estate agent didn't suggest it. There's still fingerprint dust everywhere."

"Let's start with the office," said Charles.

"You do that. I'll try the other rooms," said Agatha.

Across from the consulting room, on the other side of the small dark entrance hall, was a living room–cum–dining room. There were the usual things to be expected: television, bookcase, small table with four chairs, sofa and two armchairs, but no desk or chest of drawers. Agatha wondered whether to search through the books, but decided to leave them until later.

The kitchen was in the back. There were signs that the police had been through every food container. Agatha then made her way up the narrow wooden staircase. On the left of the landing was a bathroom. The cupboard over the hand basin was empty. No doubt the police had taken everything away. In the middle was a bedroom. There were no clothes or underwear. No doubt her brother had got rid of them. So no hope of finding anything in pockets. There was one room left, with a massage table and anatomical charts on the wall.

Agatha began to feel wearily that it was all a waste of time. The police would have been thorough in their search. There were three sockets in the house for hands-free phones but the phones were missing.

She trailed back down to the office. "Anything?" she asked Charles.

"Not a thing. Not even a phone," said Charles. "It's only in books where the detective finds something taped to the bottom of a drawer."

"Let's try the back garden," said Agatha. "With all her blackmailing carry-on, she must have needed places to hide things. I wonder if she hid that book in Jenny's desk or if kleptomaniac Jenny pinched it."

They walked through the kitchen to the back door. Charles tried several keys and then unlocked the door.

"She was no gardener," he said. The back garden was nothing but a square of weeds with a shed at the end. The day had turned very dark and as they made their way to the shed, lightning split the sky, followed by a massive crack of thunder.

Then the heavens opened and the rain came pouring down. The shed was unlocked. They dived into it out of the rain.

"Wasn't it Charles the Second who said that the English summer consisted of two days heat followed by a thunderstorm?" asked Charles.

Agatha scowled at him. She hated quotations. They made her feel more badly educated than she actually was. She looked around. Rusty garden implements were propped against the walls.

"I don't like this shed," said Agatha. "There's something wrong here."

"What?"

"I don't know."

"It's the storm," said Charles. "There's nothing here but us."

"Would she have buried things?" asked Agatha. "I mean, she thieved Tris's wallet and kept it. Perhaps she kept souvenirs of all the people she had conned. Maybe there's a loose plank or something."

"The floor looks untouched," said Charles. "There's nothing here."

"The police didn't dig up the garden," said Agatha, looking out of the grimy shed window.

"Why should they?" remarked Charles. "They weren't looking for dead bodies. I mean, Jill *was* the dead body. Look at it. That garden hasn't been touched in years."

"Snakes and bastards!" howled Agatha. "I'm sick of the whole thing."

"Never mind," said Charles. "The rain's easing off. Let's make a dash for it."

Agatha stumbled across the garden in her high-heeled sandals. One foot caught in the now muddy earth in front of shallow wooden steps leading up to the kitchen and she fell heavily.

Charles rushed to heave her up. "Look!" said Agatha.

There were three wide wooden steps and the top of one of them had become dislodged in her fall.

"There's something in there," she said excitedly. "It's a box."

"Put on gloves," said Charles.

Agatha pulled a pair of latex gloves out of her handbag. She lifted out a metal box. "I'll take it into the kitchen," she said.

She put it on the kitchen table. "It's not all that heavy. Let's see what we've got."

She took out items and laid them on the table. "We've two Rolex Oyster watches, three wallets, a big pile of notes, all sorts of currencies, sexy photographs of her in bed with various men. She must have had a partner to take these photos. What a contortionist she was! But no documents or letters."

"Anything in the wallets?"

"No cards. But family pictures in two of them."

"You'll need to call the police," said Charles.

"Do I have to?" wailed Agatha. "I found it."

"Agatha, those photos are probably from her hooking days in Chicago. You need the police to follow it up. That way, they'll find out who she was working with."

"Anybody home?" called a voice. Agatha put the items back in the box and slammed down the lid. "Who's there?"

"Me," said Simon, walking into the kitchen. "What have you got there?" He had been searching for her.

"Just found it," said Agatha. "I stumbled over a box of Jill's stuff. I'll need to call the police. There are photos she probably used to blackmail her clients in America."

"May I have a look?" asked Simon.

Agatha took the lid off the box again. "Hurry up. I'll phone Bill."

Simon carefully examined the items, his thoughts always on Ruby. He wanted the old Ruby back, the one he had been in love with. He had tried to call her that morning, but his calls went straight to her voice answering message. He knew if he left her a message about this discovery she would call him back, and he wanted to find out that the hard woman he had encountered the night before had changed back into the Ruby he wanted to marry.

"I really don't feel like waiting for the police, Agatha," said Simon. "I'm still upset about Ruby. Do you mind if I clear off?"

Chapter Seven

Simon walked down through the village to where he had left his car outside Agatha's cottage. He took out his mobile phone and dialled Ruby's number. It went straight to voice mail. "We've made a big discovery at Jill's cottage," said Simon. "If you want to hear about it, call me back."

He leaned against his car and waited. A sudden brisk breeze rustled through the leaves of the lilac tree outside Agatha's garden.

Simon felt a sudden frisson of fear. It was as if the leaves were whispering a warning. He looked along the lane. Nothing and nobody, except a discarded sweet wrapper that skittered along and stuck to his trousers.

His phone rang, making him jump. "Hullo, darling boy," cooed Ruby. "What have you got for me?"

"It's a terrific find," said Simon. "I'd rather see you in person."

"Come over. It's my day off," said Ruby.

When she rang off, she turned to her children. "I'm taking you to Granny."

"Wicked!" cried her son, Jonathan.

And Pearl said, "We love Granny more'n you."

Ruby shrugged and phoned her mother, who lived a few streets away. She fought down a small twinge of guilt. Her children spent more time with their grandmother than they ever did with her.

Simon drove to Oxford, praying that his dream of a warm and loving Ruby could be restored. He was about to ring the doorbell when he heard a man's voice through the open window of the living room, saying, "Don't you think I should stay? We're desperate for a break in this case."

"No, run along," came Ruby's voice. "The little sap is spoony about me and he might get jealous if he saw you and clam up."

"*I* might get jealous," said the man with a laugh.

"Don't be an idiot. He's just a rather boring little boy."

Simon backed off and crouched down behind a bush. The door opened and a thickset man came out. He kissed Ruby and walked off down the path.

The door closed and there was only the sound of the strengthening wind rustling through the leaves.

Simon suddenly felt immeasurably tired, silly and depressed. He crept out from behind the bush, making sure he was not observed from the windows of Ruby's house and made his way to his car and drove off. By the time he got back to Mircester, his phone had rung several times. Each time he recognised Ruby's number and finally switched his phone off.

Ruby paced angrily up and down her living room, wondering what to do. She tried to remind herself that if there was anything pertaining to the murder of Tremund, it would surely come through to Thames Valley Police and all she had to do was wait.

But she was ambitious and impatient. Simon had given her his address. She decided to drive to Mircester and challenge him.

The night was very dark. The air was sticky and humid and from far away came a rumble of thunder.

Her old car did not have air-conditioning and she was tired and sweating by the time she reached Simon's flat. Ruby rang the bell. But Simon, looking through the spy hole in his door, decided not to answer it. "The hell with her," he muttered, and went back to bed.

Frustrated and angry, Ruby decided to drive on to Carsely and confront Agatha Raisin.

Simon's flat was in a pedestrian area and so Ruby had left her car in the main square. Before she reached it, the heavens opened and the rain came pouring down. A flash of lightning lit up the square and she saw to her dismay that the back window of her car had been smashed. She slid into the front seat and tried to dry her sopping hair with some tissues. Police headquarters were beside the square but she decided against going in to report the window; they would consider that she was poaching on their territory. She noticed the streetlights were out. The storm must have caused a power cut.

Wearily, Ruby decided to forget about the whole thing and go home.

She was just about to switch on the engine when a wire was slid around her neck and viciously pulled tight. Ruby was a strong woman and tried to get her fingers under the wire without success. With one dying hand, she punched the hazard warning lights before everything turned black.

Bill Wong put up his umbrella as he left headquarters. Agatha Raisin had been released an hour before, after what Bill considered a merciless grilling from Wilkes, who seemed to persist in thinking that Agatha was impeding police enquiries.

As he made his way to his car, the rain suddenly switched off, as if some Olympian god had turned off a tap. Behind him he could hear the rumble of the police generator as it coped with the power cut.

He saw a car with flashing hazard lights and approached it curiously in case someone was in trouble. He rapped on the driver's window. He could see a dim figure at the wheel through the steamed-up glass. He opened the car door and Ruby's lifeless body and horribly contorted face slid out halfway, held by the seat belt.

Agatha Raisin was awakened the following morning by Toni with the news that Simon had been arrested for the murder of Ruby Carson. The CCTV cameras in the square had filmed her going to Simon's flat as had the one in the pedestrian area. But after the power cut, the cameras had stopped working.

Agatha swung into action, hiring a criminal lawyer, and then arrived at police headquarters to find that an exhausted Simon had just been released. The messages from Ruby, which he still had on his mobile phone, showed he had not wanted to see her. Chief

Superintendent Alistair White did not say he had been having an affair with Ruby but had said she had called him round to tell him of Agatha's find and that she was waiting for Simon.

He backed Simon's story that he had heard insulting remarks from Ruby about himself through the open window.

There was a tent over Ruby's car in the car park. Simon told Agatha the police reckoned that the murderer had been tailing Ruby and had smashed the back window and climbed into the passenger seat. A garrote had been found lying on the floor. It had been made from cheese wire with polished cylindrical pieces of wood attached.

"Surely there must be more than one person involved," exclaimed Agatha.

Despite the heat of the day, Simon shivered. He thought Ruby's dead contorted face would haunt him until the end of his days. "I feel some twisted mind is playing cat and mouse with us and knows our every move," he said.

Agatha stared at him. "Bugs!" she said. "I wonder if my cottage is bugged? We've got a radio frequency detector in the office. Go and get it, Simon, and I'll do a sweep of my home."

When they arrived, Charles was on the kitchen floor, playing with the cats. Agatha signalled him to be quiet and led him out into the garden where she told him about Ruby's murder and that they were going to sweep the cottage for bugs. "And what are my cats doing back here?" she asked.

"Doris is working upstairs," said Charles.

"What! This isn't cleaning day?"

"She thought the moggies might like to see their home again. I asked her to change the sheets in the spare room. I'd better get her and we can ask her if anyone could have got into the house while you were away."

Charles came back after a few minutes and led Doris to the bottom of the garden where Simon and Agatha were waiting. Asked if anyone could possibly have got in to bug the house, Doris wrinkled her brow, and then said, "There was only the telephone man. Some time ago it was. He said there was a fault on some of the village phones and they were checking them all. Oh, dear, I went upstairs and left him to it. Big heavyset man with a grey beard and glasses. One of them foreign accents. Could ha' been Polish."

"Anyone else?"

"Don't call anyone to mind. I'm right sorry, Agatha. Didn't cross my mind there would be anything up with him."

Agatha turned to Simon. "You'd better start sweeping for bugs. Start with the garden table and chairs."

They waited anxiously. Having finished with the garden furniture, Simon moved into the house. "Does he know what he's doing?" asked Charles.

"Yes, I get him to sweep the office from time to time," said Agatha.

"What puzzles me," said Charles, "is why you haven't been bumped off."

"You've forgotten. I was sent a poisonous bouquet."

"Maybe our murderer was sure you would recognise wolfsbane. If this place is bugged, then he would know you knew what the plant looked like. I think some psycho is playing with you, Agatha."

"That pseudo telephone man," said Agatha. "It sounds like someone in disguise. What about Tris Davent? He's got technical knowledge."

"You'd better tell the police about this, Aggie."

"What! And have to sit in that ghastly interview room again?"

"Just phone Bill. The police may have more sophisticated equipment. Still, with any luck, Simon won't find anything."

The sky above was turning darker. "I hope he finishes before it rains," said Doris.

"I'll phone Bill if Simon finds anything," said Agatha. "And how many times have I got to tell you not to call me Aggie! Jill's brother is pretty stocky. Add a false grey beard and glasses and he could be our bugger. An East European accent is easy to fake."

"'Bugger' being a good word to describe the horrible man, whoever he is," said Charles.

A warm drop of rain fell on Agatha's nose. "This is all we need," she said. "Let's get into the house and not say a word."

But when they entered, Simon was arranging four tiny bugs on the kitchen table. "All done, I hope," he said. "One in the phone, one under the computer desk, one behind the bookshelves and one behind your headboard upstairs, Agatha."

"I'll make us all a nice cup of tea," said Doris.

"Forget it. I'd like a gin and tonic," said Agatha. "Get it for me, Charles, and I'll phone Bill. He slipped me his mobile number so I won't need to be trapped by Wilkes."

Bill said to wait and he would be right over to make another sweep of the cottage.

Charles returned with Agatha's gin and tonic. She raised her hand to take the glass and Charles noticed that her hand shook. He put the glass down on the table and said gently, "Not getting the shakes, are you? Maybe not a good idea to start on the booze."

"It's not that," said Agatha. "This whole case is creeping me out. Some madman is out there, laughing at me, treating me like an amateur fool. But you're right, Charles. I am not going to start hitting the bottle. Pour it down the sink and make me a coffee instead. Are you all right, Simon?"

"That's why Ruby was murdered," he said wretchedly. "Someone listened in to everything I told you about her."

"My copies of that ledger!" Agatha jumped to her feet and raced through to her desk and rummaged frantically around. She came back and announced, "It's gone."

"So," said Charles, "the murderer must have got back inside somehow. Let's ask Doris." Doris had gone back upstairs. "I'll get her."

When Doris returned, Agatha asked, "Where do you leave the keys to this cottage?"

"At the foot of the stairs in my handbag," said Doris. "Oh, Agatha, dear. I've got a slip of paper in there with the burglar alarm code."

"So the bastard has been walking in and out when he felt like it," said Charles. "He is playing with you because he could have let himself in at night and murdered you."

Agatha phoned the security firm which had installed the burglar alarm and left a message to come as soon as possible and change the code. She then phoned a locksmith and asked him to change the locks.

The police arrived, headed by Bill and Alice, who introduced two technicians.

While the men got to work, they all moved back out to the garden, sheltering under the garden umbrella. Agatha told Bill about how the murderer had gained access to her cottage.

"You should find yourself another cleaner," said Alice.

"Never!" cried Agatha. "It was an easy mistake. No one is more honest or hardworking than Doris."

The only thing Asian about Bill were his beautiful almond-shaped eyes, now crinkled up in distress. "Agatha," he said. "Go away somewhere until all this is over. It's not safe here for you."

"What would be the point of that?" said Agatha. "You may never find this murderer who is turning out to be the serial killer of the Cotswolds. I can't leave my staff. They're in danger, too."

Agatha's phone rang. It was Phil Marshall. "I just dropped in to the office to get another camera and there is a young man here anxious to retain your services. He says he is Justin Nichols and Ruby was his stepmother during a previous marriage."

"I'd like to see him," said Agatha, "but I can't leave here just now." She told Phil what they had discovered and then said, "Give him directions and tell him to get over here."

When she rang off, she told Bill about Justin and then turned to Simon. "Did she say anything about being married before?"

"She said she was divorced," said Simon. "But there may have been another marriage before the last one. I think she kept her married name, Carson, which follows that before that marriage she could have been married to someone called Nichols."

The technicians came out to the garden to say they had finished their work and it seemed as if Simon had found all the bugs. Bill turned to Simon. "I hope you wore gloves."

"Yes," said Simon. "But if you plan on fingerprinting them, I bet our murderer wore gloves as well."

"We might be able to trace where they were bought. If you don't mind, Agatha, we'll stay on until this young man arrives. I'd like to hear what he has to say about Ruby."

Mrs. Bloxby arrived after the technicians had gone, saying she had been worried about village reports of police cars outside Agatha's cottage. Agatha told her everything that had happened. Her gentle face creased with worry. "It's as if someone is playing cat and mouse with you, Mrs. Raisin. But it does eliminate some suspects."

"Like who?" asked Agatha. "I don't see Gwen Simple being able to do anything so sophisticated as planting bugs," said the vicar's wife. "Miss Bannister is dead. Mrs. Simpson was never a suspect. Mrs. Tweedy is too old and would not have the energy or the technical know-how."

"My money is still on Gwen Simple," said Agatha. "She could have hired someone. I cannot believe for a moment she did not know what her murdering son was up to."

"We've had a watch on Gwen Simple for some time," said Bill. "She's had no strange callers, only people from the village of Ancombe. She helps out in the church and does a lot of good works."

"Humph!" snorted Agatha. "Could well be a smoke-screen."

"You're forgetting her ex," said Charles. "Davent runs a computer shop."

"How are you getting on with that ledger of accounts?" asked Agatha. She did not want to say her copy was missing, knowing that the police would not appreciate her actions.

"Don't seem to lead anywhere," said Bill. "But an awful lot of the entries are old. The ink's faded. There are very few new ones."

"Any news from America? I'll bet Jill was blackmailing one of her clients."

"It's been a laborious task checking everyone from America, particularly those with addresses in Chicago and the photos and stuff you found, but so far, nothing sinister. Not one of the men the Chicago police contacted would claim they were being blackmailed and there are ones with the wallets said they had had their pocket picked in some bar, anywhere but at the hotel. They're all married, you see."

Agatha clutched her shiny hair. "It could be anyone and we don't have a clue," she wailed. "I'm going to freshen up."

"I'm losing it," said Agatha to her bathroom mirror. "It's never affected me like this before. Get a grip!"

The day was humid and close. She showered and changed into a cool linen sheath and sandals and repaired her make-up.

The doorbell rang as she was descending the stairs. "I'll get it," she called.

"No you won't," said Bill, rushing to her side. "You don't know who is out there." Agatha stood back while he opened the door. She blinked. A young Adonis stood there with the watery sunlight gilding his blond hair. "I'm Justin Nichols," he said.

"Come in," said Bill. "This is Agatha Raisin. I am Detective Sergeant Bill Wong."

"Where's Phil Marshall?" asked Agatha.

"He dropped me off and went back to the office," said Justin.

Justin followed them into the kitchen, where the others were sitting around the table. Agatha made the introductions, urged him to sit down, took a chair herself and stared at him. His hair was naturally wavy. His skin was white and his eyes, an intense blue with thick lashes. He was wearing an open-necked shirt as blue as his eyes. He was slim but athletic-looking.

"How old are you?" asked Agatha.

"Twenty-five."

"But Ruby Carson was in her early forties. Was your father much older than Ruby when he married her?"

"Yes, he was fifty-five. I'm his only child. Mother had only been dead—she died of cancer—for two years when he met Ruby. She was only nineteen then. He was so much in love with her. But she up and divorced him two years later. He was devastated. He still obsesses about her and has commissioned me to employ you, Mrs. Raisin."

"What do you do, Mr. Nichols?" asked Alice Peterson.

"I'm a computer programmer. I'm freelance and I am taking a break between contracts. Why are you all staring at me like that?"

"Someone bugged my cottage," said Agatha, ignoring a warning signal from Bill. "Would you have the know-how?"

"No," he said innocently, "but I'm sure if I studied how to do it, I could manage, but why would I?"

"Did you like Mrs. Carson?" asked Bill.

"I thought she was a selfish, ambitious woman," he said. "But I'd do anything for my father. I resisted at first, asking why I should employ some village detective woman, but he persisted. Mind you, I did not expect to find you so attractive, Mrs. Raisin."

"Please call me Agatha." Her eyes were shining.

Surely not, thought Charles. He's much too young. Maybe it's just Agatha's maternal instinct.

"When was the divorce?" asked Bill.

"Years ago. Ruby was in sales and marketing and she suddenly announced she was going to join the police force. That was when she became insanely ambitious. All she would talk about was how she was going to be police commissioner one day. Dad hardly ever saw her. But the divorce hit him hard."

"What does your father do?"

"He's the managing director of Superfoods. That's how he met Ruby. She was doing the marketing for them."

Agatha suddenly wished they would all leave. "If you

follow me into the office," she said, "I'll draw up the contracts."

"Your secretary has already done that," said Justin.

"Look here," said Bill severely. "You are putting yourself in danger, young man. It is not only Mrs. Carson who has been murdered but other people as well! Whoever the murderer is, he seems to delight in getting rid of anyone who might help find out who he is. I strongly advise you to tear up the contracts and tell your father it is much too dangerous."

"I don't see why," said Justin. "I mean, I gather you've removed the bugs so no one will know Agatha is detecting on my behalf."

"Well, I've warned you," said Bill. "We'll be in touch, Agatha."

"I'd better go, too," said Mrs. Bloxby. "My husband will be wondering what has happened to me."

Agatha looked hopefully at Charles. "I'd better be off as well," he said. He had planned to stay, but, after all, the beautiful young man would certainly not be romantically interested in Agatha, and his presence might take Agatha's mind off her fears.

"Simon," said Agatha, "you'd better get on with that missing teenager case."

After Charles and Simon had gone, Agatha said reluctantly, "Leave it with me, Justin. Let me have your phone numbers and address. I'd better talk to your father as well."

She had planned to invite him to lunch but remembered in time that she had to wait at home for the locksmith and to have the code on the burglar alarm changed.

"It's lovely here," said Justin with a smile. "I've always wanted to see the inside of one of these old thatched cottages. Look, the rain has stopped."

"I'll be going now," called Doris from the hall.

Agatha rose to her feet and went to say goodbye.

When she returned, the kitchen was empty. She found Justin sitting at the table in the garden with the cats on his lap. "It's so quiet here," he said.

"I'm hungry," said Agatha. "Would you like to stay for lunch?"

"That would be lovely."

"Italian food okay?"

"Marvellous."

Agatha went in and phoned a local Italian restaurant that did deliveries and ordered two portions of escalope Milanese with salads and a bottle of Valpolicella.

She was just about to join him in the garden when the doorbell rang. Agatha peered through the peephole and saw Toni's pretty face looking back at her.

No, she thought. One look at Toni and he'll forget I even exist. She returned to the garden.

Agatha had never been attracted to younger men before. She guiltily remembered having a crush on that beautiful schoolteacher in Winter Parva, the one murdered by Gwen's son. Before she had always considered women who fell for men, just because of their looks, slightly . . . well . . . common. Yes, James was handsome but the same age as she was herself. Maybe Justin was gay. That was the trouble with beautiful men, they usually were.

A shadow fell across her. She swung round. Justin was looking at her quizzically. "Who was at the door?"

"I didn't open it," said Agatha. "Some salesman. I've ordered lunch. Should be here soon. Let's enjoy the garden."

Toni phoned Simon on his mobile. "Agatha's not answering the door. Is she all right?"

"That beautiful young man I phoned you about. I think our Agatha's smitten, so she won't want you around."

"That's ridiculous," said Toni.

"That's our Agatha," said Simon.

As Agatha talked about her previous cases, she decided that the attraction she felt for Justin was maternal.

Sometimes, infrequently, she thought it would have been nice to have children. She had felt strong maternal feelings for Toni, but that had unfortunately left her trying to manipulate the girl's life until she had backed off. So feeling much more comfortable, she chatted until the food arrived and they moved back into the kitchen.

Halfway through the meal, she remembered she was supposed to be detecting and asked Justin if his father had ever been in Chicago.

"I don't know if he's been in Chicago," said Justin. "I know he went to a couple of conferences in America, but that was when Mother was still alive."

"I think I had better meet your father," said Agatha. "Would this evening be convenient?"

"I should think so. I'll phone him when we've finished eating and set something up."

When Justin left, he kissed Agatha on the cheek. He had phoned his father and he would expect them at six o'clock. Justin said he would collect Agatha from her office.

After he had left, Agatha's hand involuntarily fluttered up to the cheek he had kissed. She felt suddenly lonely and old.

Reminding herself fiercely that any feelings she had for Justin were maternal, she forced herself not to change into something more glamorous. She called on Doris and gave her a new set of keys and the new code supplied by the locksmith, and set out for the office.

It was only when she arrived at the office that she realised the murderer could be someone in the crowds outside, watching to see who came and went. She phoned Justin and explained it would be safer if he just gave her directions to his home. Then she sadly opened a cupboard and took out a large box of disguises.

The frumpier the better, she thought. I must look like a worried client.

Before she changed, she took the precaution of phoning a car rental company and asked them to leave the car in the square and bring the keys and contract up to the office.

After she had paid for the car rental, she changed into a drab dress and flat shoes. On her head she put a plain dark wig that looked as if it had been badly permed. She stuffed pads in her cheeks and put on a pair of glasses. Leaning heavily on a stick, she eventually left the office, watched by a worried Mrs. Freedman.

The car was a new anonymous-looking black Ford. After studying the directions, she set off, with many nervous looks in the rearview mirror in case she was being followed.

The Nichols' house turned out to be a large mansion

on the edge of the town. A short gravelled drive led up to the house. Before she got out of the car, Agatha took the pads out of her cheeks and removed the glasses and wig. She carefully applied make-up and brushed her hair until it shone. She wriggled out of the dowdy frock, and was leaning over into the backseat to pick up her linen dress wearing only a brief lacy bra and knickers when a knock at the window made her jump. Justin was smiling in at her. Agatha lowered the window and said, "Get off with you and give me a moment. I'm just getting out of this disguise."

Justin grinned. "I was just admiring the view."

Cursing, Agatha slipped on her linen dress and a pair of high-heeled sandals, sprayed herself with La Vie Est Belle and walked up to the front door where Justin was waiting.

He kissed her warmly on the cheek. "You smell nice. Do come in. We're in the garden."

Although Agatha guessed the house had been built at the beginning of the twentieth century, the entrance hall looked dark and baronial. There were two suits of armour and beside them, two antique-looking carved chests. The floor was highly polished parquet with fine Oriental rugs placed like coloured islands across its expanse. Justin turned left and led her through a large drawing room. It somehow looked soulless, as if it had been put in the hands of an unimaginative interior designer. The carpet was mushroom-coloured, as was the velvet three-piece suite. An enormous flat screen TV dominated one wall. The coffee table had a glass showcase top holding a collection of medals. There were vases of silk flowers everywhere. French windows were open to the garden where a thickset grey-haired man sat at a table.

The air outside was heavy with the smell of roses. It was a magnificent garden with a smooth green lawn bordered by roses of every colour.

Mr. Nichols rose to meet her. He had once been a handsome man, Agatha guessed, but he now had one of those boozer's faces which looked as if the features had been blurred. His nose was thick and open-pored, his eyes a faded blue crisscrossed with red veins. He had a large drink on the table in front of him which smelled of vodka. Poor Justin, thought Agatha. Alcoholics will drink vodka, believing it has no smell.

Mr. Nichols had a potbelly, straining at the belt of his trousers.

He stood up and shook Agatha's hand. "Can Justin get you a drink?"

"It's all right. I'm driving," said Agatha. "But I wouldn't mind a black coffee."

"Justin," he ordered, "tell Mrs. Frint to make a pot of coffee and bring some biscuits as well. Now, I must find out who murdered poor Ruby. I still think about her a lot. I mean, I always hoped she would come back to me."

"You mean even after she walked out on you, you still have strong feelings for her?"

"I love her," he said.

"First I must warn you, Mr. Nichols, that there is a dangerous murderer out there. By employing me, you may put yourself in danger. This killer managed to get into my cottage and bug it. Is Mrs. Frint your housekeeper?"

"Yes, excellent lady."

"Then she must be told not to let anyone in the house—telephone, water, gas, anything like that even though whoever may seem to be carrying the right identification."

The watery, red-veined eyes of the perpetual drinker looked at Agatha with all the pleading of a beaten dog. "Find who killed my Ruby," he said.

Justin escorted Agatha out. He paused on the doorstep. "What about meeting for dinner one night so you can let me know if you have found anything?"

Agatha looked into those blue eyes and felt herself weaken. "We'd better meet somewhere pretty out of the way," she said cautiously. "I don't want the murderer coming after you."

"What about tomorrow night? There's the Black Bear in Moreton. Safe. Lots of people around. I could meet you there at eight o'clock."

Agatha's longing to have dinner with Justin fought with a dark image of murdered Herythe. Her longing won.

"All right," she said cautiously. "I'll make sure I'm not followed."

Chapter Eight

Agatha left the office early the following day, planning to spend time getting ready for the dinner with Justin. Of course, he was too young to fancy her, and surely she was too old to develop feelings for such a young man.

And yet, when she let herself into her cottage and found Charles in the kitchen, she was furious. "How did you get in?" she raged.

"Doris lent me her keys. She's worried about you being alone and so am I."

"Well, that's good of you," said Agatha, mollified.

"But I'm going out this evening and I don't want you around when I get back."

"Who are you meeting?"

"None of your business. Push off, Charles."

"He's too young for you."

"I don't know what you are talking about." Agatha made for the stairs. "I am going to change and I don't want you here when I get back."

But her plan for a leisurely hour and a half had been ruined. All the while she listened but could not hear any sign of him leaving. When she eventually went downstairs, it was to find the cottage empty and Doris's keys lying on the kitchen table.

Agatha fretted. Charles was really a good friend and had saved her so many times from sticky situations. Well, she would get him a set of keys, but after she saw how things progressed with Justin.

The evening was calm and serene, with a huge yellow moon floating above the village rooftops. Agatha remembered that blue moon. How odd it had looked. Although Moreton was only fifteen minutes away, she took a circuitous route down the backroads, past the Batsford estates office, checking all the time in the rearview mirror, but there was no one else on the road.

She hesitated outside the Black Bear. She was being

silly and all because this young man was beautiful. And by being silly, she could be putting him in danger.

"Are you going in or what?" demanded a man's voice behind her. "You're blocking the entrance."

"Sorry," mumbled Agatha. She pushed open the door of the dining room and went in.

Justin was seated at a corner table. He rose to meet her. "You look pretty," he said, kissing her on both cheeks.

No one had ever called Agatha Raisin pretty before. She gave him a radiant smile as she sat down opposite him.

Agatha had forgotten what huge servings they gave at this restaurant. She had ordered steak and ale pie and it made her waistline tighten just looking at it. Unfortunately, Justin said, "I cannot bear women who just pick at their food," so Agatha did her best and was relieved when Justin rose and said he needed to go to the loo. For one mad moment, she thought of tipping the whole thing into her handbag, but instead, she took it up to the counter and told the waitress to take her half-finished plate away.

"Good heavens!" said Justin when he returned. "I'll need to eat fast to catch up with you." He wanted to hear more about Agatha's adventures and so Agatha bragged happily, until Justin finished his meal and the waitress came up with the dessert menu.

"Nothing for me," said Agatha.

"I'm sure your son could manage something," said the waitress and Agatha could feel all her silly dreams crashing about her ears, even when Justin said gallantly, "Not my mother, my date."

Agatha suddenly could not wait for the evening to end. She thanked Justin for the meal and said she would be in touch with him as soon as she learned anything new.

Once home, she petted her cats, wondering whether to send them back to Doris for safety. But they were company and she felt lonely.

In the following weeks, Agatha and her detectives went about their work nervously, each one worried that they might be the murderer's next target, but nothing happened. Patrick reported that the police did not seem to have found anything new. Justin phoned a couple of times, inviting Agatha out, but each time she said it was not safe.

The agency seemed to be drawing in a lot of work: missing teenagers, divorces, firms who thought a member of the staff was stealing, a supermarket that claimed that liquor was disappearing, and so the list went on.

And while she worked, Agatha found her thoughts kept turning to Gwen Simple. She could not imagine Gwen having the strength to strangle anyone or to throw a body in the river, but she knew that men went weak at the knees in her company and wondered if she had an accomplice.

Mrs. Bloxby told Agatha that Gwen had started a business making silk flowers and would be selling them at a stall at Ancombe crafts fair at the week-end.

The vicar's wife said she would accompany her and they set off in Agatha's car.

"Have you see anything of Sir Charles?" asked Mrs. Bloxby.

"No, he disappears from time to time," said Agatha bitterly. "I sometimes think I could be lying dead on my kitchen floor for all he cares, and that goes for James, too. He went off on his travels and didn't even call to say goodbye. Here we are in Ancombe. Don't like the place."

"It's all right," said Mrs. Bloxby. "You've just had bad luck with some of the residents in the past. Look, you can park in that field next to the fair."

"They must think everyone drives a four-by-four," grumbled Agatha as her car bumped over the ruts in the field. She was directed by a Boy Scout to a remaining place at the far corner. "I didn't think it would be this busy," said Agatha.

"People come from all over," said Mrs. Bloxby. "They start stocking up for Christmas because you can get a lot of things here you can't buy anywhere else and the prices are reasonable."

As they wandered amongst the stalls, Agatha could not see the attraction. Did people actually give wooden salad bowls for Christmas? And if you wanted a concrete frog for your garden, how did you get it home?

"I'll find Mrs. Simple first," said Mrs. Bloxby, "and come back and let you know if she's with some man. I'll meet you in the refreshment tent."

Agatha bought a cup of tea and looked around for a place to sit down. All the tables were full. There was an elderly gentleman on his own so she went up and asked, "Is it all right if I sit here?"

"Go ahead." He squinted up at her through thick glasses. "But it ain't no use chatting me up. I'm spoken for."

"Never crossed my mind," said Agatha.

"Why?"

Agatha sighed. "You're too old for me."

"You ain't hardly a spring chicken yourself."

Agatha looked at his ancient face. "Do you mean women still chase you?"

"Like flies round a honey pot. All widders. Few of us men left down at the social club. Was married the once. Ain't what it's cracked up to be. Marriage, that's wot. Nag, nag, nag, from morning till night. When my Tilly was in her coffin I could swear I could hear her, going on and on and on."

Mrs. Bloxby came up to the table and Agatha said quickly, "Let's go outside."

Once outside the tent, she asked eagerly, "Anything?"

"She's got a very beautiful young man helping her. I'm afraid it's young Mr. Nichols."

"Surely not. It can't be!" exclaimed Agatha.

"I wish it weren't."

"I'd better have a look to make sure. No. Wait a moment. I've got his mobile number."

Agatha dialled. With a sinking heart, she recognised Justin's voice. "Don't say my name," she said. "I'm outside the tea tent."

She rang off and waited anxiously, jumping nervously when Justin came up behind her and said breezily, "Hullo, Agatha. I remember you. It's Mrs. Bloxby, isn't it?" Agatha said, "What are you doing helping Gwen Simple?"

"I'm detecting," said Justin. "Thought I'd lend a hand."

"Listen! She could be a murderess. It's not safe."

"I think she's all right. Mrs. Simple is very quiet and kind."

"She's as quiet and kind as a cobra," hissed Agatha.

"I said I would help her, so I am going back there," said Justin stubbornly. "I'll phone you later." And with that, he darted away through the crowd.

Despite the heat of the day, Agatha shivered. She had a sudden feeling of menace. But the crowds drifted back and forward, the village band played, the air was full of the smells of tea and cakes and it looked a safe, rural setting.

Later, while she waited for Justin to phone, Agatha worked through her notes. What if, she wondered, the murder of Ruby Carson had nothing to do with the other murders? And yet it had happened right after Simon had told her on the phone about Jill's book being found. She sighed. Simon could hardly go detecting in Oxford where police and detectives would be working hard to find out who had murdered Ruby.

When the doorbell rang, she went to answer its summons, expecting to see Justin but it was only Charles.

"Oh, it's you," she said. "I was waiting for Justin Nichols."

"The beautiful boy."

"I'm worried about him. He's decided to be a detective and to that end was helping Gwen sell silk flowers at the Ancombe fair."

"She's probably wrapped her coils around him."

"I tried to warn him," fretted Agatha. "Look, Charles, what do you think of this idea? What if the murder of Ruby has nothing to do with the others?"

Charles sat down at the kitchen table. The cats jumped onto his lap. "Now why do you think that?" he asked.

"Often people who are murdered are what Scotland Yard calls murderees. They set up dangerous scenarios which lead to them being killed. Ruby was having an affair with the police chief superintendent. He says he was just on a visit, but Ruby screamed of ambition and as we know from Simon, she coldly used sex as a weapon. Is the superintendent married? What if his wife knew of the affair? What do we know of the latest ex-husband? Perhaps she slept with other men to further her career and then dropped them. There is no record of her having contacted Jill Davent. It seems to me that our murderer wants to eliminate anyone who was close enough to Jill to reveal his identity."

Charles looked at her curiously. He knew, from past experience, that Agatha's seeming flights of fancy were based on sharp intuition.

"So we should start at the beginning," he said. "Let's go now and see Mr. Nichols and find out who she might have been having an affair with when she was married to him."

"I'll phone Patrick first and find out what he knows," said Agatha.

Patrick said that Ruby's last husband was a detective inspector called Jimmy Carson. He had an impeccable reputation. In fact, Patrick had been to see him. He had said that Ruby was difficult and was always throwing scenes. He had been glad to agree to an amicable divorce. He only saw his children from time to time because he was always busy.

"I didn't get a report from you about this," said Agatha.

"I was going to get round to it," protested Patrick, "but with so many suspects, it didn't seem top of the list. Also, Gwen Simple's phone has been bugged by the police for ages. Nothing there. Doesn't even get a call from her son."

"There are still such things as mobiles."

"Got that covered as well. Nothing."

"Send me over what you've got," said Agatha. "All of it. Even the stuff you don't think is important."

When she rang off, she said crossly to Charles, "I think Patrick is beginning to behave like the Lone Ranger." She told him what Patrick had said.

Charles shrugged. "Patrick's ex-police so he probably still feels loyalty to the plod. But he should have told you about Gwen's phones being bugged. Let's see what Nichols has to say for himself."

Mr. Nichols had been drinking, but was still coherent. Asked about Ruby, he went off into a paean of praise.

Agatha interrupted brutally. "Was she having an affair with Carson while she was married to you?"

"I didn't want to believe it," he said mournfully. "I wouldn't believe it, but Justin, poor little lad as he was then, was miserable. I said I'd prove him wrong and hired a detective. I was devastated at what he found out. I said I would forgive her, but she said it would be better for everyone if I agreed to a divorce. She said if I did that, I could keep Justin. If I didn't, she swore she would get custody. Justin pleaded to stay with me. What could I do? So I agreed to the divorce."

"Wait a minute," said Agatha. "She was only his stepmother. No court would give her custody."

"She said she would reveal some family secrets I didn't want exposed."

"What secrets?"

"They're secrets and that's how they'll stay!"

"So why are you still in love with this terrible woman?" asked Charles.

"Oh, she was a goddess when we were married. You don't know her. Carson seduced her. He's a wicked man. I'll bet he killed her."

"Was Justin fond of his stepmother?" asked Agatha.

"That's the sad bit," said Mr. Nichols. "He never forgave her."

"So why did he encourage you to engage my services?" asked Agatha.

"He said it was odd that we weren't getting any information from the police. He said we should try to find out something ourselves. He said it would put my mind at rest. He's a good boy and he loves his dad." Mr. Nichols raised his glass and took a large swallow of whisky.

His eyes filled with tears. "I wish I could have my Ruby back again."

They took their leave. "I think you're barking up the wrong tree, Agatha," said Charles. "Look, Ruby was garroted right after that message from Simon. That drunk in there is so advanced in alcoholism that he lives in a world of fantasy."

"Maybe he could have thought that if he couldn't have her, he would make sure no one else could," said Agatha.

"Did you have anyone else checking up on him?"

"I asked Simon to look into it."

Agatha phoned Simon. "Nichols is ex–Special Forces," he said. "You know, SAS, and they keep quiet about details."

When Agatha told Charles, he said, "That paints a different picture. He'd certainly know how to bump her off. But he's probably been sunk in booze for so long, I can't see him moving away from the chair and whisky bottle. Justin didn't say anything, but I doubt if Mr. Nichols had that job of his for a while."

When they were back in Agatha's cottage, Charles helped himself to a drink and moved out into the garden, followed by the cats. Agatha sat down at her computer and began to read everything on the murders.

After an hour, the doorbell rang. "I'll get it," called Charles. "I ordered Chinese food."

Agatha realised she was very hungry and followed him through to the kitchen, where he was placing containers on the kitchen table. "Dig in," he said. "I feel like beer. Got any?"

"No, but there's a bottle of white wine in the fridge."

They ate companionably, until Agatha suddenly put down her chopsticks and stared at him.

"Let's think about Justin," she said.

"Why?"

"Even as a child, he complained constantly about her. He must have wanted to be rid of her. What if he hated her?"

"Now there's a flight of fancy," said Charles. "Okay. I'll go along with it. Why wait so long?"

"It's a great opportunity," said Agatha. "Murders all over the place, one of them in Oxford. She's one of the investigating officers. What better time to bump her off? No one is going to look in his direction."

"But he hired you."

"What better way to find out what we know? What better way to feel manipulative power? I'll phone Simon and get him to dig up what he can on Justin."

"He'll have gone home."

"A bit of overtime never hurt anyone," said Agatha. She rang Simon. "You should ask Toni," he said.

"Are you being lazy or what?" asked Agatha.

"It's just that he came up to the office and he and Toni started chatting. Then he asked her out to dinner and a movie and she said yes."

"What movie?"

"Rerun of *Gigi* at the Arts Cinema."

When Agatha rang off, she stared at Charles in consternation as she told him the news.

"You're getting carried away," said Charles. "He's young and beautiful and so is she."

"I don't like this," said Agatha. "I'm going to hunt them down."

When Agatha entered the cinema, the film was nearly over. She blundered down in the darkness, shining a pencil torch on the faces of the audience, deaf to complaints.

She located them, sitting in the middle of a row halfway down. She found one empty seat behind them, feeling suddenly stupid. She was just thinking of getting up and leaving, when Toni turned round and saw her.

Toni experienced a flash of pure rage. Yes, Agatha had rescued her, not only from a drunken home, but from several other nasty situations. But that did not give her any reason to spy on her. She doesn't own me, thought Toni. She's always trying to control my life. The fact that Agatha had stopped doing just that escaped her mind. Young Toni often felt the weight of all that she owed Agatha a bit too heavily. It's better to give than receive—oh, thanks a bunch, Francis of Assisi—but say a prayer for the receivers, she mused.

Then common sense took over. If her date with Justin was important enough for Agatha to stalk her, always supposing Agatha was not jealous, and was not in the grip of one of her obsessions, then it followed that Agatha knew something sinister about her date.

When the film ended and the lights went up in the cinema, there was no sign of Agatha. Toni had suggested eating before the film, so, outside the cinema, she shook Justin's hand, said she would be in touch with him, refused his offer of a drink and made her way back to her flat. Upstairs, she looked out of her window and saw Agatha on the opposite side of the street, just turning away. Toni ran down and called out, "Agatha!"

Looking guilty, Agatha turned round. "Why were you stalking me?" asked Toni.

"Let's up to your flat and I'll tell you," said Agatha.

As she talked, Agatha began to feel her intuition had played her false. She had absolutely no proof of anything.

Toni listened carefully and then said, "You've had mad ideas before and they turned out to be right. Why don't we go with it? I know where Justin went to school. I'll see if I can find some of his old school friends. Say he hated Ruby, then he might have sounded off about it."

"Maybe I should do that," said Agatha. "I don't want to put you at risk."

"Don't mother me!" said Toni sharply. Then in a softer voice, she said, "I owe you a lot, Agatha, and sometimes I almost dislike you for it. Can you understand that?"

"I'll try," said Agatha, although she thought of how she had battled her way to success without help from anyone.

"Don't worry. I'll be careful," said Toni. "How old is he?"

"Twenty-six."

After Agatha had gone, Toni replayed in her mind the conversation she had had with Justin. Finally she remembered he had said he had gone to St. Jerome's School, a private school in Mircester. But he had not mentioned any school friends. Then she remembered that Simon had gone to the same school and phoned him up. After she had explained the whole thing, Simon said, "Maybe the local newspaper would have something. It's a prep school and they always covered prize givings. How old is he?"

"Twenty-five."

"So go to the local rag and look up prize givings for thirteen years ago. They all graduate when they're twelve."

Toni was a well-known figure at the *Mircester Chronicle*. She mounted the rickety wooden stairs to the editorial room and asked if she could look up the newspapers for twelve years ago. A secretary went away and reappeared with a large leather-bound book. "Not even on the old microfiche?" asked Toni.

"You know us," said the secretary. "We never move with the times, that's our motto."

Toni began to search, glad that it was a weekly newspaper. She concentrated on the July publications. She found the article and photographs of graduation day.

Justin had not received a prize. But there was a group photo. She only recognised him from his name amongst the others underneath the grainy photograph. He was wearing glasses. Those marvellous blue eyes, thought Toni. Must be contact lenses. She took notes of the names of three of the prizewinners, John Finlay, Henry Pilkington, and Paul Kumar.

Back in the office, she found a number for Henry Pilkington and called. A woman answered the phone. She said she was Henry's wife and that he worked as managing director of Comfy Baby on the industrial estate. She started to ask what it was all about but the wail of a child in the background distracted her and she hurriedly cut the call. Toni sent the information over to Agatha.

Agatha set out the following morning. Comfy Baby supplied goods for the new baby: cots, nappies, feeding bottles and clothes. The offices looked new and prosperous.

After waiting twenty minutes, she was ushered into the managing director's office. Henry Pilkington was a small man wearing thick rimless glasses. It was hard to believe he was the same age as Justin. He was bald on top and his thin brown hair was already going grey.

He studied Agatha's business card as if it were some

sort of poisonous insect. "So," he said, "she's done it at last."

Agatha looked bewildered. "Who's 'she'?"

"My bloody neurotic wife. Always accusing me of having an affair. How does she think I got this job so young? Leaving the office early? I've slaved and worked long hours to get where I am."

"I am not here because of your wife," said Agatha. "I would like to know about Justin Nichols."

His face cleared. "Oh, the golden boy. I was at prep school with him. Smarmy little creep. I'm telling you, the teachers fawned on him."

"Do you happen to know if his father's divorce hit him badly?"

"I wasn't one of his buddies. But I guess it did. I know he had long sessions with the school counsellor."

"Can you remember her name?"

"A Miss Currie."

"Do you know if she is still at the school?"

"No."

"Had Justin a particular friend?"

"I suppose John Finlay was close to him. He's working here. He's a sales rep. I'll see if he's around but he may be out on the road."

He picked up the phone and asked if John Finlay was in the building. Then Agatha heard him say, "Send him to my office."

Pilkington smiled at Agatha. "He'll be here in a few minutes. Good chap, but likes his drink."

When John Finlay arrived, Pilkington said, "You can use my office." He made the introductions and explained that Agatha wanted to know about Justin.

John Finlay was tall and handsome with thick curly black hair and an engaging smile. "I don't know if I can help you," he said. "I haven't seen Justin in ages. What's he done? Got a jealous wife?"

"Nothing like that," said Agatha, reflecting that the very name "private detective" immediately made most people think of divorce. "I'm interested in Justin's prep school days, particularly his reaction to his father's divorce."

"It hit him hard. He loathed his stepmother. Said she made his life hell, always sneering at him when she wasn't calling his father a waste of space. He was devoted to his father. He wanted to go on to Ratchett, the public school, but he did badly in the exams. His teachers intervened and managed to get him a place at Mircester High School, which is a state school. I remember now. There was a fire at the school in his final year and someone had seen him near the school on that night, but his girlfriend, Sadie Broody, stepped up and said he had been with her all night."

"Do you know where I can find Sarah Broody?"

"Haven't the faintest idea. What's this all about?"

"Nothing serious. Just checking up on something which hasn't got much to do with Justin. Thank you for your time."

When Agatha had left, Finlay was joined by Pilkington. They stood at the window and watched Agatha cross the car park and get into her car. "I like Justin," said John Finlay. "Might see if I can look him up and tell him that some detective has been asking questions about him. I mean, it was his stepmother who was murdered. Is that what she's investigating?"

Broody was not a common name and Agatha found an address for an S. Broody. Her flat was near Toni's. She rang the bell but there was no reply. By asking the neighbours, she learned that Sarah sold cosmetics at Jankers, Mircester's most expensive store.

Agatha was told that Sarah was on her lunch break and usually went to a café next door. The café was crowded. Agatha stared around at the customers. There was an attractive and elegant woman in the corner. Agatha approached her. "Miss Broody?"

The woman looked at her blankly. A woman at the next table swung round. "That's me. What do you want?"

There was an empty chair opposite her. Agatha slid into it. Sarah Broody was plain, there was no other word to describe her. She had large pale protruding eyes, bad skin and lank hair. Agatha wondered why, as she was a cosmetics saleswoman, she did not wear make-up.

Agatha explained who she was and then said she was interested in the night of the fire at the school. A red angry spot stood out on the sudden whiteness of Sarah's face. She began to gather up her things. "I have nothing to say."

"I only want to know why you lied," said Agatha, her bearlike eyes boring into Sarah's face. "It's either me or the police."

Sarah, who had half risen, sank back into her chair. "Bastard," she whispered. "Will I go to prison?"

"No, because I won't say a word," said Agatha. "It's all to do with another matter."

"He begged me. He said he would marry me if I lied for him. I would have done anything for him. I didn't sleep with him. He got hold of me the next day. I was dazzled. I said I would and I did. But the minute the schooldays were over, he dropped me. I was furious. I said I would tell the police the truth and he laughed and said I would go to prison for perverting the course of justice and he would even swear I had helped him. He's evil."

Agatha had a quick meal when she had left and went back to the office. Toni came in and asked her how she had got on and listened, alarmed. Then she said, "But why encourage his father to investigate? He was only a young boy when he was threatening her. I'm sure he's harmless."

"Look," said Agatha, "he tricked that poor girl into lying for him. He burned down the school. Murderers often start being arsonists when they are children."

"Do me a favour," said Toni. "If you are that sure he is evil, phone him up and say you have come to the conclusion that because of the huge investigation by the police in Oxford, it is hopeless trying to get anywhere. And after you have done that, phone the police and report your findings about the school fire."

But Agatha felt her report on the fire could wait. Right at that moment, she could not bear the idea of another interrogation at police headquarters.

However, she phoned Justin on his mobile and explained her reasons for dropping the case. To her relief, he took the news without protest, only saying, "I see what you mean. I'll tell Dad. He'll understand."

Agatha then turned her attention to another outstanding case and got to work. By the end of the day, she felt exhausted. The case meant she had to follow a nimble possible adulteress, on foot, accompanied by Phil with his cameras. The humid weather did not help. Nor did her high-heeled sandals. The woman in question went from shop to shop, then she dropped into a café for coffee before resuming her shopping and then blamelessly returned home to her suspicious husband, carrying bags of purchases while Agatha cursed a woman who wore trainers and never seemed to bother taking her car out.

She returned to her cottage, put a microwave meal in for dinner, fed her cats and finally settled down in front of the television, flicking through the channels to see if she could find a bit of escapism. She finally found an episode of *Morse* she had not seen before, but after the first half hour, her eyes drooped and she fell asleep.

Charles let himself in later that evening. He saw Agatha asleep on the sofa and decided to leave her and wake her later on. He went upstairs and put his bag in the spare room. He was just about to go downstairs when he heard the doorbell ring. He stood and listened. Then he heard Agatha making her way to the door, saying, "Justin! Can this wait? I'm very tired."

And then Justin's voice. "It'll only take a moment."

Charles wondered what to do. Agatha had seemed smitten by Justin, then suspicious of him. She might be furious to find him lurking around. He sat down at the top of the stairs and waited.

In the kitchen, Agatha went over to the coffee percolator and asked, "Coffee?"

"Not for me, thank you."

"I'll have one," said Agatha. "I'm barely awake." Her eyes fell on her open handbag, lying on the counter with the electric light gleaming on the edge of her tape recorder. She poured herself a cup of coffee, and, before turning around, switched on the tape recorder.

Justin was already sitting at the kitchen table. Agatha sat down opposite him.

"I had a call from the Broody female," he said. "Broody by name, broody by nature. She was sobbing and gulping and saying she had betrayed me but if I would only see her again, she would swear blind she had told you nothing. Then an old school friend phoned my dad and said you'd been asking odd questions of what I was like at the time of the divorce. May I remind you, sweetie, that you are being paid to investigate my stepmother's death?"

"I know that," said Agatha. "Look, I'm tired. Can't this wait until tomorrow?"

"No, it can't wait. You want the truth? Well, listen to this. Ruby made my life hell and she drove my father into alcoholism. I've dreamt for years of a way to get rid of her and you gave me that way. All those murders. Who would suspect me if another one was committed? So I watched and waited outside her house for an opportunity. That night I followed her to Mircester. I saw her park her car in the middle of that storm. I guessed the CCTV cameras wouldn't be able to pick up anything because of the power cut and there was another crack of thunder and I broke the glass of the back window of her car."

That beautiful face seemed to Agatha the epitome of evil. She had been trying to give up smoking but now she grabbed her packet of cigarettes and lit one up.

He grinned. "Last cigarette before the execution?"

Then he dodged as Agatha seized a milk bottle off the table and threw it at him. From his pocket, he produced a length of wire with a piece of wood at the end. Agatha jumped to her feet and made for the garden door. He seized her and bore her down onto the floor.

"Help me!" screamed Agatha as the cruel wire went round her neck.

Then suddenly he went limp. Panting, Agatha rolled out from under him and struggled to her feet. Charles was standing there with a poker in his hand.

"Got anything to tie him up?" he asked. "I hope I haven't killed him."

With shaking hands, Agatha jerked open a kitchen drawer and pulled out a roll of garden twine.

"Phone the police," ordered Charles. "I'll tie him up after I find out if he's still breathing."

While Agatha phoned, he tied Justin's hands and feet and then checked his pulse. "He's alive. Hope I haven't given the bastard brain damage or we won't get a confession."

"I got it on tape," said Agatha. Her face was chalk white and her legs seemed to have turned to jelly.

Justin recovered consciousness. "You've got nothing," he whispered. "I'll deny the whole thing."

Agatha fumbled in her handbag and took out the tape recorder. She ran the tape back and then pressed the button to play it. Appalled, Justin heard his voice coming over loud and clear.

Charles and Agatha were finally left alone, after a long night. Agatha wondered how Justin's father would survive the news. It transpired he had been sacked from his job months before for drunkenness. Agatha had not been thanked for her detective work and Charles had been grilled about whether he thought he had used reasonable force.

"Aren't you going to phone the press and tell them it was you who solved Ruby's murder?" asked Charles.

Agatha took a swig of black coffee and lit a cigarette. "I've been warned not to speak to the press. Everything is sub judice before the court case."

"I could leak it for you."

"Don't do that," said Agatha wearily. "Wilkes would come down on me like a ton of bricks."

"You're a very good detective, Agatha."

"I sometimes wonder."

"Who else would have sensed there was something up with Justin?"

Agatha scowled into her drink. She was suddenly sure that her suspicions about Justin had been prompted by jealousy when she had seen him with Gwen Simple.

She sighed. "Maybe the police would have got round to it anyway."

There was a ring at the doorbell. "Ignore that," said Charles.

"No, I'll go."

Agatha came back into the kitchen followed by Mrs. Bloxby and James Lacey.

"What's been happening?" asked James. "I've just got back and heard in the village shop about your cottage swarming with police."

"I was worried, too," said Mrs. Bloxby. "By the time the Chinese whispers reached the vicarage, I heard you had been arrested."

"I'll make a pot of coffee," said Charles, "and Agatha can tell you all about it."

"Get me another coffee," said Agatha. "I can hardly keep my eyes open."

As Agatha recounted her adventures, she began to feel the whole thing was unreal, that she had imagined it all. When she had finished, James said, "Now all you have to do is solve the other murders."

Charles entering with a tray of coffee said sharply, "I think Agatha should leave that to the police."

James laughed. "Oh, Agatha won't leave it alone. She's as tough as old boots."

"Look," said Charles, "she's just escaped being murdered. The best thing she can do is take a few days off and chill out."

Both men glared at each other.

I think they are both in love with her in their odd ways, thought Mrs. Bloxby. Oh, why doesn't Agatha get married and settle down?

James gave a reluctant laugh and turned to Mrs. Bloxby. "You must long for the days when there weren't so many incomers."

"Well, Mrs. Simple and her son had been in Winter Parva for some time. I wonder how many murders went unnoticed before all this expert technology." said the vicar's wife. "But do forget about these murders, Mrs. Raisin. Be safe."

"I'll think about it," said Agatha.

Chapter Nine

But that night, as she tossed and turned in bed, Agatha felt she simply could not let go. The murderer was out there, and, if not stopped, would kill again. The next target might be me, thought Agatha. She had kept her bedside light on to banish the fears brought by darkness. She regretted having bought a thatched cottage because nameless creatures rustled in the thatch.

Her bedroom door opened and Charles, who had been sleeping in the spare room, walked in, wrapped in a dressing gown.

He was carrying a glass of milk. "Drink this," he ordered. "And here's a sleeping pill. I picked up a prescription today for my aunt. She won't miss one."

"I don't drink milk and I never take sleeping pills," complained Agatha.

"Do as you're told for once in your life," said Charles, "or I will ram this pill down your throat."

"Oh, all right," said Agatha grumpily. She swallowed the pill. Then she said, "I never thanked you for saving my life."

"All in the day's work," said Charles. "Go to sleep."

After he had left, Agatha felt she would never sleep when she suddenly plunged down into a dream where Justin was chasing her round a village fair with an ax.

Agatha arose late next morning to find that Charles had left. Patrick Mulligan phoned her to tell her that Justin had taken poison on the road to the police station. He had died horribly. They thought it might be cyanide but were waiting for the results of the autopsy. The three officers who had been driving him to headquarters were in trouble because they had not handcuffed him. There was worse to come. The news was broken to Mr. Nichols, who had said he would identify the body. He had asked Bill Wong and Alice Peterson to wait while he changed. When they felt he was taking too long about it, they had gone up to his bedroom to find the door locked. Bill had finally managed to break it down to find that Justin's father had hanged himself.

"Where on earth does one get a cyanide pill in this day and age?" asked Agatha. "And why didn't they tell Charles that Justin had committed suicide instead of leaving him to worry that he might have caused brain damage?"

"Search me," said Patrick. "In fact, the officers are also being berated for not having searched him before they put him in the car."

When he had rung off, Agatha took a cup of black coffee into the garden and sat down and watched her cats chasing cloud shadows across the grass. The air was full of the scent of flowers. The birds were quiet as they always were in August.

Agatha finished her coffee and decided to walk up to the vicarage. With all the murder and mayhem, she had forgotten it was Sunday. People were leaving the church, stopping to shake hands with the vicar. The women in bright dresses, the happy chatter, all looked so safe. Agatha was about to turn away when she heard her name being called and swung round. Mrs. Bloxby came hurrying to meet her.

"Come back to the vicarage," said the vicar's wife, "and we'll have a quiet drink and chat in the garden."

"Won't your husband mind?"

"Alf has got to rush off to Winter Parva to conduct another service."

They started to walk towards the vicarage when Agatha stopped abruptly.

"What's up?" asked Mrs. Bloxby anxiously.

"Nothing," said Agatha. "I'm still a bit nervous." But Agatha could have sworn that just for a moment she had sensed something evil, and then decided it must be the aftereffects of that sleeping pill.

Once in the vicarage garden, Agatha sat sipping sherry instead of her usual gin and tonic. Sherry seemed such a *holy* drink and surely the God that Agatha only believed existed in times of stress would approve and not send any more frights down into her life.

"What do you get out of believing in God?" she asked abruptly.

"Comfort," said Mrs. Bloxby.

Snakes and bastards, thought Agatha, I must be going soft in the head.

"Is Sir Charles not still with you?" asked Mrs. Bloxby.

"No, he melted away like the Cheshire cat as usual," said Agatha.

"And did James call this morning to see how you were?"

"Not him. He thinks I'm made of iron."

"How did Charles get into your cottage?"

"In a weak moment, I sent him a set of keys. Just as well, or I'd be dead by now."

"Have you ever considered," said the vicar's wife cautiously, "that Sir Charles's pretty constant presence is stopping you from finding a suitable man?"

Agatha sighed. "I wish I could say that were the case. But only unsuitable men come my way and he's often been there, to save me from them." She paused. "I wonder if I should search round the village for wolfsbane."

"The police did a thorough search for that plant, not only in this village but in all the villages round about," said Mrs. Bloxby. "Try to relax and leave it all to them."

But when Agatha left, she felt she would never rest until she found out the identity of the murderer.

Once more on her own, she realised she was hungry and headed for the Red Lion. The pub had become a gastro pub, which meant the same old food with the usual gastro pub descriptions. Salads were "drizzled" with vinaigrette. There was a soup of "foraged" greens. Cheese on toast was described as "whipped goat's curd, garden shoots and pickled alliums." She ordered the "taste of Italy, home-cooked lasagne with hard-cut chips." "What are hard-cut chips?" Agatha asked the landlord, John Fletcher.

"Because it's hard to get the frozen ones out of the bag," he said.

"And you don't even blush," said Agatha. "Okay, I'll have the lasagne and a glass of Merlot."

"You'll be sitting outside then," said John, "so you can smoke."

"I've given up," lied Agatha because she wanted to join the ranks of the saintly nonsmokers.

John gave her a cynical look. "Well, if you change your mind, let me know."

"Forget the chips," said Agatha. "I'll have the shaved salad instead. What's a shaved salad?"

"I prepared it while I was shaving," said John.

"Oh, ha, so very ha." Agatha retreated to a table. A television set was mounted over the bar with the sound turned down. Richard Dawkins, that celebrity agnostic, was mouthing away about something, no doubt trying to mess up someone's Sunday, thought Agatha. Funny how Christianity bashing had become so fashionable. She waved to various people she knew but no one came over to her table. Agatha realised that once again the village associated her with murder. Was her conviction that somehow Gwen Simple was behind it the wrong one?

Her food arrived. It looked like the same old pub grub they had served before the fancy menus. She ate mechanically, turning over what she knew about the murders in her mind.

Agatha still felt shaken after the latest attempt on her life and had a longing to finish her meal, go home, go to bed and pull the duvet over her head. But, instead, she decided to drive to Ancombe and spy on Gwen.

Gwen was hosting a small party in her front garden. She was wearing an old-fashioned sort of tea gown of some gauzy patterned material, which floated about her body. Her hair was piled on top of her head. Her long thin nose and hooded eyes in her white face made her look more than ever as if she had stepped down from some mediaeval painting. Agatha stood behind a tree at the corner of the garden to shield herself from the guests. Two late arrivals walked past her and made their way into the garden.

Agatha noticed that a very handsome man was helping serve the drinks. He was as tall as James but with red hair and a tanned face. The new arrivals said something to Gwen, who looked straight at the tree behind which Agatha was hiding. She said something to the handsome man, who strode down the garden. Agatha was scurrying off to her car when he caught up with her.

"Mrs. Simple wants to know what you are doing spying on her," he said.

"I am a private detective and—"

"So she told me. What are you doing here?"

"Mrs. Simple is one of the suspects in a detective case I am investigating."

"The fact that her wretched son is a murderer doesn't make her one. She is phoning headquarters to put in a claim of harassment."

"Snakes and bastards. They'll be down on me like a ton of bricks. When that chap nearly murdered me, they treated me as if I were a villain."

He looked curiously down at her. The sun was shining on Agatha's shiny hair. She was wearing a white shirt blouse with a short skirt, which showed off her excellent legs. A faint scent of Miss Dior drifted round her.

"I've just got back from Dubai. What's this about you nearly being murdered?"

"Don't you think you'd better introduce yourself?" said Agatha.

"I am Mark Dretter. I have just taken a cottage in Ancombe."

"Look," said Agatha, wishing she had worn low heels because the straps of her high-heeled sandals were beginning to become uncomfortable, "I'm tired of standing in the heat. Can we talk somewhere more comfortable?"

"Why not? I only met Gwen today when she called on me and invited me to her party. Where do you suggest?"

"I can drive you to the pub in Carsely and we can talk there."

"You lead the way," said Mark, "and I'll follow you."

How old is he? wondered Agatha. I think he's about my age. He's very good-looking and he's got a great physique. Could he have been lying? Maybe he's close to Gwen and wants to find out what I know. Oh, I do hope Charles doesn't choose to make one of his sudden appearances.

At the Red Lion, they chose a table in the garden. To her surprise, he ordered a bottle of cold white wine.

"Aren't you worried about being caught for drunk driving?" she asked. "It's all right for me. I can leave my car here and walk home."

"I'll be quite safe," said Mark. "It's only a few miles to Ancombe and I don't plan to get drunk."

"Before I tell you all about it," said Agatha cautiously, "when did you arrive back from Dubai?"

"Yesterday. I got my sister to choose a cottage in the Cotswolds for me and I wired her the money."

"And what do you do?"

"I work at the British embassy. I'm on leave."

"Spook?"

"Not me. Just an underling. Now let's hear about this murder."

"Murders," corrected Agatha.

He listened intently as Agatha told him the whole story, ending up with Justin's attempt on her life.

When she had finished, he said, "And I was hoping for a quiet life in an area where nothing bad happens. But it seems a bit hard to suspect Gwen just because of her awful son."

"How did you hear about that?" asked Agatha.

"My sister told me."

"But not about the other murders? You get the British newspapers in Dubai. You must have read something."

"It's all coming back to me. Yes, I did read about it. For a start, I wasn't aware Carsely was so close and the other murders took place in Oxford."

With one of her sudden flashes of intuition, Agatha thought, he's lying. Gwen's already snared him and he's doing his best to find out what he can and report back to her.

Agatha rated her own appearance very low. It never dawned on her that this was caused by her previous bad taste in men. Those experiences that had reduced her self-worth. Suddenly she realised he was speaking.

"It seems to have started with that therapist," he said. "The fact that when she was in Chicago, she was a hooker makes things difficult. Look at it the other way. People in this village went to Jill for counselling. Someone was afraid that Oxford detective had found out something. Then there is the barrister. Perhaps the murderer knew from your bugged cottage that he was going to be investigated and overrated his abilities. Now we come to Victoria Bannister. What was she like?"

"Bitch. Nosy. Jealous. Spinster."

"Right. She spied on you. She may have known who went to consult Jill. Just maybe she fancied herself as a sort of Poirot and went around accusing Jill's clients, saying, you are the murderer. If it hadn't been for the Chicago connection, you would have concentrated on this village. I mean, wolfsbane suggests someone with a good knowledge of plants."

Agatha was feeling more and more attracted to Mark. But there was one thing she had to get clear. She told him about the few in the village that she knew had gone to Jill. "Why did you lie to me when you said you knew nothing of the murders? Gwen got her hooks into you when she called to invite you to her party. She told you all about her son and how this private detective was persecuting her. You were even acting as host at her garden party. Like a knight errant you probably phoned her from your car on the road here and told her you were on the case."

He gave a reluctant laugh. "Now you've made me feel like a fool. Gwen told a pathetic story and I was sorry for her. I thought I was going to scare off some hard-faced bat instead of a woman with shiny hair and smelling of summer. Look here, let's forget about Gwen and be friends."

His hair was thick and red with threads of silver shining in the sun.

"Are you married?" asked Agatha.

"No. My poor wife died of cancer three years ago. And you?"

"Divorced. Any children?"

"No. And you?"

"None either."

He smiled at her across the table and Agatha's treacherous heart gave a lurch. "You didn't answer my question. Friends?" He held his hand across the table.

Agatha shook it. "Friends," she echoed.

"Why don't we have dinner tomorrow night?"

"Perhaps," said Agatha cautiously. "Give me your card and I'll phone you. I often have to work late."

"We haven't drunk much of this wine," said Mark. "I'd better get back to the party."

"And what will you report?"

"That a charming lady such as yourself can have no evil intentions. I'll phone you."

As soon as he had gone, Agatha lit up a cigarette. The bottle was almost half full but she did not feel like

192

drinking any more. She could feel a rising bubble of excitement. Agatha often had dreams of being married. Would she need to remove to Dubai? But then reality took over. Men such as Mark did not want to marry middle-aged women. They usually wanted some young charmer of child-bearing age. She wondered what tales of persecution Gwen was regaling him with.

A shadow fell across the table. Agatha looked up. "Drinking alone?" asked James.

"No, I had company," said Agatha. "Get yourself a glass and you can have some of this wine before it gets too warm."

When James returned and poured himself a glass of wine, he asked, "Have you got over your fright of having been nearly killed?"

"Mostly. I feel I should maybe rent a flat in Mircester. My cottage just does not seem safe. But I don't like to think of my cats being stuck in a city flat."

"Then let Doris have them."

"Perhaps."

"Drink is not the solution. Unlike you to order a whole bottle."

"I didn't order it. As I said, I had company. He's just left."

"Who's 'he,' Agatha?"

Agatha proceeded to tell him the whole story, about

how she had been caught spying on Gwen and how she had become friends with Mark.

"Go carefully," counselled James when she had finished. "I've got contacts in Dubai. I'll check on him."

"He put an idea in my head," said Agatha. "If Gwen has nothing to do with it, then perhaps the Oxford murders and the sophistication of bugging my house has turned me away from the people in Carsely. You know how it is these days with Cotswold villages. There are London people who only use a cottage for week-ends. Any of them you know about?"

"I've talked to some of the wives who are left down in the village all week, waiting for their husbands to come home at week-ends. They have to find amusement to pass the time. Going to a therapist when you don't really need one is an ego trip. Just sit or lie there with a captive audience and talk about yourself."

"Any particular one you can think of?" asked Agatha.

"There's Bunty Rotherham. She's married to Oran Rotherham, who has an electronics factory in Slough."

"What sort of name is Oran?"

"It means pale green in Irish Gaelic."

"Whereabouts is his house?"

"It's just outside the village on the Ancombe road. You can't see it from the road. There is a disused gatehouse with bricked-up windows at the foot of the drive, about half a mile from Carsely."

"How do you know all this?"

"I was invited there to a party one week-end. They've got the lot: swimming pool, hot tub, tennis courts and croquet lawn."

"What sort of man is Oran?"

"Powerful and belligerent. Strong Irish accent except when he forgets to use it and bits of Cockney start creeping in. Suspected a few years ago of selling remote control devices to the Iranians, but the intelligence services couldn't find anything to charge him with."

"I'll go and call on him now," said Agatha.

"I'd better go with you," said James. "I gather you were rude to the trophy wives one evening."

"Well, let's hope Bunty wasn't one of them. I'll pay for this wine. Charles has me well trained."

But the landlord told her that Mark had paid for the wine. When she thought of him, a rosy, warm feeling enveloped her.

James suggested they take his car as Agatha confessed to having drunk two glasses of wine.

To Agatha's dismay, James had just bought a white Morgan sports car, difficult to get in and out of. James turned in past the deserted lodge and cruised up a long drive bordered on either side by tall pine trees. The house finally came into view. It was a large white fairly modern house which resembled a bathing lido. "Looks like something out of Poirot," said James. "I would guess it was built in the thirties by some architect trying to copy Lutyens. Funny, isn't it, that anything round here built in the thirties we think of as modern."

James parked the car beside a large Bentley and a Porsche. "At least they don't seem to have guests," he said.

Agatha tried to get out of the low-slung sports car and ended up landing on her bottom on the gravel.

"Bloody car," she grumbled as James helped her to her feet.

"There is nothing up with my car," said James. "If you would stop wearing tight skirts and those ridiculously high heels, you wouldn't have any trouble."

"That was what was up with our marriage," said Agatha furiously. "Always running me down and criticising my clothes."

"Oh, shut up," snapped James. "Do you want to visit this man or not?"

He marched towards the front door and rang the bell, not looking round to see if Agatha was following.

Agatha tottered after him, the thin heels of her sandals finding it difficult to cope with the gravel.

James turned round when she caught up with him. "Maybe there's nobody home."

A female voice suddenly sounded tinnily over the intercom beside the door. "Who is it?"

"James Lacey."

"Oh, darling James. Wait a moment."

The sun beat down. Looking up at the building, Agatha noticed that it consisted of a lot of curved balconies and many plate glass windows.

The door swung open and a butler stood there in a black suit, black tie and white shirt. He looked thuggish, what Agatha privately damned as a knuckle dragger. "They're at the pool," he said in a raspy voice. "Follow me."

They passed through a hall with white walls. A curving stone staircase, also white but with a black wrought iron banister, led upwards. Then into a large room where everything seemed white from the leather sofa and armchairs to the white walls on three sides, the fourth being large windows. A coffee table held copies of the latest glossy magazines. A white nude sculpture of a woman dominated the room. The windows were open onto a terrace. The man trotted in front of them. Agatha noticed that despite the formality of his dress, he was wearing trainers. Maybe he wasn't really a butler but some sort of strong-arm man. They walked down steps from the terrace to the back of the house where a man and a woman were sprawled in their swimming costumes on loungers beside a table. Bunty was wearing a skimpy bikini over her salon tan. Agatha realised thankfully that she was not one of the women she had insulted in the pub. Oran rose from his lounger and sat on the end of it. His chest was covered in a thick mat of black hair. He had a black beard and moustache. Even the backs of his powerful hands were hairy.

Bunty was the picture of a trophy wife from her pout mouth, collagen enhanced, to her painted toenails. "Roger," she said, "bring chairs and we'll all sit round the table and have drinkies."

Had Roger really muttered a four-letter word before he turned away? He certainly didn't seem to like taking orders from Bunty. But he came back in a few moments, pushing four fold-up chairs on a trolley. He opened them up and set them round the table. Bunty uncoiled from the lounger and sat at the table, waving a hand at Agatha and James, diamond rings flashing in the sun, to indicate they should do the same. Oran heaved his powerful bulk into another chair. "What'll yiz be havin' in the way o' a drink?"

"Nothing for me," said James. "I'm driving and I've already reached my limit."

"Not for me, either," said Agatha.

Bunty pouted and called to Roger, "Fix me a tequila."

Roger scowled but disappeared inside the house.

"So what's the reason for the visit?" asked Oran.

"My cottage was recently bugged," said Agatha. "Do you or your wife know of anyone in the village with the knowledge to do it?"

His eyes were suddenly hard. "Apart from me, d'ye mean?"

"Of course," said James quickly.

"Not a clue," said Oran. "If that's all you came about, you'd better clear off. Roger!"

Roger promptly appeared. "See them out," said Oran. He returned to the lounger and closed his eyes.

"That man's a villain, if ever there was one," said Agatha, after she had shoe-horned herself into James's car.

"I think he's just a rather bluff self-made man," said James.

"No, he's a villain," protested Agatha, "and that Roger is enough to give anyone the creeps."

"Okay," said James, swinging the car out of the drive and onto the Carsely road, "let's say you're right. Can you imagine him consulting Jill?"

"No, but Bunty might," said Agatha. "She's stuck in the country all week. You have to be pretty narcissistic to get all the body work she's had done. Did you notice those breasts?"

"Couldn't take my eyes off them," said James, and Agatha glared at him.

"Silicone if I ever saw it," said Agatha. "And that wind-tunnel face-lift. So she trots along to Jill to talk about herself and maybe talks too much about the shifty side of Oran's business. He gets alarmed and bugs my cottage to find out what we know."

"Agatha, I went to one of their parties and it was full of the great and the good of the Cotswolds."

"And did anyone ask about me?"

"Several people. You are by way of being a village celebrity."

"Did Bunty or Oran ask about me?"

"Not that I can remember. Here we are. I am sure you are sober enough to drive home."

This time, James came round and hauled Agatha out of the passenger seat.

"I may see you tomorrow," he said, "but I've got a lot of writing to do."

Agatha remembered Mark Dretter's invitation to dinner. "Don't force yourself," she said. "I'm going to be too busy."

Instead of going home, Agatha drove to the vicarage, reflecting that living in the country made one lazy. In London, she had walked miles. In the country, she had developed the habit of driving even short distances.

The vicar answered the door and glared at her. He

turned and walked away but he left the door open. Agatha followed him in and heard his voice shouting, "That Raisin woman is here again. Why don't you just invite her to stay?"

Mrs. Bloxby appeared. "Oh, let's go into the garden. The day has turned quite humid and there's not a breath of fresh air. What can I get you?"

"Nothing," said Agatha. "I want to talk."

Agatha sank down into a garden chair and eased her tortured feet out of her sandals. "James and I went to see the Rotherhams. I think he's a thug."

"A very generous thug," said Mrs. Bloxby. "He gave five thousand pounds to the village sports club and two thousand to the church repair fund."

"I didn't even know that house of theirs existed," said Agatha.

"They bought it six months ago," said Mrs. Bloxby. "It was nearly a ruin and they must have spent a fortune repairing it."

"Do they have any servants apart from a thug called Roger?"

"They get the cleaning done by a firm in Evesham and engage a catering company if they are entertaining. He has the most peculiar stage Irish accent."

"I wonder if he ever went to Chicago," said Agatha.

Mrs. Bloxby leaned back in her chair and closed her eyes. She looked tired. Who would be a vicar's wife?

thought Agatha. Dogsbody, nurse, therapist, always kind, always tactful. No pay and very little thanks.

"Isn't it nearly your birthday?" she asked.

Mrs. Bloxby opened her eyes. "It's tomorrow."

"Going out to celebrate?"

"I shouldn't think so. Alf always forgets."

"I've got to go. Remembered something. Don't get up. I can see myself out."

Once back in her cottage, Agatha sat down at her computer and wrote out a flier and printed off a pile of copies. The flier said, "IT IS MRS. BLOXBY'S BIRTHDAY TOMORROW. SEND A CARD TO OUR HARDWORKING VICAR'S WIFE."

Putting on a pair of flat walking shoes, she set out round the village, shoving fliers through letter boxes until she felt too tired to go on.

Returning to her cottage, she remembered she had an unopened bottle of Chanel No. 5 that James had given her for Christmas last year. She found some fancy wrapping paper in a drawer in the kitchen and wrapped it up. Then back to the computer to send an e-mail gift card. She would leave the scent on the doorstep of the vicarage in the morning before she went to work. It was a Sunday and most of the shops now closed. She could only hope that some people in the village could manage to send birthday wishes.

Mrs. Bloxby was preparing her husband's breakfast the following morning when the doorbell rang. Before she could open the door, she had to clear away a great pile of mail. When she did open the door, a florist's van was parked outside. "You've got a lot of bouquets," said the deliveryman. "I'll carry them inside for you. You'd better move all these parcels off the doorstep so I don't trip."

Mrs. Bloxby stood amazed as he carried bouquet after bouquet into the vicarage.

The vicar appeared. "What's going on here?" he demanded.

"It's my birthday," said his wife. "Look at all the flowers! And can you help me get all those parcels that are on the doorstep? I'll take most of the flowers to decorate the church. How lovely. Interflora must have been working overtime."

The vicar stood staring at his wife like a deer caught in the headlamps. Then he said, "Back in a minute."

He rushed to his study. He had recently been at an auction with a friend and on impulse had bid for a pretty gold Edwardian brooch inlaid with moonstones and small chip diamonds. He had planned to give it to his wife on their wedding anniversary in November. It came in a red morocco leather box. He took it out of the locked drawer at the bottom of his desk and hurried back with it. His wife was reading the cards on the flowers. "Here," he said gruffly. "Happy birthday."

"Oh, Alf," said Mrs. Bloxby, opening the box. "It's beautiful. How on earth did everyone know it was my birthday?"

"I think I said something," lied the vicar. He was suddenly sure Agatha Raisin was behind it and he was damned if he was going to let her take the credit. "Let's get all these parcels in."

Because the shops had been closed on Sunday, the presents were things like cakes and homemade jams.

The phone rang. Mrs. Bloxby answered it. It was Agatha to say happy birthday.

"The vicarage is full of flowers," said Mrs. Bloxby. "I feel like a film star."

Agatha's voice was suddenly sharp with concern. "Make sure all the bouquets are from the florist and no one has sneaked a homemade one in. Don't want you dying of wolfsbane."

When she rang off, Mrs. Bloxby told her husband what Agatha had said. They searched the bouquets, reading the cards, but all had come from the florist. "What a lot of thank you letters I am going to have to write," said Mrs. Bloxby.

The vicar realised for the first time that, even though it was morning, his wife looked tired.

"Look, someone's even sent a bottle of champagne. I'll open it now and then I'll help you open the presents. And I am taking you out for dinner tonight."

Mrs. Bloxby's eyes filled with tears. "You are so good to me, Alf. Isn't it too early for champagne?"

"Not on your birthday. I'll get the glasses."

In her office that morning, Agatha allocated jobs for the day. "You haven't got one for yourself," said Toni.

"I would like a quiet day so that I can go over my notes," said Agatha. The real truth was she wanted to be beside the phone in case Mark called. Of course, he could call her on her mobile number but Agatha was already fantasising about marrying him. Also, her secretary, Mrs. Freedman, had taken the day off to visit her niece.

When her detectives had left, Agatha discovered that Mrs. Freedman received quite a lot of phone calls. She longed to shout at callers to get off the line, but business was business, and so she settled down to take notes about missing pets, adulterous husbands and all the other bread and butter cases the agency dealt with. By three in the afternoon, she felt cross and hungry. She ordered a pizza to be delivered while she made herself yet another cup of black coffee.

Agatha had her mouth full of pizza when the phone rang. She picked it up. "Yes, may I help you?" she said, although because her mouth was full of pizza, it sounded more like, "Is, may elp yi."

"I would like to speak to Agatha Raisin." It was Mark. Agatha spat out her mouthful of pizza on the office floor.

"Mark!" she cooed. "It is Mark, isn't it?"

"Yes, Agatha. I wondered whether you would like to join me for dinner tonight?"

"That would be lovely," said Agatha. "What time and where?"

"The George. At eight o'clock?"

"Lovely. I'll see you there."

She had just replaced the receiver when Charles strode into the office.

"What are you doing here?" snapped Agatha.

"Why so hostile? Had a boring lunch with a cousin and thought I'd drop in on you."

"Well, I'm busy, so drop out."

Charles stared at the floor beside Agatha's desk. "Have you been sick?"

"No, it was too hot. I'll clean it up. I'm sorry, Charles, but I really am too busy."

"Who is he?" asked Charles.

"Who what?"

"You've got that travel bag of yours beside the desk, which usually means you plan to change into something slinky for a date. Good thing you didn't vomit pizza on it."

"You're talking rubbish. Oh, clear off. You make my head ache."

"Well, don't come crying to me if he turns out to be a rat."

Charles strolled off. Agatha cleaned the mess off the floor. The afternoon dragged on. Then one by one her detectives returned with their reports.

"I don't think any of this stuff warrants overtime," said Agatha. "So you can all go home."

"She's got a date," said Toni as she walked down the stairs from the office with Simon. "Any idea who it might be?"

"Not a clue. Anyway, whoever it is ought to be warned that our murderer might bump him off. Sometimes I think this murderer is out there, watching Agatha, and enjoying the fact that she hasn't got any idea who he is."

"I wonder if we should follow her, just to make sure she is safe," said Toni.

Simon laughed. "You would think we were talking about a wayward adolescent. She wouldn't thank us for interfering."

Agatha was ten minutes late arriving at the George. She had put on heavy make-up, wiped it off, tried again, decided that it was too little, and just as she decided she was happy with the result, a blob of mascara fell on her cheek and she had to start all over again.

She was wearing a scarlet chiffon jersey dress with a low neckline and scarlet red high-heeled shoes. A diamond pendant and little diamond earrings completed the ensemble.

Mark Dretter rose to meet her and Agatha suddenly felt very overdressed. The long French windows at the end of the restaurant were wide open because the evening was warm and humid. Mark was wearing a blue-and-white-checked shirt open at the neck. But he said, "You look magnificent."

"I had to deal with a very posh client before I came here," lied Agatha.

"Let's choose something to eat," said Mark, "and then you can tell me how you are getting on."

Agatha's bearlike eyes suddenly bored into him. "So that you can report to Gwen?"

He looked hurt. "Do you credit any man who invites you out for dinner as having an ulterior motive?"

"In my line of work, I'm suspicious of everyone," said Agatha. "Sorry."

"Never mind. What are you going to have to eat?"

Agatha had a healthy appetite but sadly knew that anything fattening seemed to go straight to her waistline. On the other hand, she told herself, she could start dieting the next day.

She ordered avocado stuffed with shrimp as a starter to be followed by steak and a baked potato. Mark said he would have the same and ordered a bottle of Macon to go with the meal.

"I can't help remembering having a meal here with David Herythe," said Agatha, "and then he ended up murdered. I hope I am not putting you in danger."

He laughed. "My sister is a security freak. My cottage has steel shutters on the downstairs windows, a CCTV camera over the door and burglar alarms back and front. Still, when you think about it, the murderer must have been following you. Just think. Might even be in this restaurant."

Agatha looked around the dining room. "They all look ordinary," she said. "Mind you, it's only after a murderer is caught that people say, look at those evil, staring eyes, or something like that, when in fact the murderer could be someone you would pass in the street without a second glance."

"Perhaps this murderer has given up," said Mark. "Have you got over that attempt on your life?"

"Of course," said Agatha, clasping her hands, which had begun to tremble, on her lap.

She privately thought that she would never forget Justin's attack. Her life had been threatened before and she had got over it quickly. Maybe she was suffering from an accumulation of attacks. Maybe she should get married and forget about being a detective. Maybe Dubai would be fun. She could play the hostess with the mostest at embassy parties. Would she have to wear a print dress and a large hat?

"Hullo!" said Mark. "I think you forgot I was here."

Agatha threw him a flirtatious look. "Now how could I forget such a handsome man?"

He smiled. "Easily, I should think. Why do you suspect Gwen?"

"Because her son, the baker, was serving up people in meat pies. There were the two of them living in that bakery. Don't tell me she didn't know what was going on."

"Mother love can be blind. Also, she wouldn't have

the strength. For example, you said that Tremund had been knocked on the head and pushed in the canal."

"I think it would be easy for such as Gwen Simple to enchant some man so that he would murder for her."

"But you told me the police had bugged her phone. She hasn't let anything slip. In fact, she leads a blameless life. Do eat your food. We've plenty of time to talk."

When she had finished her first course, Agatha said, "But you did think it might be a village murder and that the police are wasting their time looking at the Chicago end of the business."

"Just a feeling. Murder on such a scale would make anyone think it should be someplace like Birmingham rather than an English village. Anyway, what do you really know of that cleaner of yours?"

"Doris? Honest as the day is long."

"And Mrs. Tweedy?"

"She may be a bitch but she's pretty old."

"I bet there's someone in Carsely you haven't even thought of."

"I can't believe that," said Agatha. "Jill had consulting rooms in Mircester before she moved to the village. I wonder why she moved. More suckers to be found in a large town."

"Maybe one of her Mircester clients threatened her," said Mark. "Maybe that's why she moved. Oh, here's the steak."

Agatha was a fast eater. Mark, on the other hand, carefully cut off small pieces of steak one at a time and chewed them thoroughly before dissecting another bit.

"I'm tired of talking about murder," said Agatha. "Tell me about yourself."

"Not much to tell," he said, lifting a tiny piece of baked potato to his mouth. "Boring clerical work mostly. I might retire. There's a neighbour of yours called James Lacey. Writes books, doesn't he?"

"Yes, he's my ex."

"Didn't work out?"

"Obviously," said Agatha curtly.

"Well, I could do that. Write books, I mean."

"You'd need a private income."

"I have that."

Agatha's dream of Dubai faded. It wouldn't be the same, love in a cottage. She'd tried that with James.

"Could you possibly introduce me to James Lacey?"

"Yes, I can do that." Agatha was suddenly tired of his company. "Look, if we skip dessert and coffee, we can go now and catch him before he goes to bed."

As Mark talked enthusiastically to James about his ambition to write a book, Agatha gathered that Mark wanted to write any sort of book without knowing whether it was to be fiction or nonfiction. James found out that Mark's favourite reading was spy stories and suggested he could write one based on his experiences in Dubai. Agatha began to think there was something almost schoolboyish about Mark.

At last she yawned and said she had to go to bed. Mark reluctantly left with her and walked her to her cottage next door. To her irritation, Agatha recognised Charles's car.

"Are you going to invite me in?" asked Mark.

"Not tonight. I'm tired."

"We must do this again. I'll phone you." He kissed her warmly on both cheeks.

Agatha let herself into her cottage. Charles was asleep on the sofa with the cats on his lap. She glared at him and then went up to bed.

Would she really need to be in love with a man to get married to him? Mark was easy company. She paused. Where was the murderer now? Was she putting Mark in danger? And what about Charles and James? What about herself?

She opened her bedroom window and leaned out. A squat dark figure was just hurrying out of the lane. Agatha felt a spasm of pure dread. Whoever it was hadn't been walking a dog. There were only two cottages in Lilac Lane, her own and James's, and the lane ended at a field.

She rushed downstairs and shook Charles awake. "There was someone out in the lane," she said.

Charles straightened up, spilling cats onto the floor. "So what?"

"So what reason does anyone have for coming along here?"

He got to his feet. "I'll go and have a look."

"No!" screamed Agatha, hanging on to him. "I don't want to lose you."

He grinned. "This is so sudden." He planted a kiss on her nose. "I'll be careful."

Charles slipped on his shoes and went out into the lane. The air was damp and close and there was no moon. He ran lightly to the end of the lane. There was a streetlight at the corner. But it appeared the whole of Carsely had gone to sleep. Charles returned slowly to Agatha's cottage. He was worried about her. He had known Agatha to cope with murder and mayhem before and she always came bouncing back from every fright as good as new. But these murders were getting to her. She should get away on holiday and forget about the whole thing.

A pattering in the leaves of the lilac tree at the gate made him look up. Rain was beginning to fall.

"Anything?" demanded Agatha as he walked in.

"Nothing. Go to bed. You should go away somewhere, Aggie, and forget about the whole business. You're becoming a nervous wreck."

"I'm not going anywhere until I nail this bastard," said Agatha.

"Well, go to bed and we'll talk about it in the morning."

The grey, drizzly morning had a calming effect on Agatha. Horrors somehow seemed worse in bright sunlight. Charles was already up and on his way out. "Maybe see you later," he said.

Agatha had sometimes thought she might tell him she was turning the spare room into an office because she did not like the cavalier way he came and went in her life, but, she reminded herself, he had saved her life.

She decided to forget about the murders for the time being and concentrate on the work in hand. It was a busy week and the staff all worked hard. Agatha real- ised with delight that she would finally be able to give everyone a bonus and that news, delivered to her staff on Friday evening, was greeted with a great cheer. Agatha often worked on Saturdays with one other member of her staff, but decided that this time, as part of the celebration, they should all have the week-end off.

Agatha was sure Charles would have disappeared

again. She did not want to be alone and planned to leave her cottage and walk up to the pub. But as she arrived, she saw Roy Silver's car parked outside her door. She often viewed her former employee as an irritation. He was asleep at the wheel. She rapped on the window and he came awake with a start.

When he got out of the car, Agatha noticed that, for Roy, he was more soberly dressed than usual, wearing a business suit, but with a white shirt open at the neck, revealing enough gold chains to make an Indian woman's dowry.

"You've got to help me," he said as soon as he was out of the car.

"Come inside and tell me all about it," said Agatha. She wondered for a moment if Mark would phone and reminded herself she was not really interested in him.

The rain had stopped but the garden was still soaked. They sat in the living room. Roy asked for a vodka and tonic and Agatha helped herself to a gin and tonic.

"Now," she said. "What's up?"

"I was to handle the Leman account, you know, the Paris perfume people. Big promotion for their new perfume, Passion. Pedman gave it to that conniving bitch Maisie Byles." Pedman was Roy's boss.

"The wonderful world of public relations," said Agatha. "I'm glad to be out of it. Who the hell is Maisie Byles?"

"She only joined a month ago. Came from our rivals, JIG Publicity. Smarmed all over Mr. Pedman from day one."

"What does she look like?"

"Rabbity. Protruding eyes and big teeth."

"So how has she managed to charm Pedman?"

She found out the date of his little son's birthday and brought in a present. She offered to babysit when his babysitter let him down."

"JIG Publicity is a big powerful firm," said Agatha. "Why did she leave?"

"Don't know. She sneers at me."

"I've got a contact at JIG," said Agatha. "I'll see if I've got his home number."

She went to her desk, pulled out a drawer and lifted out a bulging address book.

"You must be the only person to still use an address book," commented Roy.

"Old numbers," said Agatha curtly. "Now what was his name? Maybe it's under JIG. Ah, here we are. Duncan Macgregor. Scottish as malt whisky. I'll phone him."

She rang a number and waited. Then she said, "No reply. I'll try his mobile."

This time Duncan answered. After the preliminary pleasantries, Agatha said, "What can you tell me about Maisie Byles?"

Roy waited impatiently, wishing he could hear what Duncan was saying.

At last, he heard Agatha say, "That's interesting. I'll bet Pedman didn't know anything about that."

She began to talk about her detective work, obviously in answer to Duncan's questions. Finally she rang off.

Agatha sat down and took a gulp of her drink and then said, "Maisie Byles left before she was pushed. She was handling Happytot baby formula. The silly cow went on her Facebook page and said that all mothers should be forced to breast-feed. Furious people at Happytot. JIG lost the account. Going to sack her but she cried and cried and said she had an invalid mother to support so instead they suggested she find other employment."

"Oh, dear," said Roy. "Do you think she has an invalid mother?"

"Not for a moment," said Agatha.

"So what do we do?" asked Roy.

"I'll send Pedman an e-mail and tell him all about it. If I do, are you sure you'll get the account?"

"Yes, it was initially offered to me but Maisie piped up and said surely it would be better if the account were handled by a woman."

"Okay, help yourself to another drink while I send this e-mail."

Agatha typed out an e-mail and sent it off.

"He always checks his e-mails, even at week-ends," said Roy. "Maybe he'll contact me."

"Let's hope so," said Agatha.

"So what's been happening in Murderville?" asked Roy.

"Quiet at the moment. I'm still sure Gwen Simple is behind it. Maybe she confessed to Jill Davent that she had helped her son with those murders."

"Oh, the Sweeney Todd case?"

"That's the one. Finish your drink and let's walk up to the pub and get something to eat. I don't feel like cooking."

"When did you ever cook, Agatha? You nuke everything in the microwave."

"Don't be rude. Let's go."

The pub was full inside but the tables and chairs outside had been wiped dry so they sat there and studied the menus, both finally settling for "sea fresh cod in golden crispy batter with hand-cut chips, mange tout and rocket from our own garden."

"They don't have a garden," said Agatha. "I hate rocket. Nasty, spidery vegetable."

Agatha lit a cigarette and blew smoke up towards the grey sky.

"Still smoking," said Roy. "It's so old-fashioned, Agatha."

"I suppose Maisie will now get the sack," said Agatha. "I must admit, that's a bit on my conscience."

"Don't worry. The cunning bitch insisted on a year's contract so Pedman is stuck with her. What if he's so enamoured of her that he does nothing?"

"He'll listen to me," said Agatha. "He'll be furious. He'll think the whole PR world is laughing at him. You know how hypersensitive he is." In the past, after she had sold her agency, Agatha had done PR work on a freelance basis for Pedman.

When their food arrived, Agatha noticed that the chips were the usual frozen ones. Between bites of food, she began to fret about the murders.

Said Roy, "Doris Simpson was one of her clients. Maybe she noticed another client, someone not on your list."

"I think she would have told me," said Agatha.

"Let's go and see her after we eat," urged Roy. "It'll take my mind off Pedman."

Doris welcomed them in. But when Agatha asked her if she had seen any other clients while she was there, Doris shook her head. "I did hear, however," said Doris, "that John Fletcher's missus had been to see her. You know, Rose Fletcher."

"And we've just come from the pub. Thanks, Doris. It's someone new."

"Won't she be working?" asked Roy as they made their way back to the pub.

"She works in the kitchen," said Agatha. "They don't serve meals after ten o'clock and it's now ten past. We should be able to have a word with her."

They went round to the kitchen door at the back of the pub. The door was standing open so they just walked in. Kitchen staff were clearing up, washing dishes and wiping down surfaces. Rose Fletcher was sitting at a table with a glass of beer in front of her.

"I want to ask you about Jill Davent," Agatha shouted above the kitchen noise.

"Outside with you," ordered Rose. "I'll talk to you outside."

Chapter Ten

Rose was a buxom woman with strong arms. She had dark brown curly hair and large brown eyes. "So?" she demanded.

"You were a client of Jill Davent, weren't you?" said Agatha.

"Yes."

"Is there anything you can tell me?" asked Agatha.

"Like what?"

"Did she try to blackmail you?"

"No," said Rose, "but she threatened to take me to court. I wouldn't pay her. I had a frozen shoulder. John told her about it. The next thing is she's round at the kitchen door saying she can cure it. So I made an appointment and went along. She fiddled about with a sort of massage. It took about five minutes or so. Then she demanded sixty pounds. My shoulder was as bad as ever so I told her to get lost.

"She said, 'I'll see you in the Small Claims Court.'

"I said, 'Why don't you do that? All your qualifications will be gone into.' She started screaming that it was dangerous to cross her. I walked away. I found an acupuncturist in Shipston-on-Stour and he was brilliant. I told everyone who would listen that she was a phony."

"When did this happen?" asked Agatha.

"The night before she was murdered."

"Did you see anyone else around?"

"Victoria Bannister. I bumped into her as I left. She was standing by the garden gate. I didn't think anything of it because Victoria was always spying on people."

"Did she say anything?" asked Agatha.

"No, she scurried off. Poor Victoria. Who would want to kill her?"

"She must have known something, or the murderer might have thought she knew something," said Agatha. "If you hear anything, Rose, let me know."

As they walked back to Agatha's cottage, Roy's mobile rang. He answered it and listened carefully. Agatha heard him say, "Yes, I'll be there tomorrow."

When he rang off, Roy did a little dance. "I've got it! I'm to be in Paris tomorrow."

"Good for you," said Agatha, but feeling suddenly low. Another week-end on her own. At her cottage, Roy said happily, "Good thing I left my travel bag in the car. Airport, here I come."

And not one word of thanks, thought Agatha as he sped off.

As she let herself into her cottage, the phone was ringing. She snatched it up. "Hi, Agatha," said Mark. "I might have found out something. All right if I call round?"

"Of course," said Agatha and ran up the stairs to her bathroom to remove the old make-up and put on a fresh layer.

Welcome to the maintenance years, thought Agatha, remembering the days of her youth when her legs felt like steel and her bras were usually limp disgraceful things because her breasts didn't need any support. Now it was all pelvic floor exercises, nonsurgical face-lifts, excruciating visits to the dentist to get the roots of her teeth cleaned, massage at Richard Rasdall's in Stow and all the other bits of hard work to keep age at bay.

She suddenly wondered why she was going to all this

trouble for a man she was not interested in, and changed into flat sandals and a blue cotton shift dress.

The bell rang as she was descending the stairs. When she opened the door, she was startled to realise she had forgotten that Mark was handsome.

Agatha led the way into the kitchen. "Take a seat," she said, "and tell me your news."

"I've been talking to Gwen," he said. "She and Jill were friends."

"That doesn't surprise me," said Agatha. "Criminals always feel comfortable in each other's company."

"Agatha! Gwen is a sweet woman and wouldn't harm a fly."

"Okay. Go on. What's the news?"

"Gwen says that Jill told her that someone had threatened to kill her."

"Yes, but who?"

"She couldn't find out."

Agatha sighed. "That doesn't get me any further."

"But don't you see? It must have been one of her clients in the village."

"Not necessarily," said Agatha. "It could have been her ex-husband. I can't believe that anyone in this village has the know-how to bug my cottage."

"But there are incomers to these Cotswold villages the whole time."

"I'll check it out with Mrs. Bloxby. But I feel sure

she would have told me if there was anyone new to the village that might fill the bill."

"I've got to dash," he said. "Maybe see you tomorrow?"

"Phone me," said Agatha.

He gave her a warm hug.

Well, well, well, thought Agatha, after he had left. It could work out. I could be Mrs. Dretter. I wish I could be married in white. I've always wanted a proper wedding. She glanced at the clock and judged it too late to call on Mrs. Bloxby and decided to see her after the church service.

Agatha really meant to go to the service but she slept late and only arrived at the church just as the service was finishing. Quite a large number of people began to stream out. Agatha waited patiently while Mrs. Bloxby talked to various villagers. At last she approached Agatha.

"Your husband's sermons seem to have become popular," commented Agatha.

"It's because he used the King James Bible and the old *Book of Common Prayer*," said Mrs. Bloxby. "People come from villages all around. The old language is so comforting in a world full of uncertainties. Would you like to come to the vicarage for coffee or something?"

"Yes," said Agatha. "I do need your advice."

"The signs are up for the Moreton Agricultural Show," said the vicar's wife. "Quite sad because it means that summer is over. I hope they get good weather for it. Some years, the field has been a sea of mud."

Agatha waited until they were both seated in the vicarage with glasses of sherry and said, "Mark Dretter called on me last night."

"The man from Dubai?"

"Yes, him. He keeps suggesting the murderer might be someone from the village. I said I didn't think there was anyone in Carsely with the expertise to bug my cottage and he said what about incomers. Know of anyone?"

"Only one fairly recent arrival, a Mr. Bob Dell."

"What does he do?"

"He is retired. I believe he was a banker. He wears frocks."

"He what?"

"He likes to dress as a woman."

"Why didn't I hear about this?" demanded Agatha. "A transvestite. It's a wonder he hasn't been driven away."

"As a matter of fact, he is popular. Even Alf has warmed to him because he brought armfuls of flowers to decorate the church. He contributes to all sorts of charities."

"Where does he live?"

"Badgers Loan. That Victorian villa, on Glebe Street at the back of the village store. It was owned by old Mrs. Dell, who died last year. She was ninety-four, very agile for her years. But her brain had begun to wander and she drove her motorised wheelchair right into the pond. She died of shock, they think. I'm surprised you didn't hear about it."

"I must have been away," said Agatha. "I think I'll call on this Bob Dell."

"You won't make remarks about his dress," cautioned Mrs. Bloxby.

"I," said Agatha Raisin, "am the soul of tact."

Bob Dell answered the door to her. He was a tall man in his sixties with a large nose and small mouth. He was wearing a blond wig and make-up and his thin body was draped in a long flower-patterned dress. Agatha introduced herself and he invited her in.

He led the way into a sitting room. The room was dominated by a grand piano covered with a fringed shawl. There were many photographs in silver frames on side tables and the floor was covered in a Persian rug. A stuffed owl in a glass case was placed in the middle of the room. One wall was lined with bookshelves. The three-piece suite was covered in bright chintz. Agatha sat down on the sofa and he lowered himself into an armchair facing her. He had forgotten to smooth the skirt of his dress under him and so he exposed a pair of long hairy legs in tights ending in white court shoes like sauce boats.

"Are you new to cross-dressing?" asked that soul of tact, Agatha Raisin.

"I only started last year," he said. "Why do you ask?"

"You haven't shaved your legs."

"I hate doing it. That's why I wear long dresses. Are you usually so rude?"

"Sorry. Just curious. You've heard about all those murders?"

"Yes, indeed."

"Know anything about electronics?"

"Can barely use the computer. I hate machines."

What you see is what you get, thought Agatha. This man is a gentle soul. But he needs help.

"Never economise on a wig," said Agatha. "That blond bird's nest you've got on your head screams fake. Phone up a firm called Banbury Postiche and get their catalogue. Aren't you getting a course of female hormones?"

"No, I'm new to all this. Are you usually so blunt?"

"Just trying to help. Where did you get that dress?"

"It was one of my mother's. She was very tall."

"Won't do. Wait a moment." Agatha took her iPad

out of her capacious handbag. "I'm just going to search for something. Ah, here we are. In Lower Oxford Street there's a shop called Trannies Delight. All sorts of clothes and things for people like you. I'll write it down."

"You are very kind. I'll go up to town tomorrow."

Agatha stood up. Having decided Bob could not possibly be the murderer, she was suddenly anxious to leave.

But she turned in the doorway and said, "Why a village like this? Wouldn't you be better off in London, where there must be lots of people like you?"

He smiled and said, "Oh, it would surprise you what you find in Cotswold villages. I am not alone."

Agatha walked away, feeling a cold breeze starting up. Soon it would be autumn. As she was turning the corner of Glebe Street, she suddenly froze. She sensed evil. She looked wildly around. Then she shrugged and walked on. Her near escape from death had left her nervous.

As she walked past the general store now closed for the Sunday afternoon, she had a sudden memory of visiting the Cotswolds as a child while her drunken parents in the grotty caravan they had borrowed from a friend bitched about how boring it all was. The child, Agatha, had found it enchanting. That was the start of her lifelong dream of living in the Cotswolds. But now there was a serpent in this Garden of Eden.

A brisk wind had sprung up, chasing the grey clouds above away to the east. In her cottage, she petted her cats and let them out into the garden and then checked her phone for messages. There was only one and it was from Mrs. Bloxby. "I forgot to remind you about the baking competition next Saturday," the vicar's wife said. "I know you will be too busy to contribute anything but there is a Sale of Work stall and I cannot get anyone to run it. Can you help?"

Agatha phoned her and said she would do it provided nothing came up to stop her attending. She was just wondering how to pass the rest of the day. She was sick and tired of studying all her notes on the murder cases.

There was a ring at the door. Agatha carefully looked through the spy hole first and saw Toni standing outside. She opened the door. "Come in. What brings you?" asked Agatha.

"Just a social call," said Toni. "I'm tired of going out on dates just to go out on dates, if you know what I mean. I hear you've got a new man in your life. Had dinner at the George."

"Oh, Mark Dretter. He's very handsome and I can't understand why I don't find him attractive. Want coffee?"

"Yes, please."

The doorbell rang again. "Help yourself," said Agatha, "while I see who's at the door."

It was Bill Wong. "What's happened?" demanded Agatha.

"Nothing," said Bill. "It's my day off and I thought I would look you up."

"Come into the kitchen. Toni's just arrived."

There was another ring at the doorbell. "If that's Simon, don't answer it," said Toni sharply. "He's started following me around again."

"Your car's outside and mine," said Agatha. "If it is him, I'll need to let him in."

But it was Phil Marshall. "I thought I'd see how you were bearing up," he said.

"Come in. Bill and Toni are in the kitchen."

Agatha reflected that nothing ever seemed to ruffle Phil. His gentle face and silver hair worked wonders at interviews. People always felt safe with him.

Toni made him a mug of coffee. "No breakthrough on the murders yet?" Phil asked Bill.

"Not a thing. What about you, Agatha?"

"Nothing."

"Wilkes had a mad hope we could pin all the murders on Justin and get the press off our backs, but at the time of Tremund's murder, for example, Justin was up in London working for a large company."

"What about Gwen Simple?" asked Agatha.

"Sorry. Nothing there. We're not even checking her phone calls now. Besides, she's alibied up to the hilt."

"I never thought she would murder people herself, but get someone to do it for her," said Agatha.

"Like her latest beau?"

"Who's that?" asked Agatha.

"A chap called Mark Dretter. Squeaky clean. On leave from the embassy in Dubai."

"He's not her beau," said Agatha. "He's been trying to help me with some detective work."

"Could've fooled me," said Bill. "They go everywhere together."

Agatha's face darkened. Had Mark only befriended her so that he could report to Gwen how she was getting on with trying to solve the murders?

"Anyway," she said huffily, "he's got some mad idea it might be someone in this village."

"Are there any weirdos in this village, Agatha?" asked Bill.

"Not that I know of. One cross-dresser but that's nothing these days."

"Oh, Bob Dell," said Phil. "It's odd. He wanted me to enlarge a photo of his niece. I often do some photo work for people in the village. I phoned him and said I was coming with it. I knocked and knocked but there was no reply."

"Did you see anyone around?" asked Agatha.

"Just some big old chap on a bike."

"I'm worried," said Agatha. "I'm going up there. He

didn't strike me as the sort of man to ask you to bring the photo and then not answer the door."

"I'll go," said Bill.

"I'll come with you," insisted Agatha. "The rest of you stay here."

"I'm sure we must be worrying about nothing," said Bill as he and Agatha hurried in the direction of Bob's home.

"All I would do is worry for the rest of the day," said Agatha stubbornly.

Glebe Street looked innocent and quiet. Agatha rang the bell beside the door of Bob's villa. There was no reply. "Phil said something about knocking," said Bill. "Maybe the bell doesn't work."

He hammered on the door.

A little breeze rustled through a clematis beside the door and then died away.

"See if you can open the door," urged Agatha.

Bill tried the doorknob. "Locked," he said.

"Break in!" said Agatha.

"I can't. I haven't a warrant. Let's try round the back. He may be in the garden."

They walked along a path at the left side of the villa. The garden was a profusion of flowers. On the patio was a garden table with a half-finished glass of wine and a book, its pages fluttering in the breeze. Draped over a chair by the table was a paisley shawl.

Agatha cupped her hands and peered in the French windows. It was the room she had sat in with Bob.

"Can you see anyone?" asked Bill.

"No one."

"We'll try later," said Bill. "I'm sure you're worried about nothing."

Agatha would not give up. Her breath had steamed up the glass. She wiped it with a handkerchief and peered in again. Then she tried the handle on the window.

"It's open," she said, and before Bill could stop her, she went into the room, calling, "Bob! Are you there?"

There was a faint sound from behind the sofa. Agatha peered over and then shrieked, "Bill!"

Bob Dell lay on the floor. His face was a mass of blood.

Bill hurried in and knelt beside him. "His pulse is faint." He phoned for an ambulance and then called police headquarters.

Toni and Phil had heard the sirens and hurried up to Glebe Street to find Bob Dell being loaded into an ambulance. Toni was worried about Agatha because Agatha's face was chalk white.

"I think you should go to the hospital as well, Agatha," said Toni. "You've had a bad shock."

"I'll be all right," said Agatha. "I feel it's got something to do with my visit to him."

Wilkes came up to Agatha. "You may go home, Mrs. Raisin, and we'll be with you shortly to take a statement."

"Look at them!" said Agatha, pointing to the forensic team, who were about to enter the villa. "Masks, heads covered, suited up, little booties. If they were on television they would have shoulder-length hair and stilettos on."

"Come along," urged Toni, putting an arm around Agatha's waist.

Back in Agatha's cottage, Toni tried to persuade her to drink hot sweet tea but Agatha stubbornly demanded gin and tonic. "You don't have any ice," said Toni.

"Snakes and bastards! Who cares?" yelled Agatha.

Toni reluctantly fixed a gin and tonic. Agatha gulped it down and demanded another. "Don't you think you ought to wait until after you've made your statement?" said Toni.

"No, I do not!"

To Toni's relief, Agatha was still relatively sober when Wilkes and a detective Agatha did not recognise came to take her statement. Then Phil was questioned and explained that he had seen a heavyset man leaving Glebe Street on a bike. "I didn't get a good look at him," said Phil apologetically. "He had a baseball cap pulled down over his face. He was wearing grey trainers and a grey zip-up jacket. He had gloves on his hands."

"We can only hope Mr. Dell survives the attack and can tell us who did this to him," said Wilkes.

"Make sure there's a police guard outside his hospital room," said Agatha.

"Don't tell me how to do my job," snapped Wilkes. "You're like the bloody angel of death, you are. Report to headquarters in the morning and we'll have your statement printed out and ready for you to sign. The same goes for you, Mr. Marshall."

After they had left, Toni said to Phil, "Would you wait with Agatha? I'll go home and pack a bag. I think I should stay with her this evening."

"I'll be all right," said Agatha.

"You'll do as you're told for once in your bossy life," said Toni.

"Then get me another G and T before you go."

"Off you go, Toni," said Phil. "I'll get it."

When Phil returned to the kitchen with Agatha's drink, she was hugging herself and shivering. "It's so cold," she moaned.

"You're in shock. Upstairs to bed with you."

Agatha drained the gin and tonic in one gulp and then allowed Phil to lead her upstairs. She sat groggily on the edge of the bed while Phil removed her shoes. Then he managed to get her under the duvet and switched on the electric blanket.

When he finally went downstairs again, he reflected that he had never seen Agatha in such a state of shock before. There was something about these murders that had got to her. Phil felt he owed a great debt to Agatha. Who else would have recognised his talent as a photographer and employed a man like himself in his late seventies?

He decided to phone Charles. Agatha had a list of numbers pinned up next to the phone. There were two numbers for Charles: his home phone and his mobile. Beside the mobile number, Agatha had scribbled, *Never answers*.

He phoned the home number. Charles's gentleman's gentleman, Gustav, answered the phone. He asked who Phil was and what was his business.

Phil said he was phoning because Agatha Raisin was in dire need of help. "I am afraid," said Gustav, "that Sir Charles is unavailable," and rang off.

Gustav jumped nervously when Charles came up behind him and asked, "Who was on the phone?"

"Someone selling double glazing," said Gustav. He detested Agatha and often feared that his boss might marry her.

Charles was aware that Gustav's eyes had a way of rolling up to the ceiling when he was lying. "So what does Agatha want?" he demanded. "Tell the truth or you can kiss your bonus goodbye."

"She's always bothering you," protested Gustav. "It was some man called Marshall said she was in need of help."

Phil was relieved when Toni and Charles arrived at the same time. Charles was told everything that had been happening and how they were frightened that Agatha was cracking up under the strain.

Now that Agatha was being monitored, Phil decided to go to his home in the village. Charles watched Toni fidgeting around and then asked, "What's up?"

"I had a date for tonight but I cancelled it."

"Not one of your old men?" asked Charles, knowing Toni's penchant for dating older men.

"No, he's a medical student. Only a few years older than me. He's nice."

"Phone him up and uncancel," said Charles. "It doesn't take two of us to baby-sit."

Agatha awoke an hour later. Her head ached and her mouth felt dry. Poor Bob Dell, she thought. Then she suddenly sat up in bed. What was it that Bob had said as she had left? *I am not alone.*

Did that mean someone else in this village was masquerading as a woman?

She slowly got up, her mind racing. Charles heard her moving about and came upstairs. "You look a wreck," he said heartlessly.

She clutched his shoulders. "Have you heard what happened to Bob Dell?"

"Yes. Bill Wong called when you were asleep. Poor Bob died in hospital an hour ago."

"Oh, how awful. But there's something else. He was a cross-dresser. When I wondered why he didn't choose to live in a town where he might meet more of his own kind, he said, 'I am not alone.'"

"So?"

"So maybe there's someone in this village that everyone thinks is a woman."

"You smell of old gin, sweetie. Have a shower and come downstairs and eat something."

When Agatha finally appeared, washed and wearing a change of clothes, she looked like her old self.

"I'm making you tea and toast," said Charles. "No more booze for you."

"I'd like a large glass of mineral water," said Agatha. "I've got a mouth like a gorilla's armpit."

"You do have a way with words. All right. One glass coming up. But eat some toast."

"Who could it be?" fretted Agatha. "I must look at my notes."

"Toast and tea first. Notes afterwards."

Agatha dutifully ate two slices of buttered toast washed down with tea. "Rats! It can't be Gwen Simple."

"No," agreed Charles. "Much as you'd like to think so. Who else is there?"

"Let's go and ask Mrs. Bloxby."

"It's getting late, Agatha."

"It's only ten o'clock."

"Still, leave the woman alone until tomorrow. And I gather from Phil that you've got to go to headquarters in the morning to sign a statement. The best thing," said Charles, "is that you put the whole thing out of your head and we'll watch something stupid and easy on television. Give your mind a rest."

They watched *NCIS* although Agatha complained that the scriptwriters obviously had a father complex as it was yet another story with one of the characters having trouble with his father. Then they watched an old

Jackie Chan movie until Charles fell asleep and Agatha took herself off to bed.

She set the alarm. She was sure she would not sleep and was surprised to be awakened in the morning by the alarm.

When she went downstairs, she found Charles awake, dressed and waiting for her. "I'll drive you in to headquarters," he said. "You're liable to think of someone, shout 'Eureka!' and drive into a lamppost."

At police headquarters, Charles waited while Agatha was led away to sign her statement for Bill Wong.

"That'll be all," said Bill. "You should take the day off, Agatha. Why are you staring at me like that?"

"You checked out the backgrounds of all the people who you knew were Jill's clients?"

"Of course."

"What about Mrs. Tweedy?"

A gatha, you need a rest," said Bill. "You surely don't suspect that old woman?"

"Listen to me. Bob Dell was a cross-dresser. When I wondered why he had chosen to live in a village instead of a town where there would be more of his own kind, he said, 'I am not alone.'"

Bill laughed. "And so you immediately leap to the conclusion that Mrs. Tweedy is a murderous transvestite?"

"Humour me, Bill. What's her story?"

"She's from a village in Oxfordshire called Offley

Crucis. She moved to Oxford and then Carsely a year ago after a tragedy."

"What tragedy?"

"Her twin brother was killed in a fire."

"How did the fire start?"

"Faulty electrics. Really, Agatha, we've gone into everyone's background thoroughly."

"What happened to Mr. Tweedy?"

"There isn't one. She said she just called herself Mrs because she didn't want to be damned as the village spinster."

"No one talks about spinsters anymore," said Agatha. "She may be old but she looks powerful and she's got strong hands."

"You've been working too hard, Agatha. Let it go."

"Agatha," protested Charles, "we can't go calling on Mrs. Tweedy and accuse her of being a man."

"I want to go to Offley Crucis where she lived, and find out about this twin brother. What if she wanted to inherit the lot and to take his identity as well?"

Charles sighed. "Can we eat first?"

"The nearest greasy spoon on the road will do."

———

Agatha phoned her office and said she was taking the day off. Then she and Charles set out, stopping at a roadside restaurant for a full English breakfast and several cups of coffee.

Offley Crucis turned out to be a very small village at the end of a one-track road. The weather had turned fine again. There were a few redbrick houses clustered around a pond. There was a small church and a general store. Apart from a few ducks bobbing about the pond, nothing moved.

"Pity there isn't a pub," said Charles. "I hate the idea of knocking on doors."

"I hope there are some people at home," said Agatha. "It's quite near Oxford and could be one of those sort of dormitory villages. Oh, look! That woman's just come out into her front garden. I'll try her."

"I'll leave you to it," said Charles lazily.

He sat on a bench by the pond and watched as Agatha entered into animated conversation with the woman. She came back and said, "That's a bit of luck. She's new to the village but she says if we go to the pub at the next village, Sipper Magna, we'll find an old boy who is a fund of gossip. His name is Barney Gotobed."

At the pub, they were told they would find Mr. Gotobed at "his" table in the garden by the cedar tree.

Agatha, who had expected to find a sort of local

yokel was surprised to find an elderly, scholarly looking gentleman in a worn tweed jacket and flannels. He had thinning grey hair and bright intelligent eyes.

Introducing herself and Charles, Agatha said, "Mind if we join you and ask some questions about the Tweedys?"

"Please do," he said. "You may call me Barney. I seem to have acquired a reputation for being the local gossip."

They pulled up chairs and sat down. "We're curious about the fire in which the brother died," said Agatha. "May we get you another drink?"

"A lager would be fine."

"Could you get it, Charles?" said Agatha. "And a gin and tonic for me."

Charles went off reluctantly. Then he came back. "I seem to have forgotten my wallet, Agatha."

"As usual," grumbled Agatha, getting out her wallet and handing him a twenty-pound note.

"So what about the fire?" asked Agatha eagerly.

"Anthony and Lavender Tweedy were twins," he began, leaning back in his chair. "Could hardly tell them apart because Lavender dressed like a man. They hated each other and lived separate lives in the same house. They had it altered, you know, so each had separate kitchens and bathrooms. Neither of them had ever had a job. The parents had been extremely wealthy; old

Mr. Tweedy owned several storage unit sites and had invested cleverly. They died when the twins were at Oxford, I believe. A car crash on the M5. To everyone's surprise, the twins chucked up their studies and returned home and there they stayed for years and years until the fire. I suppose no one thought much of it. Every village has its eccentrics. I said they didn't work? That's not quite true. Anthony was clever on the stock exchange and increased their wealth considerably. Somehow, much as he openly loathed his sister, they had joint accounts and shared the money."

Charles came back with the drinks.

"And the fire?" asked Agatha.

"The pair of them were great readers and the house was like a library. I think that's why it was such an awful blaze. It went up like a torch. Lavender was found in the garden suffering from smoke inhalation and cuts where she had smashed a window and jumped out."

"That's odd," said Agatha. "Couldn't she just have run out of the door?"

"They were both afraid of burglars and the windows were all locked and sealed. It was Anthony's job to lock the doors at night and he kept the keys in his room. Also he kept his part of the house locked. Added to that, the pair of them considered bottle gas more economical and stored several canisters and so they all exploded. The nearest fire station is some miles away and by the time they arrived, it was too late. All that was left of Anthony, I gather, were charred remains."

"Any suggestion that the fire had been deliberately started?" asked Agatha.

He raised his eyebrows. "Do you mean, did Lavender deliberately try to get rid of her brother?"

"Could be."

"The insurance company did a full investigation. It was an early Georgian house and the fire was judged to be the result of an electrical fault."

"Did you ever talk to the Tweedys?" asked Charles.

"They barely spoke to anyone. People pretty much ignored them. They became part of the village scenery."

"But you were interested in them," said Agatha.

"Since I retired from Oxford University, I found I liked studying people and speculating about them. I suppose that's how I got my reputation as a gossip. What is your interest in the Tweedys? Is it anything to do with all these murders?"

"Mrs. Tweedy was a client of that therapist who was murdered," said Agatha. "I'm just checking up on everyone."

Said Barney, "Lavender Tweedy consult a therapist? I find that very hard to believe unless she has changed considerably."

"What if she had some awful secret and she just had

to tell someone?" said Agatha. "And what if that some-one was a blackmailing therapist?"

"From what I remember of Lavender, she wouldn't have confided in anyone," said Barney.

"And the fire was really an accident?" asked Agatha.

"Yes, of course. Faulty wiring. It was an old house. A developer bought the ruin, knocked it down and built a couple of villas. There was a good bit of land, you see."

"Can you remember the name of the insurance com-pany?" asked Agatha.

Barney grinned. "You do have a nasty suspicious mind. Falcon Insurance in Cheltenham. I remember the name clearly because there was an investigator down here for quite a time."

"This really is one of your more dramatic flights of fancy," grumbled Charles as they got in the car and Agatha announced they were going to Cheltenham.

"I've got to follow this up," said Agatha. "I've got nothing else."

Cheltenham Spa in Gloucestershire has some fine Regency buildings. It has recently changed from a gen-teel town, famous for retired colonels and their ladies

251

and has become a rougher place. But it still has the pump room and beautiful gardens and those magnificent terraces of white houses. Although inland, it has the air of a seaside town and one almost expects to turn a corner and see a pier.

Falcon Insurance was situated in one of these mansions. They were passed from secretary to secretary until they were told that a Mr. Brian Dempsey would see them.

Brian Dempsey was a tired-looking grey man: grey suit, grey face, grey hair.

"I investigated the Tweedy fire," he said. "I was very thorough. Of course, all those canisters of butane gas had helped to burn everything to a crisp. The body of Anthony Tweedy was just a scorched mess."

Charles said, "I heard it is quite easy to fake an electric fault. Shred a bit of wire and put a lit book of matches next to it and clear off."

"How much was the house insured for?" asked Agatha.

"Eight hundred thousand."

They were sitting in easy chairs in a well-appointed office. Agatha suddenly sat up straight, her eyes dilated. Charles thought she ought to have a lightbulb above her head.

"The body was that of Anthony Tweedy was it?" she asked.

"Who else could it be?" Brian said. "Lavender identified what was left by the remains of his watch and one of his handmade shoes had escaped most of the burning."

"So no dental records? No DNA?"

Brian said testily, "I am very good at my job. I spent a lot of time making sure the fire was accidental. What the hell are you getting at?"

"The brother and sister hated each other," said Agatha. "Get a load of this. What if—just what if—the body was that of Lavender, not Anthony?"

Brian laughed. "You must realise, I interviewed Lavender. One very distressed old lady. I'm not a fool, you know. Also, she was the spitting image of a photograph she showed me."

"But they were identical twins," protested Agatha.

Brian rose to his feet as a signal that the interview was over. "It's been very interesting to meet you, Mrs. Raisin," he said. "Ever thought of writing detective fiction?"

"Don't be rude," said Agatha. "Come along, Charles."

"I could do with a drink," said Charles when they left the building. "I want you to sit down and tell me exactly what's got into that crazy head of yours."

They headed for the bar of the Queen's Hotel. "It's like this," said Agatha, taking a gulp of gin and tonic. "Bob Dell was a cross-dresser. He said he wasn't alone. Right? What if one transvestite recognised the man behind so-called Lavender Tweedy's disguise? What if the Tweedy woman saw me going there and got worried?"

"Well," said Charles cautiously, "what on earth can you do about it?"

"Teeth often survive a fire. I wonder if the body was buried? I should talk to Bill."

"And he will consult his superiors and Wilkes will tell you to stop interfering in police business."

"I wonder what's in the Tweedy garden?"

"Agatha, the police searched all the gardens looking for wolfsbane."

"Snakes and bastards. And it could all have been uprooted."

"What about the allotments?"

The allotments were those strips of land just outside Carsely rented by various villagers to grow vegetables and flowers.

"I seem to remember they searched those as well," said Agatha gloomily.

"Just suppose I go along with this mad idea of yours," said Charles. "Could she have got an allotment in a nearby village? Mrs. Bloxby would know if there were any available."

Agatha's face cleared. "Let's go and ask!"

Mrs. Bloxby's gentle face looked bewildered as Agatha poured out her new theory and then demanded to know if Mrs. Tweedy could have rented an allotment in any nearby village.

"Do have another scone, Sir Charles, while I think," said Mrs. Bloxby. "I'll ask Alf."

She went along to her husband's study but unfortunately left the door open. "You mean that pesky woman is here again?" they heard the vicar demand. "Hasn't she got a home of her own to go to?" Then the study door was shut.

Charles grinned. "Doesn't like you much, does he?"

"That man is not a Christian," snapped Agatha.

Mrs. Bloxby came back. "There is a village called Upper Harley. It's about ten miles from Carsely. They had allotments available last year. It's little more than a hamlet so they might allow outsiders to rent."

"I'll go over there tonight," said Agatha. "Don't want to be snooping around in the daytime."

"I can't come with you," said Charles. "Got a dinner engagement. You'd better take someone with you."

"I'll think about it," said Agatha.

"Don't be silly," snapped Charles. "There's nothing to think about. Don't go alone."

That evening, Charles talked politely at dinner while all the time his mind raced. Damn, Agatha. If her mad conjectures were right, she was putting herself in serious danger. He looked anxiously at the fading light of the evening beyond the long windows of the dining room. It would be dark soon.

At last he couldn't bear it any longer. He made a muttered excuse and found his way to the lavatory. He sat down on the pan, took out his phone, where he had all the numbers of Agatha's detectives listed. He rapidly told them where Agatha was going and begged them all to get over there. Then he phoned Bill Wong and managed to get him at home. Bill listened in amazement as Charles rapidly told him about Agatha's theory and where she had gone.

"I think that attack on her life upset her," said Bill, "or she would never have come up with this load of rubbish."

"There's something awfully convincing about it," pleaded Charles. "Can't you just get out to that allotment and check?"

"It's my night off," protested Bill. "Oh, all right. But I am really going to give her a blast."

As soon as it was dark, Agatha set out, listening to the irritating voice on her sat-nav directing her to Upper Harley. Despite the Cotswolds being such a tourist attraction, there are little Cotswold villages like Upper Harley, buried away in the wolds and seldom visited.

She kept checking in her rearview mirror to make sure she wasn't being followed, but there were several cars behind her until she swung off the main road. Her way took her down dark twisting lanes where overhanging trees blotted out the moon.

Finally she arrived, parked in the centre and got out and looked around. Upper Harley appeared to consist of a huddle of houses beside a pond. There was no evidence of a shop or pub. Agatha marched up to the nearest house and knocked on the door, demanding to know where the allotments were. "No use you wanting one," said the woman who answered the door. "Thems bin sold off for housing."

Agatha's heart sank, but she pursued with, "Where are they anyway?"

"You come by car?"

"Yes."

"Take that liddle lane t'other side of the pond. Drive slow, mind. Do be sheep sometimes. Quarter mile up on the left."

Agatha thanked her. Got into her car and drove slowly off, hoping the sheep would have gone to sleep.

There were no trees over the lane and she was grateful for the bright moonlight, thinking that otherwise she might have missed the allotments, hidden as they were behind a straggly hedge. It was only when she was driving at a snail's pace and coming to a break in the hedge that she noticed through the back a few strips of land. She collected her camera and a powerful torch and made her way through the gap.

Because, probably, of the incipient sale, many of the former allotments had been left to run wild. But there were a few sheds and a few cultivated strips. One had beans, another marrows, but Agatha was looking for flowers.

A little wind sprang up, making urgent whispering sounds. Agatha suddenly wanted to forget the whole thing and go home. She wished she had brought Toni or Simon with her. She realised dismally that for once her nerves were in bad shape.

Telling herself severely not to be such a wimp, she made her way carefully past the beds, shining her torch to left and right. At the far wall, she saw a shed behind a garden strip of flowers: hollyhocks, late roses and some early chrysanthemums. She shone the torch over the flowers. No wolfsbane. Time to go home. She was about to turn around when Agatha saw a gleam of glass behind the shed. She made her way round and found a small greenhouse. The door was padlocked. Agatha shone her torch in the window.

The beam picked out a healthy clump of what she recognised to be wolfsbane.

She grinned in triumph and took out her phone to call the police.

That was when a heavy blow from a spade struck her right on the back of the head and she slumped down on the ground.

Agatha fought desperately against the blackness trying to engulf her. Above her, she heard a sneering voice say, "You interfering old cow. I enjoyed watching you bumbling around. You're cleverer than I thought. So you just lie there while I dig you a nice grave."

Agatha's head swam. She's going to bury me alive, she thought. Let her think I'm unconscious. Or is it him? I bet it's that brother, Anthony.

She could hear sounds of digging. Blood from the wound on her head was seeping into her eyes as she made an effort to see if she could move. But that was when her strength failed her and she blacked out.

Bill and Alice Peterson were racing through the night. Bill ruefully had to admit to himself that he had been glad of the distraction. He had long fancied Detective

Alice, although relationships with colleagues were frowned on. Nonetheless, he had invited her home for supper, but his mother had been singularly rude, not that Bill saw it as such because he adored his mother and thought she was perhaps not feeling well.

"Do you really think Agatha might be onto something?" asked Alice.

"Not for a moment," said Bill. "This is just one very far-fetched idea."

"She's come up with far-fetched ideas before," said Alice.

"But this one's a stinker. Don't worry. We'll sort her out and have a coffee on the road back."

They had just parked outside the allotments when another car drew in behind them and Toni and Simon got out.

"Charles really panicked," said Bill. "Come on, you two. Let's get it over with and we can all go home."

They walked into the allotments, all shouting "Agatha!" at the tops of their voices.

A man emerged from a shed and shouted, "Wot you bleeding lot doing, stomping my prize marrows? I'll 'ave the law on yer."

"We're looking for a friend," said Bill.

"Ud that be old Mrs. Tweedy?"

Bill froze for a moment. "Where's her allotment?"

"Up back. But you're going to pay for that marrow wot you stood on."

They hurried up, Bill and Alice shining their torches. They came across a deep hole in the ground. With a spasm of terror, Bill shone his torch into it and saw, under a pile of earth, a woman's foot sticking out.

He shouted to Alice to phone headquarters and get help, and then he and Simon eased themselves down into the hole and frantically began to clear the earth away from the body underneath until Agatha was revealed, her face covered in blood.

He felt her neck. "There's a pulse," he said. "I daren't move her. Toni, there's some of that silver stuff we use for shocked people in the back of my car. Get it and we'll wrap her up until the ambulance comes."

A voice behind him made him jump. "Is she dead?" Charles stood there, his face white in the moonlight.

"No, but she's in a bad way," said Bill.

"Where's the Tweedy woman—or man, if Agatha's got it right?"

"We haven't had time to look. But Alice has phoned headquarters. They'll be a nationwide search for her."

Villagers had got wind of a fuss up at the allotments. Alice got police tape out and cordoned off the area. The marrow man was driven outside, still grumbling about his prize vegetables.

To Bill's immeasurable relief, an air ambulance helicopter soared round overhead and landed in the field opposite. Paramedics came rushing up with a stretcher.

Unconscious, Agatha was lifted up and taken to the helicopter. Charles was allowed to go with her, but Toni and Simon were told to wait behind until their statements were taken.

The surgeons estimated that Agatha's thick hair had saved her skull. When she recovered consciousness, Agatha found Bill and Inspector Wilkes beside her bed.

She gave a feeble grin. "So I'm alive?"

"We would like to take a few notes," said Wilkes. Then, as if it were being forced out of him, he said, "That was a good piece of detective work. Tell me how you figured it out."

In a weak voice, Agatha told him about meeting Bob Dell and how his remark about not being alone and his subsequent murder had started her to think of Mrs.— or as they now suspected—Mr. Tweedy. But soon her eyes closed and she fell asleep.

The next day, she was stronger and able to give a full account. When she had finished, Mrs. Bloxby came in, her kind face creased with worry. "I should never have told you about those allotments," she said.

"Just as well you did," said Agatha. "Is there a police guard on my room?"

"Of course. They haven't caught Tweedy yet."

"I bet they've been too slow to freeze the bank accounts. He could be anywhere."

"Why did we never think Mrs. Tweedy might be a man?" asked the vicar's wife.

Agatha sighed. "She appeared old and rude. Some old people lose sexuality or femininity, or whatever and people never really look at them properly. I wish they would catch her. And how did a woman who'd never had a job know how to bug my cottage? Oh, I suppose it was easy with all those little gadgets you can buy. Once she'd got in, all she had to do was spread them around. I keep saying 'she.'"

Agatha looked around the room. "No flowers?"

"Hospitals don't allow flowers these days," said Mrs. Bloxby. "People have sent chocolates, fruit and cakes but the police took them all away for forensic examination in case they contained poison."

"Where's James?"

"He's in Thailand, but he phoned to find out about you. The press have been trying to get in to see you."

"Do you know," said Agatha wearily, "I can't for once face them. And look at my poor head! All done up in bandages and shaved underneath. I'll need to wear a wig until it grows back in again."

The door opened and Charles came in carrying a brown paper bag, which he dumped on the table in front of Agatha. "Double cheeseburger, chips and coffee," he said.

"You're an angel," cried Agatha. "The hospital food is rubbish."

"Oh, Sir Charles," protested Mrs. Bloxby. "Couldn't you have brought something a little healthier?"

"She thrives on junk food," said Charles. "Look, Aggie, you'd better clear off on holiday somewhere when you get out of here."

"Nonsense. The solving of this case will bring the agency a lot of work. Can't wait to get back."

But worried Mrs. Bloxby noticed that the well-manicured hands holding the cardboard container of coffee trembled a little.

After two weeks, and on Agatha's last day in hospital, Bill Wong called to say that the body of the supposed Anthony had been exhumed and it had been established that it was in fact the sister, Lavender, who had perished and that Anthony had taken her identity.

"I'm surprised there was enough left to get DNA," said Agatha.

"Enough in a surviving molar," said Bill.

No one had told Agatha that her police guard had

been told not to allow Roy Silver admittance, everyone being annoyed that he had arrived as soon as the attempt on Agatha's life had reached the newspapers, because he had held press conferences on the steps of the hospital, bragging about how he helped Agatha with her cases. All her detectives had called daily with their reports. Charles and Mrs. Bloxby would have liked to keep them away but Agatha insisted on being kept up to date.

When she got home, Doris Simpson was waiting with her cats and watched anxiously as Agatha petted them and then burst into tears.

"Now, now, my love," said Doris. "You've got to take it easy."

"Sure," said Agatha, mopping her eyes. "I'll be all right in a day or two."

"That wicked man won't dare to come near you," said Doris.

"I hope not," said Agatha. "I suppose he didn't bump me off at the beginning because he thought I was a fool. He must have told Jill Davent something and she tried to blackmail him and set all the murders in motion. They do say that after the first murder, the others come easy."

Charles was hosting the annual village fete on the grounds of his estate. He felt his face stiff with smiling and he was bored to tears. At the end of the day, he retreated into his house and into his study while Gustav brought him a beer. He put his feet up and then remembered he had bought a lottery scratch card for a pound. He fished it out of his pocket along with a coin and began to scratch busily. He could hardly believe his eyes. It appeared he had won seven hundred and fifty thousand pounds. Found money, he thought. This demands a special treat.

Then he thought of Agatha. She badly needed a holiday. What if he bought her one? What kind of holiday would she feel compelled to take? But the elderly aunt who lived with him and Gustav should have something. He called them in.

Gustav wanted a new motorbike and his aunt wanted a big donation to a cancer society. When Gustav had left to pore over catalogues, Charles asked his aunt, "I'd like to send Agatha Raisin on holiday, a holiday she can't refuse. Any ideas?"

"Oh, that Miss Marple of yours. What about the *Orient Express* to Venice?"

"Brilliant!"

It almost didn't happen because the day after, Charles's stinginess took over. The upkeep of the estate swallowed money and he was already regretting his generosity. But he could hardly tell his aunt or Gustav that he had changed his mind. The *Orient Express* would be expensive. On the other hand, he thought Agatha was a nervous wreck, and he wanted the old Agatha back to amuse him. Still, he thought hopefully, maybe she'll turn it down.

Epilogue

At long last, after a month, Agatha decided to accept Charles's offer and, for once, all her friends were glad to see her go. She had been snappish and irritable, throwing herself into her work, slaving away long hours, and refusing all social invitations. Bill Wong had pleaded with her to go to Victim Support, which got the furious reply, "There is nothing up with me."

It was almost as if Agatha felt that living in some sort of perpetual rage might keep her fear of Anthony Tweedy coming back to murder her at bay.

Concerned for her welfare, Charles had hired a limo

driver, an ex-member of the police force, Dave Tapping, to take her to Victoria Station in London. He was a powerful-looking man and Charles felt reassured that Agatha would have a bodyguard as well as a driver.

On the road to London, Dave talked amiably about the family holiday he had just returned from in Florida with his wife, Zoe, and his two children, Harry and Hannah. He broke off as Agatha began to cry and handed her a pile of tissues. Agatha had suddenly been overwhelmed with regret that she had never managed to get married to some sensible man and have children.

"George Clooney's getting married in Venice," said Dave, trying to cheer her up. "Is that why you're crying?"

Agatha gave a reluctant laugh. "Not one of my fantasies," she said.

At Victoria, she asked Dave if he would mind parking the car and walking her to the Pullman train, which was to be her transport for the first part of her journey. She was to join the *Orient Express* at Calais.

As she settled in the dining car, Agatha thought bitterly that she must face up to the fact that she had lost her nerve and that her days of detecting were over.

But the smooth rolling of the train and a superb meal slowly roused her spirits.

At Folkstone, the passengers were met by a traditional jazz band. One matron, carried away, was bopping to the music. Oh dear, thought Agatha, Middle England out to play.

Then they were informed that because of a French rail strike, they were all to board buses to take them across the Channel by the tunnel and on to Arras, halfway to Paris. The bus was one of those with tables to seat four without enough leg room.

By the time Agatha got to Arras, she was feeling tired and grumpy but was mothered by an efficient French steward into her little cabin on the *Orient Express*. She settled for the late dinner at ten in the evening and began to unpack a few things, including a black velvet dress for dinner because formal dress was mandatory. It was a beautiful train, all shining wood and inlaid marquetry. The lavatory was at the end of the corridor, a large room and the toilet had an old-fashioned pump.

When she reached the dining room that evening, she wished she had gone for an earlier meal because the liquored-up pseuds were out in force, talking in loud baying voices, trying to outposh each other. But the food, even to Agatha's not very sophisticated palate, seemed to be the best she had ever tasted. For the first time, she began to relax and hard on the heels of that relaxation came the guilty feeling that she had been rude to her helpful friends and had not thanked Charles enough.

In her compartment was a little pile of free postcards with an instruction just to hand them to the steward for posting. Before she went to bed, Agatha wrote to Charles, Mrs. Bloxby and her detectives, thanking them all for their concern and saying she missed them.

In the morning, she raised the blind. Outside was a panorama of the Swiss Alps and Lake Geneva, benign in the sun. Agatha's heart rose and with it her hopes. Perhaps in Venice she might meet some handsome man. She settled down to enjoy the rest of the journey.

At Venice, an *Orient Express* helper led them off the train and there was a long wait while all the luggage and passengers going to all the different hotels were sorted. It was warm for late September. Then she was led to a launch to take her to her hotel on the Grand Canal, and the whole magnificent glory that is Venice burst before her eyes.

The launch cruised up the canal, past the old palaces, past the gondolas, past boats loaded with paparazzi because of George Clooney's wedding to Amal Alamuddin, and stopped at the hotel landing stage. Charles had booked a room with a balcony overlooking the canal in the hope that Agatha would have a place to smoke, but the window only opened a few inches.

She had heard the Piazza San Marco was near the

hotel, so after she had unpacked and put on a summer dress, she walked out of the back of the hotel, through several alleys, over a bridge, through a shopping area and arrived at the square. She found a table at Florian's in the sun, ordered a gin and tonic and felt as if she were coming alive again. She wished Charles had come with her. They had been on holiday together before. But she was only in Venice for four days—Charles's generosity having limits—before getting the train back. The orchestra was playing old-fashioned favourites like "La Paloma," the tourists came and went and Agatha could feel every tensed up muscle in her body beginning to ease.

She returned slowly to her room, suddenly tired, and went to bed, plunging down into a deep healing sleep.

Charles was trying to settle down in his study to read a detective story, but he was distracted by Gustav who, overcome with gratitude by his present of a motorbike, had decided to take on extra work, which meant clearing the bookcase and dusting the books.

"Oh, leave it alone!" complained Charles. "I want some peace. Sod off on your damned bike somewhere."

Gustav sulkily jammed the books back on the shelves, and as he did so, a small, shiny square black object fell onto the floor. "This yours, sir?" he asked, handing it to Charles.

Charles stared at it in horror. "It's a tape recorder. Who put it there?"

"Blessed if I know," said Gustav.

"But who could get into the house?"

"Don't let anyone. Oh, except at the fete. Some old lady wanted the loo."

Shocked to the core, Charles told Gustav to phone the police and set off for Gatwick airport.

On the last day of her visit, Agatha felt tired, "touristed-out" as she thought of it, having diligently visited all the sites up and down the canal. She had found that smoking was allowed in an open-air bar on a platform overlooking the canal.

It was late in the evening. The only other customer was a man in a panama hat, sitting by the rail of the bar. He turned and nodded to Agatha and smiled. Agatha, still on the alert, as if by some chance Anthony had followed her to Venice, stiffened and then relaxed and smiled back. He had a white beard, neatly trimmed and bright blue eyes. He was wearing a white linen suit over a striped shirt and silk tie and his build was medium, without the stockiness and burliness of Anthony.

The water flowed by. A late gondolier with a cargo

of four tourists sailed past. Because of the strong current, the gondolas moved fast down the canal and then had to labour back up. Agatha had expected the canal to smell, but the only odour was from the cigar that the man in the panama hat had just lit. He rose and went to the rail at the edge of the canal. "Well, I'm blessed!" he exclaimed. "Look at that!"

Agatha joined him at the rail. "What? Where?"

"It must be my eyesight," he said ruefully. "I'll swear I saw some fool swimming in the canal."

Agatha shrugged and sat back down and sipped her brandy. She began to feel a lethargy creeping over her body and decided it was time to go to bed. That was when she found she could not move. She opened her mouth to scream but no sound came out.

The man in the panama hat came down and sat next to her.

"It's a wonder what plastic surgery, contact lenses, a beard and a strict diet can do," he said. The only part of Agatha still working was her brain. What had happened to her famous intuition? This was Anthony Tweedy and he was going to kill her.

"I put a drug in your drink," he said. "It paralyses you. I want to see you suffer before I shove an overdose of heroin into you, you interfering horrible woman. Yes. I went to see Jill Davent. She seemed so easy to talk to and I wanted to tell my secret to just one person. She tried to blackmail me! Me! It was a real pleasure to get that neck of hers and wind a scarf round it and pull it till she choked to death.

"You bothered me, although I felt sure that all the stories about your detective abilities had been wildly exaggerated. I knew who Tremund was because before I killed Jill, I watched to see who called on her and found out who they were. He met me down by the canal because I said I had the dirt on Jill, so goodbye to him. And goodbye to Bannister, Herythe and Dell. Getting bored? I'll put an end to you soon. Oh, what is it?"

"Anything more to drink?" asked the waiter.

Agatha tried to signal something to him but even her eyeballs seemed frozen.

"No, we're fine." Anthony put his hand over Agatha's.

The waiter left them and went to tell the other staff that the nice Englishwoman had found romance. Agatha was considered nice because she tipped generously.

Anthony stifled a yawn. "I'm tired. Let's make an end of it before I bugger off to South America and forget you ever existed."

He took a syringe out of his pocket. God, thought Agatha, get me out of this and I'll give up smoking.

Anthony pulled Agatha's limp arm towards him. "Nice bare arms. Makes it easy."

At that moment, Charles, standing at the entrance to the bar, seized a champagne bottle from the drinks trolley and threw it with all the skill he had learnt playing village cricket with deadly accuracy. It struck Anthony on the head and he collapsed like a stone.

Horrified staff clustered in the doorway. "Ambulance!" yelled Charles. "Police!"

He gathered Agatha in his arms. "What has he done to you? Can't you speak? Is that Anthony with a face change?"

He waited in agony until a police launch roared up to the landing stage, closely followed by the ambulance launch. Charles insisted on going to the hospital with Agatha and said he would make his statement there, but he was sure the man he had struck down was the murderer, Anthony Tweedy, wanted by Interpol.

Charles was relieved to find out at the hospital that Agatha had a strong pulse. The doctors said they would not know exactly what drug had been given her until they did tests. But he was puzzled when the police told him they had not been alerted to any danger to Agatha. Surely, before he had rushed to the airport, he had told Gustav to phone the police.

Anthony Tweedy had suffered a severe concussion but was going to live. He had been travelling under a fake passport, but his real passport had been found amongst his luggage, although the police were waiting for the results of DNA tests to make absolutely sure of his identity.

Anthony recovered consciousness but continued to fake being unconscious. He waited until a nurse came to give him a sponge bath and a policeman unlocked the padded chain that held him to the bed. Through half-closed eyes he saw that the policeman had retreated to his post outside the door. Then he was in luck. Another nurse popped her head round the door and shouted that George Clooney and his wife were coming down the canal in a launch.

The nurse fled. Anthony eased himself up. There was a trolley of drugs over by the wall. With a superhuman effort, he made it out of bed. On the trolley, he found a syringe and bottles of morphine. He injected himself with an overdose and slowly collapsed onto the floor and died as the cheers from the crowds outside, watching George Clooney's launch, sounded in his ears.

Agatha was interviewed over the next few days by Wilkes and Bill Wong, who had flown out, and several hard-faced men from Interpol, along with Italian detectives, going over everything again and again until she felt she could scream. The paralysing drug that had been injected into her had such a long and complicated name, she could never remember it. She welcomed the news of Tweedy's death with relief. Agatha felt that, if he had lived, she would never have been free of the fear of him because she was sure he would have found some way to escape.

At last she was able to leave the hospital. She emerged into a strangely empty Venice compared to the last time she had seen the Grand Canal. George Clooney had left, taking with him all the world's press and all the tourists who had come to watch the show.

Charles had suggested one more night at the hotel, having cheerfully moved into Agatha's room because it had twin beds and he felt he had spent enough money on her. Using her insurance, he had cancelled her journey on the train back and booked flights home for them instead.

While Agatha and Charles sat in the bar on the last evening, Charles looked at her serene face and for once did not regret a penny he had spent on her. The old Agatha was back. Later, he thought of joining her in her bed, but resisted, feeling that a grateful Agatha might let him, and he didn't want that, although he wondered why he was suddenly developing a conscience. Agatha had asked him why he had not called the police before leaving for the airport. Charles had told her that he had asked Gustav to phone. "Better sack him," said Agatha. "He obviously didn't phone and could have got me murdered."

Back home in Carsely, Agatha felt rejuvenated and that nothing could ever upset her again. That was until Mrs. Bloxby called on her after the Sunday service to see how she was getting on and hear all about her adventures. Agatha dutifully recounted everything that had happened, but felt she had told her tale to the police so many times that her own voice sounded in her ears as if it were coming from an echo chamber.

"I still would have liked to get Gwen Simple for something," she said.

"Oh," said Mrs. Bloxby reluctantly, "you did miss the wedding."

"What wedding?"

"Mrs. Simple and Mark Dretter were married in Carsely church. They are honeymooning in Dubai."

"So all he was doing was cosying up to me to report back to that conniving bitch!"

"Mrs. Raisin!"

"Well," said Agatha huffily, "he was."

After the vicar's wife had left, Agatha sat and fretted. Gwen had not only got off scot-free, she had nailed the prize of a husband. There must be something on her.

What about Jenny Harcourt's desk at Sunnydale? Could there be something else in there?

Motivated by jealousy, Agatha set out for Sunnydale. Once more, she introduced herself as Jenny's cousin. "Mrs. Harcourt is at lunch," said a nurse. "If you would care to wait?"

"If I could please wait in her room?"

"Very well."

"It's all right," said Agatha. "I know where it is."

She ran lightly up the stairs in a new pair of flat shoes. She had not promised God not to wear high heels again although she had promised to give up smoking and so far had superstitiously kept to that promise.

Agatha opened the secret drawer in the desk. There was a magpie assortment of things from lipsticks to cheap jewellery. She was about to give up when she saw a square envelope stuck against the front flap of the drawer. She pulled it out and opened it. It was a CD. She thrust it into her handbag, just as a nurse ushered Jenny into the room.

"There you are again, dear!" cried Jenny.

"I brought you something," said Agatha, handing over a box of chocolates.

"How kind. Jenny adores chocolates. And Belgian, too!"

Her eyes fastened greedily on Agatha's handbag.

Agatha immediately zipped it up. She was anxious to escape. "I'm sorry I've got to rush, Jenny, but I didn't know you would be at lunch and I've got another appointment."

"No matter, dear. *Bargain Hunt* is about to come on the telly. Run along."

Once back in her car, Agatha was overwhelmed by a craving for a cigarette. "Sorry God," she muttered. Before driving off, she searched in the pocket of her linen skirt for her cigarette packet, which she carried around just in case she weakened. She looked back up at the building. Where she guessed Jenny's room was, the window was open and a thin trail of blue smoke was wafting out into the air.

Back in her cottage, Agatha put the CD in the player and then crouched forward in excitement. It was a recording of Jill's therapy sessions. There was Victoria confessing to drowning the dog, Doris complaining about her shoulders, Anthony Tweedy, not exactly confessing, but giving a long diatribe about how he had hated his "brother" and his fears that the fire might prove not to be accidental. Agatha only half listened to the next few sessions and then stiffened as Gwen Simple's voice began to sound. In increasing disappointment, she heard Gwen complaining about her son and wondering how on earth he could have done something so horrible without her knowledge. Nothing incriminating at all.

"I can't even give it to the police," Agatha said to her cats. "I can't have some of these poor people's sad little secrets exposed."

Although the Indian summer still seemed to stretch on forever, Doris Simpson had set a fire in the living room. Agatha lit it, waiting until there was a blaze and threw the disk onto it.

That evening, she put a cottage pie in the microwave, and then, when it was ready, picked at it, before giving up and throwing the remains on the smouldering fire.

Again, she was assailed by a terrible craving for nicotine. She hurried up to the pub. A damp breeze had sprung up. The evening sky was covered in thick black clouds. Far away came rumbles of thunder as if giants in the heavens were moving furniture.

She hurried up to the pub where she bought a packet of cigarettes, a glass of wine and a ham sandwich and walked through the pub towards the garden, getting rather sour nods by way of greeting. The villagers were beginning to think that Agatha Raisin's dangerous presence in the village was affecting house prices.

Agatha ate her sandwich and then opened the packet of cigarettes, extracted one, lit it and gratefully inhaled. There was a great flash of forked lightning, which stabbed down, missing her by inches.

She threw her cigarette away and fled back through the pub and down to her cottage through a burst of torrential rain.

"Coincidence," she muttered savagely, as she changed into dry clothes.

At the same time, Mrs. Bloxby heard the doorbell ring. "If it's that Raisin woman again, tell her to get knotted," shouted the vicar.

Mrs. Bloxby opened the door. A tall man stood on the doorstep, his face shaded by a large umbrella. "I'm new to the village," he said. "My name is Gerald Devere."

"Come in out of the rain," urged the vicar's wife. "Welcome to Carsely. Leave your coat on the stand there and let me have your umbrella. Come near the fire. Such a nasty evening. Sherry?"

"Yes, please."

Mrs. Bloxby returned, carrying a tray with the sherry decanter and two glasses. She paused for a moment in the doorway and studied her visitor. He had an interesting mobile face with a thin nose, fine grey eyes, and odd black brows that slanted upwards under a thick head of black hair with only a few threads of grey. He looked athletic, his slim body clothed in a well-tailored charcoal grey suit.

When the drinks were poured, Gerald leaned back in his chair with a sigh of satisfaction. "This is nice."

"Which cottage have you taken?" asked Mrs. Bloxby.

"Poor Mr. Dell's."

"Are you a relative?"

"No, I bought it from his niece. I've lived in London all my life and thought I would like to bury myself in the country. I'm retired."

"You look too young to retire," commented Mrs. Bloxby, guessing he must be in his middle fifties.

"I was a detective with the Metropolitan Police Force at Scotland Yard. I came into a good inheritance. I'd become weary of crime. I may have chosen the wrong village."

"Oh, we're all quiet and peaceful now." Here's someone for Mrs. Raisin, she thought. Gerald had an attractive, husky voice.

"Tell me about yourself," he said. "I should think you must have such a hardworking life."

Mrs. Bloxby blinked in amazement. Apart from Agatha, no one else ever seemed interested in her days.

"It's all the usual stuff," she said.

He grinned. "I know, therapist, mother's help, fetes,

disputes, and all exhausting and no thanks. Should I say hullo to your husband?"

"He's writing a sermon. I'll ask him."

She went along to her husband's study and told him about their visitor. "Can you cope, dear?" he asked. "I'm awfully busy."

On the road back, she popped into the bathroom and stared at her face in the mirror. Her brown hair with its streaks of grey was screwed up on top of her head. She loosened it and brushed it down before going back to join him.

They sat and talked for an hour while outside the storm rolled away. Mrs. Bloxby felt like a girl again.

After he had left, the phone rang. It was Agatha. "I hear there is some newcomer to the village," she said.

If I tell her, thought the vicar's wife, she'll be right round there, made up to the nines.

To her horror, she heard herself impulsively lying. "I wonder who that can be?" she said, blushing as she said it.

Agatha heard all about the newcomer from Phil Marshall in the office the next morning, but was not pleased to hear that a detective, however retired, had landed in her village. As far as Agatha was concerned, she was the only detective that mattered.

"There's one thing that bothers me still," she said. "I would like to know who inherits the Tweedy estate. I mean, there's madness in that family and I would like to be assured that there is not some relative of theirs going to call on me with an ax. Patrick, can you find out?"

She almost forgot about it until later in the day when Patrick said, "You're out of touch with what is going on in that village of yours. An elderly fourth cousin inherits and has been round to look at the Tweedy house. She's called Miss Delphinium Farrington."

"If the weird Tweedys went so far as to leave everything to her, then it stands to reason she must be as weird as they were. I thought people couldn't benefit from a crime."

"They can if they didn't commit it, or so I believe," said Patrick. "Although I think the insurance company will want their money back."

"You know," said Agatha, "when I had a dream of moving to a Cotswold village, I envisaged placid rosy-cheeked villagers whose families had been around for generations, not a series of murderous incomers."

"The old village families have all been priced out of their villages," said Phil.

"Well, they shouldn't have sold their properties," said Agatha ruthlessly.

At the end of another week, Agatha had decided to take the whole week-end off. She also wondered where Charles was, but put off trying to phone him. She wondered if he had fired Gustav.

Gustav was the main reason that Charles had not contacted Agatha. The trouble was, he thought, that no one had a staff of servants anymore and Gustav did so much. Gustav swore blind that he had called the police and had even written down the name of the policeman he had spoken to. When he finally questioned Bill Wong, Charles found to his relief that Gustav *had* phoned, but to Mircester headquarters instead of dialling 999, and the new copper who had taken the call had mistaken Gustav's Swiss accent for that of an East European babbling about tape recorders and so had not bothered to report it.

He called at Agatha's cottage, and finding her not at home, decided to visit Mrs. Bloxby instead.

He found Agatha, Mrs. Bloxby and a tall man who was introduced as Gerald Devere sitting in the vicarage garden. Agatha, he noticed, was wearing full war paint and was surrounded by a cloud of heavy French perfume. Oh, dear, thought Charles. Here comes obsession number 102.

Then his curious eyes fastened on the vicar's wife. He had never seen her wear her hair down before and she also had pink lipstick on. Surely not!

288

"Agatha!" said Charles sharply. "I hate to break up the party but I must talk to you in private."

"We're all friends here," said Agatha, flashing a coquettish look from under heavily mascaraed eyelashes at Gerald.

"It's private and very urgent," said Charles.

Agatha sulkily agreed to leave with him.

"We'll go to the pub," said Charles. "I need a stiff drink."

"Let's just hope you've got your wallet," said Agatha sourly.

Once they were seated in the pub, Charles said, "Back off from Gerald, Aggie."

"Why on earth . . . ?"

"Mrs. Bloxby's got a crush on him."

"Never! She wouldn't. She's a saint!"

"She's human and leads a dreary life. She won't do anything about it, Aggie, but let her have one little dream and stop jumping all over it with your stilettos."

Agatha opened her mouth to make a sharp retort and then closed it again. She remembered that pink lipstick and the hair brushed down on the shoulders. Also, the vicar's wife had been wearing a smart green wool dress Agatha had not seen before.

But Gerald was so, well, *marriageable*. And Mrs. Bloxby *was* married. Therefore, surely if Agatha lured

Gerald away she would be saving her friend from disaster, pain and a possible broken marriage.

Charles studied the emotions flitting across Agatha's face. "You like me as a friend, don't you, Agatha?"

"Of course," she said. "You've saved my life."

"I don't want your gratitude," snapped Charles. "I just don't want you to do anything to ruin our friendship. And competing with Mrs. Bloxby is just not on."

"Oh, all right," said Agatha. "If you say so."

It was evening before Charles took himself off. Church in the morning, thought Agatha happily. Gerald's bound to be in church.

The real autumn had come at last when Agatha set off for the church, more soberly dressed and made-up than usual, just in case Charles should take it into his head to check up on her to see if she was following orders. Throughout the service, Agatha spent the time arguing with the God she only believed in in times of stress about her smoking habit and how it was only a little sin. She could not spot Mrs. Bloxby but she did recognise Gerald's tall figure.

Agatha stood outside and waited for him to emerge. He came out at last and beside him was a new Mrs. Bloxby with her hair tinted rich brown and worn in a coronet on top of her head. *And* she was wearing a glamorous white fun fur. Her gentle face was delicately made up.

As she approached them, Gerald said, "See you later, Margaret," nodded to Agatha and hurried off.

Other parishioners came up to talk to the vicar's wife and Agatha rushed off, her mind racing. Yes, she really would be doing Mrs. Bloxby a favour if she could lure Gerald away.

She remembered Doris had baked her a lemon drizzle cake, which she had stored in her kitchen freezer. She would take that to Gerald as a welcome to the village. She took it out of the freezer. It was covered in frost and as hard as a brick. She shoved it in the microwave but forgot to turn the dial to defrost. When she took it out, it appeared to have half melted over the plate. Determined not to let this setback stop her, she firmly wrapped the hot melting mess in cling film, put it in a bag and headed up to Gerald's villa. He answered the door and stood looking down at her. "Mrs. Raisin?"

"I told you to call me Agatha," said Agatha with what she hoped was a winning smile. "I've brought you a cake."

"Dear me. What a hospitable lot you ladies are! I have so many cakes. Are you sure you don't want to keep it?"

"No, please take it."

"You must excuse me. I am in the middle of an important phone call. Another time?"

He took the bag from her, went in and shut the door.

Snakes and bastards, thought Agatha furiously. I don't believe that phone call. What if he's got Mrs. Bloxby in there?

She moved a little away, but then burning curiosity overtook her. She walked quietly up the side of his villa, hoping to be able to peer in the French windows that overlooked the garden at the back.

She moved silently up to the windows. She could see nothing in the windows except her own reflection. Agatha pressed her face against the glass and cupped her hands.

"What on earth do you think you are doing?" came a harsh voice from behind her.

Agatha jumped nervously and turned round to find Gerald staring down at her. "I was in the potting shed and saw you snooping."

"I was leaving and I thought I saw some stranger going up the side of your house. I thought I had better check," said Agatha desperately.

"As you can see, I am all right. Goodbye." He turned on his heel and strode back to the potting shed.

Agatha trailed miserably off. If only she had decided to work at the week-end. Now she was left with a long empty day to think about how silly she had been.

The phone was ringing when she let herself into her cottage. She rushed to answer it. It was Mrs. Bloxby. "Have you got time to drop up here?" she asked. "I want to consult you about something."

"Sure," said Agatha dismally. "Be right with you."

What if Gerald told her about me snooping? thought Agatha. Or how will I handle it if she confesses to being in love with him?

At the vicarage, Mrs. Bloxby ushered Agatha into the drawing room. Agatha was too nervous to accept any offer of refreshment, saying, "What is it?"

"It's the allotments."

"Those strips of land outside the village?" said Agatha, bewildered

"Yes. The problem is that they were owned by a trust which has lapsed and the land now belongs to Lord Bellington. He wants to sell the land to a developer and put a housing estate on it."

"If he has the legal right to do so, then I cannot see what anyone can do about it," said Agatha.

"But I wondered if you could engineer some publicity and start up a petition," said Mrs. Bloxby.

Agatha half-closed her eyes as a horrible memory of being nearly buried alive in an allotment flooded back into her mind.

She stood up abruptly.

"I'm sorry, but quite frankly it will be a cold day in

hell before I have anything to do with allotments again."

Mrs. Bloxby stared in dismay as Agatha went out of the vicarage and off into the village.

Agatha Raisin was not to know how wrong she was and how those wretched village allotments would lead to murder.

JOIN

M.C. Beaton
ONLINE

www.agatharaisin.com

Keep up with her latest news, views, wit & wisdom
And sign up to the M. C. Beaton newsletter

A DEAL
AT THE ALTAR